D1025934

Acclaim for Annabel Lyon's

THE SWEET GIRL

"As Lyon portrays her, Pythias is not the 'sweet girl' her father had called her, but resilient and resourceful—a survivor."

—*The Boston Globe*

"A remarkable novel, not just a pleasure to read but also a book that I expect to reread several times. . . . While Woolf's classic book *A Room of One's Own* remains a brilliant polemic, it is a mere sketch compared to the thickly and quirkily imagined world of ancient Greek women that Lyon gives us in her novel."

—Jeet Heer, *National Post* (Canada)

"Potently elegiac. . . . Lyon shows with chilling precision just how quickly a life can unravel. . . . She has a knack for intrigue, the sizzle behind seemingly ordinary remarks, and she uses this to great effect."

—*The Guardian* (London)

"Exhilaratingly original. . . . This novel thrills in its immediacy and the family at its heart, in their love for each other, is instantly, captivatingly real."

—*Daily Mail* (London)

"A provocative tale that undoes any romantic delusions a reader might hold about ancient Greek society and thought." —*Kirkus Reviews*

"Lyon does a remarkable job of making Pythias, her ancient world, and her eternal problems raw and compelling." —*Publishers Weekly*

Annabel Lyon

THE SWEET GIRL

Annabel Lyon is the author of the novel *The Golden Mean,* a bestseller in Canada that won the Rogers Writers' Trust Fiction Prize, was shortlisted for the Scotiabank Giller Prize and the Governor-General's Award, and has been translated into fourteen languages. She is also the author of a story collection, *Oxygen;* a book of novellas, *The Best Thing for You;* and two juvenile novels, *All-Season Edie* and *Encore Edie.* She lives in British Columbia with her husband and two children.

ALSO BY ANNABEL LYON

The Golden Mean

THE SWEET GIRL

THE SWEET GIRL

Annabel Lyon

VINTAGE BOOKS
A Division of Random House LLC
New York

FIRST VINTAGE BOOKS EDITION, APRIL 2014

Copyright © 2012 by Annabel Lyon

All rights reserved. Published in the United States by Vintage Books, a division of Random House LLC, New York, a Penguin Random House company. Originally published in hardcover in the United States by Alfred A. Knopf, a division of Random House LLC, New York, in 2013.

Vintage and colophon are registered trademarks of Random House LLC.

This is a work of fiction. Names, characters, places, and incidents either are the product of the author's imagination or are used fictitiously. Any resemblance to actual persons, living or dead, events, or locales is entirely coincidental.

Grateful acknowledgment is made to Harvard University Press for permission to reprint an excerpt from *Doigene Laertius: Lives of Eminent Philosophers*, Volume I, Books 1-5, Loeb Classical Library Volume 184, translated by R. D. Hicks, Cambridge, Mass.: Harvard University Press. Copyright © 1925 by the President and Fellows of Harvard College. Loeb Classical Library® is a registered trademark of the President and Fellows of Harvard College. Reprinted by permission of the publishers and the Trustees of the Loeb Classical Library at Harvard University Press.

The Library of Congress has cataloged the Knopf edition as follows:
Lyon, Annabel, [date]
The sweet girl / by Annabel Lyon.—First United States edition.
p. cm.
1. Daughters—Fiction. 2. Aristotle—Fiction.
3. Fathers and daughters—Fiction. 4. Young women—Greece—Fiction.
5. Greece—History—To 146 B.C.—Fiction. I. Title.
PR9199.3.1.98S94 2013
813'.6—dc23 2012049210

Vintage Trade Paperback ISBN: 978-0-345-80366-5

eBook ISBN: 978-0-307-96256-0

www.vintagebooks.com

Printed in the United States of America
10 9 8 7 6 5 4 3 2

for Bryant,
guardian of my solitude

And when the girl shall be grown up she shall be given in marriage to Nicanor; but if anything happen to the girl (which heaven forbid and no such thing will happen) before her marriage, or when she is married but before there are children, Nicanor shall have full powers, both with regard to the child and with regard to everything else, to administer in a manner worthy both of himself and of us. —*Aristotle's will*

CAST OF CHARACTERS

ARISTOTLE'S HOUSEHOLD

Pythias, known as Pytho: *Aristotle's daughter by his dead wife, also named Pythias*
Aristotle: *a philosopher*
Herpyllis: *Aristotle's concubine, formerly a servant*
Nicomachus, known as Nico: *Aristotle's son by Herpyllis*
Tycho: *a slave of Aristotle*
Jason, known as Myrmex: *a poor relation and adopted son of Aristotle*
Pyrrhaios: *a slave of Aristotle*
Simon: *a free servant of Aristotle*
Thale: *a free servant of Aristotle*
Ambracis: *a slave of Aristotle*
Olympios: *a slave of Aristotle*
Pretty: *Olympios's daughter, a slave of Aristotle*
Philo: *a slave of Aristotle*

IN ATHENS

Akakios: *a rival to Aristotle and guest at Aristotle's symposia*
Krios: *a city administrator and guest at Aristotle's symposia*
Gaiane: *a friend of Pythias*
Theophrastos: *Aristotle's successor as head of the Lyceum*

IN CHALCIS

Thaulos: *leader of the Macedonian garrison*
Plios: *a magistrate*
Glycera: *a widow*
Euphranor: *a cavalry officer*
Demetrios: *a slave of Euphranor*
A priestess of Artemis
Meda, Obole, Aphrodisia: *"daughters" of Glycera*
Clea: *a midwife*
Candaules: *a dog-breeder, Clea's companion*
Dionysus: *a god*
Nicanor: *Pythias's cousin*

I

The first time I ask to carry a knife to the temple, Daddy tells me I'm not allowed to because we're Macedonian. Here in Athens, you have to be born an Athenian girl to carry the basket with the knife, to lead the procession to the sacrifice. The Athenians can be awfully snotty, even all these years after our army defeated their army.

"I want to see, though," I say. I have seven summers. "If you carry the basket, you get to watch from right up front."

"I know, pet."

The next morning he takes me to the market. Crowds part for him respectfully; Macedonian or not, he's famous, my daddy. "Which one?" he asks.

I take my time choosing. It's late spring, baby season, and there are calves and piglets and trays of pullets, too. Around us, men speak of the army and when it will return; surely soon, now that the Persians are defeated and their king is on the run. I finally choose a white lamb crying for its mother and we walk it home. I hold the tether. In our courtyard, we lay out the basins and cloths and Daddy's kit.

"You'll feel sad, later," Daddy says, hesitating. "It's all right to feel sad."

"Why will I?"

He sits back on his heels, my daddy, to consider the question. He scratches his freckled forehead with a finger and smiles at me with his sad grey eyes. "Because it's cute," he says finally.

He has the lamb's neck pinned with a casual hand. Its eyeball is straining and rolling, and it's wheezing. Its tongue is a leathery grey. I pet its head to calm it. Daddy shifts his grip to the jaw. I put my little hand over his big hand and we slit its throat quick and deep. When it's bled out into the basin, Daddy asks me where I'd like to start.

"The legs are in the way," I say, so we start there.

"What am I going to do with you?" Daddy says in the middle of the dissection, looking at my hands all bloody, at the blood streaking my face. We've disjointed a leg and I'm making it flex by pulling the tendon. He's holding an eyeball between two fingers, gingerly.

We grin at each other.

"Little miss clever fingers," Herpyllis says from the archway nearest the kitchen. She shifts sleeping Nico to her hip—Nico, her blood-son, my little half-brother—so she can pull a couch into the sun and watch. I remember when he was born, though Herpyllis says I was too young. I remember his wrinkly face and his grip on my finger. I remember kissing and kissing him, and crying when he cried. I would lean against Herpyllis's knee and open the front of my dress to nurse my doll, Pretty-Head, off my speck of a nipple, while Herpyllis nursed Nico, one hand playing in my hair. I've been her daughter since I was four.

"I'll remind you of this the next time you tell me you're too clumsy to weave," Herpyllis says.

I slop some meat into the bowl she's given us, spattering droplets of blood onto my dress.

"Filthy child," she says. "Who's going to want to marry you?"

"One of my students," Daddy says promptly. "When the time comes. There won't be a problem."

From all over the world, students come to Daddy's school here in Athens, the Lyceum. Kings send their sons; our own Alexander belonged to Daddy, once. Some of them are wealthy enough to please even Herpyllis. They will see my worth, Daddy says.

"What is her worth, exactly?" Herpyllis is irritable now. Carelessly, I've spattered blood on the lamb's wool, which she wants for a tunic. She calls for water to soak it. Nico sighs dramatically in his sleep, flinging out a pudgy arm.

Daddy sits back on his heels, considering the question. I make a face at Herpyllis, who makes one back. She tucks Nico's arm in and he sighs again, more quietly.

"It's interesting." Daddy looks at Nico. "The face of a child reflects the face of both parents. Perhaps the mind works similarly? If both parents are clever, the offspring—"

Herpyllis harrumphs.

"Then, too, a philosopher might encourage her interests—"

Herpyllis yawns.

"Or not suppress them, at any rate."

"I'm not getting married," I say. Usually I'm content to listen to their conversations, but this one is irresistible.

"Of course not, chickpea," Herpyllis says immediately. "You're still my baby."

"Not for a long, long time," Daddy adds. They think I'm scared, and want to comfort me. "Years and years. Girls marry much too young, these days. We should emulate the Spartans. Seventeen, eighteen summers. The body must finish developing."

"I'm not getting married," I say again, happily. "May I keep the skull?"

"We'll boil it clean," Daddy says. "What will you do instead, then?"

"Be a teacher, like you."

Gravely, Daddy and Herpyllis agree this is an excellent ambition.

Tycho, our big slave, brings the bowl of water Herpyllis called for. I smile at him and he nods. He's my favourite. Last summer he taught me to suck mussels right from their shells, but Herpyllis reproved him. He understood: little girls reach an age when familiarity with slaves must end. She hadn't been unkind; she'd been a servant herself until Daddy chose her, after my mother died. She was harshest with me, about my manners and appearance and behaviour, and that was because she loved me so much.

I remember the feel of the mussels, plump and wet, and the salt tang. I sneak a lick of lamb's blood. It's still warm.

❦

"Daddy took the whole day away from his school for you," Herpyllis tells me later that afternoon, hacking with less precision at the parts we brought to her kitchen. She isn't displeased, though. We'll have a feast tonight, and soup for days. "You'll be keeping the bones, I suppose?"

Bones are an excellent puzzle, Daddy says. I can apply myself to them and not get bored for weeks. Daddy knows I get bored. Herpyllis knows, too, but her solutions are less interesting—embroidery, crafts.

At bedtime, Daddy comes to tuck me in. "All right, pet?" he asks.

I ask him if we can do a bird next.

"Of course." He sits down next to me. "A pigeon."

"And a bream."

"A cuttlefish."

"A snake."

"Oh, a snake," Daddy says. "I'd love to do a snake. Did you know, in Persia, they have snakes as thick as a man's leg?"

"On land, or in the water?"

We chat until Herpyllis puts her head around the door frame and tells Daddy I need my beauty sleep.

"Why?" I say. Daddy and Herpyllis laugh.

At the door, he hesitates. "What we did today," he says. "Even if you were allowed, the sanctuary isn't the place for that. You understand?"

"Why?"

His lips quirk. "Why do you think?"

I close my eyes and see the temple, the hush and the gloom and the long shafts of light with the dust motes turning in them, the piles of sacred offerings, the guttering flame, the smell of spice, the priest so cool and glorious in his robe. And outside, in the sanctuary, the stone face of the god, and the gangly-legged lamb led so simply to the feet of the statue.

"Herpyllis will always let you use the kitchen," comes my father's voice from far away. I don't open my eyes. In the sanctuary, the lamb's death is an ecstasy. The bones and the blood aren't specimens there; they're a mystery that doesn't need solving. I think of the sadness Daddy talked about, feel it rinse through me, but it's not for the lamb. It's the gods I feel sorry for. What must they think, that we opened an animal without them today? That we didn't invite them at all? I imagine their big, beautiful faces, suffused with pain. That little girl, that one right there: doesn't she love us? What are we going to do with her?

"She's crying," I hear Herpyllis say. "You horrible man. What have you done to her?"

Someone comes close with a lamp.

"Open your eyes, Pytho," Daddy says, but I keep them shut. I'm looking at the insides of my own eyelids now, all red and spidery. "Are you crying?"

"I'm sleeping."

I get a kiss on each cheek, Daddy's whiskers and Herpyllis's sweet scent. She stays after he leaves, sitting beside me on my bed. "You don't have to help him if it upsets you," she says.

"I want to."

"I know," she says.

I open my eyes.

9

"Who loves you, anyway?" she says.

"You do," I say.

She snuffs the lamp but doesn't move. We sit in the dark.

"The poor gods," I say, and then I bury my face in her lap and sob.

HERPYLLIS SCOFFS AT DADDY'S WORK, Daddy's students and the monthly symposium he hosts in our big room. His colleagues attend, plum students, politicians, artists, diplomats, magistrates, priests; Daddy's symposia are famous throughout the city.

The subject for this month is virtue. "Oh, *virtue,*" she sniffs. "Freeloaders, the lot of them. Take this, will you, baby? I'm going to drop it."

We're in the kitchen, just back from the market. I take the package of honeycomb from her and set it on the table so she can unload the rest of our purchases. I've had a growth spurt and am a hair taller than her now, though still unripe, my chest almost as flat as a boy's. We'll spend the day in the kitchen with the slaves. In the evening we'll put on our finery and sit in Herpyllis's room, eating smaller dishes of what the men are having, and afterwards weaving. Their voices will drone through the walls, muffled, occasionally bubbling up in argument or laughter. Herpyllis will try to gossip, and I'll shush her so I can listen. Eventually she'll put her finger to her lips and lead me into the hall so I can hear properly. She'll stand there examining her nails and smoothing her eyebrows while I try to understand. When we hear them rise to leave we'll run, giggling, back to her room.

"I wonder if dogs are virtuous." I spill lentils out on a clean cloth and start picking them over before I put them back in the pot on the shelf. Herpyllis likes her kitchen just so. "A hunting dog, say. You could have one that's too angry and bites everything, and one that's too shy and won't chase, and then—"

"Soak some of those, will you? Enough for ten." She pushes a strand of hair back from her forehead. "And then one in the middle that's everything a dog should be. Yes, yes, I know. And a bean that's too wrinkled, and a bean that's still moist, and a bean in the middle that exemplifies everything a bean should be. Most noble, gracious, perfect bean. A virtuous bean."

"What!" Daddy stands in the kitchen doorway. "Are you laughing at me?"

"Yes," Herpyllis and I say together.

Daddy grabs Herpyllis by the hips from behind, and nuzzles the back of her neck. "Who said you could laugh at me?"

I slip to the doorway, trying not to look at them. The slaves have already fled. We all know they like it in the kitchen.

"Beans, eh?" Daddy says.

Herpyllis's eyes are closed; she's already melting against him. Daddy's eyes are open. He smiles at me, and I know he's thinking about beans.

The guests start arriving after sundown. Tycho greets them and sees to the horses. Nico and I stand just inside the door with Herpyllis and Daddy. Nico, at eight summers, isn't really old enough to sit with the men, but Daddy lets him so long as he doesn't try to speak. Usually he eats too many cakes and falls asleep on the floor.

"Shall we play tiles?" Herpyllis murmurs to me.

"I want to play tiles," Nico says.

"And miss Daddy's party?" Herpyllis says. "Silly boy. We can play tiles tomorrow."

Nico groans.

"I don't want to play, anyway," I say, trying to help. "I want to read."

Another guest arrives, a colleague of Daddy's from the other school, the Academy. Daddy went to that school himself, when he was a young man, and is always gracious to his rivals there, though afterwards he will shake his head and tell Herpyllis their best teachers are all dead and the place won't last long.

"It's going to be boring!" Nico says. The rival, Akakios, grins at Daddy.

"Very, very boring," Daddy says.

"I only came for the food," Akakios says.

"No!" Nico realizes they're laughing at him, and stomps off.

"He's just a lad still," Akakios says kindly, once Herpyllis has gone after him. "At his age, all I wanted to do was fish and climb trees."

"For me, it was swimming," Daddy says.

"And what about you, sweet?" Akakios says to me. "Puppies, is it? Kittens?"

"All kinds of animals, really," I say.

Daddy's lips twitch, as I intended. "And she's a great help around the house," he offers.

Akakios waves this away. "You should hear him brag about you," he tells me. "A better mind than many of his students, he says. Always got her nose in a book. Should have been a boy."

I look at Daddy, who nods, smiling, flushing a little. *Yes, I said that.* I flush a little myself, with pleasure.

"Bactria, eh?" Akakios says to Daddy, changing the subject. I know that this is the latest news to arrive from the army: the king is in Bactria, at the end of the known world, calling himself Shahanshah, King of Kings, and founding city after city named after himself. Iskenderun, Iskandariya, and now Kandahar, the latest. These days, people announce the king's exploits to Daddy as though he's responsible. Daddy was his tutor, long ago, when I was a baby. It's their way of reminding us we're Macedonian and they're not.

"Indeed," Daddy says. "He's become quite the geographer."

"But maybe not such a cartographer," Akakios says. "He seems to have lost his way home."

Herpyllis returns, mock-grim, shaking her head. "We'll have to have a tile marathon tonight," she tells me. "But only after Nico practises his reading. I told him you'd help him."

I don't stamp my foot, groan, roll my eyes or spit, but all three adults laugh anyway. "She shoots sparks, doesn't she?" Akakios says.

"She gets bored," Daddy says. "It's the female aspect of the mind, I think. I was never bored."

"No, no." Akakios taps his temple with his finger. "She's got a flame in there, but it needs fuel. I get bored all the time. With lazy students, especially. That's why I so look forward to these evenings. They feed me for days."

Daddy bows; he bows back. Herpyllis manages not to snort; I hear it distinctly. These evenings are the biggest expense the household has. "The brain needs food just like the tummy." Akakios addresses me. "Your father feeds us, body and soul."

"Pompous prick," Herpyllis says after we're in Nico's room. "He brings a bag so he can squirrel food away to take home with him."

"That's a compliment to your cooking." I'm pressing my ear to the wall.

"I'm bored," Nico says, pushing his tablet away. "I'm hungry."

"You could have eaten with the men."

"Shut up."

"You shut up," I say. Mimicking him, drawing out the whine: "I'm *hungry*."

"Well, I am!"

"You're defective," I say. "Why can't you read yet?"

"Reading's hard," Herpyllis says immediately. "Please, no more fighting. Shall we go to the kitchen and see what's there?"

We follow her into the courtyard. The men's voices are clearer here, and I hang back. Daddy's speaking. I look pleadingly at Herpyllis.

"We'll be in the kitchen," she whispers.

In the past, I'd stand in the courtyard, quietly listening; perhaps creep to the doorway of the big room and listen from behind the curtains; then run fleet as a little doe back to the kitchen at the first quiver of that curtain. But something about tonight, about Nico giving up his place, about Daddy saying I should have been a boy, about Akakios's kindness, and I find myself tripping with quite a clatter over a little table just outside the big room. A moment later the curtain wings aside and Daddy helps me up off the floor. Beyond, I can see all the men on their couches craning to see who it is.

"Please, Daddy," I whisper.

Then I'm sitting in the corner that should have been Nico's, near Daddy, feet tucked up under me. The men are bemused.

"Getting eccentric in your dotage," one of them calls to Daddy. "You want to watch that."

"The lad is prettier," one of them says.

"But the girl's brighter," Akakios says.

I keep my mouth shut, and am relieved when they return to their argument.

"You cannot possibly believe all that modern nonsense you spout," an old man says to Daddy. I recognize him: Krios, a senior administrator for the city, one of Daddy's most regular guests. "The virtues of oak trees and donkeys and the gods know what else. It's all nonsense and you know it. The gods give us virtue."

"They lead by their example?" Daddy says.

"Don't blaspheme," the old man says mildly, and I see that he is used to Daddy, and too smart to be goaded. That must be why Daddy likes him, despite his antiquated opinions. "They set a better example than you'd like to admit. They would understand the presence of little Athena over there better than most of our colleagues here tonight."

He means me.

"The gods value women. They understand the power of women." Krios nods, agreeing with himself. "In their world, the greatest women are a match for the greatest men. Thinkers, warriors, healers."

"In *their* world," someone says.

"Plato, my master, taught that this world is an echo or a shadow of the ideal," Daddy says. "I'm afraid, in *this* world, our specimens are of a different quality."

I give Daddy a look that makes the men laugh.

"Not you, pet," Daddy says. "I wasn't talking about you."

"You were, though, surely," Krios says. "No offence to you, little Athena. But if we follow your argument to its conclusion, where do we get? The greatest virtue consists in flourishing to the greatest of our capacities. If we're an oak seed, we are virtuous in our vegetable growth. If we're an ass, we are virtuous in the most flourishing performance of our asinine tasks."

"Carrying saddlebags, and braying, and so on," I say.

I've thrown a pebble in their pond. There's a ripple of meaningful silence, and then Krios bows slightly, acknowledging me. "And if we are human, we are most virtuous when we are flourishing to the fullest of our capacities, the greatest of these being the intellect. That's correct, isn't it, little Athena? That's what your father teaches?"

"It is."

"You've read your father's books, haven't you?"

"I have."

"Some of them," Daddy says.

"Do you have a favourite?"

I let my mind run ahead through the conversation to come. I can see it laid out like tiles, this game of conversation the men play. I could play this tile, or that one. Daddy clears his throat, and I know he's playing the same game. I glance at him and he winks. *Quickly, Pytho.*

"The *Metaphysics*," I say. "I like the books about animals, too, and the dissection drawings, but I can read the *Metaphysics* again and again and learn something every time." I could have named any number of his books, and sent the game in a different direction with each choice, but I know few of the men here tonight have made it to the end of the *Metaphysics*, because I've heard Daddy tell Theophrastos so.

"What sort of things do you learn from it?" Krios asks.

"I've learned about change," I say. "Change in space, and time, and substance. I've learned about motion. I've learned about the perfect and eternal being, what Daddy calls the unmoved mover."

"About god," Krios says.

"About god as a metaphysical necessity," I say. "Remote and oblivious and lost in contemplation."

"You *have* encouraged her to flourish," Krios says to Daddy.

"It's getting to be a problem," Daddy says.

When their laughter dies down, Krios says, "The question, then, is whether little Athena is unique, or whether she is an example of what many girls could be, if they were encouraged by such fathers."

"Is that the question?" Daddy says. "You've hijacked the evening, pet."

"I'm Daddy's shadow," I say, because I want to tell him I love him.

"A freak." A new voice: Akakios. "Oh, I don't mean that unkindly. But how could such a great man produce an ordinary child? The tallest mountains have the tallest shadows. She's not representative of her sex. She's the exception that proves the rule."

Daddy bows, acknowledging the compliment.

"If he's right, child, you're destined for loneliness," Krios says.

"Only in the company of women," Daddy says. "She'll be all right so long as she has books."

"You'll have to find a husband willing to supply her," Akakios says.

"*If* he's right," Krios repeats.

He looks at me, and I see him thinking, *Go on, little Athena.*

"How many of you have daughters?" I ask.

Again that silence as they absorb the sound of my voice.

"Many of us," Akakios says, when it becomes clear they're not going to offer a show of hands.

"Can they read books?" I ask. "Not just household accounts. I mean real books."

No reaction.

"Could they?" I ask. "If you tried to teach them? If an ass could read, would it be wrong to teach it?"

"Would it be wrong not to?" Krios says.

"Would the ass be worse off?" Akakios asks. "Would it be unhappy?"

"Ah," Daddy says. "*That's* the question."

"Did you like that, pet?" Daddy asks when the last guest is gone.

"Very much."

"Shall our subject be animals next time?"

"Yes, please."

"They liked you," Daddy says. "You made them think."

We pause at the door to my room. He kisses the top of my head.

"Will I be lonely?" I ask.

He smiles. "Of course," he says. "Does that frighten you?"

"Are you lonely?"

"Of course."

"But you have us."

"I do," he says. "I have Herpyllis for when I'm cold, and Nico for when I want to laugh. And I have you, Pytho."

I wait while he thinks.

"For when you want to remember Mummy," I supply, finally, to spare us both.

He looks surprised. "That, too," he says. "But I was going to say: I have you, my Pytho, for when I want to think about the future."

I go up on my tiptoes and kiss his cheek. He clears his throat and stalks off to his bed.

Daddy is as good as his word, and soon Herpyllis is saying he's completely lost his reason. He arranges displays of skeletons in the big room and has Tycho stack crates of live specimens in the courtyard. It's Herpyllis's job to feed them, which means it's really Nico's and mine. Birds, lizards, frogs, rabbits, turtles, and a weasel Nico names Nipper.

"Well, don't keep sticking your fingers in." I squeeze his hand with a rag until the bleeding stops. "I wonder what he's going to do with them all."

"Dissect them, of course," Nico says.

"After he's finished, I mean."

Nico trickles some grain through the roof of the birdcage, startling the pigeons. "You're going to be soup, yes you are," he coos.

I squeeze a sponge over the frogs. Daddy says we have to keep them moist. "I wonder what Herpyllis will do with these?"

"Feed them to the dogs?"

"Feed them to Daddy's students." We giggle. "Roast frog with walnuts."

"Figs," Nico says. "I don't like walnuts. Hey, you're bleeding."

I wipe my hands on my dress. "That's yours."

"No, not there. At the back."

I twist my skirts around and see the red-brown stain.

"Mummy!" Nico hollers. "Pytho sat on something sharp."

"You great lump," I say. "It means I can have a baby now."

Nico giggles.

"Shut up," I say.

"You shut up. You need a man to have a baby. He has to stick his penis in your hole."

"Thank you, Nico," Herpyllis says, coming into the courtyard. She takes one look at me and sweeps me away to her room. "Almost thirteen summers," she says. "About time."

"I'm not getting married."

"Yes, you are." Herpyllis strips me and calls for a basin of water and clean rags. "It's straight from here to the temple. We've had a man waiting there all this past year. He's very ugly and he has very bad breath."

"Stop it."

"Well, of course you're not getting married yet." She shows me how to wind the rag around and tie it in place. "You know Daddy's views. Eighteen summers, at least. That's years and years away."

"That's ancient. Gaiane's the same age as me, and she's getting married this summer."

Herpyllis stops wringing out my bloody dress and puts her hands on her hips. "So now you *do* want to be married?"

"I didn't say that!"

"You want to argue with me, is what you want. Like every other girl your age wants to argue with her mother." I don't correct her.

The next morning Herpyllis hustles me off to the temple, with gold coins and a bottle of perfume and the good wine she was saving for Daddy's name day. Daddy frowns, but says nothing. Tycho follows a little way behind us, carrying a bag of my old toys. I wrote the dedication out myself:

> *At the time of her menarche, Pythias consecrates to Artemis the ball that she loved, the net that held her hair; and her dolls, as is fitting; Pythias the virgin, to the virgin goddess. In return, spread your hand over the daughter of Aristotle and watch piously over this pious girl.*

I had a little fight with Herpyllis this morning when I tried to keep back Pretty-Head. I don't play with her or sleep with her anymore, but my mother sewed her for me, embroidered tiny pink roses on the hem of her dress. I like to stare at the tiny complication of those roses and imagine my mother straining her eyes over the stitches. I don't really remember her, and what I do recall—a gruff woman with heavy brows and a harsh voice who carried me on her hip while she barked at everyone but me—I've been told is wrong. I don't care: I know what I know. Sometimes when I'm fierce with Nico I feel her in me, surging up, and I feel safe and strong.

Herpyllis won that fight, though. "I don't care," Herpyllis says now as we walk. "You don't skint the goddess. I knew a girl when I was young, her mother gave second-best oil, and she never had a child. Walk straight, Pytho. Everyone doesn't need to know."

"It feels like it's slipping."

"It's fine. You'll get used to it. Don't sit down, that's all, until we get home, and then it won't soak through your clothes. You have to rinse it right away and hang it to dry in your room so Daddy doesn't have to see it."

"I know."

"Listen, though." She stops in the road, puts her hands on my shoulders. "You have to thank the goddess properly. No mistakes. She'll know if you don't get it right."

I think of Daddy, his dry scepticism. "How will she?"

"She sees. Like Daddy, but without all the cutting."

I take the stopper from the perfume and sniff. "Oh, Herpyllis, no. This is your best."

"Yes, it is."

In the temple we make our offerings and pray. I do everything in the right order, and I can see Herpyllis is happy. But the ritual is one thing; my feelings are another. I find I can't be thankful for the mess coming out of me and the prospect of some pimply boy breathing his halitosis into my mouth, but I can think of Herpyllis giving up her nicest perfume on my account and find loving tears in myself that way. I kiss Pretty-Head and stroke the little stitches on her dress one last time, then lay her with the other offerings. Herpyllis kisses me when we're done, wipes her eyes and mine, and says nothing all the way home, but holds my hand in hers. Her joy spills into me. Borrowed joy, but genuine enough to please the goddess, I hope.

At home, a strange boy is rapping his knuckles on our gate. My age, roughly. He wears a pack. His feet are filthy and raw, but his clothes are decent enough.

"You have to knock harder than that," Herpyllis says. "How will we possibly hear you?"

He turns his startled face to hers. Black eyes, black hair, hurt mouth; the bruise is almost gone, but not the swelling. He looks at me.

"Fetch Daddy," Herpyllis says. Her voice has hardened almost imperceptibly; the boy won't have heard the difference. "Are you hungry?" she says.

"Yes."

Deep voice. Older than I thought, by a year or two; he's small for his age.

"Go," Herpyllis says, sharply now, because I haven't moved.

I come back with Daddy and an apple. Herpyllis is holding a letter. The boy takes the apple and looks at me again, nods. Daddy takes the letter and reads.

"And here I thought I knew all my cousins," he says after a while. "Well. Shall we go in?"

"No," Herpyllis says later that afternoon, for the twentieth or thirtieth time. "We don't have room. He'd have to sleep in the stables."

"He could share with Nico."

"Absolutely not. We know nothing about him."

"There's that empty room in the servants' wing."

"Which you use for specimens. Where would you like us to move those to?"

"Just think of him as a bigger specimen," I say.

"Now, now." Daddy stands up. "A little charity, please, both of you. Imagine yourselves in his situation, sent away from his family because they can't afford to keep him. Thrown on our mercy. He's probably terrified. Where is he now, in the kitchen? Send him to me when he wakes up."

"I've never seen anyone eat the core of an apple," I say to Herpyllis when Daddy's gone back to his room. The new boy's sleeping on a mat by the hearth; Nico's running wild somewhere with his friends, and doesn't know yet about his new brother. "Where did he come from, again?"

"Amphissa, he says."

"You don't like him."

"I don't trust him."

"Why not?"

She looks at me. "I have no idea."

"I like him," I say.

"I know, sweetheart." She stands and kisses the top of my head. "You hold on to that. I think he has a hard path ahead of him."

"Why?"

She ruffles my hair, and goes to start cleaning out the specimen room.

I go to the kitchen. He's awake on his mat, and his eyes flare when he sees me. He sits up. I ask him what happened to his mouth. He doesn't answer.

"What's your name?" he says. That unexpectedly deep voice again, music I'm still getting used to.

"Pythias."

"Your mother doesn't like me."

"She's not my mother. Are you hungry?"

"Starving."

I get bread and cheese from the shelf. "Does it hurt to chew?"

"A little. But the tooth is tightening up."

"Did it happen before you left, or on the way?"

He rips the crust off and leaves it on the plate. "Before," he says through a soft mouthful.

"What did you do?"

"Kissed a girl," he says. I laugh. He shakes his head without looking up from his plate.

"What's your name?" I ask.

"Jason," he says.

Daddy nicknames him Myrmex, Little Ant, for his black black hair and black black eyes and busy busy ways. Always this way and that, never sitting still. Daddy says he's bright. The letter says so, and over the next few days Daddy himself takes him for walks and plays tiles with him and asks him to help with his specimens and books. *Feeling him out,* he calls it. I watch from a distance. I don't think he's so bright as all that. His reading is halting and he can't do basic syllogisms. He gets bored even more quickly than I do. His main loves are horses and walking through the streets with Daddy, seeing the way people treat him. Behind Daddy's back he mocks him, to Nico and me, but in public he likes nothing better than Daddy's hand on his shoulder, Daddy's quiet word in his ear, while around him men and boys look enviously on. "My son," Daddy introduces him, from almost the beginning.

"Oh, you know Daddy." Herpyllis's dislike of the new boy has hardened into something they both have to peer through, like a piece of resin. "He'll get tired of him after a while. And he'll realize you're better with the books, baby."

"Meanwhile, I've nothing to read."

Herpyllis looks exasperated. "Just go knock on his door and ask."

"I can't. He says I have to stay away from his room until—"

Herpyllis looks blank for a moment, then her face clears. "The smell." She nods. "He doesn't like it on me, either. Never mind. You're almost done for this month. Has it changed colour yet?"

"It's darker."

Herpyllis nods. "And there's less blood, yes? There, you see. You've done very well for the first time. You haven't soiled yourself once."

That would be because I change the rag so often my room flutters like an aviary, laundry as birds. An awful thought hits me. "Do you suppose Myrmex smells it, too?"

"He's young still. He probably won't know what it is."

At my friend Gaiane's house, we discuss my new brother over our looms. "*Who* is he, again?" she asks.

"The son of some distant cousin of Daddy's. They can't afford to keep him, but he's bright supposedly, so they thought Daddy might take him in and educate him."

"Supposedly?"

I yank at a thread and it snaps.

"Jealous."

"Yes," I say. "No. Not exactly. Only Daddy can't see anyone else, at the moment. He's convinced Myrmex will run the school one day."

"What about Nico?"

"Nico's not clever enough."

"You are."

"I'm a girl. A bleeder."

"It's not all bad," Gaiane says. "You can get sick now, you know." She sets her wool down and looks at me. "Wandering womb, it's called. It gets you out of all kinds of things. You can get tired, dizzy, breathless, hysterical. Whatever you like, really. It's your womb migrating through your body, searching for moisture."

I raise my eyebrows.

"Really," she says.

Gaiane's mother, gauzy and fragrant, drifts in to check on us. "It's so nice to have you here, Pythias," she says. "It seems we hardly ever see you anymore. Gaiane's always saying how much she misses you." She leans over Gaiane's shoulder, inspects her work, and kisses her hair. When she looks at my loom, her eyebrows go up.

"Daddy's been teaching me—" I decide not to finish the sentence.

"Not weaving, he hasn't." She picks at my work, trying to correct it. "You should come here more often." I understand this is criticism of Herpyllis, whom she never mentions by name. Gaiane's parents are wealthy citizens. Herpyllis, once a servant, has never been to their house.

"Pythias started her bleeding," Gaiane tells her mother. "And she has a new brother."

"Oh!" Her mother colours. "I didn't know—" Her fingers drift through the air, alluding.

"Herpyllis wasn't pregnant," I say. They both flinch; the word is for animals. *Expecting,* I should have said, or *blessed.* "A cousin has come to live with us."

"A cuckoo in the nest," Gaiane says.

"Has Gaiane told you about the wedding plans?" Her mother rises. "I'll have them bring you some juice. It's so hot, isn't it? Gaiane can tell you all about it."

"I've offended your mother," I say after she's gone.

"Mummy lives on a cloud," Gaiane says. "She just floats along. She's never trusted you since that time she caught you teaching me the alphabet. Is he handsome?"

I bite a thread with my teeth. "Who?"

"The cuckoo, of course."

Gaiane affects her mother's sweet vagueness, but she has a sharp streak that keeps us friends. Sharpness and lust; she's told me frankly she can't wait to be married, though she pretends to be frightened, like any well-brought-up girl.

"I don't know," I say honestly.

"Do you like him?"

"I feel sorry for him. I don't think he's used to people being nice to him. When he showed up on our doorstep, his face was all bruised."

"Has he tried to touch you?"

"No. Herpyllis keeps asking me that, too."

"Too bad for you." She's told me her betrothed can't keep his hands to himself. "Well, if his being here means you have less time with your father and more time for us, then I'm all for it."

I say something nice back, like *me, too.*

When I get home, Herpyllis takes one look at my face and says, "That was a normal girl's day. Get used to it."

"Where's Daddy?"

"At the school."

"Where's Nico?"

"With him."

"Where's Myrmex?"

She shrugs, meaning *with them, too, obviously.*

"Daddy usually waits for me on the days I visit Gaiane," I say. "Why didn't he wait for me?"

Her look says, *Pytho, don't.*

I help her in the kitchen, getting ready for tomorrow's symposium. I don't slam the knives around or anything. I don't make the chicken feet do a little dance or ask to keep the beak. When the men get home, Daddy goes straight to his workroom. I follow him there. "I have a headache," he says.

"I'll make you a poultice."

"No, that's all right. You go eat with the others." He touches his forehead with his fingertips, here and there, experimentally.

"Gaiane's mother has invited me to go weaving with them again tomorrow. I don't want to go."

"Pythias, please."

"Herpyllis will make me."

"It's very stuffy in here."

"I'm not bleeding anymore."

"Pythias, *please*."

The next night, the night of Daddy's animal symposium, Myrmex is in my corner in the big room and I'm at Gaiane's house, where her mother has set her loom up next to mine. "Now, let's start simply, shall we?" she says. "It seems tricky to start, but you'll get the hang of it. You need a decent teacher, that's all."

"Is it stuffy in here?" I hold the back of my hand to my forehead and weave my head a little. "Maybe I should lie down."

Before I've even finished speaking, Gaiane's mother nods, smiles gently, and says, *Nice try*.

I should hate Myrmex. I try. The next morning I cut him dead.

"Hey," he says. "Hey, Pytho!"

He follows me out to the garden, where I commence pinching blossoms off the quince tree so the remaining fruit will thrive.

"What did I do?" he says.

I give him a look.

"They talked about you last night," he says.

I'm not asking I'm not asking I'm not asking.

"Pytho," he says, laughing. "Don't sulk."

I ignore him.

"Akakios made your father angry," he says. "He was talking about—oh, what was it? Something about plants. The difference between women and plants. Or there was no difference."

"The nutritive faculty versus the intellectual faculty," I say.

He laughs again. "You were listening!"

"I was at Gaiane's. Weaving."

"Ha," Myrmex says.

I punch him. Then we're rolling on the ground, wrestling. He's stronger, but I have no honour. I kick and bite and scratch. "You don't even care," I hiss. "You're stupid and you can't read and you might as well be a plant yourself. That party was *mine*."

"Stop." He tries to pin my hands, but I bite his shoulder and he yelps. I sense someone coming, someone big and quiet. I free a hand and manage to stick my finger in his eye and my thumb in his mouth and yank. He bites my thumb, hard, and then big hands lift me by my armpits, clean into the air.

Tycho.

"Young master," he says. "Young lady."

Myrmex's eye is red and weeping. My thumb is bleeding.

"What did Akakios say?" I ask.

"I'm blinded," Myrmex says.

Tycho puts me on the ground. "What did he say?" I demand.

"He said plants were vivified by the presence of the gods in them, and they died when the gods withdrew."

"That's dumb," I say. "What about a tree with one dead branch?"

"That's what your father said."

Tycho goes back in the house.

"Lookit," I say, and show him the ring of teeth marks at the base of my thumb.

He takes my hand and licks the blood off with his warm tongue. "Sorry."

"Sorry about your eye."

"Sorry about your symposium."

"You're not sorry."

"Well, I wouldn't rather be weaving," he says. "But I guess I'd rather be doing something else. Getting out into the city, that's what I'd like. Seeing the world."

"Daddy will let you," I say. "But you have to go to his parties. You'll hurt his feelings if you don't. Plus then you can tell me about them."

"You're weird," he says.

The bite marks will scar into a ring of white crescents around the joint.

Myrmex settles into the household. Herpyllis never warms to him. Daddy seems to pity him. Nico is afraid of his bullying. The servants treat him as a guest. But he and I, he and I. I've never held a person's weakness in my cupped hands, the way I feel I do his. Weakness and secrets: his loneliness, his hurt, his fear, his ordinary brain. He brings the world to me in pieces, the world I'm now shut out of: conversations he doesn't understand, specimens he can't name, manuscripts Daddy has set him to read that he can't make head or tail of. He even gets to attend classes at Daddy's school. I walk him through it all and help earn him Daddy's gruff love. In return, he teaches me to ride a horse and fake a fever and gamble at dice. I'm afraid for him, afraid of where he'd be without me to guide him. It's quite a responsibility.

THE KING IS DYING; THE KING DIES; THE KING IS DEAD. I walk down to the shore to watch the gulls squabble over this morsel. At sixteen summers, I shouldn't be going about alone. The trick is not to ask. Myrmex used to be my chaperone, but lately he fancies himself a strongman: hanging around the garrison, drinking with the soldiers, missing his classes with Daddy. He resents every minute he spends with the family. He carries a knife of extravagant length and detailing, paid for the gods know how. He still isn't much taller than me. He's always hefting things, trying to build up his arms. Daddy says this is a temporary infatuation, and will pass when he realizes fighting is intellectually unsatisfying.

I miss him, badly. I miss my friend, my brother. Lately, too, I miss the smell of him, and his snub nose and honey mouth and voice, the man who isn't my brother. I think it's his absence; if he were around more, things would go back to the way they were. Temporary infatuation, indeed.

I've brought the lentil pot just to have a reason to detour through the market and hear the gossip. Milk, cheese, olives, bread, nuts, herbs, fish, fruit, meat. High summer, the fat season. I wear a new muslin dress and veil and drift, listening. I feel pretty. *Babylon,* I hear. I know Babylon from Daddy's maps. *A headache, a massive headache.* Can you die of that? I don't ask it aloud, don't have to. *No, it was the guts. He was in agony for a day and a night and then he died. They buried him there. No, they're bringing him home. No, they were all wrong. He was alive. It was the double who'd died. They had a double who looked like him and appeared in public in his place. Assassins wouldn't know the difference. Poison, it was poison, but it was the double who'd died. Not the king. Not yet.*

"Now, beauty," the lentil seller says. "Red or green?"

I'm not a beauty, but I go to him in particular to hear the lie. I put the heavy pot on his table. "Green, please."

"Lucky lentils," he calls as he pours. "Favourite of the king."

Laughter all around us, not kind. Why? But of course I know why. Athenians can remember the time before Macedon, the time when they were independent and powerful and glorious in their own right. It's living memory; Daddy himself saw the battle where the king cut Athens down. They grumble and chafe and snigger and sneer, and fail to notice the Macedonian girl with the Athenian accent who understands more about democracy and empire than they ever will.

The pot's heavy; I balance it on my hip like the servant women do. I want to buy a bird, too, feeling momentousness in the air, but Herpyllis is possessive of the marketing and will find something wrong with it. I can do the heavy pots, but the party pieces she likes to save for herself.

The walk to the beach is long with the pot denting my hip. Tycho wants to carry it, but he already has the towels and lunch and waterskins and my books. We scramble over the hot rocks, away from the popular swimming spots, until we find a deserted scythe of sand at the bottom of a steep rock-dislodging scramble, sheltered by cliffs, with a little sea cave for privacy. I undress and dive into the water while Tycho sinks sticks in the sand and arranges a little oilskin tent for me. When I come out the lentil pot has disappeared, probably into his pack. He's put my food on plates, poured me a cup of water, and arranged my books in the tent, then gone to sit some distance away on the rocks, staring out to sea.

I eat and drink and pick at the blister from the lentil pot puffing on my palm. I build an obstacle course for the thumbnail–sized crab I've brought up from the water's edge and watch him negotiate sand hummocks and rivulets of my drinking water. Once I look for Tycho and see him down at the waterline, picking shells from the kelp and sucking them out. Every now and then he splashes water on his bristly skull, cooling off.

Late in the afternoon, we pack for home. My palm's seeping a little and I don't ask for the pot. We stop by Gaiane's house for a visit, but the slave who goes to her room to announce me returns saying she's indisposed. She's never turned me away before. But two babies in the four years since her marriage, one stillbirth, and pregnant again; *indisposed.* I don't think anything of it.

Sure enough, Herpyllis has felt the turbulence as I have, in the cooking part of her brain, and has bought a pheasant on her own trip to the market. Nico, twelve summers now, is in the courtyard playing Greeks and Persians with the tail feathers. Herpyllis and I make a walnut sauce.

"Do you think it's true?" she asks me, pausing the pestle.

Tycho appears at that moment to set the lentil pot just inside the kitchen doorway. I lift it to its place on the shelf.

"Yes," I say. "I think it's true."

Herpyllis shakes her head, blinking hard.

At supper, when Daddy asks me how I spent my day, I tell him some of what I heard. Some, not all. I don't tell him about the laughter.

"Never mind, pet," he says. "He's died at least a dozen times in the last year. He'll die a few more before we need to start paying attention."

Still, his long fingers fidget with a napkin. He's a bad liar but a good worrier. If he really thought the rumour were true, there'd be tears. All the same, he doesn't like to think of it; it upsets him. He was once like a father to the king, long ago, or so he likes to claim. Herpyllis is glaring at me for upsetting him.

"There was a nice breeze by the sea," I say. "Cooler than in town. We should take a picnic sometime." Her glare softens. "Just the four of us." She smiles. "We could take the cart. Spend the day."

My little brother groans.

"Absolutely not," Daddy says. "Rattle my bones loose. I ache enough as it is. Do you want to finish me?"

Herpyllis immediately does a switchback. "You could have thought of that yourself," she says to me. "You know your father hates the seaside."

"Since when?" I say.

"Why don't we eat cat?" Nico asks. Sweet, worried clown. I love his furrowed face. He holds something up on a knife. "Is this cat? It tastes like cat."

"Daddy loves the seaside," I say. "We all do."

"I have gills," Daddy confirms. He frowns at Nico's knife. "It looks stringy enough for cat." Nico giggles, but Daddy's eyes wander away and grow troubled. "Likely I'll never see the sea again," he says to none of us. He's been saying things like this more and more lately, since he passed his sixtieth summer. The number bothers him.

"What does cat taste like?" I ask Nico.

He chews chews chews gulps, dead pleased. "Sweet and salty at the same time."

"Disgusting child." Herpyllis reaches over to wipe gravy from his cheek. "You know perfectly well it's pheasant." They have the same dark hair and green eyes, the same too-wide smile. I take after my own dead mother: lighter curls, deeper voice. I have our father's eyes, though, that clear unlovely grey. Thinking is unlovely on a girl, Herpyllis has told me, though she likes to fix my hair and kiss my cheek when I'll let her. She says kissing is good for the skin.

"Never again," Daddy says again, a little sharper this time.

I reach across the table to squeeze his freckled, paper-skinned hand. "One day the sea will get tired of waiting and come to you. It'll suck itself up into one big wave and come rolling across Athens until it reaches you. It'll say, *Where have you been?*"

"Will it bring specimens?" Daddy says. "I haven't looked at new marine specimens in so long. I used to take the king looking for specimens, when he was just a boy. Did I ever tell you how I taught him to swim? He was afraid until I taught him."

"The king was never afraid," Nico says.

Daddy leans forward. "He tried not to show it, but I knew. Have I never told you that story?"

Herpyllis and I look at each other. Her lips quirk ever so slightly. I have to look away so I won't smile.

Daddy tells Nico for the fortieth or fiftieth time how he taught the king to open his eyes underwater, a skill my brother and I have had since babyhood. "It is impossible for sea water to hurt the eyes," Daddy says. "Your eyes already contain salt water. You've tasted your tears, haven't you?"

Nico nods. Daddy often encouraged us to poke and taste and smell our various excretions, to learn about the workings of our bodies. "Why does the sea sting, then?"

"Algae, perhaps," Daddy says. "Tiny bits of it. Pythias?"

"Daddy?"

"You'll stay home tomorrow, please, and help me with my books."

A job I like, the periodic tidying of his library, and the glimpse of books I'm not normally allowed to see. Plus he likes to talk about his work at such times, and show me his collections and drawings.

"Well, I'm going hunting," my brother says. He's recently made himself a lot of equipment: bow and arrows, a fishing rod, and a stick lashed to a flint blade for a spear. He and his friends set out every morning insisting it'll be rabbit for supper.

"No," Daddy says. "You'll help, too. We're all staying home tomorrow."

Nico looks at Herpyllis with do-something eyes. She opens her mouth to speak when we hear loud laughter from outside the front gate. Male, more than one. A moment's quiet, the sound of a flute, then more laughter. We hear them move off down the street, singing. *Calliope's daughter, Calliope's daughter . . .*

"Drunks," Daddy says. "No, sit down. You don't need to go look."

My brother sits back down and starts hacking at the remains on his plate. He's sulking. Suddenly he yelps. He's cut himself, drawing a bead of blood above one knuckle, black in the lamplight.

"Let me see." I make a tourniquet with my napkin and hold it tight until the bleeding is staunched. Daddy's taught me everything he knows about doctoring. I can splint a sprain, lance an abscess, bring down a fever, probably even deliver a baby. He's shown me his tools and described the process. I kiss the tip of Nico's finger and wipe pain-tears from his cheeks with my thumbs. "Stupid boy."

"Stop it," he says. "Stop treating me like a baby."

Daddy pushes his plate away. "The Athenians don't know what's good for them. I'll speak to the king when he comes home, explain the situation. If he spent more time here, if they got to know him—"

Daddy and the king haven't spoken since Nico was born, when the army left Pella and we came to Athens.

"I'll write him tomorrow," Daddy says. "The army will take it in dispatches. They know who I am."

Nico yawns. Herpyllis starts clearing the table, sorting what she can save for soup, scraping our plates onto hers.

"May I go to the garrison with you when you deliver it?" I ask. "I haven't seen Myrmex in days."

"No," Daddy says.

The next morning there's a pile of excrement in front of our gate and more daubed on our outside walls. Tycho and another of our slaves, Pyrrhaios, set grimly to work cleaning it off.

"Dog *and* cow," Nico says. "Man, too." He went to see; I wasn't allowed. The stench in our yard is everything the drunks intended. Daddy has been in his library since before dawn, Herpyllis says; he's slept poorly for years. He's told her he's working—probably on his letter to the king—and will call us when he's ready for our help. We don't know if he's smelled the insult.

Herpyllis sits in the inner courtyard, fiercely carding wool. Nico and I fence for a while with the pheasant feathers and then Herpyllis calls me over to do my hair. She has pins and combs and jewels and all kinds of whatnot. A long session then, to soothe her. I sit at her feet while she complains about the crunchy effect of salt water on my hair. She says she's going to speak to Tycho. "You shouldn't be traipsing around the beaches all by yourself, anyway. He should know better."

"How's he going to stop me?" I pick up a clip set with seashells, lovely tiny blue-brown speckled dove shells.

She snatches it from my hand. "I'll stop you," she says.

I smile to infuriate her. I'm my father's child. I do what I want.

"I'll speak to your father." She yanks and yanks again harder when I don't show hurt. "He doesn't always remember you're a girl, that's his problem. Well, who can blame him? Look at you. Have you once used that kohl I got you?"

"Once," I say.

"*And* your clothes are always dirty. You look like a goose-girl just in from the yard."

"It's only dust." I lick my thumb and rub a brown spot clear on my grey-brown foot. My hems are a little ratty, it's true.

"You should be in linen. Silk. A daughter of mine." She sticks the comb in her mouth and executes something complicated with my curls and a gold clip in the shape of a bee, one of her own. She takes the comb out, frowns, and thumbs my eyebrows smooth. "Daughter of mine."

Pyrrhaios appears in the archway that separates the inner yard from the outer, where we keep the horses. "Lady," he says.

I stand. Herpyllis gathers the hair things into her basket.

"A visitor, Lady."

"Who is it?"

"Master Theophrastos, Lady."

Herpyllis follows me to the outer yard, where Theophrastos is pacing. When he sees us, his face contorts.

"Fetch your master," Herpyllis tells Pyrrhaios. She touches his hand and he goes.

"Uncle," I say, and hug him. He's hugely tall and when I hug him my head fits comfortably in the hollow of his chest. In the past I've felt the life in him against my belly, but this time he stays soft. His shoulders shake. He lets me go and takes my face in his hands. I echo the gesture, and thumb the tears away as I did with Nico just last night. "So it's true?"

He blinks. I let him go and Herpyllis takes my place, hugging his tall skinny self, the tree-like length of him. He pats her back and kisses the top of her head but his eyes find mine. "Your father?"

"He doesn't know."

Herpyllis lifts her face from his chest and I see she's crying, too. "It's *not* true," she says. "It's not."

I look at the packed earth of the yard, the clean sky, the gate.

"What's not true?" Daddy comes stomping into the yard, his old-man stomp, with Pyrrhaios behind him. He looks from face to face. "What's happened?"

"The gate's open," I say.

Herpyllis throws her veil over her face, squats, and starts to rock, keening softly.

"Gods' sake," Daddy says. He looks annoyed. "I'm trying to work."

"He's dead," Theophrastos says.

The earth, the sky.

Daddy looks at me.

"The gate's open," I say. "We should close it."

Daddy nods at Tycho, who's come in from his cleaning. He closes the main gate behind him.

"We should lock it."

"Shut your mouth," Daddy says to me, and then he starts to sob.

Theophrastos stays the night, although his house is only a short walk from ours. At first my fears are justified: we can hear the uproar from the city, farther and nearer and farther again, and see elegant spires of smoke rising from different districts. Once our front gate is fiercely rattled, but by the time Pyrrhaios gets to the yard, whoever tested it is gone. By nightfall we can hear music and smell smoke and roasting meat on the breeze. Parties, then; celebrations. I intuit Myrmex is out there somewhere, drinking and carousing, the party mattering more than the reason for it. Shame stops us eating, speaking, until well after dark. Daddy, Theophrastos, and I lie on couches in the courtyard. Herpyllis returns from putting Nico to bed with a tray of bread and pickings from last night's bird. Her eyes look poached. Theophrastos is rolling and unrolling a set of scrolls on his lap, not reading. Daddy stares into nothing.

I make room on my couch for Herpyllis.

"Their own king," Daddy says. "They're turning on him that fast."

"They never loved him." Theophrastos puts the scrolls aside and reaches for food. He makes up a plate, not a scant one, and I'm just having thoughts about his ability to eat at a time like this when he sets it beside Daddy. Daddy looks disgusted.

"Please, Master," Theophrastos says.

When I was a baby, he was Daddy's student; now he teaches with Daddy at the school and will head it one day, Herpyllis says. His name used to be Tyrtamos, but Daddy changed it to Theophrastos because of his divine eloquence. I'm unfamiliar with his divine eloquence because I'm not allowed to attend classes. He's so tall and thin and mild and affable. He loves Daddy like a father and Nico like a little brother. He told Herpyllis once that I laugh too loudly.

Daddy had another pet before Theophrastos, a man named Callisthenes. Well, I don't remember him. He went East with the army and got locked in a cage for disobedience and died.

Daddy says Callisthenes needed a spur but Theophrastos needs a bridle. Theophrastos keeps the botanical garden at the school and curates the museum specimens. He knows a lot of collectors and has acquired my father's gift for talking to people who know more than he does and writing down what they say. I shift on my couch, reaching forward for a bite of something, far enough to see that the scrolls in his lap are in his own hand.

"Thirty-two summers," Daddy says of the king.

"We die just when we are beginning to live," Theophrastos says.

Daddy grunts and starts to pick at the plate. Herpyllis pours the men watered wine, us water. They dip their bread in saucers of olive oil and bowls of salt. There are apricots in the kitchen, but they're probably too happy a fruit for the moment. Herpyllis doesn't eat so I don't either, even though I'm hungry. I should probably try to cry. Nico cried. That's why he's in bed already: exhausted by grief.

"We'll leave the city, of course," Daddy says.

"That's probably wise." Theophrastos takes a last piece of bread to wipe the grease from his fingers, then drops it on his plate. "Just until they get the vengefulness out of them. A few days by the sea until the fuss dies down. A week or two, maybe? The girls will enjoy a holiday."

"Nico, too," Herpyllis says.

"He's a grand boy." Theophrastos pulls his scrolls back into his lap. "How about you, Pythias? Who'll miss you if you're gone a few days? I bet there's someone."

Apricots, lovely apricots.

"Leave her alone," Herpyllis says. "She's my good girl."

"We'll be foreigners here until we die," Daddy says. "No Athenian would have her. She's Macedon-born. She can't breed a citizen. We should probably just go home."

A curious silence.

"Athens is home," Herpyllis says.

"Athens is home to Athenians. We're Macedonian."

"Athens *is* Macedonian. Alexander's death doesn't change that." They look at me because I said the words aloud. *Alexander's death.*

"Antipater is still regent," Theophrastos says. "Pythias is right about that. You have powerful friends still. This outburst"—he waves a hand to indicate the sounds of singing and drunkenness that waft in from all sides—"this isn't rebellion. It's a little release, a little letting-off of old feelings, old desires. Athens is in no real position to overthrow Macedonian rule. Those days are over."

"They pleasure themselves tonight," Herpyllis says bitterly. "And they'll be spent in the morning."

"That's enough." Daddy squeezes his eyes shut and opens them looking confused, like he can't focus. "I'm a symbol. A known associate of the king. They'll kill me just as soon as they think they can get away with it. Look at Socrates."

We all look at Daddy.

"They made him drink hemlock for corrupting the youth of Athens. They kill philosophers," Daddy says, slowly and loudly, like we're all stupid. "Athenians kill philosophers." He stands. Slowly, painfully, with great nobility. "I love my king," he says hoarsely. "I am loyal to my king. We leave."

Herpyllis rises abruptly, loads the tray with our plates, and goes to the kitchen.

"Sounion," I say.

"What's that?" Daddy says.

"We could go to Sounion."

Theophrastos smiles bemusedly, as he always does when I have an opinion. *If a cat could speak,* he asked me once, *what would it say?*

I don't know, I answered. *I'm a dog.*

"Whyever?" Theophrastos says now.

"It's close," I say. "No hard journey for Daddy. And it's on the sea."

"And," Daddy says.

"It's beautiful."

"And."

"And the Macedonian fleet is there."

"Good girl," he says. "However, Chalcis is better."

"It's farther."

"And less beautiful. But it has a full garrison, and I have property there. The farm."

"Chalcis," I say. "We need to tell Myrmex."

"Myrmex is fine," Daddy says.

I raise my eyebrows.

"He sent word," Daddy says. "He got trapped on the other side of the city when the riots started. He's staying with Akakios. You remember Akakios. He'll be home in a few days, when it's safe."

I see Akakios walking slowly through the streets with Myrmex, his hand on my brother's shoulder the way Daddy used to do, speaking thoughtfully to him while around them the party continues. I see them stop at a stall to buy meat skewers and bread, then walk on, enjoying the festive night, talking about the nutritive faculty.

The next morning, Theophrastos gives my father gifts: some books he's been working on. "Something new for the journey," he says to Daddy. "This is a bibliography I've been assembling. I'm rather proud of it, actually, how much I've done these last few years. When you look at it all together like that. And then this one—"

"Ah," Daddy says. "Your plants."

"My plants," Theophrastos says.

We will see him again before we go; it's arranged. We'll visit the school in a day or so, and Daddy will give him final instructions.

"Not final," Theophrastos says. "A few weeks, maximum. Will you bring Nico?"

"If he'll come."

When he's gone and the gate is bolted behind him, Daddy says to me, "Come on. Let's take a look at these."

We go to his study and sit side by side, looking through the bibliography.

"*Juices, Complexions, and Flesh,*" Daddy reads.

"*On Honey,*" I read.

"*Animals That Live In Holes.*"

"*The Difference of the Voices of Similar Animals.*"

"Look," Daddy says. "He's written one on hair, one on tyranny, and three on water."

"*Political, Ethical, Physical, and Amatory Problems.*"

"Amatory problems," Daddy snorts, and we laugh until our guts ache. It's the first time we've laughed in days.

49

Herpyllis says when a man is at ease his testicles are tender, but when he's excited they go wizened and tight. I don't know if she's trying to give me the world or take it away.

I watch her now, standing in the courtyard next to my father as he explains the move to the assembled household, Tycho and Simon and the rest of them. Her eyes find our big slave, Pyrrhaios, then the ground.

"I will not pretend that this move will be easy," my father is saying. "I will not pretend that our life in Chalcis will be better. I'm confident it will be worse. But our way of life here is over now. We are not wanted in Athens anymore. I am not wanted. My loyalty to my students—"

His chest heaves, but he collects himself.

"We leave the day after tomorrow. Pack only what you cannot leave behind. Your mistress will instruct you about the household goods. Now, as for food. My own requirements are minimal, as you all know—"

While he drones on, I watch Simon and Tycho exchange glances. They are my father's best oxen, and they know the greatest burden will fall on them. The women have started to weep, and Olympios's child is gumming dirt again. It's a filthy little thing. Nico stands as tall as he can, listening as a soldier to his general.

Myrmex still isn't home.

I hatch a little egg of a plan: I'll take it upon myself to speak with every member of the household privately, to assure them that the move is only temporary and we'll be back in

Athens by the apple-picking. It would be natural for me to enquire after Myrmex in such a context. Even to visit his room. To penetrate his thick, hot, sour, salty-smelling room.

I start with my little brother.

"You don't pack like that, silly," I tell him. "Those'll break. You need some thorny burnet to wrap around each of them. There are lots of bushes on the road to the market. It's springy when it's dry. It'll protect them."

He puts down the little clay lion and deer and bear he's had since he was a baby. *Splotch* falls the first tear, darkening the lion's back.

"You're too old for toys, anyway," I say, ruffling his hair.

"They're not toys," he says. "They're keepsakes."

Next I visit the servants, starting with Simon and his wife, Thale. I find them in the storeroom, arguing. They stop when they see me. Simon of the yellow teeth and grey grizzlature around the muzzle; Thale the barren with her mouse-coloured eyes and greasy grey curls pinned tight to her scalp.

"Don't be frightened," I tell them. "It won't be for long." Speechless, they look at me, then at each other. I'm pleased at the effect of my words and drift away, running a finger along a shelf as I go.

Pyrrhaios is in the stables, mucking out. I've had reason to watch him lately and I lean in the doorway for a while now, silently. I've seen Herpyllis do the same. His torso is as articulated as a beetle's, I'll give her that.

"Missed some," I say finally, pointing at the straw.

He starts. "You, is it? How long have you been there?"

I say my bit about the move to Chalcis being only temporary.

"That's not what your father says."

"My father is a great man with many worries."

He laughs.

Next the other slaves: Tycho, Philo, Olympios, his toddler, and Ambracis. I find black-eyed Ambracis first, in the kitchen, chopping vegetables. She's not much older than me. She listens staring at her hands and when I'm finished says, "Yes, Lady."

"You may look at me, girl," I say.

She looks at my chin.

"Have you been crying?"

"Onions, Lady."

I look at her chopping board and see the clutter of onions. I feel a bit silly then. I find I can't ask about Myrmex while I'm feeling silly.

Olympios and Philo are in the courtyard with the toddler: clever Olympios is mending a leather harness with an enormous needle and a length of sinew; thick-witted Philo is turning carrot scrapings into the compost. The child, tethered by the waist to a column, is whining after a ball that's rolled just out of its reach. When I nudge it back with my toe the child squints up at me, little crab-hands pinching for my dress. I step back out of reach.

"Lady," the men say.

"Her face is dirty," I say. "She needs a wipe." Before either of them react I go to the barrel and dip the hem of my dress. Holding it bunched into an ear, I approach the child, who coos. I squat in front of it and wipe at the dirt and food and nose-pick on its face. It plucks at my hands, trying to get my rings.

"You must keep her clean," I tell Olympios. "She will have better health if you keep her clean. My father teaches this to his students."

Olympios bows. "Most gracious lady."

Olympios got the child on another of our slaves, who died during the birth the spring before last. My father said we were not to be angry. They did as animals do, he said, experiencing coolness and heat according to the seasons, and should not be punished for the demands of their animal natures, which were utterly involuntary. The girl was a loss, certainly, but the baby would have value one day.

How cold that sounds! In fact Herpyllis and I both wept for the girl, and Herpyllis took it on herself to find a wet nurse. The house was sombre until the baby learned to smile, at about forty days. Nowadays the toddler is mostly Ambracis's charge, though Olympios is unusually attached to it and likes to work near it when he can. We all find this endearing. My father is not a cold man, and we all take pride in the reputation of our house for indulgence to the slaves. We're known for it, for many streets around.

"Do you have questions about the trip to Chalcis?" I ask now.

His eyes stray to the child.

"Of course," I say. "We wouldn't leave her."

"Thank you, Lady."

"That's very good work, Philo," I say, and he beams. He smacks the compost a few more times with the fork, patting it down. "Ambracis probably has some more scraps for you in the kitchen." He trots off, happily. He's cheerful and good for heavy work, even if he doesn't talk much. He likes to keep near Olympios and the child.

"Where is, where is—Tycho?" I ask. *Tycho,* I think to myself. *Who cares where Tycho is?*

"Master sent him on errands. Arranging for carts, I think."

I stop myself from thanking him. I do yank a ring I've grown tired of from my finger, a cockleshell on a plain gold band, and drop it in the child's lap on my way out of the yard. It shrieks with pleasure.

I detour through the men's quarters on the way to my own room just to breathe the air, the hot leather smell.

"No," my father says, seeing the veil I've put on as he passes from his study to his bedroom, where the pot is. A trip he makes a couple of times an hour, every hour.

"Please," I say.

"No."

I take the veil off, ball it up, and throw it on the ground. Housebound, then, I must wait for Tycho, pacing up and down the yard where everyone can see me.

"Do you need something to do?" Herpyllis calls from her room.

"No!"

Nico passes by me and walks straight out of the gate. An hour later he's back with a sack of burnet. He shows it to me for approval.

"Bring everything out here," I say.

We're rolling and tying the last of his toys in the springy dried bushes, which leave long fine scratches on our hands, when Tycho returns. "I'll bring you a crate, young master," he says to Nico.

I follow him inside, to the pantry. "Why isn't Myrmex home yet?" I ask, when everyone else is out of earshot.

He shakes his head.

"Has Daddy not told him we're going?"

He looks at my face. "I'll see to it he knows."

"I could write a letter for you to take to Akakios. This afternoon?"

He removes some jars of oil from a small crate and shakes his head. "Master has jobs for me this afternoon. Let me give this to the young master and I'll go do it now."

"A very quick letter."

He bows. I follow him back to the courtyard, intending to run to my room for paper and ink, but he gives Nico the crate and is gone through the gate before I can stop him. *Oh.*

Herpyllis has closed her door, which is unusual. I can't think why she would be changing her clothes before lunch. Though if she's going out, maybe she'll take me. I hesitate, wondering whether to knock.

"Come in, and close the door behind you, Pytho," she calls. My baby name.

Her room is dark. The curtains are drawn and she's lit just one single-wick lamp. She's sitting cross-legged on the floor, her back to the door, busy with something in her lap.

"How did you know it was me?"

"Close the door," she says again.

I close it.

"I always know when it's you," she says. "I feel the fuss in the air, like a storm coming, and I smell the wild lavender that grows by the sea."

She smiles at me over her shoulder and I stick my tongue out at her. "What are you doing?"

She pats the ground beside her and I sit. She's braiding something.

"Don't you want more light?"

She shakes her head. "Your father doesn't like me doing this. It's quickly done and then he doesn't need to know. Want to help?"

I recognize it now: an iunx. She's using various threads and hairs, probably sneaked from each of us, and cups of milk, honey, and water, and a little mound of spices in the charred saucer she uses for burning.

"To protect us on our journey," she says.

I get up. "Of course I don't want to help," I say. "If my father disapproves, then so do I. That's just superstition."

"La, la, la," Herpyllis says. "I can't hear you. Shall we go out? I need some laurel to finish this. We can go to the grove near your father's school."

"Daddy won't let us."

Herpyllis draws a tiny knot tight and clips a loose end expertly with her teeth. "He can't say no if we don't ask him." She filches something fine off her tongue, looks at it, and flicks it onto the floor. "Nico will chaperone us, and Pyrrhaios will come, too. We'll be perfectly safe."

"Don't expect me to do any picking."

"Of course not. You'd spoil it anyway with your unpleasantness. The leaves would shrivel in your hands."

"That's right," I say.

"Shrivel and catch fire, probably," Herpyllis says. "I could teach you so much, you know, but you're a stubborn nut."

"That's right," I say again, and skip back to my room to retrieve my veil, grateful as a dog for its walk.

On our too-brief walk this afternoon, I got my own sackful of burnet. Despite her show of nonchalance, Herpyllis took care to have us all back far too soon. I've laid out what I want to bring on my bed. Herpyllis, passing my open doorway, rolls her eyes. "Gods," she says, but she's too busy to interfere. She and Ambracis ripped the kitchen apart after we got back this afternoon, and they're working on the linens now. We leave tomorrow morning.

First are Daddy's old surgical tools, inherited from *his* father: pipes, probes, needles, knives, spoons, forceps, clamps, extraction hooks, and the enormous vaginal dilator I've always loved for its great complicated importance. Daddy gave me the whole lot to play with long ago, saying he had no use for them anymore. They take a whole crate to themselves. Next comes my mother. She's resting at the moment, but when the time comes we'll have her ashes exhumed to be mingled with Daddy's. I keep ready an unusually small, beautiful funerary urn. Daddy said my mother loved small things, which was why he chose that particular urn. The image on it is of a mother and a little girl, who is me. I'll carry the urn on my lap until it's safely in my new room in Chalcis.

All that remains are my clothes and jewels, which I dump into the trunk at the end of my bed. I'll strip the bed linens in the morning. My collections of shells and rocks and bird skeletons and pressed wildflowers can all wait here until we return. I remember to add the little pot of kohl Herpyllis gave me; she'll notice if I leave it behind by-accident-on-purpose.

"Pytho, help!" she calls now.

I find her in the storeroom with Ambracis and Thale, all three of them sweating and dusty and struggling to hold up one end of a shelf that's somehow ripped off the wall. They're up to their ankles in shards of pottery and an explosion of dried beans. I unload the remaining pots so they can safely lower the shelf, and offer to fetch the broom and pan.

"Look in Myrmex's room," Herpyllis says. "I was sweeping there before this."

Myrmex's room smells of leather and horses and something else, something I don't know. I wonder if I've left a thread of my wild lavender smell for him.

After the cleaning of the beans and the cramming of the carts, we sit in the courtyard drinking a tonic before bed to help us sleep. Nico and I don't often get wine.

"Nicomachos and I will visit the school in the morning while you finish packing," Daddy tells Herpyllis. "I have some last instructions for Theophrastos. You'll have the carts ready in the street, please, so we can set off once we've returned."

"Take Pythias, too." Herpyllis leans forward to refill our glasses. "She'll just mooch about and get under my feet."

"Mooch," Nico says, giggling.

Herpyllis takes his glass and pours his wine into her own.

"What about Myrmex?"

Daddy and Herpyllis look at me.

"We can't just leave him," I say.

Daddy and Herpyllis look at each other. "He's been told," she says.

"Pretty one." Daddy moves to my couch to put his arm around my shoulders. "We all love him. But he's grown now. Soon he's going to start making his own decisions. Maybe even tomorrow."

"Not tomorrow," I say. Daddy holds me while I sob. When I lift my face from his shoulder, I see Herpyllis is pouring my wine into hers, too.

"Come with us tomorrow, then, pet," Daddy says. "If it'll make you feel better."

I nod, and snuffle, and feel for the pouch I've hidden under my dress at my waist. It contains the black hairs I picked from Myrmex's fur blanket before Herpyllis called to ask what was taking me so long with the broom.

Apollo of the Twilight stands just inside the gates of Daddy's school. He rests one forearm on the top of his head, like Daddy when he's frazzled and trying to think, as he leans on a tree trunk. His marble hair is braided like a child's, though he's taller than Theophrastos.

We're in our heavy travelling clothes, the clothes we'll be sleeping in tonight, and I've borrowed Herpyllis's finest muslin veil. Daddy walks ahead, saying many serious things to Theophrastos, who listens attentively, and to Nico, who does not. I trail behind. Dragonflies, poppies, tiny dandelions, light purple iris, snail shells bleached white in death. Curious looks my way.

I worked it out last night in bed. It's been four years since I was last here, ten minutes' walk from our house.

I pick up a snail shell and a small white stone to put in my pouch, later, when I can get under my dress.

Men are coming up to Daddy, touching him, hugging him, wiping away tears. Daddy looks tired. I know it's the effort of not crying himself. I slip up quietly so he can feel me near. "Pythias?" he says, starting.

I blush under my veil as the men look politely away from me, from this gross breach of my modesty: the public utterance of my name.

"So like your mother, for a moment." He touches my cheek through the cloth. "I mistook you."

I go up on my toes to whisper in his ear that I need to sit down. He looks relieved. We go into one of the lecture halls, where Theophrastos has had a table laid with food and drink. Daddy settles onto his couch with a pained groan while his students assemble around him. I whisper to Theophrastos that we might send word to Herpyllis to have the carts brought here so he won't have to walk home again. He nods. Libations, blessings, valedictory speeches.

"I'm bored," Nico murmurs to me. We're at the back of the room, out of the way, supervised by Theophrastos.

"I wonder if they do this every time he goes on holiday," I say.

"Shh." Theophrastos frowns: sternly at me, cross-eyed at Nico.

"I've been enjoying the book you gave Daddy," I whisper. "On botany."

"Ah," he says.

"The part on medicinal herbs especially," I whisper. "I was wondering—"

"It's hard to hear you in here," Theophrastos says. "Perhaps it's better if you don't try to talk."

I bow my head obediently. I've had my fun with him, anyway.

When it's time to leave, I touch Daddy's arm.

"All right, pet," he says. "It's all right. Don't be frightened. Don't be sad."

I whisper in his ear to speed us along, to spare him.

"My daughter is unwell." His voice is loud, hoarse. The men part for us.

The carts are indeed waiting in the street, loaded with our goods and our people. Simon holding the horses; Herpyllis in the first cart; Thale dandling the child; Pyrrhaios, Olympios, Philo, and Ambracis holding Philo's hand so he won't wander away; Tycho; and—leaning against the last cart—Apollo of the Twilight himself, but loose-curled, chewing on half a smile.

"Too much sun and standing," Daddy diagnoses, as many hands reach to catch me and my weak knees.

He makes me wait. He walks at the end of our caravan with Pyrrhaios. Guarding us, oh yes. Knowing he's with us, I can ignore him for the moment. The streets are busy, busier than usual, with a lot of doorway loitering and dart-eyed muttering and finger pointing. Daddy is famous. But then someone calls

"Macedonians," and "fucking Macedonians" again from another part of the street, and then a chorus of voices call other words—Herpyllis claps her hands over my ears. The cart speeds up, the horses rump-smacked by Simon, and I'm thinking of Gaiane, and I'm understanding why she wouldn't see me, or was told not to. Daddy's face is white. He takes Nico's hand in one of his and mine in the other, and sits as tall as he can.

The stone hits him in the side of the head and bounces back onto the road. A small stone. Daddy drops my hand to swat at the place, as though at a bug, and then touches his temple with his fingertips, feeling the blood there.

Myrmex is beside us now, knife drawn. Oh, he's fierce! He's shouting all kinds of things, but Herpyllis, behind me, is wiggling her fingers so hard in my ears, I can't make out a thing. Pyrrhaios is on the other side of our cart too, suddenly, saying something to Herpyllis. She pops her fingers out of my ears and wipes them reflexively on her lap. "Stand up," she tells me and Nico.

Another stone rebounds off Daddy's shoulder.

"Stand up, babies," she says. "Let them see who they're hurting."

We stand. I have to set my legs wide to balance on the bumping cart. I feel a tug at my back and air on my face and understand: Herpyllis has pulled my veil off. I take Nico's hand and close my eyes, waiting for the bite of a stone on my face or breasts, but nothing happens. We ride like that, standing, me with my eyes closed, until we leave the shouting behind.

"Sit, now," Herpyllis says.

We're in a quieter street, closer to the outskirts of the city. Daddy is lying in the bottom of the cart on a pile of skins. His entire face is an apology. I shake my head: *It's not your fault.*

"You see," he says. "I wasn't wrong."

Myrmex climbs up beside me.

"That was magnificent," he says, and then I want it to happen all over again.

We sit for a long time shoulder to shoulder, hip to hip. He pulls my veil back on himself and spends a couple of moments arranging the muslin with his fine fingers. I want to rest my head on his shoulder, as Nico rests on Herpyllis, but that might be less than magnificent, so I hold myself nobly upright instead. He keeps a hand on his knife and scans the landscape like an eagle. Gods, we are a pair!

The journey to Chalcis takes two days. We pass the first night in a field, sleeping in the carts. Herpyllis and I have a cart to ourselves, and Tycho rigs up an oilskin tent over us as he did for me at the beach. We eat Herpyllis's picnic—bread and cheese and fruit and nuts—and we each get another tonic. I read by lamplight while she tidies the camp, but I put the book away when she returns.

"What is it?" she asks.

"Poetry."

She nods, lies back, and stares at the roof of our tent. "Read me some?"

"How's Nico?"

"He's being brave. Daddy's with him. He'll sleep, I think."

"You won't?"

"Probably not." She smiles tiredly; more warmly when I meet her eyes. "It'll be good to get to Chalcis. You were brave yourself, today."

"I wasn't."

"I don't think any of us expected it to be like this."

"Daddy did, I guess."

She shrugs. "We're so used to thinking we're smarter than the smartest man in the world. Because he can never find his bath oils, or remember your friends' names. Maybe we should give him a little more credit."

I lean over to kiss her cheek.

"Read me some," she says. "There's still oil in the lamp, and I'm wide awake."

I pull the book back out and find one of my favourites, the one about the temple by the clear water where sleep comes dropping through the apple branches.

"Louder," Daddy's voice calls from the next cart, and Nico calls, "Louder, Pytho."

I hesitate.

"Pytho?" Myrmex calls sleepily.

"'Deathless Aphrodite of the spangled mind,'" I begin.

The next morning dawns pink and hot. We take turns peeing in the barley, and Herpyllis hands out apricots and sticky sesame cake to eat as we ride. The land is flat, rich, ringed by mountains; we're riding across the bottom of a vast green-gold cup. By noon, my head is throbbing and I throw up over the side of the cart. Tycho puts the tent back up. Even though it's stifling under the oilskin, Daddy says I'm sun-sick and need the shade. He makes everyone else wear hats, except Myrmex, who refuses. He's distant again today, maybe because he saw my sick-up. I'm so disgusting. I ruin everything.

We arrive in Chalcis by late afternoon. We pass gravestones along the road leading into the west side of town, and convoys of Macedonian soldiers moving to and from the garrison. They ignore us, which isn't bad. I'm sitting up by now, taking sips from the cup Herpyllis holds for me, trying to get something back inside me and keep it down.

The town straddles an isthmus that splits it neatly into two halves, like an apple. On the west side, the mainland side, the garrison dominates, set on a rocky rise. The slopes are treed with olive and cypress, and there are some nice houses set in a collar at the bottom of the hill. Officers' residences, probably. East, across the strait—forty paces or so at its narrowest—is the town proper, bustling with shops and workshops and temples and the market and smaller houses. Outside the town on the east side is Euboia, the very best farmland in the world. That's where Daddy's property is.

An hour ago, Daddy sent Pyrrhaios ahead on our best horse, Frost, named for her white socks. Now, as we arrive at the gate at the base of the road that leads up to the garrison, we're met by an officer maybe half Daddy's age. Clearly a Macedonian: he styles himself like Alexander, short hair and clean-shaven. Daddy looks pleased. "Thaulos is the leader of the garrison," he murmurs to Herpyllis. "He knows who I am."

Thaulos looks harassed and exhausted, and greets Daddy by saying, "Is it true?"

Daddy hesitates.

"They celebrate his death?"

Daddy puts his hands on the man's shoulders and shakes his head, meaning *yes*.

Thaulos squeezes his eyes shut and starts to sob. "They should be celebrating his return."

"We've come for sanctuary," Daddy says. "I wrote to you. Did you not get my letter? Is the house not prepared?"

"The house," Thaulos repeats. He looks at the rest of us, briefly, and back to my father. "The house?"

"You will see to it," Daddy says. He's gone pale again.

Thaulos hesitates, gives a curt nod. Then we're jerking slowly, painfully up the hill. The gates clang closed behind us. At the top of the hill, through another gate, he leads us to a corner of a busy courtyard just inside the walls.

"You can bivouac here tonight," Thaulos says. "Cook fires over there. Tomorrow you'll have to be out. We've got reinforcements coming. We'll need every available space."

"The house," Daddy says.

"Later," Thaulos says. He seems angry now, perhaps because we saw him cry. Slowly we all dismount, stretching our jarred, aching bodies. I whisper to Herpyllis. "I'll find us a pot," she whispers back. "We can do it in the tent."

Daddy announces he's going for a walk, as though he needs to stretch his legs after a morning's work, and simply walks away.

"Go after him," Herpyllis whispers to Pyrrhaios.

Pyrrhaios follows him at a discreet distance, leaving the rest of us to set up a makeshift camp in as small a space as possible. The shadows are already lengthening and it's too late to market. Herpyllis's picnic has run out, and she looks like she's going to cry.

Tycho whips the tent up for us and we take our turns with the pot.

"How much money have we got?" I whisper to Herpyllis when she emerges, with that grim but collected look that means success, hard-earned, in the nethers.

"A fair bit," she murmurs. "Daddy gave me all the coin in the house. It's in the bag with the salt fish."

We approach Myrmex together and explain our plan. Herpyllis gives him the leather pouch and tells him how much more to promise once the deal is made. Surprisingly he offers no argument—Myrmex always wants to put his own spin on things, add his own flair—and leaves in the direction of the officers' quarters.

He returns long after Daddy is back, long after midnight, and Daddy and Nico and the servants are all asleep and Herpyllis and I have snuffed our lamp so no one will realize we're still awake. We hear him trip over something and giggle.

"So?" She sticks her head out through the tent door, clearly startling him; he lurches heavily against the side of the cart and giggles again. The horses, tethered nearby, shuffle, disturbed.

"All taken care of." He waves at her like he's leaving on a long journey, lies down in the dust beside the embers of our cookfire, and is snoring before she has had time to refasten the flap.

67

A particularly emphatic clanging of cook-pots just outside our tent wakens me. I wish I could swim back under. Herpyllis, beside me, snuffles gently on. I imagine insomniac Daddy already off on one of his walks, and Nico rabbit-eyed in the tent in the next cart, waiting for one of us to get him.

There is scrabbling at our tent door. I whip Herpyllis's dress—the nearest thing to hand—over my face. Through the muslin I see Myrmex's unshaven face poke through the opening. "Boo."

I take the dress back off. "How's your head?"

He makes a face, then crawls in on his elbows. "Mommy still sleeping?"

"Yes," Herpyllis says, without opening her eyes.

"I found us a house."

How I love his bleary, blood-shot eyes, his awful stubbly cheeks, his dirty fingernails, his feral smell. Nico can wait a little longer. I stretch, tousle my hair to try and fluff it up a little, wonder about the propriety of sitting up with just a blanket covering my little chest. He's my brother, too, after all, just like Nico. Somewhat like Nico.

Something metal raps on the side of our cart. Herpyllis's eyes pop open and Myrmex wriggles backwards, disappearing. "You need to move this," a voice says.

Then we are working fast—dressing in our smelly travel-stained clothes for the third day, throwing everything into the carts, while Myrmex helps Tycho hitch the horses. Herpyllis goes straight to Nico, who lets her hug him. Daddy and

Pyrrhaios, as I'd guessed, are gone. Around us, soldiers wait impatiently. They arrived in the night and have been assigned our place in the camp; they want us out, now. I get busy reloading the sacks and crates we piled on the ground to make room for sleeping, and trip over a tent peg already staked by a soldier who's tired of waiting for us. "Move that," he says to Myrmex, meaning me.

Once we're back in the carts and rolling, Herpyllis leans over to Myrmex. "Where are we going?" she whispers. He pretends he doesn't hear.

Soldiers open the gates for us and suddenly we're out of the garrison and on the dirt track that leads down the hill. It's early still, the sun fingering almost horizontally through the pine and cypress. All around us songbirds are bubbling. I repeat Herpyllis's question aloud.

"I told you, I got us a house," Myrmex says.

"But how will Daddy know where we're—"

"Daddy," Myrmex says. "Daddy, daddy, daddy."

At the bottom of the hill, we bear left. The houses here are a mishmash of huts and villas crowded around the base of the hill. Above them is a tonsured strip where the trees were removed beneath the garrison walls. Myrmex looks deadly pleased with himself. We pull to a stop in front of a villa slightly more secluded than the others, set vertiginously beneath the garrison walls and veiled by a stand of cypress as tall as a man on another's shoulders. A poised, expectant silence.

"What have you done?" Herpyllis says. "We can't afford this."

Myrmex's face registers surprise like pain.

Daddy appears in the doorway, stooping beneath the trailing ivy that's encroaching on the front of the house. "We'll need to cut this back," he calls. "What do you think?"

Herpyllis eases down off the cart. "Whose is this?"

"Ours," Daddy says.

"We can't afford this." She looks angry.

"Whose is it really?" I murmur.

"Don't think about it," Myrmex says.

Nico launches from the cart like a Myrmidon storming the beach at Troy. A puppy, a fuzzy golden thing, peers out from behind Daddy's ankles. Recognizing one of his own, he muddles forward to greet Nico, tongue flopping amiably.

"Comes with the house," Myrmex says, and in his pride I see a boy like Nico and a puppy, too. I shouldn't be able to see these things, but I do. That's what Herpyllis means when she says I'm not attractive.

"Thank you," I say to Myrmex, since no one else will.

"I won it at dice."

"Oh, you did not."

"I sort of did." Myrmex thinks for a minute, frowning. "I can't really remember, actually. It's ours, though."

I want to ask where the person he won it from will live now, and about the money Herpyllis and I gave him, but he holds his hand out to ease me down from the cart and his touch wipes my mind clean.

"The grand tour," Daddy says, ushering Herpyllis and me inside.

The house is confusing. It's bigger than it looks from outside, and the rooms don't seem to stay still; we pop in and out of doors, finding and losing each other, laughing at closets that lead to rooms and private courtyards that seem utterly soundproof. I feel like Herpyllis has given me a tonic. I finally find the room I want for myself, the one with butterflies painted on the walls, but when I call out for them to come see, no one can hear me. I wonder again about who lived here before us, for what girl these butterflies were painted, and if she hates me now.

The grounds, too, are deceptively large and secluded; the whole property is walled, including the fruit trees and outbuildings, and by the large kitchen garden is a second dwelling, a liveable shed I intuit Myrmex will claim.

We settle in, which takes less time than the packing did. I find small, curious clues around the house: a wet wine-cup under a couch (but how is it still wet?); sweet green grapes, still dew-bejewelled, in a bowl on the kitchen table; a mattress still warm to the touch, as though someone just rose from it, on the bed that will be mine.

"I think you like it here," Daddy says, startling me. I had lain down just for a minute on the warm mattress and drifted off.

"Do you?"

He looks straight at me, his eyes unexpectedly clear, the haze of worry and self-absorption momentarily lifted. "It's not home."

"It is if we decide it is."

He leans down to press a kiss on my hair.

❧

In the afternoon, Herpyllis says she wants a walk into town. "We'll all go," Daddy says. His clarity has persisted, translating into a rare good humour through lunch (fresh bread from the larder—*how?*—and a salad from the garden). He arm-wrestled Nico, patted the puppy, even put an arm around Myrmex's shoulders and told him he'd done well. Myrmex blushed.

We walk away from the residences clustered at the base of the hill, while Daddy explains that the tonsured strip at the top is to prevent anyone from scaling the cliffs, and that the residents of our neighbourhood are largely Macedonian, and feel safer in the shadow of the army. The huts, he explains, were cobbled together by poor refugees, whom we should treat kindly should we encounter them. He says the word "refugees" as though it has nothing to do with us.

We stand for a while at the isthmus, watching the tide funnel through the narrowest point, then pay a man to raft us across. "Euboia," Daddy announces grandly on the other side, as though he owns the whole island. In the town proper, we visit the market. Here Daddy is whimsical, buying fish and pomegranates and cumin seed and squash flowers, imagining the ridiculous dishes Herpyllis will make of them for our supper that evening. She rolls her eyes. He buys a fishing stick for Nico and promises to take him; a vial of scented oil for Herpyllis; and a woollen cloak for Myrmex, a reward for securing the house. "And what would Pythias like?" he asks.

I shake my head. It's a happy day, but money remains a worry, surely, and Myrmex's cloak cost more than a book.

"You're a fortunate man." A large hand descends on my shoulder, squeezing. "A girl who refuses gifts. I should be so lucky in my own daughters."

"She is utterly modest," Daddy says happily. "If only I could stop her eating, I could bring her upkeep down to nothing."

The big man laughs. I take myself out from under his hand and duck under Daddy's wing, pretending shyness, so I can get a look at him.

"I know who you are," the big man says to Daddy. "Word of your coming preceded you. We're honoured, honoured, to have you among us. This is your child?"

"My child," Daddy agrees. Herpyllis and Nico hang back, far enough that the man probably doesn't know we're together. Daddy ignores them. Myrmex, browsing the stalls, hasn't noticed.

"Plios." The man claps Daddy on the shoulder. "I'm the magistrate. On my way to the courts as we speak. When did you arrive?"

"Last night."

"Perfect timing." The magistrate claps Daddy's back again, making him stagger-step. "My eldest girl is getting married day after tomorrow. We're having an informal supper before the wedding so the women can come, too. You'll join us, yes? I'll have you first that way. You'll offend me if you say no." He rubs his hands together. "A coup for me! And you'll bring your lovely, modest daughter? You can meet everyone who matters."

Daddy accepts. They exchange compliments, and the man pinches my cheek through my veil before he leaves.

"That's excellent," Daddy says. He seems unsure. He touches his temple with his fingertips, like there's a pain budding there. I exchange looks with Herpyllis, who's stepped forward again.

"Daddy's tired," I whisper to Herpyllis. "We should head back."

Herpyllis says nothing, but stalks off ahead of us, dragging Nico by the hand. Myrmex glances over, sees us leaving, and waves.

"Do you have anything to wear for a party?" Daddy asks.

"Anything to *wear*?" I look at him like he's turned into a cuttlefish.

"Girls like new clothes for parties." He says this like it's a fundamental proposition. *All x is y. No a is b. Girls like new clothes for parties.* "I'll send Herpyllis with you tomorrow to choose something."

That'll be fun, I don't say, reading jealousy in the fierce line of her spine.

At the isthmus, Daddy tugs my hand, bringing me to a stop. "Notice anything?"

I look down at the raft, up at the garrison, down at the water. I look again.

"Good girl," Daddy says.

"But it's backwards. An hour ago it flowed that way"—I point north—"and now it's running that way." I point south.

"A switchback tide." Daddy looks like Nico with the puppy. "Chalcis is famous for it. The current changes direction at the turn of the tide."

"I don't understand."

He hesitates. Then murmurs, "Neither do I."
Puts his finger to his lips; winks.

A thousand lamps send golden tongues licking in all the secret places. The air smells minglingly of meat and flowers and a loosening perfume that makes my thinking vague and my free hand unable to make a fist. The house of Plios is dazzling by twilight, scented and flickering and pretty to the ears, even, with flute girls and a blind drummer and wind chimes made of cockleshells, and the voices of men and women drinking, affectionate, old friends at ease. Daddy holds my other hand tightly, and moves through the room like a ship, parting the company in stately splendour and leaving a froth of whispers in his wake. My famous daddy! My first party! A kindly woman, her hair spangled with hammered gold flowers, hands me a cup and folds my veil back for me so I won't have to let go of Daddy's hand. "You're among friends, dear," she says, eyes crinkling. She touches a fingertip to her tongue and smoothes my eyebrows, then turns away. I take tiny sips of the sweet drink and watch the women's jewellery on the plates and shelves of their various bosoms: necklaces of gold flowers and seed pods, insects, shell-shapes, and spiral loopings of gold wire. I sip again—tiny, tiny sips—and smile shyly at Daddy. He is splendid tonight in snow-white wool, hair neatly trimmed, clean-shaven in the Macedonian style, ears and nostrils plucked hairless by Herpyllis.

She brought me home a dress from the market, thinking to

deprive me of the pleasure of choosing it, and dressed me herself. I'm wearing a girdle at my waist, my first, and my breasts are bound, and my hair is up. She yanked my hair hard, mumbling bitterly about the expense of new clothes through a mouthful of pins. But she took care that I should look perfect and expensive, as befitted our house, and kissed me before we left, carefully, because I had powder on my cheeks and the famous kohl on my eyes. I'd done that myself, to surprise her; she'd wiped it off with spit on a cloth and redone it to her own satisfaction.

"Daughter."

I snap back from the contemplation of my odd-looking self in a bronze to smile at the introductions Daddy's making. Plios pinches my cheek again and says I'm as pretty as he'd guessed. The woman who gave me the drink is back for formal introductions. Glycera is her name, and these are her daughters, three beauties in soft colours who don't speak, but smile without malice at everyone and everything. Thaulos is here, and greets my father more warmly than he did on the hill; a priestess of Artemis—white-haired, with black brows—is presented to us; also a handsome officer. I can't hear clearly over the tinkling music, and decide it's time to stop sipping. Daddy is bragging about me. "Reads, writes, keeps the kitchen garden," he's saying to Glycera. "Knows her herbs. She healed one of our slaves last winter of an infection, all by herself, no fuss. Didn't tell anybody. Lanced the abscess, cleaned it, applied a hot fennel poultice, checked the pus for—"

"Daddy."

"The body is not disgusting," Daddy says, too loudly, reproving. "As I was saying, the pus—"

"An accomplished young woman," Glycera says. "A credit to you, my dear." That stops Daddy. He's not used to being anyone's dear. "What else can she do?"

"Cauterize a cut, set a broken bone, apply leeches—"

"Weave," I say. "Embroider, a little."

"Does she sing?" the priestess wants to know.

"Like a hoopoe," I say.

The room bursts into laughter; everyone is listening.

"Dance?" Glycera asks.

Daddy frowns; I look at the floor.

"I think she loves flowers," the officer says. "I sense it. She fills the house with vases of wildflowers, beautifully arranged." I look at him gratefully. "Blue," he adds. His eyes crinkle too when he smiles, but not like Glycera's. He's young. "A bit of purple, but mostly blue."

His name is Euphranor. I ask one of Glycera's smiling daughters in the women's room, where the pots are. She smiles at the question, without curiosity; I wonder if she's drugged, though she checks her appearance carefully enough in the bronze, and corrects a smudge of colour on the lid of one eye with a steady finger. She smiles again when she sees me watching.

Back in the big room, Glycera takes my elbow. "I've offended your good father," she says. "Only I do so love dancing. My friends know this eccentricity of mine and forgive me. I'm sorry if I've shocked you. There's nothing so beautiful as a young girl dancing. So innocent. So healthy for the body. Do you enjoy exercise?"

"I swim," I admit. She covers her mouth with her hand and

her eyes go big. "Is that terrible?" I say, maybe a bit wistfully. "Will I not be allowed to swim here?"

"Utterly charming," Glycera says, which isn't an answer. She lifts my chin with a single finger and adds, "There. That's right. We wear our chins terribly high in Chalcis."

I giggle.

"Oh, we're going to be great friends." Glycera beams again. "You'll come weave with us, my daughters and me. We're a house full of women now that my dear husband is gone. Five years ago, now. We love sweet company. Anything you need, you call on me. You have no mother, I think."

"My mother died when I was three."

"Precious." Her eyes go bright and she pulls me to her, smothering me briefly in the front of her dress. "You come to us whenever you want." She glances over at Daddy, who's holding forth about something across the room. I see the men around him exchanging glances, amused at something Daddy isn't aware of. "They shouldn't laugh at him. He's a greater man than any of them will ever be," she says.

I feel surprise, and gratitude. "Will you excuse me?"

"You hold him up like a stake holds a vine. I see it. Go, go to him. You're everything to him; those men are less than nothing."

I go quickly to Daddy, slipping my hand in his.

"I was just explaining about the farm," he says. "Richest land in the world. I plan to take a much larger role in the running of it, now we're living here. I have some theories I intend to implement."

"Quite so," Plios says, loudly, patting his shoulder like he's stupid *and* deaf. "May I tempt you with a quince cake, little one?"

Before I can do anything to spare Daddy, the magistrate has led me away to a low table of food surrounded by rich-fabricked couches. "So much food." He shakes his head, gives me a plate, and takes one for himself. "You'll help me make a dent in it, won't you?"

I'm not used to eating in front of strangers. I take a few almonds, a few grapes. I expect Plios to make some joke, but he watches me gravely. I can see he's deciding something.

I wonder what grown women say to grown men. "Your house is beautiful." This sounds about right.

"It's yours," he says. "Open to you anytime, I mean. Is the villa terribly small, compared to what you had before? Are you comfortable there? I can send over whatever you need: servants, furniture. Say the word."

I thank him, tell him we're fine.

"Eat," he says. "I've embarrassed you. Eat your grapes. We help each other here, you'll see."

"Here you are." My father takes a couch and pats the spot next to him, bringing me close. I make a plate for him and he eats hungrily, cheese crumbling down his front, lips glistening with the oil he dipped his bread in. I catch his eye and touch my lips casually. He looks for a napkin.

Euphranor, the young officer, takes the couch next to ours. "I've been thinking about your farm." He pours a cup of wine and pushes it towards Daddy, across the low, food-laden table. "I could take you out there, if you like. You and your family. We could make a day of it, take a picnic. I have a small property close to where you describe. I wouldn't mind popping my head in on the way. In fact, I think we might even be neighbours. I'm terribly interested in the theories you plan to implement. Animal husbandry, is it? Crop rotation? Fertilizers?" I have to squeeze my lips together despite myself to contain a smile.

Then they're pouring the wine unwatered, and my eyes are closing, and the music is faster and louder, and it's time to go. I am pressed to chest after chest, and offers of help, anything we might need, are repeated in my ear. My great daddy is puffed up with wine and food and respect, and doesn't notice the criss-cross web of curious glances that weave around his head. Tycho, waiting at a distance to escort us, is holding an enormous basket.

"So?" Herpyllis says. She must have heard our footsteps coming up the path, and is waiting in the doorway for us.

We follow Tycho to the kitchen, where he sets the basket on the table. Herpyllis unpacks eggs, cheese, cake, wine, cold pies, fruit. Daddy grunts, kisses her and then me, and wanders off—to bed, or to work. To his solitude, anyway. Herpyllis sorts grimly through the food, finally slamming a crock of soft cheese on the table and breathing deeply through her nose. "Charity," she says. Her kohled eyes are bright with hatred. She looks beautiful.

"I want to get this off." I wriggle inside my dress.

She follows me to the butterfly room and helps me with the unpinning, unwinding, unbinding, releasing of hair, washing of face, unlacing of tight sandals designed to emphasize the tininess of my not-so-tiny feet.

"Are you going to tell me about it?" she says finally.

So I tell her about the food, the music, the perfume, the people we met, the quality. I don't patronize her by pretending I didn't enjoy it. She listens, and asks the occasional question. I see her struggling not to sneer or criticize.

"There was an officer named Euphranor. He offered to escort us to the farm, on a picnic."

She flinches slightly and looks at her lap.

"All of us," I say. "I told him all of us."

She looks up. "How did you do that?"

"I told him my father's companion was a mother to me, and I had a little brother who loves animals."

Her face scrolls through a series of emotions. Her eyes go wet.

"Stop it," I say.

"You don't understand." She wipes her eyes on her hem, leaving black streaks on the cloth. "I want all these things for you. Wine and perfume and gold and cavalry officers and—what—*cakes*." She takes both my hands in both of hers. "You're going to be gone so soon. They're going to take you from me."

"Never," I say.

"They'll take you into their world, and leave me behind in this one. Look at Myrmex."

"I'm not Myrmex," I say.

She falls asleep before I do, in my bed, curled on her side like a child, cheeks still wet, my arms around her like a mother's.

"Of course I'm coming," Myrmex says. "Why, wasn't I invited? You didn't mention me, maybe? The minor fact of my existence? Not worth mentioning?"

I open my mouth, but Myrmex is full of umbrage.

"You're ashamed of me, all of you. Well I *am* coming, and I'm going to chew with my mouth open and piss in the river and—"

"Enough," Daddy says.

"*—ask how much everything costs,*" Myrmex hisses.

Daddy and Herpyllis and I burst out laughing.

"You can ride Pinch," Daddy says.

Myrmex hesitates. He loves Pinch.

"What about me?" Nico says. "Can I ride, too?"

"It's a long way for the pony," Daddy says. "And we don't know the ground."

Nico looks stricken. "I already told him about the picnic. He wants to come."

I shake my hair down around my face like a mane, and snort, and say in a deep snuffling horse-voice, "I want to come."

Everyone laughs again, Myrmex too. "Go tell Tycho, then," Daddy says. "He'll get them ready."

"Rather Pyrrhaios, don't you think?" Herpyllis gets up and starts tidying the breakfast table. "He's better with the horses."

Soon we're gathered in front of the house: Myrmex on Pinch, Nico on Spiffy, Daddy on Frost, Herpyllis and me standing, big Pyrrhaios adjusting Nico's tack. The carts we hired to move are long gone, but Euphranor said he'd take care of everything; we weren't to bring a thing.

"You look like you're going to the theatre, not the farm!" Euphranor is suddenly just there, solidified from the shadows of the trees, with his eye-crinkling smile. "Beautiful family. Are you the one who likes animals?" This last to Nico, who's sitting painfully tall. Euphranor slaps Spiffy's neck affectionately. "You've got a fine friend here. We rarely get them this fine in the cavalry." Nico beams. "And who's this?" Euphranor smiles at Myrmex and scratches Pinch's nose.

"That's Pinch," Nico says, before Myrmex can reply.

For the rest of the day, Euphranor calls Myrmex Pinch.

He has a cart for Herpyllis and me lined with furs and purple silk cushions. He himself rides a black stallion, high-strung and fiery and snorting and head-tossing, mane like the sea and so on. Well. It's a very pretty animal, and Myrmex is very, very angry and can't do anything about it. He longs for everything Euphranor has, from his commission to his clothes to his height to his arrogance, and after the first few tongue-tied moments he can't go back and correct the mistake about his name without looking like a fool. He rides at the back of our caravan, fuming, on the horse he's now forced to hate.

The plan is to visit Euphranor's farm first—he's arranged lunch for us there—and then Daddy's property later in the afternoon. Euboia is farmland from a dream of farmland: green and golden, a long treed lane between endless fields, poppies in the ditches, birds in the branches, odd rambling houses made bigger generation after generation, each adding another room or two, all lovelied over with clematis and creeping grapevines. Chickens in the yards, dogs chasing us down the lane. We turn into Euphranor's property, where an old man steps from the shadow of a doorway to greet us. He has no teeth.

"Demetrios!" Euphranor greets him. "We thought we might swim."

"The pond's covered in scum." The old man rubs his hands. "Pollen scum. I'll give it a skim for you."

"No, don't bother." Euphranor claps his shoulder, squeezes. "Pinch here will do the honours. One mighty splash should clear it for the ladies, eh, Pinch?"

Myrmex looks at me.

"I thought we'd eat in the grove." Euphranor holds his hand out to assist Herpyllis from the cart, then me. The catch of his calluses. "Cooler there. A nap, a swim, whatever you like."

"I'd like to see your farm." Daddy's got himself off Frost and picked a branch from the ground to lean on like a crutch. I've never seen him do this before. "Are all those fields yours?" He swings the branch across the horizon, pointing—oh. That's going to get annoying.

"Right down to the river. I thought Demetrios here might escort you while I settle your family. He knows far more than I do about it all, isn't that right, Demetrios? He's been steward since I was a baby."

The old man bares his gums again in his infant's grin.

"Nico!" Euphranor has taken to barking at my little brother like a soldier, which has him giddy. He gets down from the pony and stands at attention, pale and peaky and as serious as possible, probably hoping to be asked to extinguish a forest fire or bear some great weight. Clever Euphranor slings a waterskin over his shoulder and hands him a bow and arrows. "Perhaps a bit of hunting, later, when your mother's not paying attention," he stage-whispers.

Myrmex has to come over to us; has to. Hunting! He can't be left out. He stands closer to me than usual, waiting for his assignment.

"Come, ladies." Euphranor takes a few steps. Perhaps he senses Myrmex's face hardening, because he looks back and slaps himself on the forehead. "Pinch, good man! Get that basket, would you?"

Myrmex nods at Pyrrhaios, who hefts the picnic basket and follows us at a distance. Daddy and the old man are already deep in conversation, and Daddy doesn't even notice us leave. He has that cock-headed, flare-nostrilled attention that says everyone around him is to be silent so he can learn.

We picnic in a pine grove on a horse blanket thrown over a carpet of sappy needles. Piny wine and thick, slow sunshine I can taste. "Eat your bread," Herpyllis says, but I'm not hungry. Wine and sunlight, sunlight and shade and wine. I take my cup down the slope to look at the pond, all overhung with goldenrod and forsythia. The surface of the water is thick and still and spackled with golden pollen, Demetrios's scum.

Something leaps behind me; I feel the air move.

My brother, naked; he lands in the pond with an almighty air-spangling splash, and comes up coated in gold. He floats on his back for a moment to give me a look at everything, then arches lazily and goes down smooth as a dolphin: throat, chest, softness, thighs, knees, feet, toes. The pollen has fled from the centre of the pond to limn the banks yellow, leaving a cool black hole. He surfaces again, smiles; wants me to come in. A little less golden, now, after the second dip. I feel the honey letting down between my legs. I shake my head.

"You see," Euphranor says behind me, softly. He hasn't stepped from the shadows, knows Myrmex doesn't know he's there. "That's all it needed. Cleared nicely now. Shall we go in?"

The three of us. Doors and the windows all opening. *Oh!*

"Next time."

Euphranor smiles, catching my veil as I pass him on my way back up the hill, and trails its full white length through his fingertips before he lets it go.

Shouting from the distance. Nico and Herpyllis, on the blanket, look up from their perusal of the sweets. They look at me; I shrug. Then we can make it out: Demetrios calling his master. "He's at the pond," I tell Herpyllis. "I just left him there. I'll get him."

Back down the slope, the ghost of my veil reeling me back down and in. But there's only Myrmex, supine in the goldenrod, who starts when he sees me and covers himself with his hands. The gold is gone, and instead he's pink all over from the exertion of what he's just been doing.

"You haven't seen Euphranor?"

He shudders, sighs.

Back up the slope again, where I find Euphranor listening to a puffing Demetrios, while Nico struggles to ready the horses.

"Your father is injured," Euphranor says curtly. "Where are the others?"

"Mummy went looking for mushrooms," Nico stammers. "Pyrrhaios went with her. I don't know where Myrmex is."

"Injured how?" I look from Euphranor to Demetrios. Neither is smiling.

Demetrios glances at his master, who nods. "Twist of the ankle, Lady," he says. "Already puffed up like a melon. He can't walk on it, but I reckon he'll live."

I'm moving.

"Child, wait." Euphranor hurries to catch up to me. "Do you ride? It might be faster if I were to lead you on your brother's little—"

I start to jog.

Back at the house, Daddy is sitting on a cart as though we've kept him waiting a long time. I hear Demetrios telling his master he left him inside, on a couch.

"What happened?" I climb up beside him to look.

He grunts and lifts his hem. His left ankle is a purple ball. I smell the vomit, though his face and clothes are clean. A lot of pain, then.

"Why do you sit this way?" I whisper. "You're the one who taught me—"

He lets me help him to lying, my hand supporting his heavy head. He lets me lift the good foot onto the bench, and then the bad. White with the pain, now. I scootch one of the silly purple silk cushions under the ankle to elevate it, and tell Nico to get a cold cloth. "Long enough for binding," I tell him. He nods and disappears into the house, ignoring Euphranor. Now who's the soldier?

Daddy is talking about which plant to use for the

compress. "At home," I tell him. "Right now, let's just get home."

He retches once while Nico holds the foot up and I bind his ankle. Euphranor sends Demetrios to look for the others. Myrmex appears and himself wipes Daddy's mouth with a clean damp cloth. Euphranor draws Myrmex aside and says something to him in an undertone I can't hear. I hear Myrmex tell him Daddy needs to be kept warm. They're both frowning, serious, co-operating. Euphranor touches Myrmex's shoulder and points into the house. Myrmex goes inside and comes out a moment later with a fur he tucks around Daddy, against shock. He knows without being told, like Nico and me. More than Demetrios. More than Euphranor.

Herpyllis and Pyrrhaios appear, breathless, leading the horses.

"Where have you been?" Daddy asks, looking up at her, his love. She sits beside him the whole journey home, holding his hand, gazing into his face. There's dirt on her dress and a twig in her hair. When I draw the twig out, she opens the pouch on her hip to show me her dozen creamy, dirty finds.

We will have eggs with mushrooms for supper.

"What about Daddy's farm?" Nico asks in a small voice, and Euphranor promises he'll take us another day, when Daddy's better.

"Agrimony," I tell Daddy. The plant he was trying to remember. "I'll make you an agrimony poultice for the swelling. Try not to move so much."

Daddy, pushing the fur down, says he's hot.

"No, Myrmex is right," I say. "Better hot than cold."

The rest of the ride home we are silent, chastened. I try to remember what we might have left behind at the picnic site, the pond, the field. Food, wine, the blanket, my veil. A small spoonful of Myrmex's pleasure. Herpyllis's virtue.

My sandals, abandoned in the field so I could run.

* * *

Agrimony, what Herpyllis calls cocklebur, grows like a weed along the roadside. I wrap my hands in leather to pluck the leaves, and pile some burs in the courtyard for Nico, who uses them for darts. Cooked with bran and vinegar, the leaves makes a sticky, stinky mess that Daddy soon tires of.

"Lie still," I order. He groans and squirms while I try to wrap a cloth around his pasted ankle, getting smears everywhere, until finally he demands the pot like a sulky child who suddenly can't wait any longer. So now he must stand, and I mustn't watch. I put my hands over my eyes and listen to his effortful dribble, and help him back to lying once he's dropped his clothes back over himself, smearing the poultice even further. As the days go by he complains of headaches, too, and insomnia, and whines if we leave him alone for too long. He makes Myrmex read to him, and—when Myrmex is too slow—me. Herpyllis tries sitting with us, once or twice, but she bores quickly, and Daddy complains when she starts pottering around the room, dusting or straightening the sheets or picking over the flowers she cut for him the night we got home, pinching off the dead bits. She's nervous lately, quick to tears, and when Daddy starts talking about the dead king, she bites her fist and leaves the room.

More and more he talks about the king. His grief now—clouded by the pain in his ankle, maybe—is tinctured by bitterness, until you'd think they never loved each other at all. He rants. Alexander wouldn't listen, wouldn't learn, not so bright after all, just a vicious little boy. Never a man, not really. In the body, but never in the mind.

I am not thinking of Myrmex.

Daddy wrote him letters, hundreds of letters. The army was under orders from no less than Antipater himself to have them included in dispatches, but never once a reply. That's not love, Daddy says. All that he gave him, and never once a word back.

"But he sent all those specimens," I remind him. "Fish skeletons, fossilized birds, dried flowers. To you, no one else. So something reached him."

"I don't doubt my letters reached him," Daddy says stiffly. "As I have just said."

"Not your letters." I hold a cup to his lips for him to sip. Utterly unnecessary, but he's malingering now, a week later, and demands these little services. "Your—thoughts. Your love of him. Those things reached him, and he reached back to you."

"You're a sweet girl," Daddy says.

The next day there's a gleam in his eye I recognize, and fear. With much production, he has himself carried to his study and set up on cushions, with drink and nibbles and books and pen and paper ready to hand. He insists Ambracis sit beside him in case he should need her to fetch anything, leaving all the kitchen work to Thale, who slams the pots just enough to let us know how much she resents the younger woman's easy day. Ambracis, in turn, may not move or rustle or swallow too loudly in case she should throw off Daddy's train of thought; nor may she respond when the baby calls for her. I pass by once or twice and see her sitting miserably while it screams from where Thale has tethered it to the table in the kitchen so she can keep an eye on it and do her chores, too. It quiets when Olympios stops by, but he has work to do. I try to play with it myself a bit, but it knows the difference, and is fretful all the day.

"What's he doing?" I ask Herpyllis, but she doesn't know.

By evening he's ready to show us: drawings. Designs, actually, for statues of his dead: of his parents; his brother, Uncle Proxenus, and Proxenus's wife; Daddy's little sister, who died in childbirth when her son, my cousin Nicanor, was a tot. He's with the army now, Nicanor, in the East. We assume he's alive.

"I will have them erected in Stageira," Daddy announces. "The village of my birth. And, in thanks for Nicanor's return, I propose statues of Zeus and Athena also, life-size."

Now I know he is mad.

"Is Nicanor returned?" I say carefully.

Daddy ignores me, carefully rolling his drawings.

"How big *are* Zeus and Athena?" I ask. "In life?"

"Go to your room," Daddy says.

The drawings are tentative, in Daddy's quavering old-man's hand. He intends to commission a famous sculptor, an Athenian named Gryllion, to execute them. He'll send Tycho to deliver the commission. For the next three days, he works and works on his awful drawings, and speaks of nothing else. On the fourth day, Ambracis whispers he is bedridden, and refuses to eat.

I nod, and she shakes her head. We know the pattern.

9 1

❧

Two weeks after the injury, after three days in his room, he summons me to his bedside. He's sitting up, supported by many pillows. His ankle is much less swollen, though he still affects to close his eyes and quiver when I touch it with gentlest fingertips.

"Daughter," he says. "Leave that. I have brought you here today to discuss your future."

Brought me here—as though I haven't been in and out of the room every hour, seeing to his needs while the blackness grips him. Spooning in the broth, steadying the bedpan, flapping the curtain to freshen the air. Combing his hair.

"Piffle," I say.

"You shall marry cousin Nicanor," Daddy says. "Just as soon as he returns from Persia."

A moment of utter smoothness, pure emptiness, before thinking resumes.

"I'm—you—because of—what?" I say.

"Pardon?" Daddy says.

"Pardon?"

"That's better," Daddy says. "You shall marry Nicanor. You remember Nicanor."

"Why?" I say.

"Do you remember Nicanor?"

So he has scripted this, and I must play my part. "I remember him from when I was a baby. I haven't seen him in—twelve summers?"

"What do you remember?"

Running. Trees. Arms around my waist, lifting me to reach a plum. Don't eat it. Give it to Mummy. Come on, Pytho. One for you and one for me. Come on. Hold my hand. Where's your plum?

"Nothing," I say.

"Don't be angry," Daddy says. "I had to."

He shows me the document he's written: his will.

"How many summers is he?"

"Forty-four," Daddy says.

A sound like laughter comes out of me. "No."

Daddy frowns. "Why not?"

"Why?"

He gestures at himself, the bed.

"There's nothing wrong with you," I say.

He looks at his lap.

"How do you even know he's alive?"

"I'm making enquiries."

I shake my head. "I won't."

"Who, then?"

I open my mouth but nothing comes.

"He's a good man," Daddy says. "I remember him very well. A serious, intelligent, kind man. Kin."

I think he's probably dead. I think Daddy will make his enquiries and he will find out Nicanor is dead and then we'll think about who else is kin. That's what I think. I can keep quiet until then.

"Good girl," Daddy says, when I say nothing.

He talks me through the rest of the will. For comic relief, he proposes Theophrastos as an alternative should Nicanor be unable or unwilling. (*Or dead, since he will be dead.*) I contain myself admirably and he notices nothing. He walks me through the slaves, the properties, Nico. Nico will stay with me, that's one thing. I tell him I like that.

"You see," he says, looking up, squeezing my hand.

Myrmex, he says, will be sent back to his own people. I say nothing.

Herpyllis, now.

But here he stops; his face works in pain. I hold his hand until he can talk again.

"She has been good to me," he says. "After your mother—"

He looks at his lap, shakes his head. One tear falls. Two. Two blots on the sheet. He looks back up at me. Straight at me, clear-eyed, and I see the script is gone. "You can live without love," he says. "You think you can't, at your age. I was your age, once, too."

"How do you do that?" I ask.

"You care," he says slowly. "You take care. You care for the body and the mind, you behave kindly, you are generous. You put her needs before your own. Sweet food, fresh air, clean clothes, safety. You offer these things. You offer the warmth of yourself. As to a baby. For me, it helped to think of her as a baby, or a little girl. You can offer so much affection and care, who would know the difference?"

"Is that what you did?"

He touches my cheek. "Not always as well as I could have. But if I could do it all again, I would do it that way."

"Do you not—" I begin, but can't finish the sentence.

"Love you?" Daddy says. "Did you think I was talking about you? Little Pythias. Did you think I was talking about you?"

When we are both back inside ourselves again, he tells me what he's planned for Herpyllis. He is generous: choice of properties, money, furniture, everything she might want.

"There is one more thing," Daddy says. "I want her to marry. I want her to have that, if she wants it. I want to give her what she needs, in memory of all my gratitude towards her. If she wants it."

"I think she might," I say.

"I think I'll give her Pyrrhaios, also," Daddy says. "She's used to living with servants."

Without looking at him to see what he does or doesn't know, is or isn't saying, I agree that's a fine idea.

"We shall all be brave," Daddy says. "The worst never lasts long. Especially if you've thought through all the alternatives, and you have a plan."

And that, when you think about it, is a very fine idea indeed.

In my room—twilight, curtains drawn—the brazier sends up a single thread of acrid smoke, the stink of burning hair. I do it in whispers.

> *Bring to perfection this binding spell in order that he may never have experience of another than me alone, Pythias, daughter of Aristotle; that he be enslaved, driven mad, fly through the air in search of me, that he bring his thigh to my thigh and his nature to my nature, always and for the rest of his life. Drag him by the hair and the guts to me. Burn, torch his soul, his*

> *body, his limbs. Lay him low with fever, unceasing sickness, incomprehensible sickness, until he comes to me. Take away his sleep until he comes to please my soul. Lead him, loving, burning on account of his love and desire for me, Pythias, daughter of Aristotle. Impel, force him to come to me, to love me, to give me what I want. Now, now, quickly, quickly.*

"Are you insane?"

Herpyllis stands with her hands on her hips while Daddy, happy as a dog, whaps his head vigorously to one side, trying to drain the water from his ear. His cheeks are a rude pink and his hair is still damp.

"Not at all!" he shouts, swim-deafened. "We're going again tomorrow."

When he's limped off to look for a towel, Herpyllis rounds on me. "You'll kill him."

I wring the cloth he wrapped around his parts into the plants.

"Idiot!" Herpyllis snatches it from me. "That's salt water. You'll kill my herbs. Where did you take him, anyway?"

"The beach just north of the channel. He can walk when he wants to, you know, so long as he has his stick. It's not that far."

"Swimming." Herpyllis spits onto the ground. "Give this to Ambracis. She can take it to the river when she goes with the other laundry. In the sea, in his condition."

"He gets exercise that way with no pressure on the ankle." I take the wet wad back from her. "You saw his face. It cheers him up like you wouldn't—"

"You'll kill him." Grumbling now, though, instead of angry. "Well, that'll be on your head. Does he even remember how to swim?"

I'd sat on a rock while he undressed. His skin was so pale, age-freckled, and he had soft flab in places I'd never seen. Still, it was as though the ghost of a younger man inspirited his body, guided his movements; he had the unconscious confidence of actions he'd been performing for six decades. He'd said nothing to me during the walk, a walk he didn't resist; he was too far gone. I held his arm, and he leaned heavily on me. I could smell the old-man smell of him, the must, and hear the effort of his breathing. At the beach I simply told him to undress, and he did. I told him to go in. He looked at me, then dropped his stick and limped into the surf. At knee-depth he put his hands over his head and dived. It took him a long time to come up. I made the decision not to go in after him. Instead, I dug at the sand with my toes, working my feet in and in and in until I found wet.

"Pytho!"

A long way out, one arm in the air. Holding something up. I walked down to the shore, lifting up my skirts, and he swam in to meet me and hand me his find: an anemone. Immediately he turned back, and dived down again.

I gave the anemone to Tycho and lay back on the rock, eyes closed.

"He remembers," I say to Herpyllis.

That night he calls me to his study and we dissect his specimens. He lets me slit the underbelly of an orange starfish he kept damp, and therefore alive, so I can see the contraction of the muscles, the death-wince. He shows me the anemone's mouth, a star-shaped, petalled orifice, and explains its digestion. He shucks a clam and sets me the exercise of describing it, both in words and drawings. When I bid him goodnight and gather the papers up to take to my room, he asks if he might keep them with his own notes. I go to sleep thinking about my drawings on his desk. This is the first time he's asked to keep any work of mine.

We start going to the beach every afternoon. Nico whines when we try to get him to come; he's befriended a local boy and they're off together most days, whooping through the trees with the puppy and annoying the neighbours. Herpyllis too refuses to come, though not angrily; she stands in the doorway, waving fondly, and is there to greet us with a big dry towel when we return. She bustles busily around us, ignoring the servants. Pyrrhaios is nowhere to be seen. Well. Mentally I superimpose my drawings of our specimens—the labial moistness of the clam, the petalled orifice of the anemone's throat, the spasms of the dying starfish—on Herpyllis's hole.

Daddy, basking in his new mobility, swims a little longer each day even as the weather cools. Fall is coming, singeing the trees red and prettying Daddy, who rises from the waves all steaming in the cold, holding the cloth around his parts with one hand and clutching shellfish to his breast with the other, my very own Aphrodite of the Specimens. His eyes are clearer, and he smiles sometimes. Occasionally he makes a little joke. He has a permanent limp now, but no longer complains of it; it's become a part of him. Once I watched him wade through the shallows, looking for limpets, quietly singing. Each day

I ask him how he's feeling. "Quiet," he'll say, or "Steady." Once, a day like any other, he told me he thought he felt joy.

"You think?" I said.

He shrugged. After a moment's carefully considered silence, we looked at each other and laughed.

That evening, after supper, he says he wants to swim the channel where it's narrowest. "The soldiers do it just as the tide's turning," he says. "I've watched them. Pushed one way by the current, then the other. Good fun."

"Nonsense," Herpyllis says.

"Fun *and* science," Daddy says. "It's a unique phenomenon. Awfully famous."

"You're already awfully famous," Herpyllis says. "What on earth are you going to learn from being pushed around in the current like a fig in a custard?"

"Ah," Daddy says. "But you see, I intend to dive. To observe the behaviour of the marine life during the phenomenon. I shall gather—"

"—specimens—" Nico, Herpyllis, and I say with one voice.

"—and study them," Daddy says serenely. "For my book."

Herpyllis rolls her eyes. Nico runs off to find the puppy.

"A new one?" I ask.

"A collaboration," Daddy says.

I can't imagine who with; Theophrastos is still in Athens. Then he smiles and I blush.

"You'll come watch me, won't you, pet?" he asks. "Hold my towel? Cheer me on?"

Tycho's a shadow in the doorway.

"Can Tycho come, too?" I ask.

Daddy nods. Tycho disappears.

"You like him," Daddy says. "You trust him. I think I'll amend my will and give him to you, when you get married."

I say, "Ah."

"You remind me," Daddy says. "I'll do it after my swim. Let's go check the charts for the tide."

It turns out the optimal time is dawn. "Seriously?" I say, thinking of my warm bed. "Couldn't we just wait twelve hours?"

"It'll be dark by then," Daddy says.

"Dawn's pretty dark, too."

"Lazy pet. You'll survive one early morning. Have you ever seen the colour of the sky that early in the day? The sun comes up like fine wine."

I pretend to shudder and he smiles that rare, sweet smile.

I'm woken by the tap of his fingers on my door jamb, while the sky is still black and the cock is still sleeping. I tie my hair back uncombed into a pony tail, and put on my warmest clothes. It's really cold; hoarfrost on the grass.

Once we're away from the houses and our voices won't disturb anyone, I exhale hard, like Nico trying to offend me with his garlic breath, to make a white plume in the air. "There must be fire in us," I say to Daddy. "Or something like embers. In the heart, maybe? To make smoke like this?"

Daddy says nothing.

At the narrowest part of the channel, we pick our way down the rocky slopes to the water. Daddy starts to undress.

"Ho!" calls a man passing on the near bank with a horse and cart.

"Good morning!" Daddy calls back, undressing.

"Is he sick?" the man calls to me.

I shake my head.

"Look, he's got milk," Daddy says. "Take some coins from my bag, there, and my cup, and get some for after my swim. It's early enough; it's probably still warm."

"I'll do it," I tell Tycho. *Stay with him.*

I pick my way up the slope, holding my skirts up, while the man waits, staring at Daddy. When I hold out the coin, he asks me again if Daddy is sick. I shake my head.

"Then he's an idiot." The man fills Daddy's cup with milk, which steams in the cold. I realize how stupid my idea was. Embers in the heart, seriously. That's why Daddy didn't reply. "The current's about to change. You're not from here, are you?"

"He knows about the current."

"He doesn't know anything." There's a splash and the man cries out. Daddy's in. The man says an evil word. He reaches under his seat for a length of rope and jumps down awkwardly from his cart. He hands me the horse's reins and tells me not to let go. He scrabbles down the bank, tripping once, but doesn't stop to inspect the scrape to his knee which, even from here, I can see is bleeding. Daddy is mid-channel now, treading water in what seems to be a lull. The man coils the rope, then tosses the end to Daddy. Confused, Daddy reaches for the end, but it drifts out of his reach. Now Daddy is moving, but not swimming. He dives.

The man asks Tycho what the evil word Daddy thinks he's

doing, and did Tycho and I come down here to help him kill himself, and if so we're evil words ourselves. I feel his anger on me like spit. Beside me, the horse shifts and snuffles nervously. It pulls its head against the reins, testing me, smelling inexperience. Smelling girl.

People on both banks have stopped to watch now, adults and children with early-morning business. The sky has indeed gone tender, pink and frail and fine. A shout goes up from the onlookers: Daddy has surfaced, considerably north of where he went in. He's trying to swim back to us, but the current is holding him prisoner, and he's swimming hard just to stay still. People are shouting and waving their arms, *That way, that way*, wanting him to swim with the current rather than against it. He dives again.

The crowd makes a soft, hurt sound, fist to the gut.

I scan the crowd for someone I recognize: one of the men from Plios's party, a soldier, Euphranor himself? But it's too early in the morning for the quality, and all I see are slaves, market-women, vagrants. Each face shows horror.

The milkman is beside me. "Come on," he says. "He'll wash up on the beach there." He points towards our swimming beach. "If he washes up."

I climb up onto the cart beside him and he *tchas* the horse into a trot. At the head of the beach path, he ties the reins to a stump. Tycho and I run on ahead.

The beach is empty.

"No," the man says, puffing up behind me. "No, no, no," like he's forbidding me something. My arm shoots out to point to something far out in the bay: a head. The man strips angrily to pudge-buttocked bareness and wades in, then dives. Tycho is ahead of him. Tycho swims out to Daddy and brings him back, expertly, in a kind of swimming headlock. When they're fifty paces out, I wade in myself, waist-deep, to help bring him the rest of the way. Daddy's face is white and his eyes are closed.

On the sand, Tycho wraps his own clothes around Daddy and rubs him hard all over his body. The onlookers have caught up with us now, and someone has a blanket for the milkman. I rub Daddy the way Tycho does, sitting beside him on the sand, propping him up against my body. Tycho is blue-lipped and shivering convulsively now.

Someone dumps a blanket over Tycho's shoulders, and another over my legs. Perhaps I'm crying.

"Pythias," Daddy says quietly, without opening his eyes.

The crowd exhales. The air goes white from the ember in every chest.

At home, Herpyllis proves she could have made a soldier. She has Daddy put to bed wrapped in sheets warmed with stones heated in the fire; gives the milkman a set of new clothes, a hot meal, and a bag of coins; thanks Tycho; and slaps me across the face.

She spends the rest of the day at Daddy's bedside, spooning hot broth into his mouth and singing to him like she does to Nico when he gets a tummy ache. I can hear her soft voice from my bedroom, which she's ordered me not to leave.

Daddy soon gets a cold. He snots and sneezes and aches all

over, he says, and where is Pythias? Herpyllis relents, and lets me in to see him.

"Hello, pet," he says.

I ask him how he's feeling. Herpyllis snorts.

"Fine, fine," he says, and then he coughs until his face goes purple. He waves angrily at Herpyllis to leave the room.

"It's nothing," he says, when the coughing stops. "She's hysterical."

"She's not."

He pats the bedside and I sit. "She loves us both," he says. "She knows you were trying to help."

I hold his hand for a while, his baby-soft hand.

"A child is a line cast blind to the future," he says. "Like an idea, or a book. Who knows where it will land, or what it will draw out?"

I ask him if he'd like me to write that down.

"No, pet," he says. "That's just for you."

I think we're both joking.

The cough stays with him. He begins to cough up a yellowish thickness that Herpyllis says is a good sign; it's the sickness coming out. He runs a low fever and has shivering fits. He eats little and drenches the sheets with night sweats. Still, he gets up sometimes, to use the pot or sit for short periods in the garden in the thin autumn sun. He asks for books, not to read, but just to hold on his lap. Sometimes I read to him. When he coughs, now, he holds a hand to his chest against the pain. His lips are permanently blue. Moving from bed to chair is enough to make him gasp like a runner at the end of a race. He takes to coughing into a cloth. Herpyllis does his laundry, angrily forbidding me or the servants to help. She thinks she can carry this secret by herself.

After a week of coughing blood, he lies down to die. It takes four more days. He complains of stabbing pains in his side, and his skin takes on a blue tinge all over.

"What did you see?" I ask him, late one night. I'm sitting with him so Herpyllis can sleep a bit. "What did you see down there, Daddy?"

His shallow breaths rasp like a saw.

When the cock crows, I go to wake Herpyllis. She takes one look at Daddy and sends me to get Nico, and Myrmex and everyone. The slaves, everyone. *Now, now, quickly, quickly.*

He's still breathing when we get back.

Herpyllis herself lays the coin on his tongue, and together we bathe him and dew him with sweet oil. We dress him warmly in white for his journey, and when Thale returns from the meadow with a basket of fall flowers we weave a tiny wildflower garland for his lovely head: creamy fall anemones, purple crocuses, white winter violets, pink cyclamen. Herpyllis puts the honey cake for the dog in his hand and holds his fingers closed over it until they stiffen. We wear our darkest clothes to contrast Daddy, to show we are still with the living, and the pain of that.

The next day is the laying-out. Pyrrhaios and Tycho carry the bed to the front hall and point his feet to the door. Herpyllis, Nico, Myrmex, and I sit around him, fanning away the flies. To Thale falls the coming and going: fetching white jars from the market for perfumes to keep the body bearable, sweeping up the dried marjoram and strewing fresh on the floor, trying to get the four of us to drink and Nico to take a bit of bread. Herpyllis rips her hair from its pins and lets it hang; I pull mine out, slowly, strand by strand, until Herpyllis takes my hands in hers and says enough. *Enough;* though she comes back from a visit to the pot with bloody claw-marks on both cheeks and on the tops of her breasts. When she forbids me to do the same, I know she's worried about scarring before my marriage. I touch my fingertips to her blood, instead, and swipe it onto my face, where it mixes with the tears and eventually dries. We are quiet, against tradition—no keening—but we know it's what Daddy would want.

On the third day is the procession. Herpyllis has left the body only to use the pot and put Nico to bed. Herpyllis and Myrmex and I dozed sitting up with him and are weak with hunger and exhaustion now. We set out before sunrise. Pyrrhaios, Simon, Tycho, and Myrmex carry the bed. Behind them walk the singers Thale found, sisters from Caria who know the old mourning songs. Professionals: their voices are thin and bird-like, their eyes blank. Nico and I come last, holding hands; Herpyllis—no marriage, no tie of blood—stands in the doorway, watching us go.

We walk away from the sunrise, to the road into town, to the markers we passed when we first arrived. The gravesman is waiting by a hole in the ground. Nico steps forward to help lift Daddy into the clay coffin. "On his side," the gravesman says. The only thing he says. They lay Daddy on his side like a sleeping child so that when he's lowered into the ground he'll face west. We take turns approaching him. Myrmex places the three white perfume jars at Daddy's head and hands and feet. I put a book of seashell sketches inside his clothes, against his breast, because his arms and hands are too stiff now to manoeuvre into an embrace, and at any rate he's still holding the dried-up cake. Nico is last. He has the lamp Herpyllis gave him, and a tablet and stylus of his own. I notice he glances up at Pyrrhaios as he's placing them by Daddy's hands and Pyrrhaios nods, *That's right.*

The gravesman closes the coffin and the men lower it, suspended on ropes, into the hole. They shovel the dirt over and erect the marble stone. Thale hands me the basket of olives, honey and wildflowers, which I place on the grave. Myrmex pours a cup of milk over the raw earth, and it's done.

When we get home—all but Myrmex, who peeled away from us into town—Herpyllis is holding a letter that came by courier while we were at the grave. Theophrastos will host the funeral feast for Daddy's colleagues and students—*those who were closest to him,* he writes—in Athens.

Daddy is travelling. The coin will be gone by now, and the cake. He's on his way.

We sit in the public room in the home of Thaulos, a high-ceilinged reception room with severe furniture and only a single small brazier in one corner. Herpyllis is in the middle of a couch with Nico on one side and me on the other, a wing around each of us. My hair is cropped short, like a boy's; Nico's will be allowed to grow shaggy.

"The children have been ill," she says, when neither of us answers his greeting.

She still wears her darkest dress, sweat-smelling after so many days without washing, and no make-up; her eyes are a mess. Nico drones softly to himself, a wordless keening. He's been doing this for days. I find it important not to speak. Each word feels precious, suddenly, and so many words are so utterly unnecessary.

"Your father named Antipater as executor of his will," Thaulos begins. Antipater, regent of Macedon, my father's old friend. "I stand here today as his proxy."

"I thank you," Herpyllis says.

Thaulos takes a breath to speak, then changes his mind. He rubs his forehead, reading over the paper in front of him. Finally he looks up. "It's a pickle, isn't it?" he says kindly.

We can only breathe.

"I've sent word to your father's school in Athens, to"—he squints at the paper—"Theophrastos, and to the nephew, in dispatches. His unit is still in Babylon. Nicanor, yes? Your intended?" He's looking at me.

"He's dead," I say.

"Shh." Herpyllis kisses my hair.

"Nicanor is dead."

Thaulos looks surprised.

"He's dead," I say again.

"Then you have better intelligence than I do." He smiles gently at his own joke. "I've received no such report. The army prides itself on accuracy in such matters. I wish I'd known you had such worries. I could have eased your mind."

"Is he coming home?" Herpyllis asks.

Now Thaulos frowns.

"They've been coming home ever since they left," I say. "Years ago. That's what Daddy always said. All we can do is wait."

"Your father had a unique insight into the mind of our king," Thaulos says. "I think his great wisdom guides us even now."

"She has the spark of him in her," Herpyllis says. "She always did."

I go blank for a few seconds, and when I come back they're discussing Herpyllis's future.

"Of course," she's saying, bowing her head obediently. "Of course."

"You have people there still?"

"A sister," Herpyllis says. "Cousins."

"And the boy will go to Theophrastos."

"Myrmex, you mean." Herpyllis nods.

Thaulos looks at the papers again.

"Mummy?" Nico says.

"*Nicanor shall take charge of the boy Myrmex, that he be taken to his own friends in a manner worthy of me with the property of his which we received,*" Thaulos reads. "Orphan, is he? No, I mean the other boy. This fine fellow here. Would you like to go to school? Nicomachos, is it? I'm sure it's what your father would have wanted for you."

Nico screams, a high thin sound like a hawk. Herpyllis

lets go of me to put both her arms around him. Her shoulders are shaking.

Thaulos, obviously startled, stands. I stand, too, while Herpyllis and Nico hold each other, weeping. With a look, he bids me follow him over to the window, where they won't hear us. We look out on a drill team going through manoeuvres. "And you?" he says.

I wait.

"You can go to Athens with your brother." Watching his soldiers, Thaulos stands taller with unconscious pride. "I'm familiar with your father's concerns, but I can reassure you that they were—overstated, shall we say. Macedon controls Athens. You will be safe there."

I thank him.

"I suppose you could go with the woman, alternatively," he muses. "Like a mother to you, is she? A girl needs a mother. You could wait with her in Stageira for your intended. Confidentially, I suspect the army will move quickly now to return home. Now that the king's ambitions are no longer—"

"Now that there is no longer a god to lead them," I say.

Thaulos looks at his feet.

"How long?" I ask.

"Months. A year at most, I'd guess, for all of them to return. Think about it. I have a daughter myself, though younger than you. I understand there are preparations for a marriage? Certain information to be passed on? Household management and so on? And then learning how to care for all the little ones to come?"

I think he is a kind daddy.

"I'll leave your decision to the wisdom you've inherited from your father." He gives me the paper and holds a hand towards the door, conducting us out. Nico is quiet now, and he and Herpyllis have both risen. Our interview is done. "He will guide you."

"Always," I say.

Outside, Pyrrhaios leans down to murmur something in Nico's ear. Nico stands a little straighter, wiping his face, and Pyrrhaios briefly puts a hand on his shoulder. He must have heard everything. Herpyllis walks slowly, already trying to delay the inevitable.

At home, I find Myrmex and give him the paper. He reads it slowly, then once more, even more slowly. I realize he's drunk.

"'Taken to his own friends in a manner worthy of me with the property of his which we received.'" Myrmex spits at my feet. "What property? What friends?"

"I don't know," I whisper.

He reads a third time. "There was a bag," he says slowly. "They gave me a bag to give to your father, when I left home, when I came to Athens. It was sewn closed. I bet it was money. My money."

I want to kiss him.

"Your brother'll give it to me, if you won't."

"I've been in the storeroom," I say, stupidly. "I've never seen such a bag." I stand up so he can press himself against me if he wants to.

"Tight as your father," he sneers. And off he goes to rant at poor terrified Nico, until Herpyllis flaps him away like she flaps the chickens with her skirts.

"I'll get what's mine," Myrmex says. "I'll find a way."

He clangs out of the front gate, leaving it bouncing behind him.

Herpyllis begins packing. Nico sits in a corner, his gaze following her everywhere. Sometimes he rocks a little. Herpyllis's eyes are now so raw and swollen I fear infection. She lets me examine her. I make her cold compresses with bruised mint, but, privately, I fear whatever prettiness she might once have had is gone forever.

The next morning, Myrmex still isn't back.

"He needs to grieve," Herpyllis says. "Not everyone can share grief." She puts aside what she's been doing, some last mending for Nico, and pats the couch beside her. "I've been wanting to speak to you, Pytho."

I sit.

"What I said when you took him swimming that first time," she begins. "About how it would be on your head."

I shake my head to show I know she didn't mean it that way.

"No, you listen," she says. "You're going to let me say it aloud. You didn't do this. You didn't make it, you didn't wish it, you didn't cause it in any way. You were not the cause. Neither material, formal, efficient, nor final."

I look at her.

"That was a joke," she says.

We embrace for a long time while Nico watches us silently from his corner. When Herpyllis finally releases me and I stand, he comes to take my place. I sit back down, and she and I hold him from both sides.

Herpyllis leaves for Stageira the next morning, with Pyrrhaios and everything else accorded her in the will. Some very nice furniture. While she and Nico hug fiercely, I give them the gift I've been saving to make their parting possible.

"You'll both come to my wedding," I say. "It'll only be a few months to wait, and then you'll be together again."

Herpyllis embraces me, and it's only then I realize—stupidly—she's actually leaving me, too. "Who loves you?" she whispers into my hair.

You do.

"There, that's not so bad, is it?" she says to Nico. He sniffles a smile. She kisses my cheek, crushes him to her one last time, and mounts the waiting cart. "Kiss Myrmex for me," she calls.

Nico pulls me inside to find Daddy's map of the East, to figure out exactly where his mother is going and how long until Nicanor might make it home from the wars. I play along, gravely calculating, trying to factor in rivers and seasons.

We eat a quiet supper together in the innermost courtyard, the one with the lavender. Nico will leave for Athens and Theophrastos in the morning; Thaulos has offered to convey him with some troops who are shifting there. He'll be most utterly safe at school—Theophrastos loves him like a dog loves a ball. I tell him I'll be back in Athens myself very soon, once everything in Daddy's will is wrapped up here. There are matters to be seen to, bills to be paid, loose ends to be tied.

"Where's Myrmex?" Nico asks.

"I don't know."

Nico looks at me with his big, dark, clear eyes.

We go together to the storeroom and consider the iron bars holding the door.

"Nico, he wouldn't," I say. "He'd had too much to drink, that's all. Everyone grieves differently."

"Who's got the key?" Nico says.

Thale, it turns out; Herpyllis gave it to her before she left, telling her to give it to me when I was ready.

The door swings open easily, silently; recent oiling. Bags of corn and beans and lentils and flour; seeds, dried herbs, squash; the first apples of the year. Wine, lamp oil, cooking oil, torches, wool.

"Lady," Thale whispers.

Every last coin is gone.

Who am I to be making decisions? Who am I? An orphan, a pauper. A girl. Thinking thinking thinking smiling smiling smiling. Grace matters now.

"But how did he get in?" Nico says.

"Before Herpyllis left, probably. Sometimes she left the key lying around in the kitchen, on market days when she was in and out of there a lot."

"It's not her fault."

"Of course not." I reassure Nico, reassure the servants. "Silly boy," I say, over and over, meaning Myrmex. "He'll be back."

"Lady," they say. I read their doubts, but they'll take the lead from me. There's no one else. Late at night, I count the coins I keep in my own little purse, with my clothes in the trunk in my room. I can afford a week; two, at most.

Of course I forgive him.

Once the stars are up and the house is quiet, I go to wake Tycho, who sleeps by the front gate. "Come," I say.

We walk down to the beach. I expected some objection—he's been with us so long, Tycho, that occasionally he'll risk some such—but he says nothing. Standing on the sand, we both stare into the black water.

"I should have followed him in," Tycho says. "Lady, forgive me."

I walk straight down to the water's edge, then keep walking.

The water is cold and then colder; the plunge stops my heart. I surface gasping and look back. Tycho is watching me.

I dive again, eyes open. There's a faint phosphorescence in the water that licks me greeny-gold. I sob under the surface, come up to breathe, go down again to let more tears go. I'm almost done when I hear Tycho's deep call.

"Almost," I call back. "Almost."

I chose night on purpose; no one to see me, no one to shock. Girls don't swim. But when I wade up onto the sand, my dress plastered to me, cold past feeling, I see a light back in the trees.

"Quickly," Tycho says, wrapping his wool around me. He's seen it, too.

Movement through the trees; someone walking.

We come out onto the road in silence, my wet feet chafing in my sandals. I know Tycho wants to throw me over his shoulder and carry me, like he used to when I was little. Whoever's got the lamp cut through the trees to come out ahead of us; we see the chip of light, still now, waiting. Tycho makes himself bigger—a trick he has, like a bear—and puts himself between me and the light.

"Is it Pythias?" a familiar voice calls, before we can make out the speaker.

"Stop," Tycho orders the voice.

The lamp is held up to a face: Euphranor. "I'll walk you home," he says.

He goes in front and Tycho walks behind. At our door, Euphranor says, "I heard about your father."

I nod.

"Anything at all you need."

"Nothing," I say.

He bows and vanishes back into the trees, lamp extinguished now.

I give Tycho back his smelly wool, damp now, and he settles down in his sleeping spot. In my room I strip off my wet clothes and get into bed, where I sleep dreamlessly and wake clear-headed, my hair stiff with salt water. In the kitchen, Ambracis is serving Nico while Thale feeds the baby. Nico will leave as soon as he's finished breakfast.

I ask Ambracis to prepare me a bath.

"To prepare for your journey, Lady?" Thale says.

I give Nico some coins and tell him not to spend them all on cake.

"Come with me, Pytho," he pleads. "You can't stay here without money."

And weave in my room for the rest of my life, obeying Theophrastos? I indicate the coins. "I have money."

"You'll go to your mother, then?" Thale says. "In Stageira?"

The rustic life, far from books or even the possibility of books. I shake my head. "And what about Myrmex?" I ask. "If—*when* he comes back, where else will he come back to?"

"And if he doesn't?" Nico says.

"He will."

I walk Nico up to the garrison, where the leader is waiting for us. Nico is pale but contained; I'm proud of him. I tell him so, quietly, and he nods.

"Theophrastos loves you," I say.

"I know."

I kiss him, and he squeezes my hand. He won't hug me, not in front of all these soldiers. I expect them to show him to a cart, but Thaulos asks him if he'd like to ride. A horse is brought out, a lively, pretty thing. The men's faces soften when Nico's lights up.

He'll be fine.

I walk back to the house. Tycho goes in ahead of me while

I linger outside in the garden, picking a few flowers for a vase for my room. Blue, purple, white. Athens, Stageira, Chalcis.

My husband will return, and then we'll see.

I go in and close the gate behind me. First, I'll have my bath.

II

I'm in bed. When did that happen? Thale is sitting by me with her sweet old worried face, waiting to cluck and coo and spoon broth into me.

Sometimes I sleep.

It occurs to me that I'm alone.

I get up to use the pot and stagger, dizzy; arms catch mine on either side. I'm back in bed and there is a plate of fruit slices, a cup of milk. I would rather like a tonic, but there is no one to authorize that. I lie back and feel like a jellyfish, spreading and sinking into the bed. I cry very, very quietly but they catch me anyway. Gentle wiping of my face, a cool cloth for my forehead. My nose blown for me. *Blow, Lady,* like I'm three. Someone changes the sheets; someone changes me. I keep my eyes closed. Then I'm asleep for real.

Sometimes I forget. I forget the loss of them all for minutes at a time. The mouth in my stomach opens wide and yawns and I eat the fruit slices, take the spoonfuls of broth, sip at the milk. I'm surprised that no one is surprised by me, but then I remember they've spent years caring for Daddy, and must think I've fallen to his illness.

I start to think. There is the rational mind and the animal body. The animal body forces the thoughts away, does the forgetting; I'm ashamed how often the animal asserts itself. Food! Sleep! Rubbing the parts when Thale has gone to the kitchen for a minute! I understand, finally, that Daddy suffered so because he was practically all mind and no animal; he could never forget. I am lesser. Is it because I'm a girl? Daddy would say so. But that theory doesn't account for the animal natures of Nico, of Myrmex.

O Myrmex.

I get angry. How dare he betray us? How dare he leave me?

Then I'm up. I'm up and bathing and dressed and eating a fish on the stone terrace. I'm terribly thin; I hear Thale tell Simon. The baby smiles at me in big surprise and holds her arms up to me. Uppies, uppies! I pick her up. She kicks and squirms in the air for a moment, unsure, and then I bring her in to my chest for a hug. She touches my hair solemnly, touches my cheek. She looks into my eyes. Hers are brown, clean and clear. "Who's pretty?" I ask, and she says, "Me!"

Daddy's study is neat and tidy, and I'm not sure where to begin. I call Simon to help me. He shows me where Daddy kept the household accounts, and explains Herpyllis's system of the bowl on the high shelf with the money for marketing. I know that bowl. He suggests I write to Theophrastos about Myrmex's betrayal. He tells me today is a market day, and I give him money from my little purse. He hesitates.

"No meat," I tell him. He nods.

That is my first command as lady of the house.

I'm taking an inventory of the storeroom with Thale and

Ambracis when Tycho comes to say we have a visitor. *I* have a visitor: Thaulos. Tycho says he called twice while I was sick, but they sent him away.

I receive him in the formal front room. Ambracis brings a tray of walnuts and hot tea.

"Feeling better?" Thaulos asks. It's been a month since the reading of the will.

I bow my head, assenting in silence like a lady. *Silence garlands a woman and perfumes her.* I read that somewhere.

"I'm glad of it," he says. "I was sorry to hear of your condition. Nerves, was it?"

I bow my head.

"Nerves." He nods, pooching his lips judiciously, agreeing with his own diagnosis. "Well. You're getting the pink back, though, and that's what counts, eh?" He toasts me with his tea and winks.

Poor man. He must be terribly uncomfortable. I offer him a walnut.

"I'm afraid this isn't just a social visit." He inspects the walnut before he puts it in his mouth. Chews, swallows. Sips his tea. I'm doing very well so far. "I'm obliged to bring a financial concern to your attention. A rather pressing concern. Ah, gods." He puts a walnut back on the plate. "This is awful. Only it's about the house."

"This house?" I ask politely.

"There was supposed to be—" He looks vaguely around the room, clearly wishing there was someone else he could talk to, some man.

"Money?" I say.

He looks like I've slapped him.

"Is that the concern?"

He puts his cup on the table and leans forward. "You shouldn't have to deal with all this. You're just a child."

"There's no one else."

"The fellow in Athens, your father's—"

"There's no one else. How much do we owe?"

He doesn't answer.

"Myrmex told us he won the house in a bet," I say. "That must have been a lie. How much do I owe?"

He blinks, then tells me a sum.

"To you personally?"

He shakes his head. "To one of my officers. This was his house. I explained the situation to him and he was very—"

"Did Myrmex give him anything at all?"

He shows me his empty palms.

I look at my tea. Thinking thinking.

Thaulos says, "Perhaps I should be speaking with the boy himself, with—"

"Myrmex?"

"Does he have another name? 'Little Ant.' That's a child's nickname."

"That's what we've always called him," I say. *Jason* was for me and no one else; he never even told it to Herpyllis. "He's not here."

"Where is he?"

I explain and Thaulos listens. Sometimes I can see the father in him, sometimes the soldier. He stands. Perhaps the pettiness of our domestic relationships has disgusted him. "You need your father's man in Athens to act for you," he says. "And you need a husband. I'll send another request in dispatches to find out where your fellow is. What is he, infantry?"

"Cavalry."

He's looking around the room, at the furnishings. I send my mind chasing his, and then with a rush I pass him. "How much for a first payment?"

He's looking at a little ivory owl on a side table. He looks at me. I bow my head so I don't have to see him take it.

When I look up again he's on his feet. "You need to come up with the difference." His voice is harsh. He doesn't like taking owls from little girls. "If you don't come up with the difference, you'll have to leave. You understand it's a legal matter. I have no influence."

I bow my head.

"I want to help you, but I—"

Ambracis comes in with cheese.

"I'll be off." I stand to face him. "I'll be in touch about your intended. A word of advice. If that young man comes back—"

"Myrmex?"

"Act happy to see him, then send for me."

I thank him.

"And I'll send a courier tomorrow."

My face must be a question.

"For the next payment."

I bow my head in a fragrant silence.

"And this is real Persian silk," the widow says. "Touch, go on. All these beautiful things are for enjoying. Sight is the least of the senses, I often think. We have tongues and toes and fingertips for a reason, no?"

She's already had me step out of my sandals so I can walk barefoot across a deep sheepskin rug. Now she's showing me a painted rose-silk curtain that falls from ceiling to floor. She coaxes it into my hands so I can feel the coolness of it; the tiny imperfections in the skin of my fingertips catch on the sheer surface. She takes the fabric back to rub against her cheek, then twirls her whole body in it. She makes me try. I feel the sheer cool all down the length of me, everything looking pink.

The house of Glycera smells of quince and spice. We settle into a private room, one wall open to a flower garden, for our weaving. She has a large cloth half done, and a new frame for me.

"Where are your daughters?" I ask.

She offers me a basket with many spools of coloured threads. I choose a blue. "I thought, for today, just you and me." She takes orange for herself and we begin. "How are you feeling?" she asks without looking up from her work.

It's the doorway I've been waiting for, the reason for my visit today. I tell her about Myrmex, and Thaulos, and the little owl, followed by the perfume bottle shaped like an almond, and the gold wire bracelet, and the new vase with the wrestlers on it—the one without the chip.

Glycera sets down her thread and looks at me. "You should have come to me three days ago." Cooler than I had expected, hoped.

"How do I find Myrmex?"

She does smile then, gently. "Sweetheart, you don't. He and that money are gone. *Why* do you not tell your father's man in Athens? Could he not pay?"

"He'd make me go live with him," I say. I realize how stupid an objection that sounds. "He doesn't like me. He thinks I talk too much. I'd have to spend all day indoors and eat with the women."

"That's all?" Glycera turns back to her weaving.

"He'd choose my books."

"And that's so important to you?"

I have to think about that. When did I last read a book?

"I think it is," she says. "I think it's very important to you."

"Is it?" I say. My face hurts, suddenly, from the effort of not crying.

"I can read, you know." She selects another thread, a rust. "My husband taught me. He liked me to read to him. And sing, and dance. And—talk, really. He loved to talk. We would have wonderful arguments about all sorts of things. Politics and ideas and art. You'd be surprised how many men prize an intelligent woman."

"Theophrastos doesn't."

"Then he's a boor." She sets her work down a second time and repeats the gesture from the party, lifting my chin with a single finger. "Your brows need tweezing."

She lies me down on a couch and sits beside me. She strokes my hair back from my forehead while we wait for the slave to fetch her tools. "So brown," she says. "You spend too much time in the sun. You've been a little wild thing all these years, haven't you? Going about on your own, swimming and reading books all day? Climbing trees, I don't doubt. Was it true, what your father said about healing that slave?"

I tell her it wasn't a bad infection and it probably would have healed itself. I was just a child, playing. The slave brings silver tweezers on a gold tray.

"No more talking now." She leans over me, so close I can feel her breath on my cheek. I close my eyes. She works quickly, expertly, the pinpricks arcing first below, then above the line of my brows. From time to time she presses a fingertip to my skin, firmly, to ease the pain. She smoothes a cool cream on after, for the redness.

"No, stay," she says, when I make to sit up. "I'm going to have a little lie-down, too." She takes the couch across the table from mine and together we contemplate the ceiling. "You asked about my daughters. Can I tell you a secret?"

The ceiling is painted blue with clouds. I'm not sure how to answer. "Yes," I say finally.

"I never had children," she says. "There was something wrong with me, inside. I took those girls in when they fell on hard times. Good girls, good families. But mistakes get made, accidents, misunderstandings, passions—fate can play with a young girl. As you yourself are discovering."

"Before your husband's death, or after?"

"After."

Her voice is light, high, girlish.

"I'm strict in some matters," she's saying. "My girls do as I tell them. I expect beauty and grace and cleanliness and hard work. But they are loved and cared for here. They have good food and lovely clothes and time to themselves to pursue their own interests. They have spending money and freedom, providing they use that freedom in a respectable way."

She sits up and looks at me and I understand that here comes the most important part. I sit up, too.

"All my girls can read," she says, reaching over to tap a finger on my knee. "You'd like it here."

I murmur appropriately, thanking her for her generosity, but demurring.

She cuts me off. "You don't understand," she says. "You'd be safe here."

I think for a moment, then lean forward to kiss her scented cheek.

When I pull back, her eyes are wet. "I know you're confused," she says. "Sweet girl. Think about it, that's all. And if you say no, I won't hold it against you. You'll still be welcome here. Your decisions are all your own, you see? That's what I've been trying to say."

I look at the loom she set up for me, the single line of blue all that I managed.

"I'll leave it there for you," she says. "For whenever you're ready."

"Thank you," I say again.

"Ah!" Her face lights up and she claps her hands. "Here is Meda to see you to the door."

Meda is the darkest-haired of the three, with the palest skin. I remember her from the women's room at the party. She drifts ahead of me, silently, in a dress of palest green gossamer that floats lightly behind her. Her scent is a trail of cinnamon I want to follow into a warm, dark forest, and sleep.

"Please come back," she says at the gate. "We get so lonely for visitors."

"What do you like to read?"

She smiles and touches her fingertips to her throat, *me*?

Tycho stands up from the shadows to escort me home.

❧

"Where does Master Euphranor live?" Tycho asks.

When he plays dumb like this, I want to hit him. "I have no idea," I say sweetly.

He stands there like a mule waiting for the whip.

"Ask at the garrison," I say. "Maybe he lives in barracks."

"Officers don't live in barracks."

"Tycho!"

"Lady," he says.

We stare at each other for a long moment. "Is there something you want to say?" I ask him.

"With your permission."

I nod.

"Your father would have wanted you to be with your brother."

"And Theophrastos."

He nods.

"My father took an interest in the farm. He wanted to visit it himself. He thought it could be made more profitable. I'm doing what my father intended to do."

"What he intended for himself," Tycho says.

"Yes," I say. "Let me know when you've returned. With a reply."

He picks my letter up from the table. "What if I can't—"

"Tycho!"

He goes.

Then it's morning, the next morning, and we're riding, Euphranor and I, he on his black beast and me on Spiffy, under the skeletal black trees on the long lane to the farms. The horses' hooves ring out on the frozen ground. I feel the fizz in me, the wine in my blood. We've left the cart with the lunch and the slaves far behind. He's quiet today, Euphranor, none of the jolly hostliness he patronized Daddy with. That suits me well enough. He smiles tentatively at me from time to time and I think he has a nice face. I like that he knows how to be quiet.

We stop at the entrance to the yard, familiar now: his own farm. Demetrios doesn't appear. Euphranor doesn't move to dismount or make any suggestion at all, so we just sit, silently, resting the horses. Curiosity, that fine edge, is blunted in me since Daddy's death, an irony I'm not curious enough to puzzle through. I sit feeling sad in the bright cold air, the wind moving a few dead, clinging leaves high, high up in the trees. From far away comes the sound of footsteps on gravel, running. Closer and closer. Neither of us moves or looks at the other; I like that.

Tycho appears through the trees. He stops a dozen paces away and simply stands, breathing heavily. Nothing to deliver, nothing to say. I understand he didn't like letting me out of his sight, didn't like me riding with Euphranor unescorted. I understand and dismiss the understanding, let it float out of my mind like fumes. It's not his place to worry about such things, and beneath me to notice a slave's worry. I will let it go.

"We're just over here," Euphranor says, as though he's received some signal I can't hear, like a dog. He's let Tycho catch his breath. Another thought I allow to float away. Noticing an officer noticing a slave, and liking that about him, disliking myself for liking that—it's all too complicated. I open my mind's hand and release the thought like a birdie. *Fly away, don't bother me.*

We ride a few hundred paces farther down the lane to the derelict property we would have visited had Daddy not twisted his ankle. I understand—without surprise, in my dream-like state—this place is Daddy's. Is mine. The shack in the yard has a staved-in roof. The fields are choked with dead grass. If the place has borne a crop in the last ten years, there's no evidence of it.

Euphranor helps me down from Spiffy and hands the reins to Tycho. We walk a little way into the yard. No flowers, no herbs, no kitchen patch. No hens, no pigs, no goats, no berries, no vines, no rustics working the fields, no country girls singing over their tasks. It's winter, of course, but metaphorically.

"It's bad," I say to Euphranor.

He walks around the shack, kicking the foundation stones, peering in the black windows.

"How long has it been like this?"

He waves me over. Through the window I see yellow grass longer than my hair, sprouting in the corners.

"I've done what I can, over the years," he says. "We used to bring in the fruit before the trees went bad. Demetrios tried to harvest the fields one year, but it was too much work. It's a big property. You need someone here full-time."

"I thought there was."

Euphranor gestures at the shack.

"I don't think Daddy knew."

"Not a worldly man," Euphranor says. Commiseration or contempt? "The foundation's still solid. First thing is, you get that roof fixed and get someone living in here."

"A caretaker," I say.

"A farmer." Euphranor gives me a look, long and clear and cool as water. "You want to turn a profit as quickly as possible, yes?"

Behind us, the remaining slaves have trundled into the yard with the cart, and are awaiting instruction.

"Do you have someone in mind?"

He shrugs. "I said it was too much work for Demetrios. That's without recompense, you understand. We might come to an arrangement."

"I don't understand." I kick a dead leaf from my foot reflexively. "You never made this offer to Daddy? How's he had income from the farm all these years if it's been like this?"

"Maybe he was muddled," Euphranor says. "Some men aren't careful with money, particularly if they have it coming in from many sources. It probably just got lost in the accounts."

"You never wrote to him?" I persist.

"I never knew who owned the place until your family arrived in Chalcis. Don't be angry at *me,* girl. I'm trying to help."

O he should not have called me that.

"I know the situation you're in," he says. "These things get around. I don't really see how you've got a choice."

I understand he's taking the farm.

"Are there outbuildings?"

"Worse than this." He kicks the foundation, again. I want to say, *Excuse me, please, but you don't kick that. That's mine.* "You can't live here," he says, reading my mind.

"Equipment?"

"Stolen." He nods. "I remember, a couple of years back, Demetrios telling me he'd checked the barn one day and everything was gone." He holds my look, daring me to challenge him. I know where the equipment is, and he knows I know.

"I'll buy new."

"What will you buy?" Of course I have no idea. "There's no seed, either," he says when I don't answer. "Must have been stolen at the same time."

"Must have been," I say.

We look at each other.

"Which bedroom did you take?" he asks. "The birds, or the butterflies?"

I close my eyes, open them.

"I've been kind to your family," he says softly, though there's no one but slaves to overhear. "I was assured your people were—solvent. It's a big house for one man, but I'm fond of it all the same. I've given you more than enough time to grieve. Any court would say I'd be well within my rights to take it back."

Any court is Plios, the magistrate. I could risk it, maybe.

Suddenly Euphranor's mood seems to shift. "Don't let's

fight," he says. "We should eat, instead. Things always look better on a full stomach. Come on, little one, don't look so gloomy. I'm trying to be nice to you. Still fancy that swim? I sent ahead to have Demetrios clear the pond."

"No, thank you," I say. "It's too cold."

"Oh, but I know how you love to swim."

The tone of his voice.

"You have a birthmark, lighter skin rather than darker. Just here." He touches himself. "I understand those are quite rare, the light ones. Quite—distinctive."

I blush, as he intends.

We ride back to his farm, where the slaves lay out the picnic on a table in the yard. We eat.

"Have Thaulos stop sending his couriers, then," I say.

Triumph; but he takes it quietly. "Actually, that's out of my hands." He doesn't look up from his bread. "He *was* promised a—gift, shall we say, to arrange things. By that brother of yours. The one who fancied himself a gambler."

"How big a gift?"

Euphranor tells me he'll make enquiries, and see if he can negotiate a settlement on my behalf. As the slaves are packing up, he says, "Sure you don't want that swim?"

My first kiss, there in the yard, so quick the slaves don't even look up. I manage to twirl out of it, like Glycera in the silk.

"Birds or butterflies?" he whispers.

I wipe my lips hard on the back of my hand and he smiles, but sadly. Odd.

I'm marked, now; his ghostmark on my mouth. My lips go chapped from all my licking, trying to get it off. Another loss to grieve: the first kiss should have been my husband's. Probably I'm spoiled now, and my husband will know it; he'll smell it on me. But by the time I'm his to taste, the ceremony will be over, we'll already be married, and I'll be safe. He'll be angry, though. Perhaps the way to do it will be to make sure he drinks a lot of wine, so that he won't even notice. If we can get past the first moment, then he'll have marked me with his own scent, and he'll never have to know.

I look at my mouth in the little bronze Herpyllis gave me, this way and that. Morning bounces off it onto the walls.

"Lady." Thale taps on my door frame. "The courier is here."

I hand her the bronze and tell her to give it to him. She frowns. "He'll understand," I say.

After the clop of hooves has faded away, Thale returns.

"You may speak," I say.

She suggests a visit to the temple. A thread of iron firms her jaw, and she's piled her hair on the back of her head in the style called the melon, instead of her usual skinned-back pinning. She wears her best dress, a wheat-coloured wool I remember Herpyllis sewing her for a gift. I wonder if she misses Herpyllis. She whispers, "For guidance."

I know she favours Aphrodite, but I don't.

"Tell Tycho." I get off my bed and look around for clothes. My room's a mess, lately. Thale touches her hair, meaning mine, so I let her comb it quickly and whip it into a loose approximation of her own. "What shall we take?"

Thale shows me her own offering, a pair of sandals the baby has outgrown.

"Let's take Pretty with us," I say. "She'll enjoy the walk."

Thale takes a deep breath and doesn't exhale. The next moment, she's gone to fetch her from Olympios. She'll never have a baby of her own; my father told me years ago she was too old. She's shy around Olympios's baby; awed, I think. The little girl never naturally reached for Thale, with her hard sharp angles and her nervousness and her onion smell. Thale will adore a morning of holding her chubby little hand and wiping her mouth.

In the courtyard, Olympios is lingering, making a show of sweeping the already clean ground. He looks grim. The baby is clean and neatly dressed; her hair is up. She looks serious. Olympios kneels to say a word in her ear, while Thale waits for the handover. She's practically vibrating.

I hold my hand out to the baby. "Shall we go for a walk, Pretty?"

She takes my hand on one side and Thale's on the other.

"Don't let her run away," Olympios says, so soft and terrified an order that I don't reprimand him. Tycho catches his eye and nods, and Olympios nods back. They're both such big men; I shouldn't want to laugh at their concern over a tiny girl, but I do.

Pretty walks very nicely all the way to the temple of Artemis. My choice—huntress, virgin, patron of young girls. She watches Thale leave the sandals in the massive votive pile by the gate, and unclutches her little fist to reveal her own offering: a wooden bead Olympios must have given her. Gravely she lays it next to the sandals. Both of them turn enquiringly to me.

"Take Pretty to see the lamps," I tell Thale.

When they're gone, I draw the last black hair from my pouch. I only burned two for the iunx; the third I kept, just to keep. I lay it next to Pretty's bead, where the shadows swallow it; I blink and it's gone.

"The goddess will understand, I suppose?"

A priestess. I jump, startled.

"May I make a suggestion?" Not just any priestess; the head priestess, she of the black brows, from Plios's party. "Next time, you might tie it to something so it doesn't get lost. Something shiny, to attract the goddess's attention."

"A coin, perhaps."

The priestess gestures elegantly, as though to say that's none of her business; she's above such worldly concerns. I reach back into my pouch and add a coin to the pile.

She tells me she's reading one of Daddy's books, and is learning so much. She confesses she was unfamiliar with his work before we came to Chalcis, and regrets now she did not take advantage of his acquaintance while he was alive.

"Which book?"

"The *Prior Analytics*. Oh, it's beautiful. Elegant."

"Difficult," I say, in case she finds it so.

Her face lights with interest. "You've read it?"

"I've read all my father's work."

Her hands float into the air, fingers fluttering, a mannerism I'll get to know well. It means excitement, anticipation. "But that's marvellous! And you write, too?"

"I do."

A child's voice, rising. *No, no, no!* The priestess of Artemis and I flinch simultaneously, then smile at the mirror image we make. "The goddess loves children," the priestess says. "It's a dreadful failing of mine that I so wish her supplicants would leave them at home."

I bite back a laugh.

"Unusual young woman," she says, not disapproving. "We're not all cut out for the family life, you know."

No, no, no! Bad Thale!

I catch Thale's eye, where she's struggling to keep Pretty from touching the lamps, and look sharply at the door. *Take her out.*

The priestess follows my glance, and looks back to me enquiringly.

"Members of my household," I say. "The child has never been to the temple. I apologize, I apologize. She's usually very well behaved."

Thale stoops to pick up Pretty, who's now lying on the floor, and gets a kick to the face. The priestess gestures to an attendant, who scoops up the now shrieking girl and takes her outside, trailing the weeping Thale. I touch the pain budding at my temple.

"As I was saying." With her toe, the priestess nudges into alignment the sandals, the bead, the coin. "We were not all made for the family life. Some of us need more silence, more contemplation. Devotion can take many forms, yes?"

I'm distracted by a procession of girls in matching dresses carrying votive offerings from the pile to, presumably, a storeroom in the complex of sanctuary buildings behind the temple. Young priestesses.

"Will you come and visit me again? By yourself, next time, perhaps, so you can spend more time on your contemplations?" The priestess's gaze follows mine. "I could introduce you to some of the young women who serve the goddess here. They could tell you about their lives. Might you like to know more about their lives?"

I nod, slowly. From outside rises a high, thin wail like the blade of a knife.

The priestess stoops to pick up my coin. "I think someone needs a sweet." She hands the coin back to me. "One's first visit to the temple should be an occasion of joy. A honey-cake from the market to sweeten the memory."

I take the coin slowly.

The priestess winks. "Go on. The goddess and I are old friends. I'll explain it to her. Will you come again?"

"I will," I say. Then, more warmly: "I will."

She smiles.

At home there is meat for supper; Simon and Thale, who eat with me, won't meet my eye. I don't ask. Meat, and bread and wine. I don't call it tonic anymore. It's just wine, and I drink it, properly watered, like Herpyllis did every supper time. I'm a lady now.

The next morning, I give the courier my gold bracelet with the ram's-head clasp, the one Daddy gave me. The next night there is meat again. Leftovers from the night before, must be.

"Beans tomorrow," I tell Thale, just to be sure.

"I don't like beans," she says.

She's clearing the table, just as always, and I watch her until I'm pretty sure I only imagined what she said. A bone slips from a plate onto the ground, and she doesn't pick it up. The puppy—not so little anymore—comes nosing over and gnaws at it until it starts to cough. Nico wanted to take it to Athens with him, but we guessed he belonged with the house. I get the bone away and hold it out to Simon, who pretends he doesn't see. He turns away to follow Thale to the kitchen. I put the bone on the table.

I'm cold.

In bed I pile on all my furs and lie curled tight, toes tucked behind a knee to keep them warm. Much later, deep in the night, a woman's laugh wakes me. A lovely, low, warm, tickling laugh. I know what it means; but who?

The courier arrives again while I'm eating breakfast; Simon brings him to me. "No," I say. "Yesterday was for two days. Two days at least. Probably three, probably more."

The courier says nothing, doesn't move.

"You go back and tell your master what I said."

He doesn't move.

"Go," Simon says.

He goes.

When I open my mouth to thank Simon, he cuts me off by asking what I'll give tomorrow.

I open my mouth, change my mind. "More jewellery."

"Show it to me."

An order? I raise my eyebrows.

"If you're going to give it away, you might as well get the proper value of it. Give it to me and I'll change it to cash in the market."

"I should have thought of that."

"They'd cheat you there, too. Let me see to it."

I think about that.

"Bring it out," he says. "Show me."

Then I'm showing him my special box, and he's stirring through it with one thick dirty finger. He picks out a few things.

"No," I say softly. My baby necklace with the gold wire flowers, the one from my mother.

"We need to eat."

I hold out my hand, shaking. He hesitates long enough to show me who's making the decision.

"Just that one," I say, and he gives me back the necklace. One of the flowers is already bent from its brief stay in his fist.

"Selfish little girl," he whispers.

Yes.

Over the days that follow, objects start to disappear: metals first, carvings, pots. Or have they been gone for a while and I'm only noticing now? I check the storeroom to find the winter stores alarmingly depleted; where is it all going? Then, one night, Thale brings me beans and serves herself meat. We're sitting inside, in the room for guests; it's too cold for the courtyard.

"We don't eat meat every night in this house," I say.

"You have what you wanted."

I stand. "You wouldn't have treated Herpyllis this way."

"Herpyllis is gone." She eats doggedly, without looking at me.

In the kitchen I find the slaves, also eating meat. Only Tycho stands when he sees me. I realize, with a kind of animal instinct, it would be wrong to show anger or distress of any kind. "Where's Simon?" I say instead.

Tycho leads me to the stables, where Simon is plucking a goose.

"That money was for the house," I say right away when I see him.

Simon shrugs.

"These aren't your decisions."

Simon says nothing. I feel Tycho, behind me, getting bigger.

"Was that Thale's goose?" I squint at it. "The egg goose? Why would you do that?"

I'm not here, apparently; Simon continues as though I'm just a breeze passing through.

In the courtyard, Tycho clears his throat.

"You may speak," I say.

"Your father believed too much meat to be unhealthy for the digestion."

I blink. "Yes. I know."

"You must stop them."

I touch my temple. "Yes."

He says no more, and I assume he's done. I turn away, but he doesn't follow.

"Yes," I say.

"Ambracis has a visitor," he says. "At night."

It's my turn to say nothing.

"From the house of Agapios." Our near neighbours. "One of the servant boys there. I've caught Philo spying on them."

My mind, unbidden, performs its trick of outracing his; I see Philo peeking through a curtain, rubbing himself; hear again Ambracis's laugh.

"Is she happy?" I ask.

"During the day Philo is at her, now. At her all the time. We don't know what to do."

"Keep them apart."

Tycho hesitates; nods. I go to my room with a massive pain behind my eyes, leaving the servants to their feast. Tomorrow, I will seize everything back.

The next morning, Ambracis's eyes are red and her face is bloated from weeping. She slaps my plate in front of me—dry bread—and stares at me with sheer hatred.

"Philo," I tell Tycho, when he answers my summons. "Keep *Philo* away from her, I meant. Not the other one. I don't care what she does with the other one."

Tycho frowns.

"Oh, what now?" I snap.

"Your father never permitted lewdness amongst the servants."

Herpyllis was a servant, I want to say. Instead I tell him I intend to spend the morning in my father's study, reading, and am not to be disturbed.

"May I eat now, Lady?" he asks.

"What?"

"With your permission."

"You don't need my permission."

"Bread and water, no more."

I wonder if Tycho is losing his mind.

"With your permission," he insists.

"Of course you have my permission." I shoo him away with my hand, the way my father used to when he was irritable.

This becomes a new, supremely annoying habit of his: asking permission before every meal. I understand he means to set some kind of example—for the other servants, for me—but his displays of meagre eating grate on me even more than the others' new-found passion for meat.

I spend the next day in my father's study. I'm reading the *Odyssey,* of course, reading and rereading the part about the suitors eating Penelope out of house and home while her men are away.

Finally I take up pen and paper and write the letter I've been avoiding. Salutations to my father's most esteemed colleague, gratitude for all his assistance, much affection to my little brother, and could Theophrastos offer news of the political situation? Was there the possibility of a visit? Me to him, him to me?

I send Simon on Spiffy. I intuit—correctly—a trip to Athens will appeal to him. And he likes Nico. Everyone likes Nico.

He's back, not the next night, but the one after.

Salutations to the child of his esteemed and honoured teacher, the letter says, political situation too complex to explain, ongoing attacks on Macedonian citizens, at all costs the child of his esteemed and honoured teacher should remain where she is; unsafe for her to travel.

But *you* are not Macedonian, Theophrastos; and what of Nico?

He wants me to say it straight out, I think, that I can't manage by myself. He's read Simon, the spite and the insolence in the line of his spine and the curl of his lip. He knows, he knows, and he'll let me suffer on a little more. He's punishing me for all the times I teased him about his books.

I drop the letter in the brazier. So.

A hot dream of wetness and lust, hips in a rhythm, someone moaning, and then Tycho is by my bed, touching my shoulder. *Lady, Lady.*

"Ambracis?" I say.

I follow him to the receiving room, where a big male slave waits. "My lady Glycera requires you," the new one says.

"Where's Ambracis?"

Tycho shakes his head; doesn't know.

"Thale?"

Tycho looks at the floor.

"I see," I say weakly. Animals, all of them, their lusts shimmering in the air all through the house and invading my dreams. And poor Tycho having to look and look for a woman to wake me, having to spy them at it, and finally having to get me himself and risk a whipping. I tell him, "It's all right."

"My lady says quickly," the new slave says.

Tycho looks straight at me and shakes his head, minimally.

"I beg your pardon?"

"Now." The big slave's face is bold. "She says you're to come now."

"It's the middle of the night."

"She'll be dead by morning."

I'm so tired.

"Not my lady. The young one."

"I don't understand."

The big slave actually turns and leaves the house, running home, I suppose, now that his message is delivered. And I'd go back to bed, too, if Tycho doesn't say, "It's not safe," so then of course I have to defy him and go.

We're in the street, me a little bear beside him in my furs, my breath white in the moonlight. Ice crusts the ground. Tycho walks slower and slower until finally he says, "Not this house."

We've arrived.

Tycho says, "It's a whorehouse, Lady. Everyone knows."

Someone screams inside.

"You could sell me," Tycho says.

"Don't tell me what to do," I say. "Nobody would want you, anyway. Wait here."

The big slave is waiting in the doorway. We leave Tycho behind and he leads me to a room pulsing with light and pain. Lamps lamps lamps and a girl on the bed. So many women crammed in the tiny room, so many scents all clashing in panic. The girl on the bed is naked and the baby is coming. My dream, so.

What would my father do.

"Out." I point at one girl after another. "Out, out, out."

As they flee, one steps forward. She's not like the others: scrubbed face, homely clothes, smelling of herself. She tells me she's the midwife. I see in her face judgment of me withheld. "Let me stay," she says.

I nod. There are just four of us in the room now: the girl, the midwife, me, and the woman who hasn't left, the one I can't order about. "How is she?"

"Thank you," Glycera says.

The girl screams again as the pains surge. The midwife puts a hand between the legs, checking something.

"She didn't look pregnant," I say.

"She wore a corset," Glycera says.

The midwife makes a face. "You could have hurt the baby," I say. "You must never corset a pregnant woman. My father taught me that."

"Your father is here to help us now," Glycera says to me. "I feel it. All right, now, Meda. All right. Look who we've brought to help us. It'll all be over soon."

I look at the midwife, who makes a wry face.

"I'm Pythias," I say to her. "What's your name?"

"Clea."

The girl screams at a new pitch. Something inside her is changing.

"She started early this morning," Clea the midwife says. "Want a look?"

She's twice my age, and tolerating me with a patience that tells me there's no real danger; I can't understand why Glycera summoned me. I ask Glycera for clean towels and she hurries out.

"Her daughter," I say.

"Her something." Clea shows me the dark hot mess between

the girl's legs, the pee smell and the blood and the drenched black curls. Expertly she inserts her fingers. "She's doing fine."

The girl throws up just as Glycera returns with the towels. "Water," I tell her, and she goes back out. I clean up the vomit and wipe the girl's face.

The midwife has stationed herself at the end of the bed, between the girl's legs. "We're going to push soon," she tells me.

"Meda," I say loudly. "We're going to push, Meda."

"Like using the pot," Clea says.

"Like using the pot," I tell Meda. "You're going to push like you're using the pot. Can you do that?"

"Yes," the girl says.

"When the next pain comes." Clea touches her belly, looks down below. "Ready?"

The girl screams and pushes. I feel Glycera's shadow in the doorway, but she doesn't come in. "Good, Meda, good!" I say.

"Two or three more like that," Clea says.

She pushes again as the next pains come: two, three, four times. Clea dips her fingers in a dish on the floor and massages where the baby's coming. When she sees me looking, she explains. "Olive oil."

The girl screams again and Clea's face changes; I can tell she's got the head. Joy, briefly, then not. "Once more," she tells the girl.

And the baby slides out wet and blue and cheesy. "Take it," Clea barks. I hold out a towel to receive the baby while Clea cuts the cord. It's turning pink already. It's big and has a mat of black hair. Wide blue eyes. An innocent pink snarl: a harelip.

"Pretty boy," I say, "pretty boy," for Meda to hear, and Clea for the first time shoots me a poisonous look. I hold the baby while she finishes with the girl, the cord and the afterbirth, and then she takes the baby back from me. "Clean her up, will you?" she says. To Glycera: "Lady, your daughter is thirsty."

Glycera disappears a third time.

I change the sheets and swab the blood from Meda. I wrap her in clean things and wipe her face again, and kiss her cheek, and tell her she's done very, very well. The baby goes quiet. When I turn back to Clea, she's got the baby swathed head to toe so you can't see any part of him. Even his face.

Glycera drops the cup in the doorway.

"Stillborn," Clea says. "I'm so sorry."

Glycera starts to cry. She sits on the bed next to Meda and takes her in her arms and they cry together, racking sobs.

"No," I say. I feel logic in me, cold and strong, pushing down everything else. "No."

Clea uncovers the baby's face to show me. I touch the cheek. Clea has cleaned him; no more mucus, no more cheese. She holds the little body out and I take it. I press my cheek to the little dead one, still warm.

Clea says, "Cry. Let it out." But nothing comes out of me.

We leave Glycera and Meda in the room. Clea carries the baby clutched to her chest like it's still alive. Tycho stands when he sees us.

"Where will you take it?" I ask.

The midwife shakes her head.

"Why?"

"He couldn't have latched on to the breast. He would have starved. This was quicker. Kinder."

"You don't know that."

"I do, Pythias." She tries to smile and I see that, like me, she is crying all over the inside of her face. "I've seen it many, many times. You were a great help to me tonight. I thought my lady had lost her reason, calling you, but she's always proved herself an astute judge of character. Always, and she wasn't wrong about you, either. Your grandfather was a doctor, she told me."

I say, "You've helped Glycera's daughters—many times, then?"

"Many times."

"Where will you take him?"

She looks at me for a long moment.

"I'll bury him," she says simply. "With a friend. He won't be alone."

At the gates to Artemis's sanctuary, I tell Tycho to go back to the house. "Mule!" I say, when he doesn't move.

"Yes, Lady."

"Go!"

"Yes, Lady."

He stands lumpishly until a light approaches from deep in the complex. The head priestess holds a lamp up, her face an enquiry. I can tell she was sleeping.

"Make him go." I wipe my wet face with the back of my hand. "Make him go."

She does something to the inside of the gate and it opens enough to admit me to the outer sanctuary. She closes it quickly again behind me, though Tycho doesn't move.

"Go!" I order one more time, harsh as I can, and that is the last I see of him for many days.

"You're bleeding." The priestess leads me to an alcove, where she lights more lamps from the one she's holding. My clothes are bloody from the birth and I smell of Meda's vomit. "Who did this to you?"

"No one."

More priestesses appear, silently. They want to bathe me before I go inside; then they want me to sit on the steps by the goddess and recover myself that way. I tell them what *I* want.

"Indeed." The priestess who admitted me takes my hands in hers, looks at them. Filthy. "One of your slaves?"

I shake my head.

"The baby died?"

I don't answer.

"Yes." She smoothes my hair back from my face, like Herpyllis used to. "It hurts everywhere, doesn't it?"

I spend the night on a cot in the alcove, attended by the head priestess herself. She sits by me, sometimes humming a little. She has a husband and three children at home, she tells me; she had to send a slave to tell her household she'd be away for the night. She inherited the priesthood from her mother and her grandmother before her. I try to imagine her down on the rug in front of her hearth, playing horsey, giggling with her sons. She has a kind, tired face. "I thought you disliked children," I say. "That day I first came to the temple—"

"I thought that was what you needed to hear. Sleep, now."

The next morning, she takes me into the room where they bathe and tells me to take off my clothes. She walks a circle around, tapping her lips with her fingers, while two other priestesses stand ready to assist her.

"What's this?" she asks of the scar Myrmex gave me on my thumb.

"My brother and I were fighting. It was an accident."

She runs her finger along it. "That must have hurt."

"No."

Around and around she goes. "Any pains anywhere? Ever been sick as a child, really sick? Ever had an injury?" No, no, no. "Are you a virgin?" Yes. "Will you let me see?" Yes. I lie down on a blanket the attendants spread for me, and spread my legs. She kneels down and peers.

"I didn't know you could tell that by looking," I say.

"The hole goes slack when it's used." She stands and signals I may do the same. The attendants give me back my clothes.

"It doesn't matter so much, really, virginity," the priestess says while she waits for me to dress. "We're obliged to check, but it doesn't really affect what you can do here. I think perhaps in the old days it mattered more. One of those old traditions we cling to, yes? But perhaps without meaning, in the modern world."

"I love the old traditions," I say, because I guess she does, too.

"You were honest with me, anyway," she replies. "That matters more."

We return to the big room, where a committee has assembled. The head priestess announces I am whole. "No significant blemishes, no scars. All fingers and toes."

"Not beautiful," another says. "But perhaps she can be made so."

"Clear skin," a third says. "Dark, though. She'll need powder."

Next, we talk about money. Normally my family would be expected to buy me the kind of position I'm asking for.

"Her father was renowned," the head priestess says. "She brings prestige."

They spend some time discussing my role in the life of the cult. Weaving, water-bearing, fire-tending, cooking, cleaning; each a sacred ritual. Holy housework. They decide on water-bearing. Because I have no cash in hand to purchase my position, I'm in no position to choose.

No one asks about the household I've abandoned.

The work is unexpectedly hard and I lose myself in it. I talk as little as possible. The goddess is a lamp in a labyrinth; I can't think about the darkness that is her absence. It hurts to think about much at all. My hands blister and peel; I bind them with rags and keep working. There's a spring behind the temple, and I spend my days carrying pots back and forth. I wear a ponytail and a knee-length dress and boots, like the goddess. In the evenings I sit on the steps at her feet, gazing at her. The priestesses have sewn her a dress of fawn-skin and she carries a fine bow and leather quiver of arrows. Huntress, virgin, goddess of the moon. And of childbirth.

At night, when the other priestesses are asleep, I ask her why the baby had to die. Her face is stern. I tell her they could have given him a chance to suck, they could have fed him from a spoon. Couldn't they have fed him from a spoon?

Babies drink a drop at a time, she tells me. *Their tummies are the size of grapes. He would have choked off a spoon. You know this.*

I've seen adults with harelips, though. Some of them must survive.

Many more die of starvation. Now her face is sad. *Have you seen a baby die of starvation? Have you heard one cry and then cry less? I have. You know it can take a week or more?*

She wants my tears, I think sometimes. I give them to her, weep on her feet and don't wipe them away. She puts pictures in my head and takes her price. During the day, mothers bring their sick babies to her. They leave offerings, all kinds of things. There's no set price. Gold, cloth, meat, leather, pots, coins, jewellery, beans, oil, perfume, cosmetics, knives, wheat, corn, paper, musical instruments, tools. If they can write, they write notes. The older priestesses take these things to the storeroom, a room I've never entered. They sew clothes for the goddess, wash and change her every few days. They put cosmetics on her face, anoint her, scent her, polish the gold chains that bind her hair, rub her tired feet, oil the leather quiver to keep it supple. On holy days she wears purple. I've seen her naked, all white marble and ivory, and find her most beautiful then, though the making and mending and cleaning of her clothes is one of the highest callings in the cult.

"You're happy here," the head priestess says to me one day. "Content."

"Yes."

"You work hard. I've been watching you." She picks up my hands to look at them as she did the first night. Bound now in rags. "The goddess is pleased with you."

"I love her."

The head priestess nods. We affect the seriousness of the goddess, we priestesses, and rarely smile. I hope my cousin will come to Chalcis soon. He'll pay the debt and understand that I belong to the goddess now, and can never leave the temple. Marriage is out of the question. He'll feel the spark of her in me when he touches me. He'll burn his hands. He'll understand.

At night she whispers to me and touches me. I can't make out the words. She comes when I'm almost asleep, when I'm about to let go. She tells me the baby is in another place. He can smile, now, and laugh, and gum a rusk, and drink from a cup. He has a puppy to cuddle and sleep with. She strokes my hair and kisses my cheek and holds me until I'm asleep.

I wake one night to use the pot and hear women's voices from the storeroom, hear laughter, and see light outlining the door. I go closer. Through the crack I see the priestesses filling sacks with the votive offerings.

"No, that's mine," one of them says, snatching a gold bracelet from her sister's hand. "You always take the best for yourself."

"I have four children," the other whines. "You only have two. They're expensive to feed."

"Take the meat, then," the first one says.

"It's already high."

"The salt fish."

"Oh, the salt fish. They're sick of salt fish." She makes another grab for the bracelet, but the first priestess is taller, and holds it out of her reach. The others laugh.

In the morning I ask the head priestess about what I saw. She tells me I was dreaming.

"No," I say. "I wasn't dreaming."

We sit at the goddess's feet.

"Think, Pythias," she begins. "Think about how things were when you were a baby, a toddler. Think about the people who mattered most to you. Your father, your mother, your nurse. Your love for them was huge and simple. Your love was a massive block of uncut stone. It was featureless, and nothing could shift it."

That's beautiful.

"Now think, Pythias. Think on a few years. You're a little girl now. You like some foods better than others, some toys better than others, some people better than others. You remember?"

I remember.

"That big block of stone, it's chipped away a little now at the edges. It's starting to take on a form."

It's smaller.

"It's more refined. More interesting. Now you're of age. What does the block look like now? You chip away and chip away, don't you? It takes almost all your time, all your days. You're working at it in a fever. What does it look like now?"

I look at the goddess.

"Yes," she says. "It could end up looking like her. One of her servants. Or it could end up looking like something else entirely. *You* could end up as something else entirely. Something not so lovely, maybe."

"Are you threatening me?"

She smiles. "Just a little. You have to understand, it's a privilege to be here. Would you abuse that privilege?"

"Have I?"

She pats my knee. "Only with the tip of your big toe."

"Because of what I saw?"

"Even once you've carved your stone," she says, as though she hasn't heard me, "you keep chipping away. Your love for your parents changed, didn't it, over time?"

I think about that.

"Your love for the goddess will change, too. Life is long, Pythias. Over time your love will grow deeper, or smoother, or however you'd like to imagine it."

"My father," I say slowly, "would have said you were telling yourself a pretty story to make your life bearable. That there are no gods, no blocks of marble."

"No parents?" the head priestess says, still smiling. "No children? No love?"

"It's not *such* a pretty story, surely. To think that we're all chipping away, chipping away, our loves getting smaller and smaller until we die. Is that really what you believe?"

She shrugs. "I believe in change. I believe love changes over time."

"Even for her?" I point my chin at the goddess.

"Even for her."

"Grows less."

"Grows different." She stands. "Becomes clearer."

"And deeper, and smoother."

We're both standing, facing each other now. Fighting stance.

"More forgiving," she says. "We're not very forgiving, when we're young."

"What should I be forgiving?"

She puts her palm to my cheek.

Hours later, the goddess is pale in the moonlight. I tell her I've always been lonely.

So have I.

Even with so many to care for you?

Even so.

Are my sisters in the storeroom?

Go see.

The baby, I say, tell me some more about the baby.

He's sleeping.

She's so lovely, adorned in moonlight. She needs nothing else. I reach up to finger the hem of her short dress.

Go see.

I tell her I don't want to leave her.

You will leave me, she says. *And another will take your place.*

No.

They wear my jewels, she says. *They try on my clothes. They eat my meat and drink my wine. They perfume themselves and make themselves lovely in my image. They hide my gold in their clothes and give it to their families. Where else do you think my offerings go?*

No.

You've always known.

No.

You can do the same.

No!

Child, she says. *Let me care for you. Let me feed you and clothe you. Let me shelter you. Let me love you.*

I put my hands over my ears.

Daughter, she says. I can still hear her, long after I've left the temple and am running, running, trailing the spark of her until it's extinguished behind me.

The house is cold.

Leaves have drifted into the rooms from outside. The walls are cold to touch, and damp; my fingers leave snail trails of the thinnest wet. A chair lies on its side in the inner courtyard, in front of a table crowded with empty wine cups: someone's party ended clumsily. There's no one in the kitchen, though the tables are crammed with dirty dishes. There's green scum in more than one bowl. The door to the storeroom hangs by a single hinge to reveal chaos inside, food looted and spilled. What is there to feel? They left me; I left them. We're all fending for ourselves now.

Someone is saying words in one of the rooms. Daddy's room. Primly, my ears refuse the shape of these words, keys that won't fit those locks. I follow the sound of them, though, and hold the heavy curtain far enough to one side, with a single finger, to see their fierce proclaimer: Thale, naked on the bed, Simon holding her ankles in the air at an angle that must—at her age—hurt. He's pumping her. I let the curtain go but what I've seen will stay with me for hours, flashing like after-images when you've stared at the sun: the meat of his back, the slop of her breasts, their open mouths, the rhubarb-y business I glimpse between Simon's legs on the out-stroke. Thale's hair on Daddy's pillow, and the filth she's spewing into the air he breathed when he slept, the self-same pocket of breath.

I understand only slowly that Thale is experiencing great pleasure.

I back away, then turn and—what? I don't run, because I can't feel my feet. I am soundless; there's no effort involved. Let's say I float. I float through the other rooms in the house, to find what I already know is there. Olympios, gnawing roast meat from a plate piled high with bones, grease running down his chin, while Pretty plays with my empty jewellery box.

Ambracis and Agapios's slave are in my room, Ambracis on her knees before him; I have to spy over Philo's shoulder to see them. Philo is fisting himself faster than he's ever done anything in his life.

I'm in the courtyard dying when the house explodes with the sound of their voices, from all corners, all shouting at the same time. Singing? I don't know what it's called. They all arrive together. A cloud of startled birds poofs up from a tree; somewhere the dog, no longer a puppy, starts to howl. A crack runs up one wall from floor to roof; I watch the black line of it tracing like a raindrop running upwards. High, high up, a line of dry lightning silently continues the rent. I close my eyes.

Daughter.

I open my eyes and see Tycho in the corner of the courtyard. He squats, wrapped in his great filthy horse-blanket, rocking and mumbling to himself. Has he been here all this time?

"Tycho." I go to him, put my hand on his shoulder. "Tycho, your lady is here."

He looks at me with unseeing eyes.

"Tycho." I touch his forehead, his cheek. I try to get him to stand, but he won't. "Tycho!"

He rocks, mumbles.

"Are you hungry?"

Nothing.

In the kitchen I pick through the scraps and sort out a plate of stale bread and salt fish, and a cup of water from an almost empty jar. No way to know if it's fresh. I take it back outside and set it in front of him. "Are you cold?"

He shoves it all away, so abruptly that the cup spills and the fish flips into the dirt.

I understand the goddess is punishing the house. I understand it's because of me. She is visiting her feelings upon my house: jealousy, hurt, abandonment, betrayal. All I had to do was love her.

I decide to go looking for mercy, for Tycho if for no one else. A reprieve, or a few days' rest; any crumb. At the garrison, I'm shown straight to Thaulos's quarters. He looks happy to see me.

"There!" he says. "I knew you'd solve it. Clever father, clever daughter. How was your service?"

I say, "My service?"

"At the temple."

I tell him I've left the temple.

"Profitable, though, eh? You don't have to pretend. My wife serves there. I know how it works."

"Your wife," I say.

"The army's on the move, coming home, you'll be happy to know."

I nod.

"Soon you'll be having babies. Little babies running all over, and all this unpleasantness will be forgotten. What a gift to your husband, the house all settled! You should feel proud."

I close my eyes and see Thale. I open my eyes.

"It *is* all settled?"

I close my eyes and see Simon's rhubarb. I open my eyes.

Exasperated: "But then why did you go to the temple?"

I shake my head.

"Why have you come here?"

I tell him my servants are possessed.

Thaulos laughs, incredulous. "You've brought me absolutely nothing?"

Nothing.

❧

Tycho looks up when I enter the courtyard and says, "Lady," as though he is lucid. I ignore him and go to my room. Tricks of the goddess. Fortunately Ambracis and Agapios's slave are gone. Warm clothes, the bracelet I hid under a loose stone in the courtyard. In the kitchen I'm at a loss. Water? A knife? I turn around and Tycho is there, a bear in the doorway. "Lady."

I push past him, back through the courtyard to the stables. But the horses are gone. Sold, I guess.

"Lady."

I'll sell the bracelet in the market, buy a day's food, walk at night, hide during the day. If I make it to Athens, Theophrastos will have to take me in. He'll have to.

"Lady." Tycho plants himself between me and the gate. "You must do as your father would expect of you."

"I'm going to Athens."

I see the goddess return; I see the sudden flare in his eyes. He kneels abruptly, like he's been struck on the back of the head. "No," he says.

No, she says.

"It hurts," he says.

I ask him where.

He turns his wide, crazy eyes to mine.

"You have my leave to eat," I tell him. "And drink, and light a fire. You have my leave."

"Not Athens," he says.

Not Athens.

I ask her, *Where then?*

"Think of your father," the goddess says through Tycho. Tycho's mouth and voice. "What has your father left you?"

Books. Knowledge. What, indeed?

When I come back from the butterfly room—vaginal dilator in hand—he's in the corner of the courtyard again, rocking and mumbling.

Well, what would *you* think if you saw me? Hurrying through the streets alone—morning still, the sky soft and white with cold—carrying nothing but my father's implement. The men look bemused but the women know. They shrink back from it. They clench. My hair is long and loose behind me as I stride. They part for me. I feel a bit like the goddess herself, with my implement instead of a bow, then realize she'll punish me for such thoughts. Too late. I walk faster.

The route to Glycera's house is familiar now. The turn in the road, the particular quality of light in the air just by this building here. The smell of baking, then figs, always figs. Five narrow steps up and into a quieter street—posh, elegant. The widow's house is set back from the others, right at the end.

There's a man coming out of her gate: Euphranor. He stops when he sees me.

"Where's your guard?" he asks. I don't answer. He looks at the implement and his eyebrows go up and stay there. "Really?"

I tap on the gate.

"About your farm." He's got his head on the side, studying the implement. "I know I said I could make it profitable for you, but it's winter. There will be no money coming from it before next summer at the earliest. Meanwhile—"

I tap louder.

"It's winter," he says. "Cold at night in a tent at the garrison. I need my home."

"Take it."

"No, but listen—"

I whang the gate with the implement. Now there's a sound they can't ignore.

"I've had word from Thaulos," he says. "Terrible man. He told me what happened. I'm shocked, shocked at his assumptions. That you would even consider stealing from the goddess. Paying off your debt with votive offerings. Gods, it's blasphemy. Foul blasphemy, eh, Pythias?"

Why does no one come?

"We might share the house, you know." He touches my hand. "Pythias, stop. Listen. I like you."

Thale and the rhubarb and the smell of Myrmex's burning hair and Philo peeping and Ambracis slurping and Herpyllis looking at Pyrrhaios and Daddy looking at Herpyllis and I will never touch myself ever, ever again.

Euphranor's looking down at my hand, which he's holding, breathing like he's been running, only he hasn't.

I take my hand back and two-handedly whang the implement on the gate again. The big slave finally comes.

"You're magnificent," Euphranor says. "I've always wondered how those work."

The slave closes the gate behind me.

"Think about it," Euphranor says.

I have already thought.

Glycera receives me in a room I haven't seen before, a lush cave hung with furs and hot with braziers. Her hot room, her winter room. The cushions are red and gold. She rises from her couch to embrace me. I am not thinking not thinking not thinking about how her hair is all mashed down at the back.

I don't say hello. "Clea, the midwife. Where does she live? Where can I find her?"

The thing about Glycera is she's sincere. I read empathy in the way the shoulders drop, the head goes to one side, the eyebrows furrow in concern. Her eyes slip to the implement, now dangling from my hand to the floor, and her eyes flare in horror. "Child, oh child," she says.

But I am not in the mood for her perfumed bosom.

"There are alternatives," she says. "I know women in my position usually think otherwise. But I love babies, I love them. I'd help you with it. Ask my girls! I've never put one out because of a baby. Look at Meda. Didn't I do everything I could for Meda?"

I could nod.

"How far—?" She abandons the sentence to perform the calculation herself. She looks doubtful. "Before your father died?" she says. "Quite a while before?"

"What?"

"You're at least two moons, if you know for sure. Who was it? A student of your father's? Some boy in Athens? Well, it doesn't matter. As I say, no one understands better than me the kind of troubles a young girl can face. You were right to come to me."

"I haven't come to you."

"Shall we put that awful thing away?" She seems not to have heard me. She calls for a slave and points at the implement.

I hug it to my chest. "Clea," I say. "I just want to find Clea."

"I don't understand."

"I'm not pregnant." She winces at the term, as Gaiane and her mother did so long ago. "I didn't come here to stay. Please. If you won't tell me, I'll have to find her some other way."

She stands. "Who, then?"

I don't think you can get pregnant eating it, but who knows. The lie is easier. "Ambracis. One of my slaves."

"You treat them well."

"She has no worth if she dies."

Glycera blinks, then tells me, "Clea lives in the old town, behind the market. I'll send my slave with you. Really, you shouldn't be walking out alone. Where's your man?"

"Just at the bottom of the hill. I told him to wait there."

"Why?"

I adjust my woollens around me and get a better grip on my implement. "He was getting on my nerves."

Glycera leads me out through a different door than the one I came in, into a room that is a smaller version of her luxurious cave. Small, dark, warm, all furs and cushions. "Look who's come to see us," Glycera says.

This windowless room is darker than the first, and it takes my eyes a moment to make out Meda. It takes me a moment longer to make sense of what I'm seeing: she's nursing an infant. She smiles at me, then the baby, then back at me. The baby's eyes are closed, though it's still sucking. She smiles at Glycera, who puts a finger to her lips and leads me out.

"The baby son of a local merchant." Glycera pats my shoulder. "She's working as a wet nurse while she recovers. Recovers in her body and in her mind. Usually she works at their house, but occasionally she brings him back here. It's the best thing that could have happened, really. Did you see her face just now?"

Before I can stop myself, I say, "That's horrible."

Glycera's smile sweetens further. "You're very young, aren't you? Running your own house, delivering babies, serving the goddess, knowing what's best for everyone. Not needing anyone's help. You're really extraordinary."

"No."

"Milk should never be wasted." She looks again at the implement. "You'll mutilate her with that. Maybe you don't care. Just a slave, eh? You've never had one of those up you, have you?"

"No."

"It's not for us to pick and choose the blessings of the gods. Milk is a gift. To the baby, to Meda, and to my household, which benefits from the money she brings in. I really don't care what you think of us. Follow this road straight to the market, then go up the weavers' alley. She's the seventh door on the right."

I thank her.

"Good luck," she says. "For your girl's sake. I'm sure *you'll* be just fine."

Just at the bottom of the hill is Tycho: my lie to the widow made manifest. The goddess put him on her palm and blew him here, like chaff. How else?

"Lady," he says, "Lady." He's wringing his hands, shifting from foot to foot like he has to pee. "There's a man at the house. He says he lives there."

"Yes." I start walking the straight road to the market, as the widow directed. Tycho follows. "His name is Euphranor. The house belongs to him."

"Lady," he says. Surely it's the goddess sparking in him, her spirit inhabiting his body, moving him along like a puppet. I left him past sight and speech; how else is he so quickly recovered? "Lady, he walked right in the front gate, calling for you. Laughing."

"That's not possible. I just talked to him. He was just here. How can he be in two places at once?"

We walk together for a while, not talking. I feel ragged with confusion.

"I'm sorry," I say finally. "I'm sorry I left you."

"Lady," the goddess says.

"You were kind to me. You took care of me. You deserved better from me." The goddess looks confused. "Release me from your service." Now the goddess looks afraid. "I know I still owe you a debt, and I'll find a way to pay. I will. But you have to release me."

"Lady, you're ill," the goddess says.

Odd how she can so completely resemble Tycho, with his mud-brown eyes and soldier's stubbled head, the great bulk of him, even his leathery smell. My father, in me, begins to wonder about the mechanics of divine possession. Perhaps Tycho acts as a kind of filter or shell, and something of him remains even as the goddess shines through the cracks and pinholes. Perhaps Tycho's still here, somehow—confused, terrified, but here. Perhaps I need to speak *to* Tycho rather than around him; perhaps the goddess is not as free as I thought.

I set the implement down at my feet and take both his hands in both of mine. "I free you, Tycho," I say. This is as public a declaration as any; market-goers flow around us like water, looking openly, crooked-smiling. "I free you, Tycho, from service to my father's house, as a reward for your loyalty to him and to me."

Release me, Lady.

"Lady, no." Tycho shakes his head, like I'm three again. "Your father required me to serve you until your marriage. I obey your father."

I let his hands go. "I free you!" I say loudly. Around me, people are laughing.

"Lady." Tycho picks up the implement for me. "You can't free me. A girl can't."

I snatch the implement back and run. I lose him quickly enough in the crowd, and then there's the seventh door, which opens for me just as I'm raising my fist.

❧

Clea sets me to memorizing aphrodisiacs. Not the hocus-pocus of Herpyllis's world—the iunx spells and burnt offerings and midnight mutterings—so much as the kind of science that would have pleased Daddy. Mostly, Clea explains, we prescribe seediness: quince, sesame, pomegranate. Olive oil for lubricant, honey for sweetness. I must look stupid because she says, "Not off a spoon."

I'm sent into the back room when she meets with clients, mostly well-to-do women trying to conceive, or woo back wayward husbands; sometimes young bridegrooms who can't persuade their wives to—

I listen at the door. Clea is patient, serious, respectful, never lewd. *Perhaps,* Clea says, and *Have you considered?* The clients tell her everything, quicker than I would ever have guessed. *She only likes it this way, he wants me to put my finger up there, she says it hurts, he always cries after.* They pay nicely for Clea's advice, and we sell oils and creams and other things. After, sometimes, she'll raise her eyebrows at me, knowing I've had my ear to the door. She says there's nothing she hasn't heard at least two or three times a week for most of her adult life.

She explains the business to me the night I arrive. Not sex, but the before and after: aphrodisiacs and midwifery, contraception and abortion. She is as two-faced as her work. Quiet and modest with her clients; frank and easy with her friends, the others with whom she shares her house. In the evening, they drift in: three more midwives, plus a couple of men who have no clear occupations—assistants, security, companions—it's all fluid. They sit around the big room late into every night, eating and drinking and laughing and singing and telling stories. I understand they have no family but each other. They are dregs who have drifted to the bottom and settled together.

"Who's this?" one of the men asks the first night. His name is Candaules. A pair of hunting dogs nip at his heels and he carries a new-born puppy, whose head he knuckles while it blinks blissfully.

"This is Pythias," Clea says. "She's with me."

"I thought I was with you," Candaules says.

Clea takes the puppy from his arms and kisses its face and hands it back to him with a smile. "There's lots of Clea to go around."

That first night I keep to the corners, cooking and tidying and playing with the dogs and puppies. There are always puppies underfoot, play-fighting or looking for a cuddle, reminding me of Nico. The big room is high-ceilinged and dark, smoky from the brazier in the middle of the floor, around which they lay their sleeping mats. They drink themselves to sleep. They smoke, too, from a pipe that makes them happy. One of the men whittles phalluses, life-size and a little bigger; Clea explains we sell those, too. We sleep all about on the floor around the brazier, much like puppies ourselves, under mounds of blankets in the warm puppy-smelling dark. Their voices continue even after the fire is down to embers.

I learn the language of sex, a language hidden in plain sight: *tumbling chariots, visiting the sausage-seller, the double scull, the smelter, the trireme, the lioness on a cheese grater.* They laugh and laugh. They kiss and sigh and cry out. I sleep between Clea and the wall, facing the wall while she services Candaules, who favours the *wicker basket on horseback,* and later another midwife, who shares with Clea *a sparrow's breakfast.*

"No one will touch you," she whispers over her shoulder, sensing my sleeplessness, deep in the night. "I told them you were mutilated, and in great pain."

"Thank you," I whisper.

I can't have another, I hear, more than once a day. *It'll kill me. It's too soon. It's too late. I'm exhausted. Give me something. There must be something.*

There's always something. Cheesecloth, if he doesn't mind. A douche, after. Counting the days. Clea teaches them the safe days and they nod, doubtfully. They're desperate; nothing feels safe. If it's already begun, there are teas for sale. Sometimes they'll lie down on the table and Clea will have a look, feel around, and ask me to fetch a tool she has that's smaller than my implement. There's crying then, pain and blood, and afterwards a good deep sleep while we change the laundry and prepare a child's meal of warm milk and sweet bread for the woman. Clea instructs them how to explain it to the husband: a miscarriage brought on by exertion. She is to tell him she needs rest, much rest, and no relations for—

"How old is your youngest?" Clea will ask, and the woman will say, and Clea will tell her a number of moons, and say, "How does that sound?"

They will nod, weakly.

When the women are gone, Clea cleans her equipment.

I go into private homes with her, to assist at births. I am calm and quiet and play up my Athenian accent; the grandmothers take to me. There are no live births. Each time, she sends me back to the house to tell one of the men she needs a puppy.

"Why?" I ask the first time.

"To be kind," Clea says. "We strangle the puppy and bury them together. That way, the baby won't be alone."

I join them now in the evenings around the brazier with my cup of wine.

"I had a good one today," one of the women will begin.

They tell work stories, sad stories, bawdy stories, sex stories. The brazier crackles, the puppies sigh in their sleep, the wind rages outside. While they talk, I drift into myself. I hear and don't hear their tales of the prostitute who served an entire unit in one night and walked away after; the girl who pushed out four babies, one after another, like a cat's litter; the man who tallied his lays by notching his lintel every morning upon his return, until the morning it collapsed and killed him. I hear and don't hear their tales of the newest priestess of Aphrodite, the one who has to wear a veil in the temple so the goddess won't get jealous (good advertising, the midwives agree; no one has yet seen her face, though people flock to the temple now to catch a glimpse of her; probably quite plain, though with a graceful walk; the midwives have been to see for themselves); the preternaturally beautiful baby born to Achilleus the architect's wife, who tells anyone who will listen that the pleasure of his conception was so extreme that she suspects divine interference (Achilleus the architect will nod, apparently pacifically, during these confessions, as though modestly conceding that yes, yes, it's possible he was possessed by a divine sexual fire, after all look at the infant, that hair, that skin, those eyes!, and what if he himself is a short stout bald worrying man whose wife is taller and louder than he is, what if?); the man the midwives themselves pay to cock around town, putting it wherever he can to keep them all in business.

"Really?" I say. I haven't heard about him before.

They start; they thought I was drunk, or sleeping, or in the easy shadowland between drink and sleep.

"You pay someone?" I prompt, because they're staring at me, silently.

One of the men touches the knife on his belt with one finger.

"Let's sing," I say. I hold my cup up high. "A hymn to the goddess. More wine to honour the goddess!"

"Stop it, Pythias." Clea leans back against her latest companion. "You're a bad actor. You're not drunk. You heard something you shouldn't, eh? Usually you know to keep your mouth shut."

There's a movement in the shadows behind me. Clea's a bad actor, too, with her show of relaxation.

"I don't know what I heard," I say. "I don't think I actually heard anything."

"Actually," Clea says.

The one behind me moves closer. I hear his breath. I say, "After, will Candaules kill a puppy to go below with me?"

Clea glances over my head; an understanding through glances; the one behind me withdraws, a little. After a moment of nothing, I hear the knife being sheathed.

"He came to us," Clea says. "New in town, offering his services. We laughed him off, at first. We laughed him off for nine months, until the first jump in births—we had more work than we could handle. Then he came to us again and said he'd given us nine months for free, but if we didn't start to pay him, he'd move on to another town."

"How long ago was this?"

"Five years. It's gotten so we can spot which are his. There's always something not quite right. Not quite natural. It's not just the baby not looking like the husband, though it's that, too. Though the parents don't seem to notice it; they're in a kind of daze. Sometimes the babies are deformed, sometimes too perfect. And the women all seem—dulled down, sort of. Like they can't properly remember their lives before."

I think of Meda.

"You know the health of the baby is determined by the quality of the act of conception," Clea says. "Vigorous act, vigorous baby. Unwilling act, colicky baby. I've often wondered about the ones that are his."

"Achilleus the architect's wife," I say. "But then what about the deformed ones?"

Clea nods. "We told him at the outset, the women had to be willing. I wasn't going to pay him to rape. We followed him for a few nights, too, just to be sure."

"And you were sure?"

"Oh, yes." Clea nods, shakes her head; smiles despite herself, remembering. "*Ai.* I think maybe it's that he works too hard, sometimes, and the quality of his seed suffers. That's why some of the children—well. It's not the babies he cares about, though. They're just the side effect, the by-product. It's—I don't know how to explain."

"It's the women," I say.

"It's the seduction, certainly. The hunt." Clea shakes her head. "That's not it either, though, entirely. There's something very sad about him at times."

The others nod, murmuring.

"It's more like a hunger." Clea taps her finger to her lips. "A sickness, maybe. He can't stop. He couldn't, anyway, and it suited us well enough when he couldn't. And now, all of a sudden—"

"Maybe he just needs a rest."

"That one? He'll rest in his grave."

"Does he want more money?"

Clea shakes her head. "We offered him everything we could think of."

The fire flares up, spitting sparks onto the floor; the shape behind me steps forward to tamp them out. He looks at me apologetically, shrugs; it's Candaules. He sits back in his place.

"We think he's pining," Clea says. "That he's fallen in love with some little scrap of a flat-chested thing somewhere who won't have him, and now he doesn't know what to do with himself. We'd pay *her,* if we could find her."

"What does he look like?"

They've relaxed now; they're pouring more wine, feeding the fire, whispering to each other. They're still keeping an eye on me, though. What do they think I'm going to do?

"We can't seem to agree on that," Clea says. "We think he's a bit of a shape-shifter."

"Handsome?"

"Some days." Clea holds up the wine; I shake my head. She pours for herself. "Sometimes I think he makes himself dull so he can go unnoticed. To be able to slip in and out of places without anyone looking at him twice. And then sometimes of course he's a right peacock."

"Wait, though." I sit up straight, trying to understand. "Once he's gone, surely there'll still be babies born. You seriously think this one man services the entire town? Won't people like Achilleus the architect and his wife just go back to having uglier babies?"

"We thought so, too, at first," Clea says. "At first. But haven't you noticed? They're all unhealthy now. We think he's punishing . . . everyone, really. The mothers, the babies, the families, us."

I shake my head. The room is quiet again.

"Since you came to town, come to think of it. What do you make of that?"

I shake my head. "I haven't met a man like that. No one's approached me that way. Well, except—"

"Except?" Clea says.

I shake my head.

"Except," Clea says.

"There's a cavalry officer."

The room is dirty, rough, sour with wine and dogs and lust. Clea's friends listen wide-eyed as children who know the story to come and need to hear it again anyway.

"That's the one," Clea says. "We think he might be a god."

Tick, tick, tick, the tiles fall into place like in that game Daddy used to play with Herpyllis in the courtyard, late into summer evenings.

"If you're the one he wants, who are we to deny him?" Clea says. "He'll reward us for bringing you to him."

"Gods don't behave that way," I say. "My father taught me that. God is far, far away. Not a man or a woman. More like a force."

They're listening.

"A beautiful vase," I say. "Think of a beautiful vase. Its beauty might prompt a man to buy it. That's its force. But the vase itself is oblivious. That's like god."

"What are you talking about?" Clea says.

"My father," I say. I'm trying to remember the exact words, and the sound of his voice. "My father said people lean back into the idea of benevolent gods to avoid standing on their own two feet. People lean back into each other in the same way. It's not real."

"That's a small, cold world your father lived in."

I say nothing.

"Do you live there, too?"

"I don't know," I say.

I don't have many things here, not much to collect: a change of underclothes Clea gave me when I arrived, and the implement.

"You'll bring him to us," she says, watching my tiny packing. "Or we'll find you, and we'll give you to him."

At the door, she presses her cheeks to mine and then pushes me out into the starry cold.

I wake in pain, cold and awfully cramped, in the hollow of a tree not far from the east side of the channel, in the shadow of the garrison on the hill just across the water. It was deep night when I left Clea's, black and raw cold, and my instinct had been to curl up somewhere and die on my own terms. But a knife at my throat to make more babies for the midwives to save, or not—no. I started to walk, in case they should find me in a nearby alley at dawn and change their minds.

I heard sloppy singing as I walked, and shouting, and once the shriek of a woman's laughter from an upstairs window. *Really?* I thought. *Really?* Was the world really as lewd and drunken and dangerous at night as in stories? Wasn't that a bit ridiculous? Didn't the rapists and murderers have to sleep, too? I kept moving, kept to the shadows. I kept a firm hold of the implement and walked away from any light or sound, any life. At the channel, I realized I was a prisoner in Euboia; at least until dawn, when the ferryman would come. I stood for as long as I could—Daddy had taught me the danger, the siren call of warm sleep in cold—then squatted, and finally let myself doze sitting up as the first pink wine spilled low across the sky. Pretty, brainless dawn. I hugged the implement like a puppy inside my woollens, and rested my head against the tree trunk.

I hear the ferryman's bird-like call and the *plash* of his pole. I stand and beat the pins and needles from my legs with my fists, then limp down the bank. He takes the coin I hold out. I clomp onto the raft, feet still prickling from my awkward spell beneath the tree, and sit down.

"What's that?" He unties us casually, automatically, coiling the rope while looking curiously at the implement, which I've laid across my lap. Daddy taught me to see actions learned by the body, actions so habitual the body could work without the brain. To be good at anything physical, he taught me, you had to reach that point. That was a way to judge people, too, workmen and slaves, how easily they moved in their bodies. That told you of their experience, more than words could.

"It's a dilator." My tongue refuses *vaginal.* I am a lady, still, barely. "It's for babies."

"Eh—it's not." The current is quiet; I wonder if we're almost at the change of the tide. He sets the paddle down and reaches for a pole. "I had five myself. I never saw one of those."

"Maybe your wife did."

"What wife?" His face cracks open in a delighted smile; I've fallen for whatever he wanted me to. "Five babies, five different girls." He stops in the middle of the channel, pole planted in the depths. "I've seen you before."

I'm too tired to lie. "Yes."

"You shouldn't be alone."

I don't answer.

"Tell you what." He fishes my coin from inside his clothes and holds it out. "You keep this."

I take the coin but don't put it away. If he's hoping to see where I keep my pouch, he's out of luck. He starts poling again and we crunch against the opposite shore in a few heartbeats. With the same thoughtless ease, he loops the rope around the large rock he uses for his Western cleat.

"Thank you, Charon," I say.

He shakes his head. "I've heard that joke before." He takes an unsteady, lurching step towards me, as though thrown off-balance by the bobbing raft, and kisses my mouth. I jerk back. His taste is sour, rotten. Bad wine, bad teeth. His face cracks again.

"Thank you, Grandfather," I say.

For a moment neither of us moves. Then I'm halfway up the slope and he's calling after me, *Wait, wait. Your baby-thing.*

I don't stop. There's payment, if you like: a kiss, a handful of wool where he'd hoped a bigger breast would be, and a vaginal dilator. *For you; enjoy.*

The neighbourhood, around the backside of the hill topped by the garrison, is only a short walk away now. The streets are quiet; it's early still. Lately it's always early, or late. I'm aware of my own evil smell, lank hair, damp dirty clothes, throbbing head. Fatigue has scrubbed the inside of me raw, like a handful of sand. I don't recognize the house at first and am unsurprised; the gods have plucked and replanted the neighbourhood, perhaps, or I'm addled—punch-drunk from the effort of continuing, these past few weeks. Mere weeks, only, still. I walk to the end of the street where we used to live, then back again, ticking the houses off against the map in my mind. I recognize this one, with the painted lintel; and the next, with the chickens in the yard; and the next, with the pretty gardens and the sundial; and the next, the one next to ours, with the big cypress. Our house—mine, Euphranor's, someone's—is now overgrown with vine leaves, but after a moment of staring I recognize familiar details: gate, plant pots, trees, the diagonal crack in the stone walkway.

Vines don't grow in winter.

I stand still, cautiously putting this thought together.

"Lady."

Behind me. Sitting in the street in his filthy horse blanket, a greasy cloth wound around his stubbled head. He struggles to stand. I go to him and search his face. His eyes are clear. The joy of this stabs me unexpectedly deep. "Tycho."

"Lady."

I want to touch him. It's the oddest thing.

"I've been waiting for you," he says.

"I know."

He studies my chin. "Euphranor is master of the house now."

I nod.

"He's inside."

"Yes."

We both look at the house.

"Vines don't grow in winter," I say. Like a test.

"We can't cut them down," Tycho says. "Blades can't cut them."

"It's Dionysus, isn't it. Euphranor is Dionysus."

Tycho's eyes skip over me, hair clothes feet, not settling anywhere for long. Taking my measure. He looks back at the house. "He's been looking for my lady."

"Is he—"

Tycho lets his eyes touch mine, so briefly. "No," he says. "He's brought order back to the house. It's clean and tidy and we obey him. He treats us well. He's kind. He's been building up the storeroom, as well as he can this time of year. He only insists on order, cleanliness and tidiness. That and looking for you. He sends one or other of us out every day into the city, searching."

Here, in the cold street with Tycho, these feel like my last moments of—what? The end of one life and the beginning of another. Lesser; another lesser life. That's what I fear. That's what keeps me out here, in the cold. Yet less than what? Did I have so much without knowing it? What did I have before that I don't have now, that I could possibly recover in this world? Charon, indeed.

"There's something else." Tycho runs a hand over his stubble in that familiar gesture. "Someone else, another one. He comes every day. He comes to the gate and asks for you."

A sound from inside the courtyard: horse's hooves, a whinny, the clinking of tack. Someone is coming.

"Here." Tycho leads me a little way down the street, out of sight of the gate. We step back into some trees and watch until the gate has opened and closed and Euphranor has ridden past on his big black animal, not seeing us. Heading for the garrison. Handsome, today.

"A strange young man," Tycho continues. "Every day for a week now he's been coming, asking for you. He runs, though, if he gets the least smell of the master."

"Strange how?"

"Familiar." Tycho touches his stubble, his temples, covers his eyes, uncovers them, looks at me. "Lady?"

The glaze has returned.

"You should go in now," I say, though it hurts me.

"I have to wait for my lady."

"Yes." I take from his hands the greasy cloth he used to cover his head against the cold. It's big enough to cover me. "You should wait just inside the courtyard, there. Then they can bring your breakfast."

He looks confused.

"Just inside the gate." I give him a little push. "Then you can see the street and inside the house, too. It's the best spot. Your lady wants you to wait there."

He goes in. I go, too, not far; back to the spot in the trees where we watched Euphranor pass. I wrap the greasy cloth all around me, covering my body and my hair and most of my face, and squat like a beggar in case anyone should notice me.

I spend the day in sleep's shallows, waking with a start at any sound or movement: the neighbours' comings and goings, birdsong, peddlers with their rattling carts, calling out new milk and bread and fish and trinkets and remedies and firewood and water. I buy a drink and a cake from a man who, when

I touch my throat to fake muteness, takes me for a boy. *Here, lad,* he says, and gives me my right change. Each time I think I can't sleep anymore, I'm off again, drifting, until the day's gone and it's dusk.

The street is busier now than it's been all day: people returning home, the night vendors making their supper rounds, soldiers coming down off the hill for an evening in town. I watch a beggar approach our gate, a dirty, bearded boy with a bad limp. He doesn't knock, but peers in like he's trying to stick his head through the bars. After a few moments he steps back. The gate opens minimally, then shuts with a clang. Now the beggar has a heel of bread.

He turns in my direction and I see it's Myrmex.

He passes me, close enough for me to see the limp is real, and I follow him down the hill and towards the ferry. But he turns left, along the shoreline to the beach where I took Daddy to swim in his last weeks. Down, down, down the long dunes tipped with shadows, and back into the trees, into a deep tangle where he must sleep. He could have looked back anytime and seen me; he didn't. Coming closer, I see him bending over something on the ground, working at something: a fire. I don't hesitate. When he hears the first stick crack under my foot, he jumps up and back, awkwardly, and I walk straight up to his astonished self and push him so hard he falls backwards. Down on his back and I keep coming, beating at his head and shoulders with fists, hurting him. He tries to bat my hands away from his nose and eyes, but doesn't otherwise fight back. When I stop, he's bleeding from his nose and lip, and crying a little, too.

I sit on a log and watch while he builds the fire into something usable. The light's going fast now. By the time he's done, I can't see the tears or the blood.

"Pytho," he says. Of course his voice plucks me like a lyre string.

He has a number of little packets of things, it turns out: kindling, dry clothes, dried fish, a leather roll of tiny knives I recognize as Daddy's. He worries through all these packets, looking for something with an anxious fussiness I hadn't known in him before. I accept some nuts and dried fruit without letting his hand touch mine. We sit across the fire from each other, warily eating.

"You're dirty," he says, after a while.

"You smell like pee and onions. What happened to your foot?"

He shakes his head.

"Fine," I say, and then we're not talking, again.

We finish eating and stare into the fire. After a while, he gets up and rummages around and throws a blanket at me. It hits me in the head. I wrap it around my shoulders. He sits shivering and I don't care. I'm glad.

"How's Nico?" he says finally.

"He went to Athens, to Theophrastos."

"That's good," Myrmex says. "He'll be safe there."

"Herpyllis went to Stageira," I say, when he doesn't ask. He grunts. "What happened to your foot?"

"A man put it on a chopping block. I thought he was going to cut it off with his axe, but instead he used the butt end on my ankle. I don't think it's going to heal."

The stars are out. The fire seethes, sounding like Herpyllis sucking her teeth in annoyance.

"I'm sorry, Pytho," he says. "I'm so sorry."

Let it come.

"I thought I could help, if it means anything," he says. "I took it to gamble, the money. I thought I could make more than enough for—"

Our wedding, I think. I can't stop myself. Of course that wasn't what he was going to say, but my mind makes it anyway.

"They were going to send me home," he says. "I wasn't going back there. I was going to make enough so we could choose for ourselves, both of us."

"Choose what?" I say softly.

He looks at me across the fire, utterly clear, utterly bleak. "Not that, little Pytho," he says. Again: "I'm sorry."

"You could have asked me. I would have given it to you. I would have given you everything. You didn't have to leave. You could have just asked."

He shrugs; such disinterest, now that suddenly I'm enraged. He doesn't get to choose when *my* life is over.

"Here." I hike my dress up to my thigh, rip off the pouch I have strapped there, and throw it at him across the fire. He catches it reflexively. "That's my last. That's everything I have. It's yours now. You understand?"

He's interested now. I can see he wants to look inside, to see how much is there. Instead he says, "I'm surprised Euphranor lets you carry money."

"*Euphranor?*"

He looks confused; caught.

"You think I'm living in that house with Euphranor?"

"Where else?"

I stand up. The dress falls back down over my legs; the blanket falls from my back. "Look at me. *Look* at me. Do I look to you like I've been living in a house with a man?"

He looks. I think he looks at me properly for the first time in his life.

"Come here," he says.

"Fuck you."

"Come here. I don't want this." He holds out my pouch.

When I reach for it, he grabs my wrist, and we go where we've been heading since the day he arrived: hello and goodbye in the same breath. After, he wraps us both in the blanket and holds me until I fall asleep.

When I wake, he's gone for good, with the money I carried in the pouch on my thigh, my last.

Kick, Pytho, kick.

I can't.

You can. Daddy won't let go. Kick, Pytho.

Pytho kicks. Pytho can see the bottom, the hot fine dry sand she plays in on shore now swirling, liberated by the water. Water isn't blue when you splash it or pour it from your hands, but it looks blue when you look at the whole big sea. That's interesting.

Kick, sweet.

Pytho kicks, straining to keep her chin up. Daddy holds her hands, pulling her forward while he walks backwards. He's letting his grip go softer and softer and Pytho knows he's getting ready to let go and make her do it by her own self. She crab-claws his hands with hers so he can't.

Now put your face down.

That Pytho can do. She puts her face into the water, eyes wide open, and holds Daddy's hands and kicks. She makes big splashes and wriggles her body and does silly-swimming.

Good, *Daddy says when she stands up to catch her breath.* My little fishy. You're a good swimmer.

I know, *Pytho says.*

Pytho is naked. Mummy's Herpyllis is up on the beach with the picnic and the baby. Herpyllis doesn't see why Pytho needs to learn to swim, but she isn't Pytho's mummy and she doesn't decide. Daddy and Pytho decide. Mummy is down below, but Pytho will be down below one day too, so that's all right for now. Meanwhile she's nice to Herpyllis, because Herpyllis belonged to Mummy when she was alive and Mummy was nice to her. Pytho waves and Herpyllis waves back with the hand not holding the baby. Pytho decides she will give Herpyllis a present.

Look at me! *she calls, and puts her arms over her head and dives into the water and kicks kicks kicks, all by her own self, until she comes up coughing. Daddy is right there and scoops her out of the water and holds her up to the sun, his pet fishy, and she can hear Herpyllis clapping and others on the beach too, people they don't even know, and Daddy is hugging her and telling her she's brave and strong and she did it all by herself.*

Again, *Pytho says.*

Again and again, all that afternoon, until she can swim even where her feet don't reach the sand, and Daddy never gets bored and leaves her, not even for a minute.

"Hold still," Glycera says. "This is going to hurt."

She rips the wax from my eyebrow and I say a word.

"Don't be coarse," Glycera says. "Other one."

This time I'm silent, though my eye cries from the pain. Just the one eye. That's interesting.

"Much more effective than tweezing. The redness will fade in a few hours." She picks up my hand, looks at my fingernails, and makes a face. "They'll grow back, I suppose. Still. How did you let things go that far? I've never understood girls who don't care for their bodies. Men either, for that matter. My husband always let me take care of him that way. It's who I am, I suppose. You express your inside through your outside, no? Clean and tidy?"

"Yes, Mother." It's what I must call her now.

"You always were a ratty little thing," she says, but not meanly. "Never mind. Shall we talk about your hair?"

We talk about my hair, about how often I'll be expected to wash and comb it—more than I'm used to—and the styles that are appropriate for my age and station. Nothing too complicated, Glycera says; she wants me looking young. "Nothing perverse. Just your age, that's all. You don't need to try to look older than you are. I have older girls."

Meda enters the blue-sky room with a tray of jewels, and smiles her smile.

"How is the baby?" I ask.

Glycera nods, and Meda fetches him in his rush cradle. I ask if I might hold him. Glycera smiles at me like she's going to cry, and nods again at Meda, who lifts him gently and puts him in my arms. He doesn't wake. I kiss his hair and breathe his smell.

"One day," Glycera says, and smiles again at Meda, at me. The baby sighs in his sleep.

They spend a long time over the jewels, holding them up to my cheek to check the colours. Glycera calls for the other girls to solicit their opinions. She explains that each girl has a signature colour, to show her to best advantage.

"And to stop us fighting over clothes," Meda says. The other girls giggle. This is the longest sentence I've ever heard her say.

Meda is pale green. Obole is lilac; Aphrodisia is blue. Glycera herself is orange. Yellow, they agree, makes me look sallow. Shell pink appeals to them, but I reject shell pink. Dark green? Red is coarse. Grey is dull. Brown?

The girls sniff. They don't like brown. I touch a ring, gold, set with a piece of earthy agate.

"Brown could make her skin look lighter." Glycera holds the ring to my cheek. She fingers through the tray and finds another, darker. "What do you think, Pythias?"

It reminds me of cumin, and the colour when I close my eyes, just before sleep.

"Brown." Glycera turns the word over in her mouth, tasting it. "Unusual. Well. Unusual suits you, doesn't it?"

"Yes, Mother."

I take my lessons in the big dining room, which Glycera says they use for parties. At this time of year, it's cold. Glycera says the cold will force me to concentrate; something Daddy believed also. I have dance lessons and singing lessons and lessons in the art of conversation. These are with Glycera herself, who begins by offering some opinions about Alexander's military campaigns. She can talk about tactics, formations, terrain. I tell her Daddy once accompanied the king on campaign and saw him in all his glory. Daddy had gone along to serve with the medics, I explained, and because the king himself had asked him to.

"Good," Glycera says. "That's good. Very interesting. You can use that."

We talk about battlefield injuries and their treatment. We talk about medicine more generally. She quizzes me about my cycles, and finds out what I know about contraceptives: much, thanks to Clea. She wants to tell me about the act, but I tell her I've seen animals, and Daddy has explained most everything.

"All right," Glycera says. "Only you can't keep talking about your father. Once, at the beginning of a conversation, to remind the client of your bloodline. Then you must forget. The client wants to talk to *you*."

She asks me if I have particular interests, and says I'll speak most fluently about what I care about.

Do I have particular interests? Can I speak without Daddy speaking through me?

Skeletons, I think. "Poetry," I say finally.

"Yes, dear." She pats my hand. "Recitation is a lovely skill. In my experience, though, they don't want to listen. They want to talk." I must look disappointed because she adds, "Never mind. A dreamy young girl in love with poetry. That's very pretty. A very appealing type."

Now I am a type.

"Of course you're a type," she says. "We're each a type. And after a while you'll come to see that the clients are, too, and you'll learn to respond appropriately."

"What type are you?"

"Old." She's crisp, unoffended. "I'm Mother."

"And Meda?"

"No," Glycera says. "I'm not playing this game with you. You have to learn it for yourself. Now we're going to have an argument. Are you ready? They like a spirited argument, even a bit of cheek. Always with a smile."

We argue about the relative merits of empire and democracy; the Macedonian treatment of Athens; the virtues of friendship versus erotic love. I'm guessing there's a right side to this argument, but Glycera says not. We are *hetairai*, she says, worthy companions, not common prostitutes; we are not coarse. I remember not to mention Daddy, and at the end of the lesson she says I'm very good at conversation, a natural.

"Thanks," I say.

She shoots me a look. I wonder if I'll be reprimanded for my tone, but she says nothing.

She says she needs a lie-down, and tells Aphrodisia to show me cosmetics. We powder my face white and paint my eyes. "More, more," Glycera keeps saying from her couch across the room, waving a languid hand and not opening her eyes. "She's brown as a little nut." Aphrodisia's hands are tiny and she smells of roses. The powder makes me sneeze. She rubs a fingertip of oil on my lips, to soften the chap, and says I must do so every morning and night until they've healed. In the bronze, I look like I'm wearing a mask.

My coming-out party will be in ten days. Obole and Meda work on my dress, a tan gauze with darker brown embroidery. They want ties at the shoulder, but Glycera favours the more old-fashioned gold pins. Spikes. From these kinds of details, I'm putting together a picture of the type she thinks I am: brainy, fierce, Macedonian rather than Southern. A wild young Northern thing with a chest like a boy and a brain like a man. The embroidery pattern on my dress is all geometrics.

"No flowers?" I ask, and Glycera says no, no flowers. Aphrodisia is flowers; Obole is birds; Meda is herbs and green plants and seed pods; Glycera herself is fruits. Aphrodisia is sweet and simple and pretty; Obole is graceful and athletic; Meda is lovely and sad. My party is meant to introduce my type, and a bit of myself, too: Glycera says we'll serve my favourite foods. What are my favourite foods?

"That's a lot of salt," she says, when I rattle off a list. "No sweets at all? Usually young girls like sweets."

I'm standing on a low table while they pin up my hem. "Sandals," Glycera says, considering. "Definitely sandals to the knee."

"Next you'll have me carrying a spear."

"Lippy." Glycera raises my chin with a finger, the way she does. "Have you ever been with a man?"

A question I've been waiting for. I was surprised she didn't ask within minutes of my creeping through her door and asking for sanctuary. "Three."

"All right, fine." Glycera shrugs. "I'm just trying to help. I'll give you some books to read, shall I?"

My salty, brown, spiky party is like the wedding party

I attended in Chalcis with Daddy: the same lulling golden warmth, the same rich ribboning scents of meat and wine, the same fine citizens in their finery, smiling fit to break their faces. At the last minute, Glycera decides not to powder me, and plucks all but a few pins from my hair, so it mostly hangs long and loose down my back. She almost sends me out barefoot, but decides that would be a touch too much. Her pet names for me have been evolving: now I am *orphan, waif, ragamuffin, scrap*. "Sweet little scrap," she says with her lip-biting, I'm-not-really-crying smile. "You remember the magistrate?"

I smile.

"Now, you see," Plios the magistrate says. "You've fallen on your feet, after all."

He's not the one I'm waiting for.

"Pythias." The priestess of Artemis puts her hand on my shoulder. "You have found a way."

She's not the one I'm waiting for.

He arrives late, after Glycera's speech, after the meal, after Aphrodisia has sung for me, and Obole has danced, and Meda has juggled two pears and a heavy earring, to much delighted applause. I haven't had to perform beyond a few words of thanks to the room. Glycera, in a final evolution, has turned to praising my wit. Soften them with pity and then quicken their interest; I see the scheme. We've moved to couches in the cave room. A slave announces him. Glycera leads him to the couch next to mine, and while she begins a general conversation on economics—a pre-set topic offering me opportunities to shine—he leans over and says quietly, "You're so angry, you're practically throwing sparks."

"I have a message for you. From Clea, the midwife. She wants to talk to you."

He waves a dismissive hand. "Boring."

"Mm."

He looks around the room. "What an awful party. Aren't you dying?"

"I'm dead. How's Tycho?"

"They're all fine. No fear, little Pythias. You know you can come see them any time."

I say nothing.

"You really think this is better than what I'm offering?" He means the room, the party, the guests, Glycera, my dress, all of it. "I'd take you swimming. Riding and swimming and hunting. I'd buy you books. What else?"

"My own spear?"

"Knives, spears, bows and arrows, a catapult."

I must smile because he does, too.

"Tell you what," he says. "I know how to get out of here. Together, single file, no looking back until we've reached the other side of the water."

"But who will lead and who will follow?"

He gets up and walks away. So that's how it would be.

Had he looked back, he'd have seen me moving to the magistrate's couch to challenge him—wittily—on a point of taxation.

Plios the magistrate is not a bad man. He doesn't tell me I'm throwing sparks. He comes every afternoon as the sun is going down, between his work and his home. He greets Aphrodisia with a kiss when he sees her; I'm her replacement. He takes a warm drink in one of the big rooms with Glycera and me, chatting about his day. He likes to talk about his cases and solicit our opinions. I ask the kind of questions Daddy would have, about the practical day-to-day workings of the courts. Theory is one thing, Daddy always said, but practice another. If all you know is theory, you don't know anything.

"Well, take today, for example," Plios says on his third visit. "On paper, it was an open and shut case. The woman was accused of killing her husband with an iunx. There was plenty of evidence. They found the tablet with the curse, and the bird nailed to the wheel, and the ashes, and her maids confessed to helping her."

"Confessed," Glycera says lightly.

Plios stretches mightily, groaning with pleasure. "Glycera and I have this argument," he says to me. I'm sitting next to him on the couch, holding his hand. "She doesn't believe you can get an effective confession through torture."

"An eccentricity of mine," Glycera says. "What do you think, Pythias?"

"I agree." I turn his hand over in mine and massage the meat of his palm with my thumb, the way Glycera taught me. He sighs happily. "I've seen women in childbirth who would say anything, any lie, to make the pain stop. Why is she supposed to have wanted him dead?"

"The man's brothers say she had a lover. She wanted to marry this other man. He confessed, too." I switch to his other hand. "Open and shut when I read the brief. But in court—well."

Glycera signals to a slave, who steps forward with a tray of wine. She pours Plios a cup. He takes a sip and makes a face. "You've got mice," he tells Glycera.

I take the cup and smell it. Sour, faintly fecal. I signal to the slave, who steps forward again to remove the wine. Glycera looks mortified.

"Oh, it doesn't matter." Plios stands, pulling me up with him. "I don't need wine. My good Elene is expecting me for supper, anyway. She's told me, one more late night at work and she'll let the slaves prepare my meals from now on. I can't risk it. She's got a lovely light touch in the kitchen, my Elene. Lovely clear soups. After you, my dear."

I lead him to my brown room. He wants it sitting, with me kneeling between his legs, facing him. I still gag, but he doesn't mind. I've learned a bit of pain, a pinch or a scratch just before the peak, finishes him faster.

"Why was it different in court, though?"

We're wiping ourselves and dressing again. Three times, only, and already we have habits—I hold my hair up so he can repin the shoulders of my dress.

"Well, she was black and blue. She couldn't see out of one eye, it was so swollen, and she couldn't talk clearly because of her jaw."

"The brothers?" I straighten his clothes for him, his hair, rake smooth his beard with my fingers.

He shakes his head. "Everyone agreed they hadn't seen her since the death. She was taken in almost right away. That was the one thing everyone agreed on."

"Then I don't understand."

He looks at me with his clear, kind eyes. "It has to have been the husband."

"The one she killed?"

He nods.

"Did that change your decision?"

He looks at me a little longer, without answering.

I walk him to the gate. "I can't come tomorrow," he says. "But the day after, I can stay longer. Quite a bit longer."

I say, "All right."

It starts to rain. Big, reproachful drops.

"Gods." Plios laughs. "That was sudden. It's almost painful, isn't it? Well, go in. No sense both of us getting wet. I'll see you soon."

I kiss his cheek, as Glycera says I must, and go in, but not before the raindrops have stung the skin on my bare arms and shoulders. Hours later I'm freckled there with tiny red blisters, like burns from spitting oil.

The next day, I take the coins Glycera gave me to the temple and hand them over to the head priestess. Though I go veiled, accompanied by the big slave from Glycera's house, I feel the townspeople's eyes on me.

The next day is so stormy, the sun barely comes up. The sky is black all day and the rooms are like night. Plios stays for two lamps, a meal, and another lamp. The last time, I'm on my back when something makes me open my eyes. Past Plios's ear, I see a movement in the shadows where the wall meets the ceiling. As I watch, the colour curls back on itself and rolls in a single long peel down to the ground. Then the next wall, and the next.

When Plios notices, he's delighted. "We fucked the paint off the walls!"

After he's gone, I fix my hair and strip the bed. The paint curls crumble to dust when I touch them. I go to fetch the broom and dustpan and find Obole is ahead of me, trying to clean the big dining room. Every room in the house is afflicted. Glycera and Aphrodisia are on their knees, trying to scoop up the dust in their cupped hands.

"Is it the humidity?" Meda appears in the doorway, wrapped in a sheet. They all look at me.

"I'm not sure," I say. I think of Daddy, of Clea, of Euphranor, and add—honestly—"I doubt it."

A client of Meda's, an importer named Karpos, hires us to adorn his house for an evening symposium. He's invited many prominent citizens of Chalcis. Glycera has taught me there are many kinds of intercourse between a man and a woman, and my sisters and I make our way through the room accordingly: stepping lightly on unsuspecting feet; pretending to trip and seizing elbows to steady ourselves; holding eye contact a little too long; taking a man's cup from his hand and sipping from where he sipped; occasionally licking our lips, to offer sightings of the tips of our tongues.

I glide into the courtyard. Karpos the importer made his money in wine, and the stonework is carved and painted with vine motifs. I scrape with my fingernail at a cluster of black grapes painted on a column.

"Here you are."

"Here I am."

"Hiding?"

I shrug.

"*I'm* hiding."

"I don't care."

"Course you care," Euphranor says. "Don't you want to know who I'm hiding from?"

I shrug.

"Everyone," he says. "Everyone but you."

I shrug.

"Do you want to see a trick?"

No.

"No," he says. "But I'm going to show you anyway."

He touches his finger to the painted column, where I've scored white scratches in the paint. The scratches heal.

"Very impressive," I say. "You can put paint back on as well as take it off."

"You noticed."

I turn to go back inside.

"I've been very kind to you," he says. "Very generous, very patient."

It comes then, the change. The grapes burst into reality from the paint on the columns, hanging plump and ripe from the marble; the air suddenly goes warm and druggy sweet; the god, behind me, flickers into himself like a flame catching a bit of paper. A slave passing through the courtyard sees this, hesitates, then runs into the house. As though a person could run from this.

"I'll kill Simon," the god says. "I'll kill Thale and Ambracis and Philo and Olympios. I'll throw the baby down the well.

I'll cut Tycho's throat in front of your face, so help me, Pythias. I'll make you watch."

I tell him Tycho has had enough.

"He's had enough when you decide he has," the god says. "It's entirely up to you."

Inside, I tell Glycera I have a client. I don't run; I walk.

The house is utterly overgrown with vines. It's early, still, and there's a supper laid out for us. Ambracis serves, eyes downcast, and Euphranor finds reason to summon each of the servants, one after another, on one pretext or another, so I can see they're all well, plus meek and obedient. The house is tidy and in good order; the disarray is utterly gone.

I tell him I won't do it in my father's room, and he says he understands.

I have the god in my old bedroom. I tell him what to do and he does it. I tell him what I want. It's not a matter of superior meltings or explosive joys.

"I love you," he says. Warm, naked, breathing hard. "I've loved you for so long."

I tell him he's not allowed to talk.

The next morning, I'm woken by shouting. I'm alone in the bed.

Tycho is blocking the gate, trying to keep someone out.

I wrap my fur tighter around my naked self and venture closer, barefoot.

A soldier. Filthy, haggard, knife drawn. His eyes are sunken in a way I know. His voice is deep and rough, with a bit of sandpaper in it.

"Then wake her," he's saying. "I'll wait." I step closer, and he sees me over Tycho's shoulder. "Pytho?"

I put my hand on Tycho's shoulder. *It's all right.*

"Cousin," I say.

His smile, so sweet it hurts.

III

Nicanor's ridden one horse and is leading a second. He smiles at me and sheathes his knife and dismounts and I open the gate and let him in.

"I went to Athens first," he says, looking around the courtyard. "You weren't there, but your brother was. And that tall fellow."

"Theophrastos," I say.

"He gave me all this money." He opens a saddlebag on the second horse to show me a small fortune in gold coin. "From your father's school. He said it rightfully belonged to me. Then I went to the garrison, here, and spoke to Thaulos. He said you'd be expecting me."

"Ah."

We both look down at the fur I've pulled tightly around me.

"I'd like a wash," he says. "And something to eat."

"Tycho," I say.

"Lady."

"Take care of our cousin. Give him whatever he wants."

"Will you put that lot in the storeroom?" Nicanor says to me, nodding at the saddlebags. "After you put some clothes on. You, Tycho. Lead on."

"Master," Tycho says. He's been playing his trick of keeping his big self half between us throughout this conversation.

"All right, man, I'm not going to eat her," Nicanor says. "Show me the kitchen while she sorts herself out. I want some eggs."

"This way, Master."

I lock up the bags and return to my room, where I put on the brown dress from last night. I find Nicanor in the kitchen breakfasting on bread dipped in a bowlful of raw egg. He eats standing. "Want some?"

I shake my head.

"Thaulos told me there's a man named Euphranor I owe some money to," Nicanor says, without looking at me. "Is that right?"

I nod.

"Does your family know? Herpyllis, or your brother?"

I shake my head.

"I've been on campaign for twelve years," he says. "I need rest. Your man here has explained the situation to me. It's all right, Pythias. I'm not going to tell your family. The townspeople will talk, I suppose, but that doesn't matter. I don't care. Stay home like you're supposed to, from now on, and you won't even have to see them. I'm not going to punish you."

He stops eating for a moment and looks at me to make sure I believe him.

"Oh," I say.

"Write to them," he says. "Your brother and the others. A small wedding, don't you think? Nothing too elaborate. How soon do you think they might come?"

"IS THAT WINE?" NICO ASKS. "No, not for me, I'll have water. Theophrastos has been teaching me. Water for thirst, wine for taste, that's what he says. I'm thirsty. Are these cups new? I don't recognize these cups. This is new." His cloak. "Do you like it? Theophrastos had it made for me. It's very good wool, very warm. It's almost too warm for this time of year. He's getting married, too, did you know? You'll come to Athens for the wedding? I'm best in my class in astronomy and mathematics and I'm learning to play the *kithara* now. Theophrastos says I'm really good, especially considering I started so late. I brought it with me, I can show you. It's a really good one. Theophrastos says you become a better musician if you play on a better instrument. It was actually pretty expensive. I have my own room, it's bigger than my room here. You'll see when you come to visit me. You can come visit now, can't you? Now that it's spring and the army is home? Theophrastos says it's very safe for us Macedonians now. He says Daddy was over-cautious, but it's better to be safe than sorry. He says—"

My little brother breaks off mid-thought to launch himself into Herpyllis's lap and bury his face in her dress. She laughs and runs her fingers through his hair, slowly, over and over, until he lies still.

We're sitting in the courtyard, early evening, enjoying one of the first really warm days of spring: new green, new birds, heavy clothes and winter shoes abandoned for linen and sandals. Me, Nico, Herpyllis, Pyrrhaios, Nicanor. Theophrastos is in Daddy's old room, working. I think he wants to sit with us, but feels he'd be intruding on the family. Or maybe he feels he must keep Daddy's ghost quick. Pyrrhaios is family now; he and Herpyllis married in Stageira. He smiles often, touches her gently. And Nico—I can see he wants to love Pyrrhaios like a father. Nicanor sits on the far side of Pyrrhaios, listening with his head on one side to favour his good ear, patiently answering Pyrrhaios's questions. When no one is speaking to him, he withdraws into himself, sipping from his cup. He, too, is thirsty.

I spend a lot of time watching him. I am alert to him—his body, his moods, what focuses his attention and what releases it. I find myself wanting a private glance across the table, a casual touching of hands, any acknowledgement at all. But he is cool. His eyes don't change when he looks at me. He's tired, and spends a lot of time alone in the room he's chosen for himself. He dislikes loud noise. I've seen him wince at Nico's high spirits, less in dislike than in physical pain. He has a ringing in the good ear, he's told me, and he gets headaches. After we're married, I'll see if he'll let me put herb poultices on his temples, the way I used to do for Daddy. He's already told me he'll be keeping his own room.

Herpyllis asked after Myrmex within minutes of her arrival in Chalcis. I told her the truth: that he had stolen from us, that he was gone and he would not be coming back.

"I should be surprised," Herpyllis says. But her eyes still fill with tears.

"Who's Myrmex?" Nicanor asked.

"A poor relation. Daddy took him in years ago. He was like my brother."

"What did he steal?"

"Money." I hugged Herpyllis again. She couldn't stop kissing me, all over my face. "He was a little shit."

"*Pytho*." Herpyllis looked mortified, then laughed. "Language!"

"He sounds like it," Nicanor said. "Good riddance, then. You'll excuse me."

Then he was gone to his room for the rest of the afternoon, leaving Herpyllis and me to supervise Pyrrhaios's unpacking, and generally boss him about. We laughed so much, the three of us, until Pyrrhaios looked at Herpyllis and said, "I don't care," and hugged me, too, and I let him.

"We've missed you." He put his arm around Herpyllis and the two of them stared fondly at me. "We were so worried about you."

Love had wrought magic in him, a metamorphosis; he liked me now. Herpyllis was more relaxed than she'd been in the months before Daddy's death, and her prettiness was back, in her eyes, especially. They were happy together.

Now, in the courtyard, Pyrrhaios leans over to prise Nico off his mother's lap. "I can still pin you," he says, and takes a few steps away from the table, hauling Nico onto the ground to wrestle, to prove it. Nicanor flinches at Nico's delighted shrieks but, unusually, doesn't leave. He's making an extra effort tonight. The wedding is tomorrow.

Theophrastos appears in a doorway, drawn by the noise, and watches the wrestlers with his dry smile. Neither he nor Nicanor has Pyrrhaios's tree-branch arms. Pyrrhaios gives Nico the exhilaration of the body, Theophrastos that of the mind. What, if anything, will Nicanor give him? So far, they've barely spoken.

The next day's festivities begin at sundown. A priest comes to the house to supervise the ritual. Nicanor and I exchange gifts. He gives me a bolt of pink silk and a necklace set with pink tourmalines I'll wager anything Herpyllis picked out for him. I give him a branch of snow-white plum blossoms. I wanted to give him plums, for my first memory of him, but of course it's only spring. He holds the branch without curiosity, waiting to be told what to do next.

The wedding supper is hosted by Herpyllis and Pyrrhaios. Herpyllis explains each dish as it comes. *Beans with mint, you stew it with a ham hock, and honey bread, and lamb rubbed with spices, you have to crush them first and use quite a bit of salt, and quince cake of course, seedy quince cake!* A seedy meal for a seedy wedding night; I blush, and they beam.

Nicanor sits apart from me, and sips from his cup, and listens with his head cocked, smiling his polite, dull-eyed smile. Finally it's time for the procession back to the house. Normally we would walk from my father's house to my husband's; but here, of course, there's no distinction. This morning, I asked Nicanor if he wanted to stay in Chalcis, or return to Athens, or go somewhere else altogether. He looked at me and said, "I really don't care."

Nicanor takes my hand, and together we lead the wedding party, by torchlight, on a short walk up the street and back. In the few days she's been here, Herpyllis has taken the servants in hand and had the house scrubbed to a moony glow. Even the outside walls are clean and polished. At the threshold, Nicanor turns to thank the party. Then he leads me inside.

They have prepared Daddy's old bedroom, which is to be ours now.

We stand in the doorway. Many lamps are lit, and flower

petals toast in a brazier, scenting the room. The bed's laid with silk and fur, and there's wine on the table. Nicanor moves first; he goes for the wine. I attend to the brazier with the petals, blowing them out.

Nicanor glances over. "Thanks. Perfume makes me sneeze." He takes off his clothes and gets into the bed with his cup. "This wine is decent."

"It's a wedding gift. From Euphranor, I think."

Our first married conversation.

After a blank moment, he looks up at me. "You can read, if you like," he says. "The light won't bother me. You like to read?"

"There's no book here," I whisper.

He closes his eyes.

I take a lamp across the courtyard to Daddy's old workroom. The house isn't asleep yet. Doubtless they've noticed me; perhaps they'll think he's asked me to read to him.

When I return, Sappho under my arm, he's asleep.

After the first night, he leaves the big bedroom to me and returns to the small, windowless room he claimed as his when he first arrived. There's no sneaking, no pretence; he doesn't care who knows. Herpyllis takes me aside to ask if he's injured there.

"I don't know," I say. That hadn't occurred to me.

"But the first night—"

I shake my head.

"But then you aren't married."

"I suppose not."

"Pytho." She takes my shoulders in her hands so I have to look at her. "Do you want me to ask him?"

"No!"

"Then you have to find out. It's grounds for—"

I hold up my hand, *stop*.

"We can all see he's suffering," she says. "We all have compassion for him. But we have to think about *your* future, too."

"I said I'd do it."

"All right, all right, all right, I'll stop talking about it." But something else occurs to her. "It *is* him, not you? I know the first time can be—especially if you're shy, or—"

I close my eyes and stick my fingers in my ears.

"Forget I asked," Herpyllis says.

Nico comes loping into the kitchen, where we've been having our little talk, looking for another in an endless series of snacks. Herpyllis ruffles his hair, kisses me, and leaves us alone.

"You're so tall now," I say.

"Your voice is still deeper." He sits at the table and lets me serve him, bread and dried apricots. I sit down across from him. "I've missed you," I say.

"Me, too." He eats an apricot. "Nicanor told me Daddy's will said he was responsible for me, and anytime I wanted to leave Theophrastos and come back to live with you, I could."

"Is that what you'd like?"

He looks at me steadily, with his clear, good eyes. "Not really," he says. "But I'll do it if you need me."

I lunge at him across the table, tackle him to the ground,

and tickle him until we're both breathless. "Who needs you?" I say, again and again, digging my fingers into his armpits and wiggling them. "Who needs you?"

That night, I go to Nicanor's room. I had thought to follow him, very naturally, when he first went. Early, as usual; earlier than the rest of the house. But courage failed me, and instead I stayed up, playing tiles with Herpyllis and Pyrrhaios and Nico, while Theophrastos read in his corner. We talked about their respective journeys home, the day after tomorrow, and Theophrastos's upcoming marriage, in the summer, when we would all be reunited.

"And we'll come again, the moment you—as soon as you—as soon as you need us." Herpyllis falters.

"She means when you get pregnant," Nico says. Daddy taught us both not to be mealy-mouthed.

"That will be lovely," I say to Herpyllis. And to Nico: "You won't be invited."

"Disgusting." Nico makes a show of considering his tiles. "Don't even tell me. I guarantee you, I won't want to know."

"Actually, it's a fascinating biological phenomenon." Theophrastos looks up from his book. "When we're home, we'll dissect a pregnant sheep together. It's quite similar."

"Fun!" Nico says.

"Oh, fun." Herpyllis swats at him across the table. "Disgusting, both of you. Theophrastos, you're as bad as their father was. Dead animals all over the house, and always some carcass boiling away in my kitchen so he could preserve the skeleton. Pytho, you look tired."

My cue. "I am, rather. I think I'll say goodnight."

I make the rounds of kissing cheeks and none of them quite looks at me. I wonder who Herpyllis *hasn't* told.

"I thought we'd go out to the farm tomorrow," I say. "Take a picnic."

Everyone agrees that is a first-rate idea.

I wash in the big room and change into my nightdress. By the time I'm done, the courtyard is empty. Herpyllis's doing, no doubt. I cross to Nicanor's room.

"Yes," he calls.

I open the door. The room is dark, but he's not sleeping; I can feel his tense alertness, even flat on his back in the narrow bed.

"We thought to visit the farm tomorrow, for a picnic. We'd—I'd like it if you came."

He breathes out.

"May I come in?" When he doesn't answer, I close the door behind me and place the lamp on the table. "May I sit?"

"Pythias."

I sit on the edge of the bed.

"Pytho."

"Herpyllis says I should ask if you have an injury."

"Ah."

We sit for a moment, breathing in the excellently honest silence.

"No," he says.

I touch the tie at my shoulder.

"No." He pulls my hand down, quickly, and holds it in both of his own. "I don't want you to do that."

I tell myself: he would do it if it meant nothing to him. I tell myself: therefore, it means something. He's packed in thorny burnet, still, or I am. Packed in spikes, both of us, until we arrive at a safe place.

I go back to my room.

The next morning he's there for breakfast, and supervises the packing up of our caravan. He's fast and silent at the work, and when he's done, he and Pyrrhaios go for the horses. "Will you ride?" Nicanor asks me over his shoulder.

"Yes."

We all ride, in the end, even Herpyllis, her arms around Pyrrhaios's waist. Nicanor slings the picnic in saddlebags so we won't have to bother with the cart.

"Army-style," Theophrastos says.

If this is criticism, or snobbery, it's lost on my little brother. He seems taken with his big cousin, my husband, and nips around on his pony, asking questions about army life and army style. For the moment, anyway, Nicanor tolerates him.

As for me, something happened to me last night when he turned me away. Now, when he comes back to us after being somewhere far away inside himself—a word or two in his deep voice; his sudden frail, sweet smile—I catch my breath. When his eyes pass over me, I feel it. I know this is probably only because he is indifferent to me, but there is something in that indifference that I feel in the palms of my hands. My vanity is pricked; I'm humiliated, challenged. Stumped. Where's the way in?

Demetrios is in the yard in front of Euphranor's farm with a couple of slaves, sorting through a cart loaded with bags of seed. The slaves open each bag and call out the contents while Demetrios ticks them off on a tablet. A new delivery; spring is here. Demetrios looks up as we pass, raises a hand in greeting, and returns to his work.

"What do they plant?" Nicanor is beside me for a moment.

"Wheat, barley. A few vegetables—onions, beans. Mostly it's grain, though, for export to Athens. That's where the money is. The trees are oak and chestnut. A few fruit trees."

"Vines?"

"Not on our property." I point with my chin—we're here. "It's run down." *A bit run down,* I was going to say, but that would be wrong. "I couldn't—"

He grunts, rides ahead, dismounts. Looks around. Breathes deep. Looks up at the sky through the treetops, then down at the dirt. Kicks at it with his toe; squats to run some through his fingers. Shades his eyes to look into the abandoned fields, into the sun. He's all here.

I get myself down while Pyrrhaios helps Herpyllis. I suppose I should have waited for my husband, or Theophrastos, who takes my reins with a reproving look. Ladies are unfamiliar with horses, I suppose, even getting themselves off them.

"Thank you," I say to him.

Surprised, he softens. "You ride well."

"My father permitted it."

I see in his face a tiny recalibration: his future wife will be permitted to ride, too. A wedding gift I've thrown blind at some anonymous woman; a gift I've hurled at the future, too, if he decides to write about it and influence other men that way. Perhaps, in the future, women will be taught to ride as part of their educations, all because of my lie just now, my four little words. Fun!

"Pythias."

I actually trip over my feet in my hurry to answer Nicanor's call. I see Herpyllis exchange a fond look with Pyrrhaios. They must think it happened last night.

"Will you show me around?"

I ask Herpyllis if she will supervise setting up the picnic, here in the yard. It's cool, still, even in the sun; too cool and dew-edged for the pond.

"Take your time," she says. "Blanket?" I glare at her, but she's unembarrassed. "It has to be done at some point."

She's right, of course, that and the sacrifices before the first crops go in, but luckily Nicanor is already walking, and didn't hear.

"Next time," I say. "I think right now he just wants me to show him around."

As we walk, I sketch the layout of the farm: fields, orchard, river, pond, woods. I collect specimens as we go: snail shells, flowers for pressing, a yellow and black striped millipede that I carry in my hand. It wriggles. I let it clamber from finger to finger while we walk.

"Insects, eh?" Nicanor says.

"It's for Nico. I prefer birds. Fish, too, but mostly birds. I had to leave my collection in Athens."

"Who cares for them?"

I don't understand, and then I do. He thinks I mean they're alive.

"Skeletons," I say. "I collect skeletons."

"We're behind, if our neighbours already have their seed." His mind has moved on. "I'd like to spend a lot of time here. Maybe even make the house liveable again. For me, at least. The well's still good?"

"Yes."

"I'd like to see the river." We cut through the stalks and stubble until the babble is louder. "Excellent," he says. "No crops without irrigation." He stands, hands on his hips, and looks all around again.

"You've never farmed, have you?" I ask.

He rewards me with his rare smile. "Never."

"Why are you so keen?"

He looks at his feet. "It's quiet out here," he says finally. "I can think clearly."

As we walk back through the trees to the picnic, we pass a bird's nest lying broken in the long grass. Still teasing the millipede from finger to finger, I go look. There are eggs in it still, one broken, and nearby a newly-hatched dead wren, unfletched, with a disproportionately large head and bulging eyes.

Nicanor comes to look, too. "Fell down."

I shake my head. "Starlings, probably. They're looters. Here." Awkwardly, I transfer the millipede from my fingers to his so I can pick up the dead chick. The head lolls. It doesn't fill the palm of my hand.

"What are you going to do with that?"

Back in the yard, Herpyllis has laid the picnic out on

blankets. Nico is delighted by the millipede, and everyone crowds around to see my prize.

"Filthy, disgusting children," Herpyllis says. "And I brought cold chicken for lunch."

After we've eaten, Pyrrhaios, Theophrastos, and Nicanor walk over to pick Demetrios's brains. They come back full of purpose, and immediately set about making lists. Herpyllis says she wants a nap, so I offer to show Nico the nest.

"I might have done something bad," Nico says as we walk. "I asked Nicanor to tell me about the siege of Tyre. Theophrastos said I should ask."

"Why is that bad?"

"I'm not sure."

We've reached the nest. Nico squats next to it and fingers through the broken egg shells.

At last he says, "He told me to mind my own business."

Together we pick the shards from the nest. Gingerly, Nico lifts the nest from the grass. It stays together.

"Well, I got kind of mad. I mean, that was just rude for no reason. So I bugged him a little. I mean, I kept asking. It was for Theophrastos, really."

"Theophrastos could have asked for himself." I tear a strip from the hem of my dress to wrap the nest in, so he can carry it suspended by the knot and hopefully get it home in one piece.

"I think Theophrastos is scared of him. You know he stutters, Theophrastos, when he's nervous? He's afraid sometimes he won't get the words out. I know you don't like him much, Pytho, but sometimes I feel sorry for him. He's very nervous, and he knows he'll never be as smart as Daddy."

My brother is no longer a child.

"So you pressed Nicanor. Then what?"

He shakes his head, remembering. Just when I think he isn't going to answer, he says, "He told me he'd seen men die in ways I couldn't imagine, and if I were his son he'd cripple me so I'd never have to serve in the army. I told him I wasn't a coward and he laughed." Nico flushes, remembering. "He said I didn't know what I was, and hopefully I never would. What does that mean?"

"I don't know."

"Herpyllis worries he isn't kind to you."

Kind to me. Is that what sex is?

"She worries he won't take good care of you. She says he's like Daddy used to be, always going off by himself to his room. But Daddy worked and Nicanor does nothing. She says he drinks too much."

"So does Pyrrhaios."

"Pyrrhaios is happy, though."

At home, late that night, Herpyllis finds me in the kitchen.

"I just wanted a hug," she says, putting her arms around me from behind while I tend my pot on the stove. "It doesn't seem so long 'til summer, does it, when we'll see you again?"

"Mm," I say, stirring.

"What are you making? Smells like—" She looks over my shoulder and abruptly lets go of me. "Disgusting!" she says.

When the meat has boiled from the bones, I drain the pot

and lay the bits out on a rag to cool. The skeleton has come completely apart; some of the bones are no bigger than my fingernail clippings. I'll have a puzzle in the morning.

I go to Nicanor's room. "Tell me about Tyre," I say.

He shakes his head without opening his eyes. "Go to bed, Pythias."

"Tell me about India."

He opens his eyes.

"Tell me about Persia. Tell me about Babylon. Tell me about Kandahar. Talk to me."

Harshly now: "Go to bed."

I remove the pins at my shoulders and the front of my dress falls to my lap.

"No." He actually writhes, rolling his head one way and then the other, trying not to see. "No."

"Do you want a boy?"

"No."

"Is it because of how I spent my time while you were away?"

He sits up and covers one of my meagre breasts with his palm. The nipple hardens. He's actually considering laying me. Conversation is worse?

"No." He takes his hand from my breast and touches my chin, lifts it slightly in an echo of the widow's gesture, until I have to look at his face. "Not tonight. Tomorrow."

"Really?"

He lifts my dress back to my shoulders.

❧

The next morning, I lay the bones out on a cloth in the courtyard, for the good, early light. I start easy: the skull; the vertebrae, which are tiny but distinctive; the humeri and scapulae—shoulders and arms in people, wings in the bird. Daddy taught me that.

Nico wanders into the courtyard with his bread and honey, to watch and offer an occasional suggestion. Herpyllis next, with her tea. She's enjoying the two of us together, rather than our reconstruction. Pyrrhaios appears to tell us he's loaded the carts, and Pinch is ready for Nico. We bid goodbye in front of the house. No tears this time; we are a sticky spider-web now, connected from Athens to Chalcis and Stageira, and know we cannot be unclipped from each other. We will meet again in a few weeks' time, for Theophrastos's wedding, in Athens.

Nicanor and Theophrastos appear for the final parting; they've been in some deep conversation, and embrace briefly before Theophrastos turns to me to thank me, over-formally, for our hospitality.

"Advising him on the married life?" I ask my husband without looking at him, my hand still raised, suspending the thread between my palm and Herpyllis's, as she looks back from the cart that's just disappearing round the corner at the end of our street. Nicanor sniffs hard and quirks his mouth, holding onto a surprised laugh.

"I'm funny, just so you know," I say.

I turn back to the courtyard, and my chick. At first I think he hasn't followed me, and reconcile myself to a morning alone with my project. But then he's back with a tray, and I see he's detoured through the kitchen to bring bread and tea. "I want to go back to the farm today," he says. "As soon as you're ready."

I don't answer immediately. I'm trying to fit the humerus and scapula together, those tiny bone flutes. Most of the very smallest bones I can't begin to identify. I've laid the big ones together on the cloth: skull, pubis, keel. You can see the baby's shape.

"How will you fix it together?"

I feel his breath on my ear, smell him: leather, sweat, the body, and something sweet.

"My father used fish glue."

"Ah."

He watches for another minute, then leaves again. When he comes back, he's got my travelling cloak over his arm.

"I'm busy," I say.

He sits down to wait.

I work for a few more minutes, then turn to the tray.

"Why do you suppose no one's ever seen a centaur?" Nicanor asks.

"Centaurs live in Thrace."

"I've been to Thrace," Nicanor says.

I sip my tea.

"What I *have* seen," Nicanor says, "are monkeys. In India. Do you know what a monkey is?"

"No."

"They're like little people, with hair all over them and long tails and overlong arms and legs. They chatter like they're speaking a language."

I take a bit of bread, but Nicanor puts his hand over mine to stop me.

"Pytho, listen," he says. "I've killed so many people, I lost count. I tried to keep count but I got confused. And when you torch a village, it's hard to tally. How many died, exactly? How many I was responsible for myself, and how many I would have to share?"

Figs, too.

"I saw the king. Many times. I always thought of your father. It was hard to imagine them in a room together. Alexander was so—"

I wait.

"He had the strangest eyes," he said. "When he wasn't fighting, he looked confused. Does that make any sense? And tired. He was always so tired. He seemed so old and tired and broken, but in your father's stories he was this burning boy."

"Daddy wrote him letters. He never wrote back, but he collected specimens and sent them by courier."

Nicanor shrugs. "I wouldn't know about that."

"He says he wrote the king about you. Alerting him to your presence, and stressing your relationship. Suggesting he might—make use of your talents, or your intelligence, somehow. Befriend you."

Nicanor raises his eyebrows.

"Daddy taught him to swim."

Nicanor rubs his forehead, then says, "He couldn't swim. We saw him try, in India. He wanted us to swim across the river at Nysa, to surprise the enemy from behind. He waded in and flailed around and wouldn't let anyone touch him. He looked like a cat in a rain barrel. He even tried to float across on his own shield. When he couldn't do it, he made us march to a shallower place where we could ford it. Gods, that was a long day."

"And did you surprise the enemy from behind?"

He makes a tired gesture that means yes. "Are you ready?"

I let him help me with my cloak, but I mount by myself. Tycho follows us on a donkey. I say, "I didn't know we had a donkey."

"I bought him yesterday."

"What's his name?"

Nicanor has to think about that. "Snit," he says finally.

"What?"

"Snit."

I look at him.

"I'm funny, too," he says.

We turn the corner where we'd waved Herpyllis and the others out of sight. There's the town spread out below us, the near side and the far, and the tender green farmland beyond. The sun shaves sparks off the blue water. We can see movement in the town, all the tiny people making things work, and even the ferryman with his barge and his pole, tiny, tiny.

"Snitty," I say, and he agrees that's even better.

"What *did* Daddy teach him, do you suppose?" I ask. "I mean, that stuck."

He thinks for a moment, then says we should get going.

At the farm, he tells me to wait at the edge of a muddy field. When he wades out into the middle of it with a blanket, he disappears to the ankles. Tycho and I watch him lay the blanket flat and tromp back.

"Tycho will hold your sandals," Nicanor says.

He takes my hand and leads me through the sucking mud to the blanket, while Tycho waits with his back to us at the edge of the field with our horses and Snitty and my sandals and the picnic. I lie down on my back. My husband lowers himself onto me, eyes closed. It takes a while, but finally his seed comes. He lets his full weight rest on me while his breathing recovers. When he gets off me, I reach down and wipe some of the seed onto my fingers. It's like mucus. I fling what I can into the field, and he offers me the hem of his clothes to wipe the rest on. I think of the women drugged by the god. This is nothing like that. This is bright sun, cold, mud, and my husband unsmiling. This is outdoors, daytime, bright pain, and cold. He pats my shoulder and walks away.

We return to Tycho, who's laid out the picnic. I take my sandals and a towel and tell them I'm going to the river to wash off. When I come back, they're sitting together, eating, talking. When Tycho sees me, he starts to get up, but I tell him, "Stay."

Our lunch is bread and cheese. Nicanor has rigged up a bar over a cook fire so he can hang a pot from it to heat something for us to sip. Hot water. They're talking about crops.

"My father belonged to a farmer," Tycho says. "I lived with him until my beard came in. I can tell you what I know."

Teach, he can't bring himself to say.

"I would be grateful," Nicanor says.

"I didn't know that about you," I say to Tycho.

"Lady," he says, ducking his head in acknowledgement. He hesitates, then says to Nicanor, "It's good here."

Nicanor looks up at him.

"Good air, good water, good soil." He's holding Nicanor's gaze, unusually. "Quiet."

"It *is* quiet," Nicanor says.

"A good place to come," Tycho says.

Nicanor nods.

Tycho leaves us then, ostensibly to look at what needs doing first to the farmhouse.

"A bit forward, that one," Nicanor says.

"Daddy was the one who bought him when his beard came in," I say. "For heavy work. I've known him all my life. He's loyal, but he does always find a way of saying what's on his mind."

"He wants me to farm," Nicanor says.

"Apparently."

We pack up the lunch things, and Nicanor kicks dirt over the fire.

"Well." I flutter my fingers towards the fields. "Same time next year?"

I win another smile. He slings an arm across my shoulders and squeezes, briefly. "Sure," he whispers into my hair.

Back at home, there's a commotion in front of our house. An enormous cart is tethered out front, and Olympios is supervising the unloading of a massive marble sculpture. "The other one's already inside," he says, when we come close.

They lean the two pieces up side by side in the courtyard. "Do you know about this?" Nicanor asks, while the driver waits, narrow-eyed, for his pay.

I'm blank, and it's Tycho who answers. I remember as he's saying it: Daddy sent Simon to Athens to commission statues to Zeus and Athena to commemorate Nicanor's safe return. They're to be erected in Stageira, but the cost of transport being what it was, Daddy only wanted to pay to have them sent as far as Chalcis; we'd have to take them the rest of the way ourselves. They'll watch us from now on: Zeus, big-chested and big-bearded, with the piercing eyes; Athena of the clear brow and crested helmet. Here they will remain for many months, eerie at first and later familiar, finally just furniture.

Nicanor pays the driver and says he's going to his room. He asks Tycho to send his tray there. I feel the ghostly throb of him still in my vagina, but realize we have had no easy breakthrough, and there will be no cosy cuddling in the marital bed tonight. We have done what we can to ensure agricultural good luck, and who knows what soup is cooking inside me now, but in his mind my husband is still in Egypt, Persia, Bactria, Kandahar, India, Babylon—torching villages, raping peasant girls, starving, night-marching, eternally suffering under the obsession of an eternally suffering king. Wren bones and fish glue, indeed.

I could end it here. But there is one more thing to mention: a gift I asked of my husband, a wedding gift. At first he was reluctant.

"Oh, pink cloth," I said. "Poof. Pink cloth. What am I supposed to do with that, sew myself a dress?" The chick was done by then, as done as he was going to be, and hanging from the ceiling in the big bedroom by a piece of thread. He flew in the slightest breeze. I don't see what's gruesome.

"Fine," my husband said. "But don't come crying to me when you have regrets." We weren't sharing the room—probably never would—but we used it for private conversations, particularly concerning the servants. It was high spring by then, and he was mostly living at the farm, camping out there with the men he employed. He came home every now and then for a bath and a meal, and some evenings when he'd seemed less distant than usual I'd visit him in his room, then return to my own for sleep. He'd got the good Euboia dirt grained into his hands by then, under the nails, and maybe he drank a little less. I never asked him, nor Thale neither, who kept the stores and would know.

"You'll have to come with us, to the magistrate."

"Have you considered terms?"

"As few as possible," I said. "It's what my father would have wanted."

So today we return to the home of Plios the magistrate. My husband is resentful that I've kept him from the fields; he was late getting the seed in, and his inexperience makes him anxious. But then he is proud, too, shyly proud of the pale green nubs he's already coaxed from the mud. I've begun a vegetable patch by the house so we'll have something to talk about in the evenings. The first harvest from that patch, an early lettuce, I've brought as a gift for the magistrate's wife. Tycho follows us at his usual distance, leading Frost. Nicanor plans to ride straight from the magistrate back to the farm.

"I've been thinking I might do some teaching," I say as we walk. "Girls from wealthy families. Do you remember Thaulos? He asked if I'd teach his daughter to read. Maybe a bit of math, a bit of biology. There's a fashion for it." I finger the stone and the snail-shell from Daddy's school that I've taken to carrying in my pocket, lately, as talismans. I've already started with Pretty; she can say her alphabet very nicely, and she likes it when I draw numbers on her tickly back with my finger and she has to guess what they are. Slow Philo likes to watch us, squatting on his heels, clapping his hands when Pretty laughs. Once he held up three fingers to show her and said in his thick voice, "Three."

Pretty looked at me. I told her she had two teachers now. Philo beamed.

"Not for money," Nicanor says now.

"Of course not."

"I wouldn't set them on skeletons, either," he says. "Not right away, anyway."

"I've been meaning to ask you to bring me a fox, if you find one. I've never done a fox. I know farmers kill them if they can."

"Chicken farmers," Nicanor says dismissively. Then: "I'll see what I can do. I'll ask Demetrios. He has traps."

He's made friends with Demetrios, and Euphranor, too, who is beyond deferential. Star-struck, almost, by my husband's experiences in Alexander's army, by his hard edge and remote silences. Star-struck, lovestruck. He looks a little silly, these days, Euphranor. But he's helping enormously with the farm, and says he'll put my husband in touch with an honest dealer when it comes time to sell the harvest to Athens, in the fall.

"Come, Tycho," Nicanor says. Tycho follows us through Plios's gate. A slave leads us into an inner room, Plios's office, where the magistrate rises from his desk to greet us. I'm heavily veiled; he ignores me.

"This is the fellow?" he asks, and Nicanor says yes.

"A great day for you," Plios says to Tycho.

I pay the token coin to Plios—a privilege I had particularly asked of my husband. I wanted to do it myself. I put the coin on his desk, like a lady, so our hands won't touch.

"You are no longer a slave," Nicanor tells Tycho. "But your obligation to the family will remain until your death. You will come to us three times each month for instruction. These are the formal terms. Additionally, you will owe a freedman's tax to the city. Any children you might have will be exempt from this tax. Plios the magistrate represents the city as our witness."

"Children *I* might have?" Tycho says.

"Done!" Plios says, most jolly. "Now. Do we have time for a cup?"

A slave brings a tray with a jug and three cups for the men. Tycho looks like he's going to throw up.

"Drink, man!" Plios says. "Look at him. He's terrified. Where are the others, anyway? I thought we were doing four today."

Of course, as magistrate, he's read Daddy's will: *And Tycho, Philo, Olympios, and his child shall have their freedom when my daughter is married.*

"Their terms are different," Nicanor says. "No rush there."

Outside, Nicanor mounts Frost. My hand has strayed to my belly again; I see him look, look away. "Walk her home, will you?" my husband says to Tycho. "I'll be a week at least. Your lady will explain everything to you. So." He spurs the horse and is gone, my unmoved mover: gone without a backward look.

He'll probably remember my fox, though.

"Lady," Tycho says. "I don't have money for the tax."

We walk; not home, but to the beach where my father swam and then washed up, where Euphranor saw my birthmark, where Myrmex and I fucked each other all ways. We sit on the flat rock where Daddy used to leave his clothes. "You can have the shed behind the stables," I tell Tycho. The biggest of the outbuildings. "I've been fixing it up. It's clean and dry, weather-tight. I put in a new bedroll, and a chair and a lamp, and a chest for your things. You'll keep working for us, only we'll pay you now. And you'll have free time, to do what you want."

We sit for a long time, quietly, as morning turns hot noon.

"Children," he says.

I put my head on his shoulder, and after a while he puts his arm around me.

ACKNOWLEDGEMENTS

Huge thanks to Professor Susan Downie and Professor Shane Hawkins, of Carleton University; Professor Pauline Ripat and Professor Mark Golden, of the University of Winnipeg; and Professor Maria Liston, of the University of Waterloo, for sharing their vast knowledge.

Thanks to Anna Avdeeva for her generous gift of *Medicinal Plants of Greece* and Conni Bagnall for Robert Graves's *The Greek Myths*.

Thanks to Anna Avdeeva, Amanda Holmes, Ariel Levine, and Christine Lorimer of Carleton University and the University of Winnipeg, who came to Aristotle's Lyceum with me.

The poem Pythias reads on the road to Chalcis is from *If Not, Winter: Fragments of Sappho,* translated by Anne Carson.

The iunx spell Pythias recites is a combination of four incantations cited by Christopher A. Faraone in *Ancient Greek Love Magic.*

Thanks as always to Anne Collins and Denise Bukowski, my colleagues and friends.

ALSO BY ANNABEL LYON

THE GOLDEN MEAN

A Novel of Aristotle and Alexander the Great

Keenly intelligent and brilliantly rendered, *The Golden Mean* is a bold reimagining of one of history's most intriguing relationships—that between the legendary philosopher Aristotle and his most famous pupil, Alexander the Great. Aristotle is initially reluctant to set aside his own ambitions in order to tutor the rebellious son of his boyhood friend, Philip of Macedon. Still, the philosopher soon realizes that teaching this charming, surprising, and sometimes horrifying teenager is a necessity amid the ever more sinister intrigues of Philip's court. But as Alexander grows older and becomes a man who will transform the world for better or for worse, Aristotle, like any teacher, ponders his own culpability.

Historical Fiction

VINTAGE BOOKS
Available wherever books are sold.
www.vintagebooks.com

Refusal to Submit

Roots of the Vietnam War and a Young Man's Draft Resistance

D1026084

Richard Gould

Refusal to Submit

Roots of the Vietnam War and a Young Man's Draft Resistance

by Richard Gould

Copyright ©2017 by Susan Kaplan

ISBN 978-0-9993497-0-0
Library of Congress Control Number: 2017955334

ALL RIGHTS RESERVED
No part of this publication may be reproduced, stored in a retrieval system, or transmitted in any form by any means—electronic, mechanical, photocopying, recording, or otherwise—without prior written consent.

Indexing by Judy Gordon,
www.judygordon.biz

Design by Becky Hawley,
www.beckydesigns.com

Published by:
Susan Kaplan
P.O. Box 102379
Denver, CO 80250-2379
kaplan@earthlink.net

**For information contact:
www.refusaltosubmit.org**

Acknowledgments

Richard Gould had very nearly completed this book before his death in 2013. The family felt an overwhelming need to have the book published. Our family publication team was comprised of Dan Gould, oldest brother, Alan Gould, younger brother, Sarah Kaplan Gould, daughter, and his wife, Susan Kaplan. Dan and Alan studied the manuscript and working notes to be certain that Richard's final chapter represented the conclusion he intended. Sarah contributed her thoughtful writing of the last chapter, reflecting the essence of her dad's intention and creating a bridge between her father's narrative and her contemporary social justice experiences. Susan organized Richard's notes, letters and photographs which provided insight into his process and intent.

Other family members who contributed support and guidance include Sam Kaplan Gould, Diane Tokugawa, Susan Sternlieb, Kenton Phillips, Elizabeth Gould and Paul Fitzgerald. There were many people who wrote letters to Richard in prison, which later became important references in his writing of this book. Those people included his mother Libby Raizen Gould, step father Ben Raizen, close friends Richard Frumess, Bob Tichy, Cathy Wells, Hillel Goldberg and several Spanish-speaking Mexican inmates who were in prison with Richard.

We gratefully recognize and credit all the individuals Richard interviewed, both formally and informally. Without their voices, we would have missed the richness of each of their unique draft resistance experiences and the power of a similar shared narrative:

Thayer Ashton
Paul Barnes
Celine Benavidez
Patrick Bryan
Kendal Copperberg
Hiawatha Davis
Winter Dellenbach
Geoffrey Fishman,"Jeff"
Tod Friend
Bill Garaway
Sherna Gluck
Allan Haifley
David Harris
Marty Harris
Randy Kehler
Joe Maizlish
Chester McQuery
Greg Nelson
Dana Rae Park
Jeff Segal "Bugsy"
Art Zack
Bob Zaugh

We are grateful to the students, faculty and staff of Colorado Finest Alternative High who encouraged Richard to stay with his writing. These include Chris Anderson, Bev Breshears, Jeff Clark, Peter Downie, Tom Synnott and Tom Wilson.

Lastly we honor the professionals who supported and guided us through the necessary steps to bring this book into fruition: Becky Hawley for book design, Judy Gordon for proof reading and indexing, and William Stranger for his guidance and encouragement as an agent.

Contents

	Prologue	7
Chapter 1.	Fathers and Sons	13
Chapter 2.	Why We Refused, Part I	33
Chapter 3.	Why We Refused, Part II	59
Chapter 4.	County Jail	85
Chapter 5.	Safford	103
Chapter 6.	A New Community	125
Chapter 7.	Bugsy and the Oakland Seven	143
Chapter 8.	Encountering the Empire	167

Chapter 9. L.A. 187

Chapter 10. The Road to Nowhere 213

Chapter 11. David 239

Chapter 12. Drugs, Counterculture, and the Space Cadets 261

Chapter 13. Agitating, Rule-Breaking, and Troublemaking 285

Chapter 14. Release 309

Chapter 15. After the War 321

Chapter 16. Daughters and Fathers 329

Selected Letters and Documents 335

Epilogue 341

Index 357

Prologue

Dear Sam and Sarah,

I remember sitting at the dining room table searching for the words to explain how your quiet and bespectacled father ended up in an Arizona prison not far from Grandma's house. You had come home from school, Sam—from first or second grade—having heard somewhere about all the "bad men" locked away in prison where they belong. Your mom and I looked at each other and realized it was time to tell you.

That war that got me into trouble—it must have seemed so strange and distant; it must have seemed to you like some kind of Narnian fantasy. I was afraid you might be too young to understand. Your mom, however, had grounded you early in the ethics of fighting and bullying, and you each must have carried, as well, a child's wisdom about matters of war and violence. Perhaps that made it easier for you to grasp your dad's refusal to fight in Vietnam; perhaps it made it easier to accept his criminal status and his completion of a two-year sentence with the Bureau of Prisons. We could see the confusion on your faces; you were having to learn early that the world is much more complicated than a simple division into "good men" and "bad men."

Over the years, I recall relating a few sketchy incidents here or a random prison anecdote there. I think you told your friends with a certain pride that your ex-con old man had some kind of mysterious and vaguely disreputable past. But I never told you the story from beginning to end; you would have never sat through the whole thing, anyway.

As the national memory grows hazier, popular culture has produced its own version of events, often reducing the most complex characters to mere caricatures: the selfless combat veteran defending the country's freedom, the strident and less than patriotic war protester, the hippie innocent bringing flowers to antiwar marches. Having taught twenty years in an Englewood high school, I am quite certain that *Forrest Gump* and *Rambo, Part II* impacted my students' attitudes towards Vietnam far more than a thousand thoughtful books or documentaries.

Perhaps that helps explain why a persistent unfinished obligation continues to gnaw away at my bones. Among the sacred duties relegated to parents is the task of passing down the stories from one generation to the next. Now that you're grown, it's surely past time to sit down and record, as best I can, my own memories from this window of history that so defined our generation.

My own story must necessarily weave into the stories of others whose role was generally more forthright and dramatic than mine. Together we were labeled derisively by the street and oftentimes by the media as "draft dodgers." We were nothing of the sort. We challenged the draft. We defied it. We confronted and resisted it. The legal documents of my court case charge me with "refusal to submit to induction into the United States Army."

The vast majority of us—like most of the male American middle class—could have found some way—some extended student deferment, some contrived ailment, some psychiatrist's saving letter, some "indispensable" government job, some barely active national guard unit which would have allowed us to sit this whole nightmare out and watch safely from the sidelines. You could call us crazy or foolish, masochistic, naïve, or quixotic—pick your favorite slur—but please don't call us "draft dodgers."

In reality very few of us actually ended up in those dreary federal prisons spread out in isolated spots across the country. They were little-known places: Lompoc and Terminal Island, La Tuna and El Reno, Sandstone and Springfield, Allentown, and my own temporary home outside of a desert town called Safford. Of the half million or so who clashed in some way with the Selective Service System only 3,000 of us were convicted in federal court and served time in one of those lonely prisons.

Our numbers were small; our aspirations quite large; our vision quite audacious. We meant to change the course of history. We meant to be the generation that could stop a war dead in its tracks. I think even the least political of us had a gut-level understanding of strategy: Fill the jails and we could bring the war to a grinding halt.

Ultimately the war depended upon a network of military induction centers which processed 30,000 young men a month, month after month, year after year, two million over the course of the war.

If one views the war effort as a gigantic production facility, the activities of the draft resistance movement represented our attempt to shut down the supply lines, to sever the flow of raw material, and so to strangle the operation of the plant before its machinery could inflict further damage.

The case of Muhammad Ali brought this possibility to the attention of the mainstream media in 1967. A world champion heavyweight boxer, a man who was named "Sportsman of the Century" by *Sports Illustrated* in 1999, he probably rates as the greatest stream-of-consciousness trash talker of all time. He called himself "The Greatest," taunted his opponents mercilessly, described his unorthodox fighting style by claiming to "float like a butterfly, sting like a bee." We as a generation followed the details and trivia of his life and watched his fights with the same intensity that the nation watches any Super Bowl today.

That's why what he did shocked the whole country. In 1964 Ali began hanging around with Malcolm X in Miami and that same year converted to the Nation of Islam, more popularly known as the Black Muslims. It was also in 1964 that Ali failed the qualifying test for the U.S. Armed Forces because his writing and spelling skills—the result of a segregated Louisville education—were tragically deficient. That was the year before American combat troops were shipped out to Nam; reserves were adequate then, and the military paid little attention to Muhammad Ali.

As the war heated up, however, as induction centers around the country required ever expanding numbers of raw recruits, the army scrambled to keep up. Qualifying tests were revised downward and in 1966, the world's heavyweight boxing champion was finally deemed fit to enter the armed forces.

Ali's response stunned the nation: "War is against the teachings of the Holy Quran," he stated. "We are not supposed to take part in no wars unless declared by Allah or the Messenger. We don't take part in Christian wars or wars of any unbelievers." Then he added fuel to the fire: "I ain't got no quarrel with them Viet Cong. They never called me nigger."

Muhammad Ali appeared at the Houston induction center in April, 1967, and refused three times to step forward as his name was called. An officer explained the five-year prison sentence he faced and the $10,000 fine. Once again they called his name and once again he refused. The New York State Boxing Commission stripped him of his title that same day.

The next day *New York Times* columnist Tom Wicker articulated a vision shared by most draft resisters.

> A hundred thousand Muhammad Alis could be jailed. But if the Johnson administration had to prosecute 100,000 Americans in order to maintain its authority, its real power to pursue the Vietnamese war . . . would be crippled if not destroyed. It would then be faced, not with dissent but with civil disobedience on a scale amounting to revolt.

Two leading spokesmen of the resistance movement, Michael Ferber and Staughton Lynd, described similar scenarios:

> Eventually, perhaps when ten thousand acted, perhaps when fifty, the prisons would fill, the courts would clog and the resulting bureaucratic flap would bring pressure on the federal government to end the war or at the very least, the president would have to ask Congress for legislation to make new courts and prisons and so risk a re-examination of the war and its rising costs. Moreover, the existence of hundreds and perhaps thousands of young men in prison over a matter of conscience would exert a steady moral pressure on the American public.

By 1967 resistance groups were springing up in cities across the country trying to bring this moral pressure to bear. I could never claim membership in one of those groups. I was too shy, too awkward in group settings, too lacking, perhaps, in the courage it takes to get up in front of a strange crowd and make a public stand. I was, however, one of those thousands who came out of the woodwork individually and, on our own, refused—eventually in public—to lend our bodies to the war effort.

It was a nationwide phenomenon but I can tell you here only a small part of the story, my own story and that of a number of compatriots who shared my experience in the draft resistance movement during the Vietnam War era, and who did time with me in an Arizona prison camp during the years 1968–1970. I try to cover a variety of topics in this story:

- The hopes of the movement to put an early end to the war
- The strains on our families
- The reasons we were inspired to defy the draft law
- The introduction to the county jail
- The culture of a federal prison camp in Safford, Arizona
- The struggle between a Marxist revolutionary, Bugsy Segal, and a pacifist, David Harris
- The origins of the L.A. Resistance, the primary feeder of political prisoners to Safford

I was no captain in this movement, not even a squad leader. At the time of my incarceration I had no sweeping overview or grand strategy or any sense whatsoever of what it might take to mobilize enough Americans to put an end to that war. But I did enter into a flow of history, a flow—when placed into proper context—of a great social movement, and I can offer you a microcosm of what it was like.

Chapter 1

Fathers and Sons

Dear Sam and Sarah,

The Swift Trail Federal Prison Camp lay nestled at the foot of Mt. Graham, the highest peak in the Pinaleño Range of southeastern Arizona. The mountain towered 6,000 feet over the Gila River Valley; its base marked the location where the evergreen forest abruptly turned to desert—to arid brown hills covered with prickly pear and cholla, creosote bushes and scrubby mesquite trees. It was the kind of terrain your mother, having grown up in Tucson, learned to love at an early age. I, for my part, associated the countryside with prison and exile; it was years before I could appreciate its rugged beauty.

I arrived there in chains in October of 1968, stepped out of a late-model Dodge sedan driven by two U.S. marshals and so began a convoluted journey which transformed my soul, shaped my political consciousness, and connected my life to the lives of a kaleidoscope of extraordinary characters. There were counterfeiters—the skilled tradesmen, the intellectual elite of the federal penal system. There were bank robbers and dealers of all manner of drugs—heroin and methamphetamines, the finest classes of LSD and marijuana. There were murderers, mostly from the reservations of the Southwest—Navajo, Pima, Papago, Pueblo: any felony committed on Indian land is a federal offense. There were car thieves: driving a stolen vehicle over a state line constitutes a federal offense.

Mostly there were Mexican nationals. I'd say 60 percent of Safford Federal Prison inmates were jailed for crossing the border illegally or for transporting their brothers from Mexicali or Nogales or Tijuana to factories and construction sites in L.A., to fruit orchards on the Western Slope or strawberry fields in Orange County.

There were, in addition, Jehovah's Witnesses whose religion permitted them to go to war only in the Battle of Armageddon, only under the command of Jesus, and certainly not at the whim of a president who drank and swore and ordered men to fight for worldly things. And there was a small but growing number of antiwar draft resisters—far more political, far more secular, far more attuned to the issues in Vietnam than their brothers from the Kingdom Hall.

Among the resisters I first encountered were the old man Joe Maizlish and the youngest of us, Greg Nelson. I want to begin with their stories because they illuminate so many aspects of the movement. The story of resistance is a story of politics and radical new ways of viewing the world, but it is also a story of fathers and sons, of love and conflict, of anguished mothers and strained family relationships.

The old man was twenty-six. Twenty-six was the last year you could reasonably expect to be drafted and so Joe Maizlish was senior among West Coast draft resisters. His career in the academic world had already been assured. A graduate student in U.S. history and industrial relations at UCLA, a teaching assistant who had just passed his doctoral exam, he had received an automatic student deferment every year for seven years. At age twenty-five and a half, six months away from freedom, a bright future beckoning him, he chucked the whole thing, rejected his student deferment, returned his draft card to the Selective Service System and ended up in short order in the custody of the United States Department of Corrections.

Greg Nelson had never received any deferment at all. On June 17, 1967, eight days after his eighteenth birthday, he sent the following achingly simple letter written in pencil on a blank sheet of notebook paper to Local Board Group C of the Selective Service System in West Los Angeles:

> Sirs:
> As I have turned 18 (June 9), I am informing you of my decision not to register with the Selective Service Board. I want to make it clear, with this letter, that this is an act of civil disobedience and protest, not a simple evasion of the law.
>
> I fully realize the possible consequences. However, I feel that not registering is the only thing I can do in good conscience.

> When you want me, I am available at 1018 Pacific St., Santa Monica, California. I will keep you informed of my future movements.
>
> Sincerely,
>
> Greg Nelson

"When you want me, I'm available . . ." Those words almost jumped off the page when Greg showed me that letter decades later as we shared our memories on the beach in Venice in front of Figtrees Café.

Century City

The week after he sent that letter—as his fellow seniors at Santa Monica High School celebrated graduation night riding the Matterhorn and eating cotton candy at Disneyland—Nelson made his way instead to the sleek new development of gleaming highrises known as Century City. There at the Century Plaza Hotel President Lyndon Johnson arrived to address a $500-a-plate fund-raising dinner for the Democratic Party. He would be greeted by a huge crowd—15,000 to 20,000 marchers—gathered at nearby Cheviot Hills Park to express their unhappiness with the escalating violence in Vietnam.

Joe Maizlish was also among the thousands at the park, hoping to make his voice heard. That summer night was the first time Maizlish and Nelson crossed paths. Although each was unaware of the other's presence, they would both become witnesses to a landmark event in the history of the antiwar movement as well as in the sorry history of police-community relations in the city of Los Angeles.

What Maizlish and Nelson saw might give you some sense of how polarized the country had become, how raw the emotions had grown, how the atmosphere had darkened into bitterness and fear. The American Civil Liberties Union (ACLU) was so astounded by the intensity of the event that they sent out a team of investigators whose findings eventually became accepted by even the most conservative of L.A. newspapers.

Observers there described the beginning mood as "festive" and almost "picnic-like": "the hot dog vendors, the young man flying a kite, the steady thump of tin can drums gave the gathering the air of an outing." One marcher, Dr. Theodore Munsat, said that "The mood was one of extreme friendliness

... a cross-section of businessmen, housewives, children, hippies and students. Many were there with children in baby carriages; many had older children, there were people on crutches, people in wheelchairs. All of them came with the expectation of a peaceful march." Most were attending their first demonstration. Maizlish recalls Muhammad Ali's short speech at the park as the highlight of the evening: "If there should be trouble tonight," he cautioned, "let them start it."

The Los Angeles Police Department did not share the festive mood. Their relations with minority groups over the previous two years had been marked by explosive violence. There had been, of course, the Watts riot of 1965—six days of violence and thirty-four dead during which Police Chief Parker called the rioters "monkeys in the zoo." There had been the "hippie riots," otherwise known as the Sunset Strip Curfew riots of 1966 over the closing of a night club known as Pandora's Box. (It had been the unrestrained use of night sticks against these youth that inspired Stephen Stills to write his iconic song "For What It's Worth." ". . . Stop, children, what's that sound? Everybody look what's going down.") There had been the Silver Lake gay riots in the spring of 1967.

Now came before them this crowd of middle-class dissidents that filled the streets from curb to curb. They must have seemed to this tense police force an ungrateful mob, displaying a complete lack of respect for the president and, by implication, for the young men battling in Vietnam.

The situation was not helped by the reports of a paid informant hired by the Century Plaza Hotel. Sharon Stewart, an employee of International Investigations Systems, had attended a Peace Action Council meeting a week or so before at the First Unitarian Church. She informed the participants that one of her brothers had died in Vietnam, a second had volunteered and was preparing to be shipped out. She claimed she wanted an end to the war for the sake of her brothers.

It was all a lie. Having misrepresented herself, she went on to misrepresent the nature of the meeting. Her report claimed a "detailed plan" to disrupt the Democratic dinner through such tactics as unleashing mice and roaches, setting off stink bombs, and breaking through police lines in an attempt to storm the lobby. The report failed to mention that all of these suggestions came not from the leadership but from a few individuals in the audience and that all such ideas were flatly turned down out of hand with practically no discussion.

Based on her report, however, Superior Court Judge Orlando Rhodes issued a temporary restraining order placing certain restrictions on the parade permit. The use of a sound truck was prohibited and the march had to be continuous; no one was permitted to stop along the route.

As Maizlish and Nelson marched the half mile down Motor Avenue from Cheviot Hills to the Hotel on the Avenue of the Stars they had no idea any kind of injunction had been issued. Neither did any of the other marchers. The Peace Action Council had not even been present at the court proceedings called by hotel attorneys. Council Chairman Irving Sarnoff had been given the judge's order moments before the start of the parade, had glanced at it, puzzled, and handed it to one of the council's attorneys.

The first casualty was a blue Toyota pickup, rigged with speakers and amplifiers, and intended for use as a sound truck. Police made it emphatically clear that the truck was not permitted, but not before the hapless Toyota had been engulfed by marchers and rendered immobile. Eager to enforce the letter of Judge Rhodes's injunction, one officer sprang from the police line, held his billy club with both hands, and began beating full force on the windshield, shattering windows on the front and side. A marcher, incredulous, approached, shouting, "What are you doing?," whereupon another officer "wheeled and with a violent swing drove the end of his club up into the man's abdomen." A boy and a girl who occupied the truck bed were pulled down and beaten repeatedly while a bystander shouted in horror, "The police are killing that boy; they're killing him!" It was not an auspicious start for a peaceful parade, but monitors begged the crowd to stay calm and eventually the march continued.

Marchers who reached the front of the hotel were met by 1,300 police officers in full riot gear. Clad in white helmets and shiny black boots, they formed a virtually impassable defense of the hotel lobby, three lines deep between the protesters and the lobby 185 feet away.

There was among the marchers, a small group—about twenty—that had decided to ratchet up the intensity of their protest. Their behavior and attitude were bitterly resented by many of the marchers. They came off as arrogant, provocative, and completely out of touch with the peaceful tenor of the event.

The report issued by the ACLU, however, indicates that regardless of their attitude or poor judgment, any provocation was, indeed, slight. The small band of protesters merely sat down in front of the hotel—a completely nonviolent act of civil disobedience to underscore their unhappiness with the war. The Peace Action Council had already disassociated itself from this action even while deciding not to interfere with it. Instead, they instructed their monitors to guide the parade around those who chose to sit down.

What the parade organizers did not count on was pedestrian gridlock. Police had blocked off some lanes; bystanders, spectators, and a few counter-demonstrators on the sidewalk had choked off additional passageways. The parade soon came to a complete standstill.

A Police Riot

High above the Avenue of the Stars, Police Chief Tom Reddin watched all this unfold from his vantage point on the ninth story of the Century Plaza. Claiming he saw a "bulge" in the crowd and fearing an assault on the hotel itself, the chief issued an order to Captain Louis Sporer: disperse the crowd. Sporer took the mic from a police sound truck, declared (because all motion had come to a halt) that the assembly was illegal, declared the permit null and void, and relayed Reddin's order to disperse. Hardly anyone heard. Observers testified the sound system was so distorted and garbled as to be incomprehensible.

Following a second dispersal order, one demonstrator approached a police officer and asked, "Where should we disperse to?" He just shrugged his shoulders. So the crowd remained milling about. Very few noticed when the massed police began taking off their ties and putting on their leather jackets.

Joe Maizlish stood way in the back unable to see why the parade had stopped. "For at least half an hour," He said, "I was standing right next to a policeman on his motorcycle. He didn't say to leave or anything; he was just standing there showing us the peace symbol that was either drawn or tattooed on the back of his hand. Pretty soon everyone was pushing us back, the police started to advance on their motorcycles and some people were coming from the front just running. I saw my former roommate running; he was almost crying and saying, 'Joe, they're beating people up there!' The simple order to disperse the crowd unleashed a torrent of pent-up rage within the ranks of the LAPD."

"The first police rush came as a complete surprise," said one spectator. "No warning. No apparent reason. No one had attacked the police or made any move on the hotel 60 yards away."

Page after painful page of testimony filled the ACLU investigative report: "Parents lifted children into their arms, frantically seeking a way out." Susan

Langdon, seven and a half months pregnant, approached several officers: "I'm pregnant and I want to go home. Will you please let me through?" They looked at her blankly, then pushed her and her husband back away with billy clubs. A white-haired lady was smacked across the face as she moved too slowly away from the police line. A girl who tripped over a traffic island was sitting stunned when an officer hit her over the back of the head. An observer testified that, "He raised the club over his head and came down as hard as he could."

Greg Nelson was standing a good quarter of a mile away from where the trouble started. "I was standing there with my "Resistance" sign totally unaware of what was going on. All of a sudden people were streaming by me running and I was standing there—what's going on—and then there appeared this big wall of police and some guy with a club just pushed me down to the ground. He didn't swing it at me; he had it in both hands and he hit me hard enough to knock me over and push me down to the ground. I had done nothing; I was just standing there with my sign but I had done absolutely nothing to provoke it and neither had anybody else there. That's why they called it a police riot. If there was any provocation, they went way off the deep end. It's like—wait a minute—if two or three people did something, then go get them but you don't club 10,000."

All told, five hundred people submitted statements to the ACLU. One hundred seventy-eight reported injuries. Forty reported being hit on the head. Sixteen reported blows to the back or kidneys. Ninety-seven said they were hit on the neck, arms, legs, or elsewhere on the body. Four police were injured, the most serious with a broken toe.

President Johnson, though he was a man who tended to denigrate the antiwar opposition, was said to have been deeply moved by what he saw and heard at the hotel. One report described a "visibly shaken president ... airlifted off the hotel roof." Peace Action Council Chair Irv Sarnoff claimed that the president "from that point on, could not appear anywhere in the U.S. outside of a military base."

The Press Conference

As the city pondered the meaning of the violence on the Street of the Stars, Joe Maizlish, especially, was giving some serious thought to what he witnessed.

He had grown up in a family of journalists. In the late 1950s his father, Harry, had opened up one of the early FM radio stations. FM was "not hot" back then, but his dad carried a vision that FM was the wave of the future for quality programming. His KRHM radio station (R for Ruth, his wife, H for Harry, M for Maizlish) broadcast music of all kinds—jazz, classical, folk—and quality news. Hired on by his dad, the younger Maizlish taped fifty thirteen-and-a-half-minute interviews with Mississippi civil rights workers in 1964. They were broadcast by KRHM, KPFK (Radio Pacifica), and eight other stations nationwide. Through that experience and the fact that his mother, Ruth, was writing book reviews and feature interviews for a small newspaper, Maizlish was able to obtain credentials to attend a press conference with the L.A. police chief in the immediate aftermath of Century City.

"It was a beautiful plan," declared Reddin to the assembled press. "And it was well executed."

"I thought, 'jeez, these reporters are not asking the right questions,'" Maizlish remembers. "Those police reporters, I guess, they have to develop their own relationship with the police. Because it was the chief's birthday, they even sang 'Happy Birthday, Dear Chiefie' at the end. But they weren't asking the tough questions. (Reddin) said that he was concerned that people might rush the hotel so that's why they wanted to get us away from there." Maizlish had the opportunity for just one question: "Was there ever any move by the people to rush the hotel?" he managed to ask. "At least he didn't fake his way out of the question. He just answered, 'No.'"

Later on, Art Kunkin's alternative Free Press ran an entire issue painstakingly challenging every detail of the official police version. In the face of this compelling evidence, combined with the authoritative ACLU report, even the conservative *Los Angeles Times* had to revise its original support for the LAPD.

But Maizlish was troubled on a deeper level. "Over the coming days I did a lot of thinking about this. I could feel the marchers were getting more strident," he recalls. "Not necessarily violent, although some people, not most, seemed to welcome (the violence) or want them to go in that a direction." Fearing an escalation of violence on the street, having been greatly influenced as well by the ideas of the civil rights workers he had interviewed, Maizlish began contemplating other forms of confronting the war. "That's where I came to the conclusion that we just need more actions (of a different kind). People were pouring all their intensity into mass demonstrations. If they could slice off some of that intensity and express it through changes in their own lives, they wouldn't have to bet everything on one number of the roulette wheel.

"I was beginning to think 'What is the connection of all these marchers to the war system? Are they supporting the war in some way in their daily lives? Could they be opposing it in some way in addition to the parading and the letter writing and the posters?' Then I began thinking, 'How am I supporting this war effort? Oh, of course! I'm a draft registrant and I'm a deferred one too.'" His own most intimate connection to the war effort had become obvious: his status as a draft registrant rendered him a potential warrior. "I had just read the Malcolm X autobiography and it was very challenging. It made you think; it made you say 'Okay, how am I supporting this system of privilege in some way that I can change or try to change? Well, I got this deferment. But that would be some serious consequences if I relinquished it.'"

Maizlish thought about this all summer. It was an historic summer that included a war in the Middle East and a riot that left sections of Detroit in ruins just as Maizlish drove into Ann Arbor to drop off his brother at the University of Michigan. There was a curfew that night, a gasoline shortage, and the Motor City was still smoldering. "It was a pretty crowded period there in 1967," says Maizlish.

He also met Greg Nelson and a number of other resisters. For years Maizlish had very much welcomed his student deferment and "I suppose," he said, "concern about being drafted was a factor in my charging ahead with my studies." Here was this kid Nelson, eighteen, just out of high school and ready to put into practice some of the ideas that Maizlish had been studying for years in his post-graduate studies at UCLA. By September Maizlish had made up his mind: He refused to renew his student deferment. "I looked at it; I looked at the form and said to myself, 'You can't do this anymore.'" He left the form blank.

The Elder Maizlish

Challenging the Selective Service System was one thing; talking to his dad quite another. Harry Maizlish was shaken to the core by his son's decision. To be sure, he was not particularly ashamed of Joe's moral stand. For years both his parents had admired the work of Martin Luther King and civil rights activists in the South. "These are the values you taught us," Joe told them. But the thought of his own son in a federal prison scared his father to death.

Joe's bond with his father ran deep and he harbors a rich store of family memories. "A while back, I ran out of gas one night around midnight," he recalls. "I pulled into a station and who was in the money booth? It was this girl; she had to be like ten or eleven at most. She was sleeping in a chair; her little brother was crawling around on a table. He made change for me, that little six- or seven-year-old guy. And I thought, 'That's my dad.' His dad too had lived the immigrant life, arriving impoverished from the Ukraine at age three and stepping immediately into a life of work. "On Sunday mornings he got up at 3, got on his little bicycle, went off to get stacks of newspapers that he loaded on the bike and then ran around Lynn, Massachusetts, selling them. Age six, eight, something like that. A total life of work from childhood. He was selling papers every evening. When he got old enough, he'd go sell out on the streets of Boston and then get back somehow to Lynn."

Through work, sacrifice, and community service, Mr. Maizlish had gained considerable stature in the Los Angeles community. During the '30s he became a publicist for Warner Brothers Motion Pictures. In the process of setting up large functions—premieres and theater openings—he had connected with a good many civic figures from mayors to police chiefs to aldermen. His later ownership of KRHM increased his reputation as a pillar of the community. Having worked his whole life to build some respectability and a little security, he now saw his son risking his entire future.

"He never said he was angry," says Maizlish. "But he was worried because he thought this might interfere with my career. Let's remember, he had sacrificed a lot for his family and the whole value was 'If we're gonna survive as this impoverished immigrant family everybody's gotta be working for everybody else and that any advance you can make you don't ask any questions. You got a chance for a little more income—that helps everyone.' He was concerned about the career impact."

He had one request. "Please go see my lawyer before you follow through on this."

Dutifully, Maizlish found his way to the office of Irv Prinzmetal. "I followed through and did what my dad wanted, all these things my parents wanted me to do to make it a little easier for them, to let them know I had checked in with the people they wanted me to see." Prinzmetal lifted the phone and called a federal judge, a judge in fact who was the father of one of Maizlish's high school buddies. The judge was blunt: "He'll never get a position of trust in business or government for the rest of his life."

"That was quite interesting to hear," recalls Maizlish, but no big surprise. Despite the judge's warning, despite his father's misgivings, there was no turning back.

Maizlish rejected his student deferment, then prepared the next step: he would return his new draft card—complete with a letter articulating his categorical divorce from the system. The date planned was October 16, 1967, the day a mass national draft card turn-in had been scheduled. Once again, however, his father asked to negotiate. "Don't send it in with everybody else," he requested. "Make sure it's something you would do just for yourself."

It seemed reasonable. "I figured that's a good compromise," recalls Maizlish. "It wasn't giving up on any important principle. I said, 'Dad. You want me to wait a few days, I can do that.' So I mailed mine in myself on October 20."

Mr. Maizlish took a copy of the accompanying letter, folded it carefully, and placed it in his billfold where he carried it around everywhere. "My personal experience," it began, "and what I have been able to learn from public affairs, have led me to the conclusion that mankind will make life more free and peaceful as individuals turn away . . . from the means of war . . ."

On a business trip to San Francisco, the elder Maizlish saw a familiar figure on the street in front of his hotel. Maizlish had known him years before when the man was district attorney for Alameda County. Seeking reassurance wherever he could, Maizlish ran up to the now Supreme Court Justice Earl Warren, handed him the letter and asked: "What do you think will happen to him?" The chief justice took a moment to read the statement, then looked up. "These are fine young men, Harry. Unfortunately, they're going to prison."

Greg Nelson's father didn't share the ambiguous mix of emotions that churned in Harry Maizlish's belly. Nor was there the bond that had developed between Maizlish and his father. Richard Nelson was old school, a conservative ex-marine from the Midwest, a second lieutenant during World War II who participated in Pacific-island hopping operations at places like Iwo Jima and Okinawa. When he learned of his son's refusal to cooperate with the draft, his face reddened with shame.

"He was very upset I wasn't going to go," recalls Nelson. "His whole side of the family, they were good folks but they had trouble understanding that Vietnam was different from World War II. They just thought if the government called you, you're supposed to go. They couldn't see the idea that there was a difference between being attacked and going off to try and create an empire somewhere. I remember my dad taking me to one of his old commanding officers back in New Jersey, some lieutenant colonel who tried to convince me to register."

I'm Not Gonna Register, Period

The FBI tried the same thing. In the spring of 1968, a couple of agents knocked on Lois Nelson's door in Santa Monica, informing her they just wanted to talk to her son. "I went down to the Federal Building downtown; I walked into the FBI office and said, 'I'm Greg Nelson and you guys came by to talk to me.' There were two or three guys there and they tried to talk me out of it. They were offering alternatives like giving me another chance to join or registering as a conscientious objector. They were basically telling me that I was making a big mistake, that I was gonna ruin my life and that I should obey the law. I was the young kid that they saw going astray and they were giving me a chance to change my ways. I said 'No, I'm not gonna do it. I'm not gonna register, period!'"

Richard Nelson's shame intensified when his son agreed to dramatize his stance by seeking sanctuary at the Grace Episcopal Church in downtown L.A. The Reverend William Sloane Coffin, later to be embroiled in his own anti-draft trial, summarized the history and symbolism of sanctuary in a sermon he had delivered the previous fall at a similar action in Boston:

> "Thou spreadest a table before me in the presence of my enemies." These familiar words from the 23rd Psalm refer to an ancient desert law which provided that if a man hunted by his enemies sought refuge with another man who offered him hospitality, then the enemies of the man had to remain outside the campfire light for two nights and the day intervening. In Exodus we read that the altar of the Tabernacle is to be considered a place of sanctuary and in Numbers and Deuteronomy we read of "cities of refuge," three in Canaan and three in Jordan. During the Middle Ages all churches were considered sanctuaries . . . Now if in the Middle Ages, churches could offer forty days to a man who had committed both a sin and a crime, could they not today offer an indefinite period to one who had committed no sin?

"I wasn't the kind of person who liked to be front and center," recalls Nelson. "I'm basically shy to the point where I don't deal well with people. I'm not a leader in that sense, not an organizer. I didn't bring up the idea of sanctuary but once (a group of us from The Resistance) decided, I was willing. Being shy, in fact, having this social anxiety disorder, it was one of the hardest things I ever did—to stand up in front of everybody in that church. Standing up in the middle of a room with a spotlight on me was terrifying. It was harder for me to do that than to go to prison . . . But at that point, I was willing to do anything to publicize opposition to the war. Whatever sand I could throw in the gears, I wanted to throw. If I could be on the front page of the *L.A. Times,* I wanted that because I wanted people to think 'this war's got to stop.'"

And so Nelson composed a letter to the Episcopal Church. "No court has the right," he stated, "to judge a man for what his conscience compels him to do. For this reason, it's impossible for me to recognize the power of the government to place me on trial. For we are again in a period in which government is not responsive to the will of the people, a period in which our government seems to have forgotten the principles and morality on which it was conceived. Hiding under its cloak of legality, it refuses to answer the moral imperatives of our age. Since I cannot turn to the court for justice, I turn to the church. I ask that you lend your church for the role that churches once played. I ask you to grant sanctuary."

The sanctuary was planned for the day of Nelson's trial. A local activist group had previously posted several thousand dollars in bail money, so shortly before the planned event, Nelson appeared before Judge Albert Stevenson and requested to be put on OR—Own Recognizance. That means no bail money is involved, just a defendant's promise to appear in court. His motivation, of course, was to protect his sponsoring group from losing its bail money. He was unaware of the fact that there was no danger of forfeiting the money as long as he eventually showed up in court.

"Well, the judge agreed to reduce my bail to OR," says Nelson, "but then he was really pissed off when I didn't show up for trial because of the sanctuary. He took it as a personal attack, basically. It was like, 'You lied to me; what's this about?'"

Finally, Mike Greene, a lawyer who helped Nelson with his case, was able to explain. "I wasn't trying to screw him; I just didn't want this group to lose their money," says Nelson, "and I didn't know the law. When the judge realized that he thought, 'Oh he's just a stupid kid; he doesn't know any better.' That calmed him down."

Sanctuary

Greg Nelson was late for his own sanctuary. In the old days the offender would flee to a place of refuge with his captors in hot pursuit. In this case the cops were already there by the time he showed up.

Nelson and fellow resister Bill Garaway had gone to the airport to pick up David Harris, the most notorious leader of the West Coast draft resistance movement. "L.A. traffic being what it is," says Nelson, "we got stuck. The whole church is filled with people waiting; it was supposed to start at 10:30 and here it is getting towards noon and I'm not there. By the time I arrived, the whole building is surrounded by U.S. marshals looking for me. At that time I had long blond hair and Karen Dellenbach, a leader in the L.A. Resistance, also had long blond hair and was about my size. She came out and gave me her parka and we decided that maybe I could slip in and they wouldn't realize it was me until it was too late."

The plan worked. In a symbolic show of noncooperation, a group of supporters had already chained themselves together at the wrists in anticipation of Nelson's arrival. Nelson slipped in through a side door, raced to the front of the church, and just out of the grasp of a pursuing U.S. marshal, chained himself to Mark Schneider on one side and the Rev. Harlan Weitzel on the other.

"They decided they're gonna have to get some bolt cutters to snip off these chains," says Nelson. "So a good hour or so goes by and I talked about the war, and David Harris talked about the war, and we sang songs and did all that kind of stuff. Finally the marshals show up with these huge, four- or five-foot-long bolt cutters. It was bizarre. They charged up to the front, stepping on all kinds of people and snipped the chains and dragged me off to L.A. County. I know when they finally arrested me, they were all amused. They weren't used to the idea that somebody they were trying to arrest might come in through their line to get himself arrested."

The marshals never realized that in his haste, Nelson put his chains on so loosely, they could have just slipped them off over his wrists and dispensed altogether with the giant bolt cutters.

Despite the comic overtones—despite the lateness, the sneaky dash to penetrate the police line, the loose chains about Nelson's wrists, the ridiculously outsized bolt cutters—the scene at Grace Episcopal Church ended in high drama. The place was filled to the rafters. The press was there. The clergy was there. The chains were wrapped around the holy altar at the center of the sanctuary. As the marshals dragged this slender eighteen-year-old manchild out of the church to meet whatever fate awaited him in federal prison, an audible gasp filled the room. The power of the state—generally closeted in the background—revealed itself in open display. Cameras flashed. The story did indeed appear on the front page of the *Los Angeles Times.* A friend of Nelson's serving in the army in Vietnam saw it in the news over there. Greg's story reverberated across the Pacific.

The sanctuary at Grace Episcopal delayed Nelson's trial for only a day. Official documents from the United States District Court for the Central District of California presented Nelson as a kid with no means of support:

- Average weekly income: none
- Cash on hand and in banks: none
- Number of dependents: none
- Property owned: none

Assistant U.S. Attorney John Lane had only to perform three embarrassingly menial tasks to get the conviction. He had to prove Greg Nelson was over eighteen. He had to prove he was a resident of Santa Monica and thus obligated to register at the local draft board. And he had to prove he had failed to register for the draft. It was like nursery school for lawyers.

An American Mother's Nightmare

Step one was to call Nelson's mother to the witness stand and have her testify to the authenticity of his birth certificate. Lois Nelson was living an American mother's nightmare—1960s style. Her eldest son had just been sent to Vietnam and spent his first days there walking point—the most dangerous job in the infantry. Now her youngest was facing five years in a federal prison and they wanted her to assist in putting him away. It was all too much for Mrs. Nelson. She refused to testify. Of course the prosecution could have insisted, but they backed off. It might not sit well with a jury to force a mother to testify against her own son.

They turned instead to his dad, Richard. Richard and Lois Nelson had been divorced for fifteen years and lived on opposite sides of the country. Father and son were practically strangers.

"My father was willing to testify. They flew him all the way out from back east. I remember my father accusing me of doing all this because I was wanting attention." Nelson whose social anxiety is still evident today in his hermetic lifestyle and his fear of crowds was thinking, "Dad, you don't know me. You really don't know me. (Attention) is the one thing I hate." "He was only on the stand for a few moments," recalls Nelson. "It was an annoyance, but I was never really close to my father anyway." It seemed that last phrase left a lot unspoken.

Step two, proof of residency. The state brought in Archibald Leech, vice principal of Santa Monica High School, which Nelson had attended the previous spring. He thought he would have an easy job of it; he just needed to testify that Nelson was living in his school district at the time he was supposed to register. He brought forth a school roster with Greg Nelson's name on it as well as his address which showed him to be a Santa Monica resident. He thought he was done.

Nelson, who represented himself throughout the trial had other ideas. Nelson had been dating Lynn Fielder, a young lady two years his junior who was still attending Santa Monica High. She had been refusing, on a variety of grounds, to stand for the Pledge of Allegiance and Archibald Leech countered continually by calling her into his office, questioning her patriotism, and harassing her, she claimed, because of her failure to respect the flag.

Nelson had done his legal homework. He discovered a 1943 Supreme Court decision, *West Virginia State Board of Education vs. Barnette*, which found mandatory pledge of allegiance in violation of the First Amendment. The challenge had come from Jehovah's Witnesses who maintained that pledging allegiance to any flag defied the prohibition in Exodus against worshipping graven images. "Thou shalt not make unto thee any graven image" (Exodus 20:4, 5). The court's ruling, however, was broader and held unequivocally that "No official high or petty can prescribe what shall be orthodox in politics, nationalism, religion or other matters . . . or force citizens to confess by word or deed their faith therein."

With this ammunition in hand, Nelson set out to impeach the testimony of Archibald Leech on the grounds that the character of a man who routinely violated the United States Constitution was unworthy of credibility in the courtroom.

It was a high school rebel's dream. Instead of the student waiting anxiously for the reprimand in the vice principal's office, for a brief moment the tables were turned. Not only could the former student interrogate the authority figure at will, he could defend the honor of his girlfriend in the process. A fairly tolerant Judge Stephens permitted the questioning to proceed.

"Are you acquainted with a Miss Lynn Fielder?"

"Have you ever had occasion to discipline Miss Fielder?"

"What were your instructions to her in regard to the Pledge of Allegiance?"

"Are you familiar with the Supreme Court decision in the *West Virginia State Board of Education vs. Barnette* case?"

"It was kind of fun for me," says Nelson. "He thought he was just gonna testify to the fact that I was living in this school district. He had no idea he was about to get drawn over the coals for harassing my girlfriend and here I was impeaching his testimony. He didn't take kindly to it."

After ten minutes, Judge Stephens finally interrupted. "All right. Enough. I've had enough. Let's get back to the issues at hand here."

The issues at hand were a forgone conclusion. When Mrs. Alma Whisenant, executive secretary of Local Board Group C of the Selective Service System took the stand, she produced Nelson's letter which declared his open defiance of the draft. That was all the prosecution really needed. During a prison visit later on, Sherna Gluck, one of the key L.A. Resistance organizers told him of the aftermath of his trial. The jurors were upset, she told him. They took no pleasure in convicting Nelson but the law was clear and they felt they had no choice. The court reporter was so shaken, she left the courtroom in tears. But by that time Nelson had already been whisked away to a holding cell in the Federal Building awaiting shipment to the Los Angeles County Jail. Lane got his easy conviction and Nelson got his three years.

By early spring of 1968, some months before Nelson's trial, Joe Maizlish had already been reclassified and called to serve. He and a friend, Christian Hayden, decided not to enter the induction center but instead to stand outside and announce to the world their joint refusal to submit to induction. Maizlish, who had been at that corner dozens of times, leafleting young men and asking them to consider their own positions, stood with a sign proclaiming "Today I'm Refusing Induction What Will You Do?"

Hayden carried a similar sign. Both of their fathers were present.

A Hollywood Dad

The presence of the two Haydens brought the press out in force. Christian Hayden was the son of actor Sterling Hayden who couldn't walk down the block without generating publicity. A striking six foot five inches, the elder Hayden had been dubbed by Paramount Pictures "The Most Beautiful Man in the Movies" and the "Beautiful Blond Viking God." He had played leading man in *The Asphalt Jungle*, and a score of other popular but lesser known films. More recently he had appeared in a fierce satire of the Cold War, *Dr. Strangelove or How I Learned to Stop Worrying and Love the Bomb*. In the 1964 film, Hayden had played Air Force General Jack D. Ripper, a delusional nutcase who managed to unleash a nuclear strike in order to thwart a communist conspiracy to "sap and impurify our precious bodily fluids" with fluoridated water.

The actor's personal life was more dramatic, perhaps, than his professional one. He joined the marines during World War II, then transferred to the Office of Strategic Services or OSS, the secret intelligence agency that preceded the CIA. Awarded the Silver Star for gallantry, Hayden shared a similar story with your Uncle Hi (Haim Barmack). Both parachuted behind German lines to fight with the Yugoslav partisans against the Nazis. Hayden's admiration for Marshal Tito and his communist guerrillas went so far as to inspire him—briefly—to join the Communist Party after the war.

Then in the early '50s—with the McCarthy era in full swing especially in Hollywood—Hayden was subpoenaed to appear before the House Un-American Activities Committee. There the "Viking god" buckled under questioning. He confessed his former ties to the party, then he "named names," that is, he revealed the identities of those he associated with during his communist period. In all likelihood those names were already in the hands of the committee, but Hayden left the hearing profoundly humiliated. "I don't think you have the foggiest notion," he later wrote, "of the contempt I have had for myself since the day I did that thing."

This surely set the context for the interview broadcast on the evening news of March 5, 1968, the night of Christian's refusal to report for induction. Asked for his reaction to his son's open defiance of the draft law, the decorated former marine captain stunned his listeners: "This is the proudest day of my life."

Maizlish's father remained ambivalent and tormented. "He started crying," recalls Maizlish, "because he was looking at the other families where everyone was saying goodbye to each other—tearful good-byes and hugs—and he told me he was thinking, 'What is all this for?' He just didn't quite understand this war or feel quite right about it and he was getting the idea that it's important to stand up against it. But he was still quite worried about the way I was doing it and the expected consequences. It was very valuable to me that he took the trouble to go down there with me."

Maizlish's trial was just as easy for the prosecution as Greg Nelson's. He too had brazenly defied the law, offered no apologies, stood ready to face the punishment. He too acted as his own counsel. At his arraignment before Federal District Judge Manuel Real, he refused to enter a plea, feeling not particularly guilty on the one hand, but unwilling to deny he had violated the law on the other. Judge Real was not happy. "He seemed to be irritated with everybody, anyway," says Maizlish. He soon gained a reputation among area draft resisters as the harshest judge in the L.A. District Court. Gruff and arbitrary, he was the judge most likely to hand out long sentences. Defense attorneys described him as "imperious" and nicknamed him "Maximum Manny." Of Hispanic heritage, he took offense to anyone using the two-syllable Spanish pronunciation of his surname: Ray all. "It's Reel," he would insist. "My name is Reel."

Meditating in the Courtroom

Judge Real was particularly irritated the day of Maizlish's arraignment by the presence in the courtroom of Greg Nelson whose trial date had yet to be set. Nelson showed up that day just to be supportive to Maizlish. "Back in those days," says Nelson, "in my hippie days, I wasn't religious, but I was into meditation in a vague sense, and I was sitting there kind of folding my hands with my head down trying to give out good vibes. Judge Real looked down and saw me with my head bowed and decided I was on drugs. He pointed me out to the bailiff and said, '86 that guy out of here; he's stoned.' I looked up and said 'What are you talking about, I'm not stoned I'm just meditating.' '86 him!' he said. It was the first time I ever heard that term. '86? What is that?' I'd never been to a bar or anything. Next thing I know the bailiff's hustling me out of the courtroom and I'm being thrown out."

Maizlish was not unhappy to have his trial reassigned to Judge Stephens, but the change made little difference. Prosecuting attorney Arnold Regardie so outmaneuvered the inexperienced Maizlish as to render any moral aspects of the case off limits. Maizlish wasn't even permitted to describe his state of mind on the day of the offense. When the final gavel banged, Joe got three years.

Maizlish recalls a minor slip up when Judge Stephens neglected to order him to report immediately to the marshal's office. Without contrary instructions, Maizlish simply filed outside the courthouse followed by a few supporters who sat down in the plaza. Someone pulled out a guitar and songs of farewell filled the air. Two burly marshals, realizing that this was unacceptable, quickly moved in to place Maizlish into custody.

It was at this point that Harry Maizlish, touchingly naïve, came over to aid his son. "It was a very moving moment actually," says Maizlish. "He said to the marshals, 'Perhaps if I put the handcuffs on, they wouldn't hurt so much.'"

Who was this guy? The marshals looked at him in disdain, placed a hand on his chest, and shoved him roughly away. They seemed to be saying, "Get serious, old man. Your son belongs to the Bureau of Prisons now."

Maizlish, who had been ready to walk peacebly, looked at his father, looked at the marshals, and then went limp. "It was in response to them pushing my father. They carried me into the courthouse and one of the marshals mutters, 'If this hurts my back, I'll sue you.'

'Hey, I'm not asking you to do this,'" responded Maizlish.

They found a wheelchair and wheeled him down to the holding cell in the U.S. marshals' office as Joe's parents gazed helplessly down the corridor.

They would never see their son again outside of federal custody.

Chapter 2

Why We Refused, Part I

Dear Sam and Sarah,

I suppose I need to address the obvious question: how did we reach such a state of moral desperation that we might risk five years in a federal penitentiary? Given the way we all grew up in 1950s America, it was, for most of us, a long and complicated process.

I'm sure you noticed the conspicuous absence of my own father from the previous chapter. Your grandfather David—as you well know—died of a massive heart attack when I was thirteen and in the eighth grade. I honestly have no idea how he might have reacted to my decision to defy the draft. He had been an officer in the Medical Corps during the Second World War but he was no zealot; his politics leaned left of center and I have no reason to think he might have disowned me, as Greg Nelson's father had. More likely, he would have suffered a broken heart from my withdrawal from formal studies and my reckless abandonment of any chance at a solid career.

Your grandmother Libby was generally sympathetic to the rising sentiments that opposed the war, but even more so, she was protective and full of maternal anguish. She went out and purchased a small sculpture, a little round polished ball enveloped on one side by a larger, similarly smooth stone. The obvious connotation was that of a mother figure cradling her son and sheltering him from the outside world. I was embarrassed no end by it but I understood her need to express how desperately she wished to protect me.

Your great-grandmother Rose (Barmack) was the most understanding in the family because the circumstances seemed to fit within her historical experience. The Jewish shtetl in Romania was full of tales about how the boys in neighboring Russia scrambled to avoid conscription into the

Tsar's army. To be drafted meant a twenty-five-year stint in service of a much despised government. Hatred of the draft was part of the social fabric. At least according to family lore, it was not unheard of for the *mohel* or the *shochet*—the ritual performer of circumcision and the ritual butcher, respectively—to slice off the finger of a young male in order to make him undesirable to the imperial army. To oppose the draft just seemed natural to my grandmother.

But how my father would have reacted to his son's rebellion remains a mystery. It was not that I didn't seek out surrogate fathers after your grandfather's death. There was an art teacher, Mr. Rankin, who I had in the ninth grade just months after my father passed away. He was a tall, bald man with a kindly look and a pleasant tolerance toward those of us who showed no artistic talent whatsoever. My clay pencil holder was the only project in the class that managed to blow itself up in the kiln. I had no clue what Mr. Rankin was really like as a man, but there was something about him, some inexplicable air, that made me want to bask in his paternal warmth.

One day he came into class and failed to unlock the closet doors where our art supplies were stored. He unpacked a tape recorder from his briefcase as the class leaned forward in anticipation that something out of the ordinary might happen.

"Some things are more important than teaching the techniques of art," he explained. "I need you to listen carefully to these tapes for the next couple of days because I consider them of the utmost importance."

We listened. Out of all the topics my art teacher might have chosen to emphasize, he played for us a tape-recorded lecture about American POWs during the Korean War. I'm not sure to this day why this particular topic merited the cessation of our art class, but if Mr. Rankin thought it important, so did I.

I recall few details from that tape. I remember we were told the first thing we must do if we ever found ourselves as prisoners of the communists was to dig a latrine so as to maintain sanitation standards within the camp. I remember we were to offer only our name, rank, and serial number if interrogated by the enemy. I remember we were advised to maintain chain of command at all times and to continue to follow orders only from our own superiors.

Mostly I remember the shame of those Americans who went over to the dark side. I remember that those who caved in to the torture and brainwashing techniques of our communist enemies did so because they were weak, that they possessed little intelligence, little education, and no backbone. At fourteen I knew I never wanted to let Mr. Rankin down.

Of course I had been exposed before to the doctrine of anticommunism. You didn't have to be conservative in those days for that. The most liberal politicians in the country drew the line at the Iron Curtain that separated the free world from the darkness of the other side.

Masters of Deceit

My eighth-grade social studies teacher, Mrs. Lockhart, swore by the J. Edgar Hoover book entitled *Masters of Deceit: What the Communist Bosses Are Doing to Bring America to Its Knees*. Hoover had been director of the FBI since its inception in the 1930s and had accumulated enormous power simply through collecting information on every politician and controversial figure in the country. I knew I would please Mrs. Lockhart if I chose his work for a book report. Its cover was bold with big red letters and a big red splotch of blood bleeding out to the margins. "Every citizen," it began, "has a duty to learn more about the menace that threatens his future, his home, his children, the peace of the world." It went on to describe how communism "tears out a man's soul and makes him a tool of the party." It concluded that communism would lead to the destruction of Western civilization, the destruction of the American way of life, and that it would "roll history back to the age of barbaric cruelty and despotism."

I have to admit that neither Mrs. Lockhart's nor J. Edgar's warnings were viscerally convincing on every level. Hoover focused primarily on the danger from within—the danger from those communists living in America. During the 1950s, the Communist Party, riddled with FBI agents and staggering from Nikita Khruschev's 1956 revelations of Stalin's atrocities, had become an empty shell.

Years later, Bob Zaugh, one of the L.A. resisters, told me about a professor who very much influenced him at El Camino Junior College. "The Communist Party USA," he would tell his students, "is so weak, it couldn't overturn the coffee table in my living room." Even at fourteen, I sensed this; I couldn't quite buy Hoover's fear of an internal threat. Like every Jewish family, we had our own eccentric communist, Uncle Bill, tucked away in New Jersey. He was a nice guy, certainly not a threat to anybody's security, and I couldn't really connect him to any kind of serious conspiracy to overthrow the government. I was able, somehow, to separate Uncle Bill from all the other communists and from my acceptance of Hoover's basic assessment of the red menace: They were liars. They were ruthless. They were trained in deceit. They were alien. That was just part of the times; that was just part of the oxygen an American kid breathed in. I embraced this outlook even as I carried no particular fear of some takeover from within.

The Chinese. Now they were a different matter altogether. If the Communist Party, USA was not much to worry about, the "yellow peril" was. Somehow, from some movie in the distant past I had acquired a vision of zombies with tommy guns charging out of the snowy Manchurian plain. That's why Mr. Rankin's tapes touched a nerve. Somehow the approval I so wanted from Mr. Rankin was wrapped up in these primeval fears of communism and in my desire to be a good soldier.

There was also the "John Wayne thing." Fiercely anticommunist, John Wayne had starred in dozens of Hollywood cowboy movies and war films, emerging as the icon of masculinity for an entire generation of American males. David Harris, the guy who made Greg Nelson late for his own sanctuary, named that phenomenon and wrote about his impact in the book *Our War*. "We were to say few words, keep a hard jaw and a tight ass, not snivel, stifle feelings, take orders, never cry, dish out punishment to the bad guys, fire from the hip, know we were right just because we were Americans, always win, but die like heroes if our luck ran out."

Anticommunism for us young men was not just some abstract political ideology. It was part of an emotional jumble bubbling deep inside us—sometimes conscious, sometimes not. It colored how we related to our sense of patriotism, how we felt about our duty to be good soldiers, how we won approval from our fathers and our peers. It was part of our sexual identity. It was part of how we defined our manhood.

These attitudes seeped into the souls of even the most peaceful of us as we grew up. Joe Maizlish remembers himself as a preteen, applauding the execution of Julius and Ethel Rosenberg, two Communist Party members convicted of espionage in an extremely controversial trial during the 1950s. Even his parents were shocked to hear his callous attitude.

Bob Zaugh recalls listening to inspirational lectures in a California junior high school by Dr. Noh Young Park. They were entitled "Red Cloud Over Asia," and designed by the South Korean speaker to work up anticommunist sentiment to a fever pitch. "Our school was happy to have him," says Zaugh.

"He just whipped you into a frenzy. It was like you wanted to bolt from the auditorium and find someone and accuse him of being a communist . . . He got me rolling. I was looking for communists everywhere after I heard him."

Only a year before his refusal to register for the draft, Greg Nelson had begged his mother to sign the papers which would allow him to join the navy before he was eighteen. Nelson was fascinated with scuba diving and aspired to become not some kind of Gandhian draft resister but an underwater demolition expert.

Dana Rae Park, a Hawaiian resister, whom I met on my first day at Safford, believed as a high school student that we should drop the atom bomb on Vietnam. "All these stupid restrictions on bombing the North, that was obscene," he had thought.

I remember arguing with a peace advocate in my senior year of high school that if the French weren't going to fight the communists in Vietnam, then someone had to.

In his book *The Arrogance of Power,* Senator J. William Fulbright quoted a report filed by UPI correspondent Joseph Galloway to convey how our attitudes might play out in battle. It was during Operation Utah in 1966 when about thirty U.S. marines managed to isolate a lone communist soldier and chase him up a hill. A group of reporters and soldiers could see the chase from the next ridge over. "We stood on the hill," wrote Galloway and cheered and whistled and shouted advice:

> "Kill the son of a bitch . . . Get him . . . what's the matter with you jarheads?" It was like watching a ball game from the upper deck of Yankee Stadium. We . . . could see every move clearly. (The marines on the ridge across the way were below their target and could not see him well. They fired time and time again at him.)
>
> Suddenly one of the bullets struck. The communist dropped to the ground. He lost his rifle as he fell. "They breezed him, they breezed him," one of the cheering section beside me shouted. "Naw, there he goes," another marine said.
>
> "He's up and running again . . . get him . . . get him."
>
> Another bullet knocked the communist off his feet and a second time he got up. He was moving slower when the third and fourth bullets slammed into his body and knocked him

> down again. But still he moved, crawling up and over the crest of the hill. Nobody could tell whether he lived or died. The marines chasing him went no further than the ridge top.

The senator added: "What Mr. Galloway described in his dispatch was the killing not of a man but of something abstract or something subhuman, a 'communist' . . . The possibility that he may have regarded himself as a patriot fighting to free his country from foreign invaders would never of course have occurred to anyone in the 'cheering section.'"

At the dawn of the war most of America sat in the cheering section. It was, after all, how we were brought up.

On March 8, 1965, as I entered the last stage of my senior year at George Washington High School, 3,500 United States marines disembarked from amphibious landing craft onto the beach at Da Nang. They were our first combat troops in Vietnam. The war—or at least America's overt and dominant role in it—had begun in earnest. The photographs of those young men, holding their M-14s over their shoulders to protect the weapons from the ocean spray, were quite extraordinary. If you looked past all the gear and weaponry, if you looked closely at the faces underneath the marine combat helmets, you could see who they were: they were kids. They were maybe a year older than me.

We all thought they'd kick ass and be out of there in a few months.

I had already registered the month before at the Englewood draft board on Bannock Street near Cinderella City. I was two or three weeks late. It wasn't some kind of political statement like Greg Nelson's. I just hadn't got around to it. I was nervous as I passed through the door, knowing that having failed to register on my birthday, I was in violation of the law. The clerk, Wanda Story, looked down at the driver's license, then looked up at me. I didn't know what to expect. She looked down at the license again and said: "Oh, you boys," then handed me the forms to fill out.

Other than that short trip down to Englewood, I can't say many of my fellow students gave much thought to the draft in the spring of 1965. George Washington at that time was an overwhelmingly middle-class school. Everybody was going off to college in the fall; very few faced the dreaded 1-A classification that made you immediately subject to the draft.

I was one of the exceptions. I can't say I had read *On the Road* but I had tasted expresso at the Green Spider Coffee House on 17th and gotten infected by the spirit of Jack Kerouac. I was enthralled too by the album cover of a young folksinger who was accompanied as he walked down a Greenwich Village street by a beautiful young woman clinging tightly to his elbow. The album was titled deliciously *The Freewheelin' Bob Dylan*. Somehow, I thought, if I could embrace that freedom, if I could feel the wind at my back on a lonely highway or wander the cities of industrial America, I could partake of that same free spirit that captivated Dylan and electrified Kerouac. Maybe I could even get an attractive young lady to cling to my elbow. University of Colorado held no magic for me. My dream was the search for America.

Searching for America

In June of 1965, I packed a small bag and began the journey, hitchhiking over the Continental Divide in the days before they had drilled the tunnel straight through the granite mountains beneath Loveland Pass. Aspen might seem an unlikely place to start a search for America, but in 1965, Aspen had not yet become the upscale glitterati-infested town it is today. People who worked there could actually afford to live there. You could get a spot at Red's Beds for fifty cents a night. You could live nicely at the Independence Hotel for twelve dollars a week. I stayed in the Chitwood Apartments across the street from the Jerome Hotel for twenty-five dollars a month. Just below me was the Epicure Restaurant where I hired on for the summer, making omelettes and slinging hash browns for a dollar an hour. Crazy Frumess (Richard Frumess) was up there washing dishes at the Red Onion. So was Neuschatz, tall and skinny, contentious as ever. Anne Silver—sad-eyed and long-haired, the secret love of a hundred would-be intellectuals including myself—was cleaning rooms at the Independence. Kathy Swiers waited tables at The Lodge, and Matt Wells worked at the sawmill. Aspen was the place to be for me and all my high school buddies in the summer of '65. We could drink beer at Pinnochio's while listening to the incredibly suggestive lyrics of the Rolling Stones "Satisfaction." We could drive Matt's old yellow Chevy up towards Maroon Bells. We could sit around the wood stove at the Quadrant Bookstore, admiring Ivan Abrams, the pipe-smoking owner, who we were sure had read every book in the shop. Kathy remembers walking Aspen Mountain on beautiful moonlit nights, thinking, my god, we're on our own now; we're really adults. It was intoxicating and scary all at once.

Hitchhiking from Denver on my first jaunt to Aspen, I caught a ride outside of Idaho Springs from a black GI just back from a stint as an advisor in Vietnam. I thanked him for his service and he just replied, "It's not what you think it is. It's not what you think it is over there." I tried to coax out a little more of his story, but that's all I could get. He wouldn't talk. That tiny exchange was perhaps the first hint I got that something unsettling was happening in Vietnam.

Even so, all through the summer, all through the fall and early winter of 1965, I managed to keep the draft out of my mind even as U.S. troop levels climbed to 51,000 then soared towards 125,000. But as I journeyed through the country, I was beginning to see a side of America that, perhaps indirectly, made me more receptive to a critique of what our country might have been doing in Southeast Asia. I was beginning to see parts of America that showed me that we were not in every case "The Land of the Free."

Historians generally contend that one cannot overestimate the impact of the civil rights movement on the emerging antiwar movement. Many white leaders of The Resistance got their early political schooling from the movement for equality.

Joe Maizlish, like most of us, had a basic visceral instinct that the struggle against segregation "just sounded right. People aren't allowed to vote? What? People can't sit on the bus? What? It just wasn't right." Maizlish had a direct line to some of the most courageous civil rights workers on the frontlines of the struggle through his radio reports on KRHM. Many of the fifty weekly programs occurred during the tense "Freedom Summer" of 1964 and most of them would contain a few minutes of phoned-in reports from Mississippi. There was always a sense of urgency. "Once in the middle of the report someone ran into (the office) in Sunflower, Mississippi, and reported that the Freedom House in the next town over was on fire and burning down. They had to interrupt the report to run over and learn what was going on." The reports were aired on KRHM, then sent to the newly forming KPFK Pacifica Radio and to KGFJ, a local black community-interest station. Maizlish was twenty-two and very much aware he was reporting history in the making. "It was quite a privilege to hear some of those stories."

It was at this point in Maizlish's life that he began to question the credibility of official government versions of anything. "One of the civil rights workers," he recalled "made some remarks on the air about the FBI and the misbehavior of a particular agent in Mississippi. She said she had not exactly been threatened but that the agent had spoken badly to her. So I figured What the hell, I'll send this recording to the FBI and ask them what they had to say about it. They came out, visited my parents' house, left their card. When I called them back they said we want you to put a retraction on the air of what you said about our agent in Mississippi. I told them, 'It's not what I said, it's what the civil rights worker down there said. But if you have anything for me to read, any denial or anything, absolutely, I'll put it on the program.'

'We just want a retraction,' insisted the agent.

'Well, what was true? What did the agent say?'

'We're looking into it.'

'Wait a minute. I said my offer is whatever you folks send me I'll read on the program.'

'Well, we don't do that.'

"Later on I called the agent back after confirming one side of the story and I gave him the name of the agent in Mississippi (who was accused of the misbehavior). The agent I called couldn't be less interested. I didn't think they were looking into a damn thing. So I got the feeling that with these guys, whatever the quality of their work personally, the reputation of their organization was number one for them. Truth would come in somewhere; I don't know in what order truth would finish, but it sure wasn't up there with reputation. It made it kind of hard later to believe the remarks of the government about war and peace, or about what was going on in the Gulf of Tonkin or anyplace else. Even if you've studied a bunch of history, when you personally encounter these kinds of lessons, it's a big disappointment to realize that the organization's reputation is way ahead of the truth."

Two of the original founders of the draft resistance movement in California, Dennis Sweeney and David Harris, lived in the midst of the war zone that was Mississippi in that summer and fall of 1964. Sweeney organized for months in the town of McComb located in Pike County southwest of Jackson. Harris wrote that "McComb had the reputation of a rabid dog. Before the summer was over two-thirds of the state's seventy-odd racial bombings would happen within a half hour's drive of the place." Sweeney's life was changed forever as he experienced the community's trauma. McComb's Freedom House was bombed and then in short order, according to Harris: "A rabbi in Clarksdale was bludgeoned with steel bars. A car full of whites fired guns into a black church in Moss Point, wounding a nineteen-year-old girl. The blacks who chased after the assailants were arrested and charged with assault. In Browning, the Pleasant Plain Missionary Baptist Church was burned to the ground. So were the Jerusalem Baptist and Bethel Methodist Churches in

Natchez. Two blacks trying to use the white window at a drive-in in Laurel were stabbed. In Kingston, three more black churches were bombed."

When nine whites were later convicted of these crimes, they were sentenced to five years and then had their sentences immediately suspended. "They were just getting started in life," explained the judge. "They came from good families . . . and were unduly provoked by outside agitators, some of whom are of low moral character, some of whom are unhygienic."

Harris drove down from Palo Alto that October and was assigned by SNCC (Student Nonviolent Coordinating Committee) to Quitman County in the heart of the Delta. It wasn't two days before a pickup truck pulled up beside his car. In an instant he faced two young men, both of them armed, the driver pointing a shotgun at Harris's chin. "Nigger lover," he told him, "we're givin' you five minutes to get out of town." Harris and his friend Morse hurried on to the next town.

Harris, like Maizlish, had his first encounter with the FBI while advocating for civil rights. When his buddy Morse, a fraternity man from Stanford, was beaten bloody in Marks, Mississippi, the FBI was sent to investigate. When Harris answered the door, the agent said: "Well, nigger lover, what seems to be the problem?" A day later the beleaguered Harris was informed that he was under suspicion for the assault on Morse. "That was too much for us," wrote Harris. The next day the two of them headed back for school. Much later, Harris found the following inserted into his FBI file in response to allegations of misconduct by the Mississippi agent: "This whole matter arose as a result of an insidious effort on the part of these individuals to create a situation designed to harass and embarrass the agents who were conscientiously engaged in their duties."

My experience was much less dramatic. I wasn't trying to change any systems or right any wrongs as I worked my way across the country. But I was paying attention; I was taking everything in.

It was in St. Louis when I first got the idea to head south. It seemed serendipitous at the time, but looking back, it was only natural—being utterly without ties or responsibilities—to seek warmth before the winter set in. I had just finished a day's work unloading a boxcar full of cartons of Carnation Milk and was heading back to the Bondel Hotel—a dollar-a-day luxury residence where I had resided the last two weeks. Just outside the warehouse district, the Missouri State Department of Casual Labor had placed a sign outside its office window: ORANGE PICKERS NEEDED IN FLORIDA. BUS LEAVES MONDAY.

A cold autumn wind blew down the back of my neck just as I passed and that sealed it.

Before dawn on Monday morning I boarded a dilapidated yellow school bus along with thirty-eight other men and red-haired Wendy, whose toothless smile added a good twenty-five years to her appearance. About half of us were white. I learned later that the "BWIs"—the British West Indians and Jamaicans—who normally worked the Florida citrus groves had been barred from the country by the repeal of the Bracero Act of 1964. The Mt. Dora Growers Coop had roamed far afield recruiting a replacement labor force.

We pulled into Memphis late morning, stiff from the hard-backed seats, hungry, and relieved to see the driver pulling into the parking lot of a crowded restaurant. We filed out of the bus with instructions to keep our orders to less than seventy-five cents.

American Apartheid

Then we divided up. It was automatic; no one had to ask questions. The whites marched in through the front door greeted by the manager with a friendly smile. I went toward the rear and peeked around the corner. There were my black coworkers waiting patiently to give their orders to the cook through the back door of the kitchen. The vision hit me full force. Of course I had seen Whites Only restrooms on TV, but they were just fleeting images on a screen. This line in the back of an all-American drive-in was alive and breathing. The tired faces of these men embarking on a thousand-mile journey in a Bluebird bus for a subsistence level job, then prohibited from setting foot in the door of a cheap hamburger joint—these faces became for me the embodiment of an American apartheid. I returned to the bus, having lost my appetite and my innocence. There I waited for everyone to come back, too scared to join my black brothers, too ashamed to join my white brothers.

There were other faces as I journeyed through the South. There was the twelve- or thirteen-year-old boy, near tears in rural Lake County, Florida, trying to enter the main floor of a movie theater a full year after the Civil Rights Act had passed Congress and been signed by the president.

"But they let me sit down there in Tampa," he pleaded.

"You not in Tampa, boy."

There was the dignified face of the man at the take-out window of the Royal Castle where I worked as a short-order cook in Metairie, Louisiana, just outside New Orleans. The take-out window was not for drivers; it was for blacks. They would regularly walk around to the side window to order our sixteen-cent hamburgers with a dime side of fries. I remember this particular gentleman, weary from the day's work, politely ordering a burger and cup of coffee.

"Would you like cheese on that burger, sir?"

"No just the burger and a cup of coffee. No cream." I filled the order and took his twenty-six cents.

Then came the shift supervisor, a curly haired man who hit on the waitresses and had just instructed me on how to water down the root beer. "You ever call a nigger 'sir' again, you out the door, boy, you hear?"

I had been flat broke, just got out of the Salvation Army Mission where enduring "ear-beatings"—sermons each night to get a ration of baked beans and a hot dog bun—had been the daily routine. That's what went through my mind as I kept my mouth shut. The real truth was I hadn't the courage to tell him to fuck off.

We all grew up believing fervently in America's essential righteousness, but coming face to face with that segregated underside of America's soul, we began looking at the world a little differently; we began to see the imperfections and examine the basic assumption that, as a nation, we were incapable of wrongdoing.

Of course, the thinkers and organizers of the coming antiwar movement saw far deeper than I did. Guys like Harris and Sweeney and Maizlish had witnessed the power of civil disobedience that had given rise to a virtual social revolution in the South. They saw that real social change might require putting your body on the line, maybe even your life on the line. They saw also that when Vietnam intersected with race, minorities took the full force of the impact: disproportionately assigned to combat, disproportionately killed.

Among the earliest sentiments for draft resistance was a flyer out of Pike County, Mississippi, where Sweeney had worked with SNCC. When John D. Shaw was killed in Nam in July of 1965, his friends in McComb, raw and angry, fired off a leaflet:

> No Mississippi Negroes should be fighting in Vietnam for the White Man's freedom until all the Negro people are free in Mississippi. Negro boys should not honor the draft here in

> Mississippi. Mothers should encourage their sons not to go. No one has a right to ask us to risk our lives . . . so that the White American can get richer. We will be looked upon as traitors by all the Colored People of the world if the Negro people continue to fight and die without a cause.

When Julian Bond, just elected to the Georgia State Legislature, expressed sympathy as a SNCC staff member "with those young men who could not respond to the military draft," his fellow lawmakers went apoplectic and voted not to seat him.

"By the fall of 1966," wrote Michael Ferber, "when white students were beginning to sign 'We Won't Go' statements, induction refusal by blacks had become a widespread phenomenon."

Haunted by this vision of black suffering and black courage, some of the white leaders of the antiwar movement began to seek out ways to emulate what they had seen and experienced in the civil rights movement. Guys like Sweeney who had faced death in McComb, who had faced jail and physical assault, who had faced brutal police and shamelessly biased judges sought tactics that could embody the kind of risks blacks had been taking for a decade. They were looking for ways to replicate the intensity of commitment they had seen in the fight against segregation.

I arrived in New Orleans on New Year's Day of 1966, drawn mostly by the knowledge that the legal drinking age in the state of Louisiana was eighteen. I knew my time was running short; I knew that upon turning nineteen, the Selective Service System would soon call my name. After settling into a run-down apartment on Marigny Street a block away from Elysian Fields and after nailing down a night shift job at the Royal Castle, I resolved that I better find out just what was going on in Vietnam. It was time to do some reading.

Reading at the Café du Monde

I can't recall the bookstore, but somehow I found a slender copy of a background report by a Pulitzer Prize–winning journalist. The title of the book—*The Making of a Quagmire*—was intriguing, but I was drawn to it mostly because it was skinny.

Many radicals, I later learned, couldn't stand David Halberstam. The idea of a "quagmire" might imply that the United States, as one scholar put it, "stumbled into Vietnam accidentally rather than as a consequence of a deliberate and misguided policy," an idea anathema to some radical thought. More important was the fact that he wanted us to win the war. He shared with Kennedy and Johnson the Cold War bias that got us into the war in the first place. He believed that however miserably executed, the war, at least in its beginning stage, was worthy of support.

All these subtleties were over my head. I just wanted some background from a credible source and Halberstam's credentials as a *New York Times* correspondent on the scene since 1962 seemed credible enough. Had I suspected he was some kind of radical, I never would have picked up the book. I was not ready for left-wing analysis.

I began reading one morning at the Café du Monde near Jackson Square, world-famous for its chicory-flavored coffee and the steamy hot, sugar-covered pastries they called *beignets*:

"I arrived in Saigon at a time of singularly bad feeling toward foreign correspondents." From the first sentence, Halberstam conveyed a sense of the opaque cloud that hung over the truth concerning everything that happened in Vietnam. The thing that struck me continuously—as it might for any nineteen-year-old kid—was the dishonesty and self-deception that permeated the entire war effort from day one.

I'm afraid most of the particulars have been forgotten over the years, lost in the mists of the past. One of the national narratives that consequently arose is that we who opposed the war, at least those who weren't out and out traitors—hey, we were hippies, dude; we just wanted peace and love and everything to be groovy—we were living in a Fools' Paradise.

The truth is we had done our homework. We had read and researched; we had listened carefully to the reports filtering home and to the stories of our returning soldiers. We concluded that if anyone suffered from delusion, it was the generals and presidents, the national security advisers and cabinet secretaries who sent us off to die. Most of us in prison shared a common knowledge of the war's roots. It was often the details that moved us. I'll try to convey some of what I learned from my own reading with the hope you might better understand the source of our motivations and the reasons for our passion.

The *Making of a Quagmire* centered on South Vietnam's first regime. Its president, Ngo Dinh Diem, was a Roman Catholic aristocrat ruling a country 90 percent Buddhist and 90 percent peasant.

After the French had been driven out during the First Indochina War, after the Geneva Accords of 1954 had divided the country in two, the United States cast about looking everywhere for an anticommunist to rule the southern half of Vietnam. There wasn't a lot of choice. Having led the resistance to French rule, the communists had successfully identified their cause with the surging nationalistic feeling that coursed through the country. Anticommunists, almost to a man, had been tainted by association with their former French masters.

Diem, fiercely anticommunist, a man whose brother had been murdered by the communists, had sat out the last years of the war in exile in New Jersey and New York, managing, in the process, to distance himself from the French colonial regime. Those slim qualifications were enough. Beginning in 1955, he received unlimited support from an Eisenhower administration that saw him as their only hope. One journalist coined the slogan: "Sink or swim with Ngo Dinh Diem."

For a few brief years, it seemed to work. The *Saturday Evening Post* called South Vietnam "the Bright Spot in Asia," and *Life Magazine* called Diem "the Tough Miracle Man in Vietnam."

David Halberstam arrived in Saigon in time to document Diem's painful descent.

First was the retreat into the presidential palace, into a surrealistic world separated utterly from the reality of Vietnam. An aloof man, a man who valued tradition over everything else, Diem systematically rejected counsel from anyone outside a tiny circle of insulated family members.

"The test used by the Ngo government in evaluating a man," wrote Halberstam, "became not what he had done for Vietnam, but what he had done for the Ngo family." Most influential among advisers was Diem's brother Ngo Dinh Nhu and his sister-in-law Madame Nhu. Halberstam described Nhu as a "born intriguer." "Under Nhu," he wrote, "the men who rose to power were of a kind. They were from the same geographical area and the same religion as the Ngo family . . . men who understood the vast security systems of the country and who had little compunction about telling the brothers anything they wanted to hear." Incredibly, Diem placed his best-trained military units, not out in the countryside fighting Viet Cong but along the perimeter of Saigon where they could protect the president from coups and palace intrigues.

Shortly before Diem's downfall, I remember watching news reports on TV about the bitter conflict between Buddhist monks and the South Vietnamese government. Nobody here really knew the background, but Buddhist resentment had smoldered for years under Catholic rule, first under the French and then under Diem. After watching a Vatican flag wave during a public celebration honoring an archbishop in Hue, Buddhists discovered just days later that they were prohibited from flying their own religious flag on the Buddha's 2,587th birthday. When they protested, government troops came in and mowed them down, killing nine in the central square. Of course, the protests escalated, then repression escalated until one morning in 1963, Quang Duc sat cross-legged in front of the Xa Loi pagoda in Saigon, watched calmly as a colleague doused a gallon can of gasoline over his monk's robes, then lit a single match. It was astonishing.

Images of those few seconds were all most Americans ever saw about the whole Buddhist crisis. Perhaps that should have been a wake-up call for me, for all of America, but at fifteen, maybe sixteen, I think I reacted like most Americans: who is this lunatic with the shaved head and the orange robes?

Then Madame Nhu, stunningly beautiful, perfectly manicured, cold as ice, appeared next day at a press conference and delivered her impression of Marie Antoinette: the gruesome immolation, she said, was a "barbecue. Let them burn and we shall clap our hands." She offered to pay for fuel for anyone who wanted to use it on Western correspondents who she believed responsible for showing her country in a bad light. Again my reaction was typically American: who is this bitch? But, at sixteen, that's as far as my questions went. The whole thing was not yet comprehensible.

Now, a couple of years later, reading this skinny book at the Café du Monde, I was beginning to sort things out.

Defending Democracy in Vietnam

I read on as Halberstam summarized the state of democracy in South Vietnam under Diem:

> There were elections though no opposition candidates were permitted. There was a legislature but it was the rubber stamp kind . . . there was a cabinet whose ministers had responsibility but no power and who lived in mortal fear of Madame Nhu . . . In the 1963 Assembly elections, Ngo Dinh

> Nhu representing Kanh Hoa Province received 99.98 percent of the vote; Madame Nhu running as a candidate from a district in Long An, almost totally controlled by the communists received 99.4 percent.

When Halberstam questioned her about this, she responded, "I am becoming a popular figure, which is very encouraging because I have no public relations."

The same disconnect and clinical denial that ultimately destroyed the Ngo family was echoed by the American military command. These men, the men who supervised the 20,000 American advisers to the ARVN (the Army of the Republic of Vietnam or South Vietnamese Army), constituted the Military Assistance Command, Vietnam or MACV. They were, according to Halberstam, obsessed by multi-colored arrows on maps in the Saigon briefing rooms, by the count of enemy dead, by the number of secure villages created by a massive peasant relocation project called the Strategic Hamlet Program. All the numbers showed we were winning.

They wore these numbers like some kind of body armor. No burst of reality could penetrate their wall of statistics.

Many guerilla war experts, for instance, maintained that the increase in the Viet Cong body count actually indicated an increase in guerilla activity and represented a sign that we were losing the war. "In a successful counterinsurgency," wrote Halberstam, "when you are doing well the casualties do not rise; they drop and the war simply goes away."

Then there was the obvious notion that strategic hamlets actually created more enemies than friends. Again Halberstam wrote:

> All too often this meant relocating people from an area which they loved and had held for many generations to a region for which they cared not at all—in order to fight an enemy they did not really consider their enemy. By and large, the population of the (Mekong) Delta had been on the fence, but the very act of relocation turned thousands of peasants against the Government.

For Halberstam, the symbol of accumulated illusions manifested during a battle in 1963 in Dinh Tuong Province south of Saigon. The two sides, the 4th Corps of the Seventh ARVN Division and the 514th Battalion of the Viet Cong met near a small village called Ap Bac on the edge of the Plain of Reeds.

In command of the Seventh Division was Colonel Huyn Van Cao, a classic example of ARVN leadership under Diem. Catholic, a native of Hue, the son of an aristocratic family, he had been promoted not for his success on the battlefield but for his loyalty to Ngo Dinh Diem during a coup attempt in 1960. His accounts of enemy casualty figures were so fanciful that reporters developed the "Cao Formula" to determine the number of enemy dead: "Take his figures, subtract the announced Government casualties in the same action, then divide by three for a figure approaching reality."

For years the Viet Cong had been masters of the hit-and-run, eluding government troops with such success it drove American advisors half mad with frustration. "If we could only make them stand and fight," was the continuing refrain. At Ap Bac the guerillas of the 514th were surrounded on three sides in broad daylight by superior ARVN forces employing helicopters and amphibious armored personnel carriers, highly mobile in the soggy rice paddies. The fourth side to the east was left open because the terrain was so bare that any fleeing soldiers could be cut down by artillery and aircraft fire. In a captured report afterwards, the VC commander had written: "It is better to stand and die than run and be slaughtered." "The standing battle the Americans wanted," wrote Halberstam, "was about to take place."

As dusk approached after the day's contest, American advisors surveyed the results. Five U.S. helicopters had been downed by small-arms fire. The ARVN officer in charge of armored personnel carriers had at first refused to deploy them, then moved so slowly as to render them virtually useless. Infantrymen held weapons over their heads and fired blindly. Troops on the southern flank remained out of action because provincial chiefs refused to take orders from division commanders. In the confusion of battle, a small firefight broke out between an ARVN airborne battalion and an ARVN reserve unit. The Viet Cong held their ground and maintained discipline. As night fell, they quietly escaped along the canal system to the east under cover of darkness.

MACV called the battle of Ap Bac a victory. "Yes, that's right," stated General Paul Harkins, "It was a Vietnamese victory. It certainly was." Madame Nhu concurred.

And so the Ngo family pretended to run a democracy and the MACV pretended to win a war. ARVN officers, having created the illusion of victory, now feared contact with the VC more than ever, since an increased casualty rate would expose their previous falsified reports. While they continually avoided combat, guerilla forces grew steadily. By summer of 1963 Viet Cong battalions commonly had 500 troops or more. Government weapons losses in the delta had risen by 20 percent while parallel VC losses had dropped by 100 percent.

While Diem, Ngo Dinh Nhu and his lovely wife, MACV and the State Department inhabited their respective dream worlds, the Viet Cong was out in the delta winning the war. David Halberstam expressed no love for the VC, but months of slopping through rice paddies with ARVN assault units had left him with an appreciation for their lethal effectiveness.

Halberstam's lengthy *New York Times* article of August 15, 1963, began:

> South Vietnam's military situation in the vital Mekong Delta has deteriorated in the past year, and informed officials are warning of ominous signs . . . These military sources say a Communist Viet Cong build-up is taking place in the Delta. They find it particularly disturbing because it has persisted since an American build-up (began) twenty months ago.

Halberstam told the story of two American officers in the Mekong Delta who tried desperately to file honest reports of what they saw in the field. Lt. Colonel John Paul Vann, for instance, had written that the number of ARVN or South Vietnamese troops received by a particular zone was determined not by the need for combat troops, but by the province chief's relationship with Diem. Thus provinces teeming with communist guerrillas got no help while those with little need received troops in abundance. The reports were suppressed at every level by General Paul Harkins. All the numbers showed we were winning the war. Veteran guerrilla war experts argued that high enemy casualty rates were actually a sign of weakness—that in a successful counterinsurgency the number of guerrilla casualties decreases and the war simply goes away. The pessimists were ignored. I think Halberstam's description taught me how to read a newspaper or at least to read between the lines of the kinds of articles I had read in the *Rocky Mountain News*. Most of the articles simply detailed the number of casualties suffered during a skirmish in some unpronounceable village in the delta or the central highlands. The description of Ap Bac actually put some flesh on to the statistics.

American officials from the president to the secretary of state angrily denied Halberstam's allegation and presented the usual barrage of statistics refuting Halberstam's report.

Of course, we finally rid ourselves of Ngo Dinh Diem in November of 1963. He was too much of an embarrassment. An officers' coup drove him from the palace, arrested him and his brother in Cholon, then executed them both in the back of an armored personnel carrier.

By that time, however, the tide of the war had already turned. It was clear that the government of South Vietnam was reeling; indeed, it lay withering on its deathbed. Its survival required life support; it needed to be kept artificially alive. The technique we chose was a massive transfusion of American troops, tens of thousands at first, then hundreds of thousands. By 1968 we had half a million men in our national Lazarus project trying to bring South Vietnam back from the dead.

The antiwar movement tended to oppose the war on grounds of morality first and then politics. I would come to these positions soon enough. But on this first reading in New Orleans it was the futility of the war and the dismal performance of our allies in South Vietnam that set my mind to spinning. Explain to me again now: just what kind of government is it you want me to die for? And who were these little bastards in black pajamas who fought so bravely, whose bodies we were counting as "enemy dead" and whose cause we were saving the world from? These were the questions swirling around in my brain as I decided to continue my reading.

The Longer View in Vietnam

The next book was simply a compilation of documents and analyses and it was titled simply *Vietnam*. Edited by a radical New York professor named Marvin Gettleman, he seemed to choose his historical analysts from across a wide political spectrum. I recall reading portions of it while riding the famous Desire Street bus on my way out to flip hamburgers for the Royal Castle in Metairie.

Several passages jumped right out of the pages.

There was, for instance, the disgraceful behavior of French forces in the aftermath of World War II. France had ruled Vietnam rather harshly for nearly eighty years before the Japanese marched into Southeast Asia and imposed an even harsher occupation in 1940. Armed resistance to the combined Japanese and Vichy French rule was led by the Viet Minh, our wartime ally in Indochina. It was a communist organization—in many ways a predecessor to the Viet Cong—headed by Ho Chi Minh. a man who had lived in Harlem, who had worked menial jobs in Manhattan and London, who had studied revolution in Marseilles and Moscow and Canton. By the time the Japanese surrendered in 1945, the Viet Minh had established enough political and military presence to seize power in Vietnam.

It was a hopeful time for the colonized world—a time when the whole system of colonial domination seemed to be crumbling. France—having just been humiliated by the Nazis, having just been saved by the Americans—could not bear the thought of giving up even a small corner of its fading empire. They mobilized Japanese soldiers to help them take back Vietnam.

Even the conservative General Douglas MacArthur railed against the French: "If there is anything that makes my blood boil, it is to see our allies in Indochina and Java deploying Japanese troops to reconquer the little people we promised to liberate. It is the most ignoble kind of betrayal."

The French assault initiated the First Indochina War and introduced eight years of bloodshed between the Viet Minh and France. The United States was forced to choose between the French version of anticommunism and the anticolonialism embodied by the Vietminh.

We threw our support—massive financial support—behind the French.

Subverting the Peace

When the fighting was all over, when an exhausted French army surrendered to the communists in 1954, all participating parties met in Geneva to hammer out what they called a "Cessation of Hostilities." The Geneva Accords set down what were supposed to be the guidelines for a viable peace after almost twenty years of continuous warfare.

What I learned about the Geneva Accords and what happened in their wake, was, for me, breathtaking. I believe, likewise, that when my peers began to discover the contents of that agreement and its subsequent betrayal, America began to lose a generation of previously loyal and patriotic youth. A basic familiarity with the terms of Geneva soon permeated the campuses and became part of the common knowledge, the "cultural literacy" of the period. Of course, not everyone—not even the majority—took the trouble to inform themselves, but those who did would constitute the most dynamic segment of our generation. And they numbered in the millions.

The Geneva Accords were relatively straightforward. They divided the country in two at the 17th Parallel: North Vietnam headed by the communist Ho Chi Minh and South Vietnam, soon to be ruled by Ngo Dinh Diem.

They acknowledged the nationalist sentiment that pulsed through all of Vietnam and recognized the desire by the vast majority to unify North and South.

They called for general elections to implement the new unified government in July of 1956 supervised by an international commission.

It was here that the United States saw the writing on the wall. There was no way our side could win an election in Vietnam. Ngo Dinh Diem had no following whatsoever except among a small minority of Catholics.

Ho Chi Minh had been around after World War I begging the West for independence. He fought the French in the 1930s, the Japanese in the '40s, the French again in the '50s. His years of suffering had made him an old man before his time. He lost his teeth in a Chinese prison. He grew gaunt, "painfully thin" from years of hard living in the mountains on the Tonkin frontier along the Chinese border. One American historian wrote:

> His name became universally known throughout Tonkin, Annam, and Cochin China. It became synonymous with the most dogged and persevering attempts to create and keep alive kernels of resistance to French rule. (He) was like a shadow across French mastery in Indochina. His presence was reported everywhere. His name was spoken in whispers. His influence stirred young people in the villages and towns.

Ho Chi Minh, indeed, implemented a brutal land reform in the North, one which he himself would call excessive. Nevertheless, for the mass of Vietnamese people, he was the revered "Uncle Ho;" he was the liberator, the George Washington of Vietnam. He could no sooner have lost that election in 1956 than George Washington could have lost one in 1789.

Walter Bedell Smith, our representative in Geneva, was well aware of this. Secretary of State John Foster Dulles knew it and so did President Eisenhower.

And so the French signed the Geneva Accords and the North Vietnamese signed. The United Kingdom, the Soviet Union, Laos, and Cambodia all signed. South Vietnam and the United States refused. Diem cancelled the elections.

The guiding principle seemed to be: if you don't think you can win an election, cancel it. You can win by force of arms what you can't win through a vote. For anyone proud of America's democratic legacy, the whole cynical episode seemed a betrayal of the fundamental principles we had been taught as children.

In Eastern Europe Joe Stalin had cynically set up the sleaziest, most chilling police states— governments whose only claim to legitimacy was submissiveness to the Soviet Union. There was little affinity between the unfortunate people of Poland or East Germany or Czechoslovakia and their respective governments. But Vietnamese communists had fought decades for their legitimacy, had won over the most vital and patriotic sectors of the population, had gained the respect of massive numbers of people, and were willing to put their fate on the line in an internationally supervised election. It seemed a different breed of communism than what I had been brought up to fear.

I also learned about Law 10/59. Passed by the Diem government, it essentially institutionalized an ongoing manhunt of anyone in the South who had previously fought in that war for independence against the French.

After the Geneva Accords, a reshuffling of the population took place in Vietnam. Catholics—hundreds of thousands of them—fled from North to South, fearful of persecution by the communists and attracted as well by the possibility of choice positions with the Diem government. Most Viet Minh soldiers native to the North returned to their homes above the 17th Parallel. Many Southerners who fought with the Viet Minh stayed in the South after the war, awaiting the election that would never happen.

According to the French historian Philippe Devillers, Diem made a fatal mistake around 1957 when he turned on these former Viet Minh soldiers of the South. He tried to root them out employing methods resembling a reign of terror. Hundreds were harshly rounded up and sent to concentration camps.

Around 1958 the communists began to fight back. They shot informers as well as village chiefs who cooperated with the government manhunt.

Then, wrote Devillers:

> Diem's police saw their sources of information drying up one after another. To make good the lack, they resorted to worse barbarity, hoping to inspire an even greater terror among the villagers than that inspired by the communists. And in that fateful year of 1958 they overstepped all bounds. The peasants, disgusted to see Diem's men acting in this way, lent their assistance to the communists . . . going so far as to take up arms at their side.

When Southern communists asked for help from Hanoi, they were told that the timing was wrong. "The overriding needs of the worldwide strategy of the Socialist camp," continued Devillers, "meant little or nothing to guerilla fighters being hunted down in NamBo. It was in such a climate . . . in 1959 . . . that the Communist Resistance came to the conclusion that they had to act, whether Hanoi wanted them to or not. They could no longer continue to stand by while their supporters were arrested, thrown into prison, and tortured . . ."

Here was an origin story for the Vietnam War markedly different from the one handed down by our government. It seemed we had turned everything on its head. It seemed in every way the rationale for our presence in South Vietnam rested on rotted-out flooring.

As I turned the pages of *Quagmire* and read through the analyses of Gettleman, a rising fury welled up inside. It was an inarticulate anger, to be sure. At nineteen, I struggled and stammered to express outwardly the feelings that were growing and the thoughts that were germinating within. But on the inside I knew. I understood the issues; I could see through the flimsy rationalizations.

Having pored through books, articles, and documents, there were things that stood out in vivid relief.

It was clear that the war in Vietnam was a civil war.

It was clear that the enemy had far deeper roots within the population than did our allies in Saigon.

It was clear that to the extent outsiders were vying with men, guns, and money for influence within Vietnam, the United States was the primary actor.

It was clear, finally, that America's freedom was not at stake nor was her national security.

Mutilating the English Language

As much as anything, the mutilation of the language fed our rage. Here was MACV manufacturing inflated numbers of enemy dead and telling us we were "winning the war." Here was the State Department trampling on an international peace agreement and accusing our opponents of "aggression." Here was our government creating a dictatorship out of thin air and sending us off to die for the "free world." Here we were subverting an election and calling ourselves "defenders of freedom." It all represented a complete inability to search within ourselves, a refusal to explore our national soul. When you ripped off the mask, when you exposed the cruel mythology for what it was, they were all empty slogans. They were sorry reasons for which to die.

In the winter of 1966, as I waited in Louisiana to hear from the Englewood draft board, I had pretty much made up my mind. The previous summer I had carried the vague feeling that something was wrong in Vietnam. Now those feelings had crystallized. This was more than just "something feels wrong;" this was a political and ethical fiasco. I wasn't quite sure of my next step, but, no, I would not fight in Vietnam.

Sometime in February a letter arrived in an official-looking envelope with a return address: 3400 South Bannock St. Englewood, CO. I was shaking. I opened it up and removed the wallet-sized white card from the envelope. There it was, the new Selective Service classification in small letters: 1-S. 1-S?! I could hardly believe my eyes.

Everybody knew the coding system. There was 1-A and 1-Y, I-O, 4-F and 4-D, 1-S and 2-S. It was a virtual alphabet soup, what might all seem to another generation as a lot of secret mumbo jumbo. But we knew the details, at least the important ones: I-A, Uncle Sam would take you right in. 2-S, college student—a deferment. But 1-S? High School student? Somehow Wanda Story or some angelic secretary over in Englewood thought I was still in high school. That wrong stroke of the typewriter key gave me six more months.

I was in heaven. Maybe this meeting with destiny didn't have to happen at all. I was getting sick of filling short orders for the after-bar crowd in Metairie, anyway. I was sick of unloading boxcars, picking oranges, cabling up barges on the Mississippi for a dollar and thirty cents an hour. And for all my travels, there were no young ladies in my life clinging to my elbow and reveling with me in discovering the soul of America. I was ready to go back to school. When the draft board next heard from me, I'd be in college studying history and philosophy inside the red sandstone buildings of Boulder, drinking mugs of 3.2 beer at the Sink or gazing up at the Flatirons that hovered over the most idyllic town in Colorado. Life would be good.

Chapter 3

Why We Refused, Part II

Dear Sam and Sarah,

Does all this reading in New Orleans sound too mental or too bookish? Do people really make life-altering decisions based on some book they read in a coffee shop? I'm still not sure how weird or peculiar I was. I was definitely a loner, sometimes desperately lonely. I was definitely introverted, sometimes painfully so. I could mull over what I read as I scrubbed down the hot grill with a grillstone or cleaned up the coffee machine (or watered down the root beer). The introspection could provide a nice escape from the tedium of fast-food life.

There were other—more social—ways to get in touch with the views and ideas I had read about in books. In parts of America, especially on campuses and in the emerging youth ghettos, you could feel almost viscerally those ideas permeating the atmosphere. It was part of the zeitgeist, part of the spirit of the times.

Of course we were famously barraged nightly on the TV news by scenes from the war. They depicted the fear, the body count, the emotional intensity; they made the war a presence in our living rooms with GI interviews punctuated by gunfire or footage of medics retrieving the wounded. At least in the earliest years, however, these images provided no framework for this war and therefore no context for the meaninglessness and dumb brutality of it all. Nowhere did they provide analysis of how we got involved. Nowhere were we shown the true impact of the air war that literally rained fire on the Vietnamese population. Nowhere on these programs did we hear examination of the failed strategies of the U.S. military.

To get context you needed to turn to other sources: the church, or more often, for those of us who confronted the draft, the college campuses. The war in Vietnam became part of the national conversation at college dining halls, at the fountain next to the Memorial Center in Boulder, at the courtyard in front of Sproul Hall in Berkeley, at a thousand outdoor plazas on campuses across the country.

Walk through the north lobby of the UMC in Boulder and you would certainly find the literature table of the Student Peace Union, staffed all day with volunteers and brimming with brochures and flyers. Pick up a copy of the student-run *Colorado Daily* and you would invariably find an article on the war offering a perspective entirely different from the *Rocky Mountain News* and generally providing much more depth as well. Walk out to the fountain area and you would, likely as not, hear a member of the Students for a Democratic Society (SDS) speaking out against the war at the top of the west stairs and urging you to do something about it.

We tended to pay close attention, to weigh the arguments, consider the nuances because for so many, the specter of the draft stalked us; its nightmare vision haunted our innermost thoughts. The draft was the Queen of Spades; the draft was the Bitch, the card in the deck we wished would go away.

Most of the universities had their "teach-ins." They sometimes stopped normal classes and devoted the entire day or evening to the subject of Vietnam. Historian Tom Wells described the very first one in Ann Arbor in the early spring of 1965. Attended by 3,000 students, it lasted through the night until 8:00 the next morning. A midnight bomb threat sent everyone scurrying outside in 20-degree weather, but nearly everyone returned. "It was such a powerful event," recalled one of the organizers. "The campus was now alive with debate on Vietnam. It was impossible to avoid the controversy whether one wanted to or not." From Michigan, the teach-ins spread "like wildfire" to over 100 campuses that spring semester. It was the beginning of a sea change, a climatic transformation of student attitudes toward the war.

That draft resistance was a middle-class phenomenon is largely true but rather overstated. Within a month after my arrival at Safford I found myself among only half a dozen or so resisters. One of them grew up in the drab, noisy public-housing projects of the Kalihi Valley neighborhood in Honolulu. One was raised in the East Denver ghetto close to Five Points before the word "gentrification" even existed. The father of a third worked the assembly line at Samsonite Luggage across Broadway from Gates Rubber in south Denver. The father of another was a sheet metal worker at the huge Lockheed aircraft plant in the San Fernando Valley.

They were all working-class kids. What separated them from their peers who marched off to war was somehow acquiring that long view, that sense of history that a college atmosphere can so often impart to you. Each of them had tasted the intellectual life; each had developed a thirst for knowledge and each had had his world broadened by that roiling marketplace of ideas that can define the college experience.

Marty Harris (no relation to David) who joined me at Safford in 1969 grew up in the town of Gardena, California, a neighbor of Bob Zaugh. His father had an egg route. Zaugh's dad managed a grocery store half a mile from home until he told the family one night, "I'm going out for pork chops; I'll be right back." He never returned. Zaugh's mom ended up sorting rivets at Hi-Sheer down the freeway in Torrance for a dollar and a quarter an hour. "She went right to the bottom of the barrel," says Zaugh. "It just became really dark. There were no family dinners, just work. TV dinners had just been invented and we started eating nothing but TV dinners." Zaugh started drinking and disrupting classes; his grades plummeted and he barely graduated from Gardena High.

Harris and Zaugh's lives both centered around the bowling alley at Rose Lanes. They bowled on the same team; both made the all-star team. Zaugh would go down to Rose for both the early and late session of league play to keep score. "He had to scrape quarters and dimes together," says Harris. "He had to keep score even to buy school clothes." "We bowled every day after school," adds Zaugh, "and on the weekends round the clock. We drank together and we bowled together. In the summer Marty and I would get up and plan out a route. We'd hitchhike to five or six bowling alleys all over L.A. County and even Orange County."

When their teammates graduated from high school most of them drifted off to war. "Dave Trojan went to Nam," recalls Harris. "Trojan was a little wild. He was one of those guys that got in trouble—a stolen car or something like that and the judge says, 'Well, you want to go in the marines or you want to go to jail?' 'Well, I'll go in the marines.' Mike Deans went to Nam. Jerry Hurst and Tom Chavez went to Nam. Jim Chavez didn't go there, but he flew over it as part of an air force squadron. Ellis Pease. There was another one went to Nam."

Harris and Zaugh ended up instead at the junior college in Torrance. There on the conservative campus of El Camino Junior College they enrolled in the class of a political science professor named Dr. Carney. It turned their world upside down and challenged every political and historical worldview they ever grew up with. Carney was the kind of professor the administration wanted to get rid of. He would say things intentionally provocative to incite spirited discussion: "Why don't you grovel at the feet of the great gross capitalist and beg him to exploit you?" When he got angry, he would whisper instead of yell. Zaugh liked it. He switched his major from psychology to political science.

Harris became part of a peace group that caused a major stir on campus around winter break. Every year at Christmas time student clubs would decorate the big glass windows in the student lounge with a holiday painting. Harris's group put up a painting—eight feet tall—of a fork-tongued Santa Claus serving Campbell's Cream of Poverty Soup. It was not the most popular art project in the cafeteria. To protect Santa, they had to bring security in at night when conservative students threatened to throw chairs through the windows.

For all his controversy, Carney was no communist, nor did he advocate much in the way of political action. He created instead an openness within which one could accept a radically different worldview. "It wasn't like he was an activist, urging you to run the gauntlet," says Zaugh. "When Marty and I both started heading down the path of resistance, his position was 'Don't put your head in the meatgrinder. Don't do it.' And he was real strong on that." Regarding Vietnam, it was other influences that swayed the two poli sci students.

Harris recalls a crucial turning point. It was shortly after he received a student deferment from the draft in 1966 that J. William Fulbright, chairman of the Senate Foreign Relations Committee, conducted televised hearings on Vietnam. The senator labeled the hearings "an unprecedented experiment in public education." Harris recalls rushing home from class and turning on the TV. There he watched Fulbright, the senior senator from Arkansas, the most prominent dove in the country, locked in battle with Secretary of State Dean Rusk, the man charged with justifying the war to the whole nation. Harris remembers Fulbright asking Rusk point-blank about the origins of the war. About the Viet Minh's struggle for independence. About our failure to sign the Geneva Accords. About the popularity of Ho Chi Minh and the certainty of his victory in the hijacked election—the election that never happened—in 1956. Certainly in Harris's mind, the secretary failed abysmally to respond to any of the senator's questions.

"I had heard some of this before," Harris said, "I had professors that told me these things, but I didn't know if it was the truth, you know what I'm saying? You know, sometimes you can't believe everything anybody tells you. But here was Fulbright! Fulbright and (Senator Wayne) Morse! They brought it all up in Senate committee and nobody refuted them. Rusk (was) all mumbly mouthed . . . To me, (the non-election of 1956) was the crux of the whole war. That was everything. I said to myself, "Man this it it. Now it's gonna be headlines in the paper the next morning . . . It was like the truth is out. This war was gonna be over in a couple of months. If people knew this, why would we continue?"

So I rushed out the next day. It was like the *L.A. Times* or something. The headline: "Westmoreland Says Communists Control Antiwar Movement." And I'm going, "Is there something wrong with me or is there something wrong in our system?"

From that time on, I was 100 percent antiwar. And from that time on I never really cared about the particulars of the war. Zaugh will tell you about (*L.A. Times* Vietnam correspondent) Jack Foisie who was a great chronicler specifically of what was going on. That the pacification program wasn't working or that this is what really happened in that battle and Bob would really latch on to these things and say, "See, this is why the war's wrong." And I'd always say, "Bob, we don't need to worry about these details. We know from the beginning the war is wrong."

The White Paper

In February, 1965 as the U.S. geared up for all-out war, Mr. Rusk and the State Department circulated a much anticipated "white paper" entitled "Aggression From the North: The Record of North Vietnam's Campaign to Conquer South Vietnam." Its design was to justify the war, to ease the mind of any of us who required a rationale for sending 100,000 young men to fight in a little-known country across the Pacific. The title spoke for itself and was by and large successful in bringing the general public aboard. As a high school student, I'm sure I didn't read the whole thing but I was aware of its basic thrust and pretty much bought into it. It was essentially a compilation of all the weapons that had been shipped down from the North and all the enemy soldiers who had infiltrated South Vietnam from above the 17th Parallel.

Greg Nelson remembers reading the response to that white paper at the informal study group that formed at Greg McGlaze's house across the street from Santa Monica High School. Nelson describes McGlaze's mom, Marcy, as the kind of woman who Joe McCarthy might have blacklisted, the kind of woman who had grown up with Franklin Roosevelt's ideas of the world instead of Richard Nixon's. The kids used to come over and shoot baskets at lunch and Marcy McGlaze encouraged them to read the magazines she had around the house. She must have been a remarkable woman to get six teenage boys to discuss articles about the war during their lunch period. "We basically got educated about the war right there," says Nelson. Perhaps it was the forbidden fruit of periodicals like *The Nation* and I. F. Stone's *Weekly* that lured them.

Izzie Stone was an eminent journalist with the *New York Post* for two decades before he started his own independent journal in the 1950s. In no time he made a complete nuisance of himself, driving Washington power-brokers crazy with challenges and precise analyses. It was he, alone, who first questioned President Johnson's version of the Gulf of Tonkin incident in 1964—a version which later proved a complete fabrication. It was he also who ripped apart the State Department's 1965 white paper with a scathing reply within weeks of its publication.

First he broke down the weapons shipments. 15,000 weapons had been captured from the Viet Cong between 1962 and 1964 according to Pentagon statistics. Stone tallied up all the communist-manufactured submachine guns, recoilless rifles, carbines, and rocket launchers listed in the white paper. They added up to 179. Two and a half percent of the total. The remainder of the 15,000—M-14s, M-16s, Browning automatic rifles, bazookas—had been captured by VC from South Vietnamese forces. It appeared the principal suppliers of both ARVN and Viet Cong were American arms manufacturers.

Stone then turned his attention to the allegation of infiltration by military personnel from North to South. He turned to the appendices in the back of the white paper and found that the total number given is 19,550. "One way to measure this number," he wrote, "is against that of the military we have assigned to South Vietnam in the same years. These now total 23,500 or 25% more." He scrutinized those same appendices for the provincial homes of all captured infiltrators from the North. There were six; the rest were native-born

Southerners. "It is strange," he wrote, "that after five years of fighting, the White Paper can cite so few."

"None of this," he concluded, "is discussed frankly in the White Paper. To do so would be to bring the war into focus as a rebellion in the South, which may owe some men and materiel to the North but is largely dependent on popular indigenous support for its manpower, as it is on captured U.S. weapons for its supply. The White Paper withholds all evidence which points to a civil war."

Nelson's reading of I.F. Stone and everything else he could get his hands on led him inexorably to the same conclusion millions of others were also coming to—the same conclusion I had come to in New Orleans: the case for U.S. intervention in Vietnam ranged from feeble to nonexistent. And faced with this, the president, the State Department, and the Department of Defense were, to put it civilly, less than forthright in their presentation of the facts.

David Harris experienced this lack of candor face to face at a meeting he attended at the State Department in 1967. At the time Harris was president of the student body at Stanford and along with student body presidents from four other colleges, he was given the privilege of a private briefing on the "Vietnamese situation" with Secretary Rusk himself.

"When he talked, it was with an air of self-satisfaction," wrote Harris years later. "His manner showed that he clearly assumed this was something we should be grateful to get. The American effort had, he said, 'turned the corner ... stabilization of the countryside' was now 'in sight.' The recently resumed bombing of North Vietnam was yielding 'great returns.' ... The 'enemy' was experiencing 'great difficulties.' It was only a matter of time before American presence would begin being curtailed ...

"All of this," Rusk pointed out with a biting look in our general direction, "had been necessitated by 'North Vietnamese aggression.' It was the North Vietnamese who were 'sending troops into their southern neighbors.' It was, the secretary continued with a motion of his hand on the tabletop to emphasize his point, the North Vietnamese who 'were supplying tons of weapons and ammunition.'"

When the secretary paused to check his notes, Harris, "incensed by his hypocrisy," had only a split second opportunity to interject: "We aren't sending any weapons and ammunition over there, are we?"

"Rusk looked up and snorted," continued Harris. "One of the security officers by the door came over to the wall behind my chair and stood there for the remainder of the secretary's presentation."

Channeling

During the Civil War, if you could come up with $300 cash, you could buy yourself a substitute and purchase an exemption from the draft. During the Vietnam War, if you could afford tuition at the university, you could get yourself a student deferment and avoid the draft for at least four years, maybe more.

With my admission to the University of Colorado in 1966, I entered the ranks of those protected from the war by order of General Lewis B. Hershey, director of the Selective Service from 1948 to 1970. He called it "Manpower Channeling." In Hershey's mind, his job was far broader than just supplying healthy bodies for the U.S. military. It was rather to allocate human resources where the country most needed them.

"Delivery of manpower for induction ... is not much of an administrative or financial challenge," he said. "It is in dealing with other millions of registrants that the Selective Service System is heavily occupied, developing more effective human beings in the national interest." With this in mind, Hershey set himself up as the national guidance counselor and, under the influence of his gentle persuasion, millions of young men voluntarily enlisted in the armed forces, remained in college, or entered such professions as teaching, engineering, or work in the defense industry.

The secret to his persuasiveness, according to Hershey, was "exerting 'pressurized guidance' to encourage young people to enter and remain in study, in critical occupations, and in other activities in the national health, safety, and interest ... From the individual's viewpoint, he is standing in a room which has been made uncomfortably warm. Several doors are open, but they all lead to various forms of recognized patriotic service to the nation ... The club of induction (could be used to drive men) out of areas considered to be less important to the areas of greater importance in which deferments were given."

We were rats in a gigantic Skinner box. In this grand system of operant conditioning we, as college students, received the greatest of positive reinforcements: we got to stay 10,000 miles away from Vietnam. If we strayed down the wrong corridor of the rat box, the negative reinforcement would kick in soon enough and we all knew what that was. But as long as we stayed in school, we were primary beneficiaries of Lewis Hershey's manpower allocation scheme

If I could get Cs indefinitely in Western Civ and English Lit, I might get to watch the rest of the war on TV. I could drink pitchers of beer at the Sink or listen to the Moonrakers at Tulagis all in the "national interest." What a deal. We all knew it was a scam, but it was awfully difficult to pass up. Of course some other poor bastard would have to go in our place, maybe Olie Nygaard or Bob Sickels, maybe Norm Pacheco or Eddie Scott. But who said life was fair? Besides, the poor had always fought on the frontlines. They were used to it.

Even Lyndon Johnson was troubled by the lack of fairness. When the boyfriend of his older daughter, Lynda Bird, received a deferment, the scandal gained national publicity on a scale that personally embarrassed LBJ. Hollywood actor George Hamilton, who drove around town in a Rolls-Royce, got a "hardship" deferment to support his mother. Republican Congressman Alvin O'Konski complained that all the recent draftees from his Wisconsin district came from families with annual incomes under $5,000. "The system is undemocratic and un-American," he said. "It nauseates me."

Even so, large numbers of students remained comfortable with their privileged status even as they worried about losing it in the future. A 1966 poll at Harvard revealed that "65% believed they deserved draft deferments 'solely because they were students.'"

I don't think one resister could be found among that 65 percent. With a few exceptions (Greg Nelson, for instance), most of us did play the deferment game at one time or another. We yanked on the response levers in our Skinner box and pellets dropped out in the form of draft deferments. We avoided the punishing electric shocks, at least for a time. But the inequities weighed heavily on us all.

There was the issue of collaboration, always present in antiwar discussion, sometimes as the elephant in the room. If General Hershey factored the lives of college students into the overall equation of military strength and military preparedness then where did that leave us? If we accepted our place of privilege within the system were we all unwitting accomplices to those things being done in Vietnam?

As to fairness and disparities within the system, there wasn't even debate. Inherent in the very values of the draft was bias—naked and shameless—against the poor, against minorities, against the children of the working class. Under the system of channeling, their lives simply had less value than mine. Their lives were expendable; mine was not. Even a Republican congressman from Wisconsin could see that.

You could hide from Vietnam at the university but you could still feel its pulsating presence, breathing heavily, enveloping the surrounding atmosphere. The evidence for the war's congenital derangement kept piling up wherever we looked.

Joe Maizlish, whose systematic study of Gandhi and SNCC, Thoreau and King led him early on to a nonviolent orientation, continued to ingest the troubling flow of information.

At UCLA he met the daughter of Truong Dinh Dzu who ran for president of South Vietnam in 1967 on a platform to negotiate with the communists. For his peace efforts he was jailed after the election by Vice President Nguyen Cao Ky, the air marshal with the ever-present purple scarf, later accused of using CIA planes to transport opium and heroin out of Laos. Even Assistant Secretary of State William Bundy recalled that Ky and his coruler Nguyen Van Thieu "seemed to all of us the bottom of the barrel, absolutely the bottom of the barrel." The election had been fixed in any case: Ky had stated that if a civilian won, he would respond militarily because "in a democratic country you have the right to disagree with the views of others." Dzu's daughter, Monique, told Maizlish that her family remained so well connected that "she went to some kind of party with a lot of government officials. She had this dance with Air Marshal Ky and took the opportunity to complain about her father's being in jail. 'Well, in politics,' he said, 'sometimes you have to do things you don't like.'" It provided Maizlish with insight into the intimate repression that defined Saigon's internal politics.

Returning Soldiers

Reports from sadly disillusioned GIs added to Maizlish's sense of urgency. Thousands went to save the Vietnamese from the evils of communism and came back shaking their heads. Walking L.A. neighborhoods handing out flyers, Maizlish met one veteran recently returned as he knocked on the door. "It's like hitting your head against a brick wall," the guy told him. "They hate us over there. You walk through a village during the day; everybody's smiling and waving at you. You go back through at night, they're shooting at you. We don't belong there."

By far the most influential veteran in the early years was Sergeant Donald Duncan of the Special Forces. Maizlish read his articles in *Ramparts Magazine* and then heard him speak on the UCLA campus. As a Green Beret since 1956, Sgt. Duncan embodied the military ethic: loyalty, dedication, courage, and a fierce sense of anticommunism. By the time he completed his stint in Vietnam, he was publicly writing, "the whole thing was a lie."

As a trainer of counterguerrilla forces within Vietnam, Duncan discussed in detail his own training as a Green Beret. "Emphasis was placed," he said, "on the fact that guerrillas can't take prisoners. We were continuously told, 'You don't have to kill them yourself—let your indigenous counterpart do that.' In a course entitled Countermeasures to Hostile Interrogation, we were taught Soviet methods of torture to extract information . . . for example, the cold water–hot water treatment or the delicate operation of lowering a man's testicles into a jeweler's vice. When we asked directly if we were being told to use these methods, the answer was, 'We can't tell you that. The mothers of America wouldn't approve.' . . . I was later to witness firsthand the practice of turning prisoners over to ARVN for 'interrogation' and the atrocities that ensued."

Duncan was stationed in Germany in 1956 when Soviet tanks crushed the uprising in Hungary. The proximity heightened his awareness of communist oppression and inspired in him a greater commitment to Special Forces. After his eighteen months in Vietnam, working with the ARVN and watching the Viet Cong, he could only write, "We aren't the freedom fighters. We are the Russian tanks blasting the hopes of an Asian Hungary."

At CU, in the shelter of a student deferment, I was assimilating my own set of observations. Even as I enrolled in Physical Geography to satisfy a science requirement and Intro to Philosophy, I continued my own reading on the war. There was Bernard Fall, the Austrian-born journalist and historian who understood, as no American general ever did, the primacy of politics over military superiority in determining who would emerge the winner. I even read St. Augustine's *Confessions* to try to discover his criteria for which wars were "just" and which were not. (I have to admit the early unsuccessful battles against his own sexual urges made for far more interesting reading.)

Senator Fulbright's book *The Arrogance of Power* came out that year and, like Marty Harris, I was impressed with the credibility he carried with his title: chairman of the Senate Foreign Relations Committee made him the most powerful legislator in America in the realm of foreign affairs.

He seemed to look at revolutions with a long view. "An examination of past revolutions," he wrote, "the English, French, or Mexican Revolutions—may suggest that much of what we find shocking and barbarous (in communist regimes) may have more to do with a particular stage of revolution than with communist ideology." He said that revolutions were not static, that at a certain point there is a "coming back to earth, an abatement of fanaticism . . . and a return to everyday living."

He saw different shades of communism. In Mrs. Lockhart's social studies class a communist was a communist was a communist. The senator pointed to diversity within the communist camp—to the independence of Yugoslavia and Romania, to the differing national interests of the Soviets and the Chinese. The Vietnamese communists, who embodied the nationalist sentiment of a country emerging from colonial domination, were a whole different animal. "Far from being unified in a design for world conquest," he said, "the communist countries are deeply divided among themselves." In Fulbright's view, a Third World revolution—communist or not—need not represent a threat to American security.

For the previous two decades any president, any secretary of state or FBI director could count on the Pavlov effect in addressing the country on national security issues. Mention the word "communist" and we dogs would salivate—our reason suspended, our response conditioned and automatic. Fulbright's book—along with his committee hearings—were encouraging Americans to think, to make distinctions, to analyze the specific conditions. Many of us were learning not to slobber at the mention of the C-word.

Perhaps as much as the reading, the atmosphere on campus was pulling and pushing, dragging me into taking some kind of stand. Somewhere in my sophomore year the Students for a Democratic Society (SDS) began making its presence known in Boulder and Denver. A couple of scholarly graduate students in philosophy, John Buttny and Bruce Goldberg, provided the initial leadership. Both had buried themselves in study at Norlin Library for two years before they felt compelled to convert what they had digested from books into political activism on the streets.

Goldberg had been roommates at Penn State with Carl Davidson, a fellow philosophy major, who had moved on to the University of Nebraska for graduate studies. In 1966 Davidson was elected president of SDS largely by virtue of a mimeographed paper he authored and distributed at the organization's conference that summer in Clear Lake, Iowa. In "A Student Syndicalist

Movement," he likened the university system to a "knowledge factory" producing the talent and "know-how" upon which the "corporate state" depends. Among the commodities produced were AID officials (who ran civilian operations in Vietnam), military officers, CIA operatives, segregationist judges, corporation lawyers, politicians, welfare workers, managers of industry—a litany of roles necessary for the maintenance of an unjust society and increasingly militaristic society. He proposed in response a union of students—a union to struggle not just for better conditions on campus, but for "student control." "What we want is a union of students where the students themselves decide what kind of rules they want or don't want . . . Only this kind of student organization allows for the direct participation of students in all those decisions daily affecting their lives."

The next spring Davidson showed up in Boulder driving "a big old black hearse," full of clothes, SDS literature, and the galley proofs of a new book by former SDS president Carl Oglesby entitled *Containment and Change.* "It was a pretty heady stew," recalls Goldberg. When Davidson asked the CU grad student to accompany him as he drove around the state addressing crowds in Greeley, Ft. Collins, and Pueblo, Goldberg couldn't resist. "It convinced me that now was the time," Goldberg says. "It was time to stop interpreting the world and start changing it."

Buttny, a navy veteran and a former deacon at a conservative Baptist church, was engaged in an exhaustive study of the French existentialist Maurice Merlau-Ponty. The Frenchman's final work ended with the quote: "You cannot will your own freedom without willing the freedom of all men." "It fit in very nicely," says Buttny, "with the idea of moving off into political activism. Bruce and I both decided that this is what we wanted. This war was wrong and we've gotta take a stand."

In many parts of the country SDS would clash with those who called themselves The Resistance. I became aware of this only after many months of incarceration at Safford. In Colorado the SDS and The Resistance were essentially one and the same. "I remember we used to joke that the two different organizations made it look like there was more going on than there really was," says my friend Allan Haifley who was sentenced to Safford after I was released. "It turned out it was all the same people."

The Boulder SDS made regular appearances handing out flyers at the U.S. Customs House at 20th and California where busloads of young men were transported for induction and where eventually my own showdown with

Selective Service would take place. "We periodically got up at the crack of dawn to go to the induction center," recalls Buttny. "I remember those early morning rides to Denver and seeing the first beginnings of smog in the city, those first little clouds hanging in the air. One time Bruce and I played a little trick on the FBI. We called each other on the phone and planned an 'induction center event.' We didn't tell another soul. Then just the two of us drove down and walked up to the induction center. The FBI was out in force. We just waved to them and walked away."

In the summer of 1967 the Boulder SDS, along with one University of Denver student began preparing for a national draft card turn-in day in the fall. Mendel Cooper, the solitary DU student, provided the most dramatic moment of the action. Slight, pale, fragile-looking at five foot five inches and 110 pounds, Cooper's thick glasses highlighted his bookish appearance. Amidst a crowd described by the *Rocky Mountain News* as "bearded, hippie-types," the clean-shaven math major wore a coat and tie for the occasion. Deliberately, he removed his Selective Service card from his billfold, lit it on fire, then extinguished it just before the flame could devour his signature. He explained to the crowd quietly that he wanted to "preserve the portion of it which bore his signature that the government might have evidence of his deed." He carefully placed the charred but easily identifiable remains into a white envelope addressed "To Lyndon With Love." The whole scene was caught in a large front-page photo the next day in the *News*. When the photographer asked him to identify himself, he responded, "I am Mendel Cooper, that's M-e-n-d-e-l. I'm twenty years old. I live at 2275 South High Street and I attend DU."

Like other draft card burnings, it was an electrifying performance—the epitome of raw defiance. The burnings tended to drive some Americans wild. A year and a half prior, a mob of seventy-five high school students in South Boston had beaten four card burners bloody in an act of uncontrollable rage. Personally, I had my hesitations about the burnings. I thought the act too brash and shocking, too iconoclastic to be effective. When I heard about how Mendel had pulled it off, I had to admit, however, to a strain of admiration: What balls.

I knew a number of SDS members, respected them all, and tended to like them individually. They were a colorful bunch. John Akeson used to recite Bob Dylan lyrics to passersby at Boulder demonstrations: "Something is happening, but you don't know what it is/Do you, Mr. Jones?"

Draft Card in a Steel Block

Dick Roth turned in his draft card in a steel block he had welded up in his dad's garage in Aurora. It consisted of six one-inch steel plates welded together and weighed about fifteen pounds. "I remember I used almost a whole box of welding rod on it. I always thought there must be a file cabinet somewhere in an FBI office with that block in the drawer."

Looking at them as a group, however, I felt out of place and uncomfortable. To be sure, I felt awkward in any group, but these guys struck me as a bit abrasive, a bit too militant for my personality. For a shy, introverted soul, they were a little much. I thought their style would drive ordinary Americans away. They had a self-assurance that I never possessed. I was not a "Hell No, We Won't Go" kind of guy. I envisioned whatever confrontation might be in store for me as a polite one: "No, sir, I will not go." Of course, I had no historical knowledge of what kind of organization or what configuration of personalities it might take to get a social movement started. And perhaps I was just too scared to express my deepest feelings in front of a crowd.

At any rate in those days before my imprisonment, the FBI never counted me at an SDS action. I would come into draft resistance later from out of the blue. But the SDS guys were always there—prodding and challenging, goading everyone to take a stand.

In the summer of 1967, as SDS prepared for the draft card turn-in, I took a more modest step towards an activist approach. Gar Alperovitz, a former State Department aide, sensed intuitively that a reservoir of antiwar sentiment among "silent Americans"—Americans who were "deeply worried about the war"—had been left untapped by the mainstream peace organizations. To bring them in, he proposed a massive canvassing campaign to bring the issues to the doorsteps of Middle America. He envisioned Americans taking "little steps" against the war—signing a petition or just engaging in a dialogue. "They'd climb up the ladder," said Alperovitz, "but let them take the first step to the level they're comfortable with."

Twenty-six thousand volunteers answered the call for Vietnam Summer and I was one of them. As a canvasser, I was a disaster.

I knocked on doors in the Mayfair neighborhood of east Denver under the guidance of Susie Stark, a long-time peace activist from Kentucky and the mother of three young kids. I was a bumbling door-to-door salesman, hesitant and inarticulate. The few signatures I got, the few phone numbers I collected I attributed more to acts of mercy than to anything else.

The Air War

But Susie Stark did put me in touch with a circle of Denver activists whose conversation always included news about events in Vietnam and who emphasized the growing urgency of opposing the war. That was the summer I learned about the air war.

In 1965 General Curtis LeMay, U.S. Air Force Chief of Staff, went on record threatening to bomb North Vietnam "back into the Stone Age." President Johnson countered with "Operation Rolling Thunder," a more graduated and measured response, but one which, nevertheless, represented an awesome display of power above the 17th Parallel. In the South the display would prove equally ferocious. When the smoke cleared at the end of the war, the U.S. had dropped three times the tonnage of explosives in Vietnam than were dropped in all of World War II, in both the European and Pacific theaters.

The reports that drifted back took particular note of the lethal types of ordnance. There were antipersonnel cluster bombs known also as fragmentation devices. These were canisters filled with hundreds of lethal bomblets which shot off randomly in every direction like popcorn shells exploding over the length of two football fields. There was white phosphorus, which burns the flesh down to the bone and which can't be put out with water. There was napalm, the gasoline jelly incendiary which flowed into irrigation ditches and bunkers alike, torching whatever it touched, sticking to the skin, continuing to roast the flesh slowly for up to ten torturous minutes. The GIs called its victims "crispy critters."

The B-52 bombers from Guam and Okinawa attacked in waves which shook the earth, which shattered eardrums from half a mile away. Their payloads of 750-pound bombs left an awesome swathe of destruction and mile-long craters all over the Vietnamese landscape.

The common denominator of all these weapons was indiscriminate slaughter. Villages were destroyed in response to a single Viet Cong sniper. Psychological Warfare Operations would send laughable warnings to the women, children, and old men who still inhabited an assaulted hamlet: "From now on, chase the Viet Cong away from your village so the government won't have to shell your area again." Free strike zones were established in many regions of South Vietnam. In North Vietnam *New York Times* correspondent Harrison Salisbury documented extensive bombing in civilian areas.

A few military counterinsurgency experts who understood the importance of "winning the hearts and minds" of the populace condemned the indiscriminate nature of the attacks. General Edward Lansdale wrote:

> The most urgent need is to make it the number one priority for the military to protect and help the people. When the military opens fire at long range whether by infantry, artillery or air strike, on a reported Viet Cong concentration in a hamlet or village full of civilians, the Vietnamese officers . . . and the American advisers who let them get away with it are helping defeat the cause of freedom. The civilian hatred of the military resulting from such actions is a powerful motive for joining the Viet Cong.

Nevertheless, the tonnage of American bombs dropped in Vietnam surpassed even in 1967, the tonnage dropped in the Pacific theater during all of World War II. In a secret memo to the president shortly before he resigned, Secretary of Defense Robert McNamara wrote: "The picture of the world's greatest superpower killing or seriously injuring 1,000 noncombatants a week, while trying to pound a tiny backward nation into submission on an issue whose merits are hotly disputed, is not a pretty picture."

Much later in the war Daniel Ellsberg, a Defense Department and Rand Corporation analyst with top-secret clearance (and cousin of Frumess [Richard Frumess]), covertly xeroxed 7,000 pages of a secret study ordered by Defense Secretary Robert McNamara which exposed many of the fundamental deceptions surrounding the war. Before he released what became known as the Pentagon Papers in 1971 to the *New York Times*, however, he anguished over the consequences of revealing them. Seeking her advice, he showed excerpts to his wife, Patricia, who took them into the bedroom and read them over. She returned shaken, and turned her husband's attention to the language of the strategists: "the need to reach a threshold of pain;" "DRV pain in the North;" "VC pain in the South;" "Fast/full squeeze option" versus "Progressive squeeze and talk"; "the hot-cold treatment"; "one more turn of the screw." "This is the language of torturers," she said. Her eyes were filled with tears. "These have to be exposed. You've got to do it." Readers of the mainstream media gasped in disbelief when they read about the web of disinformation the war entangled us in. The new information certainly confirmed some suspicions and exposed some inside dialogue, but basically we had known for years that the whole operation was based on manufactured myth and disinformation. The Pentagon Papers filled in some gaps, but we resisters knew the gist already.

In the mid '60s, we were unaware of the backroom talk of the generals and political strategists, but we were already cognizant of the devastating results of their decisions.

The air war added a whole new moral dimension to Vietnam. It hastened us to greater commitment; it compelled us to consider more emphatic strategies to bring what now looked like utter insanity to a halt.

In January of 1967, before leaving Miami on a month-long vacation to Jamaica, Martin Luther King picked up a copy of *Ramparts Magazine* and "froze" when he turned to a page of color photographs. The article was on child victims of napalm; the photos showed their "horribly disfigured" features. One of his colleagues described his reaction: "Martin just pushed the plate of food away from him. I looked up and said, 'Doesn't it taste any good?' and he answered, 'Nothing will ever taste any good for me until I do everything I can to end that war.'... That's when the decision was made. Martin had known about the war before then, of course, and had spoken out against it. But it was then that he decided to commit himself to oppose it."

In the face of repeated warnings that his stand would jeopardize twelve years of credibility, twelve years of unprecedented progress in the civil rights arena, King declared to a crowd in New York's Riverside Church that the war "was extracting resources from America's poor 'like some demonic, destructive suction tube.' The U.S. government, he concluded, was 'the greatest purveyor of violence in the world today.'"

The Call to Civil Disobedience

Here was the marriage between the civil rights and antiwar movements longed for by so many peace activists. The Reverend King's decade-long embrace of civil disobedience—his repeated arrests and dignified defiance of the law—tended to reinforce the growing idea that nonviolent resistance could effectively challenge the war. His example provided inspiration to many in the resistance movement.

There were other sources of inspiration as well, both contemporary and historical. I met no resister, for example, unfamiliar with the story of Henry David Thoreau. Convinced that the Mexican War of 1846 was fought to extend slavery and hence, the power of the slave states into the American

Southwest, Thoreau refused to pay taxes in support of the war. It was his "duty," he wrote later, it was the duty of all citizens to disobey an unjust law. "Under a government which imprisons unjustly, the true place for a just man is prison . . . Cast your whole vote," he urged, "not a strip of paper but your whole influence."

For his trouble he ended up in the village jail of his hometown in Concord, Massachusetts. The story goes that his friend Ralph Waldo Emerson, the great man of American letters, came in the night to visit him. "Henry," he said, "what are you doing in there?" To which the hermit of Walden Pond responded: "Waldo, the question is what are you doing out there."

One of Thoreau's most renowned metaphors—bringing the machinery of state to a halt—echoed in a 1964 Berkeley speech that also resonated with those in the draft resistance movement. Addressing a crowd supporting the Free Speech Movement at the University of California, Mario Savio expressed the anger and frustration of dealing with a rigid and often duplicitous bureaucracy:

"There is a time when the operation of the machine becomes so odious, makes you so sick at heart, that you can't take part; you can't even passively take part, and you've got to put your bodies upon the gears and upon the wheels, upon the levers, upon all the apparatus and you've got to make it stop . . . you've got to indicate to the people who run it, that unless you're free, the machine will be prevented from working at all."

In 1967 David Harris began traveling the circuit of California colleges, up and down the West Coast, fusing the ideas of King, of Gandhi, of Thoreau, and of Mario Savio, applying them directly to the war and to the draft.

"Students kept talking about how they had no tools to stop war with," he wrote referring to a speech he delivered in Oregon. But I contended, "Your life is a tool . . . Without your allegiance, the government cannot, in fact, wage war. All the government needed from students was their willingness to play the game, holding deferments and making their separate peace with the Selective Service. With that cooperation it then raised armies for Vietnam. We could not afford to be passive government property any longer. If jail was the price, then we would have to pay it. It was time we used our lives to grind the machine to a halt."

"You have no right," he told a crowd in front of White Memorial Plaza at Stanford, "to send others out to do your butchering." The time had come for "massive resistance," he said and urged them to "join me in jail."

At Kezar Stadium after a huge march in San Francisco he again addressed the crowd: "We are mistaken if we call this war Johnson's war or Congress's war. This war is a logical extension of the way America has chosen to live. As young people facing that war, as people who are confronted with the choice of being in that war or not, we have an obligation to speak to this country, and that statement has to be made this way: that this war will not be made in our names, that this war will not be made with our hands, that we will not carry rifles to butcher the Vietnamese people, and that the prisons of the United States will be full of young people who will not honor the orders of murder."

Paul Barnes, who showed up at Safford in 1969, was home watching the news on a local L.A. TV station when he saw an appearance by Harris and fellow resister, David Bolduc. They had both refused induction that week and were interviewed briefly as to why they had done so. "It was an awakening for me," says Barnes, "in that up until that time I didn't see any alternatives. What do you do in the face of a draft and a war going on that you're gonna end up in at some point along the way? . . . For the first time I realized there were people out there who simply said, 'Look, I'm not gonna participate in this.' In the face of penalties, in the face of jail and fines, these guys were taking that on and saying 'Hey, we're not gonna cooperate; we're not gonna participate; we're not gonna allow ourselves to be inducted.' It was the first time I had ever heard that kind of statement and seen that kind of stand taken.

The effect was electric. When Bob Zaugh recalls hearing Harris speak at UCLA, he describes something akin to an epiphany. "Harris explained that you have a voice in this thing. You have your body. You can use it . . . If you saw that guy speak inside a building, inside where none of the energy could escape, out comes the draft card. You just had to do it. And so I made a decision." "If I'm able to make any meaningful decisions," he wrote in a letter to his draft board, "I must reject the sanctuary of a 2-S deferment."

All this defiant talk had created quite a clamor in the highest circles of government. Since Congress discovered the draft resistance movement in 1965, both Democrats and Republicans had weighed in on just exactly who we were, vying with one another for the most bitter invective.

Senator Thomas H. Kuchel, Republican, California: the "infamous" anti-draft movement is "vicious, venomous, and vile . . . replete with so-called conscientious objectors and beatniks."

Senate Majority Leader Michael Mansfield, Democrat, Montana: draft resisters "show a sense of utter irresponsibility and lack of respect . . . what these people have done is furnish fodder to Hanoi, Beijing, and the Viet Cong."

Senator Frank J. Lausche, Democrat, Ohio: the movement is headed by "long-whiskered beatniks, dirty in clothes worn down, seemingly, by a willingness to look like a beatnik . . . The point I am trying to make is that, substantially, these demonstrators are the project of communist leadership."

Senator Everett Dirksen, Republican, Illinois: "It's enough to make any person loyal to his country weep . . . where in the name of conscience is their sense of history?"

Senator Richard B. Russell, Democrat, Georgia: "I have said on the floor of the Senate that the fact that people in high places had encouraged campaigns of civil disobedience . . . in other cases (i.e., the civil rights movement) would bring home at other times under other conditions campaigns of civil disobedience that would be much more far-reaching and dangerous."

Representative Gerald Ford, Republican, Michigan: resisters are "shameful and disgusting."

Representative Robert F. Sikes, Democrat, Florida: "America has been shamed by the spectacle of organized treason and blatant cowardice . . . this sort of thing is encouraged by half-baked professors, communist sympathizers, and professional agitators . . . crackpots who have little comprehension of world problems or American responsibilities."

We were the scum of the earth.

The Moral Dilemmas

David Harris's stirring speeches failed to reach inside my insulated studio apartment just outside downtown Denver. Having transferred to the Denver campus of CU, I somehow managed not to hear a thing about what Harris and his band of peaceful rebels were doing on the West Coast. I did, however, keep reading and listening, listening to the growing mountain of evidence about the horrors in Vietnam.

I was also considering the moral dilemmas:

There was the vision, for instance, of Kitty Genovese, murdered outside her apartment in Queens in 1964 during my junior year in high school. The *New York Times* had reported that thirty-eight of her neighbors witnessed the crime over a thirty-minute period and had done nothing to intervene. The story touched off a national dialogue about moral responsibility, about growing apathy among Americans, and about the "bystander effect"—the idea that we can lose our decisiveness and courage by melting anonymously into the group.

There was the ghost too of the "good German"—the ordinary citizen who pursues ordinary duties as his country spirals downward into madness. Having grown up Jewish, it was axiomatic that the Holocaust and rise of the Nazis served as the bar with which to measure norms of evil and immorality.

It's not that I equated Vietnam to the Holocaust or ever have. I have never used the word "genocide" to describe our policies in Indochina. I have always cringed at the easy misuse of the term "Nazi" or "fascist" to describe every kind of malignancy that festers in a nation's heart or guides a nation's behavior. I knew instinctually that in fascist countries political dissidents—as I had begun to define myself—tend to get shipped off to secret prisons from which they never emerge. The America I knew was no fascist country.

Nor could I condemn violence for its own sake; I was no pacifist. Having chosen the Holocaust as the standard for immoral behavior, having been grateful to World War II veterans for defeating the Nazis, having taken as heroes the fighters of the Warsaw ghetto uprising, I could not repudiate the right to self-defense, national or otherwise.

Still, the idea of the "good German," the idea of the passive bystander, the indifferent witness to evil continued its haunting presence. It doesn't require a Holocaust to present us with individual moral dilemmas. Perhaps Vietnam failed to measure up to the unapproachable bar of immorality set by the Germans. Perhaps America could never rival European evil in sheer numbers and malevolence. But that seemed of little importance. Vietnam seemed to represent a peculiarly American brand of evil, perhaps smaller in scope, perhaps with better intentions, perhaps layered with a veneer of idealism.

But the corpses, nevertheless, were piling up fast, as were the twisted rationalizations. In the summer of 1967 I needed only a little shove to push me over the edge.

It was David Bentley who unintentionally provided that last shred of evidence. He was Frumess's (Richard Frumess's) roommate up on the Hill in Boulder, a handsome, dark-haired mountain climber with a pair of hearing aids that emitted a shrill high-pitched whistle at random intervals. Almost totally deaf, he had thrown himself—when he wasn't scaling cliffs or chasing feverishly after women—into the silent world of books and literature.

He consumed indiscriminately works on history, sociology, geography, and politics. "I think you really should take a look at this," he told me one day as he pulled an issue of *The New Yorker* out of his back pocket.

The New Yorker had deemed Jonathan Schell's book-length report on "The Village of Ben Suc" significant enough to devote its entire July 15 issue to. I brought it back to my place and began reading that night.

The Village of Ben Suc

The village of Ben Suc was located in the Iron Triangle, a Viet Cong stronghold twenty-five miles northwest of Saigon, whose proximity to the capital represented a standing insult to the U.S. military. In January of 1967 the 173rd Airborne Brigade, in conjunction with the 1st Infantry Division and the 196th Light Infantry Brigade, began Operation Cedar Falls to root out the enemy in Binh Duong Province. It would be a two-phase operation. Phase one was to kill and capture enemy soldiers and destroy VC-dominated villages and infrastructure. Phase two was to resettle remaining civilians and win them over to our side: winning "hearts and minds" was the operant phrase. "We realize you can't go in and then just abandon the people to the VC," said Major Allen C. Dixon. "This time we're really going to do a thorough job of it: we're going to clean out the place completely . . . and then we're going to move everything out—livestock, furniture, all their possessions. The purpose here is to deprive the VC of this area for good."

Phase one proceeded efficiently enough. Some of Schell's descriptions sounded biblical, something like what Nebuchadnezzar might have done to some unfortunate Judean city. First came the B-52s. Then came the M-2 flamethrowers to torch each of the grass-roofed village structures. Then came the hogjaws—sixty-ton bulldozers—to scrape away what was left of the village and then to flatten out the jungle in fifty-yard swaths on both sides of Route 13. Then finally came the air force jets once again to "pulverize for a second time the heaps of rubble, in the hope of collapsing tunnels too deep and well hidden for the bulldozers to crush—as though having once decided to destroy it, we were now bent on annihilating every possible indication that the village of Ben Suc had ever existed."

As always, identifying apparently unarmed Viet Cong was tricky, especially when American lives were at stake and instant decisions were required. Schell cited one bicyclist clad in a black peasant garment gunned down as he pedaled rapidly away from a village center. "That's a VC for you," said one soldier. "He's a VC alright. That's what they wear. He was leaving town. He had to have some reason."

"Okay," said Major Charles Malloy, "so some people without weapons get killed. What are you going to do when you spot a guy with black pajamas? Wait for him to get out his automatic weapon and start shooting? I'll tell you, I'm not." When a captured villager walked by during the interview, Malloy added, "There's a VC. Look at those black clothes. They're no good for working in the fields. Black absorbs heat. This is a hot country; it doesn't make any sense. And look at his (bare) feet. They're all muddy from being down in those holes (tunnels)" Then he added thoughtfully, "What're you going to do? We've got people in the kitchen at the base wearing those black pajamas."

After the killing and the demolition, the resettlement program began. Known by the army as the "other half," the nonmilitary half—it involved trucking 6,000 villagers from Ben Suc and the surrounding area down the road to the village of Phu Cuong and then to Phu Loi. There they were greeted upon their arrival by a sign hanging over the barbed-wire coils which read in large letters: "WELCOME TO FREEDOM AND DEMOCRACY"

Inside the barbed-wire fence were their new homes: half a dozen nylon cloth canopies, each about 100 feet long draped over bamboo poles, constructed over the bare earth without floors or walls. Beside these was a temporary mass toilet: two fifteen-yard ditches clearly visible from the camp entrance, which no one used because of the lack of privacy and the difficulty of leaning over its edges.

Schell wrote:

> When (the people) climbed down from the backs of the trucks, they had lost their appearance of healthy villagers and taken on the passive, dull-eyed, waiting expression of the uprooted. It was impossible to tell whether deadness and discouragement had actually replaced a spark of sullen pride in their expression and bearing or whether it was just that any crowd of people removed from the dignifying context of their homes . . . and dropped, tired and coated with dust in a bare field would appear broken-spirited to an outsider.

In contrast to the demoralized villagers stood Lt. Col. Kenneth J. White, on loan from the military to the Office of Civilian Operations. Bounding around the camp, he displayed, according to Schell, "unflagging energy and almost unclouded high spirits, not unlike an eager camp counselor managing a large and difficult but highly successful jamboree."

Brimming with pride at the speed with which the shelter had been constructed, he exclaimed, "This is wonderful! I've never seen anything like it. It's the best civilian project I've ever seen ... You know, Phil," he continued to the AID official at his side, "sometimes it just feels right."

Operation Cedar Falls represented all that was wrong in Vietnam: the awesome and devastating destruction of U.S. firepower. The capacity and the willingness to annihilate villages and jungle alike, to remake the very landscape of the countryside. The abysmal ignorance of the language and culture of the people we claimed to be saving. The hubris of believing we could rip out the country's social structure in its entirety, then remake it magically in our own image. The disconnection from reality. The endless ability to deceive ourselves.

The Stench from Vietnam

Learning of the decimation of Vietnamese village, Ben Suc, reinforced what I had already known: We had fallen over the edge. Maybe Vietnam represented our own peculiarly American brand of evil, less malevolent, perhaps, less cynical. Maybe some of its architects were well intentioned, even idealistic. But, whatever the motivation, our country, my country, had lost its way. We had long passed any measure of justification for continuing this slaughter. We had fallen over the edge.

The whole war was based on a rotten foundation—a set of fabrications like so many faulty rotting floor boards. The phony statistics from MACV. The phony numbers of enemy dead from the ARVN. The subversion of the an international peace agreement at Geneva. The attempt to call aggression where no aggression occurred. Suspend any reason. Say communist, and the dog will salivate.

The mutilation of the language. The Vietnamese communists had fought for their legitimacy, had gained the loyalty of massive numbers of people, and had won a mandate from their people. The Americans set up a dictator in South Vietnam and disregarded any chance for elections in Vietnam, yet called ourselves defenders of freedom and democracy. The truth was turned upside down. The hypocrisy, the double standard took our breath away—mutilation of the language horrified us.

It outraged us. The whole thing was madness.

I was certainly no scholar of history; I was twenty. But I think for most of us who refused, there was a certain sense of history: that opposition to this war was our generation's burden, that a narrow window of time existed during which we had to act and that in failing to do so, we would choose to turn our backs on our own history, to become malleable, passive spectators of our own times.

I think we sensed that when the moment came, the choice of inaction would stay with us the rest of our lives. Those of us who began to question the war were accused of disloyalty. The antiwar movement was accused of being unpatriotic bordering on treason. But I believe we turned against the war precisely because we were Americans. We, who were nurtured on the idea that America's place in the world rested on the side of democracy, of fair play and simple honesty, were sickened when we saw those ideals violated in Vietnam, by what was being done in America's name.

Our teachers had taught us well. If we reacted passionately it was because it pained us so to watch helplessly while the very principles we were taught to cherish were betrayed.

I set down Bentley's copy of *The New Yorker* a little dazed, certainly troubled but still uncertain how to proceed. I'm sure there were more reasonable things to do, more effective things to do. But the disparity between what was in my heart and how I was living my life was too much to endure. Within the month, I wrote a letter to the Englewood draft board, informing them I would no longer accept a student deferment. It was time to confront the draft; it was time to face the Bitch head on.

A year or so later Crosby, Stills, and Nash came out with a line in a song that seemed to capture perfectly my own feelings as well as the feelings of everyone else in the antiwar movement. In a beautiful rendition of "Long Time Gone," they sang out the words: "Speak out, you've got to speak out against the madness."

It was time to stop the madness.

For God's sake, it was time to stop the madness.

Chapter 4

County Jail

Dear Sam and Sarah,

About ten years ago I experienced persistent swelling of lymph glands in my neck and Dr. Dodge referred me to the Kaiser Franklin Building for an MRI. At first glance, the machine, an elongated tube surrounded by housing for a huge circular magnet, seemed innocent enough.

"Are you claustrophobic?" the tech asked.

"No, not me." I could take it.

"You have to stay perfectly still," he warned as he settled me into a sliding examination table.

"No problem."

Then he slid me into the enclosed cylinder, the narrow dark chamber where I would spend the next forty minutes of my life. It was a casket. They were sliding me into my tomb. *You're kidding me*, I thought. Then the coils in the magnetic field were activated with radio frequency waves. The chamber exploded with repetitive blasts of 120 decibels—a jackhammer pounding and reverberating through the entire cylinder.

I was claustrophobic after all. I was white as a sheet by the end, flailing, shaking, gasping for breath.

That evening I dreamed, as I would dream nightly for the next couple of weeks, that I was back in my cell at Denver County Jail. It had been two decades since I'd given much thought to my first intersection with the Bureau of Prisons. But when the latent memories were unexpectedly released, they came out in a torrent that left me lying awake in a cold sweat.

For most of us, the immersion into county jail was our initial introduction into the strange new world we would live in for the next couple of years. Whether in Halawa Jail in Honolulu, L.A. County—Old or New—the Santa Rita complex in Alameda County or the Denver facility at Smith Road and

Havana, we slept at times on concrete floors in overcrowded cells, ate cold bologna sandwiches on stale white bread, and heard the terrible clang of steel on steel as cell doors crashed shut with dreadful finality.

In Halawa some superpatriot in a six-man cell appointed himself to head the welcoming committee for Dana Rae Park. He lit a wad of toilet paper and threw the flaming roll at Dana Rae whose picture had just been splashed over the pages of the *Honolulu Advertiser.*

But Park's most vivid memories came after his first plane ride carried him to the mainland—a culture alien to anyone born and raised in Hawaii. The *U.S. News and World Report* doesn't rank the best jails in the country as they do colleges but Park claims L.A. County had to be one of the worst. "I don't know where it could be much worse. Maybe Washington, DC. Maybe someplace down south. But as far as jail rankings are concerned I don't know where it could be much worse than L.A." A few years ago at his home in Kelseyville I asked Dana Rae if he could recall his first impression—a Rorschach impression—of L.A. County. He didn't hesitate a second: "Jesus Christ, get me outta here!" "L.A. County Jail, God, that's where the nightmare begins. That's where it gets all Kafka."

(Kafkaesque: "marked by a senseless, disorienting often menacing complexity.")

Yes.

(Kafkaesque: "marked by surreal distortion and often a sense of impending danger.")

Yes!

"L.A. County, that's where it gets all Kafka," repeats Park. "L.A. County Jail where the lights are always on. I remember being processed forever going from one cell to another cell to another cell to another cell. And finally after twenty-four hours you end up in the place where you're gonna be held and you sleep on the fucking floor because there's no bunk for you in there. Four bunks and two on the floor. Four beds and six people, yeah! Always overcrowded, always overcrowded. I remember on weekends more people would get swept in because of the drunks and whatever. I always slept on the floor."

Of course there were some educational opportunities. One inmate convicted of burglary taught Dana Rae how to lift up and put down a chair without making a sound.

Joe Maizlish, having left his folks at the Federal Courthouse, ended up in L.A. County about the same time as Dana Rae Park. He is sure he was singled out for harassment. Of all the people booked on that grueling first day, he was the very last, conspicuously passed over and left in holding cell after holding cell for interminably long periods. A deputy sheriff assigned to search inmates for drugs or weapons made Maizlish pound his shoes absurdly against the wall for a full five minutes. An inmate mouthed off at a guard and was escorted out to the hallway. He came back bleeding from the mouth. When Maizlish, who was being fingerprinted, glanced over, he was asked, "Do you want to go out there with your buddy?"

National publications had run several articles in the recent past about overcrowding in the country's jails. Ronald Goldfarb, for instance, had toured the facility in Washington, DC, and written a piece for *The New Republic* entitled "No Room in the Jail." Because it housed double its original capacity, Goldfarb labeled the place a "human stockyard" and referred ominously to studies of Sika deer on a Chesapeake Bay island. When the population had reached a certain density, the deer began dying off for no apparent cause except that their adrenal glands had swollen up to abnormal size. He referred obliquely to other studies: John B. Calhoun had done the classic research on the bleak effects of overpopulation on rats and mice. Calhoun coined the term "behavioral sink" to describe the aberrant patterns of 2,600 mice stuffed into a nine-foot-square steel box.

At the end of his processing, Maizlish found the L.A. County Jail packed as solid as the DC Jail. "The whole place was paved with mattresses," he recalls, "They had at least three in each cell, then they put in a fourth, then two more out front in the runway. They just brought in a whole bunch of people and said, 'Put 'em in there.' And so we were overstuffed. There was a general outcry and I joined in along with everybody else. I think they took enough out so nobody had to sleep in the corridor. But the problem wasn't walking the corridor. You still had to step over people in the cell to get to the toilet. It was just too many people for the number of toilets."

Paul Barnes, another Safford alumnus, arrived in Old L.A. County above the County Courthouse some months after Park and Maizlish. "There were thirty-four inmates in a cell block designed to hold sixteen," he recalls. "It was very tense. Out of the thirty-four guys, I was the only one who knew how much time he had to serve. Everyone else was sort of in the process of prosecution and trial and hearings. Trying to get lawyers. Trying to get witnesses. There were people who'd been there already for a year and hadn't gone to trial yet. So it was very tense . . . I witnessed three attempted suicides just in the area where I could observe. One of them was successful. The guy cut his veins open lengthwise instead of crossways. He was very serious about it. He wanted out; he got out.

"The rape I witnessed was a set-up kind of situation. Gay people—obviously gay people—were usually segregated in county jail and put into an area out of population. But this particular gay guy had been thrown into our module and had been paired up in a cell with a man who—I'm sure the guard knew—would abuse him. That night they locked three guys in the cell; everybody else was sleeping out on the floor behind a barred wall. We heard this guy screaming, yelling, getting slapped, getting beat, getting raped. Everyone out there knew it; everyone in the module knew it. The guard at the end of the module knew it. He didn't do a thing, didn't do a thing at all. This guy had obviously incurred the wrath of somebody for some reason and this was his punishment.

"I remember the day I was discharged. The (federal) marshals had come to pick me up and I was walking through a hallway in the basement of the courthouse building on the way to the parking area. As I'm walking out, there's a door on my right, an open door. Inside this room there's a man sitting on a chair, obviously bruised, with two L.A. sheriffs beating him. I turned my head to take a look. Just a quick little flash of the scene, but I could tell what was happening. I turned my head and kept right on walking."

Our New Home

I would be less than honest if I told you the draft resisters fit immediately in to the boisterous, street savvy culture of the county jail. Most of us worked hard at it—eventually successfully—but in the beginning we looked on wide-eyed and walked cautiously into the strange and unfamiliar surroundings.

At least, I did. I had, after all, graduated from George Washington High School in 1965. The student body in those pre-bussing days consisted of 3,000 students, four of whom were black, two Mexican. Not exactly the kind of school that might prepare me for the realities of county jail.

Maizlish, as a young boy, had attended B'nai Reuben Hebrew Academy. The grandfather of Ruth Maizlish had come to the United States in 1870, studied at yeshiva for a year and then returned to Poland with the concluding remark: "My children would not grow up to be Jews in America." With this vision in mind, the Maizlishs sent Joe to an Orthodox school where he donned skull cap and prayer shawl for half a day while studying Torah and

Talmud in the original Hebrew. It was a poor school in a struggling neighborhood, but a universe away from the streets where the California correctional authorities recruited the bulk of its population. One of Maizlish's teachers sent him a copy of the Hebrew Bible which Joe would read occasionally in his jail cell. The image stays with me: Joe on a bunk next to a lidless toilet in a dank cell reading this ancient alphabet, this sacred text—a striking contrast with the din and clamor of L.A. County. The guards must have wondered why he was reading backwards.

Reunions occurred frequently. A fraternity of sorts, an inner brotherhood, had incorporated over the years on urban streets, juvenile halls, and state correctional facilities. A new inmate would wander in and half the tier knew him from the street. "Hey wussup, cuzz; whatchoo been up to? Where you stay now?" The street banter rolled continuously. "What's up with the silk underwear, man?" "Hey, I'm not gonna have nothin' next to my ass, but silk."

One seasoned "fraternity member" approached Maizlish and asked what he'd done on the street. "I talked a little about my alleged crime," remembers Maizlish, "and that I was a student and a teacher in my former life. When he found out that I'd never been in jail before he said, 'You twenty-six years old and this is your first time in jail? Where you been?'"

"It was quite a society they had in there. I was just trying to adjust," says Maizlish, "to figure out, okay, this is gonna be the way I'm living for a long time. It was a funny bunch, this all-male society, mostly somewhat younger than me. Just seeing that we weren't attacking each other or fighting each other (was reassuring). That wouldn't have made sense; that would have just been hell for everybody all the time . . . If you didn't go in with a judgmental attitude about who was who and who did what, you could get along with most everybody."

Louie Vitale, an activist L.A. priest, visited Maizlish from behind a glass window in the first days. Besides extending friendship and solidarity, he had an ulterior motive: to find out what side of the jail Maizlish was housed in. Old L.A. County, unlike the new one, had windows that could actually open. Next night Maizlish looked out the window from his twelfth-floor cell and there stood his buddies from the L.A. Resistance, setting up a sound system. Rich Profumo led a round of "He's Got the Whole World in His Hands." The prisoners went wild, cheering and yelling at every peace song offered. When

Maizlish's then girlfriend yelled up "Good night, Joe," they went wild again. "They loved that," says Maizlish.

"The deputies didn't like it at all." It wasn't long before two U.S. marshals showed up in a Volkswagen Bug and transferred him over to Ventura County, much farther removed from the dangers of folksingers and girlfriends.

For Greg Nelson, L.A. County was relatively easy time. Since he acted as his own lawyer, they gave him his own cell with access to the law library. With his transfer a month later to the federal holding facility in Florence, Arizona, Nelson's life changed for the worse. Inmates greeted him with leering catcalls, whistles, and high-pitched voices, mocking him for his long hair. "In the next cell over," he says, "there was this transsexual guy who'd been attacked and burned with cigarettes."

But most of all he remembers the noise. Poet Richard Shelton once visited Cell Block 2 in the state prison at Florence and wrote, "It was as if I were inside some huge drum being pounded on mercilessly . . . I felt assaulted, as if by some huge animal who was pressing against me, sucking all the air out of my lungs and squeezing my head between its terrible paws." The federal facility at Florence consisted of four different units on one floor with twenty to forty inmates in each unit. The units were separated by bars but no walls which might keep out noise from the surrounding cells. Each of the four dayrooms had its own TV, each tuned to a different channel with the volume turned up full blast. Country and Western music blared in from the loudspeakers. Clamorous voices blasted in from one cell to the next. The final mix produced a cacophony of disconnected and discordant sound, deafening and disorienting for the most social of inmates. For the shy and reclusive Nelson, the ceaseless noise represented a Dantesque scene from *The Inferno* that kept his head continuously throbbing.

The Tet Offensive

Shortly after Maizlish, Nelson, and Dana Rae Park entered L.A. County, I walked into the second tier of the CAPIAS section of the Denver County facility on Smith Road. CAPIAS: Court Appointed Prisoner Is Awaiting Sentence. We were—all of us—convicted felons, but despite the lengthy title, most of us had already gone through sentencing. We were all waiting, waiting in limbo, for transfers to the more permanent institutions whose mission was to process, punish, and rehabilitate us all. Most had gone through the state system and were destined for Cañon City or Buena Vista.

I had been sentenced to two years by the Honorable Judge Alfred Arraj, whose daughter Sally had been a high school classmate of mine three years before in Dudley Enos's English Lit class. I was awaiting transfer to some unknown federal facility, the uncertainty of which racked my thoughts day and night.

My trial in Judge Arraj's courtroom had been, for any spectator, an exceedingly dull affair. It was open and shut: did I refuse to comply with the Selective Service Act or did I not?

The facts demonstrated that the crime did indeed occur on February 2, 1968.

As it turned out February 2nd proved to be a turning point in the war. Throughout the previous year the Johnson administration had assured the American public that we were indeed winning, that the tables had turned, that there was "light at the end of the tunnel." On January 31st the Viet Cong shattered that illusion. They launched the Tet Offensive—a wave of attacks on thirty-six provincial capitals and five major cities, which extended even into the heart of Saigon, even on to the grounds of the U.S. Embassy. On February 1st a Viet Cong captive was marched through Saigon streets and handed over to the custody of General Nguyen Ngoc Loan, chief of the national police. The captive, dressed in civilian clothes, a plaid shirt, unruly hair, was handcuffed, his wrists tied securely behind his back. It was alleged, though never proven, that he was part of an assassination and revenge squad capable of perpetrating his own atrocities. General Nguyen appeared very casual as he pulled out a small-caliber pistol, placed it six inches away from his prisoner's temple and pulled the trigger. On hand to catch the whole sequence of summary execution was Associated Press photographer Eddie Adams along with NBC cameraman Vo Suu. Journalists labeled it the "shot seen 'round the world." It became an icon of the war.

The photograph which stunned the world was hitting the morning papers on February 2nd, the morning I was ordered to report for induction into the United States Army. Historians now call the Tet Offensive the pivotal event of the war. Gone forever was the illusion of military victory, gone—for those shocked by Adams's photography—any pretense of moral superiority. As I walked up the stairs on the 20th Street side of the U.S. Customs House, I had only the vaguest awareness of the significance of events that had occurred that week. But I had made up my mind months ago.

Part of the plan was thwarted in the first moments. A lower-grade officer greeted me at the door with a checklist of routine questions. The final question left me dumbfounded: "Do you intend to refuse induction today?" The obvious aim was to isolate any draft resisters from the general population of draftees. Should I lie in order to make my stand more public? I had only a split second to decide. I'm not sure I had enough brains to be a good liar. "Yes," I blurted in a decision I regret to this day. I was incapable of lying, incapable of shedding this damnable honesty, even for the greater good of speaking truth in public.

They ushered me into a private room and brought me before the inducting officer, a Captain Ferkhins, I believe. He towered over me. I had no idea if he had already completed a tour of duty over there or if his special contribution to Vietnam was simply to send these young men off to war. He directed me to stand in front of the painted white line on the floor. I felt all alone.

"How old are you, young man?"

"Twenty-one."

"We can make a good soldier out of you," he said. "A fine soldier."

"Not for this war." My heart was thumping. There was no defiance in my tone, just quiet, almost polite, resolution.

"I'm going to order you to take one step across the line. When you do so, you will be in the United States Army. If you fail to do so, you will be convicted of felony refusal to submit to induction. You will be sentenced to five years imprisonment and a $10,000 fine. When you complete your sentence, we will draft you again and again. We will draft you until you submit to induction. Do you understand?"

"Yes, sir." (*He's bluffing*, I thought. *Isn't he? About the second time around, the second induction, I mean. I hope he's bluffing.*)

"Now. I order you to take one step forward."

I didn't move.

"I order you again. Take one step forward."

Silence.

"I order you once more. Take one step forward."

"I won't go."

The captain took pains to have me write out a simple statement: "I refuse to be inducted into the Armed Forces of the United States." I signed and dated it.

"Very well. The next word you hear from us will be delivered by the FBI."

I turned and walked away. I have no idea what I did the rest of the day. Who I saw. What I said. Perhaps I should have felt relieved. Perhaps proud. Perhaps I should have found my way to the White Mule for a drink. I think mostly I just felt lonely and uncertain, waiting anxiously to hear what the FBI might say.

Within the legal community surrounding the U.S. District Court in Colorado, Judge Alfred A. Arraj has always held the highest reputation for fairness and straight talk, a reputation of such stature they named the federal courthouse for him after his death in 1992. I have no doubts as to the man's integrity, but I can't help but ponder on the trivial issues that emerged as the focus in his courtroom. In the fall of 1968, as another thousand GIs were cut down, another couple of dozen villages torched, another few hamlets bombed into oblivion, another few thousand civilians caught in the crossfire, there was no acknowledgment in Judge Arraj's courtroom that perhaps some moral dilemmas existed. There was no acknowledgment on the part of Assistant U.S. Attorney Milton Branch—a young lawyer who surely sensed in my case an easy conviction for building his career—that perhaps there were matters of conscience involved.

On my lawyer Bill Reynard's advice, I had applied for something considered quite bizarre at the time in Selective Service circles: a selective conscientious objector status. That implied that an American citizen might actually have the right to choose the war he would fight in. Some wars, it implied, probably the vast majority of them, were not worth fighting at all. I knew, of course, that this concept was way over the line but it did give me a chance to articulate some of the things I had learned over the last three years. Having expressed my belief in our country's right to self-defense, having outlined in some detail my objections to the government in South Vietnam, to the futility of pacification, to the folly of opposing a nationalist revolution, to the inhumanity of the air war, I wrote that "I will not be a mercenary for the Thieu government, nor will I contribute to our effort in Vietnam by submitting to military authority."

Perhaps it was my lack of skill as a witness, but none of these objections ever saw the light of day in the courtroom of Alfred Arraj. The issues that came forth included: Did the correct number of Selective Service officials actually sign my order to report? Did Wanda Story type my I-A classification accurately? Did I really fail to cross that thin white line that separated me from military service? Yes, to all of the above and American justice could relegate my case to a criminal act, rather than a political or moral one.

Milton Branch got his conviction without working up much of a sweat. The jury did their duty. Alfred Arraj brought down his gavel with finality. I found myself the next day on the second tier of one small section of the massive complex of Denver County Jail.

Denver County

CAPIAS had three tiers of cells stacked one on top of the other, about twenty cells to a tier, at least two inmates in each cell. There were no windows. The bottom tier was preferred; it had something like a concrete yard extending maybe twenty yards beyond the iron bars of the cell line. This provided additional space for some pretty lively handball games. Tiers 2 and 3 had catwalks—corridors about a yard wide extending beyond the line of cells. A black iron railing, maybe chest-high, prevented you from falling on to the hard concrete floor of the first tier below.

Every few hours a guard opened up the doors of all the cages simultaneously and each inmate had a decision to make. Do I spend the next few hours pacing along the corridor in the company of others or do I choose to stay in the relative privacy of my cell? The cells were maybe ten feet long, eight feet wide, eight feet high, each equipped with a double bunk bed, a U.S. Army blanket and an aluminum toilet minus the lid. High on the west wall above the concrete yard was a single TV set, which could be viewed by prisoners from the runway of all three tiers. I believe around nine o'clock the catwalk was cleared and the cell doors clanged shut for the night. The utter lack of control and constrained mobility are what kept recurring in those nightmares I dreamed years later. My memory is a little hazy, but I think we were marched outside to the yard about thirty minutes a week for sunshine and exercise. Here the gun towers and coils of thick barbed wire created well-defined borders to the view of the sky above.

As I entered the walkway, two prisoners on the first tier had broken, in perfect harmony, into their rendition of the Righteous Brothers: "You are my soul and my heart's inspiration. Without you, baby, what good am I?"

It was stunningly beautiful, achingly sad. It reminded me of the live primal blues that wafted through the citrus groves in Florida; I could listen to the plaintive tones from atop my tall wooden ladder as I gave the stems a quick twist and dropped the fruit into my canvas bag. I had no idea how long these two beautiful gray-clad brothers might be behind bars—how long it might be before they might touch the woman who so inspired their heart and soul. I thought of Linda C., my high school sweetheart, at least for a few short blissful months. I thought of Jeannie who had broken my heart that summer at the Family Dog and of Teri who had so graciously relieved me of my virginity in her Cheesman Park apartment. Then I walked on down the runway.

My cell partner would become as good a mentor as anyone could expect, at least for a week until they shipped him off. "What you doin' here, man?"

"Draft."

"You federal?"

"Yeah."

"That's me too. *United States of America vs. Charles Jackson*. Try an' make you think the whole muthafuckin' country's against you."

I never found out what criminal act, what crazy or tragic series of life decisions had brought Charles Jackson into CAPIAS, but he had been around. He was in his mid-twenties and he knew the system.

"You know you go to a youth joint, you gonna have to fight, boy." The youth prisons—El Reno, Englewood, Sandstone—were set up for those aged eighteen to twenty-three. I didn't quite get the point of concentrating all that testosterone in one facility and in CAPIAS those youth institutions carried a mean reputation. "You go to a youth joint, somebody's gonna test you real fast and you gonna have to fight." My thoughts drifted back to Leonard Morgan who in two seconds had knocked me senseless one night on Monaco Parkway in the only real fight I'd had in high school. I did not look forward to time in any youth facility.

"Adult prison. Now you gotta chance there. You just do y' own number and they might leave you alone." "Do your own number." "Mind your own business." I heard that piece of advice at least a dozen times.

Of course, embedded in doing your own number was the Iron Law: Never, never, never, even think about ratting someone out. It's a jungle in there and you're on your own. "You get labeled a snitch," said Charles Jackson, "someone even suspects you a snitch, you a dead man, you hear? Do y' own number."

"Stay clear of the TV. They be more killin' over a TV channel than drugs, or sex, or money."

Paul Barnes got a similar warning in L.A. County, particularly concerning competing channels that might reflect racial preferences in music or cultural tastes. He heard the story—maybe just prison lore, but certainly within the realm of possibility—about the California inmate who switched a channel in the middle of a song, then sat down on his folding chair in the front row. From two rows back, another inmate leaned over the man directly behind the offending channel changer. "Excuse me," he said to the guy in the middle, as he drew a shank from his pants and brought it down full force directly through the top of the offender's head.

Barnes was in the holding tank with an older white convict and several L.A. Resistance buddies who had been sentenced for contempt of court during Barnes's trial. Having listened a few moments to their conversation and having spent a few moments observing their faces, the old man went around the group and spoke to each one. "He told us which of us would make it and which of us wouldn't," said Barnes. "Who could handle this and who couldn't. When he came to me he said, 'You'll make it. You'll handle this alright.' He had obviously been in jail a long time and in many different institutions. He had a sense for who could do it and who couldn't. Actually I think I was the only one he said would make it. 'The rest of you guys are going to have major trouble.'"

I asked Paul if that reassured him, and he answered, "Well, to some extent I was, you bet. I would have been a lot more nervous had he said, 'You haven't got a chance in hell.'"

Nothing that Charles Jackson talked about in that two-man cell was particularly reassuring to me. But I was happy to have him as a cell partner.

That Sunday night I recall walking to the west end of the catwalk close to the TV where a large group of inmates gathered on each of the three tiers. Having just listened to Charles's advice, I approached cautiously. Everything seemed peaceful; everyone seemed entranced. There on the screen were the four Beatles singing their hearts out on the *Ed Sullivan Show*.

"Hey, Jude, don't make it bad . . . "

I had no idea the song was written to John Lennon's son to help him through the divorce of his parents. I had no idea why the melody struck such a melancholy chord deep inside.

"Take a sad song and make it better . . . "

I had no idea why this song could tap into all the emotions that had built up during the previous week.

"Remember to let her into your heart; then you can start to make it better."

I had no idea how much beautiful music might pass me by in the federal prison over the next two years.

"Na, na, na na na na na. Na na na na, Hey, Jude."

A single tear slid down my cheek, then another. A moment of shameless self-pity and then I returned abruptly to sanity. I didn't need Charles Jackson to teach me this one. You don't show weakness in the county jail, you dumb shit. You don't let anybody see tears in CAPIAS. I managed to hide my eyes as I turned and walked back down the corridor.

I lost myself in chess to pass the time. My lit teacher at George Washington, a truly eccentric and theatrical lecturer named Dudley Enos, had entranced us all with readings and interpretations of T.S. Eliot's imagist poetry. This was decades before I had any inkling of the controversy over Eliot's anti-Semitism and I, like everyone else in the class, was won over by the sounds and rhythms of "J. Alfred Prufrock," of "Preludes," and "The Wasteland. "The Wasteland" had a whole section entitled "A Game of Chess," and somehow my mind kept wandering back to the few fragments I had memorized:

"I think we are in rats' alley where the dead men lost their bones."

This was followed a little later by:

"And we shall play a game of chess . . . waiting for a knock upon the door."

I can't say I had any idea what T.S. Eliot meant by those lines, but somehow they resonated there on the second tier of rats' alley as we played game after endless game of chess on frayed cardboard with cheap plastic pieces, as we waited for the marshals to come and take us away. Perhaps I should have been dreaming of steel bars and concrete walls, but I distinctly recall dreaming instead of chess moves. In particular was my opponent's white bishop who repeatedly sped diagonally across the entire field of play to capture my helpless rook, my castle which I had stupidly left completely vulnerable. That bishop ripped me apart night after night.

My first opponent was Nathan Young, a black kid from Five Points who had dropped out of Manual High School early and lived hard ever since. I had always thought chess a game for intellectuals; I pictured the competition at the Green Spider Coffee House between hip young men smoking pipes and sipping cappuccino, listening to Beethoven in the background. I thought I could take on Nathan pretty easily. I had attended an excellent high school and completed two years of college. Nathan had dropped out in the ninth grade. Surely that gave me the advantage of acquiring the analytical and reasoning skills necessary to win a game of chess.

Nathan Young kicked my ass. Checkmate—I don't think it took ten minutes. Ten minutes later—checkmate—I succumbed a second time, and then a third. That series of defeats helped prepare me for the days ahead. It forced me to reassess Nathan's intelligence and more importantly to examine my own hidden presumptions. Here was a jumble of social-class distinctions and differences all entangled and intertwined with race. For bigotry and racism in general, for social snobbery and condescension I had no tolerance, but deep within were buried judgments and preconceptions I didn't even know existed. They were intimate and subterranean. They had remained unexplored even as I watched the whole country grapple with equality and civil rights. Listening to the talk radio shows today, I think many of us have left those latent sentiments unexplored for decades. For me, the jail in Denver County was as good a place as any to begin exploring them.

T.C. was one of the handball players on the first tier. We, on the second-level cell block, were always a little resentful of those guys because all we could do for exercise was to pace like lions in a cage, whether in the cell or on the catwalk. We were expected, in addition, to serve the handball players below us. Most of us congregated on the walkway outside the cells for much of the day and, thus, most of the cells were locked up but unoccupied for hours at a time. Whenever a handball bounced into one those unoccupied cells, it was our job to retrieve it. Somebody had rigged up a gadget—a rope made of rags and T-shirts that could stretch all the way from the front of the cell to the rear. Tied to the end was a rolled-up newspaper that was used as a scoop. When the ball bounced into a cell and settled on the floor beneath a bunk or beside the toilet, one of us would toss the rag-rope through the bars and use the newspaper to drag the ball toward the catwalk where we could grab it, then throw it back down to the first tier. When the errant balls flew frequently into our cells, it could get a little annoying.

That afternoon a stray handball flew into an empty cell, bounced once on the floor, then landed with a splash directly into the toilet. We were helpless, unable to retrieve it, and, relieved of our tiresome duty, the whole second tier broke out into spontaneous laughter. We were temporarily freed from servitude toward the privileged handball players below us.

T.C. stormed over to the edge of the catwalk. He was huge, maybe six foot four inches and I stood on the second tier only about four feet above him. I looked down and took in every detail of the contorted muscles of his face. "Anybody laughs again," he raged, "you're a dead man! I done killed two muthafuckers already, ain't nuthin' to kill another."

There was absolute silence. Here we were, everyone of us a convicted felon and no one said a thing. Most of us were car thieves or burglars, dope sellers or heroin users. There were some convicted of manslaughter, some for aggravated assault, one or two for murder, another one or two for rape. But no one said anything to T.C.; nobody was in his league. The most hardened cons knew to keep their mouth shut. I stole a look and saw murder in his eyes. I looked beyond those eyes and saw within a boundless hatred, an uncontrollable, psychopathic rage. I backed away, as did everyone else, and made a mental note: don't ever mess with his handball.

There was a singular message here: life is fragile in Denver County Jail.

I met Sugar Bear in the first week, a short young man with an Afro, waiting to get shipped off to the state youth joint at Buena Vista, which everyone called "byoonie." He was friendly enough, talked smooth, played a lot of five-card stud on the walkway to pass the time. When I first saw him, he was on a roll; he was winning most of the penny-ante hands—straights, three of a kind, full houses—he was on a roll. His luck changed later in the week and that's when he came to me. "Hey, man, five dollars is all I need. Spot me five and I'll get it right back."

I wavered. "C'mon, man, five dollars is nothin'. I'll pay you back."

I don't know why I gave in. I'm sure white guilt played its part. I was weak. I was brand new. Above all, I wanted approval from somebody in this strange new world. "Alright, bud. Five bucks. I'll back you up." Of course he lost it all in less than an hour to some petty dope dealer named Johnson.

Cash was contraband on the cell-block floor; all financial transactions took place on Thursdays at the commissary. There from a window on the landing near the cafeteria you could use your account to buy peanuts, combs, candy bars, toothpaste, and most of all, cartons of cigarettes. Everybody got a free pouch of Prince Albert's tobacco—they didn't want inmates under stress having a nicotine fit. Nevertheless, the manufactured goods from R. J. Reynolds and American Tobacco were in high demand. With smokes in hand, you could go out on the floor and buy all kinds of stuff. All currency was based on the tobacco standard, a system which easily outlasted the gold standard abandoned by Nixon in 1971. The Mexicans in Safford would say

"Pacas hablan, Ricardo," cigarette packs talk. I had about twenty dollars on my commissary account so I could easily cover Sugar Bear's losses.

On Tuesday before commissary a slender inmate from Tier 1 approached me in the cafeteria.

"William is hearing rumors that you can't cover your debts."

"Who's William?"

"He's the man you're in debt to."

"I don't owe William anything. I owe five dollars to Johnson."

"You're wrong there, man. Everybody owes William. He's watchin'. You don't come through, you could find yourself splattered all over the handball court."

Shit. They're threatening to kill me for five dollars? Shit.

I made sure Johnson got King William his carton of Camels that Thursday. Afterwards, Sugar Bear discreetly pointed him out to me so I knew just who it was who got my money and apparently everyone else's money as well. I saw him that weekend in the mess hall—a fleshy hulk of a man—eating breakfast right next to his skinny "assistant," a self-congratulatory look on his broad face. There he was, king of CAPIAS, small-time master of a small-time black market. He had about a dozen link sausages on his plate and what looked like another dozen scrambled eggs piled high. He was shoveling it all down with a big spoon; forks and knives were forbidden in Denver County.

The images of T.C. and William are etched in my memory, icons of the veiled threats, the gloved hands, the implied violence that permeates the air and rules, from the shadows, the behavior of the residents at the county jail. Years later, driving the night shift at Yellow Cab I would sometimes relive those feelings. There the veiled threat of violence was also ever present, sitting in the darkness behind your right shoulder like some big grinning serpent from the underworld.

And so I played chess and watched TV, read from the Book of Exodus, listened wide-eyed to the stories of my new peers, and learned what it really meant to "do time." Another line from Eliot kept recurring, this one from the "Preludes," number three:

> And when all the world came back and the light crept up
>   between the shutters
> And you heard the sparrows in the gutters,
> You had such a vision of the street as the street hardly
>   understands.

I was certainly, from that second-tier cell, gaining a new vision of "the street," a new meaning for "the street." "The street" meant hard living, scratching for every penny, staying forever alert to danger. But from the cell block at Denver County, from the jail at Santa Fe, from the barracks at Safford, the real meaning of "the street" was clear to everyone: "the street" meant freedom. I would come increasingly to appreciate this new vision, to yearn for it, to live for it.

I think many of the resisters began their experience in jail with a broader sense of compassion and social responsibility than I did. Joe Maizlish was protesting overcrowding in L.A. County the day he arrived. David Harris helped lead a food strike in Alameda County for better medical care. I have to confess that my weeks in Denver County were focused on my own survival; I was hanging on for dear life.

I did learn a few things, though. Do your own number. Don't loan out any money. Don't judge a man's intelligence by his appearance or social station. Find out who runs the cell block and don't do anything to rile him up. Put some distance, if you can, between you and the psycho-men. Watch your step around the television. Don't mess with T.C.'s handball.

It wasn't a bad start.

Chapter 5

Safford

Dear Sam and Sarah,

Like our beloved hometown of Denver—Queen City of the Plains—the Swift Trail prison camp at Safford sat at the edge of two entirely distinct ecosystems. Sierra and arid lowland, pine forest and scrub mesquite, mountain and desert. The surrounding desert—though absent the regal saguaro which defines the area around Tucson—constitutes a northern border of the Sonoran Desert, a wilderness which stretches deep into Mexico.

The place used to be Apache territory. Geronimo was born fifty miles to the northeast and roamed all over the landscape, conducting fierce guerrilla raids, and riding at times into the southern reaches of the Sonoran on the Mexican side. Cochise, for whom the adjoining county was named, led the Chiricahua band on similar migrations and expeditions. The San Carlos Apache Reservation lies fifty miles northwest of Safford, established after the two great leaders succumbed to relentless pursuit. Mt. Graham, in whose shadow we lived, was one of the four holy mountains of the Western Apache and considered sacred by all the Indians in the area.

Even as a child, your mother loved everything about the desert. It was her refuge and solace, her playground and homeland. She's told me the desert taught her about listening and paying attention because its changes are so subtle and ephemeral. She loved the sweeping horizon, the deep blue skies set against the changing colors of the mountains—purple with ever-shifting shades of gray. She loved the big rolling cumulus clouds with their shifting formations and brilliant reflections of sunlight. "I love the call of the mourning dove," she told me, "and the amazing numbers of birds that migrate through the area. There are those that fly overhead—hawks, mourning doves, finches, and hummingbirds, and those incredible birds on the ground—the roadrunner and the quail. There's inspiration in how desert plants and animals live—the plants with their roots extending far out underneath the ground to absorb the water. There's the distinctive smell of the creosote bush when it rains, the tiny leaves of the mesquite trees fluttering in the breeze, and the red blossoms of the barrel cactus contrasted with the deep lime-green of its base. In the desert you have to watch where you put your feet because you're looking for snakes. The action of watching your feet invites you to notice where you're walking: the plants, the lizards, the rocks, the curve of the land."

Joe Maizlish also appreciated the desert's beauty. "I'd been visiting deserts since I was quite young, maybe three or four, and I always liked it." He told me, "I liked that Gila Valley area; there were certain things about it that were outstanding. The thunderstorms you could see from afar, way out there in this big upper valley we were in. Then sometimes they'd come through right on top of us and I can right now imagine the very fresh air smell—maybe it was from a lot of negative ions or the sage getting all wet, but something caused this terrific, fresh scent. And then immediately after the storm passed, things felt dry again—short intense rain and then nothing, absolute calm. That was always a treat. And I remember the effect of the scattered clouds and the sun on the hills across the valley some fifteen or twenty miles away."

I'm a bit ashamed to confess that a good deal of this beauty passed right over my head. I tramped at times through mile after mile of the Gila Valley and the upper Sonoran fighting brush fires whenever the Bureau of Prisons farmed us out to the U.S. Forest Service. I did see a lot of burning bushes, but I never saw God out there, nor the ghost of Geronimo, nor was led by the Holy Spirit. I did see a lot of rock and prickly pear, but I never developed the eye of the painter Georgia O'Keefe or the poet Richard Shelton. What I saw, in my insensibility, was a lot of brown dirt, a lot of scraggily vegetation, and a few rattlesnakes.

But the panoramas—those stunning views of mountain range and distant horizons—any dunce could see that. I was grateful—we were all grateful—for the panoramas after our sunless existence in the county jail. And yet the panoramas and landscapes could be double-edged. Sometimes their very presence, their seductive presence could inspire in us more yearning, more frustration than appreciation for Nature's handiwork.

The federal prison camp at Safford was a minimum security institution. A stone wall, not more than three-foot tall marked the perimeter and separated us from the free world. There were no gun towers, no coiled razor-edged wire. We could, at any time, have crossed over the perimeter and attempted to flee the hundred and fifty parched miles to the Mexican border or to hide ourselves in the youth ghetto of any large American city. What constrained us was not a physical barrier. It was the near certainty that our capture would bring us an additional five years imprisonment for escape—this time in a maximum security facility. Either that or a life-long exile, the life of the eternal fugitive. The V-shaped notch they cut in our boot heels—designed for easy tracking of footprints in the desert—reminded us of the risks of escape.

Besides, we were all short-timers. Our two- and three- and four-year sentences might at times have seemed like eternity. But relative to the men at Leavenworth or Atlanta facing ten years, the men at Marion or Terre Haute looking at twenty-five or thirty years, we were short-timers. The veteran convicts among us were all coming off long years of confinement and only had a few years to go to mandatory release.

And so after months in county jail or years in the penitentiary, we were—all of us—relieved to arrive at Safford. But not that relieved. As preferable as Safford was, you still better watch your step. As my usually good-natured friend, Kendall, reminded me: "They could fuck you up." They could set your life spiraling downward for years to come.

The big stick they held over your head was called La Tuna, the medium security facility across Interstate 10 on the Texas-New Mexico border. La Tuna had the gun towers and the razor wire. It had the hole and the segregation cells. Step out of line at Safford and your first destination was La Tuna. There you could lose your "good time;" you could lose your shot at parole. If you were unlucky enough to get caught with contraband or get into a fight you could even get some extra years tacked on to the sentence you already had. La Tuna was the Big House; La Tuna was Siberia hanging over your thoughts and guiding your decisions.

Dana Rae

The first inmate you met at Safford would be Dana Rae Park. He clerked in the Administration Building on the west side of the complex, which faced Mt. Graham and the Coronado National Forest. Dana Rae was half Korean, half Portuguese, all Hawaiian. He once told me how he had missed—unconsciously—the faces of his Asian compatriots so prevalent on the island.

"I remember arriving in Hawaii after my release," he said. "I remember my sister being there; I remember her face. I remember all the Oriental faces I had not seen for so long. I grew up all my life seeing Oriental faces. Japanese people. Chinese people. Korean people. How distinctive their faces were and how unique Hawaii was." I had never heard of a Haoli—a white boy in the native Hawaiian tongue—until Dana Rae called me that and then had to explain what it meant.

He had learned to type in high school and thus was qualified—perhaps overqualified—to work the office. When prisoners arrived, an inmate photographer would place a number on your chest (mine was SA 4209) and snap your picture. Dana Rae would type up receipts for the marshals to sign, officially transferring us from their custody to the custody of the prison. It was all very formal.

Working in the office gave him access to everybody's file except his own. "I was aware of who was coming in and what their jacket was. I remember people asking me what the scuttlebutt was. 'Who is this guy? Where's he from?' I remember even getting advance notice of people coming in and advance notice of parole board decisions."

For draft resisters, Dana Rae had received the worst possible sentence: "the Zip-Six." It was supposed to be some kind of progressive reform for young offenders under the Youth Act. Under its terms, the inmate was eligible for parole on his first day of incarceration if he could convince the board he had rehabilitated himself. Hence the "Zip," meaning zero time served. Absent a personal reformation, he could spend up to six years in lock-up. What constitutes rehabilitation for a draft resister? Omar Rios, the caseworker, told him he could always change his mind and join the army. "I had no idea what a Zip-Six was until Rios explained it to me. When I found out, I said, 'Fuck this; I'd have been better off sentenced to the maximum five years . . . What was bad," he told me with a laugh, "was seeing people like Richard Gould come in and then seeing people like Richard Gould get out and I was still there." More than any of us, Dana Rae had to walk the line. A disciplinary hearing for him could mean some serious time.

What Dana Rae brought to us was music. Indeed, music helped push him along a twisting, tortuous path toward resistance.

Brought up in a Honolulu housing project, he describes his parents as "churchgoers to a fault. My father was a deacon. I remember going to three services every freaking Sunday. Sunday school, morning service, evening service. It was terrible. It was a nondenominational church, one of those 'nobody else gets it right but us' kind of church. Methodists got it wrong. Catholics, of course, got it wrong. Rock 'n' roll was a sin. Going to the movies was a sin. Makeup for my sister was a sin. I didn't dance. I remember getting some sort of note from home excusing me from dance. It was fire and brimstone, weeping, and gnashing of teeth.

"High school began an evolutionary process that was part of liberating myself from my home life which was oppressive and Christianity which was intellectually oppressive. If my parents could have fed my intellect and talked about questions—'Are Catholics Christians?' 'Why do people go to hell?' 'What happens to babies in hell?'—There were so many questions their minds were closed to. Instead, they said, 'We don't talk about that.'"

The first crack in the structure came from the Right. "I was very taken with Ayn Rand," he says. "*Atlas Shrugged, Fountainhead*. The idea of the individual versus society. The idea of selfishness, the idea that you live and do things only for yourself."

Much later, he could acknowledge the role of his religious roots in his evolving political and ethical outlook. "With the religious upbringing I've had, I've come to see the very strong underpinnings of pacifism in Christianity."

But there was none of that in high school; he had to make a break. "(Ayn Rand) helped me to distance myself from the church, to push the church away. The church doesn't have any control of your life; you decide your own life. I'm the master of my fate, the captain of my fate, the master of my soul."

And so the Parks began to lose their son. They watched as he grew his hair long and listened in horror as he told them "I don't want to go to your stupid church." In high school he tried to start a chapter of Young Americans for Freedom, a conservative, radically anticommunist youth group quite in line with the objectivism espoused by Ayn Rand. That's when he went around talking about dropping The Bomb on Vietnam. "But the YAF was a very small window," he said. "You rebelled from the church; you rebelled from home; you rebelled from orthodoxy. Once liberated, it was easy for me to find my equilibrium." The drift to the right was just a blip, just a short-lived phase.

The music was much more enduring. He picked up the guitar later in high school and began practicing what became a life-long passion. "I couldn't play rock 'n' roll," he claims, "so I turned to folk music."

I suspect rather that he turned to folk music because he was always the outsider, always the lone rebel looking in from the periphery.

"Folk music was part of the fabric of the peace movement. Peter, Paul, and Mary, Joan Baez, Bob Dylan. They became associated so strongly (with the movement) that I thought every single folk singer was necessarily pacifist and antiwar. I mean, right-wing folk singers? I think Dylan was the first folk singer to resonate with me. "The Times They Are a Changin", yeah, that was an anthem. "Blowin' in the Wind" is a song that's sung on every continent; I would think in every single language. I think you could go to China and hum the tune and I think you'd find people there who'd recognize it and probably sing it in Chinese. It'll become a true folk song in that people will sing it and not know who wrote it, and it wouldn't matter.

The Battle for the Guitars

The long fingernails Dana Rae preferred for guitar picking had been shorn by order of the Los Angeles Sheriff's Department in the county jail. Hungry to get back to his music, he discovered a couple of government-issue guitars upon his arrival in Safford. They were in sorry shape. "They were just wrecked," he said. "The strings had been broken . . . they were actually tied in knots. They would just cut your fingers to pieces."

Any personal request to prison authorities required filing a form we called a "copout sheet." "Copping out" implied that we agreed to submit to the prison rules, to abide by the decisions made by the caseworker, Omar Rios, Chief Correctional Officer Thomas Lanier, or Camp Administrator J.J. Kennedy. Of course, we all filled out copout sheets because that was the only way we could receive visitors, make emergency phone calls, or change work assignments.

Dana Rae's struggle to get his own guitar sent in from Hawaii provides some insight into the subtle dynamics of power within the prison system. There was this giant bureaucracy with its giant bureaucratic inertia; there was also their perplexity and uncertainty over how to deal with this new breed of prisoner, these unrepentant political rebels who scorned their punishment and rejected the very concept of rehabilitation. "I mean we were political prisoners in essence," says Park. "They couldn't say we were gonna go back to our life of crime."

We were weird; they didn't understand us at all.

Dana Rae wrote out his copout sheet: "Request to bring in our guitars."

"No, no you can't do that," Dana Rae described the response. "Personal property, blah, blah, blah. Can't do that. We allow that and then everybody else will want . . . blah, blah, blah."

In normal times the request would have stopped right there. Rios, Lanier, Kennedy, they ran the show. There wasn't anyone around looking over their shoulder or questioning their decisions. It was all internal; they were unaccustomed to inmates who could bring public pressure to bear on these everyday, routine decisions. They were unaccustomed to anyone who could rally outside supporters to lobby on their behalf.

As the first resister on the island to face imprisonment, however, this nineteen-year-old kid with a Zip-Six had emerged from Honolulu as something of a celebrity. I think there might have been a three-sentence blurb on page 55 of the *Rocky Mountain News* about my conviction in Denver, but in Hawaii Dana Rae Park was front-page news. When he went to trial "the press was there, the TV channels were there, the courthouse was packed with my supporters, and there was a demonstration out front. I was ready to go to the clink. I had wrapped up all my affairs; I had pleaded guilty. It was kind of through a fog and a haze that I walked down the line and thanked everybody, shook their hands, and went into the courtroom. I remember getting up and making my statement which was reprinted in the paper in its entirety. Very short. A six-sentence statement. Then the judge, this first-class aku-head . . . accused me of having 'antisocial tendencies' and gave me the Zip-Six." Surely, refusal to kill must be antisocial. Even after his lockup, the *Honolulu Advertiser* sent in a reporter to talk to him on the telephone through the glass.

Within the storm of publicity and commotion, a network of support had sprung up around him. He was not your ordinary prisoner.

"We had guardian angels looking after us," says Dana Rae. "People that care about you. People that love you. They come out to visit and bring you letters. They'll have a place for you to stay when you come out. They'll welcome you back."

We all knew lots of older convicts in Safford coming off of twenty or twenty-five years in the federal system who never got a visit. Dana Rae said, "I realized right away in Halawa Jail, a lot of these guys are on a one-way street with no social network for them, no social net to catch them . . . But we had our guardian angels.

"You know Hawaii wasn't all that gaga about Vietnam. I mean we had a very cosmopolitan population, a lot of Asian people, a lot of Filippinos, a lot of Chinese. I don't think there was a lot of fear of communism; I don't think there was a lot of fervor to go to war. Come on, in Hawaii? I think people are liberal on the coasts. You get the sunshine; you get the ocean; it's a good life. It's gotta take a lot to motivate you and get you all upset about Ho Chi Minh and what's happening 4,000 miles away. I mean there are other things on your mind. You're going to the beach and getting a suntan. Hawaii's pretty much a liberal place, you know. People learn to get along with each other."

Eccentric geopolitical theories notwithstanding, the at-large congressional district of Hawaii elected one of the U.S. House of Representatives' earliest opponents of the Vietnam War. Patsy Mink, the first Asian American woman in Congress, became the angel-in-chief for Dana Rae Park. When he failed to appear on time at Safford because he was stuck in the detention center at Florence, supporters, wondering where he was, called up Patsy Mink. "They would appeal to her . . . and say 'He was supposed to show up at Safford. He left L.A. County but he's not at Safford. Where is he?' When I finally got to Safford, they said, 'Oh, you're the guy!"

Later when Dana Rae informed a visitor that his guitar request had been turned down, Rep. Mink was called once again. "We had to lobby Congress just to get our guitars in," he recalls.

You can imagine the consternation at the Bureau of Prisons when they kept getting calls from a U.S. congresswoman about some kid down in Arizona. Who else in this vast system of forgotten convicts had a member of Congress looking after his well-being? Perhaps it was annoying, but bureaucracies, by their nature, abhor publicity. Dana Rae's Fender guitar soon came in from Hawaii packed in a hard case purchased by his friends for safe shipping. Other guitars soon followed as the whole policy on musical instruments was revised. "Then I asked for a recorder and they said, 'No, you can't have a recorder.' They thought I was talking about tape recorders. No a recorder is a wooden flute; it's one of the oldest instruments in the world. Here's a picture of it from the dictionary. 'Okay, okay, you can have your fucking recorders too.' So the recorders came in.

"My guitar took a beating in Arizona," he said, "and it's checkered to this day because of the humidity in the case. But it helped; it helped a lot."

And so Dana Rae brought us the gift of music. I retain a vivid memory: Dana Rae on the compound before the late-afternoon count, strumming chords on unbroken strings in the Arizona heat and singing softly. His favorite song, one that he repeated often, was a Joni Mitchell tune:

I've looked at life from both sides now
From up and down, and still somehow
It's life's illusions I recall;
I really don't know life at all.

I remember on occasion singing it along with him.

Years later Dana Rae told me a story whose image also lingers in my memory. He was working as a stock clerk at the Food Land supermarket on the outskirts of Honolulu while living in the Palolo Valley. He had been telling the store manager and his fellow workers that he would soon be arrested; no one believed him. He was working up front one afternoon when they called him back into the stockroom. And there they were: two FBI agents in suits. They were polite. The store manager was there. The assistant manager was there. All of his coworkers looked on in disbelief. "How quickly can word spread through the store that you have FBI people in the back room?" he says. They were polite but they put the cuffs on firmly and led him out the back door to the car. The employees watched with astonishment as he disappeared through the exit. "I don't remember the details very vividly, Richard. I just remember the handcuffs. Handcuffs are pretty vivid."

After he posted bail, he returned to Food Land headquarters to pick up a check and close out his employment. "I remember this Chinese guy coming out of an office and giving me $50. He said, 'I think you did the right thing.' He was a complete stranger."

Journey to Safford

A few years ago, your mom and I were walking a couple of blocks back to the car after attending the Dairy Theater in Boulder. Just west of Folsom Avenue on Arapahoe we passed a common-enough late-night scene in the city. Under the flashing lights of a Boulder police car a young man had just been arrested. We were maybe twenty yards away when I heard the sound of several clicks as the officer fastened the handcuffs and tightened them down. The sound of those barely audible clicks ran through me like shots from a pistol. I winced inwardly, caught my breath, felt my heart rate quicken. The reaction was visceral. Your mom looked at me like I was crazy, like "What happened to you?"

Listening to Dana Rae's story of the arrest at Food Land or passing by this chance encounter on a Boulder street corner could easily jolt me back years to my own journey from Denver County to the federal prison in Safford.

The order to transport us was sent by teletype from Washington to U.S. Marshal W.H. Terrill in Denver. Two marshals picked up three of us from CAPIAS and drove us across town to the Englewood facility, one of the youth joints that Charles Jackson had warned me about. I groaned inwardly, as we pulled up to the building on Quincy and Kipling, thinking my time for a mismatched boxing bout had come. To my surprise, they unchained Gary Lane Benton from my side and told the two of us who remained that we should wait inside the car with the second marshal. Benton was kept at Englewood for observation, but his place was taken by another prisoner from the youth facility to be transferred at least as far as the jail at Santa Fe.

I don't remember the names of my two partners; I just remember the cuffs and the shackles which attached the three of us together. The cuffs dug into our wrists. Nobody asked, "Is this too tight; does this hurt?" They just clicked till they couldn't click anymore, till they clamped hard against the bone. The three of us were chained together at the waist, chain-gang style, livestock style, chattel style. The cuffs, in turn, were attached to the waist chains—a short leash—preventing us from lifting our hands more than six inches above crotch level. The shackles rattled and clattered whenever we moved.

At Walsenburg we pulled into an old-fashioned drive-in for lunch. That's when the public saw us dragging our chains. As the three of us filed out the car on the way to the restroom, the customers at curbside gawked and stared open-mouthed. It's not often you see people walking around in chains in modern America; it's quite the spectacle. We stared back. I'm not sure if I scowled but the scene stirred up in me a whirlpool of contradictory feelings. There was humiliation, of course, but mixed with a wave of defiance. For a moment we felt cool. We—two small-time drug dealers and a shy draft resister—looked "badder" in chains than we could possibly live up to in normal attire.

Humiliation prevailed a moment later when we returned to the back seat of the car. Still manacled at the waist, we were forced to hunch over, stripped of any shred of dignity, to eat the cheeseburgers we could not lift above our laps.

The experience was instructive. If you want to wrench someone out of the realm of civil society and place him solidly into the criminal world, if you want to complete the process of marginalization, try parading him around in public, his wrists tied to the chain around his waist, then shackle him securely to the next slave down the line.

Following some days' layover in the Santa Fe jail, a new set of U.S. marshals arrived in midautumn of 1968 to drive us south through piñon and juniper country then west along Interstate 10 and finally northwest into the Gila Valley on Arizona State Highway 70. No one told us where we were going; that was classified. But upon swinging west towards Deming and Lordsburg, I pretty much knew our destination. There was a moment of panic when I began to notice strings of wispy cottonballs blowing along the road. My god, did they bring me down here to chop cotton? Finally, in the afternoon we turned sharply left at the Swift Trail junction on Highway 366 and our journey was complete.

Dana Rae was there to meet us. His partner took my mug shot—the one you found a few years ago in my FBI file—and sent all over the Internet to your friends. I was happy to be unchained.

I barely remember the routine processing.

The clothes. Military issue—a pair of khaki trousers with matching shirt, a pair of brown work fatigues. A pair of work boots with the distinctive V cut into the front of the heel. I had never worn boxers before; that felt funny.

The haircut, buzzed short.

The housing assignment. Six cinderblock barracks, three on each side of the Administration Building were our living quarters. With the Ad Building to the west and the mess hall opposite, with a laundry on the south and a medical clinic on the north, the structures formed a rectangle facing inward toward a dirt compound in the center. I was assigned to Dorm 1 just northeast of the Ad Building, bed 46. Each barracks contained fifty-two beds squeezed tightly into four rows. Home, sweet home.

The work assignment. Kitchen duty. Surely, they were impressed by all my experience at the Royal Castle in New Orleans. They issued me a set of extra clothing—all whites—required for working in the mess hall.

I soon realized there was no lack of vitality within the perimeter walls. There was control, yes. The BOP controlled the tiniest details of your life. They tell you when to get up in the morning and when to go to bed. They confine you to barracks after nine and switch off the lights at ten. They restrict your movement. They count you twelve times a day and make you line up bedside for morning count and afternoon count. If you slept with your head under the sheets during night counts, they'd rattle your bed, pull down the cover, and shove a flashlight directly into your eyes. They tell you what work detail you're on and pay you nothing for your labor. They read your letters. They read your mother's letters. They tell you who can visit you and when. They frisk you before and after a visit and pat you down. They censor what you read. They determine what you eat. They write you up for trivial infractions. They peer into the private things in your locker, searching for contraband. Occasionally, they conduct shakedowns, ripping out the books and papers, the socks and cans of toothpowder, leaving everything in your locker in disarray. They watch you close. There is not a shred of privacy. You're crammed in with fifty-one other men for the duration of your sentence.

And yet within the tyranny of prison regulations, the place was pulsating and full of life. There were card games and music, handball and dominoes. There were tattoo artists and smuggling schemes; there was bartering for contraband, a whole underground cigarette-based economy. One guy carved delicate little monkeys out of peach stones; another made belts out of rattlesnake skin. A third crafted purses, wallets, and carrying bags intricately woven out of used cigarette packs. A former contractor created a beautiful, elegantly curved, rock wall near the officers' quarters. There was homebrew, shared books, and illustrated pornographic fiction written by a creative genius right on the premises. There were stories and endless conversations as subcultures and nationalities traded merchandise, talked Spanglish, worked side by side, and rubbed shoulders. It was, as Joe Maizlish said, quite the society.

The Strangers

The majority were Mexican. Most were "pollos"—chickens—men who had come up from the other side in search of work and been arrested by Immigration as "illegal aliens." A few were "polleros"—chicken haulers—who transported the pollos across the border. When they weren't called "aliens," they were wetbacks, mojados. In turn, they called us "gabachos"—white boys—a shade more derogatory than "gringo." Gallegos called us "seabacks," implying that we gabachos had come over the Atlantic "sin papeles," without papers, in the same manner that Mexicans had crossed the Rio Grande.

From my second-tier cell in Denver County I had just completed reading the Book of Exodus, which presented an interesting perspective on how I should view my new companions. Within the story of liberation, within the intricate listings of ancient Halachic Law was a decree to the freed slaves repeated time and again in Exodus as well as later on in Leviticus: "You shall not oppress the stranger for you yourselves were strangers in the land of Egypt" (Exodus 22:9). Watching firsthand the criminalization of these strangers would in time weigh heavily on my own worldview.

There was a background here, an historical context to the lives of these men imprisoned along our Southwestern borderlands. I can't say I understood much of this going in, but I would gradually begin to fill in some gaps. I might have grasped much more, I might have seen far more deeply had I been aware earlier of the contours of this mass migration, this northward movement that left such an imprint on the country and so shaped the American working class.

The story of the men in Safford was a migration story quite distinct from the story of those millions who streamed in from Europe. It was vastly different from the story of your great grandparents who came from Russia and Romania in the early part of the twentieth century.

The Bracero Act symbolized one of these distinctions. The law took its name from the root Spanish words "brazo" or arm and "bracero" or laborer. It was passed in 1942 as America mobilized for the war and sent millions of young men to the European and Pacific theaters. Employers in the Southwest cried out for help, complaining of a massive labor shortage.

The government turned to Mexico and in September of that year, 500 Mexican contract workers made their way to Stockton, California, to work the sugar beet fields. Here they chopped and thinned the beets with a short-handled hoe about twelve to eighteen inches long. They called it "El Cortito," the short one, and claimed it was designed by the devil himself. When I was in Florida I worked with a man, a white guy, just released from the notorious Tucker Prison Farm in Arkansas, who told me he had once worked those beet fields in California. "We called that short-handled hoe the 'West Coast Motherfucker,'" he said. At the end of a twelve-hour shift it was nearly impossible to stand up straight. Practically every betabalero—beet worker—suffered chronic life-long back pain. They could have used a regular hoe, but growers insisted the short-handled one could be more easily controlled and less damaging to the plants. They insisted all the way to the state supreme court which finally ruled El Cortito illegal in the 1970s.

Those first beet workers were soon followed by thousands more. Mexican farmers from the interior flooded into the now-swollen border towns, into Tijuana and Juarez, and contracted on to work in America. They worked the big farms but they also took jobs on the railroad, repairing track, and in the smelters and factories of the cities. By 1947 nearly a quarter million braceros worked under contract. American employers loved it and lobbied successfully to extend the Bracero Act far beyond its emergency wartime origins.

Its sudden repeal in 1964 had impacted my own life when the Mt. Dora Growers Coop had to drive their yellow buses clear to St. Louis looking for workers to harvest the orange groves for twenty-five cents per ninety-pound box. I had no idea of its implications at the time, but the repeal of Bracero was emblematic of the entire history of labor relations between Mexico and the United States.

Together with their Mexican American cousins, Mexicans had formed the backbone of industry in the Southwest. Their labor on the California vegetable farms and fruit orchards, in the Colorado coal mines and Arizona copper pits, on remote stretches of railroad track, and on Texas ranches had helped transform an arid, windblown region into a land of prosperity. Inside these engines of economic growth, the labor force was disproportionately brown. They were welcome—legal or illegal—when employers needed extra hands. Welcome, at least, if they agreed to live invisible lives in the shadows of American society.

Whenever the economic engines began to slow, however, or the political winds began to change, it was time to send the Mexicans back to Mexico. Thus, during the Great Depression upwards of 400,000—many of them U.S. citizens, many of them legal residents for decades—were deported to clear the way for white employment. Again in the 1950s Immigration deported over a million through a program they called Operation Wetback.

Under the terms of the Bracero Act, the operating word was contract worker. "Guest" workers enjoyed few rights under the contract; they could not legally change jobs regardless of abuses suffered or wages offered. And when the contract was done, when their services were no longer needed, they were expected to go home. The repeal of the Bracero Act signaled to Mexicans that once again under the law, they were neither useful nor welcome.

Of course, the reality was different. You can imagine what foremen at the Mt. Dora Growers Coop thought when they sized up their forty new recruits just in from St. Louis. The majority of us were running from something we wanted to forget: a tragic boating accident, a long prison record, a broken heart. There was a lot of binge drinking. Some of us drank Sterno—canned heating fuel—sifted through a T-shirt. Some of us couldn't get up in the morning. Some of us had trouble slinging our twenty-four-foot wooden ladders from tree to tree. We left fruit up on the treetops and had to climb back up a second time to retrieve it. We left fingerprints on the dew-covered oranges and picked far too many grapefruit not yet up to standard size. I generally picked about forty to fifty boxes a day; the Jamaicans the previous year had averaged ninety to one hundred. Maybe they drank their share of rum too, but they could get up morning after morning and pick their ninety boxes. The coop wanted their immigrant workers back. Finding enforcement of the current law nonexistent, they, like their fellow employers all over the country began hiring agricultural workers once again without asking questions about legal status.

The Swiss playwright Max Frisch described the European equivalent of the Bracero Act, a series of laws which would bring to northern Europe temporary immigrants from places like Turkey and southern Italy. "We called for workers," he wrote in 1965, "and there came human beings." The human beings actually tried to make a life for themselves in the countries that alternately lured and then discarded them. That is what men like Fernando Cota from Mexicali and Perfecto Diaz from Coahuila had tried to do when I first met them at Safford.

An Economic Transformation

There were monumental forces at work, gale forces prodding and pushing these men. A new variation on the global economy was in the making and with it the emergence of a new international division of labor. Increasingly, workers from the South and workers from the Third World would fabricate and assemble our products—here and abroad—feed our elderly, work the back kitchens of our restaurants, pour our foundations, tile our roofs, and clean up after our children. More and more workers in the North would exchange blue collars for white ones to sell real estate, adjust our insurance claims, counsel our personal investments, design electronic components, and create new programs for software. It was a transformative time.

There was, for instance, the impact of winter vegetables. In the late 1950s Mexican agriculture became the source of 50 to 60 percent of the tomatoes or cucumbers, bell peppers or eggplant that you might find at your local

Safeway store from November to mid-April. Just as Americans' insatiable consumer demand for marijuana and cocaine spawned today's murderous drug cartels, so too did the massive demand for fresh tomatoes in the middle of February set in motion the economic forces that would change the very face of Mexican society. Who could imagine that a minor change in our consumer preferences and expectations might reverberate with such potency on our southern neighbors?

In the Culiacan Valley in the state of Sinaloa, modern farms requiring more machinery than men sprang into existence overnight. Their technology was state of the art: irrigation systems, crop dusters, refrigerators, tractors, and temperature-controlled packing sheds. It was a boon for Mexican exports.

It was also expensive, all these fertilizers and pesticides, sprinkling systems and harvesters. The small farmers, the growers of maize and beans who had made Mexico self-sufficient in grain production were soon crowded out by the large commercial enterprises. They failed to get loans; they frequently overextended themselves; they sank deeper and deeper into debt. As Mexico exported peppers and cucumbers for Americans, it began importing grains to feed its own people. As incentives for growing corn disappeared, as rural debt rose, as rural income plummeted, the traditional farmer began to abandon the land.

Between 1950 and 1970 the number of landless farm workers soared from 1.5 million to 14 million. They trekked to the cities. Tijuana's population multiplied eight times over and Mexicali's growth topped 600 percent in that same twenty-year period. Here in the colonias, the displaced and uprooted poor searched for work wherever they could find it, borders be damned.

In early October of 1968, as I paced the catwalk in CAPIAS at Denver County, thousands of Mexican students gathered at the Plaza de las Tres Culturas in the Tlatelolco section of Mexico City. They came to protest a government willing to disburse $150 million for the international Olympics, but unwilling to lend a hand to its struggling students or extend a loan to its struggling farmers. Police and military forces from the Olimpia Battalion opened fire and gunned them down by the hundreds.

For the world, the massacre at Tlatelolco revealed the dark underside of the PRI, the Institutional Revolutionary Party, which had ruled Mexico since 1917. It was ruthless and on the take. It tolerated no dissent and had lost touch with its original constituency. It showed little regard for human life.

I don't think many of the pollos at Safford even heard of the massacre in Mexico City. But those who did would not have been shocked. They had long ago lost hope that their government, now bloated and corrupt, might be of any assistance to them.

They were on their own, caught in a giant trap. Like other trapped and uprooted populations, they would make handy scapegoats. Driven from the land by invisible economic forces, abandoned by their own government, lured by recruiters in the border towns, welcomed by American employers for their work ethic and their acceptance of meager wages, shunned by Immigration and the new Bracero rules, they were pushed, pulled, and battered by political and historical winds over which they had little control.

And so they piled into the trunks of Ford Galaxies and squeezed into the backseats of Chevy vans. They migrated to the North in search of work and ended up in and out of the federal prison system. They were no angels but neither were they inclined to crime. They were farm boys mostly, used to hard work, and they worked circles around us gabachos.

I have to admit that my first contact with the Mexican population was shamelessly self-serving.

Leaving behind the fear, the threats from T.C. and King William in the county jail, I thought I could relax a bit and breathe a little easier in my new home. It must have been the second day; I had just finished my first early-morning shift in the mess hall. Four thirty to 2:00; I had the whole afternoon off and was walking the compound, taking in the sights. I passed the handball court south of the laundry.

Johnny Lara was just leaving the court. Short and muscular from long years lifting weights in La Tuna, he had recently transferred from the Texas prison. He was one of the Duke City boys, an Albuquerque native. I guess the city was named after some titled Spanish nobleman in the eighteenth century and the Duke City nickname has stuck ever since. They pronounced their hometown "Ahl—bor—kay." I had seen Johnny in Dorm 1 the day before and had felt his eyes following me for a brief moment.

Now at the edge of the court his eyes bore down on me again. "I like you, kid," he said. "I really like you." He put his hand on my shoulder. "Meet me in the bathroom. Midnight tonight." Then his voice softened almost to a whisper. "I don't find you there, you'll find a shank in your back before morning."

I envisioned bed 46, Dorm 1, empty the next morning, sheets soaked with blood. I thought I had left behind the terror in CAPIAS but here I was, heart pounding once again, throat parched, mind racing. We walked off in opposite directions, my head reeling, lungs gasping for air. There was a full hour of panic, a full hour before I regained my composure. I returned to bed 46 for afternoon count, my mind now searching for a strategy. How could I approach this high-stakes chess game? What defenses might I erect for my own survival? What pieces existed in my personal armory? What strengths did I have at my disposal? I wasn't coming up with much.

Miss Royce's Survival Skills

I walked down to the mess hall for supper. There at the end of the line was Fernando Cota, another resident of Dorm 1 whom I had noticed earlier in the day. Then it dawned on me: there was one small skill in the arsenal I hadn't considered. Miss Royce had been my Spanish teacher for three years at George Washington High School. She had me pegged right away for a lousy student and rode me for the last year for my too-literal translations. But at least she gave me some basics. In truth I could speak just enough Spanish to be misunderstood and when these guys shifted into rapid fire I could barely follow every tenth word. But that was enough. I think any gabacho who even tried to speak to Mexicans in their own language was given a qualified welcome, at least for curiosity's sake.

I knew Johnny Lara spoke no Spanish. He was Chicano—American born and raised—what they sometimes called a *pocho*, a man who's forgotten his native language. I would learn to value and appreciate Mexican culture from both sides of the border, but right now I reached out for whatever help I could get. Johnny was relatively new and walked alone. It was clear that in Safford the Mexican nationals, not the Chicanos, had the numbers. Spanish was everywhere. If I could convince Johnny, I had some support, some crucial support, maybe that would be enough to turn the tables.

"Hola," I said to Cota, "¿como estás?" Kindergarten Spanish.

"¿Qué pasó, ése?"

What? Miss Royce never taught me about "¿Qué pasó." I might have to learn a whole new language here. ¿Qué pasó, ése? What's happening, dude? That was my first vocabulary lesson at Safford. Then, ¿quiúbole carnal? What's up brother?

Cota introduced me to Perfecto Diaz. "A sus ordenes," he said, "at your service." Such a polite young man in the middle of a federal prison. Then came a few guys known only by their mundane nicknames: Chaparrito,

Shorty. Flaco, the Skinny One. Gordito, the Pudgy One. I talked Spanish—or at least my abbreviated version of it—all the way through supper in the mess hall. I talked Spanish in the compound after supper. I talked Spanish in Dorm 1 till lights out. Every now and then I saw Johnny Lara glancing my way and I talked Spanish all the louder.

That evening I slept not a single moment. Guys would walk down the corridor to pee and I'd stay coiled up, ready to spring, ready to fight, ready to run like hell. Guards would walk down the corridor for count; my eyes were wide open. Midnight came, one o'clock, two o'clock. I stayed wide awake. Johnny Lara never came by. At four o'clock when Officer Kenski came to round me up for breakfast duty, I put on my whites and reported to the kitchen, exhausted. The long night was over.

Over time, I learned a great deal from these new companions. Oscar Lewis in one of his classic anthropological studies of Mexico City once described a tenement, the Casa Grande, in which he said many of the residents spent their entire lives. Within a three-block area, they worked and shopped, slept and played. They never left the neighborhood. That was not these guys. These guys were intrepid. They were adventurers, wandering far from home, separated from their families, crossing borders they barely recognized. Most of all they were workers. Cut them loose on the road crew on Mt. Graham clearing a pilot trail, they would fell trees at four times the rate of anyone else in camp. Put them on brush-fire patrol with a shovel or Pulaski, they'd be chopping at smoldering cactus till the last wisp of smoke disappeared.

I think it was Flaco who told me about the chilitos encurtidos I could buy at the commissary. Hot chili peppers soaked in pickle juice: magic in a glass jar. They changed my culinary habits for life, preparing me for the cosmic experiences we all shared later at the Chubby Burger Drive-In on Denver's north side. It was the best way to survive the fare in the prison mess hall. Mashed potatoes with chilitos encurtidos. Bologna sandwiches with chilitos encurtidos. Bread and butter with chilitos encurtidos. Canned peas with chilitos encurtidos. The contents of those jars could turn the blandest, sorriest meal into something tolerable.

They told me about the hero of northern Mexico. The gabachos called him Pancho Villa, but the Mexicans knew his real name: Doroteo Arango. When they said "Viva Doroteo Arango," they knew that no American would have the slightest idea what they were talking about. Arango's story is so shrouded in legendary song and mythology that I don't think anybody knew his real history. I do think I know what he symbolized to these men: he represented a man who fought for the poor, who gave away land—Robin Hood–style—to struggling farmers during the revolution. He represented too a man who could challenge the Colossus of the North, who could take on the United States and thus assuage latent feelings of powerlessness in their relationship to America.

When President Wilson in 1916 abandoned Pancho Villa in favor of General Venustiano Carranza, Doroteo Arango led his troops in a raid across the border, attacking a U.S. Cavalry detachment in the town of Columbus, New Mexico. He stole a hundred horses, burned down half the town, killed seventeen people, (losing eighty of his own), then headed back to the other side. A livid President Wilson dispatched General John J. Pershing and 12,000 troops in pursuit. Pershing chased the Mexican general all over the state of Chihuahua before finally giving up in exasperation nine months later. The whole thing gave rise to countless "corridos"—legendary ballads along the border which completed the lionization of Pancho Villa.

Later on I would learn more about the dark side of Doroteo Arango: his reckless disregard for human life, his arbitrary brutality, his flagrant racism toward the Chinese Mexicans whom he slaughtered in pogroms. These actions would perhaps have stained his reputation save for the endless corridos and oral stories which glorified his name. Certainly among the prisoners at Safford—especially those with roots in the North, in Durango, Chihuahua, Sinaloa, and Sonora—Doroteo Arango was a true revolutionary hero and a true nationalist.

Chato, the kid with the pug nose turned out to be the chief balladeer. He used one of those broken-down government-issue guitars to accompany his country music and sometimes drew a crowd at dusk along the margins of the compound. I can't say I understood all the lyrics, but I did hear some verses about the Doroteo Arango raid, about bandits in the backcountry and killings committed in a jealous rage. They were often melancholy. They were lonely men in a foreign land, far from home, far from Mom, sin amor—without love. Cota taught me the words to a couple of sad songs, to Rosita Alvirez, the story of the prettiest girl in Saltillo shot dead upon refusing to dance with Hipolito, a jealous loner, hurt deeply by her scorn.

> Su mamá se la decía, Rosa, esta noche no salgas.
> Mamá no tengo la culpa que a mi, me gustan los bailes,
> que a mi me gustan los bailes.

Her mother told her, "Rosa, please don't go out tonight."
She responded, "Mom, it's not my fault I love to dance."

Cota also pulled me aside a couple of times and taught me how to let loose those high-pitched, laughing, coyote-like howls and yips—the gritos—that punctuate the verses and permit communal participation in the singing—that long string of aye, aye, ayes. "Come on, Ricardo, no como un gabacho, not like some white guy." After a few lessons, I could do a passable aye, but I think the gabacho in me gave me away every time.

They taught me to swear. They taught me all the "hijos," all the "sons of" that lay at the heart of Mexican swearing. Son of this. Son of that. You could label your target, if you chose, not just the son of a whore, but the son of the archetypal whore, the son of the Jungian mother of all whores. You could say Hijo a la Gran Puta Madre, Son of the Great Whore Mother. I could see it in capital letters, the great maternal whore in the sky. You could revel in blasphemy with "Hijojesu!," Son of Jesus! All one word and guttural from the top of the throat. It pre-dated *The DaVinci Code* by decades; it harkened back, for all I knew to the anticlerical fervor of the revolution. It implied the Great Mother Whore might have been Mary Magdalene herself. For me, Mexican swearing brought swearing to a new grand level; it soared into another realm.

Fernandez once revealed to me the lowest, most dismal moment in his life. I have no idea how he got himself into this situation, but he was driving the streets of Tijuana, four in the car, his old girlfriend in the backseat. He was still in love, but she sat nestled against his buddy's shoulder. The two embraced, lost all restraint, and in no time, tore into each other right there in the backseat. Fernandez drove on helplessly, glancing at this horror scene, catching fleeting glimpses through the rearview mirror. He was near tears here in these lonely all-male suroundings, as he finished the story. "Qué mala es la vida," he said. How bad life is, how miserable is life.

I heard that expression—and its opposite—repeatedly from a few of my new companions. A guard would brusquely waken the breakfast crew at four in the morning: "Qué mala es la vida." A cool breeze would deliver a moment's comfort to a scorching afternoon and someone would say, "Qué buena es la vida." How good life is. Chato's singing might inspire the drifting off into childhood memories: "Qué buena es la vida." A brilliant sunset hovers over Mt. Graham: "Qué buena es la vida."

Somehow this penchant for taking the details of everyday life and broadening their meaning, placing the moments into the bigger picture—somehow this seemed to me something to strive for. Looking back, I see those statements—"Qué buena es la vida"—as steps toward a more spiritual outlook, as a recognition and awareness that those tiny particulars have a greater context that might lead to a greater appreciation of life. Qué buena es la vida was almost a prayer.

In those first few weeks the words "Qué buena es la vida" took on particular significance because Johnny Lara never showed up at my bed after midnight with that shank he promised me. I don't know if my association with Cota and Diaz, Flaco and Chaparrito played any part in his decision. It's quite possible the whole thing was just a test: if he could terrorize me into submission with the mere threat of murder, he could have his own personal punk without risking much of anything. As it was, for whatever motive, Johnny Lara never said another word to me.

Chapter 6

A New Community

Dear Sam and Sarah,

I never mentioned Johnny Lara to anyone until years later. By and large, few inmates at Safford faced threats of murder or physical harm. I thought it must have been something I had brought on myself, something in the way I carried myself, something in the way I walked, perhaps some sign revealing a lack of confidence that brought me to Johnny Lara's attention. So I kept my mouth shut.

I found out much later Dana Rae experienced trouble on his first night. He was young, slender, good looking. "I think this guy was on the baseball team," he recalls, "an old white con who had gotten drunk. I was some sort of new fish and a draft resister—the two lowest possible things. It's not likely you're gonna forget when some guy comes up to your bunk in the middle of the night. He grabbed me, yeah, and pulled me toward the urinals." Dana Rae managed to wriggle loose and bolted toward the compound. He made it to safety and was put up in the infirmary for the night. The next day Lt. Lanier assigned him to Barracks 6, the dorm reserved almost exclusively for Jehovah's Witnesses. They had their own little peaceful community in there.

"I did feel much more secure in the JW dorm," he said. Referring again to his "guardian angels," his support system on the outside, he added: "I think the administration feared that if I got hurt, there'd be hell to pay."

Greg Nelson, likewise, survived a couple of incidents, but they occurred after he had time to integrate himself into prison culture: "There was this Arnold-Schwarzeneggar, muscle-type guy, lifted weights constantly. He and his buddies were in the shower one day while I was taking a shower. He threatened to rape me right there. I told him you could probably do it 'cuz you're big and your friends are big. But I got friends too. I mentioned Sisco." Jerry Sisco was six foot five, a hulking formidable man serving time for car theft. He could have ripped the weightlifter's head off. "He was the nicest guy in the world," says Nelson, "but you wanted him on your side. 'Oh, you know Sisco?' said the muscle man. I mentioned some other big guys too; I mentioned enough people that he backed down.

Nelson recounted,

"The other incident was a just a weird misunderstanding. I was working in the library, and there was a fellow that cleaned up in the front area, an old guy named Rubio, a Mexican and part Indian. I was alone in the library with another Indian, a convicted murderer from one of the Arizona reservations. He was a nice guy; I had a good relationship with him till that day. Rubio had once told me that he called him 'Chief,' and that he really liked that. Well, I made the mistake of calling him 'Chief', 'Hey, Chief, how you doing?' Well, I didn't know. That was the wrong thing to say. I didn't know when a white guy calls an Indian 'Chief,' it's an insult. He really got pissed. Next thing I know he's got his hands around my throat, squeezing. I had to do some fast talking. I said 'Wait a minute, I'm not trying to insult you. Rubio says you liked being called that. What do I know?' He eventually realized I wasn't trying to be malicious. Then he finally let go."

Sooner or later most of us got acculturated and learned to breathe a little easier. Joe Maizlish, whose journey took him to eleven different federal prisons and three city jails said, "I guess you develop a certain confidence that after being transferred around to a lot of different places—every time you go to a new place, you kinda worry—but eventually you get some confidence that you can adjust."

Even so, some inmates carried secret fears for a lifetime. Salter lived directly across the compound from me in Barracks 2. Short, barrel-chested, sandy-haired, he was fierce-looking with enormous biceps and tattooed forearms. You expected from him a sailor's language, but "Goodness!" was the strongest word I ever heard him say. He had done something like twenty or twenty-five years for bank robbery, most of it at the penitentiary in Atlanta. I don't know what he did in that Georgia prison or who was after him, or why, but a story made the rounds at Safford. In the evening the night-shift guards, flashlights in hand, walked the corridors every hour for count. They say when Salter heard the footsteps, he flung himself forward, sat bolt upright and made certain the dark form passing by was a uniformed federal guard, not an assassin seeking vengeance or justice. Every count, every hour, every night, year after year, decades of sleepless nights, a sleepless life, a life marked by exhaustion.

Most of us could breathe a little easier, but you could still make a stupid mistake. Three or four months after my arrival, a new transfer in from Leavenworth joined me on the kitchen crew. It must have been four in the morning; we were bleary-eyed, both of us. I started mopping the tile floor near some of the big soup and potato vats. He grabbed a mop too and started working the other corner. What really needed his attention was the bakers' area, that is, if we wanted to make the most efficient use of time. I didn't even know who he was, but, at least, as far as the kitchen crew was concerned I was his senior. "Go mop under the bakers' table and along the ovens," I told him. "I'll finish up over here."

He was quick as a cat. He hurled me backward toward the mixer and pinned the base of my throat against the wall with a thick, wooden mop handle. "My name is Joe," he said. "Joe Rodriquez. You don't even know my fucking name and you telling me what to do? If you wasn't such a stupid motherfucker, I'd kill you here and now."

He was right. I was a stupid motherfucker. Who was I, four months in jail, acting like some kind of supervisor? I hadn't known him for three minutes. He could have run me through with that warrior's mop handle he held in his hands.

"You're right," I said. "I wasn't thinking. I won't let it happen again." His eyes were still burning, still raging, but he lowered his weapon. Rodriquez, like all of these men on society's margins, was hungry for respect. Neglected, overlooked, disrespected by judges and prosecuting attorneys, by public defenders, by cops and guards, he was at least entitled some respect from his fellow inmates without some twenty-year-old kid telling him where to mop the floor. In prison I learned a lack of courtesy could cost you your life. I should have introduced myself.

The Witnesses

In those early days the number of draft resisters was very small unless you count the Jehovah's Witnesses. As Dana Rae soon found out there was a whole barracks full of them, at least fifty strong, probably more. I had a great deal of respect for these guys, especially after I learned about their legacy in Germany during the Nazi years. When loyalty required the Heil Hitler salute, the Witnesses refused to raise their arms. When the draft was instituted in

1935, the Witnesses refused to join the Wehrmacht. In contrast to the sorry legacy of German Lutherans and Catholics, alike, Jehovah's Witnesses displayed astounding courage and faith. Ten thousand were rounded up and shipped first to Sachsenhausen, then Buchenwald and Dachau. As the Jews wore their yellow triangles, the homosexuals their pink ones, the Witnesses were issued the purple inverted-triangular patch for identification as "Bible Students." There in the camps they were offered the opportunity to escape persecution by renouncing their religious beliefs. Almost to a man, they refused. Between twenty-five hundred and five thousand perished.

They were not pacifists. As soldiers in Jehovah's army, they simply would not bear arms for any nation. Jesus had said, "Render unto Caesar the things which are Caesar's," and, for the Witnesses, these things clearly excluded their bodies for national military service. They were not pacifists; they waited to face the armies of Satan in the Battle of Armageddon, and thus, they remained ineligible for conscientious objector status. They wanted, instead, ministerial deferments but Selective Service balked because their ministry was only part-time. And so during Vietnam they were jailed by the hundreds.

The Department of Justice finally figured out a way to avoid the cost and embarrassment of incarcerating these religious objectors. Judges began sentencing them to alternative service, to work in hospitals under court order. The JWs could not accept alternative service granted by the military draft, but they could accept a sentence imposed by the court system. By the time I left Safford in 1970 the number of Jehovah's Witness inmates was practically zero.

I worked in the bakery with a group of Witnesses for a month or six weeks. They were kind enough at work but beyond that our social contact was limited. I resided, after all, among the sinners. As I understood it, the book of Revelations told them that only 144,000 anointed ones would enter heaven. I didn't expect to be one of them.

They tended to stay in their own barracks; if they reached out to you it was for predictably evangelical purposes rather than for mutual comfort. Joe Maizlish recalls attending one of the Bible studies they conducted. "I said, 'Yeah, I'll do some of that with you' and so I met some of them once. They asked me; they kinda checked out their assumption: 'You do believe that Jesus is the son of God, don't you?' I said, 'Well, like all the rest of us; we're all sons of God.'" There was dead silence. "They thought I was from some other world. They knew there was not much hope that I would join their group and so I didn't last long with that reading group."

I read their small purple book, *The Truth That Leads to Eternal Life* and several periodicals that the Watchtower Society published. Their independence from mainstream Christianity was quite intriguing. They rejected Christmas as a pagan holiday. They rejected the trinity. They rejected allegiance to any nation. They rejected the concept of hell on the grounds of God's merciful nature.

But otherwise there was little enough common ground. They held to the absolute literal interpretation of the Bible, scorning the theory of evolution, scorning even the idea that the earth might have existed more than 6,000 years ago. They held that theirs was the one true faith; all other beliefs were false doctrine—those beliefs represented the Harlot as envisioned in Revelations riding atop the Beast. Intellectually, Dorm 6 was a separate universe. I, like Joe, soon began politely to refrain from any discussion of theology and I suppose I was quickly written off.

The other draft objectors—there were less than ten of us in 1968—had followed completely different paths. All of us had struggled individually with our consciences. We were modern-day rebels without a script. None of us were certain what God wanted; none of us were assured a place in heaven, nor did we particularly want one.

Hiawatha

Senior among us was Hiawatha Davis. An African American from Denver, he grew up in the Cole neighborhood near Five Points around the corner from that pulsating east side block anchored by Daddy Bruce's Barbeque and Duke's Tavern. He carried a reputation for black power militancy. One newspaper account, looking back on his life, labeled him an "angry young man." Perhaps that was true, but I never saw that side of him.

Like all of us, he agonized over his decisions, and his letters to Selective Service Clerk Mildred Hamlin were proper and polite. He had been in San Francisco working as an airline clerk and community organizer when Local Board #2 called him back to Denver for induction. He ignored the notice and Ms. Hamlin sent him another one, this time for October 17, 1966. When he failed to appear once again, the clerk sent his file over to the U.S. attorney. The FBI soon talked to his parents in east Denver, then tracked him down to an apartment near the Haight-Ashbury District. There they had what must have been an extraordinary conversation.

"During the questioning," he wrote to his draft board, "I finally came to the conclusion that I will not be going into the military service. This decision is the result of an internal conflict that has been going on within me for the last four or five years."

Then, remarkably, the FBI agent conducting the interrogation turned draft counselor and offered him some advice:

"During the interview with the agent, continued Davis, "he advised me to inform you of my decision and request an application for CO. I believe it is Form Number 150. If it is possible I would like for you to send me the application if you possibly can.

"There is a strong chance I imagine that I may be going to jail because I won't involve myself in or with an organization whose sole purpose is to destroy and kill. I know how difficult it might be too for me to explain to God why I took something from someone that I could never return. That something is their life. The only real reason I could give would be to say I was told to do it. I don't think God would accept that answer because He gave me a mind to decide for myself."

Mildred Hamlin never sent Davis Form 150 because the case was already in the hands of U.S. Attorney Lawrence Henry. Hiawatha had violated the law twice; it was too late to stop his momentum towards jail.

Across the bay in Oakland during that time, the Black Panther Party was beginning to exhort the young people of the community to "pick up the gun." I'm not sure how Hiawatha picked up his militant reputation, but his letter to the draft board shared little in common with the fiery writings and speeches coming from Bobby Seale or Stokely Carmichael. Upon his release, Hiawatha involved himself first in community-organizing projects as director of the East Side Action Center, then later in local electoral politics as a city councilman. Those who worked with him in those years remember him not as a militant, but as a peacemaker.

There was his role, for instance, in attempting to establish a civilian police review board, an endeavor which spurred more than a little hostility from the police. "The more hostile other people got, the more calm he got," recalls one coworker. He could de-escalate a situation just by the tone of his voice."

That low calm voice is what I remember. I only met him a couple of times; his sentence was nearly complete by the time I arrived. He resided in Dorm 3 adjacent to my own with a bed next to John Banks, a tall, slender Black Muslim with a voice even quieter than Hiawatha's. It was clear Hiawatha had devoted his prison time to scholarly pursuits. He was studious, reserved, very focused on his reading. When I first introduced myself as a fellow Denverite, he was finishing one of the twelve volumes of Arnold Toynbee's *Study of History*. It was a weighty analysis of the rise and fall of civilizations, the patterns of ascendancy and decline from the beginnings of recorded history to contemporary times. A far cry from the few Louis L'Amour and Mickey Spillane novels he might find in the prison library. His reading choices were a testament to his seriousness and I must admit, for me, a little intimidating. Toynbee seemed way over my head.

Kendall

One of the other resisters remained unfazed by Toynbee. Kendall Copperberg, a long, lean, dark-haired young man from Pacoima in the San Fernando Valley had already borrowed a couple of Hiawatha's books. He was off-beat, a little antisocial, fiercely independent, lived a bit in his own world. His approach to the draft had been more individualistic than most of us and contained an element of impulsiveness. "I was not an active resister," he said. "It was a surprise to me that I actually did it."

Having spent three restless years as a theater arts student at Los Angeles Valley Junior College in Van Nuys, Copperberg faced the draft in 1965, early in the war. "I didn't know what the hell I wanted to do. I didn't want a desk job so I got into theater thinking maybe I could go into the movie business as a laborer of some sort. I had no direction; I was just sort of waiting, working part-time as a stagehand. I tried to leave home a couple of times, but couldn't afford it so I always had to come back. I commuted on a motorcycle; a Honda 350 was all I could afford. It was falling apart; I had to push it to start it, but had no money to get it fixed. Pretty pathetic actually.

"I knew the draft was happening but I didn't know what to do about it. I was totally passive about the whole thing. I even thought the military would probably be good for me. Give me some discipline."

His instincts, however, were clearly antiwar. "I was antiwar in general. I was thinking, 'Wait a second. We just finished World War II, we had the Korean War, and now there's this other thing and something was starting to happen in the Middle East.' The news is always the same. Two thousand years of recorded history of nothing but wars. Why the hell can't politicians get out of this cycle? Why can't anybody solve this; why can't anybody stop this? As long as I've been alive there's always been a war someplace; just the location has changed. It never ends. Even in junior high I was sick of it. The futility of war was obviously in my head and I didn't believe this war was actually gonna solve anything.

Nevertheless, Copperberg found himself still ambiguous at the induction center. "I was thinking maybe it'll be good to go in; maybe it'll be good for me. Then this kid in this uniform got up in front of us and just started barking at us like we were grammar school kids. Do this, do that. Lift up that pencil, fill out that form, march down that hall. I don't know who the hell he was. He was a kid in a uniform barking at us. I was really put off. I was put off with the whole process—being treated like a cow and herded through stuff. I'm very passive, but at a certain point, I will just say no. I was just not good with the idea of blind authority. I wasn't even aware of that until it happened. It was kind of a spur-of-the-moment thing. I said, 'To heck with this, I'm not gonna put up with this crap.' It was a very visceral and emotional thing that told me, 'This is wrong.'

"If an older person with some sense of real authority and gravitas had been there instead of some eighteen-year-old kid, if there had been some sense that here's some personality I should probably follow for a good reason because they know what they're talking about, I might have behaved differently. But the only day in my life I got to dig in my heels and be stubborn was the day that happened. Jesus, I didn't think I had it in me.

"We went into the (induction) room and some guy in front of me refused to step across the line. Then the guy in charge said, 'Is anybody else in this room planning on refusing today?' And two, maybe three others of us raised our hand. Then we were taken off to another room to write our statement.

"You refuse to go in. You write a statement. Then you wait for three years to see what they're gonna do to you. There was a lot of worry. What's everybody gonna think? I'm gonna be a felon. I'm gonna have to walk around now with this over my head for the rest of my life. I didn't walk out of there saying, 'Oh boy, I stuck it to The Man or anything.' It was just 'Okay, I did it. Now I'm screwed.' I was sorry that the best way to serve my country at that time was to refuse fighting a war I didn't understand or believe in. What a lousy way to serve my country. You'd think they could have given me something else to do."

Copperberg has only vague memories of his trial and his time on the witness stand. He'd been assigned a public defender who didn't really want to go to trial. "The prosecution says, 'Well, here's what this jerk-off wrote. He was fool enough to fall for and actually incriminate himself 'cuz he didn't know any better. And here it is. Did you write this?'

"'Uh. Yeah. It needs some editing.' I was thinking, Oh my God; this sounds terrible. God, don't I write any better than that? And in my mind I'm saying, 'Wait a minute, that's my defense. That's my defense for why I didn't go in.' But here they are reading it to me as part of the prosecution. Shit, I don't have a legal leg to stand on, do I? They're reading my defense as a case for the prosecution. I'm doomed, aren't I? The judge, I don't remember his name. Just a judge. Bored stiff at having another one of these jerk-offs go through his court. Just listen to this poor schmuck and see what he has to say. 'You wrote that, huh? Did you write that?' 'Yes.' 'Okay. You're guilty.'"

Mendel

Mendel showed up in the spring. He looked fourteen in his new crewcut, downright scrawny with a boyish face and those big Harry Potter glasses. When Sisco saw him he stopped short and said, "I wonder if they let him bring his model airplanes along." He must have brought out all the paternal sentiments the old cons had because as far as I know, nobody messed with him.

The Justice Department had wasted little time serving him an indictment after his draft card burning performance. Just ten days after his action, Mendel Cooper was charged with "Mutilation and Willful Non-Possession of a Selective Service Certificate" and directed to appear before Judge William E. Doyle in Denver. His trial proved as dramatic as his behavior at the U.S. Customs House on October 16. His counsel, Walter Gerash, was the flashiest, most theatrical that Denver's legal community had to offer.

"Ladies and gentlemen of the jury," began his opening statement, "this is the case of David versus Goliath."

The drama lay as much in Mendel Cooper's past as in his controversial actions. Cooper had been born in a displaced persons camp in Kassel, Germany, the son of Polish parents who had survived the Holocaust. Gerash stated: "The evidence will show that Esther Cooper hid with her child (before Mendel was born) for six days while 5,000 Jews were shot. The evidence will show that she was captured and with five other people put in an open grave and shots rang out; a six-year-old child was killed and the mother fell among the dead. Three hours later she came out and a Polish Christian family who used to play with her child gave her asylum and she hid for two years underneath the kitchen floor. The evidence will show that Joe Cooper fled and joined the Partisans and he fought the Nazis in the hills, in the dales, in the swamps for four years ... And after four years, all of Mrs. Cooper's family were dead, all of Mr. Cooper's family were dead—brothers, sisters, aunts, uncles, everyone."

Gerash had to maneuver, and wheedle to bring Cooper's father, a shipping department employee for Samsonite Luggage, to the witness stand. "I know why you're trying to do this," Judge Doyle told him in chambers. "You're trying to draw a parallel between police states. I'm just not going to let you do that; that's all. You're trying to show that this is a National Socialist–type government. I'm not going to permit that ... It's not relevant to this case."

Gerash persisted. "The father has imbued upon the young man to be wary of wars, to be wary of persecution, to be wary of the destiny of his people in time of turmoil and this is the very thing that the defendant experienced when he burned his card ... It goes to show his state of mind. It goes to show his intent."

The defense called upon character witness after character witness. Mendel was a good boy, a model of virtue. He had won a prestigious National Merit Scholarship Award and been photographed with the mayor. He had won a scholarship from the AFL-CIO since his father was a member of the United Rubber Workers. He had chosen to go to University of Denver, in spite of offers from more prestigious schools, in order to stay close to his family. His father testified in heavily accented English that he tended to believe everything his son said because "He never said a lie."

All these were presented as mitigating circumstances. The core of Cooper's defense was the constitutionality of the law which forbade the burning of draft cards. "This type of crime is what we call a malum prohibitum crime," stated Gerash. "He didn't commit any robbery, mayhem, or disturbance, and I'm sure the facts will show not even a misdemeanor or what we know as a common law breach of peace ... And yet it's elevated to the status of a felony punishable by five years." Repeatedly, he asked questions like those he addressed to Special Agent Carter who was present at the scene of the crime.

Q. And none of the speeches inflamed any of the people on the street to the degree that there was violence or cussing or anything like that?

A. No.

Q. Would you say it was a very quiet gathering?

A. Yes.

Q. No policemen were there either, were they?

A. Not that I saw.

Q. And there was no necessity of having any policemen there?

A. In my opinion. No.

Referring to the fact that Cooper had requested a duplicate draft card and had received one, Gerash stressed that even the existence of the certificate was redundant and unnecessary. "Now that the evidence is in, we know that there exists at the local board all the information necessary to make Mendel Cooper and all young people his age amenable to the draft. There is no evidence that the function of this card, SSS Form No. 2, is in any way vital to the functioning of these United States or the drafting of men to be sent overseas ...In fact, the evidence is contrary. Communications were sent. They know where he is. I submit that there must be ... a reasonably connected function to this piece of paper that is valueless ...I submit that the legislation directed to this piece of paper is an abridgment of the First Amendment because when it was passed, it was passed specifically to stop protestors, characterized as beatniks and hippies and people who differ from what Congress feels is our grand mission in Vietnam. The evidence now shows overwhelmingly that the action of Mendel Cooper was ... a symbolic effort."

Neither judge nor jury were impressed, of course. In their minds neither character, nor intent, nor the right to dissent were at issue. As for the press, the *Denver Post* had already written off Cooper's character; they labeled him, "childish and show-offish ... an immature exhibitionist." "Draft card destruction in public is designed to express contempt for the draft laws," said Judge Doyle in discussing Cooper's conviction.

In the entire country only thirty-three young men were convicted of destroying their cards; practically all received lengthy sentences. Mendel had joined an elite group who became targets of what amnesty expert Lawrence Baskir termed a "deliberate Justice Department policy of selective law enforcement designed to end a dramatic form of public protest."

As the new President Nixon prepared for a savage escalation of the air war over Vietnam, Judge Doyle sentenced Cooper to two years in a federal penitentiary and referred him for psychological examination because presentence reports showed that his "basic philosophy was destructive."

They had no idea at Safford what to do with Mendel Cooper. He spent most of his spare time pumping iron out near the handball court and doing whatever he could to annoy Lt. Lanier and Caseworker Rios.

One Halloween he and Terry John painted their faces, converted blankets into capes, grabbed a couple of pillowcases and went trick or treating among the inmates. Everyone laughed at the absurdity and offered a cigarette or any little sweet they could find in their locker. The guards were dumbfounded. It was a clear violation of prison regulations: you couldn't give or receive gifts; neither could you change your appearance. You just can't do this in a federal prison. The two man-child rebels were mocking the whole dreary structure that set the code for prison behavior. The administration couldn't conceive of trick or treating in a penal institution.

But nothing happened. It was so far beyond their universe, they just shook their heads.

The Current of Nonviolence

Gandhi's autobiography, *The Story of My Experiments with Truth* made the rounds among a few of us quite early. I think Gandhian nonviolence had become a major, if not the major intellectual current among the tiny band of resisters, mostly through the influence of the three most prominent of us: Dana Rae, Greg Nelson, and Joe Maizlish.

Dana Rae had met Catholic theologian James Douglass in Hawaii and had been favorably impressed by his work. In fact, Douglass's later book *Resistance and Contemplation* was dedicated to Dana Rae and another Hawaiian, Nick Reidy, who joined us later. Dana Rae was intrigued by the Catonsville Nine, a group of nine Catholic activists in Maryland led by the Berrigan brothers who broke into the draft board building, ripped out hundreds of files, and burned them in the parking lot with homemade napalm. The action may well have occupied the outer fringe of Gandhian nonviolence, but Father Dan Berrigan cogently characterized it as "the burning of paper rather than children."

That first Thanksgiving Dana Rae asked me, surely in the spirit of Gandhi, to participate in a fast against the war. I thought it a futile gesture out here in a remote desert far from any media that could transmit our message and among inmates we were barely getting to know. I turned him down and opted instead to feast on a dinner of dry turkey and pasty dressing. I regretted the choice later; solidarity with a friend should have trumped my dreams for a Thanksgiving dinner.

Greg was becoming a strict vegetarian under trying circumstances. Gandhi was a zealot on diet and wrote extensively of his austere experiments, describing his food intake as "limited, simple, spiceless, and if possible uncooked." His ideal food was fresh fruit and nuts, goat's milk, bananas, dates. Safford was not the best place for pursuing the Gandhian ideal. They cooked with a lot of lard back in that steamy kitchen; Greg recalls his common fare as canned string beans and corn "boiled for two days." John Banks, the camp's only Muslim was enduring a similar fate. It took another of those minor bureaucratic skirmishes—copout forms, letters to the Bureau of Prisons, and outside pressure—to get dried, roasted soybeans available at the commissary. Jars of blessed protein—it seemed Greg forever carried a jar of soy nuts in his hands after that.

Maizlish, the scholar, naturally was the most intellectually grounded in the principles of nonviolence. It hadn't always been that way. At age sixteen, upon his entry into UCLA in 1959, he signed up with the Air Force ROTC, a requirement for all male students at land grant colleges. He never gave it a second thought; you had to be a Quaker, anyway, he believed, to qualify for conscientious objector status, and he was no Quaker.

In truth, he fit in well with ROTC. He wore a uniform once a week. He got along well with his teachers. He issued orders as a drill instructor and was pretty good at it, even to the point where he feared he might enjoy it too much. He liked the World War II movies on air power and the visits to Oxnard Air Base where the food in the cafeteria was excellent and you could eat all you wanted. He enjoyed the ride he got on a big transport plane where each candidate rode for five minutes with the pilot in the cockpit. He was fascinated at Oxnard by the fighter planes that could take off on three minutes' notice to defend against enemy bombers coming in to attack the United States.

One class period his favorite teacher wrote down the air force's four national objectives on the blackboard.

- Number One: We should have sufficient power to deter and to severely damage or destroy any enemy that attacked us.

- Number Two: We should have standards and guidelines for when we would employ that force.
- Number Three: We should communicate to the opponent what things they mustn't do that would cause us to deploy our deterrent force against them.
- Number Four: We should create an atmosphere of peace.

"Now my hand went up, he recalls. "I wasn't ready to reject deterrence. 'I understand' how these numbers one, two, and three—the deterrents—work, but I just don't think that if you're ready to do all that destroying you can create an atmosphere for peace. You won't be able to do that.

"The instructor didn't understand my question," continued Maizlish "He just repeated one, two, three, and four. 'Obviously, you're deterred, so nobody's going to be attacking anybody. So then you can create peace.' But I didn't get it. I wasn't rejecting deterrence or warfare or anything like that but it just wasn't adding up. I didn't think people were like that. It was quite fascinating. I liked the instructor, actually; I still think about him in a positive way. He was very earnest in trying to clarify it and he probably couldn't understand why I didn't get it. The more I reflected on it, the more I thought, 'Well, he's not nuts and I'm not nuts; it's just that we're not connecting.' I wasn't quite sure why I didn't get it except that it just didn't feel right."

The seventeen-year-old Maizlish had intuitively embraced the meaning of Albert Einstein's famous quote: "A country cannot simultaneously prepare for and prevent war." That exchange in a UCLA ROTC class marked a milestone in Maizlish's journey toward a pacifist orientation. It was a journey that would put him in contact with civil rights workers in Mississippi, with the Student Nonviolent Coordinating Committee, with Martin Luther King, with the riot at Century City, with David Harris, and ultimately the prison at Safford where Gandhi's autobiography was making the rounds.

Doing Time

One day rolled seamlessly into the next. The community was endlessly fascinating: Cota and Perfecto, Rodriquez, Sisco and Salter, Hiawatha and Kendall, Greg, Joe and Dana Rae. "A unique brotherhood," Dana Rae called it.

And yet time hung over the whole camp like an oppressive summer heat wave, like one big throbbing communal migraine. A lot of guys could talk trash about doing time. "Two years? I could do two years standing on my head." "You down to just six months? Six months, shit. I could do six months standing on my head."

Maybe a saint or mystic could focus constantly on the immediate moment, could fix each thought on the present, and lock out from his stream of consciousness the dreams of the street, the dreams of release, the dreams of a freedom that was just out of reach. I knew no saints at Safford. And I never saw anybody standing on his head, either. We didn't talk much about it, but time weighed heavily on us all. Sometimes I think Salvador Dali must have done time. The art critics say "The Persistence of Memory," Dali's surreal painting with the four clocks melting in the sun, must symbolize Einstein's Theory of Relativity—the collapse of a fixed cosmic order—or Freudian psychoanalysis or death or female genitalia. But for me, those drooping watches hanging from a naked tree branch like a limp pizza, draped over the edge of a table, or wrapped around some one-eyed fish-like fetus must represent Dali's awareness of the grotesque, bizarre, and oppressive nature of time as it hangs perpetually over the lives of convicts secretly marking off the days.

Sometimes when the count went wrong we could feel the guards getting keyed up and excited about the possibility of chasing down an escapee. Usually it was just a mistake; somebody miscounted one of the dorms and the whole camp would sit around for half an hour until they came up with the right number. Every once in a while, though, the count really was off and then the guards got to spring into action.

Dana Rae remembers one guy jogging through the compound and the baseball field getting himself into shape for the big break. He waited till the weekend when movies would delay the lights-out count by an hour, thus giving him an extra edge, an extra bit of time to create some distance. He was methodical and scientific. "I remember it being a real event for the guards," says Dana Rae. "They'd get a chance to break out the guns and have something to do. It was an interruption of the routine." We had heard that a couple of guards were experts in tracking and that they had dogs for the pursuit. They'd follow those little V-cut footprints across the desert and usually get their man.

One day a postcard written in Spanish to a Mexican inmate arrived in Dorm 3 where Maizlish and Hiawatha lived. It was postmarked Puebla, Mexico, a town with a substantial Japanese Mexican population. The note was just a routine "Hello, wish you were here" scribbled on the back of a photograph of "El Reloj," a famous clock tower that overlooked Puebla's central square. The card was signed "Jesus Uchira Watanabe," who happened to have escaped from Safford the previous week. Obviously, the censor that night—the guard who was supposed to monitor the mail—wasn't paying much attention. He let the thing go through, oblivious to its true meaning. Within moments the news of a successful escape spread through the entire camp. At least for a brief time before dinner, everyone walked around with a smile.

Brush fires in the northern Sonoran would also break the routine on occasion. The guards trucked us out to join the Forest Service and the tribal members of the Tohono O'odham who were expert firefighters. They would issue us a paper sleeping bag, a box of K-rations full of little tin cans, and a shovel or a Pulaski. A Pulaski was a special firefighting tool that combined an axe and a pick on opposite sides of the same head. You could dig soil with the broad blade of the pick or chop wood with the sharp edge of the axe. We'd hike miles sometimes searching for clumps of burning or smoldering cactus which we were then supposed to pulverize till the wisps of smoke were no longer visible. Our job was the "mop-up" operation and I think they paid us about thirty cents an hour. I remember coming over a ridge and looking down for the first time at the brush fire below us. Brush fire, not forest fire. It was like 5,000 individual campfires flickering in the night, each one fueled by a single cactus or mesquite shrub. They brought to mind a movie I had seen as a kid, *Helen of Troy*. Here I was atop a city wall gazing down on Achilles's army camped out on the Trojan plain. It was eerie and beautiful.

Some of the prisoners played mind games with the civilian firefighters. "Watch out for Begay," they would tell them. "He was a triple axe murderer over in Gallup. You never know when he might lose control."

I would fantasize as we trekked over this rugged country, Pulaskis in hand, that some young lady from Thatcher or Oracle Junction, some angel in search of adventure would appear suddenly at twilight at the crest of a desert hill. I think I really convinced myself it could happen. She would select me from among all the firefighters and together we would keep each other warm under our paper sleeping bag.

Despite our brotherhood, despite the friendship and vitality within the compound, it was loneliness that gnawed away at us. One-time Black Panther Eldridge Cleaver wrote from Folsom Prison that "those things withheld from and denied to the prisoner become precisely what he wants most of all." Precisely what we longed for was female companionship. Becky Newman wrote me a letter one week, and I fell in love with Becky Newman. The next week Donna Smitherman wrote and I fell in love with Donna Smitherman. Then it was Kathy Taylor and I fell in love with Kathy Taylor. I barely knew any of them.

A Transfer to Terminal Island

Sometime in November of 1968 Maizlish was ordered to the control room to receive a phone call from his brother. George Turner, the guard on duty, listened in. The illness which Ruth Maizlish was currently suffering, Joe learned, was actually a return of the cancer she thought she had defeated four years previously. She was sinking fast. Harry Maizlish had corresponded with the Bureau of Prisons and managed to secure a transfer for his son to the Terminal Island facility to be closer to his family.

Turner heard the whole story. We had several choice epithets for the guards; mostly we called them "hacks." Most of them were doing time, like us, waiting in limbo for retirement. Some were on the take, but there were others like George Turner—a pretty decent fellow. He pulled Maizlish aside and apologized for having to listen in. It was just part of the BOP rules, he explained. "I wanna tell ya," he said, "I just went through a similar thing with my mother. She was dying in Seattle. I went up there and stayed a week or two at her side and realized I couldn't do anything for her. But I know what you're going through and how hard it is."

Maizlish was moved. Here was a guard and an inmate reaching out to share their common humanity. It appealed to Joe's Gandhian sense of morality. He had once attended one of David Harris's hearings in San Francisco and met folksinger Joan Baez in the courthouse hallway. Someone had said, "Gee, here we are among the enemy" because so many attorneys and cops were scurrying through the corridor. Baez had said, "We have no enemies," and Joe was struck by her response. "I thought it was charming," he said. George Turner's sympathy represented the same sentiment. "He was somebody who understood the circumstance," recalls Joe, " and was just talking to me person to person without regard to our different statuses."

Terminal Island—what a name for a prison. It lay at the edge of the San Pedro district of Los Angeles close enough for Harry Maizlish to visit his son on weekends. Joe was granted two days leave to sit at his mother's bedside just before she died. The elder Maizlish must have felt empty and heartsick—his wife no longer living, his son in a federal prison. Harry Maizlish passed away three months later. His son still faced two and a half years in jail.

We thought Joe might return eventually to Safford, but that was not to be. His unexpected departure for Terminal Island represented for him the first step in an incredible coast-to-coast odyssey through the U.S. prison system. He might have mentored several of us had he stayed; he surely had the depth and the teaching ability.

With Joe transferred and Hiawatha released shortly thereafter, I may well have quietly served out the remainder of my sentence, just doing time. Tumultuous events in 1969, however, brought two powerful personalities to the camp, two players from the national stage. Bugsy and David were first-class organizers—the kind of men who molded and shaped history. They were wildly different in style: the latter bold, charismatic, and extroverted, the former quiet and shrewd, more comfortable operating in the background. They had their political differences and occasionally found themselves at odds with one another. But each left an imprint on the times. Certainly their impact on the course of my own life and a number of my compatriots was pivotal.

Chapter 7

Bugsy and the Oakland Seven

Dear Sam and Sarah,

Bugsy arrived sometime in the spring of 1969. His real name, Jeff Segal, did not sit well with the first friend he made in the holding cell at the Federal Courthouse for the District of Northern Illinois. Newly convicted for failure to report for induction, Segal found himself locked up with the thin, graying, wiry convict everyone called Mousie. Mousie was an "independent entrepreneur," one who clearly had some shadowy connection to the Chicago Mob. "Jeff Segal?" he said. "What kind of name is that? You got to have some kind of nickname in the joint. Segal, Segal. Let's see. What about Bugsy?" And so Jeff Segal instantly became Bugsy Segal after the Jewish mobster Benjamin (Bugsy) Siegel. The original Siegel had been a cold-blooded killer, an early founder of Las Vegas, and a compatriot of the greatest of all Jewish gangsters, Meyer Lansky. Perhaps it was a bit pretentious to take on such a name, but our Bugsy seemed to wear it well enough. The original Siegel hated the nickname because it derived from "bugs" which meant "crazy." But our Bugsy enjoyed the moniker immensely. Besides, it didn't hurt to carry a Mafia nickname into a federal prison.

SDS

Since 1964 Segal had worked with the Students for a Democratic Society—that cauldron of creative energy that transformed the climate of hundreds of college campuses in the mid '60s. SDS became practically synonymous with the New Left in America.

Early on, SDS had convened in a small Michigan city and hammered out in 1962 its declaration of basic principles, the Port Huron Statement. Ideologically, that was light years before the political madness took hold in 1969. "We are people of this generation," the statement began, "bred in at least modest comfort, housed now in universities, looking uncomfortably to the world we inherit." It went on to elaborate in great detail the things that troubled them:

"The declaration 'all men are created equal' ... rang hollow before the facts of Negro life in the South and the big cities of the North."

"Hard core poverty exists just beyond the neon lights of affluence."

"The most spectacular and important creation of the authoritarian ... structure of economic decision making in America is the institution called (by former President Eisenhower) the military-industrial complex ... "

"Our pugnacious anticommunism ... has led us to an alliance inappropriately called the "free world." ... It has included through the years Batista, Franco, Verwoerd, Salazar ... Ngo Diem, Chiang Kai Shek, Trujillo, the Somozas—all of these nondemocrats separating us deeply from colonial revolutions."

"Loneliness, estrangement, isolation describe the vast distance between man and man today. These dominant tendencies cannot be overcome by better personnel management nor by improved gadgets but only when a love of man overcomes the idolatrous worship of things by man."

"Some would have us believe that Americans feel content amidst prosperity—but might it not better be called a glaze above deeply felt anxieties about their role in the new world?"

Racism, poverty, Cold War, alienation. The Port Huron Statement constituted a far-reaching critique of American society. It proposed the establishment of "participatory democracy": a system governed by the idea that "the individual shares in those social decisions determining the quality and direction of his life."

SDS took pains to separate itself from the "Old Left," from the Socialist Party and the Communist Party. The former was too dogmatically anticommunist to respond humanely to the tide of revolution sweeping the Third World. Furthermore, its persistent charges of "communist" or "communist infiltration" had long been used to rip apart the fabric of organizations on the frontlines of social change.

The latter was stodgy and authoritarian. Some of its members talked funny in stilted rhetoric that nobody listened to. Worse, it was beholden to the Stalinist monstrosities erected in the Soviet Union and Eastern Europe. The Old Left counted on the industrial working class to rise up as the primary agent of change; the New placed its hopes on the students, the emerging class of white-collar workers, the poor, and minorities.

With this new vision the SDS set out to revitalize a movement for social change in America. Its founders focused on civil rights and poverty issues, but many of the local chapters tended to concentrate on campus issues: the relevance to real life of academic curriculum, the connection of universities to the defense establishment, Puritanical dress codes, and paternalistic curfew rules.

Then Came the War in Vietnam

SDS called for the first mass antiwar demonstration in April of 1965 and astounded even its own leadership by drawing 20,000 people, mostly students, to the Washington Monument. SDS President Paul Potter closed the rally, stating "We will build a movement that will find ways to support the increasing numbers of young men who are unwilling to and will not fight in Vietnam."

Carl Oglesby, another early SDS president, described the subsequent change of direction. "Vietnam," he wrote, "imposed its own imperative, and SDS became in effect a single-issue antiwar organization . . . I cannot say we had much freedom of choice. There was no way the SDS could have avoided the war. Like everyone else, we came upon the war as a terrible accident burning in the road, an event without logic, but inescapably right there in front of us. We just had to jump in and do what we could."

Despite Paul Potter's bold speech in Washington, the SDS adhered to no single position in regard to the draft. The organization proceeded to hesitate, waver, plunge ahead, and then backtrack on its position on draft resistance.

For a short time it considered a perfectly legal program encouraging its members to apply formally for conscientious objector status. That was quietly dropped because few SDS members could qualify as true pacifists and because, despite its moderation, the policy was viciously attacked by the administration and press alike. Columnists Rowland Evans and Robert Novak accused SDS of developing a "master plan to sabotage the draft," while

Attorney General Nicholas Katzenbach said the organization was moving "in the direction of treason."

Since SDS's constituency remained on campuses, the matter of student deferments was a touchy one. One leader claimed that "the national committee kept being too scared to say anything firm because it feared that most local chapter people weren't ready yet." Another who was urging chapters to oppose student deferments estimated that only about 20 percent of his listeners agreed. "It's really hard to start a movement when the very first thing you do is ask someone to go to jail," said Boulder's Allan Haifley.

Despite the hesitation, the national committee did come forth with an unmistakably clear statement in 1966:"SDS believes that a sense of urgency must be developed that will move people to leave campus and organize a movement of resistance to the draft and the war, with its base in poor, working-class, and middle-class communities. SDS therefore encourages all young men to resist the draft."

Jeff Segal became the leading antidraft coordinator for SDS. For some years he had worked out of the national office in Chicago's south side close to where he had grown up and attended the South Shore Reform Temple. One SDS leader described the chaotic nature of that office on 63rd Street in the middle of the Woodlawn ghetto. "Weeks of chapter mail," he wrote, "piled up at our chronically understaffed pigsty of a national office." The state of the office reflected the chaotic state of organization within the SDS. "Because things were fairly loose," recalls Segal, "I decided on my own what I was doing, where I was gonna go, when I was gonna go, how I was gonna do it."

Segal had already been convicted in 1966 for failure to report for induction. Originally he had planned just to do the time and get it out of the way. Then Judge James Parsons told him his behavior was destructive to troop morale, implied he needed to set an example, and handed him a four-year sentence. With that, Segal resolved to do two things: he would appeal his conviction and, while out on bond, he would redouble his efforts to build SDS's antidraft program. "His attitude," Segal told me, "was to give me a heavy sentence so people wouldn't do what I had done. My attitude was to become a public example of what you should do."

Ultimately that's why Jeff Segal showed up in Berkeley during the summer of 1967. The aim of his appearance in the Bay Area was to lend a hand to the most militant confrontation with the draft the nation would experience during the entire Vietnam era.

Background to Confrontation

Understanding Segal's role in these events requires some background and a broader overview of the draft resistance movement. October 16, 1967—the date that Mendel Cooper had burned his draft card in Denver, the date Dick Roth had encased his card in a steel box, and the date Allan Haifley had turned his in to the attorney general—that date was a much bigger deal than I was aware of the day I heard about it back in Colorado.

Early in the war, scattered outcroppings of opposition to the draft tended to originate from long-established pacifist organizations—The Central Committee for Conscientious Objectors (CCCO), for instance, or the War Resisters League. They tended also to come from tiny numbers of individuals.

Exceptions to this occurred in the black community where members of the Student Nonviolent Coordinating Committee encouraged in some areas of the South mass defiance of the draft. There was the SNCC statement that got Julian Bond barred from the Georgia State Legislature in 1966 and the McComb statement in Pike County, Mississippi, which urged blacks not to fight in Vietnam for the "White Man's freedom." That same year, Atlanta saw twelve blacks arrested for repeated demonstrations at the induction center. Six were convicted and received three and a half years for "interfering with the administration of the Selective Service Act." Another got three years on a Georgia chain gang for "insurrection."

The Burners

It was The Burners, however, who brought the idea of defying the draft to the national scene. Congress could watch—apparently without flinching—some unfortunate soul in the Central Highlands set aflame by napalm jelly. It could watch an entire thatched-hut village in the Mekong Delta torched with a Bic lighter in what the GIs called "Zippo Raids." But light up a Selective Service card—set afire that little wrinkled up piece of paper we were all supposed to carry in our billfolds—and there would be hell to pay.

Chris Kearns from the *Catholic Worker* newspaper did exactly that in July of 1965. The incident in front of the Whitehall Induction Center in New York was captured by a photographer from *Life Magazine* and within weeks an incensed Congress added the destruction of draft cards to the list of felonies one could commit under the Selective Service Act.

David Miller, another radical Catholic pacifist, was the first to respond to the new law. At an October, 1965, rally in New York, Miller followed a lengthy opening speech with a two-sentence speech of his own. "I believe the napalming of villages is an immoral act," he said. "I hope this will be a significant political act, so here goes." The political act that followed those two sentences cost him two years in prison.

When four conservatively dressed young men lit up their cards at the South Boston District Courthouse on a frigid day in March, 1966, the hostile crowd that surrounded them went wild. "Shoot them! Kill them!" they yelled, then proceeded to punch, kick, pummel, and break bones.

Cornell student Bruce Dancis remembered his feelings just before the massive Spring Antiwar Mobilization in 1967 at Sheep's Meadow in Central Park: "that the antiwar movement had to become much more serious. That the days of writing postcards to congressmen and taking part in demonstrations were already growing short." Dancis and fellow student Tom Bell hoped to see 500 young men burn their cards on April 15, but the day before, the doubt began to set in. At a meeting the night before at the New York Free University, a much smaller group discussed their plans. "We decided that fifty would be the minimum number of burners to make it an important political act," said Marty Jezer, one of the participants. "There was a tense moment when Dancis asked 'How many will burn their cards if fifty do it at the same time?' Hands shot up around the room. The count was fifty-seven."

The next day that small core stood on a knoll in the corner of the meadow and set their cards afire. Suddenly—profoundly moved by the spectacle of resistance—another hundred surged forward spontaneously, each with a burning card which he deposited in an empty Maxwell House Coffee can passed around as a collection box. Among them was Gary Rader, a uniformed Green Beret who everyone thought had come to cause trouble. He stunned the crowd by taking out his own card, lighting it, and then placing it into the tin can with the rest. "Not to have burned your draft card on April 15," said Jezer, "would have been tantamount to living in Boston in 1773 and not to have dropped tea in Boston Harbor."

Perhaps the burning cards infuriated millions; perhaps they polarized the nation. But for those growing numbers of Americans who fervently opposed the war, who had marched and rallied and prayed to no avail, each flaming card represented a challenge—a challenge to take another step, to move, as the slogan went, from "dissent to resistance."

"With the draft card burnings and the furor they stirred," said one peace activist, "a line of demarcation seemed crossed, and looking backward, one realizes that The Resistance was born."

The Resistance

The name and the time for a national day of resistance came out of the Bay Area. At a ramshackle communal house on Cooley Street in East Palo Alto, David Harris and Dennis Sweeney met with two radicals from across the bay in Berkeley, Steve Hamilton and Lennie Heller. In March of 1967 they announced to the world their formal name, "The Resistance," with a capital T and a capital R. They drafted a leaflet headlined in bold letters "We Refuse to Serve." "We will renounce all deferments," it began "and refuse to cooperate with the draft in any manner . . . " Then they set the date, October 16, 1967, the first national draft card turn-in day. They urged all American males of draft age to sever on that day their relationship with Selective Service.

Harris and Sweeney set off on a tour up and down the West Coast to spread the word. Heller traveled to the Midwest and the East. Hamilton stayed in Berkeley. "Early on, as we were organizing," recalls Harris, "it became apparent that a lotta people wanted to support us who didn't have draft cards to turn in. They were older men or they were women and weren't subject to the draft. At that point the idea we came up with was 'Let's do an action around the Oakland Induction Center.' Dennis and I were trying to get things started in L.A.; Lennie was headed East. So we reached an agreement that at the end of the summer we'll be back together and figure out what to do with this other (Oakland) demonstration."

On the East Coast, distinguished intellectuals—men and women far beyond the age of draft eligibility—composed and signed "A Call to Resist Illegitimate Authority" in support of the resisters. Each signer risked five years imprisonment for "counseling, aiding, and abetting" draft resistance. Dr. Benjamin Spock—the preeminent pediatrician who advised an entire generation of mothers and fathers on how to parent their children—put his name to the document. The Rev. William Sloane Coffin, chaplain at Yale University, signed it as did Rabbi Arthur Waskow. Noam Chomsky, Denise Levertov, Mitchell Goodman, Marcus Raskin—respected scholars, poets, and writers—all signed. Poet Allen Ginsberg wrote back, "I can't recommend the humorless prose. You'd be better off telling people to goof off or fuck off from the draft than all this gobbledygook which takes too long to read. But I'll sign anyway." In all, 2,000 individuals defiantly signed that illegal and subversive document.

As October 16, 1967, approached, as the National Mobilization Committee organized tens of thousands of demonstrators to "Confront the War Makers" that same week in Washington, as Abbie Hoffman and Jerry Rubin conspired to levitate the Pentagon, turning it orange and driving out the evil spirits therein, thousands of draft-deferred college students anguished over what to do with their own ties to the Selective Service System.

Most of Bugsy's SDS work dovetailed nicely with the activities of The Resistance. He had busied himself building "antidraft unions" on campuses all over the country. Union members were signing "We Won't Go" statements and pledging to return their draft cards to local boards with notices of refusal to cooperate "until American invasions are ended." Segal and Jezer reported that by June of 1967, sixty antidraft unions had been established nationwide and at least 2,000 men had signed "We Won't Go" statements. "Those statements were essentially the same kind of statements that Dr. Spock et. al ended up getting charged with," says Segal. "The antidraft unions also engaged in day-to-day activities. Many would go down to induction centers to leaflet and provide counseling. There was a vast network being built of draft counselors, of doctors, particularly psychiatrists who were willing to write a letter that would be appropriate to get some guy out . . . I was just a little piece of it, but there was, at the time, a massive civilian effort around this." These were the same types of things The Resistance was involved with.

Stop the Draft Week

But in Berkeley—Mecca of the Left, a roiling kettle of radical activism—in Berkeley they aspired to raise the ante much higher. The Oakland Induction Center stood in the midst of downtown Oakland on 14th Street between Clay and Jefferson Streets. It was there that draftees from all over Northern California, from Oregon and half of Nevada were bused in, day after day, examined by army doctors and inducted into the armed forces. It was a central staging ground for shipping out soldiers to Vietnam.

Radicals in Berkeley eyed the Oakland Induction Center, assessed its significance, and set out to shut it down. They formed an organization—an off-shoot of the October 16th event—called STDW, Stop the Draft Week. "Shut the Mother Down," became the slogan of the season.

Jeff Segal had arrived in Berkeley earlier that summer dressed in the uniform of the day: jeans and a denim workshirt with black engineer boots he had bought cheap in a surplus store in Chicago.

Antidraft unions aside, the SDS position on the draft had grown increasingly murky during the previous year, particularly with the emergence within the organization of a rigidly Maoist sect called the Progressive Labor Party or PL. In one of its position papers PL stated: "While we must oppose the (student) 2-S deferment as a divisive and class-racial discriminatory system, we have to do this on the basis of collective struggle, not by individual sacrifice." They sneered at Harris and his fellow resisters: "You guys are just going to martyr yourselves," they said, and labeled them "bourgeois moralists."

Resistance leaders chafed at the rhetoric and saw through it as a transparent excuse to do a lot of talking without taking any action. Harris still seethes with anger when he recalls that kind of criticism. "We thought that the strategy and the morality were the exact same thing," he says. "They (SDS) had a standard line about draft resistance: 'we're too important to the movement to go to jail.' And our line was if you've got a draft card, you're part of the war, for Chrissake. You wanna be against the war, put your money where your mouth is. And they didn't want to hear that . . . They were great at making speeches and trumpeting ideology, but when it came down to getting their shit on the line, these people weren't there and never were."

In certain respects, Segal's position echoed the rhetoric of Progressive Labor. "I was critical," he told me many years later, "of what became organizationally The Resistance that Harris led. The position we developed as the SDS approach was to say that we needed to support and encourage mass resistance and institutional resistance, not burning your draft card in public and individualistically opting out of the system. At least in my thinking, instead of doing those kinds of demonstrations, what we needed were demonstrations to close down the system. We were gonna do, at least symbolically, whatever we needed to do to keep people—particularly working-class people who may not believe that they had alternatives—from being drafted." It implied inherently a rejection of Harris's creed of nonviolence.

This reflected the thinking of most of the STDW members in Berkeley. Much of their literature aimed at "involving young people who are facing conscription: black people, high school students, the unemployed, and young working people." "The dominant group in STDW," wrote Michael Ferber, "perceived nonviolence as an obstacle to reaching working-class youth." He quoted one STDW member: "The gentle, almost timid tone of peace demonstrations has left many young people—black and white—feeling they have no place in the peace movement."

If Segal's position approached, in some ways, the line of Progressive Labor, his path, in other ways, was decidedly different. For one, he had already been sentenced to four years for draft resistance. His Marxist politics remained relatively free of orthodoxy and, true to its New Left origins, stood fiercely independent of Russian and Chinese communists alike. He was horrified at the thought that some tiny little in-group like PL might try to impose its will and its politics on an organization as open, vibrant, and varied as the SDS. Finally, he was about to engage in an action that might cost him many additional years in the penitentiary.

Few of his SDS compatriots were to be found in the Bay Area; the organization had established little presence there. On the other hand, he had no trouble finding any number of Marxists, socialists, and independent radicals around campus who shared his views on the draft and what should be done about it. He moved in with two friends, Karen Jo Coonan and Terry Cannon (editor of a SNCC newspaper called *The Movement*), and as he put it: "lived off the land . . . I got food. I got shelter. What else did I need?"

During that late summer and fall, the radicals of Berkeley pieced together a steering committee to direct the activities of Stop the Draft Week on the East Bay. No one could foresee then the magnitude of the legal charges they would face within the next year.

Preparations

Segal's special task was tactics. Nobody really had any idea how to shut down the operation of a major government institution. "I'd been reading, among other things," said Segal, "some police crowd- and riot-control books . . . I had some book learning, but you know I'd never done this before either. The other folks that were out there thought I knew more than I really knew . . . But I did develop what we referred to as the 'military strategy.'

"It would not be the run-of-the-mill demonstration. We figured we needed to train people as much as we could.

"We decided, first, that we were gonna train what we called 'monitor squads.' Three to four people: a leader, a deputy leader, and a communications person. We would instruct them on the basics of police crowd and riot control so they would need to know something about tear gas and CS gas and what to do about it. Because we expected that kind of stuff to happen. People were told to bring kerchiefs and things to cover their noses and mouths and to water those things down and to use Vaseline around their faces which helps ward off the gas . . . Some people were told to bring gloves and given some rudimentary instruction on what the canisters were and how to pick them up. The canisters were hot and people were instructed to throw them back, which we consider to be defensive. It's the kind of stuff people do to this day.

"About a month or a month and a half before the demonstration, we put out a call for people who were willing to be part of these monitor squads. We had—I don't know—fifty, sixty, seventy people in a park in Oakland that we were gonna train. I advised that this locus of groups be the center. If we had these groups of a couple a hundred demonstrators under some kind of leadership on the street, we would have the mechanism for stopping traffic, for bollixing up traffic in order to keep the buses from getting to the induction center. So the instructions were to have these couple of dozen groups assigned to specific places where they could do things to tie up traffic. If the police came, they were instructed to split. Only if police were ahead of buses were they instructed to stay. Each of the monitor squads was given a walkie-talkie to stay in touch with the central command, if you will.

"We also trained our monitor squads on how to defend against batons and the like. People were told to bring as much as they could of things like helmets and foam wrapping. I also got a couple of hundred bucks from the till and pulled together several guys to make shields. Not all of the steering committee would have been happy about this, but we made dozens and dozens of plywood shields. So that there would be some way at least minimally of protecting against cops wailing on folks."

This "military strategy" is not what David Harris and his nonviolent friends in The Resistance envisioned. They were under the impression that the action in Oakland had been theirs to direct. "Our plan," says Harris, "had been to come up with an idea: 'Okay, this is the action we're gonna do,' then call a meeting and recruit people for this specific action . . . Especially in Berkeley where there were four thousand political groups and more bullshit than you can shake a stick at." When their own Steve Hamilton broke ranks and invited in all of Berkeley's sundry radicals, Harris was furious. To his way of thinking, the radicals had hijacked a Resistance demonstration.

The subsequent infighting turned bitter. I don't really know what was said in those Berkeley forums leading up to the action, but I can imagine there was a lot of reckless and self-righteous posturing in those times.

That summer had seen massive rioting in ghettos throughout the country, particularly in Newark and Detroit where the casualty rate had counted sixty-nine dead. Over in Oakland, the Black Panthers were calling for armed revolution and practically goading the police to engage them in gun battles on the street. Their Minister of Information Eldridge Cleaver was saying things like, "We shall have our manhood. We shall have it or the earth will be leveled by our attempts to gain it."

Many white radicals were entranced by this kind of talk and saw the Panthers as the driving force of the revolution. Other radicals tended to glorify the working class—white, brown, or black—and held the belief they had to prove their toughness to win over the working population.

Harris had patience for neither the rhetoric nor the accusations hurled at The Resistance. "Our response," he said, "was this: I mean who's kidding who here? This entire meeting is full of middle-class people. Who else goes to the University of California or Stanford or any of these other places? . . . We're all middle class. The only thing different is that we acknowledge we're middle class and we've set out to organize the middle class which is gonna be the difference between whether this war continues or not. And you guys are out here pretending to be Black Panthers, talkin' like you grew up in the ghetto. That's bullshit; you didn't grow up in the ghetto. You're just as middle class as the rest of us."

Segal's response is equally impassioned. It expresses the frustration on the part of many radicals that strict adherence to traditional techniques of nonviolence was simply not sufficient to end the war, that more forceful methods were required to get the attention of Lyndon Johnson, Robert McNamara, and Dean Rusk.

"The position of the Stop the Draft Week," said Segal, "was we will do what we thought necessary to close down the induction center and prohibit buses of inductees from getting through. This was not a pacifist demonstration. The people in the Berkeley antidraft union—while by and large, they were not military crazies—they were not, as a matter of principle, nonviolent . . . We weren't out to have some kind of violent confrontation. The end was to close the induction center. It wasn't like from our end we were out to do battle with the authorities . . . It's just we weren't going to not do battle if the circumstances required it."

That might seem a little like splitting hairs. The protestors who marched from Berkeley down to Oakland knew very well the Oakland cops, the Alameda County Sheriffs, and the California State Patrol had no intention of allowing the closure of the induction center without a fight.

On the other hand, those marchers were unarmed. The police carried side arms, cuffs, gas masks, chemical spray Mace, twelve extra rounds of ammunition, and hardwood riot sticks with a density greater than baseball bats. One officer testified that some men had individualized their batons with carvings and notches, and others had them inserted with lead. Among their thousands, the protestors had a few scattered motorcycle helmets and several dozen plywood shields.

"You end up in one way," says Segal, "with a false dichotomy because it wasn't a choice between pacifists and armed revolutionaries. Even, as it was, that many of us thought the country might end up with some kind of armed insurrection, we certainly knew at that point that we were not at that stage in the development of the political struggle . . . When people were told to bring helmets and foam wrapping, that was characterized on the part of Harris and The Resistance, as planning a, 'violent demonstration' . . . They ended up painting us as these violent crazies and attacking us in public . . . They could command some press attention. Reporters from the *San Francisco Chronicle* . . . would talk to Harris so they could get a quote. (Those public attacks) in part created the circumstances and the environment from which the police perceived what was going to happen and what they were gonna do about it."

As the summer wore on—over across the bay in San Francisco, they were calling it "The Summer of Love"—the tension between contending parties in Berkeley reached a breaking point. Only a few attempted to reach out across the gaping chasm of mistrust. Frank Bardacke, a radical steering committee member wrote that:

> Although most of the Left admired the passion and eloquence of The Resistance leaders, they disapproved of burning and turning in draft cards as an antidraft tactic. They claimed that the Resistance was moving back to a position of apolitical moral witness and they demanded to know what was the political purpose of spending five years in jail.

> Never has the Left so thoroughly missed the point. The Resistance made Stop the Draft Week possible. Young men burning their draft cards on Sproul Hall steps changed the political mood of the (UC Berkeley) campus. This example and that of hundreds who turned in their draft cards gave the rest of us courage.

Any attempts made at conciliation, however, fell flat. In the middle of one acrimonious meeting, Harris finally stormed out. "I thought these guys were off the wall," he said. "I didn't want to be associated with them."

Some of the long time Bay Area pacifists stayed and eventually worked out a compromise: They would implement a nonviolent action on Monday, October 16, with a sit-in in front of the induction building. The rest of the week belonged to the radicals.

Street Fighters

And so on Tuesday, October 17, the day after 1,500 young men nationwide collectively defied the Selective Service System by returning their draft cards, 3,000 thousand people, twenty of whom were undercover police agents, gathered at the Oakland Induction Center to shut it down.

That day was a disaster. "There was a large multistory parking garage kitty-corner from the induction center," recalls Segal. "The Oakland police had commandeered the garage. We thought they were gonna come in from outside, but they were already there." When they poured out en masse from the garage, it was the Oakland Raiders versus the Claremont Junior High School flag football team. The walkie-talkie communication system broke down. "The machines worked alright," says Segal, "but nobody was calling in with information. They had other things to do. So it was pretty ragged getting communication both ways." Meanwhile, the cops showed little mercy.

"The street was dotted with blood, broken glass, and ripped clothing," wrote the *Oakland Tribune*. Protestors limped back to Berkeley, smoldering, demoralized, licking their wounds. Their confidence shaken, they even questioned whether to return the next day. A divided steering committee recommended a rally at the university chancellor's office—Berkeley cops were much gentler than the Alameda County Sheriffs' deputies.

Following a late-night meeting on the UC campus, the crowd finally voted to return peacefully the next morning to downtown Oakland. Both Harris and Segal argued forcefully for a return to the induction center. For the next two days—Wednesday and Thursday—nonviolent pickets assembled at the downtown site once again.

By Friday they were ready to try again. Still chafing from the beating administered earlier in the week, 10,000 protestors gathered in Berkeley to try once more to shut the center down. Mobile tactics and spontaneity were the order of the day.

"It all started at some God-awful time—three o'clock in the friggin' morning," remembers Segal, "because the army started at dawn to do its thing with the inductees. We bagged the walkie-talkies; they hadn't worked on the first day. Given our experience on Tuesday, we decided not to converge on the induction center. People were assigned corners. They would move from corner to corner and build barricades to whatever degree they could, at streets around the induction center. Maybe eight blocks or twelve blocks out. The area we were dealing with bordered on the ghetto so one of the things we consciously wanted to do was to be careful about that border. We didn't want to invite the cops into the ghetto by our activities. So we were pretty careful about not going too far."

"Typically," said Segal shortly after the demonstration, "a group would march into an intersection and form a moving circle in the area of the crosswalks. They would then come out and start to paint things on the streets and sidewalks. The paint was really the original catalyst that loosened people up and led to many other great, beautiful things. Once this loosening process had taken place, small groups of demonstrators would break out of the circle and begin to move all kinds of objects into the streets.

"People ... built barricades from whatever they could find handy—benches, large potted trees, parking meters, garbage cans, cars, trucks. These were placed in the middle of the streets and the air let out of the tires. People would run up behind buses and rip the ignition wires out or would climb into trucks and steal the keys.

"People in the neighborhood got into it too. They would bring out old couches and washing machines and the like and help build barricades."

"It was soon evident," wrote Karen Wald in the SDS publication "New Left Notes," that there were more of US than THEM, and this combined with our mobility, enabled groups of demonstrators to carry out actions unimpeded by the police ...

"The real change came about when one line of demonstrators, instead of simply backing up before a line of police, dispersed to the sidewalks—then quickly, instinctively, converged on the streets again behind the line of cops The cops suddenly, uncomfortably, found themselves surrounded . . . Nervous and demoralized, the cops stood there, shuffling their feet, looking worried and unhappy . . . For the first time demonstrators, unarmed, saw police lines in retreat in front of them. It was our first real taste of victory."

"I remember quite clearly," says Segal, "watching the news that night and seeing a dozen people or so being attacked by a couple of billy-club-wielding cops at the entrance to a store on the street. And there was this guy—I have no idea who he was—holding these cops off with one of our shields. I mean standing there with the cops banging away and him taking the blows with the shield."

At the end of the morning on that Friday, weary protestors roving the streets around the induction center looked around and realized what they had done. They had shut it down! For four hours the processing of young soldiers bound for Vietnam had stopped dead in its tracks. The protestors were jubilant. They had shut it down!

Governor Ronald Reagan had to mobilize the National Guard to clear the streets.

"We had come prepared to tussle with the police," says Segal. "We had not come prepared to fight the National Guard. It was time for everybody to go . . . I mean we had stopped the buses for the day . . . We declared a victory and went home. Good grief, we weren't stupid. We may have been reckless but we weren't stupid."

The Controversy

Neither Bugsy nor David talked much about Oakland while I was with them at Safford, at least not that I ever heard. They had both moved on to the more immediate realities they faced in prison. I was spared at the time from having to sort out some of the thornier controversies that arose from the battle.

Certainly within the context of Vietnam, fending off cops in downtown Oakland with a plywood shield doesn't register the tiniest blip of violence on the Richter scale. Likening the use of napalm and cluster bombs, B-52s and Browning automatic rifles to some guy wearing a motorcycle helmet and pulling a wire from a distributor cap strips the term "violence" of practically any meaning. If pulling up a park bench or ripping out a parking meter could more speedily end the mass killing in Vietnam, then who could harbor moral qualms about some minor property damage? More at issue than the morality was the wisdom of the action. Was that kind of militance truly effective in ending the war?

Even within the draft resistance movement, itself, there was widespread disagreement. Three of the four original founders of The Resistance—the four who set the October 16th turn-in date—ended up approving the action in Oakland. Steve Hamilton served on the steering committee and was later indicted for his role in Stop the Draft Week. Lennie Heller was enthralled by it. One writer described Heller's reaction: "Speaking in Washington on October 20 after flying in from the West Coast, his eyes still smarting from the tear gas, (he) was obviously more excited by the mobile tactics planned in Oakland than by the draft card turn-in he had done so much to organize."

Dennis Sweeney, Harris's co-organizer at the Cooley Street commune, began to rethink his position as the week's events unfolded. "The Resistance's decision to boycott Stop the Draft Week had been a serious error . . . History was being made," he came to believe, on the streets of Oakland.

Of the four, only Harris maintained his original opposition. "I thought 'mobile tactics' were self-indulgent and bullshit," he said. "Running through town turning over a garbage can? C'mon. Rupturing the tires of local buses? It may make you feel powerful—what the hell does it do? . . . That bus wasn't taking (its riders) to the army—that bus was taking them to work."

Even from a distance, measuring the isolated impact of Oakland as distinct from all the rest of the craziness of 1967 is an impossible task.

Oakland represented one of the innumerable variables, a tiny component of the weights and counterweights, pressures and countless intelligence reports which played into President Johnson's strategic decisions in 1967.

Generals and admirals clamored for escalation: more ground troops and more bombings, fewer restrictions on targets, more free-fire zones, more attacks on enemy sanctuaries, and "relentless application of force" including invasion of North Vietnam. At the same time, some of his advisors warned of the dangers of broadening the war: Chinese troops pouring over their southern border as they had done in Korea or a heightened confrontation with the Soviets which might lurch out of control.

But also among the major factors in Johnson's deliberations was domestic opposition to the war in all its wild diversity. Even as he believed the antiwar movement riddled with communist dupes and communist sympathizers,

Lyndon Johnson remained extremely sensitive to public opinion. The accumulated forms of dissent—the peaceful rallies, the civil disobedience, the increasing defiance of the draft, the turmoil in the streets all weighed heavily on the president's thoughts. At one point, Department of Defense officials who advocated unlimited bombing of Hanoi and the port city of Haiphong presented Johnson with a computer study calculating how many American lives had been saved by dropping the atomic bomb on Japan during World War II. Responding to the presentation, LBJ demanded further information: "I have one more problem for your computer—will you feed into it how long it will take five hundred thousand angry Americans to climb that White House wall out there and lynch their president if he does something like that?"

After consideration of the entire set of complex particulars, Johnson refused to order American ground forces into the North, into Laos, or into Cambodia. He turned down, as well, General Westmoreland's request for additional troops in South Vietnam. In 1967 Johnson placed limitations on the scope of the war.

Perhaps, then, Segal and the Berkeley radicals had found a timely and effective method of sending a powerful message: escalate the war and America's streets would erupt in turmoil and rebellion. There would be a price to pay for increased violence in Vietnam.

There would be a price, however, for the Left, as well. Though Segal's tactics in the Bay Area had a specific and well-defined goal—shutting down the induction center—some radicals across the nation drew the most simplistic lessons from Oakland: Street-fighting and "kicking ass" might be the path and the strategy to revolution and social change. Within a couple of years those superficial conclusions would contribute to paroxysms of self-destructive behavior on the Left.

The Trial

The higher profile leaders in Berkeley faced high-stakes legal consequences. They were charged with conspiracy to violate Section 602(j) of the California Penal Code (Trespass) and Section 148 (Resisting Arrest or stopping a police officer from properly discharging his duty). For this, they faced five years to life in prison.

The 1960s were famous for political trials involving multiple defendants: the Chicago Eight, the Catonsville Nine, the Boston Five. Bugsy and his friends became, naturally enough, the Oakland Seven. In addition to Segal and Hamilton, Cannon and Bardacke, charges were filed against Reese Ehrlich, Bob Mandel, and Mike Smith. All were members of the steering committee; five of the seven were former students at the university. Bugsy, having traveled in from Chicago, was the sole "outside agitator."

It was the word "conspiracy" that ratcheted up the charges. Trespass is a misdemeanor; resisting arrest is a misdemeanor. But under California statute, agreeing with one other person to commit a misdemeanor constituted a felony. By playing the "conspiracy" card, Alameda County DA J. Francis Coakley unabashedly injected politics into the legal process. "The indictment procedure in such instances," he said "is a new one, a new policy we have adopted and (it) should serve as a warning to people who would violate the law by so expressing themselves." Coakley had thrown down the gauntlet.

Throughout the three-month-long trial, Bugsy resided, courtesy of the U.S. government, in the Alameda County Jail. Convicted as a draft offender in 1966, his bail—pending appeal—was revoked in 1968 because his travel as SDS antidraft coordinator had left a series of civil disruptions in its wake. Oakland was only the beginning. He traveled to Duke in April, 1968, with the Southern Student Organizing Committee and students in Durham seized the university president's private home. They demanded minimum wages for college employees and the president's resignation from an all-white country club. He traveled to Athens, Georgia, that same spring and students seized a university building in protest of repressive and discriminatory curfew and drinking rules on campus directed primarily towards women. He flew back to New York and took part in the occupation of several buildings at Columbia University with students protesting the school's ties to the war and the university's plans to build a gym on public land in Morningside Park adjacent to Harlem. "I mean 1968 was a good year," recalls Segal.

Of course, all this turmoil would have occurred with or without Bugsy's presence, but in the eyes of the U.S. attorney general, it looked like he was running wild. They could put an end to that by revoking bail—put this boy away and get him off the street—and that's exactly what they did.

He certainly looked wild enough. His dark unshorn hair, frizzy and wavy, spread straight out in an oval above his head and brushed against his shoulders. "A Jewfro," he called it because it resembled the natural Afro hairstyle popular in the mid-'60s. His parents never questioned his political ideas, but they had little tolerance for his appearance: "Don't you think you could do what you're doing better if you cut your hair?" When he first appeared at the Springfield Federal Prison Facility in Missouri to begin his sentence, his hair remained uncut and unruly. One inmate stared at him in disbelief: "Goddam," he said, "they just busted Jesus Christ." Then they shaved his head.

In the late winter of 1969 as the trial of the Oakland Seven opened, Segal shipped out to Alameda County. On the day of his arrival he rode the elevator—filled to capacity with gray-clad inmates, hardened on Oakland's meaner streets—up to the seventh-floor cell block. "What choo here for, man?" asked one of them. "I told 'em I was busted for closing down the Oakland Induction Center," said Segal. A cheer rose; arms raised up. "Yes!" they shouted, and the creaky elevator reverberated with applause.

Each day during the trial Segal underwent a strip search at the end of the elevator ride. Then, by permission of the court, he put on a suit—the same gray suit day after day—so that the jury would never know he was a convict as he sat in the dock with his fellow defendants. When the court recessed for lunch, Segal would return—again unknown to the jury—to a jail cell adjacent the courtroom to eat his bologna sandwich.

The Trial Was Quite the Spectacle

During the week of protests Karen Jo Coonan and Segal had been given the task of building a defense apparatus. "Primarily Karen put together a manual for mass defense," says Segal. "So, for example, when we were at the staging area everybody got phone numbers to call up if they got arrested so we could bail them out. Then we went around and got commitments from lawyers to do trials including felony trials. It included recruiting law students to be legal observers. It also included recruiting people to set up emergency first aid. So yeah, we had this whole apparatus worked out. As a result when the seven of us did get arrested on felonies, we had several lawyers we could go to, all of them fairly experienced."

Most prominent among them was Charles Garry, chief counsel for the Black Panther Party, an attorney known for flair and theatrics in the courtroom. Together with attorneys Mal Bernstein and Dick Hodge, the defense team hammered away on multiple fronts, including the voir dire process—the process of jury selection.

It represented an early use of the technique of thoroughly investigating potential jurors. "For each and every one on the jury panel," remembers Segal, "people went out and got their background, so we knew some significant amount of information with which to probe . . . Charley got up with the first juror and took like half a day and really tore into this guy. He finally got him to volunteer prejudicial attitudes like, 'I think these long-haired hippies deserve whatever they get' kind of stuff. First off, that's what got him bounced from the jury. But the rest of those on the jury panel learned that if there was a problem, if there was something lurking, it would get ferreted out. They preferred not to go through what the first guy did, so they would volunteer prejudicial attitudes or the like right off the bat.

"Then there was a guy who we agreed to seat who was a retired World War I colonel. Prosecution knew that and evidently thought he was gonna be a good guy for them. What we knew was that he was working part-time in a bookstore around the corner from the induction center, that he lived in sort of a more working-class section of Berkeley, not up in the fancy hills, and that there was a Proposition P sign—a peace initiative—posted in his window. So, taking account his military background, prosecution didn't ask any questions, but we figured he was gonna be good for us.

"We went through a good couple hundred people—the voir dire must have lasted a good month and a half—before we ended up with a jury we thought we could work with."

Undercover

For his key witnesses, prosecutor Lowell Jensen relied largely on the team of undercover plainclothesmen that Oakland and Alameda County had inserted inside the mass of protestors. Some had been discredited even before the action began. Segal recalls discussing the existence of these infiltrators at the first training meeting for monitors.

"We knew these guys were floating around," he says. "In fact we got the CB system from one of them . . . I didn't know most of the people there because I hadn't been living in the (Bay Area). So I came up to Terry (Cannon) and Reese (Ehrlich) and said, 'If you had to choose, what three people would you identify as cops?' They picked the exact same three guys that I picked. So we had them followed. One of them went home and the name on the mailbox was not the same name he had given us. One of them was discovered calling the police department from a phone booth. I mean people did a good job of following these guys around and so we were pretty confident of who they were. They looked like cops; I mean it was really intuitive. They were all pretty young. They looked and acted like cops. We had a serious discussion in the steering committee about this, and we decided as long as we knew them, we would not expose them. We thought we'd be able to control what they learned. And if we exposed them, the cops could send in some more guys who we might not be able to identify.

"There were serious concerns . . . that once the demonstrations started that they would become agents provocateurs. Because one of my cousins was a drummer for (the rock band) Country Joe and the Fish, I had arranged—it wasn't very difficult to do—for the group to perform at a predemonstration rally. So the Fish did their thing and a couple of hundred people showed up and there were some refreshments and the like. The three cops, each of them—I was not involved in this—ended up getting coffee laced with LSD. They were taken off into the Berkeley hills and dropped off at what was for them unknown territory to wander around for a while in an LSD-induced euphoria. That got them out of the way and avoided the possibility of them becoming agents provocateurs."

One of the undercover men was Robert Wheeler, alias "Roster," the man who provided Segal with the walkie-talkies. Perhaps it was the brand-new jeans that he bought for the assignment that got him identified as a cop. Shortly before the first demonstration, Wheeler was sent by STDW organizers to Palo Alto to deliver a letter written, he was told, in secret code. Thinking he had discovered something of crucial importance, he steamed open the letter and read, to his great disappointment, that its contents contained no code at all, but merely stated in plain English that he'd been identified as a cop. "I then hitched home," he testified at the trial, "and reported back to my superiors that we'd been burned."

Despite their bumbling, the prosecution team was able to testify to "overt acts committed in furtherance of the conspiracy:" chartering buses to take people to Oakland, distributing leaflets, opening an account at the Wells Fargo Bank, transporting loudspeaker equipment, making speeches, walking around downtown Oakland with a "monitor group," renting a meeting room at the Wesleyan Foundation Hall.

For the defense, Garry and his team countered with forty witnesses of their own, all of whom testified to the spontaneity of the events that occurred that week in downtown Oakland.

"How did you come to hear about Stop the Draft Week," asked Jensen of several witnesses. Mostly from the *San Francisco Chronicle*, they responded. One learned about it at the office of the Episcopal Peace Fellowship, another through Women Strike for Peace. An English teacher answered: "How do you know there is going to be a football game on Saturday? Well, that was how I knew about the demonstration."

"What did you have in your hand when you crossed the street by the induction center," one witness was asked. "Just my girlfriend's hand," he responded.

One young woman testified, "I came to the demonstration to protest the forced induction of my boyfriend. I felt a moral obligation to oppose the war and put my body in between." A Stanford professor of Victorian literature came with a colleague because "we felt we could help the students. We felt that professors could act as buffers between the police and the students."

The Verdict

"It was really a cross section of life," commented the court bailiff on the composition of the jury. Four housewives, two post office clerks, a retired marine colonel, a statistician, a carpenter, an assembly line inspector at General Motors, a defense plant tool and die maker, and a construction supervisor at a radiation laboratory listened intently to all this testimony.

They listened as prosecutor Lowell Jensen delivered his closing arguments: "This moral righteousness is an outrage. Everyone of us is neither above nor below the law ... We do not want the problems that exist solved on the streets."

In delivering his closing argument, Charles Garry boldly threw the principle of "jury nullification" into the brew of conflicting ideas. Jury nullification was an American tradition, he said, which allowed juries to acquit defendants accused of violating unjust laws or laws that were unjustly applied. New England juries, for instance, often refused to convict abolitionists charged under the Fugitive Slave Act with harboring runaway slaves before the Civil War. In this case, said Garry, even if the jury believed that misdemeanors had been committed, the U.S. Constitution, in guaranteeing free speech and assembly, trumped the California state criminal code. If the state code was misused to curtail First Amendment rights, then the jury had the obligation to uphold federal constitutional rights.

It was radical ground he was treading on and he fired off all the theatrical flourishes. He referred to the defendants as "these demonstrators, God bless them." He quoted from the words inscribed on the Statue of Liberty.

He reminded the jury that "This beautiful country of ours was founded by leaders who were outlaws."

For three and a half days, they deliberated, twelve hours each day. Late in the evening of March 28, 1969, they returned to a tense and expectant courtroom to deliver their verdict: Not guilty. The defendants and all their supporters exploded with joy and relief. Not guilty. The prosecution's decision to escalate the charges in order to send a message to future demonstrators had backfired.

Surely the performance of the undercover agents failed to impress the jury. With all their numbers the agents never managed to penetrate the steering committee where any evidence of a true conspiracy might have been discovered.

"In the interviews we conducted afterwards," recalls Segal, "the jurors all said they believed we had conspired to close down the induction center. They did not believe we had conspired to commit these misdemeanors—the trespass and resisting arrest . . . A lot of what happened certainly grew from what we (on the steering committee) established. But classifying that stuff as being 'planned' has a connotation of having a lot more consciousness about it than what actually happened . . .

"And they bought the jury nullification argument: that the case was being prosecuted for the purpose of chilling our rights to free speech and assembly . . . It was quite an achievement from a legal practitioners point of view."

As the rest of the Oakland Seven celebrated into the night, Segal was escorted back to his cell in Alameda County. "What happened, man, what happened?" they asked him as he passed through the seventh-floor walkway. "Not guilty!" And the whole cell block erupted in cheers.

Chapter 8

Encountering the Empire

Dear Sam and Sarah,

It's not that Bugsy gave much thought beforehand to bringing the revolution into the federal prison system. He did, however, carry some essential ingredients. As a student at Roosevelt University, he began calling himself a Marxist in the early '60s before anyone had even heard of Vietnam. An urban commuter school near Grant Park in the bustling Chicago Loop, Roosevelt provided fertile ground for leftist thought. It was the kind of place you might likely meet the son of a packinghouse worker still active in the Communist Party or a radical foreign student from Brazil, seething over the poverty in his nation's shantytowns. These were exactly the people who schooled Segal in his early college years. He honed his politics at the student paper, *The Roosevelt Torch*, a hotbed of radicalism constantly under attack from conservatives in the Business School and from worried officials in the administration. "We figured we weren't doing our job," he recalls, "if at least once a semester there wasn't a committee from the Business School to reform the *Torch*."

Years later when Segal arrived at Safford, he came with an organizer's mind and an organizer's eyes. That mind-set, to me, was a thoroughly novel concept. I came to prison with survival mind. I surveyed the place cautiously, trying to figure out how to best get along. Bugsy's thoughts occupied a different strata altogether. Here's Oscar Sanchez from East L.A. and I would think, "What a good guy, friendly, affable, a veteran of prison culture, and a good teacher, besides." Bugsy would think, "What a natural leader. What could I do, what set of incentives could I offer, what appeal could I make to his intellect to nudge him in the direction of political activism?" Here's Sisco selling some kind of ripped-off contraband in the mess hall and I would think, "What a hustler, but what a lovable teddy bear." Bugsy too would see the hustler in Jerry Sisco and think, "How might that man use his talent and street savvy to further the revolution?"

So shortly after settling into Dorm 1, not far from my own bunk 46, Bugsy began assessing the situation in ways that had never remotely entered my mind. "I thought we ought to at least try to figure out," he said, "if there was an ability to organize and politicize some of the inmates." He began looking for opportunities to introduce subtle changes into the prison environment, all the while pushing inmates to consider the unthinkable—to push them slowly towards the brink of revolutionary thought.

Just down the row from Bugsy was Patrick Bryan, a slim nineteen-year-old kid who had followed the same path as Greg Nelson: on his eighteenth birthday he had paid a visit to the attorney general's office in San Francisco and presented a paper explaining why he would not so much as register for the draft. I believe it was Patrick with whom Bugsy first shared his subversive ideas for stirring up the pot in the prison camp.

Bryan was a military brat, a kid who had traveled the world from base to base: from San Angelo, Texas, to Japan, from Pennsylvania to France, from Oklahoma to Fort Wainwright in Alaska and finally to the Bay Area in California. His father's career spanned from the Second World War to Vietnam. Lt. Col. Frank Dean Bryan was a Quartermaster—"Sustainer of Armies" according to the Quartermaster's Creed—an officer in Logistical Support in the U.S. Army Transportation Corps. That's why the family ended up on the West Coast. It was the Oakland Army Base Terminal that provided the primary supply line to ports like Da Nang and Cam Ranh Bay in South Vietnam.

The idea of war hovered over Patrick even as a child. "You're always preparing for war in a military environment," he recalls. "In France at the height of the Cold War, my father was off playing intense war games. Sometimes they would go on Defense Readiness and call an 'alert status.' They would grab my father out in the middle of the night and get everything ready for combat. I was always aware of what could potentially become World War III.

"My dad was in West Texas when he enlisted in the Great Cause. He spent World War II in Europe and for most of his career he remained—like many in his generation—convinced of the Great Cause: in the war against Germany, in the Cold War, in standing up against the Evil Empire.

"I don't know if he believed in the Vietnam War, but people in the military also have allegiance to the institution. It's like the Marine Corps slogan, Semper Fi, always faithful, forever loyal. My dad's allegiance was to the army, to the institution, and the army was good. That army had freed a people and that army, in his experience, was a positive force. You can compare it to the church. The church can make mistakes; the church can be imperfect, but the loyalty remains. To his last days, he was an army guy."

You can imagine what kind of pain the entire family suffered when Patrick began questioning the war for which his father was shipping materiel to supply the troops. Patrick got in with the wrong crowd—the art and drama crowd—at his high school in Pleasant Hill just outside of Berkeley. He and his sweetheart, Gayle Garver, would cut class, borrow a car or hitchhike the eighteen miles to Berkeley to attend lectures or drama productions. All the resources for rebellion against the military ethic were nearby. In Berkeley there was the War Resisters League, the Free Speech Movement, the civil rights movement. In "that subversive organization called the public library," he discovered the Central Committee for Conscientious Objectors.

"With Dad," he says, "there was no discussion. In my home life, it was classical: he was the officer; I was supposed to be the obedient son. On Vietnam, I was just wrong. End of discussion. My father was not engaging; he did not explain things. He was not going to discuss things.

"By senior year of high school, it was clear the path I would be taking. I was over the edge and both my parents had given up on me. My father was fed up and, for me, I didn't care. My father was out of my life. He was an angry guy, but there was nothing he could do about it. We had the usual argument one night before I even finished high school and I said, 'That's it.' I left. I went off to friends in Berkeley and never even graduated."

Events in the year before the trial followed the same stormy pattern that marked his departure from home. He tried to block the shipment of napalm to Vietnam with a group called the Port Chicago Peace Vigil. He knocked on doors all over the East Bay with Vietnam Summer. He heard Bugsy speak at Provo Park in Berkeley the day before the rallies began at the Oakland Induction Center. He showed up next day for the peaceful demonstration in downtown Oakland. On all of these endeavors, Gayle accompanied him.

She was not with him, however, on the second day—the day the violence began during Stop the Draft Week. "I was involved with this guy who had strong opinions about what I should do," says Gayle Bryan. (The couple married shortly after Patrick's release from prison.) "We went the first day—the peaceful day—but decided not to go the second day. Then he lied to me and went where he shouldna been. He got his face smashed in." "If you were unlucky enough to get pushed down to the ground," says Patrick, "the Oakland cops used the tools at their disposal: mace, clubs, boots." When he returned to Gayle that afternoon—bleeding—the truth came out.

The Farm Workers

The future affinity with Jeff Segal, however, stemmed not from the blood Bryan left on Oakland's streets but from the couple's decision to work with Cesar Chavez and the United Farm Workers Organizing Committee. The Farm Workers aspired to bring dignity to the hardest working, most underpaid, most unprotected, most invisible workers in the American workforce. "We the Farm Workers of America," stated the preamble to the union's constitution, "have tilled the soil, sown the seeds, and harvested the crops. We have provided food in abundance for the people in the cities, the nation and the world but have not had sufficient food for our children." Many of the workers were the kind of guys—with roots in Zacatecas or Michoacan—who ended up with a jail sentence in Safford. They fed the country in return for barely subsistence wages, a bunk bed in a rundown dormitory, and a sometimes murky immigration status.

Chavez, a devout Catholic and equally devout student of Gandhi, created a movement that blended union organizing with civil rights and a religious campaign for social justice. As such, the union's headquarters in Delano was deluged with youthful volunteers. Gayle and Patrick hooked up with the grape boycott in Oakland, shuttled back and forth to Delano, then traveled to New York, Kansas City, St Louis, and L.A. as part of a massive operation to use the boycott as a weapon to force growers to recognize the union. The volunteers got five dollars a week along with their room and board.

With the Farm Workers—at least in its early years—Bryan sensed a level of organization he never experienced during his short time in the antiwar movement. Chavez first learned his trade as a grassroots organizer with the Community Service Organization, a group founded by Fred Ross. Ross, in turn, had worked closely with Saul Alinsky, the recognized genius of neighborhood and grassroots organizing from Chicago. Together the two had virtually written the book on tactics and strategies for organizing the poor and disenfranchised.

For a year before his draft conviction, Bryan came into contact with many of those who had faced the raw power brought to bear in isolated regions of rural California: picketers—followed by local cops and rival Teamsters—sometimes beaten, often harassed by arbitrary court injunctions. In the cities he met the Old Left: communist longshoremen and electrical workers who truly believed in their hearts in the spirit of workers' solidarity. They were the Farm Workers' staunchest supporters. Mostly he was steeped in the details of organizing: picketing at Safeway for the grape boycott, reaching out to churchgoers, doing precinct work, and going door to door for voter registration.

Bryan was awed by the charisma of Cesar Chavez who came to his draft trial and even visited him at Safford. But he was most impressed—perhaps this came from his military upbringing—by the attention to detail and the level of organization. "I realized the only way to significant social change," he says, "was to get at the grassroots. For that you need framework and mind-set. You need to develop talent. You need training, discipline, and leadership. When I worked with the UFW, I thought, 'These people have their act together. They're gonna rock the world.'

"I came to Safford," he said, "a bit taken with myself and my organizing skills. I was ready to change the world. If you volunteer to go to prison, you can be effectively silenced. But you ask yourself how do you carry on the struggle from the inside? I believed we were gonna carry on."

Band-Aids and Peanut Butter

Bugsy determined early on that making himself useful to other inmates was an essential first step to organizing in prison. He did little things to motivate fellow prisoners to seek him out. Even in Alameda County he had taken extensive notes on the background of jurors who were rejected at his own trial. Those people returned to the jury pool and were eligible to serve on other trials. Segal would return each evening to the cell block and share his information with inmates who had upcoming trials. Most of the inmates had public defenders who had neither the time nor inclination to do research on each juror. Bugsy could give cell block brothers the heads-up on jurors who might reveal their prejudices under interrogation by the Oakland Seven's legal team. That knowledge and his willingness to share it made him a popular man on the seventh tier and a respected one as well.

Following the trial in Oakland, Segal's radical reputation followed him all the way to Safford, then stuck with him after he arrived. Segal, the Red. The guards—having learned in advance of his notoriety—referred to him as "The Commissar." That, he believes, actually helped his cause. "As time went by, I discovered that some of my best advertising came from the guards. I learned this afterwards because guys that I became friendly with told me that one or the other guards would tell them not to associate with me because I was a troublemaker. So that led a number of folks to say, 'Hey, maybe I need to talk to this guy.'"

Nevertheless, Segal took pains to take care of the details. Band-aids, for instance. Derrick, the med tech assistant in the health clinic treated prisoners with disdain, tended to discount our ailments and pains, and sometimes attributed our illnesses to illegal drug use. Going on sick call almost always ended in humiliation. The MTA was universally despised by inmates across all ethnic groups and universally avoided except as a last resort.

Bugsy found in this an organizing opportunity. He began collecting Band-aids and aspirin from outside contacts. Then inmates began supplying him because they found out Bugsy was distributing free medical supplies. Little boxes of gauze or rolls of adhesive tape missing from the prison clinic were likely to end up in Bugsy's locker. "I had a little dispensary," he said, "for guys who didn't want to go to The Man."

Then there were snacks. After Segal started working in the bakery, his locker became a distribution center for things like peanut butter, saltines, and extra cookies that might easily be sneaked out of the kitchen. Those commodities might not measure up to the kind of jobs, for instance, that a Chicago politician could dole out in a precinct ward, but the cookies were appreciated all the same.

So was the tutoring. Several inmates were studying for GED exams and Segal made himself available to help them out. "We were reviewing math," recalls Segal, "and one evening we were dealing with conversion from U.S. standard measuring units to metric. I think maybe it was Freddy Flores. He'd been dealing drugs on the streets of Albuquerque before he got busted. We were doing some little math exercises converting pounds to kilos when all of sudden he stops short. 'Sonuvabitch!' he says. 'The sons of bitches were giving me pounds and charging me for kilos.' He had just figured out how massively his suppliers had been ripping him off. Of course in my role as academic, I had to seize the teachable moment. 'You see? You see why it's important to know math?'"

Perhaps Bugsy's most-valued service stemmed from his role, at least for a time, as the principal source of a very critical item: yeast. "As a baker, I would get like a one pound cake of yeast and so it was no big deal to shave off a couple of ounces. It would just take a little bit longer for the bread to rise. I gave it out to whoever wanted it as long as I had it."

The end result of course was homebrew, sometimes called "pruno" by its manufacturers, sometimes misnamed "applejack." A few potato peels, a little sugar, a little yeast, and a little time for fermentation—it could produce a potent concoction, indeed. I tried it just once. "Echa un pisto, Ricardo," Ramirez told me in the darkness near the right field line of the ball field. "Take a shot." One "pisto" left me short of breath, embarrassed, and nearly choking; the stuff was over my head. Some of the guys were left reeling after a few chugs, a few "tragos." You could forget where you were. The still operators were often the pillars of the community—Sisco was always getting yeast from Bugsy and so was Sanchez.

In providing these services and in quietly becoming a central player in the social life of the camp, Bugsy carried a much bigger picture in mind. He hoped to parlay that social position, that respect within the community that came from taking care of business into political leverage. He would be sought out, yes, but he would also be listened to.

He met Patrick Bryan in the first days. "He had some significant organizing experience with the Farm Workers," remembers Segal. "It was easy enough once we got familiar with each other to sit down and think some things through. Here was a circumstance which neither of us were particularly familiar with but for which we could apply organizing principles into a new situation."

One of the more subtle if more ambitious items on the political agenda was to strike a blow at the heart of the market economy that existed in prison.

"Patrick and I, and a couple of others," says Segal, "we decided on some principles we wanted to adhere to if we were gonna have some impact on the lives of the rest of the inmates . . . We decided—however effective or not—we would go after the base of the inmate economy."

The inmate economy was a highly capitalistic one based on the cigarette currency I had first witnessed at the Smith Road facility in Denver County. You want a burrito instead of a bologna sandwich? That can be arranged for a couple of packs of Camels. You want a tattoo? You might need a carton of Marlboros. A couple of packs of smokes could get you a slightly more personalized haircut in the barbershop. You want to get high? That can be arranged as well. "Pacas hablan, Ricardo." Cigarette packs talk, ése. Money talks.

"Several of us," recalls Segal, "decided that we weren't gonna do that, that we weren't gonna buy and sell stuff. To whatever degree we could, we would try to foster some kind of solidarity." So the yeast was free. The Band-aids were free. Joel Armstrong, the barber, stopped charging for a cut above the normal prison hairdo.

I don't know how many people understood what the overall plan was, but for the Red Baker, these things represented tiny steps towards a hopefully brighter future.

Building Ties to the Free World

Integral to organizing plans was the need to nurture networks of support on the outside. Dana Rae had already pioneered this art, using his congressional guardian angel to get him his beloved guitar. He had also established contact with several peace groups in Tucson who came to visit some of the resisters on weekends.

Bugsy and Patrick both understood the advantages to this setup and sought to expand the existing network. They both sensed the profound isolation of the average inmate lost in the wasteland of the Bureau of Prisons. They both realized how our separation from the outside world contributed to a debilitating sense of powerlessness. Like Dana Rae, they understood the power of an outsider from the free world who could bring a spotlight to the workings of a normally closed system.

Gayle Bryan had moved to Tucson in the winter of 1969 to be close to Patrick and to offer any support she could. She had no money, no job, no friends. Just a contact, Lisa Spray, from the Central Committee for Conscientious Objectors (CCCO). "It was youthful love" that brought her down there, she says. She drove down from Pleasant Hill with Patrick's folks who were on their way to visit family in Texas.

"I barely knew them," she says in remembering the painfully long, awkward drive from California. "They didn't speak to me. Our perspective on everything was totally alien to each other. I didn't know them. They didn't know me. But they blamed his politics on me." 'Whatever you do, don't marry him,' his mother told her in a burst of unexpected communication. 'He's just like his father.'"

Despite the endless miles of silence, the mere fact they let her in the car represented the first step, the first reaching out in a long healing process between father and son. (It was a step never taken by Greg's father, Richard Nelson.)

The Bryans dropped Gayle off at an old U-shaped trailer court on Tinsdale Street near the University of Arizona. They immediately called Gayle's parents with an urgent warning and an alarming description of her new surroundings. Lisa's residence was located in the back of the U right next to an unlit alleyway. "My parents called me right up and told me to 'get out of there right away; you're going to be raped.'"

Gayle survived those first nights in the trailer court, was welcomed warmly by the peace community in Tucson, and would play a key role in the prisoners' support network. "It always seemed odd," she recalls, " that we weren't smuggling things in. The prisoners were smuggling things out. We didn't have anything, and in the winter we were freezing. They smuggled gloves out for us. You'd have visitors walking out the door in military (prison) garb." Patrick gave Gayle his jacket since he could easily replace it from the laundry where he was assigned to work duty.

Kept warm and army fashionable, courtesy of the Bureau of Prisons, she visited Safford every weekend and delivered messages from inside the prison. She spoke about our presence at local antiwar rallies. She welcomed the wives of prisoners who came to live in Tucson. She kept in touch with Frank Buismato, the official visitor from the CCCO. (Since World War II days the CCCO had negotiated an agreement with the BOP to allow a representative inside, a sort of Red Cross–type arrangement in which he could communicate with draft objectors and check up on the treatment they were receiving. Frank was allowed to walk inside the compound until, I learned later, he made too much a nuisance out of himself. After that his visits were restricted to the visiting area.) She contacted a Tucson lawyer. "I learned from the Farm Workers," she said, "that the first thing you did was to find a sympathetic lawyer. And they were always out there."

Bugsy also kept in touch with lawyers, and carried on regular correspondence with at least three of them. There was the Tucson legal firm that Gayle had connected with, and there were higher profile ones as well. The Center for Constitutional Rights, prominent for its role in defending the civil rights movement in the South was handling his draft violation appeal. Fay Stender, a partner with Charles Garry, was becoming widely known for her defense of various Black Panthers in the Bay Area. As Bugsy was sending her letters from Safford, she catapulted onto the national stage early in 1970 through her defense of George Jackson. Jackson, an inmate in California's Soledad Prison would soon electrify the nation with his revolutionary writing from inside Soledad's maximum security wing before he was shot dead in 1971.

Omar Rios, the caseworker in the Prison Ad Building, was quite aware of the extent of Bugsy's correspondence with this impressive array of lawyers. He was, after all, reading Bugsy's letters, especially Segal's descriptions of life inside the prison. Periodically he would call Segal in to challenge him and ask him why he would write anything negative about the Swift Trail prison camp. Rios knew, however, he was on shaky ground as were Lt. Lanier and Camp Administrator Kennedy. They had been accustomed to making arbitrary decisions in the remote Arizona desert without some slick San Francisco lawyer second-guessing them. They could look over Bugsy's shoulders by reading his letters but they also knew some aggressive, nationally known attorneys were looking over their shoulders as well. They were naturally hesitant to make any decision likely to bring in adverse publicity.

Subversive Literature

So censorship, or rather free access to radical literature, became a key issue in the attempt to organize within Safford. When the time came, Bugsy had already lined up his legal guns on the outside.

Censorship tended to be quite capricious at Safford and generally left to the whim of whichever guards happened to draw the night shift. I assure you they didn't read with any particular zeal, but pictures would often attract their attention. Frumess (Richard Frumess) once sent me a Picasso sketchbook full of line drawings, some of which contained some innocent-looking nude subjects. Picasso didn't make the cut. On the other hand, they allowed in a copy of *Soul on Ice*, Eldridge Cleaver's scathing indictment of race relations in America, which included a call for violent revolution as well as something of a rationalization for raping white women. I doubt Officers Kenski or Thomas read any of the contents once they noticed that the cover described the work as a "spiritual and intellectual autobiography."

Segal had experienced the censor at the Alameda County Jail during the Oakland Seven trial. He had obtained a subscription to *Ramparts Magazine*, the leading left-wing periodical of the era, but somehow the copies never arrived at his seventh-floor cell block. One of his lawyers hauled the sheriff to court, subpoenaed all the voluminous material that had been withheld from Segal, and began his cross-examination. "What is your objection to this?" he asked, as he pulled a *Ramparts* out of a pile of Bugsy's undelivered mail. The jailer obviously hadn't read any of it but as he leafed through the pages, he chanced upon an ad with small reproductions of artwork for sale, including a tiny copy of a Modigliani nude. The sheriff pointed the ad out as a rationalization for censorship. "The judge thought it was so stupid," says Segal, "that he ordered the sheriff to give me every bit of my mail."

With this success recently under his belt, Segal addressed a letter to the *Monthly Review Press* shortly after he arrived at Safford. *Monthly Review's* editor Paul Sweezy, a Harvard economics professor, would later be described by the *New York Times* as "the nation's leading Marxist intellectual and publisher during the Cold War and the McCarthy era." The first issue of his magazine came out in 1949 with its lead article "Why Socialism?" by Albert Einstein.

Bugsy's request evidently moved the people at *Monthly Review*: he asked them for books—as many as they could spare. "I think my letter initiated the prison program they had there for a number of years," says Segal. "They gave out free books to prisoners everywhere." Segal had to spar with Rios on occasion to have the books sent in, but he won nearly every battle, unless there were cartoons or pictures involved. Soon his locker was overrun by dozens of books coming in from New York City.

A Lending Library

He now had something much more subversive than peanut butter and yeast to share with his fellow inmates. He now had a little Marxist lending library that soon began circulating among some of the inmates throughout the camp.

That library represented a new beginning in my political education. During the '60s and '70s, virtual colleges—underground universities for the study of revolution—had sprung up throughout the prison system in America: at Folsom and San Quentin, Soledad and Attica. For me, the Marxist study group that formed around Bugsy and his library was irresistible. Here we were—right under the noses of the prison authorities—reading, examining, talking revolutionary politics. It was far more intoxicating than the homebrew Oscar was bringing in from dark corners around the compound.

The sense of rebellion wasn't the only attraction. I was twenty-two, thrown into a cauldron of competing ideas with a multitude of twisting life paths to choose from. The feverish youthful search for identity does not stop at the edge of prison walls. I was still searching. The readings Bugsy offered opened up new vistas to explore. On the street I had picked up a couple of left-wing periodicals and found them impossible to digest. Every third word was "bourgeois" or "imperialist," or "revisionist." Bugsy, on the contrary, tended to speak plain English, and the stuff he gave us to read tended, likewise, to avoid orthodox rhetoric. Joining the Great Study Group Conspiracy was invigorating and stimulating. It helped fight off the numbness that sometimes envelopes prison life. It wasn't a bad way to do time.

Though Bugsy was clearly the mentor, the first book given me—a book that marked a turning point in my political thinking—came from Bradley Littlefield. Brad was a short, chubby, very affable, sometimes self-deprecating, often quite brilliant kid from Tucson. He was one of those draft card burners whose symbolic speech had incurred the wrath of both Congress and the justice system and got him sentenced to eighteen months at Safford. Once inside, he had gained local notoriety, when, as a cook, he had turned out some of the worst, rock-hard biscuits the camp had ever experienced. Kendall and Patrick smuggled a few out of the kitchen, ambushed Brad in the dorm, and pelted him with his own miserable creation.

Bradley had cornered me a couple of times in Dorm 1 and at the chow hall, trying to explain his position on one of the great debates, one of the great divides within the antiwar movement. It was the liberals versus the radicals and one of the burning questions that emerged was this: Exactly why did we get ourselves involved in Vietnam in the first place?

The liberals said it was a big mistake. We misjudged the commitment of the communists and their willingness to endure punishment. We misread the extent of nationalist sentiment within the communist camp. We underestimated the venality and incompetence of our South Vietnamese allies. We compensated for our lack of popularity in the countryside by unleashing an indiscriminate barrage of air power. We had no idea how long this war might drag out and how many lives it might cost. In trying to do the Vietnamese a favor, our miscalculations and blind ignorance had turned the endeavor into a nightmare. The war was immoral, to be sure, even an atrocity of needless bloodshed, but nevertheless, it was a mistake. We had stumbled into the swamp by accident.

With much of this critique, the Left had no quarrel, but the origins of our military campaign in Vietnam, they said, was no mistake. The war was built into the system. It was a natural and inevitable extension of decades-old policies designed to protect and expand the American empire.

Empire?

What empire? What array of possessions and colonies could possibly afford us the status of empire? Guam? The Virgin Islands? You've got to be kidding.

Nevertheless, the implications of the radical position were not very comforting. If half the world, as they claimed, truly belonged to America then might we be condemned to war after endless war in defense of the empire? Like the Roman legions scattered in the far corners of Europe and North Africa, might our soldiers remain dispersed throughout the world for decades to come? If the radicals were right, the war in Vietnam would not be the last.

I had never had reason to consider these implications, but Brad Littlefield, in his good-natured manner could get pretty dogged when it came to political dialogue. One afternoon he pressed a book into my hands and half insisted, half begged that I read it. *The Tragedy of American Diplomacy* was written by William Appleman Williams, a University of Wisconsin professor who had attracted a large flock of loyal graduate students and exercised considerable influence on the New Left.

Necessarily, the framework through which I followed his line of reasoning had been rooted in the basic fundamentals of Mr. Jordan's and Mr. Walker's high school history classes at George Washington High School. That framework included an orthodox perspective of our founding fathers: Washington and Jefferson, Adams and Franklin had transformed themselves in less than a generation from loyal British subjects to rebels against one of the greatest empires the world had ever known.

Tea taxes and stamp taxes surely came into play, but in their hearts, the founders recoiled at the thought of being ruled from afar—being ruled by foreigners from 3,000 miles across the sea. The shot heard round the world reverberated not only because it represented a blow against the king's tyranny but a blow, as well, against the primary imperial power of the day. It represented the modern world's first anticolonial revolution. Our heritage, our origins, and founding documents placed us squarely at odds with nations that dared colonize the world. True, we had picked up a few colonies—the

Philippines and Puerto Rico—at the turn of the twentieth century, but that period represented merely an aberration.

By contrast, British possessions had circled the globe. French-held territories spanned the Mediterranean, and reached across the Pacific. British West Africa, British Guiana, British East Africa. French Equatorial Africa, French Guiana, French Indochina—the very names left no doubt as to who was in charge. These were real empires. Compared to these, America's meager little colonies and territories amounted to no empire at all. With a couple of minor exceptions, we had remained true to our anticolonial heritage.

An Empire without Colonies

To this widely held American view, William Appleman Williams offered a sober and persistent challenge: You needn't have colonies or possessions, he asserted, in order to amass a great empire. You needn't appoint viceroys or governors; you needn't create a foreign civil service bureaucracy to run an empire.

What you need is economic control. What you need is dominance over the financial levers of subordinate states. "When an advanced industrial nation," he wrote, "plays or tries to play a controlling and one-sided role in the development of a weaker economy, then the policy of the more powerful country can with accuracy and candor only be described as imperial."

He quoted one presidential economic advisor from the 1930s: "Our economic frontiers," stated William Culbertson, "are no longer coextensive with our territorial frontiers." "No one ever offered," added Williams, "a more succinct description and interpretation of the single most important aspect of twentieth-century American diplomacy."

The mechanisms of economic control have surely undergone considerable change since the 1960s when Williams offered his startling analysis of U.S. history. In those days when America produced its own radios and telephones, its own punch presses and stamping machines, the formula for economic dominance was perhaps a little more straightforward than today: take an emerging country struggling to dig itself out of feudal and colonial poverty. Sell it American grain from Iowa and Kansas to feed its people. Sell it steel from Pittsburgh and Cleveland to build its railroads. Extend to it foreign aid with which to buy products from American companies. Offer it loans so its middle class can purchase the items necessary to achieve modernity. Shower it with investment capital channeling development into desserts for American consumers—into the export of chocolate or sugar or coffee. The earnings, from Dole pineapples, for example, or Standard Brand bananas would be paid out as dividends to American stockholders. Credit, debt, imports and exports, investment capital—control these things and you can maintain the grotesque imbalances of power, wealth, and resource distribution that have long characterized the imperial systems of the planet. Control these things and you can dispense with the trappings of direct political power. Pacas hablan, ése.

To this new definition of empire, Williams added a couple of corollaries. In Mr. Jordan's tenth-grade history class I had heard about the great historian Frederick Jackson Turner who advanced the thesis that the vitality of American democracy and the source of its prosperity stemmed from the country's continuous westward expansion into the vast frontier. It was us Westerners at the cutting edge of U.S. history; we were where the action was.

While acknowledging this dynamic, Williams emphasized the economic pressures that pushed and prodded the country ever outward, ever westward. Further, once that westward march had reached the ocean, once the destiny of the country had manifested itself on the shores of the Pacific and begun filling in the open spaces between the coasts, the pressure for continuous expansion and economic growth did not cease. Williams quoted leader after leader, decade after decade concerning the perpetual need for new investment opportunities and new markets:

> "As our manufacturing capacity largely exceeds the wants of home consumption, we shall either have to curtail the same by shutting up a great many establishments or we shall have to create a fresh outlet for export." Iron Age, 1877

> "American factories are making more than the American people can use; American soil is producing more than they can consume. Fate has written our policy for us; the trade of the world must and shall be ours." Albert J. Beveridge, senator from Indiana, 1897

> "Our industries have expanded to such a point that they will burst their jackets if they cannot find a free outlet to the markets of the world . . . Our domestic markets no longer suffice. We need foreign markets." Woodrow Wilson, 1912

> "We must finance our exports by loaning foreigners the wherewithal to pay for them . . . Without such loans we would have the spectacle of our neighbors famishing for goods which were rotting in our warehouses as unusable surplus." John Foster Dulles, 1928

> "We have got to see that what the country produces is used and is sold under financial arrangements which make its production possible...You must look to foreign markets." Dean Acheson, assistant secretary of state, 1944

Blessed as the country was with amber waves of grain; blessed as it was with a genius for industrial production, its economic arteries clogged periodically without an outlet to the outside world.

What the nation required to keep the arteries flowing, according to Williams, was the Open Door. Originally the term referred to a U.S. policy toward China in 1900. All trading nations would agree to compete on an equal basis for Chinese markets and concomitantly a prostrate and helpless China would "agree" to allow all the economic giants equal access to her markets. Williams extended this particular policy of Open Door into a global metaphor reaching even into contemporary history. Some British historians labeled the concept "free trade imperialism" or "informal empire." "Based on the assumption of . . . 'America's economic supremacy,'" wrote Williams, "the Open Door was designed to clear the way and establish the conditions under which America's preponderant economic power would extend the American system throughout the world without the embarrassment and inefficiency of traditional colonialism."

As long as subordinate countries behaved themselves and played by the rules, the informal empire functioned quite smoothly, thank you, without the need for armies of occupation or military coups. It was only when struggling nations searched for paths of development outside the boundaries of the Open Door, only when they jeopardized debt payments or crossed the line respecting private property rights of the powerful and privileged that we had to orchestrate a military coup or send in the marines.

A Pattern of Intervention

Such was the case in Guatemala where a hapless president dared to distribute uncultivated land to his nation's dispossessed. The title to the unused land belonged the United Fruit Company which sealed President Jacobo Arbenz's fate. He was deposed unceremoniously in a CIA-engineered coup in 1954.

Such was the case in Cuba where—before he turned to the Soviets—Fidel Castro first expelled the American Mafia from Havana's casinos and confiscated large tracts of agricultural land owned by U.S. companies. For his independence, he won the enmity of the United States—replete with proxy invasions, assassination attempts, economic sabotage, and embargoes—for the next fifty years.

Such was the case in 1965 when President Johnson dispatched 20,000 plus marines and paratroopers to the Dominican Republic to ensure that the reformist president Juan Bosch would never return to power after a military coup had stripped him of his office two years before.

Such was the case in Haiti, Nicaragua, and the Philippines, in Iran, the Congo, and Indonesia, all of whom attempted at one time or another to navigate a course independent of U.S. economic control.

And then there was Vietnam whose rebel leaders saw in the American model merely a continuation of the suffering their people had endured under the French.

Although the various spins, contexts, and meanings are fiercely contested today, most of the basic facts of these interventions have been confirmed over the years with the release of intelligence and State Department documents. Generally the purpose of those interventions stretched far beyond achieving access to a particular resource—to oil in the South China Sea or rubber in Binh Long Province. This was far too simple and mechanistic an explanation. Rather they were aimed instead at keeping the whole global playing field open for business.

For some on the Left this was old hat by 1969, but for me, the literature stashed in Bugsy's magic locker together with the revelations in Brad Littlefield's book offered a totally new perspective, a new window through which I viewed the world. They challenged me to peer beneath the Cold War rhetoric that rationalized every single aspect of American foreign policy—no matter how sordid—as a response to Soviet aggression. Certainly the fear of communist expansion was real and perhaps, on the part of many, the inclination towards empire was unconscious. Did politicians who bemoaned the "loss" of China, for instance, or who warned of the "loss" of Vietnam even realize that they were implying that China and Vietnam were ours to lose? Perhaps not. Nevertheless, I was learning to search beneath the fear for the hidden strains of self-interest, the smug embrace of the status quo, and the naked pursuit of economic privilege.

I would never claim any great depth of economic expertise. I slogged and struggled through some of the stuff Bugsy lent out. And I suppose the lens through which I viewed his material was colored by my surroundings. The faces, personalities, and life histories of my immediate neighbors made certain truths achingly clear. Flores and Ramirez, Armstrong and Watkins, Sanchez, Salter, and Begay—these guys all grew up on mean, heroin-infested streets in L.A. or El Paso, in impoverished villages in Guanajuato or Coahuila, or remote reservations in Arizona and New Mexico. There were no rich men in Safford save for one bewildered individual named Max Gitman busted on some shady embezzlement scheme.

It was plain for anyone to see. Justice in America exonerated—even celebrated—the pathological behaviors of those who sent us off to war, of those who accumulated vast wealth producing napalm jelly and phosphorus bombs in a defense complex that represented the single largest industry in the country. But find some lost soul in East L.A. sticking a needle in his arm and the courts would grind him to bits. Justice in America rested on a mountain of racial and social inequality. It was easier for a camel to go through the eye of a needle than for a rich man to end up in a U.S. prison.

From my vantage point at the bottom of the American barrel, the books in Bugsy's locker quickly began to resonate. In a rather short time, I came to believe that the Marxists, the New Leftists, and the radicals were right: we had transformed as a nation from a band of revolutionaries against the world's greatest empire—think Luke Skywalker—into the guardians of our own new and mighty empire.

As an American, I found this whole idea profoundly unsettling. As a Jew, I recoiled all the more. Jews and great empires never much got along. Though much of the world might think "pyramids" in its first Rorschach association to the Egyptian empire, the first reaction of Jews is never in doubt. We are instructed every year at Passover to taste bitter herbs and cry bitter tears in memory of the slavery and captivity to which we were bound. "Remember that you were once slaves in the land of Egypt" (Deuteronomy 15:15).

Though Greek civilization might conjure up images of democracy, beauty and soaring philosophical dialogue for much of the world, we Jews are reminded every year at Hannukah it was the Greeks who erected a statue of Zeus in the Temple and who desecrated the holy sanctuary with the blood of pigs. It was the forcible Hellenization of the world—cosmopolitan though they believed themselves to be—that incited the Maccabbees to begin their guerilla war against the empire.

Though much of the world might recall Rome as a builder of roads and an empire that bestowed a republican form of government upon the world, the memory of Rome for Jews invokes, instead, the final destruction of the Second Temple and the forced exile of the Jewish people throughout the ancient world—the beginning of an endlessly painful diaspora.

Surely there were Jews capable of identifying with a great empire—Henry Kissinger never had any trouble—but it would require a great many mental, ethical, or theological contortions to reach that point.

I considered my resistance to the war an act of patriotism.

I didn't quite know what to do or where to go with this newfound understanding; I had no idea how to integrate these studies into my life. But as the patterns and connections fell increasingly into place, as the need for systemic change became increasingly apparent, the word "revolution" began to creep into my vocabulary.

Chapter 9

L.A.

Dear Sam and Sarah,

One by one during that same spring of 1969, more characters from the L.A. Resistance began emerging from the shadows of L.A. County Jail and arriving inside the compound at Safford. Dana Rae, with inside access to the prison files, anticipated each of them before they even showed up. Paul Barnes. Tod Friend. Marty Harris. Art Zack. Bob Siegel. Geoff Fishman. The main pipeline of draft offenders into Safford originated in Los Angeles and so the group known as the L.A. Resistance became the core of the resistance community in Safford.

They were distinctly L.A. If East Coast resisters favored coats and ties, slacks and Ivy League shirts, short, well-groomed hair, the folks in L.A. were quick to embrace the countercultural hippie look—at least before their hair was shorn and military fatigues issued at Safford. If East Coast resisters attracted as their supporters Ivy League intellectuals—Chomsky and the Rev. Sloane Coffin—the L.A. Resistance tended to attract rock bands and Hollywood writers. If East Coast resisters steeped themselves in the philosophy of Marcuse, the analysis of C. Wright Mills, and later on the writings of Lenin, the L.A. guys more likely read Timothy Leary's *Psychedelic Experience* or *The Autobiography of a Yogi*. They left quite an impact on our prison culture. They were a colorful bunch—crazy in their own peculiar way—and slowly, imperceptibly at first, the political and cultural climate began to change with their presence.

The peace movement at UCLA spawned the early roots of the L.A. Resistance. The man responsible for its launching was Professor Donald Kalish, chairman of the Philosophy Department, an earnest teacher who regularly gave out his home phone number to everyone in his classes with instructions to call him any time, day or night. He was just beginning to gray, a tall man with unkempt hair who looked a little like Einstein. Winter Dellenbach, another formative figure in the organization, recalls that "he was known back then as a luminary of the peace movement. At the big marches they would put these people literally in the front row behind a banner so that when the media had their cameras on them they would see sober, respectable people in business suits. God, yes, they would dress up. He was of that echelon, of people like Benjamin Spock and the Rev. Sloane Coffin."

Dellenbach grew up in the small working-class, citrus-growing town of Pomona about an hour east of UCLA. As a kid, she had been a "Nixon Girl" during the 1960 presidential campaign. Dressed in white skirts and white blouses, wearing red, white, and blue ribbons attached to straw hats and sewn diagonally across their chests, the teenage "Nixon Girls" got to shake the candidate's hand at the mall just outside of town.

Despite that adolescent thrill, she yearned for something more than a small agricultural community by the time she graduated Pomona High School. "I had vague notions, very deeply felt notions that I wanted to discover in college the world of the mind, the world of the intellect. I thought if I became an art student, that those people got to be weird and odd and associate with all different kinds of people . . . I became part of the UCLA art department and it was everything I was looking for."

UCLA was no Berkeley but it was beginning to change in the mid-'60s. Don Kalish began holding silent vigils against the war once a week on a main walkway leading to the Student Union. Dellenbach soon began joining in. "It was about as mild as imaginable," she said.

Then one day in 1967 word went out that Dow Chemical—maker of napalm—had sent a corporate recruiter to the campus placement office. A small peace organization—the Vietnam Day Committee—set out to prevent the interviews. "The Vietnam Day Committee—holy cow—they were actually gonna have a sit-in. It was a huge leap what they did.

"I thought, well, if I believe in this, I should do something," recalls Dellenbach. "If I had beliefs about war and suffering and this corporation is getting rich off napalm, then I have to do something . . . I went over there just spontaneously. I walked in and sat in one of the chairs with about a dozen other people from the committee . . . In fact, the sit-in prevented anybody from being interviewed that day. The dean of students came in and said 'if you don't leave right now, you put yourself at risk of arrest and suspension from school. And we'll call your parents.' Everybody got up and walked out. And

I thought, 'Where are they going?' I mean this is their sit-in; why are they leaving? I thought it through. I sat there and I consciously thought it through. I can't not do something. And if somebody threatens me, that doesn't change the reasons that put me here. The (departure of the others) is not a reason to not do this."

Sitting Alone

"So I continued to sit there. I sat there until the place was gonna close for the day, 5:00. There was a lot of publicity; I mean it was on the news; it was a big deal—the first direct action at UCLA. I was the only one—within the administration's definition—at risk of being thrown out of school or put under arrest. But they didn't do that. I'm five foot four inches, 110 pounds. I'm a young cute coed. Blonde. And I'm wearing a miniskirt and Italian slingback heels—little short heels like three-quarters of an inch high like Jackie Kennedy used to wear. And fishnet stockings. Fashionable. It's what everybody was wearing. I mean they weren't gonna arrest some cute little coed sitting there all by herself with all that media—the TV, the *L.A. Times*—trained on the door of the placement center.

"Then the dean came back and said, 'We're closing now; it's closed. Nobody has been interviewed since this began. Are you planning to stay here for the night or are you gonna leave?' And I said, 'No, if it's closed, there's no point; I'm out of here.'"

When the Vietnam Day Committee was called in to face disciplinary hearings by the university, Dellenbach was not among those subpoenaed. She was never a member of the committee. The hearings were a mess. "It was a kangaroo court," says Dellenbach. "The administration was horrible, disgusting, and rude. The students were disorganized, rude, and really immature. I mean everybody was young and dumb and this was the first demonstration anybody had done. At one point a man stood up and it was Don Kalish, and he said, 'I wish that girl that was sitting in the other day were here.' And I stood up and said 'I am here. I'm that person.' And so that was that.

"As we walked out, he came up to me, and he says, 'Listen, can I take you out for a drink? I need to talk to you.' He took me to a big high-rise on Wilshire Blvd. in Westwood—a huge high-rise, very plush with all these business people and we had drinks, and he said, 'Listen, I have money from Martin Luther King's Vietnam Summer and I'm looking for a full-time organizer to open a draft resistance office in West L.A. I'd be willing to pay the rent on the office, pay the utilities, pay for the phone as long as is needed, and I would pay you $30 a week to work full-time and put it together.'"

A couple of others came in early to the mix. There was Jerry Palmer, from the physics department at UCLA, a big blond-haired guy with "twinkley eyes, a bouncy step and a Santa Claus demeanor." His political roots lay in UCLA's SDS, even, I'm told, with the faction sympathetic to Progressive Labor. To say that The Resistance clashed with SDS contains some truth, but the reality was far more complex. The reality included shades of differences shifting with the peculiarities of geography, the unique composition of groupings in different cities, and the chemistry of various personalities. Viewed from a national perspective, Palmer was not the only SDSer to play a role in the formation of The Resistance. He was handy and had a knack for fixing things around the office, "a genius," recalls Bob Zaugh. The group had trouble finding printing companies willing to run off antiwar literature so Palmer bought a printing press cheap—an aging A.B. Dick. It was just a big box of parts. He painstakingly assembled the miscellaneous parts and, together with Zaugh, the two gradually taught themselves how to run a press. It would soon become known as Peace Press, an institution that printed alternative literature for the next twenty years.

Sherna Gluck also found her way to the office on Braxton Street. She climbed the terra-cotta steps to the second story, opened the door, and saw Jerry Palmer doing silk screening on the floor, making the little red hands that became a symbol of The Resistance. She joined him that very moment—stencils and ink in hand—and soon made herself indispensable. A longtime activist in the anarcho-pacifist community, she was attracted to an organization whose very essence was defying authority.

"She wore wrap-around skirts and sandals and sleeveless blouses with beads—lots of beads and earrings," remembers Winter Dellenbach. "She ran two steps toward beatnik. Thank God for Sherna. Being a few years older, she was married, owned a house with her husband, Marvin, in Topanga Canyon, and had a level of experience that most of the rest of us didn't have. She was able to think in a way that we weren't so much able to think in because of her experience . . . She had ideas about how we could meet up with other people and I'm sure she was behind the idea of having meetings in the evenings with supporters—with grownup people with families and houses and mortgages. She was very good with strategy and thinking things through and she was key."

And so the office—"the Draft Resistance Office"—opened for business in the spring of 1967 in a beautiful old Spanish-style building in the heart of Westwood Village adjacent to the campus. David Harris, with his buddy, Dennis Sweeney, soon paid a visit from Palo Alto, and began talking to students in the Free Speech Area at UCLA. That's when things began to really kick in.

"Talk about an idea whose time has come," says Dellenbach. "There wasn't a male of that age anywhere who wasn't thinking about the draft. We became the 'L.A. Resistance.'... and once there was a place called L.A. Resistance, there was a place to go." An early core group of young men—Maizlish and Nelson, David Bolduc and Dennis Durby, Rich Profumo, Mike Swartz, and Jack Whitton began to pass through the doors. Malcolm Dundas, who'd already served his time in prison also appeared. "People just started to come in," says Dellenbach. "I mean the fact that we had an office, the fact that the office was a safe place to come to, the fact that there were always people there, that there was activity and energy and goals because we had the next draft card turn-in or the next speaking engagement—it was really happening. Louie Vitale and some of the ministers came in, people in the community, obviously students from UCLA and the West L.A. area, but also working-class people from Inglewood and Gardena and places like that. It was fabulous . . . I mean L.A. Resistance was the most amazing organization I have ever been involved with by far."

One of those eventually recruited into this beehive of activity was Bill Garaway, a UCLA transfer student in political science from Pepperdine. "We had been together as an organization for quite a few months," says Dellenbach, "and one day this guy walks in the office wearing huaraches, blue jeans, and a dark blue wool pea jacket. He had a big Zapata mustache and huge, huge brown eyes—almost like Rasputin brown eyes. He's very good looking. Extremely good looking. He walked in and introduced himself. 'Hi, I'm Bill Garaway and I just wanted to see what was happening.' And so he started to be around."

Garaway had traveled to Europe and North Africa in 1965 on one of those cheap student fares and by happenstance crossed paths in Algiers with an Indonesian journalist from a rather distinguished magazine. Curious as to the attitudes of a typical American student towards Vietnam, he interviewed Garaway at length. "I started telling him stuff I had read in the newspapers and heard on television," says Garaway. "He saw that I was completely ignorant on virtually everything. And so he started giving me the history of what happened."

That episode set in motion a whole series of chance encounters. At a UCLA teach-in on the war, David McReynolds of the War Resisters League challenged the crowd by declaring that the draft constituted involuntary servitude, that it was un-American and that no one should submit to it. At the back of the crowd, Garaway—somewhat casually—lit up his card, and dropped it into a trash can with a smoldering pile of other cards. When he heard of Bruce Dancis's plan to initiate the mass card burning at Sheep's Meadow in Central Park that spring, Garaway wrote the Cornell student and informed him, "I don't have my draft card because I burned it a while back, but you can put me on the list of people who turned them in."

Criterion for Organizing

That list is how David Harris got his name and that's why Harris and Sweeney called on him at his apartment in the "hippie house" in Ocean Park near the beach in Santa Monica. They had driven down from the Bay Area in Harris's aging Nash Rambler. It was the week after the police riot at Century City and the L.A. antiwar community was still in shock. Harris was looking for organizers for the nationwide draft card turn-in October 16. "The Resistance had one rule for its organizers," Harris wrote. "No one got anybody to do anything he wasn't doing himself. Convincing people to risk long imprisonment was a heavy responsibility, and the only insurance against bullshit was to make everyone put his own life on the line first."

At least on that criterion, Garaway was eminently qualified, but for the moment he had other plans. Harris departed from L.A. a bit discouraged even though he had sown a few seeds. Garaway left for the East Coast to explore grad school possibilities, which is why he found himself in New York for the October 16 draft card turn-in. Having already cut his ties with Selective Service, he was asked to speak at an auxiliary rally that day at Fordham University.

"Speech was the only class I ever got a D in in college," he remembers. "I couldn't stand up in front of large groups of people. I can't even think about how terrible and inarticulate I was. But just the fact that I had turned in my draft card and was risking arrest—it just kind of didn't matter what I said."

That moment proved a turning point; he soon agreed to return home and organize full-time for the L.A. Resistance. His area would extend through much of the Southwest—Southern California, Arizona, New Mexico, even southern Colorado. There was no hierarchy, no formal structure of leadership; in fact, any attempt at formal leadership and titles was conscientiously shunned. But Garaway soon emerged as the informal leader, the natural leader. His speaking talents blossomed from a college D to C for charismatic.

"Harris kind of gave his pitch to me, his standard rap," he said. "He was a pretty compelling speaker; he was excellent. After a little while, I had it down, and I could make his speeches almost as good as he could. Once I had my rap down, instead of worrying about what I was gonna say, I could pay attention to what people were doing, how they were responding, what they were saying and that changed everything. Up until then I was just petrified . . . But when you know your subject really well, there's only so many questions you're gonna get. You'd hear 'em over and over and over again, so you wouldn't be worried about what anyone's gonna say because you'd already thought through how to respond to it. So then you can relax and you're fully engaged and that changes the whole thing."

He had a sort of frenetic energy and a commanding presence. "Bill was energetic," says Winter Dellenbach. "He could talk. He was hip enough that—hey—he'd be off rolling a joint and passing it around and talking about resistance and going off on fifty-seven tangents and rolling another joint and then—hey—'Let's go walk over and get some ice cream,' and then we're in Venice so 'Let's go over and watch the ocean,' and they'd be watching the ocean. I mean it was just a circus all the time. It was a sideshow. Resistance was the main thing and then there was the sideshow. And the sideshow then kind of evolved: The Resistance was the political work, and the sideshow became the cultural revolution."

The chemistry of culture and politics, the dynamic mixture of personalities, the spontaneity and enthusiasm resulted in a burst of creative energy surrounding the activities of the L.A. Resistance. "Celebrate Life, Resist Death," became the group's adopted slogan.

A number of members lived together in communes—the Omega House on St. Francis Street around the corner from the First Unitarian Church, another place in Topanga Canyon, and a third in Redondo Beach. They shared food together—sometimes potlucks, sometimes the day-old bread thrown away from the Van de Kamp Bakery, sometimes pastries salvaged from the Dumpsters outside the Alpha Beta grocery store. Some of them helped set up a sort of underground railroad, guiding AWOL GIs and civilians alike through safe houses into western Washington where they would slip over the border to safety in Canada. They shared dope. They shared risk. They shared the fear of FBI infiltration, the fear of public speaking, and the fear of prison.

At the L.A. Induction Center—the old Occidental Petroleum Building near the heart of downtown—they became a virtual fixture. As the kids from South Central and Watts, East L.A. and Inglewood, Van Nuys and Gardena—as they filed out of the bus for physicals or processing, the L.A. Resistance met them with flyers and leaflets, flowers and donuts. "Don't Go!", they pleaded. "Don't le 'em lead you off to the slaughter!"

"They'd get off these buses," recalls Winter Dellenbach, " and they'd file out the door, looking grim, half of them hostile toward us, particularly early on, and most of the rest looking shell-shocked. Usually a few guys—two or five or seven—would want to talk, but of course the Selective Service people would come out—'Hey, get in here right now; get in and stop talking to those people.' You know when you think about it, very few people are gonna make life-altering decisions on the spot unless they're almost there anyway. And we did get a few people that way. But often people would come out after their pre-induction physicals and that's when they'd sometimes go, 'Who are you people? Where are you located?' We got a lot of people involved that way."

The flyers, printed on the ancient press restored by Jerry Palmer, included analysis of the war and the draft as well as details about draft refusal. Marty Harris remembers a favorite leaflet, "Generals against the War," which featured quotes from Marine Commandant David Shoup, Airborne Commander General James Gavin, and even General Dwight Eisenhower. "We had all their quotes," says Harris. "'Never ever get involved in a land war in Asia.' That was Eisenhower. And 'Vietnam has no more to do with our national security than Timbuktu.'"

"Here's how you refuse induction," recalls Paul Barnes on the topic of one of the flyers. "The truth is you could go in there and talk all day about how 'I'm not gonna go in,' but once you're in that final stage where you're sworn in—if you take that step forward whether you raise your hand or recite the oath, it doesn't matter. You take that step forward, you're in the army. That's the critical moment for you and we explained that in our literature. And there were things like here's where you get help; here's where you get lawyers. Here's where you go for draft counseling and legal advice; here's phone numbers and addresses."

When the time came for one of their own to refuse induction, they showed up in force and tried to make a celebration out of it. "A celebration of the confrontation with Selective Service," said Bob Zaugh. "Dale Oterman, a very accomplished artist, would come down and draw mandalas—concentric circles with spiritual significance from the Hindu tradition—or other huge pieces of art in colored chalk on the sidewalk . . . There were balloons and free baked goods, guitars and singing. It was like a celebration. It was like a party. There was a guy named Calypso Joe who dressed up as General Hershey Bar—head of Selective Service—and then Don Dunphy created this persona, General Waste More Land (after the commander of American forces in Vietnam). They'd put on these uniforms and show up with plastic bombers glued to their sleeves and do street theater. When Dunphy was inducted, he conducted a 'pope-in.' He had himself declared pope and put on this big flowing robe. He had a scepter that he used for invoking people as bishops so they wouldn't be subject to the draft."

On draft card turn-in days The Resistance strived for distinctive and memorable ceremonies. On April 3, 1968, for instance, at MacArthur Park, Oterman again provided some color. He created a collage on a giant draft card—four or five foot tall—with images of the Detroit riot, helicopters, napalm, peace signs, marchers. Twenty-six resisters tore their cards in half, glued them on to the collage, marched downtown, and tried to turn it in to the U.S. attorney. The Justice Department flatly refused to take in the unwieldy piece of art, but Zaugh claims the FBI subsequently broke in to Norman Witte's house and confiscated their symbol of defiance.

Paul Barnes's sentencing by Judge Manuel Real took place on his twenty-second birthday. The courtroom ceiling was covered with helium gas balloons, the walls decorated with banners and happy birthday wishes. Billy Spires was playing the bongos and everyone was singing when the judge came out of chambers. Ten supporters refused to stand for the judge as he pronounced a forty-two-month sentence, then proceeded to lock up Paul's friends for contempt. "We were occasionally testing the limits in ways we shouldn't have," admits Zaugh, "because it was disrespectful."

The College Circuit

Zaugh recalls making the rounds of colleges in the area—Santa Monica City College, El Camino Junior College, Long Beach Community College, Fullerton Junior College, L.A. City College, Orange Coast College in Costa Mesa—and setting up speaking engagements on each campus. "I'd just drive out to the school," he says, "walk out on to campus and find somebody with long hair. Sometimes I'd reach into a bag and ask if they'd like some marijuana, but always I would ask 'Who are the liberal teachers at this school?' Then I'd walk in and ask them, 'Can we speak in your class about the war and the draft?' And they would always set up a time and let us come in.

"Sometimes David Harris would come down from Palo Alto to speak and sometimes I'd bring down Jeffrey Shurtleff, one of Harris's really good friends. He was a great singer, sort of country folk who used to sing Dylan songs and who even sang at Woodstock. He was also a Buddhist, a serious Buddhist. I brought him to L.A. and I'd take him to schools; I remember him at El Camino. He'd be sitting in the lotus position in some classroom and people would just start smirking. Then this guy would open up his mouth to speak about the draft and he'd pick up his guitar and sing, and people were stunned. He was so good. It was shocking how good a singer he was with this crystal-clear voice.

"We also did a unique demonstration at one of the Claremont colleges. We went out there and they were having a graduation ceremony on a Sunday morning. There were like 400 people in the class, and when they went in the church, we showed up and pounded 400 white crosses into the ground. When they came out, there was a grave for each of them." The reality of war intruded, symbolically, upon a serene campus.

Paul Barnes remembers the trip he and Rich Profumo made to another of those outlying L.A. suburbs where the two addressed a small crowd at Rio Hondo Junior College in Whittier. "A year or two later," Barnes says, "I'm in Safford and here comes David Moore." Moore had attended the same high school as Barnes and Profumo—St. Paul High, a small Catholic institution in Santa Fe Springs just outside Whittier. He had known about Barnes and Profumo earlier because they had been notorious Young Democrats in high school who questioned the dress code, the gender segregation, even what time should be set aside for lunch. Upon turning eighteen, Moore had applied for conscientious objector status, but because Catholics had no formal tradition of pacifism, he was turned down by the draft board. When Barnes met the younger resister inside the prison camp at Safford he asked: "How did you end up here?" To which Moore responded: "I remember listening to you and Profumo at Rio Hondo Junior College."

"I had no clue," says Barnes, "that he was making those decisions and doing the same thing that I had done. I had no clue about how I might be influencing the folks I talked to at those speeches. One of the things we talked about often in The Resistance is that everybody has a constituency; everyone's got family and friends and workplace relationships or school relationships, teachers and that sort of thing, and what you do and say has an influence on those folks. The truth was if everyone just addressed their own constituency, then at some point, virtually everyone in the country is gonna hear what we're talking about. And essentially that's what we tried to do."

The Lawyers

Lawyers played their own crucial role in the L.A. Resistance. Key among them was Bill Smith, a Marxist attorney ("a sweet huggybear Marxist," according to Winter Dellenbach) with the radical National Lawyers Guild. Smith operated out of the drab Community Storefront Law Office in the struggling Echo Park section of Los Angeles. His colleagues credit him with virtually inventing the defense system against draft law in the United States. He initiated the Guild's Selective Service Law Panel which provided legal assistance to indigent defendants free of charge, and published a newsletter, "Counterdraft," which had 3,000 subscribers nationwide. "Bill successfully translated," said fellow lawyer Gary Blasi, "the abstract language of federal statutes, regulations, and case law into terms that could be understood by everyone . . . If he had put his mind to work as a tax lawyer for Union Oil, he would have been one of the richest lawyers in Los Angeles." Instead, he put his mind to work training lawyers and lay draft counselors in the fight against Selective Service. The presence of trained draft counselors in the Westwood office—guys like Barnes and Profumo—helped to bring in a stream of young men seeking advice from the L.A. Resistance.

Blasi once asked his three-year-old son, Jeremy, what he wanted to be when he grew up, expecting the usual reply of basketball player or firefighter. He answered instead, "I want to be a draft lawyer like Bill Smith. He helps people. He's nice. And he's funny."

In cases involving core activists from the L.A. Resistance it was the two Michaels—Michael Panzer and Michael Greene—who tended to provide legal assistance. Most resisters acted as their own attorneys, but Panzer or Greene were generally available with free advice, sometimes acting as co-counsel. "They took care of us phenomenally," says Bill Garaway. Both were libertarians. Admirers of Ayn Rand's objectivist philosophy and proponents of individual liberty, they both viewed the draft as involuntary servitude.

There was some money to be made representing draft defendants in L.A. and Michael Greene, especially, jumped into the market with entrepreneurial enthusiasm. A former prosecutor, he churned out one legal victory after another with industrial efficiency. If a client reached him early enough in the draft process, legal success was practically automatic. He built his practice on volume but also saw a market in Los Angeles celebrities who wanted, at any cost, to avoid the draft and the inconvenience of the war in Vietnam. Later on Greene threw a huge party at the Shrine Auditorium in appreciation of all his clients. "He had all the L.A. rock groups as his clients," recalls Garaway. "The Doors, Steppenwolf, The Byrds, The Nazz, which became Alice Cooper. It was like a who's who of the L.A. rock scene. They were all his clients to get out of the draft. He got all those big bands to play and he invited everyone on his client list. Over 5,000 people came to that thing."

Greene's office reflected his success and his flamboyant personality. "There's green grass growing on the floor," says Dellenbach. "You go into the office to consult with your attorney and you sit on pillows on the grass floor. Michael's at his elevated desk which is part wooden desk and part grass and there's a stream of water flowing around it."

There was also the XKE. Bill Garaway and Winter became a couple in 1968 and moved in for a time with Michael Panzer at his place on the beach in Venice. But it was Greene who often provided the ride. "He bought a brand new Jaguar XKE," says Dellenbach. "He took it right off the lot and to the body shop and said, 'Paint it like a rainbow.' I remember going down Sunset Strip sitting on my boyfriend's lap with Michael Greene driving this rainbow-colored XKE convertible. The Beatles' *White Album* ('Revolution Nine' and 'While My Guitar Gently Weeps') had just been released and we had it on a cassette listening to it, going down the Strip on a beautiful L.A. night. It was one of those moments where everything falls into place and life is just too groovy."

This wasn't just any resistance; this was L.A. Resistance.

Dark Nights of the Soul

Along with the crazy antics and rock 'n' roll, along with the confrontations and celebrations came a great deal of soul searching, of private anguish and lonely nights—what some Christian theologians have called the dark night of the soul. Ultimately, each individual had to make a set of life-altering decisions on his own.

Bill Garaway, for instance, had a serious asthmatic condition, an arthritic condition called Reiter's syndrome, and flat feet. He wouldn't have been drafted in a hundred years. He could have submitted to an army physical at any time, received his 4-F deferment, and walked away. Bob Zaugh, likewise, had rheumatoid spondylitis, a long-term disease that causes the joints between spinal bones and the joints between the spine and pelvis to swell up. He had a letter from his physician which would automatically exempt him, but chose instead to refuse the physical examination by an army doctor. Joe Maizlish could have studied quietly until the coming of his twenty-sixth birthday placed him out of the draft's reach. Rich Profumo could have kept his 4-D, his deferment as a divinity student. Paul Barnes remembers narrowing down the options once he decided not to go to war. He could change his name and go underground, go into hiding and take his chances, trying to steer clear of cops and FBI. He could cross the border into Canada and if he were lucky, get landed immigration status. Or he could do the time. "I decided the strongest statement I could make in opposition to that war was to do the time," he said. Greg Nelson steeled himself to face his worst fear: the public spotlight on the day of his sanctuary at the First Unitarian Church.

Like several others, Zaugh lived in mortal fear of public speaking. After completing El Camino Junior College, he was accepted both at Long Beach State and UCLA. UCLA required four years of foreign language; Long Beach one semester of public speaking. "I'll go to UCLA," he recalls. "I would do anything to avoid speaking in public." His terror loomed especially large as the trial approached. He had chosen to act as his own attorney and dreaded addressing the entire courtroom.

"My dad had left; my mom had no comprehension of the issues; I was on my own," he says. "I had seen Marty Harris and other people I'd known a long time transform themselves for their trial. I'd go up Topanga Canyon and read Walden to get my mind prepared. I knew that in order to be effective, I had to speak without fear; I knew I could not be nervous."

Perhaps in other regions, Zaugh's choice of literature to guide him through the legal process might have seemed odd, but in the culture of the L.A. Resistance, it fit right in. *The Autobiography of a Yogi* is a mystical work rooted in the age-old Kriya Yoga tradition of India. Written by the

Paramahansa Yogananda, its pages are filled with sudden appearances and disappearances of Hindu saints who materialize and then dissolve at will, who communicate mysteriously from afar and who drift into blissful altered states they call "God Realization." They focus on the breath, attune themselves to the rhythmic vibrations of the universe, and seek out the vision of the mystical light of cosmic creation. It was to this book that Zaugh turned for comfort in the weeks before his trial.

"When I went to court," says Zaugh, "I carried *The Autobiography of a Yogi* in and that's what I read to study for my trial because I knew I had to speak the truth. If I was nervous, I knew the words would not make it across the courtroom; they would have no force at all. So I prayed not to be nervous. The night before the trial I had everything prepared but my closing statement. I went to sleep and in my dreams, a closing statement appeared to me and was just deposited in my mind.

"I went downtown the next day for my trial and got up there, and they said, '*The People of the United States versus Robert Zaugh*' and I felt like this bolt of fear hit me—and then it was gone. Just like that. I was no longer nervous or fearful . . . I was not afraid . . . In my mind, I would like to think that I got up to the podium and defended myself. But I prayed to have help in my trial and I was given some kind of spiritual support from Yogananda or God or something. I recognize that, appreciate it, and need to remember that that's where my defense came from. Not from my own ego."

Whatever the source of inspiration, the defense was apparently effective. "If you were trying to defend yourself on moral grounds," says Zaugh, "the prosecutor would go, 'I object.' And if you had somebody like Judge Real: 'Objection sustained.' Case over. I was lucky enough to draw Judge Harry Pregerson and Pregerson says, 'I'd like to hear what Mr. Zaugh has to say.' So I presented my case."

He told the judge about the letters from his doctor and the fact that he had been classified 1-Y—ineligible for the draft except in the case of national emergency. He told him about the people lined up around the corner in Las Vegas waiting to get married to avoid the draft. He told him about all the people having children, not for the love of family but from fear of the draft. He told him resisters did not dodge the draft. "We have chosen to do this because we cannot cooperate with the war and I cannot accept a deferment of any kind."

"So Pregerson—I remember he started to face away from me, but I had enough force in what I was saying and enough confidence in what I was saying that literally—as I saw it—he couldn't face what I was saying. He literally turned. In my mind, I saw the judge turn away because he just couldn't face this."

When the time came for sentencing, Zaugh got two years probation and, amazingly, was allowed to continue his work with Peace Press, printing literature for the Black Panthers, for the Communist Party, for Daniel Ellsberg, for Timothy Leary. "He was tired," speculates Zaugh, "of sending people to prison over this issue. And so he stopped with me."

A Marriage Proposal

The question of marriage played a role in some of these solitary struggles. A couple of incidents in the months leading to Marty Harris's court date caused him some uncertainty as to the viability of a long-term relationship with his girlfriend, Kathy. There was the car incident, for one. Harris drove around in an old clunker, a '51 Chevy upon which he had painted the message: Get Out of Vietnam Now in large letters on the side door. One evening another motorist ran him off the road, forcing him into an abrupt halt on the side of the freeway. To say the least, it brought home the stark reality of the position he had staked out. Then came a minor drug bust. Harris sat in the back seat of a Volkswagen bus with four other resisters when the vehicle was pulled over. Police found one tiny vial of pot in the front and hauled all five of them off to jail. Since it was a Friday night—the Ides of March of 1968—it was five days before they got bailed out.

"At that point," says Harris, "we were having a little bit of a tough time figuring out how do we keep this relationship going when I'm gonna be going to jail, and that drug bust brought it all home to me. Yeah, five days in the county jail made me think 'Hey, I'm gonna be here for a long time and what does Kathy think of me? Is she gonna be able to take this? Does she really wanna be with a convict?' Can this really happen? Everything had been right up to then, you know what I mean, but I could sort of see something slipping away already. And I just had to clarify it. So I went to her and said, 'If I go to jail and have this record, would you still marry me?' And there was no hesitation; she said 'Of course, I would.' She said 'Yeah,' and I said, 'Okay. Let's get married.' We got married May the 10th and I refused induction May the 13th." They've been married now over forty years. Marty Harris stayed married to Kathy; so did Patrick Bryan—the only two marriages to survive.

Noncooperation

As members of the L.A. Resistance began to drift into Safford that spring in 1969, they tended to bring with them—like Greg Nelson and Joe Maizlish before them—an abiding faith in the principles of Gandhian nonviolence. Some of them advocated, as well, pushing another Gandhian concept farther to the limit: noncooperation. Indians, said Gandhi during the struggle for home rule, "could not simultaneously oppose the government and work with it." According to Gandhi's biographer, Louis Fischer, all activity had to be evaluated according to the criteria of noncooperation: "To boycott British exports was inadequate; they must boycott British schools, British courts, British jobs, British honors; they must non-cooperate." They must sever all ties that might support the system which they opposed.

For some in the L.A. Resistance, those criteria necessarily included noncooperation with the prison system itself. Gandhi, himself, tended to be a model prisoner. The page of his criminal file entitled "Prison Offenses" generally remained blank. He cooked for his fellow inmates and "performed hard labor—digging the earth with a shovel—which blistered his hands."

Nevertheless, several generally accepted informal rules seemed to militate in favor of some form of noncooperation in prison:

1. Never make it easy on your oppressor. Never fit nicely into an institution which plays such a vital, coercive role in prosecuting the war.
2. Maximize as much as possible the government's financial burden for carrying out its war policies.
3. Your obligation to resist does not end with your incarceration. Resistance must continue within the prison boundaries.
4. A simple matter of personal pride requires you to make yourself a pain in the butt to those who would deprive you of your freedom.

The freewheeling and anarchistic style that characterized the L.A. Resistance dictated that most of the decisions concerning noncooperation remained a matter of individual conscience. The lines which divided cooperation from resistance were vague and undefined; there were no prescribed rules.

However, the L.A. Resistance, I believe, brought a sort of ethic with them, a standard to which many aspired. It came out in some of the stories they told, stories that would eventually be passed down about the men they looked up to. They tended toward stories about powerful personalities who stood up tall and defiantly against a guard or a warden or a judge.

Joe's Odyssey

The odyssey and quiet strength of Joe Maizlish fell within this framework. Maizlish had not intended in the beginning to practice noncooperation. "At Safford," he recalls, "I was a fairly agreeable guy. I was assigned to the kitchen as an assistant cook for the daytime group which meant finishing lunch and getting dinner ready." An ex-marine named Kenneth—a World War II veteran who served in the Pacific—took him under his wing and taught him the basic principles of institutional cooking. "When I was learning to cook," he told Maizlish, "my instructor said remember one thing and you'll never go wrong. Garlic the shit out of everything." And so Maizlish spent his first months in prison crushing garlic, slicing potatoes, and chopping up twenty-five-pound bags of onions. He even got a promotion to food service clerk, due to his ability to type. "When I knew I was gonna leave," he said, "I offered to make a list of the duties I was doing. I made this two- or three-page list of all the zillion little things I was doing, and the food administrator appreciated it very much because that would help him orient the next person."

It was only after his transfer to Terminal Island to be closer to his dying parents that things began to shift. Shortly after the death of his father and shortly before his expected reassignment to Safford, an inmate strike broke out at his new prison in San Pedro.

The source of the strike was a little hazy as is often the case when tension erupts inside a prison. It started in the women's division which stood adjacent to the men's facility. Maizlish suspects it was inspired by a couple of female antiwar activists incarcerated at TI for spilling blood on the courtroom floor of the Presidio military installation in San Francisco. The women were protesting the court martial of twenty-seven soldiers accused of mutiny for sitting down in the Presidio stockade in opposition to the war and protest of conditions within the prison. These women activists had apparently explained to their sisters at Terminal Island about the existence of antiwar sanctuary houses on the outside. The women's division at TI consisted of several houses within the prison compound so that when the strike began, the women all gathered in front of one of the houses as a makeshift sanctuary.

In the men's division tensions already ran high because of the recent death of an inmate—a Mr. Ho—who, the prisoners believed, had been denied medical care other than aspirin for several days before he was shipped to the county hospital. There he had succumbed to pneumonia. Then the men heard news through the grapevine over an inter-prison telephone system that the women next door were being physically mistreated by the guards. The men gathered together a set of demands to present to the authorities. Attempting to squelch the fire before it raged out of control, the administration summarily singled out three leaders—one white, one black, one Latino—and placed them in segregation.

At a tense meeting held in the yard one inmate asked, "What's gonna happen to the people in segregation?" The warden replied, "Well, we'll look into that." It was the wrong thing to say. "We all got so upset," recalls Maizlish. "I stood up and walked out as did a lot of other people. Right then they rang a bell so everybody was supposed to go back to their dorm rooms. They figured we weren't sitting there quietly and listening appreciatively." That's when the strike began, and save for a few scattered threats by individuals, the action remained a nonviolent affair.

In the night they grabbed Maizlish out of bed in something like a military-precision-type raid on his dorm. Four guards, forcing his arms backwards and upwards, dragged him out to the baseball field and handed him over to two others wearing gas masks and full riot gear. He feared he might be beaten senseless at second base. They stuffed him into a bus with a couple of dozen other inmates and sped them off through the desert towards El Paso and the La Tuna Federal Correctional Institute. One of his companions was the wrong Lopez. The right Lopez—one of the strike organizers—was a Mexican American, a militant who had initiated Chicano studies groups inside the prison. The Lopez who they shipped out by mistake was a bewildered Mexican national who spoke no English and had no idea why he'd been dragged from his bed in the middle of the night.

It was on that drive over Interstate 10 that Maizlish began readjusting his attitude toward the Bureau of Prisons. It was, after all, a nonviolent protest, he reasoned. Even the guards who drove him toward La Tuna had observed how unusual the situation was. "'Whenever we come pick people up on some kind of incident,'" Maizlish remembers them remarking, "'they're usually all beaten up and bloody and a mess.' We weren't bloody cuz there wasn't any fighting." In addition, Maizlish had had very little to do with instigating the strike; he had taken no leadership role.

"I thought it was treachery on the part of the administration that they should attack us and (ship) us out in this terrible, frightening way . . . I became disgusted with the whole system." It was on that trip to La Tuna that Maizlish's willingness to chop onions or sweep floors or cooperate in any way with the BOP melted away.

He first began fasting, ingesting only water for ten days or so until he landed in the prison hospital. At that point, he decided to eat once again, but his days as a worker within the prison were done. "I wasn't gonna participate in any work program." That translated into a total loss of "good time," which set back his release date and a permanent placement into the prison segregation block. "I had no parents," he said. "My parents are dead by now. I didn't have any reason to rush out of prison."

Eventually the grand journey of Joe Maizlish would take him on a tour of half the federal prisons in the United States. The impetus for this tour appeared unexpectedly when charges were filed in New York City against a former friend of his father's. When Assistant U.S. Attorney Richard Ben-Veniste (later appointed to the 9/11 Commission) learned that the suspect in a fraud and corruption case had been friends with the elder Maizlish, he sent word to the Justice Department to bring Joe in for questioning. "Since I was in federal custody," says Maizlish "he didn't have to subpoena me or extradite me or anything like that. They said, 'Well, he's now owned by the Department of Justice' . . . so they just ordered me sent to the Manhattan Federal Jailhouse in West Greenwich Village." Maizlish knew next to nothing about his father's friend and even less about any corruption scandal. However the round trip—some 8,400 miles—in the constant custody of two federal marshals allowed him—before his release in 1971—to view the scenic insides of three county jails and eleven federal prisons.

He recalls the highlights. At El Reno he caught a glimpse of the Terminal Island guard accused of abusing the female prisoners during the strike. Apparently his behavior had got him transferred from California to the hinterlands of Oklahoma.

At Leavenworth he saw some of his old buddies from TI busted for selling heroin and carrying cash inside the prison. (No cigarette packs for these guys.)

He remembers the foreboding castle-like architecture at Lewisburg.

He experienced Terre Haute with its "strange rules:" walking down the hallway with hands in your pockets, for instance, was prohibited. The policy required no warning; no guard would come and tell you, "Get your hands out of your pocket, bud." They would come instead to grab your arm forcefully and wrench the offending hand out of your pocket. "Yeah," says Joe, "my arm got grabbed . . . Other prisons didn't care about hands in pockets, but that was the rule in Terre Haute. Same system, different rules."

At Springfield, which includes a hospital for federal prisoners, they threatened to place him in the psychiatric ward for his uncooperative behavior. That Soviet-style punishment truly frightened him until a psychiatrist on the unit refused his admittance. "No way," he said, "uh,uh. If we keep him, we'll get 'em all." The doctors wanted no part of a stream of intransigent draft resisters in their department.

In his cell block in Manhattan Maizlish spoke through the bars with Sam Melville, the man later convicted of bombing, among others, the Grace Pier Building owned by the United Fruit Company, the Whitehall Street Army Induction Center, the Standard Oil offices in the RCA Building, the Chase Manhattan Bank headquarters, and the General Motors Building. Destructive and self-defeating it certainly was, but he sure knew where the sources of American power were. (Two years later he was cut down—along with thirty-eight others—in a hail of gunfire by New York state troopers during an uprising at the Attica penitentiary.)

The Pet Rat

In addition to Melville, Maizlish chatted with the eight other prisoners in the cell next to his. Desiring a pet to pass the time, they had captured a rat, which they kept in a shoebox. "It's not a rat;" they said, "it's a mouse." "But I knew what it was," says Maizlish. "It was a rat."

After Joe's release, he visited Stuart Z. Perkoff, a beat poet who some described as "the heart and soul of the Venice West beat scene" on the beach in West L.A. Perkoff had done time in the same Manhattan jail years before for refusing to register for the draft. "Those rats," said the poet "were probably descendants of the rats that were in that place when I was there in 1948."

Upon returning to Texas, Maizlish completed his entire sentence in the segregation unit at La Tuna. With no outdoor yard privileges, with never a moment's exposure to sunshine, Maizlish got paler and paler. One day without warning, he and Tod Friend, who had been transferred from Safford were granted permission by a guard to leave their cells and take a little time in the yard. Puzzled because the others in segregation remained in lock-up, the two L.A. resisters reveled in a few precious moments of daylight. They wondered why they were so favored and felt awkward about the companions they had left behind.

Next day it all became clear. They received notice in the mail that a representative from the American Friends Service Committee would soon visit them and surely inquire about their well-being. "The administration didn't like how extreme white we must've looked" says Maizlish, "and we realized 'Oh, that's what this is about.'" When the guard came that afternoon and said, "Friend and Maizlish, you guys get to go outside to the yard for a while," the two of them refused outright. "We'll go out," they said, "but we won't go till these other transferring prisoners—they'd been there like a week or ten days—we won't go till you give them a chance too. It's not gonna feel right for us to go without them. The other prisoners were saying 'Don't do that, you guys; they'll never let us out anyway. You just go ahead and get your sun.'"

But the two held fast. It wasn't long before the administration gave in. Grumbling and muttering under his breath as he escorted all the inmates to the yard, the guard whined that the two resisters had told him what to do and how to do his job. "We didn't tell you what to do," replied Maizlish. "We just told you what we weren't gonna do."

Sometimes the little power games were subtle, but for those who played it right, they could win a tiny victory here and there.

During the whole grand tour of the prison system from TI to New York City and back to Texas, during the final stretch of his sentence upon returning to La Tuna, Maizlish never once backed down in his refusal to work for the BOP. From the time they ripped him from his bunk at Terminal Island until his release date, he did his entire time in one segregation unit or another. It was the kind of noncooperation that was revered by L.A. Resistance and would pass into resistance lore.

Lompoc

Situated 150 miles north of Los Angeles in Santa Barbara County adjacent to the Vandenberg Air Force Base, the Lompoc Federal Prison carried a rough-edged, mean reputation among draft resisters in Southern California. (Marty Harris called it a "Gladiator School.") At least three of them from L.A. Resistance—Rich Profumo, Mike Swartz, and Jack Whitton—landed there after sentencing by Judge Harry Pregerson, and all three chose paths similar to the one Maizlish followed. At a reunion years later Profumo and Whitton described their experiences.

"I didn't like Lompoc very much," remembers Profumo, who had spent half a year as a novitiate in training as a Franciscan monk before joining The Resistance. "They gave you an IQ test on the first day and I got a good score. They were gonna train me to be an x-ray technician . . . On the second day I went out on the lawn and started sunbathing. The captain of the guards soon came up: 'What are you doing?' he demanded.

'Tryin' to catch a few rays before the sun goes down.'

'No, no, no, no,' he says. 'What about your job?'

'That's not gonna happen,' I said. 'I'm not gonna do the job.'

'What do you think the other prisoners will think,' he says, 'if they see you out here sunbathin' and they're out there workin'? Why would they work?'

"And I said, 'Now you got it. That's it.'

"So bang! Into the hole."

Profumo, who would spend close to a year in solitary, remembers discovering that at a particular time each day in the afternoon, he could glimpse the sun shining through the window in the ceiling. "If I partially closed my eyes, it refracted the light into a rainbow. That daily routine became my only real escape from the experience of solitary confinement."

By this time, the strain of the war—the daily reports of violence, the dogged persistence of the opposition, the occasional internal pressure from families—was beginning to seep into the personal lives of many in positions of power. Secretary of the Army Stanley Resor, for instance, had two sons, and Under Secretary of the Army Ted Beal a daughter, who became committed antiwar organizers. Attorney General Nicholas Katzenbach suffered fierce criticism at the dinner table from his son, Chris. Most famously, the son of Secretary of Defense Robert McNamara became a peace activist at Stanford. By 1967 McNamara was described as "increasingly tired and depressed, persistently thin." President Johnson wondered if his secretary stood "on the verge of cracking up." McNamara would sometimes cry at work and hide his tears by turning away and pretending to look out the window. "An emotional basket case," the president called him.

It's difficult to assess how much this nationwide inner turmoil impacted the Honorable Judge Harry Pregerson in Los Angeles. (I tried to contact him once by phone and through the mail, but received no response.) We do know, however, that as a long-term resident of the hole in Lompoc, Profumo's correspondence was severely curtailed; one of the few permitted to see his letters was Judge Pregerson. Profumo apparently decided to go for the jugular. He says he wrote Pregerson a blunt letter and told him "You know, Harry, you're like me. You watch the news every day and you see all the people getting killed in Vietnam. Well, the reason they're getting killed is that the people who are doing it don't want to be here where I am. So when you go to sleep tonight, remember, Harry. You're the guy that's killin' the babies, not these guys out there with the guns."

A few days later (following an administration threat to ship Profumo off to the psych ward in Springfield), Profumo was informed of an unexpected visit. Emerging from the hole after months of solitude, the appearance of Judge Pregerson must have seemed like some kind of apparition. "You're a middle-class guy," said the judge, "you're not so bad, you know. I can get you out of here . . . I could give you alternative service. You could work in a hospital or some sort of government job."

"I said, 'Wow, that's great; get me outta here. But I'm not gonna be working for you under any circumstances.' Pregerson sort of rolled his eyes, then gets up and turns around toward the Venetian blinds. He cracks a hole in the blinds, looks out and says, 'Well you know, nobody's free.'

"Well, I'm takin' a shot at it," replied Profumo. He was soon escorted back to the hole.

A couple of months passed before a guard appeared at the cell door and said, "Get your things; roll 'em up; I'm takin' you outta here." "I'm thinking, 'Oh no, they're gonna send me to Springfield," says Profumo. "They're gonna do the electrodes-on-the-brain trip. This is the end of the line; this is freaky."

The bus with several other prisoners headed south, however, towards Los Angeles, and again the mind of the prisoner ran wild: "They're gonna charge me with a second offense," he feared. "Totally a bummer."

As Profumo entered the courtroom, he saw Kent Ten Brink, the marshal who had brought him to Lompoc. He saw Matthew Byrne, the prosecuting attorney. He saw Judge Pregerson. Approaching the bench, he listened to the judge read off in a monotone what appeared to be endless sections of unintelligible legalese. Then these words rang out: "Defendant indicted illegally. The court is vacating the sentence." The judge had researched the case and discovered a technical loophole. Profumo was free. "The next day I was at a corner on a pay phone somewhere in downtown Los Angeles trying to get a ride home."

A Hindu Story

Jack Whitton was the next to tell his story at the reunion. He had consciously embarked on a spiritual path prior to prison. At a resistance commune called The Land outside of Palo Alto, he had taken classes from a yogi of the Hindu tradition, Sri Rivan, who told him, "If you ever go to prison, I want to come see you." In a county jail in Bisbee, Arizona, he had been given a copy of *The Tibetan Book of the Dead*, which he carried with him into Lompoc. The ancient work is designed to guide one through the visions and hallucinations, the "clear light of reality" that one experiences during the interval between death and the next rebirth.

"By the time I reached Lompoc," he recalls, "I don't know if it was Malcolm Dundas or Ed Tripp, but someone who had gone there before told me: 'If you're weak, they'll take you over. If you're strong, they'll fight you. But if you're crazy—if you're crazy, they stay the hell away from you.' I decided at that point that I was gonna be crazy. I was already halfway there anyway.

"And so from the very beginning I refused to work. When the guards came down for count at A & O, at Admissions and Orientation, everybody else was standing up straight beside their bed. I would not make my bed, and instead of standing straight, I'd lay on it.

"For three days, they couldn't figure out what to do. They had never had anybody actually demand to be taken to the hole. The first time I walked down the aisle, they gave me a sponge for cleaning and I said, 'No way. Take me to the hole. I demand you take me to the hole.'"

Whitton's Resistance brother, Mike Swartz, was already in the hole and his wife, Kelley was worried. There had been no communication for some time and she wanted someone to see him. "So I took it upon myself," said Whitton. "And anyway, I wanted to have these guys—the prison administration—on their heels."

The administration, however, threw him a curve ball. "They came to me and said, 'Look, if you don't start cooperating we're gonna take away television for the whole unit.' If I had known there was an organization called Western Prisoner and Support Service (serving as a conduit of communication to the outside world), I would have called their bluff. But at that time I didn't know anyone was out there watching . . . So I settled." Whitton wanted no part of responsibility for collective punishment. "I said 'Alright, I'll do something for ya.'" They offered him work in the kitchen.

"I will not work around the carcasses of my dead brothers," he countered. "I had put on my initial application I was Hindu. I'm Hindu and I don't eat meat. I won't work around those carcasses." When they offered him a cleaning job—fifteen minutes of pushing a broom around the tier three times a day—he finally agreed.

The arrangement was short-lived. Whitton's need for noncooperation quickly overcame his prior hesitation and once again he set out to test the limits. He refused even the minimal sweeping job. This time Lompoc dispensed with the empty TV threats and just threw him in the hole.

It was yoga and the teachings of Sri Rivan that kept him sane.

"The worst thing they think they can do," he said, "is put you in a cell with you—to put you in a cell where you must see your mind dashing about in duality." The overwhelming aloneness, the endless time, the fear. "And yet there was a you they didn't know about—a singular nature. I couldn't do all (of the yogic teachings) . . . although I could do a few things. The main one was the breath—watching the breath. You know when there's a trauma and somebody comes over and says 'Take a deep breath,' there's an understanding. There's a relaxation and a calmness that comes over you when you are hooked up with that original—I would have to say—primal vibration."

"There was one point when I refused to shave in jail and there was this nasty guard who had pictures on his desk of him holding up three Viet Cong heads to show how tough he was. He said, 'Whitton, you're gonna shave' . . . And he grabbed me out of the cell and he started dry-shaving me with a straight razor. I was sitting there and I was grinning—grinning like an idiot. I was not gonna let him know that this got to me. Halfway through, he looked at me and said, 'Whitton. What are you, some kind of masochist?' And I said, 'Well, what does that make you?' And at that moment, the guy softened; I watched his eyes soften. And he went over and got some shaving cream and finished the job. He treated me with respect from that point on because he knew there was no fear."

The warden appeared once at Whitton's door in the hole and said, "Whitton, what can I do to get you out of here?"

"Well, my friend, Sri Rivan, is coming to visit," he replied, "and he's willing to teach yoga to the inmates for three weeks for free. If you let him in here, I'll come out."

"I won't do a quid pro quo," said the warden, "but if you come out, I'll see if I can get him in."

"I said, 'Okay,'" recalls Whitton. "But as he was leaving, I said, 'You know, I can come back here any time I want.' It was a way of wresting that power and that fear that they beat you with."

Being in the hole was the "beginning of me conquering. I knew I was gonna go through some fearful situations in Lompoc and I did. There was no fear. What were they gonna do, beat you up? If you're gonna be dead, you're gonna be dead. They're gonna throw you into prison and throw you in the hole to be with yourself? What horrible thing is that? How out of touch are we with our own selves that we cannot be alone? All I can say is through the help of Sri Rivan and through the help of those techniques, I was able to keep my sanity in that place. And actually turn it to my advantage time and time again. The whole thing is when you are determined to do something . . . it's like all the forces in the universe back you up."

It was these confrontations—one man standing up against the whole system—that would become the stuff of legends within the L.A. Resistance.

Chapter 10

The Road to Nowhere

Dear Sam and Sarah,

I can't say I knew quite where I fit in with these ideas hovering in the Arizona air: Gandhian noncooperation and Marxist revolution. I didn't have near the confidence of a Jack Whitton, the certainty of a Rich Profumo, or the determined resolution of a Joe Maizlish. I also didn't want to end up in the hole. There were times, I must confess—perhaps most of the time—that I felt like a little kid buffeted about by powerful personalities. Here I was, twenty-two years old—a grown man, a convicted felon in a federal prison still trying to figure out who I was. Not that I could afford to let on. Most of our young men in the prison system—ready to go to blows at the slightest perceived affront—really have no clue who they are. But that's not something you tell to anybody in the joint.

A certain degree of overlap existed between Bugsy's embrace of the class struggle and the L.A. folks' inclination towards nonviolent resistance. It was the interplay of these ideas—coupled with the capricious realities of involuntary servitude—that impelled me to reconsider my relationship with the Bureau of Prisons. My deteriorating attitude is clearly reflected in the monthly work reports filed with the camp administrator.

The first report, filed by Roy Connor, the kindly, white-haired culinary supervisor who everyone called "Smilin' Roy," is dated November, 1968. Mr. Connor placed a checkmark in the appropriate column for each and every category of my evaluation as an A.M. Cleaner (mopper of kitchen floors, scrubber of dirty pots):

- Quality of Work: Outstanding.
- Quantity of Work: Outstanding.
- Attitude to Others: Above Average.
- Care of Equipment (the mop and bucket): Above Average.

"A sturdy and dependable worker," he wrote. "Puts forth his best effort on the job." Connor's nemesis in the kitchen, Food Supervisor C. W. Parkerson (who Connor occasionally described as a "goldbrick") filed my next evaluation as a Baker's Helper with a similar set of checkmarks. "An excellent worker," he wrote.

When I came up for early parole in the spring of 1969, my "Parole Progress Report" looked pretty impressive even though we, as draft resisters, knew that we had a snowball's chance in hell of early parole. We showed no remorse for our crimes and remained decidedly un-rehabilitated. Nevertheless, the report asserted that Gould "maintained a clear conduct record," "and reportably (sic) does an outstanding job and always helps out wherever he is needed. In recognition of his favorable performance, he has been granted a Meritorious Service Award ($5.00 a month for cigarettes) effective 02-01-69. Gould is presently quartered in Dormitory # 1 and has adjusted quite well to the population. He reportably spends his leisure time reading and conversing with the Spanish-speaking people at this institution in an attempt to further his knowledge of the Spanish language."

This generally compliant demeanor would begin to change over the next few months as I began to listen closely and internalize the ideas brought in by Bugsy and some of the new breed of resisters from L.A. There was also the arrival of Sidney Sexton who transferred in to replace Roy Connor as supervisor of the Culinary Department. The personal and emotional qualities of the prison staff ran the full gamut from kindness to cruelty, from trivial harassment to total indifference. Most of whom we referred to as "hacks" were just putting in their time till they could retire. The new culinary supervisor, however, had higher ambitions and occupied a class by himself.

Kendall Copperberg, who generally enjoyed his cook's job in the kitchen, viewed the new arrival with a good deal more amusement than I ever did. "He held himself like a little bantam rooster," he recalls. "Straight back like he had a rod up his ass. A by-the-book military type, or pseudo military type. 'Yessir, we're getting this meal out! Great meal today! Color, texture, eye appeal! Let's go! How you coming with that? All right, lookin' good!' Then he'd strut himself on down the line."

Dressed in his gleaming white kitchen uniform, bowtie, white guard's hat, spit-shined shoes, he tried to take charge of us cleaners, dishwashers, cooks, and cafeteria line servers as if the oatmeal we made were the essential ingredient for storming Pork Chop Hill. "The guards," says Copperberg, "that's all they were ever gonna be. But Sexton had a career path in mind. He mentioned that once or twice. He was on his way up; he was working his way up to something bigger. 'In a couple of years I should be here and another couple of years I should be there.' He was trying to do a good job; he was just fine for what he did—dedicated to putting out acceptable meals from the navy cookbook, which is what we used. But he was a cocky little administrator. Always strutting around. If swagger sticks were legal, I think he would have used one. It would have been a nice prop for him."

Inmates assigned to culinary responded in a variety of ways. Most of the older cons just rolled their eyes, shook their heads, and kept doing what they'd been doing for years. Some, like Copperberg, watched with amusement. Mexicans looked the other way, exchanged knowing glances, and feigned ignorance of the language. Some of us put in for transfers.

Mountain Road Crew

Although I was ready for a change even before Sexton's arrival, the new atmosphere he introduced explains, in part, my flight from kitchen duty. It explains, in part, why I filed a copout form, requested a new work assignment, and ended up that spring up on the mountain. They told us the road we were building, the road that traversed the pine and aspen forests of Mt. Graham would serve eventually as a logging road. It was a joint project: the State of Arizona provided the equipment, the supervision, and the expertise; the feds provided the labor. That was us.

In the summer we drove up top in canvas-covered flatbed trucks peering out the back as we sat—huddled together—upon benches bolted to either side of the truck bed. To the lead crew (to which I sometimes belonged) they gave axes to clear out a new path through the forest before the snows came to the high country. Winters we spent on the lower section where the weather remained milder.

Paul Barnes who worked on several of the mountain crews remembers a variety of assignments: "Originally I was on a scaling crew where the road's already been cut. There's still a lot of loose debris up along the sides of the roadcut. We were knocking down rocks and taking out brush. Wind and rain will come; something changes; something loosens and falls and maybe hits something else. So all that loose material needs to be scaled off the roadcut. We'd use big iron bars—beveled at the bottom—to pry the rocks loose or we'd use picks and shovels. We also built headwalls for culverts that diverted running water under the road. The headwall at the top of the culvert where the water enters we made with mortar and whatever rocks we could pick up in the area."

In truth, no one seemed particularly interested in finishing the road. The men from the state highway crew lived nearby and seemed in no hurry to leave the mountain they loved. "They were basically getting a good living working on the road," says Greg Nelson, "and they had no interest in finishing it because they weren't gonna have a great job anymore if they did. Sisco, who was a very outgoing guy, introduced me to one or two of them and they were nice guys . . . But the prisoners didn't care and the state crew had no interest in getting it done. So it moved very slowly and there wasn't a lot of progress."

As for the guards, Mr. Flegler insisted on working us, but the others—Mr. Kenski, Mr. Jones, Mr. Merrell, or Mr. Lovely—they were content to drive us into the hills where they could mark the days till retirement and we could feign productivity. Bugsy remembers the existential absurdity of raking leaves in the middle of the forest. As for Camp Administrator Kennedy, he would have had to find something for us to do had it not been for that road on Mt. Graham where half the population could safely disappear for the day.

It's possible that Judge Arraj imagined—when he pounded his gavel and pronounced sentence in the Denver District Court—that he was shipping me off for two years of hard labor. But up on that mountain, I can't say I labored very hard. "The road was decaying and deteriorating," recalls Geoff Fishman, "faster than we were building it. It was surreal." "It was never gonna be finished in our lifetime," adds Dana Rae. When Allan Haifley arrived on the mountain a full two years after my release, they were still calling it the "road to nowhere."

Leniency, however, did not change our essential status. Leniency did not make us forget who we were. Hard labor or soft, we were prisoners. What labor we did was slave labor, the fruit of which would never pass our lips; no incentives drove us to finish the road to nowhere. We did just enough to keep ourselves from getting shipped off to the Big House in La Tuna and stuffed in the hole. Which wasn't very much.

As a Marxist, Bugsy viewed the whole system of imprisoning the most impoverished in the country as part of the ongoing war against the poor, as part of the centuries-long class conflict. But we draft resisters had an additional role in the conflict: we were prisoners of war and should act accordingly. For us, the Justice Department and the BOP represented one more arm in the prosecution of the war in Vietnam. If we could gum up the works—if we could make the prosecution a little more difficult—it was our responsibility to do so.

Consequently, Bugsy and a few others implemented the One-Tool-a-Day Plan. "When we scattered into the forest," he said "we would take a tool—a pick, a shovel, a rake, whatever—and dump it in the woods. Over the course of time, we'd end up with fewer and fewer tools. The guards were reluctant to get more, because they would have to admit they had no control over the crew. So over time we would do less and less work."

Sisco, the lovable car thief, would pee, from time to time, into the gas tank of the work truck if he thought—after cautiously looking in every direction—he could get away with it. At six foot four, he was one of the few who could pee at gas-cap level. As Segal saw it, this act of mischief represented a tiny volley (or trickle?) in the class war—a gut-level act of incipient class consciousness. It was part of that instinctive rebellious spirit that refused to cave in to the authoritarian control that lay at the heart of the prison system.

There were other acts of resistance. There was the dynamite story, for one. I have no idea why anyone would give federal prisoners access to dynamite, but on the road to nowhere, a lot of things were possible. "In the fall," an L.A. resister told me, "the crew switched to the lower piece of the road. The road was cutting across a side hill of a steep portion of the canyon . . . You'd blast the highs along the road where the mountain was high in relation to the course of the road. Then we'd use these old World War II D-8 caterpillars to drag earthmoving cans through the rubble and scoop up the blasted rock. You'd make a turn and take it to a low in the road and fill in that low. So you're blasting the highs and filling in the lows to make the roadbed.

"There was a lot of drilling of holes into the rock with what was called a Woodpecker—a ten-foot long bit operating on a framework that had two Cat tracks. It had controls where you could position the Woodpecker and angle that bit in almost any direction—180 degrees—to drill the hole. And of course these holes were stuffed with dynamite. Sixty percent nitroglycerin is what we used.

"We did a lot of that drilling and we also stuffed the holes with dynamite in prep for a blast. I remember we had finished a series of holes that we'd been drilling for several weeks on this one particular high. We had drilled many, many holes—maybe 100,a hundred-plus—holes. We were told to put ten sticks of this nitro in each hole. Well, we—me and a couple of other guys who were doin that work—stuck these holes with as much dynamite as we could get in. Way more than ten sticks. It was probably charged two or three times more than it should have been charged . . . We just wanted to make a big bang, a great big explosion.

"We stuffed each hole with a primer cord coming off it and the state explosives expert—he comes in and finishes off all the wiring. He connected all this stuff up and took it back to their control box. They'd never blast while the inmates were there on the job. We'd always load up in the trucks and then after we were headed down the hill back to camp, that's when they'd execute the explosion. So we're going down that long grade, looking back up from out the truck, intently watching because we knew this was gonna be one hell of an explosion."

They blew the hill to Kingdom come.

"We looked up and there was rock flying everywhere. We figured we're gonna blow up this mountain, let's do it right. It was an incredible explosion. Rocks flying all over the canyon. It blew a hole far greater than the low they originally wanted to fill. It was great fun.

"No one ever said anything to us. There was nothin' to say; it was all done. The next day, we went up and I'm on the Cat. We had to pick up those rocks and put them back where they came from."

Another incident recalled by Paul Barnes illustrates the nature of relations between prison authorities and inmates: "We were coming down from work detail on the mountain one afternoon and the guard who was driving was irritated with us. I don't remember who it was or why he was irritated, but he was driving very fast. He was going around corners and trying to slam us around in the back of the truck. The back of the truck was arranged so that the food canisters that we'd haul up every day for lunch were hooped in a little framework set up on either side of the truck. Joe Crampton got up from the bench and undid one of the hooks. He threw that lunch canister out the back on to the highway as we were going sixty, sixty-five, maybe seventy miles an hour. It landed with a big crash which demolished the canister. The guard had to come to a halt and pick it all up. Of course, no one ever said a word and he knew better than to ask what happened. He knew what we would've said: 'Hey, it just fell out, man, what can I tell ya? You were just goin too fast, man.' And he did slow down."

The One-Tool-a-Day Plan, a shovel hidden in the bushes, urine in the gas tank, the overstuffed holes of dynamite, the metal lunch barrels crushed on the highway—these were all part of the game, the covert hostility, the testing of limits, the intricate back-and-forth match of power plays that defined the relationship between authority and inmates, between the two natural adversaries of the prison environment.

The Hogan

Before the winter snows came to Mt. Graham, we built a shelter up the hill from the lower road to protect us from the weather. Everyone associates Arizona with the desert heat, but it could get bitter cold up on the mountain. I remember shivering at times even wearing a U.S. Army parka and an olive-drab winter hat with huge ear flaps of synthetic fur.

I think it was J.C.'s idea to build a Navajo-style hogan. J.C.—Joe Crampton—was this stocky muscular, barrel-chested guy finishing up a ten-year-plus sentence for drug sales in Albuquerque. Barnes remembers his bullish physical strength: "I remember one night we're in Dorm 4 where there was only one table for playing cards. A group of us—Joe, Dana Rae, myself, David, maybe one other guy used to play pinochle and so did this counterfeiter who had his own group. That night we approached the table at essentially the same time and both groups were wanting to play some cards. So Joe and the counterfeiter agreed they were gonna arm wrestle to decide who got the table. It was an epic battle. They sat down. They locked wrists. And we watched this go on and on. Neither of these guys would give up. You know Joe; he had major strength and this incredible chest, but so did this other guy. He was bigger and much taller than Joe, but Joe never gave an inch. You could see their chests and their arms just bulging. And at some point along the way Joe begins gaining. And gaining. And gaining a little more. It just took incredibly long—one minute, two minutes, three minutes. The other guy never really gave up, but finally Joe forced his arm all the way down on the table. So we won the table that night. The counterfeiter got up in kind of a huff. He didn't like losin' the table. He was a very, very strong man, and he didn't like losin'. But Crampton beat him and that's when I realized how strong U.S. really was. He told us once he wrestled a bear, you know, one of those circus bears that was muzzled and declawed. He wrestled this bear twice and the bear kicked his ass both times, but he was one of the few in the crowd who dared go in there. That night in Dorm 4, I could see and believe how he took on that bear."

The counterfeiter escaped shortly after the Great Pinochle Arm Wrestling Match of 1969. "He had come from another institution; I think starting in Leavenworth," says Barnes. "He had done maybe eight, ten, twelve years and finally earned his way down to a minimum security camp where he doesn't have more than about two years to do. And one day he walks off. He had made arrangements apparently for somebody to pick him up on the road. He walked into the desert, got a vehicle, and drove away. I couldn't believe it. He had two years left on probably a 1fifteen-year sentence. And he just couldn't wait anymore. He just disappeared.

"At any rate," continues Barnes, "Joe Crampton—he was really sort of psychologically a father figure in some ways. He really liked to head a family and gather people around him. He sorta saw himself as a protective mentor, a father in some respects and very streetwise. He knew what you could get away with and what you couldn't."

So when J.C. got the idea to build a hogan, it caught on right away. He knew the basics of its construction; he knew its sacred nature; he knew to place the entrance facing east so as to welcome the rising sun. We put wood posts in the ground, built an oval-shaped rock wall, stretched branches over the top to serve as a ceiling. We gathered more rocks from around the site and Tod Friend put in a stone floor. Someone stole a drop-cloth canvas from the paint shop for the roof. The heavy axle grease rubbed into the tarp for weatherproofing created different shades of color and a sort of psychedelic light show effect from the inside when the sun shone through the canvas. Someone else salvaged an oil drum from the highway department to convert into a stove.

"It was a good place to hang out," says Barnes. "And to the guards' credit, we weren't botherin' anybody; they knew what we were doin and they just sorta let it be. They didn't hassle us about it at all. Never confronted us about any of the kind of obvious shit we had stolen outta the camp to do this thing with. It was a sort of a hands-off attitude." A couple of the more heavier-set guards would have struggled to climb the hundred or so yards up a steep path to inspect the hogan. So they didn't even try.

Of course, if you give a bunch of jailbirds access to a private hangout in the mountains, they're not likely to turn the place into a church chapel or a meditation room. The hogan soon flourished with drugs—weed and a variety of hallucinogens—and became a staging area for another form of illegal substance: home-cooked meals. A couple of guys from Tamaulipas set up a burrito kitchen to augment the one already in operation near the rock crusher inside the camp. The original they called El Restaurante de Tres Piedras—the Three Rocks Restaurant. The one up on the mountain remained nameless as far as I knew, but both got their shipments of flour, lard, beans, a little potato, a little cheese, and a little meat sneaked out of the pantries and refrigerators of Mr. Sexton's mess hall. Sometimes they added the flesh of rabbit caught in the desert and sometimes the meat of rattlesnake snared fearlessly with a stick, then smashed on the head with the nearest handy rock. The chiles they must have gotten from the commissary. The burritos sold for a couple of packs of smokes each and they were usually pretty good.

We sometimes skipped breakfast in camp in favor of omelettes served hot off the ninety-gallon stove in the hogan up on the mountain—cheese, onion, whatever we could scrape up for the breakfast du jour.

Since I had transferred from the kitchen and since I knew a little Spanish, I sometimes acted as the intermediary for the trade and commerce between kitchen crew and mountain crew—for the contraband smuggled out beneath the aprons of the cooks and bakers and cleaners.

It's not that I'm proud to tell my kids about the petty theft operations that occasionally engaged my time—about my violations of the Eighth Commandment. But at times the rewards and incentives for moral behavior get turned upside down in prison. We were quite sure that substantial quantities of food—big boxes of meat and forty-pound cartons of butter—were going out the back door of the kitchen and ending up on the street in surrounding southern Arizona towns. We suspected one or two of the guards, but no one ever got caught, at least, not while I was there. In our case—in the inmate arrangement—we were transporting food out the front door of the kitchen, the one leading to the compound. We were recirculating food, preparing it in more palatable form and feeding our fellow prisoners.

I'm not sure that really sounds persuasive as an ethical rationale for theft, but I don't think I gave much thought to the ethics of eating an occasional burrito on the mountain as opposed to chipped beef in the mess hall. The real motivation lay in winning approval from the brotherhood of fellow prisoners. Being too timid to pocket a lousy bag of pinto beans for the Burrito Kings on the mountain would have been a disgrace.

One morning in the hogan, as J.C. finished off a plate of eggs, he daydreamed about the next meal. "You know what I really crave," he said, "what would really be nice, is some sauteed mushrooms in the omelette." That very afternoon after work someone from culinary—I think it was Romero—approached me in Dorm 1: "Hey, Ricardo," he said, "quieres hongos?" He slipped out two small cans of chopped mushrooms from his pants pocket. "You're kidding," I replied. "Cuántas pacas?" He held up two fingers; I went over to my locker and retrieved two packs of Lucky Strikes. What timing! Next morning I entered the shelter as U.S. began cracking eggs for breakfast. I removed the two cans from my jacket pocket, picked up a miniature P-38 can opener—one of those they gave us on firefighting duty to open K rations—and slowly made a circular cut around the lid of the container. Without a word, I dumped the contents on to a makeshift cutting board. J.C. hardly said a thing; I think he might have said, "Thanks, bud." But I knew I had won some respect, and that was vitally important.

The Grand Dragon

I believe it was that spring of 1969 that the Grand Dragon arrived. Robert Scoggins had appeared earlier before the House Un-American Activities Committee for interrogation as leader of the Invisible Empire, United Klans, Knights of the Ku Klux Klan of America, Inc., Realm of South Carolina. His other titles over the years included Grand Titan and EC—that's Exalted Cyclops—of Unit 21. Who could possibly pass up the opportunity to be addressed as "Exalted Cyclops"? All this failed to make him quite the equal of Imperial Wizard Robert Shelton, head of the UKA—United Klans of America—but he was pretty far up there. His testimony in front of HUAC consisted of one sentence repeated over and over: "I respectfully decline to answer for the reason I honestly feel my answer might tend to incriminate me in violation of my rights as guaranteed by Amendment 5."

Chief Investigator Donald Appell responded repeatedly with a stock phrase of his own: "I put it to you as a fact and ask you to affirm or deny the fact." Some of the facts he posed to Scoggins for confirmation were cause for great concern: "Were you aware of the fact when you were there in

November, 1964, that there had been a bombing of a residence of a Negro family in Jacksonville, Florida?" (I respectfully decline to answer.)

"Were you aware that a Mr. Rosecrans was arrested and confessed to the fact that he and some others had conspired to bomb this residence because the young Godfrey boy was the first Negro to attend public schools as a result of a court order?" (I respectfully decline to answer.)

"During that time you were staying at the Capri Motel where Mr. Rosecrans stayed, did you participate in discussions with respect to Rosecrans?" (I respectfully to decline to answer.)

Scoggins, a plumbing and heating contractor from Spartansburg, South Carolina, was sentenced to a year in prison for contempt of Congress when he refused to provide documents and records that HUAC had subpoenaed from him. They sent him to La Tuna and then Safford, presumably because they reasoned he stood a better chance of survival among all the Mexicans in Texas and Arizona than in places with the large black inmate populations like Atlanta or Marion.

Dana Rae recalls Scoggins's first days in Safford. "The Klansman, yeah, I remember him. A small, mousy kind of guy. I remember the black barber, Joel Armstrong, made it be known that he was not gonna cut this motherfucker's hair. That was cool with the administration. They didn't force him to do that." Which was probably fortunate for Scoggins.

Paul Barnes particularly remembers the man's cane. "He used to walk around with a cane that was painted with red, white, and blue stripes. He used to spend half of his time hanging out in the control room because he was such good friends with the guards. The rest of the time he would make the rounds of the camp killing frogs and tarantulas with the end of his cane. Whatever he could kill. He was just that kind of a guy."

Greg Nelson remembers the anthill. "I was walking along in the compound and there was the Grand Dragon with a couple of his buddies. I'm wondering what they're doing so I walk over and he's throwing bugs into an anthill to watch the ants tear the bugs apart. It was so weird. I'm thinking, 'Does this guy have all his cylinders firing?' This was his entertainment—watching the ants ripping apart these bugs. That was the mentality the guy had and it was just very, very strange."

The resisters made friends with most everyone in the camp, but none of us approached Scoggins. When we returned from the mountain every afternoon there he was walking the compound—a portrait of pent-up hatred—destroying the lives of whatever sundry creatures crossed his path on the desert ground.

Another Struggle in Denver

Absorbed with daily life on the mountain and inside the compound, perhaps I lost track of many events unfolding on the street. I remember watching Tom Jones on Saturday mornings bringing a very commercialized form of rock 'n' roll to the TV screen. For a while it was the only way we could keep abreast of current music unless we listened to the tinny sounds of mostly country music through headphones provided by the BOP. I don't recall watching TV news. But several things occurring out in the free world should have attracted my attention.

In Denver, Ernesto Vigil appeared in Judge Arraj's courtroom in October of 1969. I had met Ernesto briefly once while canvassing door to door for Eugene McCarthy's peace campaign during the 1968 Democratic primaries. Ernesto belonged to the Crusade for Justice, perhaps the most influential of the nationalist Chicano organizations that arose in the Southwest in the 1960s. Its origins lay mostly in Denver's east side barrio, but I believe, at the time, its headquarters stood in the near west side on 12th and Cherokee. Since I was living downtown, their building was in my precinct; it was my assignment to try to win their support. That task was completely over my head. If I recall correctly, I ran into Ernesto on the sidewalk leading to the building's entrance. Over the previous two years the Crusade had undergone a bitter and irreconcilable divorce from the Democratic Party. No one was about to let some inarticulate white kid talk to them about which white Democrat they ought to be voting for. I don't think my conversation with Ernesto lasted three minutes. Neither one of us knew at the time that the other was facing a prison sentence for draft resistance.

Mexican Americans had fought with great valor in the Second World War and in Korea. In Vietnam they had already suffered an excessively disproportionate number of casualties. While my friends at George Washington were attending college in Boulder, the kids from West High School and North were being shipped overseas. The GI Forum—a group of returning war veterans unwilling to accept racial discrimination after shedding blood in Europe, in the Pacific, or along the 38th Parallel—had emerged as a leading Hispanic civil rights organization. Those roots might help to explain why sentiment in favor of the Vietnam War was widespread in Mexican American neighborhoods when Vigil returned his draft card to Selective Service in 1967. "Opposition to the war in the Chicano community," he wrote, "was equated with cowardice or communism."

For support, then, Vigil turned to the Crusade—an organization far more radical and militant than the GI Forum. Spurred by the unequal sacrifice of its Chicano constituency, the Crusade came out early in opposition to the war in Vietnam. The group's leader Corky Gonzales—a former Golden Gloves champion and professional boxer who literally punched his way out of poverty on the east side —had steeped his organization in the ethic of struggle, the ethic of fighting for the smallest victories. In taking up Vigil's cause, the Crusade brought a more militant edge to the face of the antidraft movement.

Ernesto attempted in numerous ways to escape the draft. On the advice of the Crusade, he sought counsel from the American Friends Service Committee who recommended he apply for conscientious objector status. He did so, but stated only his political and ethical objections to the war. Because he failed to package these objections in religious beliefs, he was not surprised when his application was rejected. At his physical, he tried unsuccessfully to fail a vision and hearing test, then decided to lie on the psychological interview they conducted. "I told them I used many drugs," he wrote in a book entitled *The Crusade for Justice*, "and once overdosed on barbiturates in an attempted suicide due to depression." Despite this ruse, the psychiatrist concluded that the "Registrant is mentally, morally, and physically qualified for military service." On Corky's advice, he considered fleeing to Canada, but concluded finally it was too cold and "there weren't enough Mexicans there."

At wit's end, he concocted a scheme—Plan A, he called it—to collaborate with an older Crusade member who owned a jewelry store. He would put a rock through the store windows the night before induction, then wait to be arrested for attempted burglary—a charge which would make him ineligible for the draft. Then by pre-arranged agreement, the store owner would drop charges at the last minute. Instead, at the last minute, the store owner backed out of the plan.

And so a discouraged Vigil and a couple of buddies drank into the early-morning hours of February 27, 1969—the day of his scheduled induction. They woke up with hangovers, and then came up on the spot with Plan B. It was quite the plan. Assuming that "Selective Service would not want to induct a dope-smoking subversive," Vigil showed up five hours late at the U.S.

Customs House smoking a joint and carrying an armful of antiwar literature. He was accompanied by his friend, Gilbert Quintana.

In an act of incredible denial, avoidance, or naivete—take your pick—the recruiting officer never gave the smoldering joint a second glance. Nor did he acknowledge any peculiar fragance. He merely lectured them on their tardiness and instructed the young men to proceed to the next office down the hall.

They must have created quite the scene in that hallway—shrouded in a cloud of marijuana smoke and passing out communist flyers to potential draftees. Officer Milton Johnson threatened them with ejection from the building for "interfering with the orderly processing of inductees," then opted to pass the problem on to his superior, Captain Thomas Cooper. As more and more recruiting personnel and filing clerks gathered in the hallway to watch, Cooper demanded a halt to the illegal distribution of "unauthorized" literature and demanded that the material be surrendered to him.

"It's not illegal and we're not surrendering any material," asserted Vigil and Quintana. Their activity, they insisted, was protected by the United States Constitution. That's when Captain Cooper called the U.S. marshal's office across the street in the Federal Building and requested their assistance. In a slapstick move reminiscent of the Keystone Cops, the responding marshal rushed right by the two stoned revolutionaries, looking all over for the disturbance. When finally redirected toward the scene of the crime, he placed Gilbert Quintana under arrest, only to be challenged by Vigil. "If Quintana was arrested," wrote Vigil, "the marshal should take me too since we were both involved in the same activity. We would accompany him peacefully but would not surrender our material, and did not want anyone to lay hands on us. He agreed. Plan B seemed to be working, though not exactly as planned. The goal was to be rejected by the military, not arrested by a marshal."

This is when the comedy began to shift into serious drama. A recruiting officer rushed over to inform the marshal that Vigil was scheduled for induction and should not be arrested. Only Quintana should remain in custody. Captain Cooper's outrage must have been building up because, according to Vigil, he grabbed Quintana by the neck to pull him away from the scene and separated him from Vigil. Quintana—not one to suffer such treatment lightly—fought back. The melee at the U.S. Army Induction Center had begun: seven soldiers and a U.S. marshal versus two subversive Mexican radicals. "One of them pinned (Quintana) to the floor," says Vigil, " I grabbed the marshal who was also on top of Quintana and attempted to pull him off." When it was all over the two found themselves handcuffed in a holding cell in the Federal Courthouse charged not with misdemeanor disturbance but with felony assault on a U.S. marshal. The Crusade lawyers—Gene Deikman and Harry Nier—had their work cut out for them.

Judge Arraj ruled that Gilbert Quintana's arrest was unlawful and he had, therefore, the right to resist. He was acquitted. Vigil's case, however, was beyond salvage. He was found guilty and ordered—after a two-year appeals process—to serve a three-month "pre-sentence observation" period at the Federal Correctional Institute in Englewood.

Vigil writes appreciatively of the all-out support given him by the Crusade. During his confinement for observation, "The Crusade campaigned for my release, and slogans were painted on barrio walls throughout Denver. The graffiti were noticed by the authorities, and prison administrators held meetings in anticipation of riots and demonstrations. The prison guards were trained at nearby Camp George West and automatic weapons were issued to the watchtower." When the tense three months were over, Judge Arraj blinked. He sentenced Vigil to three years probation, at the end of which his record would be expunged under the provision of the Federal Youth Corrections Act.

That sentence, maintains Vigil, represented a tremendous success for both the Crusade and the antiwar movement. "Activists," he wrote, "packed the courtroom every day of the trial . . . The lawyers' strategy was to bring the war in Vietnam into question and into focus and to have the courtroom serve as a classroom . . . Motions were entered based on the Treaty of Guadalupe Hidalgo, the treaty that finalized the invasion of Mexico by the United States. Though the judge could reject the motions, everybody had to listen as they were made. Though a conviction resulted, the war in Vietnam and the guilty verdict itself were still subject to the ongoing tribunal of public opinion. And slogans condemning the war appeared on the walls of every barrio in Denver."

His original resistance in 1969 represented one step towards a greater awareness in his community about Vietnam. Eventually that awareness would lead to a massive demonstration—the Chicano Moratorium—in 1970. Twenty to thirty thousand Mexican Americans turned out for the antiwar rally in East Los Angeles that summer. The Chicano Moratorium would become the closest the country ever got to a mass movement of working-class and minority civilians against the war.

The Demise of the SDS

It was many years before I ever saw Ernesto again, and certainly his struggle with the draft board passed right by me during my time in Safford. It wasn't the only thing that passed me right by. Perhaps I should have paid closer attention to other events on the street.

One of them culminated in the demise—or rather the suicide—of the Students for a Democratic Society in 1969. That registered barely a blip on my radar, but for Bugsy, it represented something akin to trauma. He had helped nurture the organization lovingly for five or six years, then had to stand by and watch helplessly from prison as the thing self-destructed.

"It was a tremendous frustration," he recalls. "I mean SDS essentially destroyed itself and there I was, unable to do anything but write letters to people asking, 'Why are you doing this?' Not that I would have necessarily made any difference; I mean just one person, but yeah, it increased my sense of helplessness. Now that I think about it—in a way, that was the worst part of being locked up—unable to engage in what was going on out on the street at a time that appeared to be significant."

Segal had seen the warning signs before he went to prison. He watched with alarm as the Progressive Labor Party gained increasing influence in SDS. Progressive Labor touted itself as a Maoist party—the disciplined vanguard party that would lead the American working class into the revolution. They had a bible—the Little Red Book entitled *Quotations from Chairman Mao Tse-tung*—which they cited excessively. I assume this provided some of the inspiration for the last line in the Beatles' "Revolution" song: "But if you go carryin' pictures of Chairman Mao, you ain't gonna make it with anyone anyhow."

Dogmatic to the extreme, PL went so far as to criticize North Vietnam—under ferocious aerial attack at the time—for entering peace negotiations with the United States. The Vietnamese people, it stated, were "driving out the oppressor" until the "revisionists in Moscow and Hanoi agreed to sell them out to U.S. imperialism."

Progressive Labor's message to its members consisted of a constant refrain: Go forth and organize the industrial working class. Kirkpatrick Sale—the chief chronicler of SDS history—wrote that the "New Left style that was coming to be associated with the hippies was held (by PL) to be unpopular with the working masses and denounced as 'bourgeois;' marijuana smoking and drinking were discouraged, couples living together were asked to get married, beards and long hair were frowned upon, casual blue jean attire was renounced." At the same time, internal discipline within the party was ratcheted up and rigidly enforced.

There was a hitch, however, in PL's message. The riveters and metal assemblers, the phone operators and seamstresses, the tool and die makers, and over-the-road truckers who were supposed to follow PL into the revolution, failed to respond to the call of its vanguard party. In the vacuum this created, Progressive Labor turned its eyes, instead, towards the SDS.

"The thing that we were looking at," says Segal, "was that PL operated within SDS as a cadre organization. They had their positions figured out beforehand and they'd pack meetings. We're talking about an organization that was not internal to SDS. It was an external organization whose members were operating within SDS and attempting in one way or another to control it . . . You gotta remember that by that point there were bunches of political organizations that nibbled around SDS, because, at least among young people, SDS was the game. But the principal problem and objection we had was that this was an external organization trying to take over SDS."

Some of the older SDSers termed PL's move "The Invasion of the Body Snatchers" after the wonderful 1956 horror film that depicts extraterrestrials—from the outside—taking over the bodies and ultimately capturing the souls of human beings.

Just before his imprisonment, Bugsy and Neil Buckley concocted a proposal they hoped would counter PL's growing influence. The idea was to out-organize PL and retain control by creating a new organizational structure. The new arrangement would include four national secretaries and fifteen field secretaries in various regions, all of whom would be full-time paid staff. "The key aspect of Neil's and my proposal," says Segal, "was that we would build on the year or two years of work that had already been done. We had already brought a bunch of people to the national office in Chicago and put them through organizers' training. What we were looking to do was to bring together full-time organizers who would then become the backbone of efforts to maintain SDS as an independent entity. It was also a way of beginning to build a nonstudent organization—an adult organization. That was necessary for two reasons: (a) that we needed something for our members when they got out of college, and (b) because if we were looking at truly building a mass entity, it could not be confined to college campuses."

The Segal/Buckley resolution, presented at the 1968 summer convention, was a bit oblique, its purpose perhaps not entirely clear to new members of the organization. Some delegates reveled in SDS's tradition of decentralization. PL condemned it as a "power grab" by the national office. In any case, Bugsy was already locked up in the Springfield penitentiary and the plan received insufficient support from the membership. The fact that the proposal went nowhere, however, did nothing, to resolve the growing crisis in SDS. The polarization process continued full steam and Progressive Labor's opponents—still fearful of being devoured from the outside—began to prepare for the next battle.

The problem was that PL's opponents turned out to be as crazy as PL. Those opponents formed a group within SDS and called themselves the Revolutionary Youth Movement (pronounced rim). Early on, the RYM divided itself—mitosis-like—into two rival factions—a set of twins they called RYM I and RYM II.

One of them followed a path resembling Progressive Labor: RYM II fancied itself the leader of the proletarian masses, although it placed its emphasis on young workers. Segal used the term "fetish"—an unreasonably excessive reverence—to describe the attitude of both RYM II and PL towards their perceived images of the working class. It was almost like working people were Martians—so strange and mysterious were they to this new crop of party activists. Out of their mouths came some of the same hackneyed rhetoric that characterized orthodox Marxists from China or Vietnam: "enslaved masses," "running dogs," "lackeys of the ruling class."

In addition to this, RYM II had jumped the gun. It lacked any organic development which might spring from years of filing grievances on factory floors, debating resolutions at Knights of Columbus/union halls, or playing pool at neighborhood bars. Or perhaps just listening. From out of the blue, they stood and declared themselves the leaders of the revolution. They had the "correct" reading of the scriptures and, therefore had received a mandate from Vladimir Lenin himself.

Segal would have loved to see the transformation of SDS into a revolutionary party. But not yet. "Even if I thought it would make sense to do that eventually, there was a lot of work—years of work—that needed to be done between then and (the formation of a party). So sure we could have declared ourselves a party of revolutionary socialist youth, but it would have meant diddly squat." There existed a gaping hole between the militant Marxists in the national office and tens of thousands of students on disparate campuses across the country. Sale writes of one angry student from the University of Nebraska responding to SDS President Carl Davidson's scorn for the idea of setting up literature tables at student unions rather than engaging in more militant action. "In case you don't know," he said, "sitting behind an SDS literature table involves taking a very large step if you happen to be a Nebraskan fresh off the farm and don't even know who Marx is." Segal, who had visited the University of Georgia just prior to his incarceration, insists that "the kids in Athens, Georgia—the SDS members—would have had no idea what we were talking about (had we brought up the idea of a revolutionary party). There was a large chapter there that was active, that was relevant, that was doing good stuff, but talk of a socialist revolutionary party would have been like talking Greek to them."

The third faction in this new constellation—the most famous and legendary one—called itself the Weatherman. Its name was a stroke of genius, stemming from a stream of consciousness fragment in Bob Dylan's "Subterranean Homesick Blues": "You don't need a weatherman to know which way the wind blows." The wind blew obviously in 1969 towards revolution and the Weatherman called for armed guerrilla struggle in the streets of America. They adopted the slogan "Bring the War Home" and over the next year began assembling explosives and collecting firearms. They engineered confrontations with cops on the streets and thought they could attract working-class kids by proving their mettle as street fighters. After all, just the previous year the Rolling Stones had come out with *Beggar's Banquet*, and its lead song "Street Fighting Man." "Summer's here and the time is ripe for fighting in the streets, boy."

Most renowned of Weatherman actions was the gathering in Chicago for the Days of Rage in October of 1969. Called to protest the ongoing war and the conspiracy trial of the Chicago Eight, organizers of the Days of Rage expected to draw thousands of angry youth to the city where police had rioted the year before at the Democratic National Convention. There was a lot of talk of "kicking ass" in the streets.

The first night they gathered, shivering, around a bonfire on a cold autumn evening at Lincoln Park. They numbered barely 300. Around 2,000 Chicago police clad in full riot gear surrounded the park. "This is an awful small group to start a revolution," declared one of the protestors. Nevertheless, at a pre-arranged signal, the group charged south into the Gold Coast neighborhood along the lakeshore smashing windshields in automobiles and shattering windows in retail stores. Peace activist David Dellinger noted "that a disproportionately high percentage of the cars wrecked were Volkswagens and other old and lower-price cars" and that other targets tended to be "small shops, proletarian beer halls, and lower middle-class housing." The Chicago PD—nightsticks in hand—made short work out of the affair. The whole thing ended in half an hour with sixty-eight arrests, clouds of teargas, and an unknown number of injuries suffered on streets strewn with broken glass.

In disassociating his own organization from the Weatherman, Black Panther leader Fred Hampton termed the action "Custeristic," invoking the image of General George Armstrong Custer leading 200 riders of the 7th Cavalry into the waiting arms of 1,800 warriors from the Lakota, Northern Cheyenne, and Arapaho Nations. Other criticisms were equally severe: "You don't need a rectal thermometer to know who the assholes are," said one SDS member from Wisconsin. And former SDS leader Greg Calvert added that Weatherman's actions "did more to set back the development of a meaningful American left than anybody else in the country."

In the aftermath of Days of Rage, Weatherman abandoned the national office of SDS. It changed its name to the Weather Underground and disappeared from public view to carry on the revolution with altered identities from clandestine cells. "One of my principal objections to the Weather people," says Segal, "is that you only go underground when you have to go underground, when you get outlawed. Pick anybody historically. They went underground when they had no choice. Otherwise, they would have stayed out on the streets to organize and agitate. You don't choose to screw up a mass organization that you're responsible for, for no reason. The purpose of going underground is a strategic move in response to changing conditions. Weatherman's application of guerrilla warfare of the Maoist variety was not, at least at that point, applicable to the United States. So what Weatherman did seemed to me to be both idiotic and irresponsible, particularly when they had been responsible for growing a national organization."

I asked Bugsy years later if he believed that the street fighting and mobile tactics he helped organize in Oakland tended to inspire Weatherman two years later to engage in ultra-confrontational actions. "Yeah," he replied.

"Yeah, I'd agree. I wouldn't be surprised if the Weather people were encouraged by Stop the Draft Week. But they drew the wrong conclusions from the facts in Oakland . . . The message that we had in Oakland was compatible with the tactics we were using. We had a specific target; our object was to close down the induction center. So when you talked to people, you could say that a minor inconvenience—driving around the blocked off streets—was reasonable when stacked up against keeping people from getting shipped off to Vietnam and getting killed. Whereas blowing up buildings or intentionally instigating fights didn't adequately communicate or sympathetically communicate these things to a wider audience."

"I saw the best minds of my generation destroyed by madness," wrote Allen Ginsberg in the opening line of "Howl" in 1955. I'm not sure who the best minds of our generation really were, but certainly those folks in SDS were among the most sincere, the most passionate, the most committed to justice. Although vilified mercilessly in the press, when the Weatherman did turn to bombs, they scrupulously informed authorities beforehand so as to avoid casualties. No one was ever killed by a Weatherman bomb, save for three of their own when a bomb they were constructing accidentally exploded in a Greenwich Village townhouse.

But the madness of the sects lay in their hubris; it lay in the lack of humility that drove them to fight among themselves, to judge one another, and to conclude that their chosen path and theirs alone was the only path to social change. It lay in their willingness to sacrifice an entire mass movement in order to carry out their own romanticized and delusional visions. It lay in the fact that they could not read their own student constituency and that they had lost touch with American reality. They were the Left's political equivalent of today's religious fundamentalists: more revolutionary than thou and in sole possession of the word of God or Marx or Lenin or Mao.

By the time Weatherman slipped into the underground in December of 1969, by the time RYM II declared itself the vanguard party of the revolution and Progressive Labor returned home to its strongest base in Boston, the Students for a Democratic Society—a diverse organization 100,000 strong the previous year—was no more. It had been shot down in the crossfire of sectarian warfare.

I don't recall that he showed any outward signs, but down the line in Dorm 1, where he kept his revolutionary library in a small prison locker, my friend Bugsy was heartbroken.

Peace with Honor

What framed all these events, what loomed over everything that played out in the streets and in our little prison subculture, as well, was the inauguration in January of 1969 of Richard Milhous Nixon. Nixon intimated during the presidential campaign that he had a "secret plan to end the war." He called the conflict "a bone in the nation's throat" and promised to end it quickly. Although the details of the "plan" took several years to unfold, its general outline soon became apparent to anyone who was paying attention.

The goal was "peace with honor," and in that last word lay the rub. In order to achieve "peace with honor," we could not abandon our South Vietnamese ally. We could not allow the collapse of the Thieu regime in Saigon. We could not allow a Viet Cong takeover of the South. We could not allow the reunification of the two Vietnams under communist rule. To do so, we would have lost the war and Nixon "would not be the first American president," he told a group of congressmen, "to lose a war." In short, to achieve "peace with honor," we had to persist in pursuit of the exact same goals we had when the war started in the first place. And so the war rolled on.

Looking back, we can identify a number of different tactics envisioned by Nixon in his plan to end the war. The first was offered by Secretary of Defense Melvin Laird who proposed the strategy of "Vietnamization." According to the plan, we would reduce the number of American combat troops and replace them with greater numbers of South Vietnamese soldiers. Thus Nixon pulled 20,000 troops from Vietnam out of half a million early in his tenure. The reduction in American casualties, he hoped, would divide the peace movement here at home by dissuading its more tepid elements from criticizing the government.

For South Vietnam, the new policy meant total mobilization for war. A new law in the South allowed the Government of Vietnam (GVN) to induct all men from eighteen to thirty-eight into military service and order seventeen-year-olds and men from thirty-nine to forty-three into the newly formed self-defense (militia) forces. By the end of 1970 the armed forces had reached a staggering 1.1 million—one of the world's largest armies. Naturally, the rapidly expanding military required huge supplies of M-16 rifles, M-60 machine guns, M-79 grenade launchers, heavy mortars and howitzers, ships, planes, helicopters, jeeps, trucks. "It meant," wrote journalist Frances Fitzgerald, " that the GVN had mobilized about half of the able-bodied male population of the country into the armed forces . . . It meant the United States was arming, and in one way or another, supporting most of the male population of Vietnam—and for the duration of the war."

Even so, Nixon knew better than to depend solely on the ARVN to "end" the war.

There was the rapid growth, for instance, of Operation Phoenix. Directed by the CIA and Special Operations Forces, the Phoenix Program aimed at destroying the Vietcong infrastructure in villages throughout South Vietnam by "neutralizing" VC officials. During a four-year period ending in 1972, over 26,000 were permanently "neutralized." It's not that the Vietcong were any better; they had a civilian assassination program of their own. But as the details of Operation Phoenix trickled out, they belied—once again—the hollow claims of American moral superiority.

Cambodia and Laos too were entwined in Nixon's plan for peace. Through the rain forests of Vietnam's western neighbors ran the legendary Ho Chi Minh Trail—the principal supply route from the North and the principal path through which North Vietnamese soldiers marched into South Vietnam. Two hundred and fifty miles long, the "trail" actually encompassed thousands of miles of swirling double loops and triple bypasses designed to provide a multitude of alternate routes so that trucks could proceed unimpeded by B-52 bomber raids. Caught in the withering crossfire between giants—China and North Vietnam, the United States and South Vietnam—Cambodia's neutralist Prince Sihanouk danced desperately on a highwire, trying to keep his tiny country from getting sucked into the war. Lyndon Johnson, fearful of an ever-expanding war gone out of control, had declared Laos and Cambodia off limits.

Richard Nixon shared no such qualms. Within three months of taking office, he ordered Operation Breakfast, the beginning of 3,600 B-52 raids over Cambodia, the beginning of 100,000 tons of bombs dropped on the country, the beginning, as well, of the unraveling and destabilization of the Cambodian government. It was a "secret operation," except that the raids could be seen and heard so easily by journalists in Saigon that the *New York Times* reported it in a front-page story in March of 1969. The next year, of course, saw a full-fledged invasion of Cambodia, which Nixon called an "incursion."

Operation Breakfast, followed by Operations Lunch, Dinner, and Dessert fell right in line with what Nixon, himself, called the "Madman Theory." The president long held a reputation for zealous anticommunism stemming from his days on the House Un-American Activities Committee in the midst of the McCarthy period. Nixon believed he could parlay that reputation into a strategy of intimidation. Speaking with H.R. Haldeman even before his inauguration, he explained the strategy to his future chief of staff:

> I call it the Madman Theory, Bob. I want the North Vietnamese to believe I've reached the point where I might do anything to stop the war. We'll just slip the word to them that "For God's sake, you know Nixon is obsessed about communism. We can't restrain him when he's angry—and he has his hand on the nuclear button—and Ho Chi Minh himself will be in Paris in two days begging for peace."

The new president even ordered the National Security Council under Henry Kissinger to draw up plans—labeled Operation Duck Hook—to deliver "savage, punishing blows to North Vietnam including massive bombing attacks on major cities, a blockade of the ports, and even possible use of tactical nuclear weapons in certain 'controlled' situations."

Over the next several years, as the communists refused to cave in to Nixon's ultimatums, the president would implement most of the elements of Duck Hook, albeit, not immediately. The withdrawal of American combat troops was generally accompanied by an increase in the ferocity of the aerial war. "The bastards have never been bombed like they're going to be bombed this time," said Nixon, as he ordered the execution of Operation Linebacker in 1972. And later that year he warned Admiral Thomas Moorer, chairman of the Joint Chiefs of Staff: "I don't want any more of this crap about the fact that we couldn't hit this target or that one. This is your chance to use military power to win this war, and if you don't, I'll consider you responsible."

And so the harbor in Haiphong was mined, the civilians in Hanoi fled to refuge in underground shelters, the tonnage of bombs climbed ever higher. And though—as time went by—fewer Americans could be found among the faces of the dead, the death rate in Vietnam continued to soar to one million, two million, probably three million before the violence finally stopped.

Twenty-one thousand additional American troops were sent to their deaths in Richard Nixon's quest for "honor." Another quarter of a million Vietnamese soldiers—NVA, ARVN, VC—died during those years, along with untold numbers of civilians. Nixon's honor did not come cheap.

Madmen and political assassinations, the bombing of neutral countries and escalation of the air war—they seemed a funny way to end a war. From our confinement at the Swift Trail prison camp during all of 1969 and the early months of 1970, we certainly didn't know the full extent of Nixon's plans for ending the war. But we knew about Vietnamization; we knew that the carpet bombing of the B-52s, and the fire from helicopter gunships continued without cease. We knew the pacification of Vietnamese villages intensified, that American soldiers continued to shed blood fighting to take jungle hills of no strategic value. We knew exactly what "peace with honor" meant. Peace with honor meant war with no end.

Nixon's continuing war provided the subtext for what we tried to do; it provided the context for whatever little rebellions we tried to foment, for whatever steps we took to try to inch forward some sort of revolutionary change. It was either that or succumb to helplessness.

Chapter 11

David

Dear Sam and Sarah,

David Harris walked into the compound in August of 1969 and settled into Dorm 4 across the yard from my own Dorm 1. Barely a week later, his wife, Joan Baez, stepped on to the stage in the drizzling rain at one o'clock in the morning and faced the crowd—400,000 strong—at the Woodstock Music Festival. "I see my light come shining," she sang, "from the west unto the east. Any day now, any day now, I shall be released." Her words were Bob Dylan's. Her voice was high and pure—"an achingly pure soprano." Jeffery Shurtleff, one of David's best friends—the man who sat in the lotus position at junior colleges and universities across California setting the stage for David's speeches—sang with her and accompanied her on the guitar. "Any day now, I shall be released," they sang, and then Joan told the story of her husband's arrest. She told about the sheriff and the U.S. marshals arriving at the commune on Struggle Mountain above Palo Alto. She told about the last-minute hugs, the handcuffs, the "Resist the Draft" bumper sticker surreptitiously plastered above the license plate of the sheriff's car. At two o'clock in the morning, as the rain intensified, she finished the final song of Woodstock's first day: "We Shall Overcome."

What I remember about David's first day at Safford was how he carried himself—how his bearing manifested an aura of supreme confidence. He was six foot three, sandy-haired, athletic-looking despite the scholarly-looking rimless glasses he wore. My first steps into that compound had been tentative and cautious, carefully trying to conceal my fear and apprehension over new and strange surroundings. David came in like a lion, looking like he owned the place. He was not to be intimidated.

David and Bugsy eyed each other in the yard early on. "I was shocked to see Bugsy," recalls Harris. "He had been part of the group in Oakland that had been openly badmouthing The Resistance—calling us martyrs and middle class. I had certainly clashed with him then and I was surprised to see him in prison. Seeing Bugsy doin' time on a draft offense—you know I never expected to see this guy here."

Segal's case had followed a different route from the classic resistance advocated by Harris: he had not defiantly turned in his draft card in order to openly court prosecution. He had, instead, dropped some courses at Roosevelt University and become a part-time student, rendering him eligible for the draft. Segal says that documents he received later under the Freedom of Information Act indicated that Roosevelt had informed the draft board of his altered status because of the bitter antagonism that had developed between him and the administration. The draft provided an easy way to be rid of him. He moved to New York, tried an array of delaying tactics, but in the end, was summoned to appear at the Whitehall Induction Center—the same one made famous by Arlo Guthrie's ballad of "Alice's Restaurant." There, in the same building where Guthrie told the story of his isolation on the "Group W bench"—the bench reserved for those convicted of crimes—Segal told a clerk that he too had been arrested. His case from a recent bust at the Chase Manhattan Bank during a protest over South African apartheid was still pending. The clerk told him to go home until the case was settled. Segal never took a step beyond that clerk's station.

The FBI, however, was never informed of the clerk's instructions, and, consequently, issued a warrant for Segal's arrest for failure to report for induction. So Bugsy's draft case was clouded in a mixture of misunderstanding and confusion. Had he been able to document his conversation with the clerk, he surely—in his words—would have "mickey moused around" further to delay his induction as long as possible. Under no circumstances, however, did he have any intention of entering the army. Though his was not the classic case of resistance, his harsh four-year sentence reflected his intense opposition to the draft.

"He came up in my estimation just from the fact that he was there," says Harris. "I didn't have any clashes with Bugsy in the joint 'cuz we were both prisoners together."

Nevertheless, an undercurrent of unspoken tension continued to define their relationship. Differences in personality surely underscored the already existing differences in their strategic and philosophical orientations. Harris was a charismatic figure—a brilliant, fiery speaker, magnetic and outgoing, possessed of a commanding presence, and nationally prominent. Bugsy was quieter, more methodical in his speech, more systematic in his thinking, more comfortable planning strategy in the background, and certainly less well known.

Neither had forgotten their previous clash in Oakland. Even now, Harris reveals a streak of anger when he discusses his past relations with SDS. "I'm obviously still impassioned," he says, "'cuz I'm still pissed off."

Nor are Segal's memories of Harris particularly warm. "It wasn't much of a relationship," he recalls. "I don't think we communicated very much. From my end of it, he was the celebrity, not me. And sort of, he was the white knight and I was the black knight. He was the darling of the antidraft movement and I was the worker. And I was this evil, violent revolutionist. I mean that's how I conceived it. We never had a direct conversation about it or an argument, so those are totally my perceptions. But yeah, I could feel some tension."

That tension, however, never flared at Safford into anything resembling a confrontation. They both agreed on Vietnam. They had both fought in their own ways against the draft. They were both essentially political prisoners in the federal system. There was no reason to carry old disputes with them into jail.

The synthesis David Harris carried into the movement—the fusion of Gandhian ideals, of nonviolent traditions, of a home-grown American anarchism rooted in Joe Hill's Wobblies and Jack Kerouac's wandering beats, all melded into the boisterous and rollicking American youth culture of the 1960s—it was really quite remarkable.

As a nineteen-year-old student at the Crozer Theologicial Seminary in Pennsylvania, Martin Luther King had borrowed a professor's copy of *Gandhi: That Strange Little Brown Man of India*. Particularly striking to him was a passage from Gandhi's writings: "Through our pain, we will make them see their injustice." Over time, King came to embrace the Mahatma's strategies and viewed them as applicable to the struggle for civil rights in the American South. "Gandhi was the guiding light," wrote King, "of our technique of nonviolent social change" during the Montgomery bus boycott.

Gandhi's ideas, however, were not imported mechanically from Gujarat to Alabama. King wove them into the already existing fabric of the black church and adapted them to church culture. Alongside Gandhi, King invoked the prophets: "Let justice roll down like waters and righteousness like a mighty stream" (Amos 5:24). He invoked the nonviolence—the love thy neighbor as thyself—ethic of Jesus and the lyrical tone of the old Negro spirituals: "Thank God Almighty; we are free at last." He especially employed the metaphor of the Exodus—the slaves' liberation from Egypt and the view—from the mountaintop—of the Promised Land.

In a similar way, Harris tried to adapt Gandhian concepts to the American middle-class culture—to the West Coast college-student culture—from which he sprang. East Coast draft resister Michael Ferber wrote that Harris and his buddies injected into the movement a worldview that derived "neither from religious pacifism nor from revolutionary political theory . . . but from a unique California blend of cowboys, Nietzsche, drugs, Jung, motorcycles, and Gandhi."

Harris was a Stanford boy. Stanford even in the mid-'60s remained a largely conservative campus, especially compared to its rowdy neighbor, UC Berkeley—thirty miles up Highway 101 to the north. Nevertheless, Harris began to drift in his sophomore year towards the radical minority. He drove down to Mississippi in the fall of 1964 and glimpsed the war over black suffrage. He worked with the Vietnam Day Committee to stage a teach-in in 1965 and that same year worked briefly with the United Farm Workers' grape strike. He advocated for student control in a dispute with the Stanford administration over how to run Wilbur Hall.

In the spring of 1966, his fortunes turned drastically when a Stanford senior—the leader of a "tiny" radical caucus in the student senate—approached him with a request that he run for student body president in the upcoming university election.

"I don't want to be student body president," he answered.

To which the senior responded: "It'll just be an educational campaign . . . You just give a few speeches and that's it. You don't stand a chance of winning. This is Stanford. We just want to raise some issues . . . You'll be lucky to get 200 votes."

So Harris and a few compatriots began passing out campaign buttons printed with the slogan "Hind Swaraj" which happened to be the words Gandhi used in his campaign against English colonialism. The words meant "Indian home rule." Harris translated the Hindi simply as "home rule," and distributed a second button with the words "Community not Colonialism." Together, the buttons clearly implied that Stanford administrators ruled the campus like a crew of English viceroys, reducing the role of students to that of powerlessness. The Hindi language added a touch of mystery, and the buttons must have become cool because Harris's campaign, unexpectedly, began to take off.

His was certainly a different campaign. Six other clean-shaven candidates wore suits and ties and campaigned like traditional politicians. Harris, according to the *Stanford Daily*, wore "a coat, tan moccasins without socks, blue jeans, and gold wire-rimmed prescription spectacles. His hair, beatnik style and straw-colored, crowns his neck, and he has a moustache."

When it began to look like Harris might actually win, he began to panic. He began stressing "those of my beliefs that I thought would give the allegedly conservative Stanford student body both compelling reasons and a special incentive to turn out and vote against me.

"I talked about the war," he wrote, "and how wrong it was. I argued that the two qualities essential for education were 'equality based on a pure democratic model' and 'freedom bordering on anarchy.'... I hinted that I had once been interrogated by the FBI (the Mississippi incident) without mentioning why."

On the eve of the final vote, Harris's campaign sponsored just two events. Stanford's only blues band, "most of whose members ranked among the scruffier of the campus LSD set," played for an hour at White Plaza. Harris had been friends since freshman year with Peter Kaukonen, the brother of Jor Kaukonen, who was lead guitarist for the Jefferson Airplane. "To get amplifiers," wrote Harris, "the lead guitarist (of the Stanford band) and I had gone up to the Jefferson Airplane's house in Haight-Ashbury and traded a lid of weed for the rental of theirs."

Later that day the candidate appeared before the Interfraternity Council—a bastion of inherited privilege, of blackballing exclusivity—the kind of cliqueishness that would later be described as institutional racism. Their first question: "What is your attitude toward fraternities?"

"I think fraternities are a crock of shit," he answered.

It's no wonder, then, that he took 56 percent of the vote in the largest election turnout in Stanford history. His election would cost Stanford several million dollars in alumni contributions. It also became national news. As reports of campus turmoil hit headlines throughout the country, David Harris emerged as a symbol of the rising student rebellion. That national prominence would follow him as he emerged as the most-visible leader of the movement to resist the draft.

The first skirmish occurred at the convention of the National Student Association at the University of Illinois the summer after Harris's election. There *Time* magazine identified him as the leader of a small radical uprising and featured his photograph in its coverage. "With scraggily hair that had not been cut all summer," he later wrote, "with a thick beard, and heavy shadows under my eyes, I came out looking like one of (*Time* publisher) Henry Luce's nightmares." The convention considered three resolutions on Selective Service: a conservative one merely recognizing the draft as a necessary reality, a liberal one critical of the war, and finally one from the upstart radicals. The draft and the policies it was used for were "unconscionable," stated this third proposal. It called on the NSA to organize "civil disobedience" among college students, and for the first time Harris spoke publicly about "noncooperation." The resolution was defeated by one vote. "Using a spontaneous, unorchestrated strategy," he said, "the radicals had, out of nowhere, made themselves a force to contend with."

Increasingly, however, Harris's energies were drifting away from college and moving inexorably towards a total commitment to organizing resistance to the war. He lived off-campus in a commune of a dozen young men in the grittier part of East Palo Alto. They were a tight-knit group—adventurous, idealistic, open to experimentation with drugs, and looking to live life to the fullest. They were a strange breed of hard-riding bikers saturated through with existentialist thought; not quite outlaw bikers, they constituted a band of Zen/intellectual bikers.

"We were all into the motorcycle thing," says Harris. "Jeffery (Shurtleff) had a big Triumph 650. At the beginning of the summer I bought an old Broyle-Enfield 750 . . . It is the most existential position possible . . . I have a conception of what you do in emergencies that's gained from motorcycles. There is no defense on a motorcycle. The brake is meaningless if you're in trouble. If you go for the brake, the back end of your motorcycle swings right around and you're flat on the pavement. I remember hitting corners, and hitting gravel, and the bike starting to go out from under you. The only defense you have at that point is open up your accelerator and hope your bike develops enough torque to pull you through. We were riding life like a motorcycle, on top of it, opening it up as far as it would open."

All this while reading Kierkegaard and Nietzsche—the early founders of modern-day existentialism—and the sometimes mystical psychologist, Carl Jung. I can't even pretend to say that I've read any of these guys so I'm not sure how all this reading—probably reading while stoned—might have influenced the young men at the Cooley Street commune.

Nietzsche shocked nineteenth-century European Christianity with the phrase "God is dead," thus bringing to the fore the idea that life's purpose might be less easily graspable in our modern secular world—indeed that life itself on our tiny and isolated planet might well be absurd. That individuals must create their own meaning from this deep well of uncertainty—their own purpose, perhaps their own approach to morality follows closely from this absurdist existential corollary. At any rate, I believe that's what Harris and his friends were trying to do: create their own meaning within a life-affirming moral structure and living life full throttle at the same time. Harris described noncooperation "as a means of expression of the lives we were trying to do. We were into the idea that your life was your art."

"The curious thing about my own attachment to nonviolence," Harris told Michael Ferber, "is that it came in the same period when I was reading Nietzsche, riding motorcycles, and visiting women late at night by the back door. It came at a time when I was gobbling up experience. The nonviolence came as a function of a vision of adventurous, hell-bent, Wild West manhood. (After my election as Stanford student body president, the *Stanford Daily* described me as 'swashbuckling.') What brought me to it, and keeps me pursuing it, was the idea of 'truth' itself as a force. I saw truth as rugged, solid, and big chunks, which was the way I wanted to live. To me it appears that a man must be twice as strong to do truth, and what else would the young reader of Nietzsche want?"

Harris recalls his decision to turn in his draft card as something of a religious epiphany—an almost mystical vision. His reading at the time focused on Jung and his theories on dreams and the collective unconscious. It opened him to the notion of trusting intuitively the instincts of his inner voice.

"I was in the city," he says, "staying in the apartment of a girl who was gone for the weekend, and I was sitting and watching the sun go down over San Francisco. And then sort of out of nowhere, in my mind, whatever the voice your mind talks to you with, saying, 'You're going to refuse to cooperate with the draft.'"

A strange synchronicity reinforced this decision. His partners, Jeff Shurtleff and Dennis Sweeney, came to identical conclusions independently at almost exactly the same time. Harris swiftly mailed in his card to the draft board in his hometown of Fresno in central California's San Joaquin Valley.

Not long afterward, Harris resigned as student body president of Stanford and then in March of 1967 came that momentous meeting in East Palo Alto that marked the beginning of The Resistance.

Lennie Heller and Steve Hamilton came down to the South Bay—to the Cooley Street commune—from their home in Berkeley to hold council with Harris and Dennis Sweeney. Heller was far more brash even than Harris. Michael Ferber saw Heller speak in Boston that summer, and recalls thinking that he "practically declared to the females present: 'If you girls want to sleep with me, you can form a line over there.'" He presented himself with a "manly swagger," and stated that men unwilling to turn in their draft cards "had no balls." Hamilton, quiet and soft-spoken, a Maoist who had once counted himself a member of Progressive Labor, would soon stand trial with Bugsy for the events at Oakland. Sweeney had been a committed and highly respected civil rights activist, a veteran of the violent years in McComb, Mississippi.

"Lennie and Steve were two cats," said Sweeney, "who were talking exactly the same idea that (David and I) had the previous summer, and not only were they talking about it, but they had some literature which they'd already printed up and it had this name: The Resistance. They wanted to know when would be the first day. The feeling I had that day was yeah, now is the time."

Harris remembers the general atmosphere. "They came about eight o'clock in the morning and we sat around and talked. The talk was life-sharing. We all wanted to get a feeling of what kind of people the other people were. We smoked a lot of dope and everybody was rapping about their hopes and dreams, and what they did every day, and what kind of music they liked; and we played some of our music and they talked about some of their music. It was almost like a cultural exchange, a meeting of two gangs. Hamilton was very quiet. He sat behind Lennie; Lennie did all the talking; Lennie was the front man. I remember digging Lennie. We all dug each other and we said, 'Well, we're going to do it.'"

The next month they distributed their founding document—the one entitled "We Refuse to Serve."

> We will renounce all deferments and refuse to cooperate with the draft in any manner, at any level ... The war in Vietnam is criminal, and we must act together, at great individual risk,

> to stop it. Those involved must lead the American people, by their example, to understand the enormity of what their government is doing . . . To cooperate with conscription is to perpetuate its existence, without which the government could not wage war. We have chosen to openly defy the draft and confront the government and its war directly.
>
> This is no small decision in a person's life. Each one realizes that refusing to cooperate with selective service may mean prison . . . To do anything but this is to effectively abet the war . . . We prefer to resist.

The group now had a statement of purpose and soon from resisters on the East Coast, they had a symbol: the Greek capital letter, omega. Omega stands for ohm—the unit of electrical resistance. "It suggested to draft resisters," wrote Staughton Lynd, "the very metaphors they had been using—friction in the machine, attrition of the supply lines, turbulence in the conduits to Vietnam." Introduced by resisters at Harvard, the omega was soon adopted by groups from coast to coast.

From the moment the lives of those four young men from the East Bay and South Bay intersected, Harris threw himself into organizing like a mad demon, galloping at a pace that approached frenzy. His activities in Los Angeles provide one example of his grueling routine. "Typically I would fly into L.A.," he told me, "and Garaway would pick me up at the airport. In three days, we'd do like seventeen or so speeches, plus radio shows and maybe a television show if we could arrange it. Then he'd drive me back to the airport and I'd fly back to San Francisco or fly on to Portland or Seattle or whatever. Local chapters would set up a bunch of gigs for me and I'd come down and do the gigs and we'd use those to recruit people. So that was the kind of routine I had; it was just endless speaking. In the last year before I went to the joint I think I gave 500, 600 speeches. Every time I turned around." It was the kind of grinding schedule that made him chafe all the more when militant groups criticized him for being more a martyr than an organizer. Whatever differences the various factions might have had, David Harris was organizing his ass off.

In the course of this frenzied activity, he met Joan Baez. Actually, he was assigned to meet Joan Baez. The Resistance—like every other movement group—forever teetered on the edge of financial ruination and one of

David's tasks was to find a wealthy donor who might pull the organization back from the abyss.

With the famed folksinger's longtime commitment to pacifism complemented by a sizable disposable income, Joan Baez met all the necessary criteria. As early as 1959, at the age of eighteen, she had begun her climb to stardom with an appearance at the Newport Folk Festival. Appearing as an unannounced guest with Bob Gibson, she performed two religious pieces—"The Virgin Mary Had One Son" followed by "Jordan River"—and stunned the crowd. "I looked and sounded like purity itself," she wrote in her autobiography, "in long tresses, no makeup and Bible sandals. No wonder the press labeled me 'the Madonna' and the 'Virgin Mary' the next day. Within three years she produced two gold albums for Vanguard Records. *Time* magazine featured her on its cover and she jumpstarted the career of an unknown Bob Dylan by bringing him on board her national tour and introducing him to audiences as large as 10,000.

Her pacifism was pure as her voice. Raised in a Quaker household, she first heard Martin Luther King at age sixteen during a Monterey conference of the American Friends Service Committee. At age seventeen, she met Ira Sandperl at a Quaker Sunday meeting, who for the next several decades would mentor her studies in nonviolence. He was a serious scholar of Gandhi.

"Ira adhered to nonviolence with a kind of ferocity which would eventually come to me as well," wrote Baez. "People would accuse us of being naïve and impractical, and I was soon telling them that it was they who were naïve and impractical to think that the human race could continue forever with a buildup of armies, nation states, and nuclear weapons." Together, Sandperl and Baez would found in 1965 the Institute for the Study of Nonviolence, first in the Carmel Valley and later up on Page Mill Road in the hills above Palo Alto.

David Harris first visited Baez in Carmel Valley. "We met at her home on a hill overlooking the valley," he wrote. "Custom-designed and built, it must have cost at least a quarter of a million dollars (a small fortune in 1967). There was a brand new Jaguar sedan in the driveway; she dressed expensively and displayed nothing of the scruffy quality attributed to her by the cartoonists of the day.

"I told her what The Resistance had planned for October 16 and claimed that we were the most viable available representatives of her kind of politics.

She agreed, but apparently was not all that impressed with me personally. She didn't like my clothes or all the hair on my face. She also thought I smoked too much and was too 'impressed with myself.'

"For my part, I found her more than a little impressed with her own self and culturally distant as well. She didn't smoke dope or live close to the ground; more than that, she carried herself with a celebrity's air that made me uncomfortable. Seeing her fancy house confused me. At that point, I only knew it didn't jibe with her record covers.

"Even so she gave The Resistance a check for $3,000. It was the largest block of money I had ever seen. When I returned to the commune, everyone cheered and wanted to look at it."

He visited her once again, this time at the Santa Rita Rehabilitation Center where Joan had been jailed for sitting in at the Oakland Induction Center. Perhaps it was those new surroundings—so far from her stunning home in Carmel Valley—that caused the two of them to reconsider the initial feelings that had surfaced from their original meeting.

"He was handsome and bright and appealing," she later wrote. "He was clumsy, messy, and sweet. Most of all, he shared my passion for nonviolence. He was a brilliant speaker. He spoke of eliminating the draft in this country, and then tackling the military here and around the world. The military, as he put it, was a house of cards. America owned most of the deck. If you pulled out her cards, the house would automatically fall. He had a lovely mouth. When he stopped preaching long enough, it was a kissable mouth. *Maybe he's what I need*, I told myself. Someone as strong as me, or stronger. Someone I don't just crave because his hair falls a certain way and his lips have a cupid's curl."

For Harris's part, what he termed "infatuation" quickly overcame any judgments he held about Joan's weakness for fine clothes and elegant cars. She was beautiful. "Having a woman everyone else seemed to want," recalled Harris, "was—at the age of twenty-two—an overwhelmingly seductive proposition." She was fully committed to the ideals that David held dear. About her early career she wrote, "My mere existence as a rebellious, barefooted, antiestablishment young girl functioning almost totally out of the context of commercial music and attaining such widespread notoriety designated me a countercultural heroine, whether or not I understood the full import of the position." She had stood courageously with Martin Luther King in Grenada, Mississippi, and sang "We Shall Overcome" at the massive march for civil rights in Washington. She appealed for peace in Vietnam to the vast audiences who flocked to her concerts. Rather than reveling in celebrity for its own sake, she used her fame to advance the great causes of the era.

Not that David didn't take a lot of flak from his friends at the commune. Baez had little tolerance for David's "blue-jean look," and accompanied him to San Francisco for a shopping spree. "(Afterwards) I drove down to Cooley Street to see Dennis and the rest of the commune," wrote Harris. "I arrived in my superstar girlfriend's Jaguar wearing $50 bell bottoms, a $30 shirt, a $150 leather jacket, and $60 boots. Dennis Sweeney took one look at me and walked out of the room."

And again later when Harris moved into Joan's lavish home in Carmel Valley, Sweeney called him on the same issue. "How can you do this, David?" he asked. "I mean look at all this."

"I knew exactly what he meant," wrote Harris. "The incongruity of my politics and my new physical situation haunted me, and Joan and I had already fought over the question dozens of times. 'What can I say?' I answered. 'I'm going to have to work all this out with her. Now I'm just trying to deal with it as best I can.'

"Dennis snorted through his nose. 'In the meantime, you're living like some kinda fucking king up on top of a hill in a palace.'"

There were differences over drugs as well. "I brought her back to the commune where I was living up in the mountains at the time," says David. "Walking around on her own, she found a bag full of weed. We had just scored like a pound of weed or something like that. It was more than a lid; it was like a pound! And she flushed it down the fuckin' toilet! I said, 'You did what!?' People were pissed! She did end up paying for it."

Differences aside, Baez and Harris teamed up on a whirlwind speaking tour. She warmed up the crowd with song and then David spoke about the draft. "The kids would get mesmerized," Baez wrote. "I thought David was going to turn the world around singlehandedly, and if he could have done it with charisma alone, it would have been done overnight." Harris wrote his own take on the tour: "Where I, alone, might draw a crowd of 200 if I was lucky, having Joan on stage with me multiplied those numbers by at least four to five times. Where I, alone, might get short mention in the back pages, as her political partner, I was part of a feature story with pictures. She was treated as a legend wherever she went, and I was swept up in the charisma."

They were two young people in love when they married in New York City in the spring of 1968. But it was a marriage, as well, of two highly charged personalities—of two complementary bundles of light and electric energy eager to build something new in this war-torn world. "We were public creatures," stated Harris. "Sweet-voiced heroine of a generation joins with young knight advancing in the battle for peace in our time. Without the intoxication of those roles and the image they fostered, I doubt whether the relationship would have ever come off."

They embodied the hopes of a whole generation of rebels, hippies, and radicals out to change the world. *Time* magazine labeled it the "Wedding of the Century." They had a lot to live up to.

For David, transplanting the teachings of the holy man from India on to the landscape of the California coast required necessarily an unorthodox approach. This was, after all, the land of Hollywood and Disneyland, of Haight-Ashbury, Telegraph Avenue, and Marin County. I had read Gandhi's autobiography early on and even I could tell that a lot of those ideas weren't going to fly in America—especially not in the California youth culture of the 1960s.

For one, there was his zeal around food and diet. Interestingly, Gandhi had experimented with meat as a young man. The notion that the English ruled over India because they were a nation of meat eaters was prevalent among India's young. "We are a weak people because we do not eat meat," claimed one of Gandhi's friends.

"Behold the mighty Englishman," wrote the poet Narmad, "He rules the Indian small/ Because being a meat-eater/He's five cubits tall." So the young Gandhi stole out in the night on several occasions to partake of goat's meat—tough as leather. He suffered nightmares the first time. "Every time I dropped off to sleep, it would seem as though a live goat were bleating inside me." In the end, he couldn't bear telling lies to his parents who were staunch members of the school of Vaishnava—among the strictest of vegetarians.

That decision launched a lifetime of ascetic and puritanical experiments in dieting. He fasted often, eschewed spices and seasonings, and insisted that diet should be limited only to sun-baked fruits and nuts, although he consented to drinking goat's milk during a serious illness. He often quoted the Indian proverb "As a man eats, so shall he become," and what Gandhi sought to become was a man in a state of purification. "For the seeker who would live in fear of God," he wrote, "and who would see Him face to face, restraint in diet both as to quantity and quality is as essential as restraint in thought and speech."

Gandhi's quest for purity stemmed from the concept of Brahmacharya: conduct that leads one to God through absolute control of the senses. "If he did not curb his passion for food," wrote biographer Louis Fischer, "how could he curb stronger passions: anger, vanity, and sex?" In the Indian tradition, Gandhi married at age thirteen and struggled mightily with "carnal lust," which as a young man, he says, usually got the better of him. He experienced trauma at age sixteen when his father passed away while Gandhi lay in bed with his young wife, Kasturbai. He describes the "shame of my carnal desire even at the critical hours of my father's death . . . Although my devotion to my parents knew no bounds . . . it was weighed and found unpardonably wanting because my mind was at the same moment in the grip of lust." At the age of thirty-seven, Gandhi vowed to Kasturbai, to remain celibate for the rest of his life. Thus, he thrust off the "shackles of lust" and extolled the "joy of chastity." It sounded a little like the pope.

"The chaste life apparently reinforced his passion and determination to sacrifice for the commonweal," wrote Fischer. "Less carnal, he became less self-centered. He seemed suddenly lifted above the material . . . Storms continued to rage within, but now he could harness them for the generation of more power."

The embrace of the ascetic life surely served Gandhi well and fit nicely into the fabric of much of India's cultural heritage. But try selling a diet of fruit and nuts to a generation of Americans accustomed to reaching for a box of Screaming Yellow Zonkers or a can of Pringle's Potato Chips after a night of blowing dope through a glass waterpipe. Try talking chastity to a population of college students who, having recently discovered The Pill, having recently cast out restrictive curfews and oppressive dress codes, were now reveling in their newfound sexual freedom. For that matter, try talking to the sex-starved inmates at Safford Federal Prison about the virtues of abstinence and see how far you get.

On the other hand, the political Gandhi, the revolutionary Gandhi—the Gandhi who sparked an insurrection without arms, the commander who could mobilize 50,000 to march to the sea and illegally extract its salt, who could fill the British jails with tens of thousands of Indian patriots—this Gandhi might well resonate deeply among the millions of Americans searching for a more peaceful world. It was the principles of this revolutionary

Gandhi that David Harris espoused during his speaking tours along the Pacific Coast.

Foremost among them was the invented word, "Satyagraha": soul force, truth force, or love force. During Gandhi's campaign against discrimination in South Africa, he used the term "passive resistance" to describe the tactics. That term, he wrote, "was too narrowly misconstrued, that it was supposed to be a weapon of the weak, that it could be characterized by hatred, and that it could finally manifest itself as violence." He went so far as to hold a contest in search of a new word. His second cousin offered "Sadagraha"—truth firmness—and thus, won the prize, but Gandhi modified it slightly into its final form. "Satyagraha is the vindication of truth, not by infliction of suffering on the opponent, but on one's self. The weapons of the Satyagrahi are within him." The word implies that Gandhi was anything but passive. "Where there is only a choice between cowardice and violence," he once wrote, "I would advise violence." But nonviolence requires more bravery than violence, he said, and "forgiveness is more manly than punishment."

The second key principle originated in the Sanskrit word "Ahimsa," which literally translates as "not hurting," or nonviolence. It expresses the Hindu doctrine that all living creatures are sacred and should not be harmed.

The corollary to these principles was the political weapon Gandhi called "noncooperation"—a term he invented in 1919, as Muslims and Hindus in India together searched for a plan of action against British rule. "His idea had an instantaneous, mighty appeal because it was so simple," wrote Fischer. "You must not reinforce the wall of the prison that encloses you; you must not forge the fetters that will bind you."

In short, you withhold your support from institutions of oppression. This was the message Harris tried to convey to his young compatriots. It required sacrifice and discipline and action.

Gandhi once said that a "man . . . who takes a pledge and breaks it forfeits his manhood." He was referring to a different kind of manhood than what I had learned in Mr. Rankin's class in the eighth grade and what we had all learned from the John Wayne movies as we grew up. It was often to this sentiment of Gandhi's, to this new definition of manhood that Harris tried to appeal. From this new definition, Harris drew some of the strands of his synthesis.

"Part of what made The Resistance different, Harris explains, "was that we weren't traditional pacifists . . . We were coming out of a different culture.

A lot of us had been athletes in high school or college. We used to ride motorcycles for a while and there was just kind (of the idea) that you don't have to be a milquetoast to not want to kill people.

"I guess what I was really responding to was the sense that in a lot of nonviolent circles there was a kind of concentration on their own demeanor as opposed to the larger political issues. And you know we had a different kind of emphasis. We didn't talk about why it was important for you to personally give up all forms or seeming forms of violence. We concentrated on why it's essential that you don't allow the state to commit the violence that it's committing. And you know, hey, if I'm in the joint and somebody jumps me in the shower I'm gonna bust him in the fucking chops. That was my attitude and I didn't feel like there was any great contradiction between that and my nonviolence.

"But on the other hand, I'm not gonna go pick fights with people. It was more concentration on the big issues of policy and the violence embedded in those, than a kind of hyperconsciousness of my own violent attitudes (with the assumption) that you had to correct those first before you try to correct the larger picture. I was ready to start with the larger picture and work my way back.

"Joan was more of a traditional pacifist than I. She was raised a Quaker and had been in to pacifism before she was into the issue of Vietnam . . . I had a lot of dealings both with Quaker meetings and the (American Friends) Service Committee. One of the places we found support in the beginning was from our local Quaker meeting and I have great respect for them; I liked the Quakers a whole lot. I almost became a Quaker myself just because I was so attracted to their religious demeanor and the process of the Friends meeting . . . But I guess we were saying you didn't need to be a Quaker or act like a Quaker to be nonviolent. You could be rowdy and boisterous, and whatever without denting your nonviolence.

In an interview that took place before his imprisonment, Harris stated that, "For me to adopt 'pacifism' (meaning a whole style) would have meant giving up my neo-juvenile delinquent past, my days as a football player, and in many ways my love of people, not to mention my childhood fantasies. (I think my decision for nonviolence was to be a Gary Cooper who didn't need guns.) I think of all these things as strengths, and out of them brewed up the style that makes sense to me. Out of them, I've found a truth that is stronger without weapons than with. (In the gang I ran with in junior high school, carrying a weapon was considered 'chickenshit.')

"I had to find a way to reconcile my nonviolence with my long-held childhood dream of being a cowboy. What I came up with is as far from "pacifist" circles as it is from the Black Panthers.

"I . . . am for salty, rugged (Marlon Brando in *On the Waterfront*) virile nonviolence. What is gentleness without strength? I agree with Gandhi that the only true nonviolence is, in itself, an evidence of strength and is only a tool of the strong."

So Harris reached out for a Gandhi that young men like Tod Friend, the starting defensive safety for the UCLA Bruins might embrace—an essential Gandhi acceptable to a red-blooded American male. Looking back, perhaps it was a bit self-conscious and perhaps he pushed a little far at times. The women's movement, after all, was virtually unknown when we went to prison, but had become the cutting edge of social change when we got out. Joan Baez created a seductive poster and coined the phrase "Girls Say Yes to Boys Who Say No" before her husband got shipped off to prison. When he got out, she soon tired of all his "macho prison stories about all the seedier and most violent times" he'd lived through.

Nevertheless, given the militarist notions of masculinity that had nurtured us, given the straitjacket of "manhood" we had grown up with, the synthesis Harris developed and brought with him into prison was quite timely and necessary. "Where our fathers had become men at war, charging a hill with a rifle in their hands," he wrote, "we were trying to do the same thing by dropping the rifle, stopping the war, and saving the hill. We had no models to go by, and it took courage to fly in the face of everything John Wayne stood for."

I believe an atmosphere of near-palpable anticipation filled the air when Harris walked into the compound on that hot August day. We had no idea exactly what he had in mind, but we sensed that something would happen, something would change as a result of his presence among us. There was a sense he would usher in some kind of revolutionary change at Safford, and most of us welcomed the opportunity to be part of that change. Dana Rae recalls thinking then about the prevalent idea that "the struggle didn't stop at the gates of Safford Federal Prison."

Harris had just come off a strike in San Francisco County. He was on A Block when a man in 3 Tank began having trouble breathing because of a pleurisy condition. The inmates yelled for medical assistance, but for an hour and a half no one came to help. When lights went out at 10:00, the men in A Block began banging tin cups on the bars in the dark. "Suddenly the lights went on," wrote Harris later, "and eight cops in riot gear rushed down the hallway to our tank." They moved the sick man to another cell and then announced that all of A Block would lose visiting privileges because of the disturbance we had created." An eight-day food strike began the next morning when everyone in the block refused to eat any jail food until their visiting rights were restored. Naturally Harris was labeled the instigator and eventually shipped off across the bay to Oakland before the marshals arrived to take him to Safford.

Like Bugsy, David had no preconceived notion about what kind of organizing might be possible in Safford. "I didn't really have a plan," recalls Harris in regard to his arrival "but the mind-set was to continue to resist on some level . . . So I had all those pictures, and the other picture was how to integrate into the prison population . . . It was important to me that draft prisoners be prisoners in the sense of prisoner culture and not try to establish our own culture. But that's as close to a plan as I got.

"Obviously, we as draft prisoners, had impacts and brought stuff to convict culture that hadn't been there before us. A kind of defiance. Or a willingness to be defiant. We weren't constantly defiant. We obviously were going with the program most of the time; that's what you do. But that noncowering confidence in yourself and who you were—I think that was part of what we brought there. And a kind of rebellious sensitivity; I mean we weren't afraid to stand up and complain or to engage in overt actions if we thought there was some injustice being done. I think we also brought a lot more books than had been there before and a lot more thoughtful discussion, I suspect, than was part of the culture left to its own devices. Just because of where we were coming from culturally. And we were rambunctious. If a guard said, 'Do this," we as a group were predisposed to say 'Why?' Or 'Who are you to tell me this?'"

(Perhaps it's presumptuous to say that we introduced "defiance" into the prison system. There have always been defiant prisoners and they always—as happened to many resisters—end up in hole. Surely we brought some books into the system, but so, too, did the Black Muslims and so did the black liberation movements. What we did bring was a different sort of articulateness and a support system on the outside that made prison officials uneasy.)

On the inside, Harris must have harbored a whir of confusing emotions pulling him in different directions. There was Joan; she was pregnant when Harris was convicted in the spring of 1969. Harris expected an eighteenth-month sentence—the average time for draft resisters in liberal San Francisco. The judge, however, threw him a curveball and gave him three years. I mean, really. They weren't going to let David Harris—renowned architect of mass defiance to the draft—they weren't going to let David Harris off with some kind of lightweight sentence.

The young couple now grappled with a difficult dilemma. Harris had appealed his case, which could have dragged out for another couple of years. By that time, however, their son would have been a toddler and more acutely aware of his father's absence. If David dropped the appeal and began his sentence immediately then Joan would face pregnancy isolated and alone, without the presence of her husband. "The choice we made mutually," says Harris, "was to go in earlier and get out earlier. I dropped the appeal . . . She had to go through childbirth by herself and I think that was traumatic for her. It was a mutual decision, but she paid the price . . . I was not there for her." With Joan waiting on the outside, Harris was reluctant to do anything too provocative on the inside.

On the other hand, the relentless criticism of his stand to openly court imprisonment—even embrace it—intensified the pressure on him to continue to organize from within. That the militants and many in the SDS accused him of "martyrdom" and abandoning the movement was painful enough, but not unexpected. As his trial approached, however, his best friend turned on him as well. Shortly before his scheduled court appearance, Dennis Sweeney, one of the four original founders of The Resistance, asked him, "Why go to jail? Organizers are needed on the streets, David. You're just throwing yourself and the movement away in jail."

Sweeney suggested using a legal technicality to escape conviction and Harris recorded the following exchange:

"You're not supposed to let them take you, David. You're supposed to stay out however you can."

"I don't believe you're saying this, Dennis. If I felt that way I'd still have a deferment. I've given all kinds of speeches telling people they ought to join The Resistance, and there are people in jail for doing what I told them to. If I let them go to jail while I stay out, that makes it all just so much hypocritical bullshit."

"No," Dennis insisted, "that's not true. As long as you keep organizing. Otherwise you're just being a martyr, and we martyrs are no good to anybody."

"You sound like Stop the Draft Week," I snapped.

"You sound like Joan Baez," he snapped back.

"We glared at each other for a minute, and the conversation never went much further."

Harris noted an additional incident between the two—this one even more bitter than the first—as they drove home after the second day of David's trial. "Dennis steadily mocked what I was doing," Harris wrote. 'Fucking David,' (Sweeney) said, sticking his arms out and lolling his head to the side like a man crucified . . . He repeated the gesture over and over and laughed harder with each repetition."

In the face of that kind of belittlement, Harris offered two responses: First, the iron rule of The Resistance: "You can't organize people to do it," he said, "unless you're doin' it yourself."

And second: "I considered our presence in jail to be organizing. In the larger culture, the fact that we were there had an enormous impact on people."

Mere presence, however, would not suffice. It was clear that Harris had committed himself to carrying on some kind of resistance, some kind of agitation, some kind of struggle once inside the prison walls.

In 1968 Marty Harris attended a local TV talk show in Los Angeles—the *Les Crane Show*—where David appeared as a guest. In the late '60s, Les Crane—the public personality—was wearing turtlenecks and mocassins and using words like "groovy" on the air. It was one of those early audience-participation shows and Marty raised his hand to ask how David envisioned the prison experience.

Marty recalls David's response as something along the following lines: "We're going to liberate the jails." Not liberate them, of course, in the sense of storming the Bastille, pikes and pitchforks in hand. But through strikes and resistance. Through talking to the jailers. Through talking to the other convicts. Liberation in the sense of introducing humanity into an inhuman institution. Marty says he was looking for some kind of leader in prison as he waited for the arrival of David Harris—some kind of leader commensurate to a Hamilton or a Madison—a leader capable of bringing a new kind of revolution—beginning with the draft and the prisons—to American society.

David's arrival put the authorities—Camp Administrator Kennedy, Lt. Lanier, and the caseworker Rios—on edge. They could see the political realities shifting beneath their feet. "We had connections to the street," says Harris. "I mean most convicts didn't have those connections. Maybe somebody shows up to visit them once a month, whereas we had left functioning political organizations behind, which occasionally showed up to visit or make their presence known, so that changed the equation somewhat. We had a kind of political visibility or impact that wasn't the case with the average prisoner and which the Bureau of Prisons recognized. I mean that's why to move a draft prisoner from one place to another, you had to get permission from headquarters in Washington. When they wanted to ship a resister from Safford to La Tuna, they had to call DC and ask permission. For anyone else, all they had to do was call La Tuna, and say, 'Hey, you gotta cell?' I think all that, in effect, was to politicize the environment in a way that it hadn't been."

It was one thing to have the lawyer, Fay Stender, advocating for Bugsy. It was bad enough to have Hawaii Representative Patsy Mink asking pointed questions about Dana Rae Park. But Joan Baez opened up a whole different universe. She was a bona fide celebrity with instant access to national and even international media. Mess with David and the whole world would learn about it the next day. All that was needed was for Joan Baez to get up on stage in front of 10,000 people and say a few words about her husband. The press would latch on to every word. Joan Baez could focus the attention of half the country on to our little rinky-dink prison in the middle of the Arizona desert.

Harris brought in no set framework for operating within the parameters of Gandhian noncooperation. "You know, I thought (total) noncooperation was an individual choice," he said. "The two guys I knew personally who were non-cooperators were . . . Joe Maizlish and Tod Friend . . . I thought theirs was a brave decision and certainly one that prolonged their stay. I respected it as a personal decision, but—as an abstract principle—it wasn't what I was prepared to make." Instead, Harris viewed the question of when to withhold cooperation as fluid and situational.

Dana Rae Park did sense one general rule Harris carried with him. By virtue of his ability to type, Dana Rae had been assigned to clerk in the office. Dana Rae provided Harris's first contact with a federal inmate; it was Dana Rae who processed him in. "Yeah, he saw me right away," says Park.

"I definitely got the vibe from David that he thought that my working in the office was something that, one, he wouldn't do, and, two, that he didn't think any other draft objector should do. That I was somehow 'co-op-erating' too much with the system, 'co-op-erating' with The Man—that I was doing The Man's work."

"Our attitude" says Harris, "was if you're in jail, they've got your body. The issue is whether you give them your mind or not. I was determined not to give them my mind, to make it clear that I wasn't their man and to respond to the situation the way we had responded in San Francisco County Jail, which was to stand up for ourselves."

Chapter 12

Drugs, Counter-culture, and the Space Cadets

Dear Sam and Sarah,

Except for the sexual revolution, we had our own little microcosm of the 1960s right there in the midst of the prison. We had our Marxists and Gandhian pacifists, yes, but we had also our seekers of Eastern wisdom, our greeters of the dawn, our New Age pioneers, our believers in Gestalt therapy, our devotees of psychedelic rock, our drug dealers, and our voracious consumers of psychoactive drugs. We had all the makings—for better or worse—of what came to be called the counterculture—that brew of cultural rebellion through which many in our generation sought to define a life outside the boundaries of respectable mainstream society.

Some proponents of the counterculture believed we could reshape the world by building our own insular society, "building the new society within the shell of the old." I don't think I heard that theory articulated with any great frequency among the draft resisters and youthful drug dealers at Safford. But we certainly had our share of individuals who wanted to be left alone—free from politics—to pursue their own path to happiness. There were those who sought refuge from the insanity and constraints of the "straight world," those who just wanted to live life, to celebrate life. And inside the camp there were plenty of life paths to explore.

Geoff Fishman, one of the L.A. resisters, cautioned me in writing about our Safford experience, not to forget the "craziness of life, the surrealism, the One-Flew-Over-the-Cuckoo's-Nest aspect of it all. "When I remember

Safford," he said, "I remember guys making peach brandy out in the arroyo, and some of them making runs to the liquor store. I remember drinking up on the mountain and even one of the guards drinking with us. I remember one of the Mexicans crossing himself when that same drunken guard took the wheel to take us back to camp. The insanity of the whole thing. Watching those incredible electrical storms. Watching the nuts ripen on the pecan trees in the administrator's quarters just outside the perimeter wall and finally smuggling in an illegal salad with contraband pecans and fresh-picked fruit. There was Flaco who played a Malagueña—a folk song from southern Spain—that just knocked my socks off. Just beautiful music coming out of that guy. And the road on the mountain decaying faster than we were building it. It was all weird and surreal."

Marty Harris recollected the strange, almost apparitional dance that occurred at dusk one Saturday night out by the right field pole on the baseball diamond. Most of the camp sat watching movies in the auditorium, but out on the ball field stood Terry John—the same free spirit who befuddled the guards on Halloween by trick or treating with Mendel. "There were four or five others," recalls Marty. "I think Joe Crampton, maybe Michael Vane, a guy from Mexico, Cervantes, and you were there too, Richard. But it was Terry John that incited us."

One of those desert electrical storms crackled in the sky. And then the group of us—a tough drug dealer from the Albuquerque streets, a Mexican campesino, and three or four draft resisters crossed over a forbidden line and reached out to hold hands—men holding hands, convicts holding hands—to dance, crazy, around a rusty pole like a bunch of maniacs. The dance stopped suddenly when the storm stopped, then started again just as suddenly when the lightning returned. And then—as thunder rumbled like kettle drums in the sky—the pole sizzled. There was dead silence. "It was sorta like somebody speaking to us," says Marty, "like you're drawing too much energy here, like all the frantic dancing was drawing the lightning towards us." More likely, any voice from the sky would have been saying, "Get out of the storm, you idiots! And for God's sake, get away from that pole!" Which we did.

Marty began his time at Safford searching for a revolutionary leader but soon found himself traveling a different path. He befriended Terry John, a skilled clarinet player on the street, a young man with a passion for life, but little interest in politics or revolutionary social change. Terry John washed dishes in the rear of the mess hall and often talked about the close relationship and intimate conversations he shared with his work companion, Hobart, which happened to be the brand name on the dishwashing machine.

Marty befriended Larry as well—tall and skinny in his kitchen whites and wire-rimmed glasses—a one-time brilliant student—a PhD candidate in philosophy who abandoned the academic life for the psychedelic world, and got himself busted selling LSD. He loved the Beatles. He had a beautiful wife who got him off once in the visiting room by using her key to rip out his pants pocket, then slipping a soft hand quietly, quietly through the hole and down the inside of his leg. At least, that's what he told us. He exhibited a certain joy for life, but don't ever mention anything resembling political action around him. I remember once watching the veins in his forehead bulge with rage when he heard some us talking about a boycott of the chow hall. He just wanted to do his time, get out of jail, rejoin his wife, and follow Voltaire's simple formula for contentment: "Cultivate your own garden." I'm told he bought a farm in Utah upon his release and started growing organic herbs just as the market began to rise and flourish.

Marty began to see his time in prison as a "spiritual journey, a spiritual proving ground." "Growing up in the city," he said, "you feel disconnected from the environment, from the sun and the moon." Among his most poignant memories, then, was the stunning beauty of Ladybug Saddle—a wooded gap up Stockton Pass where he went with the mountain crew while building the "road to nowhere." Mr. Jones, the guard, explained the ladybugs' habit of gathering by the hundreds of thousands to spend the winter among the rocks on the high pass above Sulphur Springs Valley. The prison experience, concluded Marty,"is about a personal quest. It's about who you are. What am I here for and what am I going to accomplish?

"All the books—it was like a Mecca of education. I read more books in Safford than I ever read in my life. They were eye-opening. Larry introduced me to Herman Hesse's books and I read them all: *Steppenwolf* (the story of the deeply alienated and suicidal Harry Haller—the lone wolf of the German plain—searching for meaning inside the phantasmal doors of the 'magic theater'), *Siddhartha* (the story of the Buddha's journey toward enlightenment), and *Beneath the Wheel*. They were all about a personal quest."

Much later, after the change in the prison administration, after the arrival of a new, more-liberal warden, Marty—along with a half dozen or so others—turned to yoga and meditation. Kendall—Ken Copperberg—whose quest for personal growth in prison had opened up new worlds he had never even considered on the street, was another of those who joined the group. Earlier on, Kendall had kept a journal every day, had studied the art of celestial navigation from a book—from the *Whole Earth Catalog*—had discovered the geodesic domes of Buckminster Fuller in the same publication, had read the poetry of Kahlil Gibran and learned the basics of welding and the rudiments of guitar. Now he joined Marty and Geoff Fishman, Bradley and Terry John and a few others—shivering at five in the morning—to practice the sun salute, to practice asanas—the yogic postures and positions: the cobras and the down dogs, the half moons and the curling cats—out by the baseball field as the sun rose. Perhaps in today's prisons, there's an easier acceptance of yoga, meditative breathing, and the techniques of the Indian saints; I don't know. But I can tell you in those days, the spectacle of ten hippies saluting the sun in a federal prison camp was something quite incongruous.

"We had this one guy," recalls Kendall, "who came to teach us early in the morning for a while. He was a traveling sheik or something, Sri Rivan, who approached the administration and said, 'Can I come teach your inmates in exchange for food and a shower?'"

"He was a freaky looking guy, a white guy with long hair and a beard," adds Geoff Fishman. "He seemed old, maybe late forties or early fifties. Drove around in a pickup truck with a camper out in the desert. He came every morning for a while to teach classes on yoga and meditation."

"He had some great stories," says Kendall, "about how he used to be a soldier and how he narrowly missed death and had narrow escapes. But then he saw the truth in his teacher, Sri Baba—(a Hindu mystic from the Madras province in India)—and now he was spreading the word. His magic was to go around and things would materialize in his hand—little gifts he would give to people. 'Here's a rock that my teacher gave me. It was touched by Sri Baba and this is my talisman.'

"We'd go through the asanas. Then we'd see him eat breakfast and he'd take a shower and then be gone. It was bizarre that the prison officials let him do this."

As you might expect in this era of cultural rebellion, sometimes the search for enlightenment, sometimes the personal journeys, and flights from the boredom of prison routine arrived in the form of capsules or tablets, plastic bags of mushrooms, or decorated shapes of blotter paper smuggled in from the street. It was the contraband of mad visions and magical vibrations.

The search for the delicate balance between personal exploration and political activism is a difficult one, but, looking back, I think the lure of drugs might have pushed us a little off course. As a group, we might have gotten a little out of hand with the drugs.

My own experimentation leaves me in no position to judge anyone else. There was the century plant, for one. I think it was Perfecto Diaz—the gentleman—who harvested the flowers of one of the spiny, succulent plants that grew in the desert just beyond the perimeter wall. He offered me some as a gift; it was just too awkward to turn it down. I remember little reaction at first except a sort of dizziness that followed me through the afternoon. Then that night I placed my hands—palms down—in front of my eyes and stared. My fingers had swollen up weirdly, as if infected, as if sprained from punching through a wall; each of them puffed up with water. It was plain to see: I had taken on the characteristics of the desert plant I had consumed; I had become a century plant, retaining the water necessary for survival in the desert. A trip to the clinic translated automatically to a ticket to the hole in La Tuna; I decided to keep my mouth shut and ride it out. I stood in front of the urinal for a minute, three minutes, five minutes. Nothing passed. I was a moisture-retention machine; I think it was three terrifying days before I could pee.

That should have been sufficient warning, but not long after, one of the cooks from the kitchen returned to the barracks and surreptiously pulled a can of mace from his shirt pocket. "This is great stuff," he said, of the fruit of the nutmeg tree native to the Spice Islands in Indonesia. He pored a generous portion into my palm and urged me to swallow it whole like you might consume a shot of tequila in one quick gulp. The nausea hit instantly. "I'll never do that again," I said to myself, as my stomach convulsed and turned inside out. "I'll never do that again," I repeated as I began to float slowly upward—Alice rising—toward the ceiling of the dayroom. My head never hit the ceiling; it was all too ethereal; that is, my self—wherever it was—was too amorphous, too vaporous to bang into anything concrete. I remember looking down and I saw—my God—I saw myself down there writhing around in pain from the cramps. That metaphysical separation, the eerie out-of-body sensation, lasted minutes. The nausea went on for hours.

The last straw was the mescaline. I thought it might provide a temporary escape, a journey away from the routine and the loneliness. Perhaps a journey to another realm, a world of magic, an altered consciousness. For me, it intensified everything about the prison reality. There were distortions of shapes, to be sure, scattered, disorganized thoughts and intensely vibrating waves of heat and sunlight and wind. But mostly I remember the exaggerated presence of the guards, the gargantuan presence of Kenski, now a Greek monster, striding through the dorm for count, the sinister presence of Proto—L'Avispa, the Wasp—transmitting great waves of negative energy, looking for a bust to build up his file and his ego. I had "guilty" written all over my face; I was sure these two pulsating malevolent creatures could see right through me. The drug served merely to highlight my natural paranoia. I'm not saying I remained pure the rest of my life, but as far as prison and drugs were concerned, I was done.

Others were more fearless than I. Others reveled in the game of putting one over on The Man. "I had the finest, best drugs in my entire life while I was in prison," recalls Dana Rae, "and never had the equal ... Great acid. Great acid! They shook down the prisoners, but they didn't shake down the visitors. Sometimes visitors would just bring drugs right in there and put them in Coke bottles—mescaline capsules into Coke bottles—and you just drank the Coke."

Dana Rae employs a famous scene from the movie *Exodus* to describe his take on the guards' reaction to all this. Peter Lawford plays a British naval officer bragging that he could "spot a Jew a mile away" when Paul Newman, playing a Jewish officer, asks him to check his eye for a cinder. Lawford looks him right in the eye, then walks away oblivious to Newman's mockery. "I remember how we thought all the guards were so stupid," says Dana Rae, "so unaware that they couldn't tell whether we were stoned or not. I mean it was pretty obvious to me walking around looking at people and their bloodshot eyes that you would know that this guy is high and he's flying around. And yet we'd look them right in the eye like Paul Newman in *Exodus* and they would have no idea, not a clue.

"I remember staying up the whole night once and being paranoid ... But it took the monotony off of prison life. I mean, come on. It was something to do. I mean, my god, there's a damn desert out there; what else can you do?"

It was Larry who took Kendall aside, slipped him some blotter acid, and guided him through his first trip. "It was a life-altering experience," he recalls, "but I had done my homework long before. I'd read what the stuff was, knew what the effects were, knew what the preferred environment was, knew how long it was gonna last. I knew you were gonna feel like you were gonna go crazy, so I was prepared to die before I took it. I was gonna go with it and I wasn't gonna be afraid. And if I was gonna die, that's fine. There was nothing else going on in my life . . . Here I am in prison, you know; what have I got to lose? So my mental state was correct; I was in the proper frame of mind . . . And it was just dandy, as pleasant as can be . . . Your mind is going places it's never been before. The novelty of seeing trees breathe and clouds breathe. It was just a phenomenon of the eyeballs focusing on things, but it looked like these things were pulsing.

"I found out what is was like to be first an animal, then a little child. I was out in the woods and I heard a rustle in the bushes and I just froze. Just stock still like an animal. I stayed that way for a couple of minutes; I said, 'I'm not moving. I'm just sitting here quietly taking in as much of my surroundings as I can . . . An animal on the planet—here I am amongst all the others.' It was some deep low-level instinctive thing that I was completely unaware of in my psyche; it was a revelation . . .

"And then, seeing everything like it was brand new, like a child might see it. There was an awareness there; I was saying, 'Oh, I think this is really looking at the world with fresh eyes.' After x number of hours, it lost its novelty, but all in all, the experience was—well—mind-blowing. It was very nice; it was a great day. And I always thanked Larry for that."

L.A. Goes Countercultural

Out on the street the L.A. Resistance had already veered sharply down the countercultural path. Just as David Harris had clashed with Bugsy in Oakland, so The Resistance in Los Angeles harbored a bitter relationship with some of the more dogmatic Marxists in L.A. Bob Zaugh, who painstakingly built the Peace Press, claims that the SDS at UCLA "would come in and use the press and then not take the ink off. They would use paper that we bought.

They wouldn't clean the press which can ruin a press and then they'd just leave. But they (said) they 'represented the masses' and we didn't. We'd lock up at night . . . and once or twice they would just take a crowbar and break off the padlock on Dennis Blvd., come in, use the press, and just leave . . . So I've never forgotten that.

"(Later on) they had these book studies and everybody was supposed to pick a book to read. They'd bring this to the group and we'd all read it. It was like *Das Kapital* and the *Communist Manifesto* and Mao Tse Tung's

Little Red Book. So when it came time for me, I picked *U Needa Comix* by Robert Crumm with a story about Honeybunch Kaminsky, the drug-crazed runaway . . . I thought this comic expressed some of my political views. Boy, were they pissed off!"

Bill Garaway recalls debating with Marxists and ending up so frustrated, he'd go and walk outside in the rain. "The basic principle of the ends justifying the means," he says—"I was not interested in that at all . . . I mean I had friends in SDS, and I don't want to generalize too much, but these guys saw nothing wrong—no problem—with going into a store and ripping it off. They were shoplifting all the time, because, 'Hey, these are capitalists.' . . . It's not gonna produce good fruit and I didn't want anything to do with it . . . They'd argue about everything, ad infinitum. I couldn't stand sitting at meetings just going on and on and on . . . Get me outta here."

So as the L.A. leftists dug deeper into political rhetoric, the L.A. Resistance plunged deeper into the counterculture. You could see it in the changing physical appearances. When Bill Garaway first appeared before Judge Jesse William Curtis in the U.S. District Court for the Southern District of California, the closest he came to a hippie look was a prominent mustache. His lawyer, Michael Greene, a Harvard Law School graduate and former prosecuting attorney in Los Angeles, displayed his Ivy League style with a three-piece suit and button-down collar.

Greene had come up with an innovative strategy. Garaway, he claimed, was "psychologically unable" to submit to induction given his upbringing and personality. An individual who is conditioned or reared with the belief that all killing is evil, contended Greene, cannot help but refuse induction. Garaway's was a case of "moral compulsion"; his refusal was neither willful nor done with criminal intent. He put Garaway on the stand; he put Garaway's mom on the stand; he brought in expert testimony from psychologists and psychiatrists.

Judge Curtis remained unimpressed. Garaway's confession of draft refusal, he insisted to the jury, required a conviction. When they returned obediently—guilty verdict in hand—Curtis handed down a five-year sentence. Criticized for the excessive punishment, the judge responded with a letter to one of Garaway's friends, John Buchanon. "I have two sons in Vietnam," he wrote, "both of whom have about the same feeling that Bill Garaway has about war in general and the Vietnam war in particular . . . They do however, have one thing more and that is a mature overriding conviction that as a citizen of the United States, they have a responsibility to obey the law, all the laws, even those which they may dislike . . . I am concerned when anyone for any reason, takes the law into his own hands and, especially, where he sets out on a determined effort to destroy the law, not by constitutional means, but by breaking it and urging others to do likewise."

Garaway appealed, claiming Judge Curtis's instructions to the jury stripped him of his right to invoke the principle of "jury nullification"—the same principle Bugsy and the Oakland Seven used to beat their conspiracy rap. When the court of appeals ruled in his favor, Garaway faced a retrial and was ordered to appear once again before the court of Judge Jesse William Curtis. It was a different scene this time.

Attorney Michael Greene, the former Ivy Leaguer, showed up all in white. White pants, white shirt, white coat, white boots, white cowboy hat. His hair flowed down beneath his shoulders. He was, Garaway claims, totally stoned on mescaline. Garaway himself revealed a new look as well. "I was wearing loose pants that I made myself," he says, "with a sort of drawstring. I had a psychedelic shirt that had seventy colors. My hair is down below my shoulders. My beard must be down to here," he added pointing toward his chest. "I had a huge beard."

The physical appearance of defendant and defense attorney standing side by side in an L.A. courtroom told a story in itself. It told the story of the roads the L.A. Resistance had traveled in the year and a half between Garaway's two trials and hinted at the journeys they would undertake in the near future.

Garaway was able to continue this strange journey because on this second trial, the state essentially dropped the charges. It's impossible to know exactly why. Garaway finds part of the answer in his extraordinary private meeting with Judge Curtis in the judge's chamber. I told him, "Your honor, I need to apologize to you. I was talking a lot about nonviolence (at the first trial), but I realize my attitude and spirit were not nonviolent . . . I was arrogant and angry. If I was really nonviolent, I wouldn't be angry. I wasn't practicing what I was preaching. And I really want to ask your forgiveness for that." We can't be sure how the judge received this apology, but we do know that Garaway's charisma ran deep.

Winter Dellenbach speculates further that as the war dragged on, as the body count climbed, fewer and fewer people could deny how senseless the whole thing was. "Assistant U.S. Attorney John Hornback was very uncomfortable now prosecuting draft resisters. Even during the first trial, he was refusing to raise objections, no matter what was said. The judge would sometimes turn to him and go, 'Mr. Hornback?' But he wouldn't object to anything. So the second time around, it's like, holy crap, this is about the last thing I want to do is be prosecuting Garaway again."

Most importantly, the judge's sons were back from Vietnam and their experience and alienation from the war evidently impacted their father profoundly. "He told me in his chambers that his sons came back very much against the war," says Garaway, "and they appreciated what I was doing."

It became clear that both Hornback and Curtis were open to discovering any legal loophole capable of preventing Garaway's imprisonment. As the trial began, the Assistant U.S. Attorney delivered a motion referring to what Garaway called the Bruce Dancis precedent. "His draft board," explains Garaway, "had never sent him a conscientious objector form, even though all his correspondence indicated that he was a conscientious objector. And so the court said the draft board was negligent in not considering that based on the information they had. I had done all the same things Bruce had done so the judge came back in after a recess and announced: 'I've considered your motion and it's granted. Case dismissed.'"

The packed courtroom exploded with joy. "We love you, Judge Curtis," shouted resistance supporters from behind the front-row picture of the Guru Sri Baba they had attached to the gallery. "After the first trial when he gave me five years," says Garaway, "he stamped his gavel and he was gone. This time, he's standing there in the courtroom smiling, and people are screaming, 'We love you Judge Curtis.' It was unbelievable."

Garaway's legal victory allowed him to return to the countercultural highway that the core of the L.A. Resistance—at least, those not already in prison—had been traveling for some time. In 1968 novelist Tom Wolfe had just finished chronicling the drug-soaked adventures of author Ken Kesey and his band of Merry Pranksters as they embarked on a rollicking eastward journey in a psychedelically painted bus they called "Furthur." Wolfe's book, *The Electric Kool-Aid Acid Test* was reviewed in the *New York Times* as "not simply the best book on hippies . . . but also the essential book." Not long after *Kool-Aid's* publication, members of the L.A. Resistance began their own magic journey in their own painted bus. They called it "The Medicine Show" and set off on the road to preach the gospel of draft resistance and alternative values in the hinterland. "I was talking about nonviolence as a way of life," says Garaway, "and I'd be talking about how we have to model that. Bob Zaugh was kinda my conscience . . . He'd ask me, 'Well, Bill, you keep talking about this stuff, but what are you doing? So we ended up moving to Arizona to start some type of community where we could practice the sort of things we were talking about . . . Have people travel together, get along together, sing and dance and play music. Healthy eating. Healthy living."

If the core of alternative culture involved peace, nonviolence, communal living, rock 'n' roll, embrace of Eastern spirituality, and drugs, The Medicine Show certainly embodied its share of each.

Seeking to be near their imprisoned brothers, The Medicine Show and its participants drifted towards Safford, then up into the Chiricahua Mountains on the New Mexico/Arizona border. "Are you guys from Paradise Ranch?" asked a young man along the road. "No, what's Paradise Ranch?" "Well, you look like the guys from Paradise Ranch. You ought to go over and check it out." And so the bus ground through twenty-five miles of dusty dirt roads off of Interstate 10 outside of Rodeo, New Mexico, until it came to a stop at the ranch just past the town of Paradise. No one was there. A sign on the door read, "If you're hungry, come in, and help yourself to food in the cabinets. If you need to get cleaned up, help yourself to a bath. If you're tired, take a rest. Treat this house as you would your own in the brotherhood of Jesus Christ. If you need help, call this number." "We went, 'Wow!'" says Garaway.

The phone number belonged to Peggy Hitchcock Bowart, heir to the Mellon banking family and wife of Walter Bowart, editor of the *East Village Other*, a competitor to the alternative weekly, *The Village Voice*. She had previously loaned out a Mellon estate in Mill Brook, New York, to Timothy Leary where he conducted his LSD experiments. When the L.A. Resistance called her in Tucson, she invited them to be caretakers at the Paradise Ranch and they accepted.

There they entered into the movement of rural hippie communes—intentional communities along the lines of Wavy Gravy's Hog Farm in Llano, New Mexico, and Stephen Gaskins's "The Farm," in Summertown, Tennessee.

From Paradise they could visit their friends in Safford, an hour away, and at least, once, serendaded us with a concert from the road beyond the perimeter wall. They encouraged Sri Rivan to go and teach yoga and the ways of his guru, Sri Baba, inside the prison. They played music up on the ranch; Billy Spires's guitar was professional and inspirational. They sometimes used the *I Ching*—the ancient Chinese Book of Changes—to make decisions.

"When there was a decision to make," says Bob Zaugh, "sometimes someone would say, 'Let's throw the *I Ching* . . . Some people weren't into it; you know Greg Nelson wasn't gonna throw the *I Ching* and Joe Maizlish certainly wasn't gonna make decisions based on a Chinese oracle in a book. But other people were. We'd throw it all the time . . . You take coins or yarrow stalks, you ask a question, and you throw the *I Ching* six times and it will give you two sets of numbers which you then look up in a book . . . It can be pretty accurate. C.G. Jung wrote the introduction to the Wilhelm Banes translation we used."

When Garaway's appeal came up in the Ninth Circuit Court, they all returned to California for a time to crowd into the courtroom. "Nobody goes to an appellate court hearing," says Winter Dellenbach, "maybe four or five people and three justices up on the bench . . . This time the whole courtroom was packed. Everybody was holding hands and we were breathing together. I was so concentrating on the white light that I didn't hear a single word of the appellate arguments when Michael Greene was doing his thing. Michael Greene could have been up there half naked and I wouldn't have noticed. Because I was into the white light."

With all the white light and Taoist trappings, it was drugs that financed a healthy portion of The Medicine Show's expenses. There was some support from wealthy donors, to be sure. Joan Baez supported specific projects. The Playboy Foundation donated some money and some of the Playboy Bunnies even came to the trials. Garaway landed a supporting actor's job in Michelangelo Antonioni's widely panned movie, *Zabriskie Point*. But Garaway maintains the major portion of the finances came from drugs.

Garaway went down to Mexico with a young pilot, a real character named John, who had quit his job as dean of students at the John F. Kennedy College in Wahoo, Nebraska. Smuggling marijuana in a small airplane evidently generated much more excitement and cash than finessing student problems and sponsoring the flying club in Wahoo.

"I brought him down the first time," says Garaway, "and introduced him to everyone he needed to meet. After that I didn't need to go down there." That first meeting took place in the small town of Chapala in the state of Jalisco not far from Guadalajara. Garaway's brother knew an American down there who had married the daughter of the town's mayor. "We had our whole supply chain (starting) in the mountains in Zacatecas . . . We picked up this super high-quality stuff. It was kind of a cosmic thing. When we were about to go to Mexico, people would just show up at our house and give us money to buy marijuana. Then we'd come back and distribute it . . . I didn't actually sell it; I wasn't out peddling marijuana. I just organized the whole thing. (We) had no trouble ever with the quality of the stuff we had and the prices were so reasonable, it wasn't even like a selling type of thing. It was just a simple income-generating activity that took very little time. (There was a set group of customers) we knew who would take everything."

The drug focus sometimes diverted the L.A. Resistance from its original purpose. It ended up fighting drug cases as well as draft cases in the courtroom. There was the bust in Whittier, for example. With Garaway driving ten people in his van, he got pulled over after a sanctuary action from which they were followed by the police. They had their entire stash of drugs in the car: LSD, mescaline, cocaine, marijuana, hashish. "Not in huge quantities," says Garaway, "just our personal stash." They ended up beating the rap, but only after a drawn-out court battle involving a battery of lawyers, countless hearings, testimony, affidavits, letters, the whole courtroom drama.

They beat the rap too in Paradise. They offered weed and LSD to a couple of undercover agents at the commune, and a few nights later the sheriff and deputy sheriffs of Cochise County had circled the house, using loudspeakers to order them out of the house with their hands up. "Instead of coming out," recalls Garaway, "we sat down and started chanting 'Om.' They thought we were violent SDS revolutionaries or followers of Timothy Leary (who had lived at the house prior to the L.A. Resistance). They were armed to the teeth and they had all this hostility. But there was nowhere to place it because there we were—all these peaceful hippies on the floor . . . They came up to me and said 'Stop that chanting,' and I said, 'I'll tell you what. We'll stop chanting if you take your guns out of the house.'

"When they took the guns out, we said 'Would you mind if we get some instruments?' They said, 'No,' and so we started playing music and by the end of the evening, the girls were there dancing with all the sheriffs . . . They thought they were going to arrest everyone so they had a whole booking unit set up for taking fingerprints and pictures. They had the whole thing set up, but they ended up finding just a tiny bit of marijuana, which they could tie to only three of the people living there at the commune. They arrested (Winter and Billy and Evie Spires) and let everyone else go. At the end of the evening, the person that was supposed to be taking all the mug shots did a group photo of all the sheriffs and all of us with our arms around them. We were singing (the kundalini yoga farewell blessing) 'May the longtime sun shine upon you.'"

Billy sang to the cops on the way down to the jail in Douglas and they say he even sang to the mayor and chief of police from the city jail. They say when he broke his guitar strings they went out and bought him new strings.

Life was good for the L.A. Resistance traveling with The Medicine Show and living on the commune. They had love-ins in towns like Thatcher, Arizona, and sing-ins at the prison. They had run-ins with residents of what Zaugh called "gun rack territory" and always escaped unscathed. Garaway never got convicted. Arizona dropped charges against Winter and the Spiers. It was a charmed life, a magical life, and almost everyone who took to the road looks back fondly at those crazy times with the L.A. Resistance.

Fondly, but not uncritically. "We were all looking for enlightenment," says Bob Zaugh,"and we didn't find it in an LSD capsule." Bill Garaway found Jesus in the early '70s, turned his back on the drug life, and became an evangelical preacher. Marty Harris evaluated the period by claiming that Sherna Gluck and Winter Dellenbach—two women who had a lower public profile because they never went on trial—represented "the soul of the L.A. Resistance." "(They) were level-headed and had their eye on the ball." "(They) weren't just there to get stoned and have a good time. They were the real leaders of The Resistance as far as I could see, but I didn't realize it until twenty years later."

David Harris expressed considerable ambiguity about L.A.'s countercultural drift. He watched the growing rift between the "politicos"—most of whom were Marxists from Northern California—and what he and his buddy Dennis Sweeney termed the "space cadets." Bill Garaway maintains that Harris proclaimed him "the leader of the 'space cadets.'" "David would affectionately call me that," he says.

Affectionately and sympathetically perhaps, but Harris also expressed a great deal of concern. "Garaway was a dynamite organizer," says Harris. "He walked a thin line between political organizing and space cadetism. Space cadetism in my mind was a lifestyle emphasis: that the important thing was to live with peace and love and everything would work out . . . They were into being hippies and living peace as opposed to organizing. It was a lot of communal stuff and one of the emphases we made in The Resistance was on community and building communities. There were people who took that and kind of ran with it . . . who took Haight-Ashbury and ran with it . . . The point was to make a counterculture and that was what was gonna change America. While I had my own connections to Haight-Ashbury and certainly dropped a lot of acid and smoked a lot of dope and partook of the lifestyle ... ultimately, to me, the point was to organize people and that there were political realities that had to be addressed.

"(Garaway) really got into 'space cadetism' about the time I was leaving the streets for prison ... I remember he was basically into vibrations. He had two separate trials in L.A., one for draft and one for dope. He got off on both of them and he was convinced they flooded the courtroom with all these great vibes ... The extreme form of space cadetism (happened) about the time I went to the joint and Garaway got into flying saucers. I never figured out what, but they were gonna make a flying saucer or greet some flying saucers; I can't remember exactly ... So that was Bill, and we'd laugh about it. But he kept setting up gigs and was a great Resistance organizer."

In his book *Dreams Die Hard* Harris writes of his personal frustration which peaked at a resistance conference he and Joan attended just prior to his imprisonment in 1969. "The conference," he explained, "had split into two mutually antagonistic groups:

"The first faction, the proto-Leninists, wanted to give up draft resistance organizing and turn to something more 'militant' and 'working class.' They were now into theories of 'oppression' and 'imperialism.' The second faction, the space cadets wanted to give up draft resistance organizing in favor of 'alternative life styles.' They talked about founding communes in New Mexico and co-ops in Mendocino County and commencing the new world immediately. The space cadets had complicated everything even further by ignoring the conference rules.

"Each resistance group was supposed to send only two representatives and all of them had complied except this New-Age lobby, virtually all of whom were from Los Angeles. They brought up two dilapidated school buses full of people who spent much of the conference consuming immense amounts of brown rice, chanting 'oooommmm' in unison or piling on top of each other in thirty- and forty-person heaps. All of these activities were put forward as a means of emitting 'peace vibrations' into the atmosphere.

"After six hours of the conference, Joan and I split," Harris continued. "At least I don't have to worry about the organization falling apart after I go to jail," he joked morbidly as they drove home.

Clad in our army fatigues, our faces clean-shaven, our hair cropped short, the resisters imprisoned at Safford missed this particular drama, but all of us—despite our military appearance—drank at least to some degree from the countercultural stream. The counterculture was everywhere in the late '60s and early '70s. We occupied our various positions somewhere along the continuum from strait-laced to tripped-out hippie, although most of us resided somewhere in the middle of that strange spectrum.

Even Bugsy had his countercultural ties. He had arranged for Country Joe and the Fish to play a concert during the Berkeley antidraft activities and was not above dropping a hit of acid from time to time. He recalls once in prison watching a Frank Sinatra movie while stoned, but—bored stiff—he ended up back in Dorm 1 reading something like E.P. Thompson's *Making of the English Working Class*, or the *The Eighteenth Brumaire of Louis Napoleon*. "One of the inmates came along," he says, "and was totally amazed. I mean who, but Jeffrey Segal would get stoned and read Karl Marx?"

David Harris spent a couple of formative years frequenting countercultural hotbeds in San Francisco's Haight-Ashbury as well as the Stanford campus in Palo Alto. The Grateful Dead began its career at Magoo's Pizza in Menlo Park and were soon joined by a sound technician Owsley Stanley. Owsley, whose name came to be associated with some of the finer grades of LSD, manufactured something like a million tabs of the stuff before it was outlawed in California. "To me," says Harris, "it was just part of the general experimentation . . . It was part of the great voyage of self-discovery. I read *The Tibetan Book of the Dead* before I took acid the first time. It was kind of a spiritual journey thing that was going on...I think there was obvious danger in drugs in the sense that it's pretty easy to get distracted into that. And certainly people did. But I didn't feel like they interfered with our movement at all."

Whatever illegal substance made it past the guards was freely shared. I doubt this exerted much impact on the free enterprise system within the prison, but it did encourage camaraderie among diverse groups of prisoners, excluding, of course the Klansman and his small circle of intimates. Marty Harris recalls being on the receiving end of a small batch of LSD capsules. They were left in the chapel and picked up by Oscar Sanchez whose job cleaning up the visiting area gave him a little flexibility. "Oscar gave it immediately to me," says Marty. "I mean it was like a football play . . . and he's the one who actually made the handoff." It was an act of selflessness on Oscar's part. He risked his neck and a lot of prison time just to help out a fellow inmate. "I do remember afterwards," says Marty, "that somebody came up to me and said, 'Oscar wants to know if he can try some of it.' I said, 'Of course he can; he's the one that brought it in.'"

Early on, the L.A. Resistance provided the outside supply, but later, the professionals arrived. "That's when we had that one fellow that had the Orange Sunshine," says Greg Nelson. "That one fellow was in jail for dealing acid, and his friends would come by and give him some. He had, like, tons of it . . . He had bottles of it."

"That one fellow" was Jamie, who resided, I believe, in Dorm 4. On the street, in Laguna he had worked with the Brotherhood of Eternal Love, otherwise known as the "Hippie Mafia." The Brotherhood got its start as a commune led by John Griggs in Orange County. Regarding drugs, they were downright evangelistic, producing and distributing their Orange Sunshine aggressively with the aim of ushering in a psychedelic revolution nationwide. It was the Brotherhood who cornered the acid market in the entire western region of the United States. It was the Brotherhood who hired the Weather Underground for $25,000 to spring Timothy Leary from a California prison and spirit him away to Algeria.

Safford had received modest amounts of psychedelics from the L.A. Resistance. "But this Jamie was on a whole different level," recalls David Harris. "When he came in, all of a sudden, the place was flooded . . . with all these orange triangles of acid . . . On Mondays after visits, people'd be jumping off of work trucks running to the stash box." Even the traditional drug users—the guys inclined toward heroin, the ghetto drug of choice in the 1960s—were getting high on Orange Sunshine. "Remember that dude from Phoenix we'd sometimes call Jewell?" says Harris. "I remember Jewell being all fucked up on that acid walking around the compound."

On Christmas Day of 1969, Safford was swimming in drugs. Marty Harris claims that twenty-five, thirty, maybe thirty-five guys were wandering through the dorms and out on the compound, eyes glazed over, completely obliterated on Orange Sunshine. Christmas cheer in a 1960s prison.

Counting on holiday disarray among the guards, a couple of guys jumped the perimeter wall in broad daylight and sneaked the half mile or so down to the liquor store on Highway 191. They might have slipped away and returned unnoticed, except for the quick count, the unscheduled count that caught us all by surprise. We were all ordered back to our bunks and Kenski or Thomas or maybe it was Jones or Lovely swiftly identified the missing inmates, apprehended the two runners and shipped them off—chained at the waist as usual—to La Tuna.

Blame for the incident quickly centered on Tiny, an immense new inmate from the Midwest serving time on a Zip-Six. Paul Barnes worked with him in the kitchen. "He was a big fat snitch," said Barnes. "I remember him chumming up to me, sorta digging me for info . . . seeing if he couldn't come up with something he could go tell the guard. Yeah. The rule was, you didn't talk a lot about other people anyway. I just didn't talk about (other people) until I knew somebody real well. And I never trusted him. In fact it turned out, he was there for snitching, for protection. He had started his time somewhere else, and ended up getting shipped to Safford for protection because he would've been probably killed where he was."

Several folks claimed sightings of him making a beeline for the control room as soon as word got out about the liquor store run. It was Tiny's betrayal, went the consensus, that brought the heat down into the dorms and caused the surprise count. The Mexicans used the word "dedo," or "finger" to connote the idea of a snitch; a snitch will "finger" a violator of prison rules for the cops—for "la chota." It was pretty clear to everyone that "un dedo" must have been at work.

The counterculture could be mellow and groovy, yes, but there was a hard edge to it. It was Jamie, the apostle of the drug revolution, the disciple of the Brotherhood of Eternal Love, who determined that the snitch should not go unpunished. It was Jamie who really pushed it, but I know at least three draft resisters who were involved in the retaliation as well.

"Jamie came up to me," said one of the resisters, "and said 'Let's high dose the guy; he's a snitch.' I asked if he was sure and he said, 'Yeah, he's a snitch.' And I said, 'Well, I think you're right.' I was the one who had the acid; it was given to me in a salt shaker and it was Orange Sunshine. (Another resister) had gotten a piece of pastry for Christmas that had a maraschino cherry on top of it. I gave him four hits of acid and he took that maraschino cherry off and pushed those four tabs down and then put the cherry back on."

"(Tiny) wolfed down that muffin," recalls a third resister. "He never even thought to chew it; he just wolfed it down. And he got wasted . . . I mean he took those four or five hits at once and just freaked out." Induced psychosis. Tiny ended up in the clinic where the med tech proceeded to counteract the overdose with exactly the wrong medication.

"He thought he was dying," said Kendall Copperberg, who spoke to Tiny some weeks later, "and the stuff they (the medic) gave him didn't help any; it just made him stay awake longer and feel it more . . . I heard J.C. say, 'I'm gonna go tell him.' And he did. Crampton thought that was the conscientious thing to do."

So Joe Crampton, the street-savvy dealer who knew more about drugs than anyone around, marched across the compound to the clinic and knocked on the door. Just his presence there put him at risk for a disciplinary write-up, but it was the humane thing to do. "Give him Thorazine," he told Derrick. No one really knows what Derrick did with the advice, but at least J.C. tried to do the right thing, and Tiny ultimately recovered, maybe even a little wiser.

Kendall recoiled at the whole operation. "As far as I know, it was an unjustified accusation," he asserts. "When (Tiny) talked to me, he said, 'These guys think I did this (snitching), but I didn't.' . . . He thought some guy overheard part of a conversation and completely misinterpreted it. It could have been he was just too stupid to know what he was saying . . . In any case I was put off by the fact that these guys were taking the law into their own hands. Something I've never appreciated ever since my days as a kid of watching Roy Rogers in vigilante justice . . . I thought these guys were crazy for doing it."

I don't know anyone else who swallowed the idea that Tiny might have really been innocent of ratting out his brothers. At the same time, I think everyone approved of Joe Crampton's act of kindness and mercy. Not many of us were out for the jugular on this issue, but neither did we appreciate a snitch. Of course, turning in a murderer or a rapist brings up a whole different set of ethical issues than turning in someone for making contraband burritos, drinking applejack, or sprinting down to the liquor store on Christmas Day. Protection of the inmate community and its norms requires a series of situational ethical decisions. But the high-dosing of Tiny did reveal that some of us resisters were hardening with the prison experience. We, as a group, might have changed prison culture, but prison culture was changing us as well.

The drugs, the spiritual journeys, the self-discoveries, the Gandhian nonviolence, the Marxist revolution—they all constituted a confusing thicket of convoluted pathways for a young man to wander through and find his direction.

One of Dana Rae's friends and mentors from Hawaii, James Douglass, wrote a book called *Resistance and Contemplation* which he dedicated to

Dana Rae and Nick Reidy. "The full truth of liberation," he wrote, "is, like the Tao or the Way, realized through a yin-yang movement in all things . . . If resistance is the yang of the Way of Liberation, then contemplation is its yin . . . 'Now yin, now yang; that is Tao.'"

I'm not sure I've grasped the whole of Douglass's meaning, but I read it like this: Resistance—the yang—requires a participation in the political struggles of our time; it thrusts us into the turmoil of political life. Contemplation—the yin—beckons us into realms of self-discovery, into the private world and the search for individual fulfillment. We are mistaken to pit the political life and the private life against each other; they are both necessary parts of the whole.

The contemplative life devoid of participation in the public sphere, oblivious to the suffering around us, blind to the hunger for social justice, leads to a life of self-indulgence, a life that lacks connection with our fellow humans. It leaves an emptiness in the soul, a hole in the heart. Conversely, choosing the political path without attention to matters of the individual soul leaves its own form of emptiness and impoverishment, its own denial of the fullness of life. Douglass quotes the radical activist Julius Lester who was mourning the suicide of his friend and fellow activist Bob Starobin:

> Revolutionary politics should have within it the nourishment and comfort necessary to sustain us when we enter the inevitable dark nights of the soul. And the fact that these politics could not sustain Bob Starobin is the most serious indictment possible of those politics.

Of course, that's all hindsight. As I watched the decade wither and transform into the '70s, as I turned twenty-three in that Arizona prison, I saw no need for balance or for seeking wholeness. I'm not sure I have ever found that balance, but by the winter of 1969 and 1970, I had gravitated solidly towards Bugsy's circle of revolutionaries.

It's not that the contemplative life never called me. I recall, just as Marty Harris recalled, the discovery in my high school years of *Siddhartha*—Herman Hesse's story of the Buddha's journey. I remember the exhilaration in learning of secret saints who appear—like Elijah—in humble garb when they're least expected. I remember Vasudeva, the ferryman, who gained enlightenment simply navigating his vessel and learning the currents and intricacies of the river he traversed daily. (Indeed, in later years, my thoughts sometimes dwelt on Vasudeva as I navigated my Yellow Cab night after night, year after year through the streets of Denver. Could I find enlightenment picking up fares at Ritchie's Tavern or Sid King's Crazy Horse Bar?)

By that winter, however, I had come to the realization that the contemplative life, for me, was no longer a possibility, nor was the scholarly life at the university. The turbulent history I was living through had ruled those options out. Quiet personality or no, it was no time for the quiet life.

It was not the advocacy of violence that attracted me to the Marxists. I had great respect for David and his brothers from the nonviolent Resistance. We were all headed in generally the same direction. On the philosophical plane, my views on violence hadn't much changed from the days prior to Safford. I believed before prison, and still believe today that if the Nazis are knocking on your door, if the Hutu militia is coming to burn down your child's school, if the Klan is approaching your house with a hangman's noose, or a conquering army is invading your shores, then you have the right to fight back. But philosophy and theoretical situations aside, I could not envison a group of American revolutionaries taking on the U.S. Army or, for that matter, even the Denver Police Department. What worked in China or Vietnam or Cuba could not be imported thoughtlessly to America.

In certain respects, my thoughts may have resembled David's more than I suspected at the time. Many years later I asked him about his level of commitment to the abstraction of nonviolence—to the concept that nonviolence represents an absolute value, never to be transgressed.

"I believe in situationalism," he responded. "When the parole board asked me that question—it's one of the standard ones they ask you—I said, 'Look, I take my wars one at a time. You only asked me to do one, and that one sucks. You got another war you want me to participate in? You come to me and we'll talk about it' . . . I kinda rebelled against the abstract principle, although I thought I was totally committed to nonviolence . . . I didn't feel the need to answer the abstract question before I ventured out into the world to deal with things. My father fought in World War II. My brother was a captain in the 82nd Airborne Division and myself, I wanted to go to West Point when I was a kid. So I wasn't bringing some traditional pacifism to the situation. Whenever you went around giving a speech about draft resistance, you always got that question: 'Are you against all wars? And if you're not, are you a hypocrite, or if you are, are you an idiot?' And my answer was the one I gave the parole board. 'Take 'em one at a time. We know what's on the table here and what I would've done in World War II is maybe an interesting parlor game, but it has nothing to do with reality.'"

"But . . . at that time in the movement in the late '60s, there was all this kind of neo-Marxist bullshit going on. 'We gotta fight The Man. We gotta off some pigs.' All this kind of rhetoric that I really disliked. So in those situations, I was always the guy saying, 'No. Nonviolence is it.'"

Regardless of philosophical nuance, what attracted me to Bugsy and his Marxist approach was not the violence, but the economics. I'm sure we paid homage to the theoretical need for self-defense, but that's not what we talked about in those subversive study groups in the day room of Dorm 1 and that's not what I read about in the stash of *Monthly Review* books hidden away in Bugsy's locker. We talked about social classes and inequalities, dog-eat-dog economic systems, and the relentless necessity for endless growth, inevitable depressions, and equally inevitable wars.

What drew me to Bugsy was the realization that the needle-sized hole in Watkins's arm, that Freddy Flores's tawdry drug deals in Albuquerque's South Valley, that the desperate border crossings by Saul Ramirez in search of a subminimum wage job, that Sisco's self-destructive scams around stolen automobiles—these things all cried out for institutional change, for systemic change. To be sure, my fellow inmates may have made, individually, some dumb decisions. But each chose his course within the narrowest framework—a framework of meager life choices bound by grinding poverty. They were a poor man's crimes, prosecuted by the comfortable to maintain a social order that served the comfortable. Compare theirs to the rich man's crimes: the quarterly dividends from the manufacture of cluster bombs. The healthy return on investment in banana plantations where discontented workers and union organizers were gunned down in the night. The black ink on the ledger books of oil companies and mining operations sharing profits with dictators installed by the CIA. The executive decisions to spray Agent Orange wholesale across the Vietnamese countryside. If you want to enter the world of crime, it's quite clear you should run with the rich and powerful. The benefits are far greater, the risks to life and limb generally borne by someone else.

It was the naming of the system; the recognition of the great chasm and often hidden clash between the social classes; the clear-cut analysis of market capitalism and its far reaching impact that finally swayed my head and my heart. What I gained from Bugsy was the understanding that so many of the injustices I had learned about these last few years were inextricably woven into the very fabric of our vaunted economic system. Repairing the world would require an upheaval—a sea change in material conditions, a turning, and total transformation within the economic realm.

Both Johnson and Nixon had turned their worst fears upside down: they thought the antiwar movement infiltrated by Marxists. Actually their own policies were taking antiwar activists and turning them into Marxists. There was certainly a Marxist influence in the antiwar just as Johnson and Nixon charged. But it wasn't caused by insidious infiltration from Moscow money or Chinese influence or Cuban subversion or what was left of the communist party. It was caused by the brutality of Johnson and Nixon themselves.

Chapter 13

Agitating, Rule-Breaking, and Troublemaking

Dear Sam and Sarah,

In the spring of 1969 Bugsy, Don Watkins, Max Gitman, and I shipped out for a short time to La Tuna. Your grandmother, Libby, nearly flipped out until she learned from my letter the reason why. Passover was fast approaching and neither the 300 inmates at our Arizona prison, nor the Mormon population in the town of Safford were able to produce a minyan. The BOP—in deference to the First Amendment—kindly transported us 250 miles along Interstate 10 to the more cosmopolitan institution in Anthony, New Mexico-Texas, just outside El Paso. There we arrived in chains to celebrate—behind the gun towers and the coiled rows of barbed wire—the liberation of our people. There in the chapel adjacent to Cell Block A, with a rabbi from El Paso we broke matzah, cried over the bitter herbs, washed down charoset with grape juice, and filled a wine cup to welcome the wandering prophet, Elijah, whose spirit remained undaunted by the barrier of prison walls.

La Tuna was more crowded—600 inmates—more agitated, more dank, more dangerous, more suffocating than Safford.

For the short time we were there, the prison celebrity was Joe Valachi. Valachi had long been a soldier in what became the Mafia's Genovese family headed originally by Charles "Lucky" Luciano. While serving time for trafficking in heroin, Valachi—for reasons still debated today—turned state's evidence at a U.S. Senate subcommittee hearing on mob investigations. When Valachi spilled his guts about the internal operations of "La Cosa

Nostra," it represented the first time in history that any insider had testified against the mob. It shattered an iron law, an unbreakable taboo. It was unheard of. Vito Genovese put a $100,000 price on his head. In one of the harder core joints on the East Coast or Midwest—Lewisburgh or Marion, for example—Joe Valachi would have been dead meat in five-minutes time. In La Tuna, a medium security institution half a continent away from the New York mob, he might have lasted fifteen minutes. That's why they installed him immediately in his own isolation cell, an invisible but looming presence among the general population.

Paul Barnes, who ended up eventually in La Tuna, remembers looking through a window and seeing Valachi exercising in his own private courtyard. "The way La Tuna was arranged," he says, " it had a main body and wings that ran perpendicular to it . . . In between two of these wings on the third floor was a little grassy lawn area accessible by just one door. There was a high chain-link fence with a lot of barbed wire on top that closed the little courtyard off. That was his personal exercise yard and otherwise, he lived up in his room. The word was he had his own TV and radio, and those kind of amenities. But yeah, he was there and he was still there when I left."

La Tuna was rougher than Safford, but the demographics—save for the lack of draft resisters—were about the same. Mexico lay fifteen miles to the south. Within its catchment area were the Mexican American cities of Albuquerque, Las Cruces, San Antonio, and El Paso, and the nearby valley of the Rio Grande cuts through border towns on both sides of the river.

When Reies Tijerina arrived there not long after we left, he could have had a field day organizing the Mexican inmates with his militant sermons in eloquent and rapid-fire Spanish. Tijerina had organized New Mexicans in Rio Arriba County around the issue of stolen land. He claimed the real estate there had been granted to Mexican Americans under a system of land grants issued by the Spanish and Mexican governments before the Americans brought their armies into the Southwest. In 1967, he had carried out an armed raid in the town of Tierra Amarilla where he boldly attempted a citizen's arrest of the district attorney "to bring attention to the unscrupulous means by which government and Anglo settlers had usurped Hispanic land grant properties." When authorities finally convicted him of destruction of federal property and assault on a federal officer in regard to an earlier incident in the Carson National Forest, they locked him up in the segregation unit in La Tuna. They weren't about to let him loose and talk his stuff among the general population. He was only there a short time before they transferred him to El Reno.

Besides Tijerina, a couple of other notable inmates wound up in the La Tuna lock-up not long after we left. There was Joe Maizlish who completed his national prison tour in the segregation unit at La Tuna. There was Randy Kehler whose influence would soon reverberate far beyond La Tuna's walls. Maizlish recalls asking Kehler about a visitor the latter received late in 1970. "I know I asked Randy, 'Who was your visitor?' and . . . he said it was a guy who was trying to figure out a way to make sure the American people learned what had happened in Vietnam and would never permit it to happen again . . . (He told me who the visitor was) but I forgot his name by the time I got out of prison in 1971."

The *New York Times* headline in June of 1971 jolted Maizlish's memory. Kehler's visitor at La Tuna was Daniel Ellsberg—the man who finally and forever exposed the web of lies—the covert American support for the overthrow of Diem, the deliberate fog created around the Gulf of Tonkin incidents, the suppression of LBJ's true intentions during the 1964 election campaign, the inflated body counts of Vietcong dead— that got us entangled in Vietnam in the first place. Ellsberg had surreptitiously copied 7,000 pages of a Pentagon study ordered by Secretary of Defense Robert McNamara, then released the material to the press in a devastating exposé entitled the Pentagon Papers.

It was the East Coast draft resister, Randy Kehler, who had provided Ellsberg with an inspirational turning point. Ellsberg met Kehler at a 1968 War Resisters League conference in San Francisco. As Kehler addressed a small crowd about his feelings toward his upcoming imprisonment, Ellsberg underwent an epiphany—a moral awakening that left him sobbing uncontrollably. "What I remember most vividly," wrote Ellsberg, "is not the content of what he had said but the impression he made on me as he spoke without preparation from the platform . . . I was experiencing a feeling I don't remember having had in any other circumstances. I was feeling proud of him as an American. I was proud, at the end of this conference, that this man on the platform was American . . . The auditorium was filled with people from all over the world. I was thinking as he spoke, I'm glad these foreign visitors are having a chance to hear this. He's as good as we have . . .

"When he mentioned his friends who were in prison and remarked that he would soon be joining them, it had taken me several moments to grasp what he had just said. Then it was as though an ax had split my head, and my heart broke open . . .

"We are eating our young . . . we are using them, using them up, 'wasting' them. This is what my country has come to. We have come to this . . . What I had just heard from Randy had put the question in my mind: What could I do, what should I be doing to help end the war now that I was ready to go to prison for it?"

Sensing the results of Kehler's impact on Ellsberg, stunned by the headlines in the *New York Times*, Maizlish too stopped to think about the way unpredictable connections can produce unforeseen ripples. "In some small way," he said, "or maybe some big way, Randy's posture helped encourage Ellsberg to go farther with what he was doing . . . The effects that your actions have—you just never know."

Besides Tijerina, besides Maizlish, besides Kehler, events at Safford would send several more of our brothers to La Tuna within the next year.

My redacted prison record delivered by the Department of Justice years later under the Freedom of Information Act indicates that the first minor round of confrontation occurred late in October of 1969. My own memory of what led to the incident is hazy and so are the recollections of several of my fellow inmates. In order to get a more complete picture, I tried to search out archival information kept by the Bureau of Prisons. I communicated with Misty Thompson at Safford, with Wanda Hunt at the Department of Justice, with Omar Herren at the BOP, with Eugene Morris at the National Archives and Records Administration. It all came to a dead end. Ms. Hunt informed me that all available records were located at the NARA facility in College Park, Maryland, but NARA, in turn, claimed that Safford records after 1967 were missing and possibly destroyed. So I'll try to reconstruct what happened as best I can from various accounts I gathered decades later.

If you recall, Marty Harris arrived at Safford itching to participate in a movement to change the prison system before he experienced the change of heart that led him on a more spiritual journey. Marty remembers a meeting one early evening on the bleachers of the baseball field in which a number of draft resisters discussed their ideas for organizing inside the prison.

"Somebody said maybe we should go talk to the Jehovah's Witnesses," recalls Marty. But no one really trusted any of them. "Everybody said, well I'm not gonna go to 'em," says Harris. "So I says I'll talk to 'em. In fact, I'll go talk to Robert Brown, one of the hundred and forty-four thousand . . . that were gonna go to heaven forever . . . I went over to Robert Brown and I said, 'You know, we got this thing going on here and we think you ought to join in.' I can't even remember what (the issue) was because all the things were so insignificant, Richard . . . I remember in the beginning . . . they said you could only get three books, and we called a couple of people and the next thing you know we were getting hundreds of books; we were getting as many books as we wanted . . . So we had some (other) little issue and I went over to the Jehovah's Witnesses and I had this long talk with Robert Brown trying to convince him that because they were people of Jesus that they should act in coordination with us.

"Within twenty minutes of having that conversation, I think it was Mr. Lanier who called me into the office and accused me of trying to organize the Jehovah's Witnesses and creating a riot at Safford."

When I asked Marty years later about the details of what happened, he replied, "Well, yeah, I got called in on the carpet . . . I do remember them telling me if there's any problem here, we're gonna send you to La Tuna and we don't need troublemakers here. It was never like we're shipping you out tonight or anything . . . (But) they probably threatened to send me to La Tuna; they probably did. They probably threatened to send me there . . . Maybe I wasn't around for a few hours, and so you know how things are. You know, somebody disappears for a couple of hours and (someone goes) 'Wow, I wonder if they sent him off already' . . . I guess I was the talk of the camp for a day or something."

That was indeed true. The talk on the compound was flowing fast and furious. And most of us did think—rumor or no rumor—that Marty Harris was in the lieutenant's office waiting to get shipped out—singled out unfairly as the camp agitator. Some of us thought his destination was not La Tuna but Springfield—location of the psychiatric facility. This doubled the danger since a psychiatric evaluation could cast him into a black hole from which his ascent out could get very difficult. "We found out one morning," claims Paul Barnes, "that yeah, Marty was rolled up and on his way to Springfield."

Our response took place that morning on October 24, 1969. After the 7:30 count, as the camp mustered for work detail, as the mountain crews lined up to board the transport trucks that carried them up Mt. Graham, eight draft resisters refused to report for duty. Eight of us sat down on benches under the pavilion in the middle of the compound and refused to work until we knew about Marty's status. It was a line in the sand—blatant defiance of the prison rules. We were sure we'd all be shipped off en masse that afternoon. David remembers giving away all his books to Joe Crampton in preparation for the expected transfer.

I don't know what issue Marty was discussing with Bob Brown. Some say we might have isolated ourselves by protesting trivial grievances. But the issue on October 24 was clear enough: it was solidarity with a fellow draft resister. We may or may not have been mistaken as to Marty's exact status, but our message was significant and straightforward: You don't pick us off one at a time while everyone else stands around and watches.

It was Dana Rae who had the most to lose. Dana Rae was serving a Zip-Six; he was facing six long years of prison unless he showed some signs of rehabilitation. He'd already been in trouble once. When Dana Rae worked in the office, one of the inmates asked him to smuggle out a letter outside of normal channels to circumvent any censorship from the guards. He tried to pass the letter on to Nick Reidy's wife, Pam, and got himself busted. Lanier stripped him of some good time and transferred him out of the office on to one of the mountain crews.

Now, here he was under the pavilion facing the loss of more good time and putting his chances for parole in jeopardy. "It was very scary, that strike," he says. "I don't know if I was shamed into doing it or if it was a rebirth of some of my convictions . . . I remember the guards coming down or maybe it was Lanier telling us to go report (for work) and our saying, 'No, we weren't gonna do that'. I remember the count taking place and the trucks going off . . . and our being there after the trucks left . . . We were expecting the worst. That was my singular proudest moment at Safford. I potentially had 365 days times six years plus being shipped off to La Tuna. I didn't want to do this. I didn't want to do more time. But sometimes you gotta plant the flag and say 'Here I stand,' come what may." Dana Rae just kept playing his guitar: "I've looked at life from both sides now/ from win and lose/ and still somehow/ it's life's illusions I recall/ I really don't know life at all." Geoff Fishman was there beside him, strumming along on the banjo.

When Fishman went up later for parole, he found out he had been pegged as a ringleader. He had no idea why; he was not an activist by nature. "I'm not a very politically committed person," he says. "I was pretty cooperative except for the strike. I pretty much played by the rules."

David Harris, of course, was always presumed guilty in anything that smelled of confrontation. The administration got that one wrong too. "David actually was reluctant," says Paul Barnes, "because he had made a promise to Joanie that he would not get involved in anything too stressful for her. She was pregnant at the time, expecting Gabriel, and he said he wouldn't do anything crazy until after Gabe was born. But we're sitting there at the table (in the pavilion) . . . and when it was time to line up at work sites, David didn't . . . He acknowledged us, said he had never crossed a picket line and never would."

If someone had to identify an instigator, it was probably Nick Reidy. Nick had joined The Resistance at the University of Hawaii and had gained a reputation as a man with a fiery and uncompromising demeanor—one not prone to waiting for consensus before taking action. Fishman recalls, for example, an incident that occurred while the two were out on firefighting duty together in the desert. "We had hiked in," he says. "We walked in at night—a whole crew of about fifteen guys—with little lights shining out from our helmets. When we were done, a military helicopter from Fort Huachuca came in to take us out . . . Reidy was a very interesting guy, a person with a lot of principle. If something didn't feel right, he didn't have any qualms about standing up for it . . . He wanted nothing to do with the military and refused to get into a military helicopter. The guard didn't know what to do. But in the end, all of us ended up walking out."

"Nick was not shy about voicing his opinion," adds Dana Rae, who first met Reidy in Hawaii. In Barnes's recollection, it was Reidy who was the principal organizer of the strike. He wrote up a statement and served as spokesperson for the eight of us who refused to work. As near as any could remember, the tiny group of strikers included Reidy, Dana Rae, Fishman, Terry John, Barnes, David, a guy from the kitchen named Emmett Hollander, and myself. If anyone else was there, I apologize for my faulty memory. Greg Nelson? Art Zack? Robert Siegel? Tod Friend? I just can't remember.

My own role remains a confused blur, as well, but some of it was captured in the personal BOP files I was able to obtain. Dana Rae says that one or two "idiots" left the group on the compound and ended up in the control room.

A disciplinary report filed by Sidney Sexton indicates that I was probably one of the idiots. The food service administrator accused me of "Refusing a Direct Order" and "Resisting an Officer." "At approximately 0800," wrote Sexton, "inmate Gould was ordered by Mr. Lanier to wait in the Assembly Room of the Administration Building. He flat refused to move from the hallway in front of the Control Room and stated that he was going 'out there' which inferred (returning) to the compound . . . It was necessary to physically remove him as he was resisting physically and verbally every request by Mr. Lanier. When we had reached the Assembly Room where I handed over the prisoner to Mr. Lanier, Gould jumped up from his chair to make a lunge at me. He was detained by two other officers of the camp who had interceded. His attitude was most hostile and contemptious (sic)."

I can't describe the frightening impact of Sexton's imaginative piece of fiction. Assault on a federal officer could potentially tack on eight more years of prison time to my sentence. I fired off a letter to the Department of Justice—CC'd to Warden Moran in La Tuna and to Alan Cranston, a sympathetic California senator—in order to give my version of the story.

"Immediately after the 7:30 count," I wrote, "one of the eight inmates was called to the control office. He entered the control room and several minutes later, I followed him in order to find out what his situation was.

"When I arrived, the inmate's discussion was over . . . (and) the two of us began to leave the control building. At this point, the other prisoner and I were ordered to go into the visiting room, which is about twenty feet down the corridor from where we were. When neither of us moved, four officers converged on us to carry us into the room . . . Two officials took hold of my arms and walked with me through the corridor into the visiting room. I offered no resistance and walked with them at their own pace. The man who took my left arm was Mr. Sidney Sexton, the kitchen supervisor."

The letter describes Sexton's comments in the hallway (the need to get rougher with "these people"), the threatening tone, the apparent attempt to provoke a fight.

"Upon entering the visiting room," continues the letter, "the official on my right released my right arm. Mr. Sexton then turned me around, and threw me violently against the wall. He then took me by the shoulders and threw me a second time against the wall. After being thrown twice against the wall, I instinctively raised my arms in order to protect myself. However, I immediately lowered them. At this point, another corrections officer intervened by stepping beside the two of us and calming the situation."

Except for generalized fear and anger, it's difficult to bring the details back into my field of memory. Was I an idiot to follow Emmett Hollander into the Administration Building? Should I have meekly obeyed the order to file into the visiting room? Was I rude or arrogant? I don't know those answers, but I can tell you that the charges of "lunging" or "resisting an officer" were a total fabrication by my former boss in the mess hall.

Whatever the truths were, things looked gloomy sitting in the visiting room, facing new felony charges and a quick shipment off to the hole in La Tuna.

Then within hours, the outlook—for all eight of us—shifted 180 degrees: a complete turning of the day's events. The word came down from the Ad Building: no one was going anywhere. Not Marty. Not Dana Rae. Not David. And no one said a further word about anyone resisting an officer. (The camp administrator later reported that "As far as the Gould incident is concerned, I cannot find anyone who is willing to talk about it . . . The report was filed in his Central File and no action was taken." I suspect that meant that even the guards weren't backing Sexton up.)

"That's when we learned they had to have permission from Washington to move a draft prisoner," says Paul Barnes. "We discovered—maybe via Joanie to David—that there had been a directive from the head of the federal prison system that the resisters were not to be provoked. Just let 'em do their time, sort of a hands-off laissez-faire approach to dealing with us."

Apparently, they didn't want the publicity. They didn't want the radical lawyers and the liberal U.S. representatives breathing down their necks. They didn't want to deal with political prisoners. They just wanted us out of their hair.

The victory of the mini-strike went a step further. Camp Administrator J.J. Kennedy was soon shown the door. J.B. Clendening took his place as acting camp administrator and by Christmas a new leader appeared—a modern reformer named Charles Benson. He must have arrived about the same time thirty-five or so inmates were wandering around the compound ripped on acid. He was a nice enough guy—the guy who allowed Sri Rivan, the yoga instructor in, the guy who allowed a stereo donated by Joan Baez into a listening room next to the library. I guess he wanted to keep us happy. I'm sure a lot of the old school guards were pissed off.

The mini-strike may well have constituted a victory for draft resisters, but a victory for draft resisters only. The results brought us no closer to creating the kind of environment envisioned both by David and Bugsy, the kind of movement in which prisoners of all types participated to change the conditions in their own lives.

Inmate Council

The inmate council must have been Bugsy's idea. The concept was vintage SDS, at least the kind of thing SDS would have engaged in its earlier, saner years. Prisoners for a Democratic Society: an attempt to give voice to those who previously had none, an attempt to give the disenfranchised the smallest taste of power. The new man, Benson—to his credit—was willing to experiment though I'm sure he aimed to keep it on a tight leash. As it was, it wouldn't last long. The idea of the inmates running the asylum was just too far off the map.

I somehow kept a copy dated February 8, 1970, of a committee report proposing the structure for the council: fifteen members with each dorm represented by a designated number of delegates elected every three months. Provisions for recall elections upon the request of any five inmates in a particular dorm. Bilingual meetings held at least once every two weeks. "As the primary avenue of communication with the administration," it read, "the inmate committee shall divide itself into three subcommittees, each dealing with an area of camp life: 1) recreation and visiting, 2) work and education, 3) facilities.

In its language, it sounded mundane to the extreme, but within the context of the top-down hierarchy of the prison environment, the implications were radical. Here were men raised on ranches in Guanajato or Tamaulipas, on barrio streets in East L.A. or Phoenix grappling with the ideas of bylaws, recall elections, and committee delegates—grappling with the very vocabulary of self-governance.

"It was an attempt to deal—relatively speaking—with institutional change," says Bugsy. "So we had our election that Lanier and Rios were not very happy with. And then we had some early meetings in which one of the issues that council members pushed—most of us at any rate—was to have bilingual meetings . . . It was a principal matter of contention . . . which they balked at. They were really not happy about that . . . I remember they did produce one of the guards to translate, and I think we had a meeting or two in which we started to talk about issues. And then they stopped calling the meetings and it sort of died. I don't know whether it was because they were afraid we might be getting into real stuff . . . I did not have a really long list of issues but rather expected issues . . . to come out of the people on the council. We did get some Spanish books for the library, not a whole lot, but there wasn't a whole lot in the library to begin with. And we got some Spanish movies.

"Once a week—I think it was Wednesdays—we would have films. For a brief period of time, they started to show very overtly anticommunist propaganda films. I suspect somebody had the bright idea that they needed to counteract the influence of us Lefties. The one I remember in particular was this film called *Communism on the Map*. It starts out with a map of the world and various countries in shades of red and pink to show which are commie-influenced or commie-infiltrated or commie-run. As I remember, South Africa and Taiwan were the only ones that were all white, which showed that they were (free of communist influence). Everybody else had some color—even the United States. I mean it was John Birch–like; (it represented the point of view of those) who accused Dwight Eisenhower of being a communist sympathizer. So those were the films.

"There were a lot of John Wayne movies ... and as I remember a fair amount of 1950s science fiction. Then after some pressure from a number of us, we got them to agree to bring in some Spanish-language films."

One of the films they brought in sounded almost Spanish, almost comprehensible, but nobody could quite follow what was going on. People began to mutter, "What in the hell is this?" Then it all became clear: the movie was made in Brazil, its Portuguese dialogue frustratingly familiar, but not quite graspable to our Mexican audience.

Dark Shadows

Bugsy was involved in the formation of another organization, as well—this one secret, covert, and underground. Early on, he had given up going to dinner, finding it both unsatisfying and unhealthy. Instead, he walked over to the TV pavilion on the compound to watch the early evening news. Sometimes, he would catch the last five or ten minutes of what he called a "weird program"—weird enough to stimulate his interest and induce him to arrive early enough to watch the show from beginning to end. The program turned out to be "Dark Shadows," a melodramatic soap opera featuring the vampire Barnabas Collins and a medley of werewolves, zombies, witches, and warlocks inhabiting a world with time travel and even a parallel universe. Bugsy was soon joined by a half dozen of Safford's own weird collection of characters, and "Dark Shadows" developed something of a cult following. Someone—it was probably Bradley Littlefield, who possessed a wonderful sense of the absurd—came up with the idea of initiating an organization: something akin to a mock fan club or a group of Trekkies. They elected Bugsy, who had discovered the program, as president. And so was born the organization, "Sons of Dark Shadows."

It wasn't long before word got back to Bugsy that the guards had grown uneasy. They had learned that the dreaded SDS was lurking in their midst right there in southern Arizona. They kept on heightened alert, watching for suspicious activity. What they didn't know was that SDS stood not for Students for a Democratic Society but for Sons of Dark Shadows. Bugsy says that every now and then, they'd put out the word on the grapevine that SDS was organizing a demonstration just to keep the guards on their toes.

"I don't remember all the details," he says, "but this sort of thing happened prior to one of the World Series games. As a consequence, they kept everybody in camp . . . because they were afraid something was going (to happen) up on the road . . . So everybody got to watch the ball game."

Power Games

Even with the new administration, a number of issues hovered in the atmosphere in the aftermath of the work stoppage. They gnawed away at any chance for goodwill and eventually resulted in another minor clash—this one involving the vast majority of the camp.

There were a lot of little penny-ante things played out in the complicated scheme of relations between guards and inmates. David Harris, for instance, played on the camp basketball team that used to go to places like the state prison at Ft. Grant and play the guards. He was six foot three, a pretty good shot, and had definitely earned a spot as a starting forward. One game he got hot and scored thirty points. The following game Joan Baez came out to see her husband play. "My wife had never seen me play basketball because it wasn't a big part of my life on the streets," says Harris. "So she was coming out and was gonna go to one of the games . . . Kenski benched me the whole game. He was the official coach because we had to have a cop play that role . . . He didn't know anything about basketball but he made sure I didn't play. I think he was currying favor with his superiors. Let's fuck with this guy; you know how they do it." In the big scheme of things, it's nothing, but in the daily grind, the petty little power games can eat away at you.

Geoff Fishman was always looking for knickknacks he could use for arts and crafts. While on firefighting duty, he came upon a few empty shell casings, scooped them up, and deposited them in his locker. He figured he'd hammer them, beat them—do something with them. They found them during locker inspection and wrote him up for contraband like he was assembling some kind of arsenal. He found out later, the incident cost him some parole time.

At meal times, dormitories were sent to the chow hall on a rotating basis so that each barracks had the opportunity to be first in line. Because some guys were sneaking into whatever dorm was assigned to go first, the guards posted a notice in each building warning of disciplinary action for chow-line violators. Saul Ramirez came over after count and asked me to come over to Dorm 3 to translate the new regulation. The notice was written only in English and there was, Saul told me, some confusion over what it said. That's when I got caught in the Great Safford Chow-Line Raid. Anyone not authorized to be in Dorm 3 got rounded up by Officer Thomas. He assigned the offenders on the spot to go clean the corridor of the Administration Building. I usually can't think too quickly on my feet, but this time I was on it: a violation of due process, I responded. I wanted the opportunity to defend myself and explain my presence in Dorm 3 before being summarily punished. Thomas wrote me up for "Out of Bounds, Failure to Do Assigned Task, and Insolence." (On the disciplinary report form, Thomas wrote down "23" in the space provided for my "Age" and a question mark under "Mental Age.") Within the vastly unequal realm of guard-inmate relations, it didn't take much to be labeled "insolent." Insolence was a catch-all phrase. If they couldn't hang you on anything else, they could always get you on "insolence." I did get my trial and Lt. Lanier even wrote that I appeared before the "Adjustment Committee" not with insolence but with a "good attitude." Attitude or no, they gave me an extra day's cleaning duty in the mess hall.

That same winter, the men who ran Tres Piedras—The Three Rocks Restaurant out by the rock crusher—got busted and shipped off to Texas. They had taken their chances and lost, but nevertheless, their punishment ratcheted up the tension one more notch. Ramirez and Cota took that one especially to heart.

Don't Get Sick

Of greater importance was the issue of basic medical care. It was a system wide failure. Recall that the strike that got Joe Maizlish shipped out of Terminal Island was ignited in part by the death of Mr. Ho who had been given aspirin for days to cure the pneumonia he eventually succumbed to. Recall that the hunger strike in which David Harris participated in San Francisco County exploded because an inmate with pleurisy was left lying in his cell as he struggled to breathe.

After Paul Barnes was transferred to La Tuna, he decided, along with Randy Kehler and a couple of others, to document the specific individual complaints of their fellow inmates. "We spent weeks," he says, "going around and talking with everybody who had a story and who would talk to us about it. There were all kinds of complaints...People who had ulcers who could never get medication for them. People who had chronic pain that was never seriously addressed. People with respiratory problems ... (We asked them) how long it took to get care and attention. How were they treated at the hospital.

"When I went to jail, I was in the process of having root canals and three teeth capped. I wasn't looking to have this work completed in jail. But my teeth—a couple of them got infected, and it was so painful and so bad I had to go to the dentist at Safford. The way they deal with it, they don't fix your teeth; they just pull them. These two teeth right here, they just yanked right out of my head. No anesthetic. I damn near passed out.

"But La Tuna is even worse ... The kind of medicine practiced in the prison system is just very poor and very slow. And we documented this. It was my job the day I was released to smuggle out of prison a report on medical conditions and deliver it to a local lawyer in El Paso ... We made arrangements to leave the documents in a folder, and we got one of our inmate friends who worked in the administrative office to type it all up. So it was all looking real sharp.

"As you exit La Tuna out the front doors, there's a little anteroom entrance and off to the right were toilet facilities for visitors. We made arrangements to have the documents hidden in that bathroom. As I left the institution, I walk out the barred gates and then through another set of doors and I go right into that bathroom and grab the documents that have been hidden behind the water tank of the toilet. I stuffed "em down the front of my pants, under my shirt, and walked out ...I still have one more set of doors, down a set of steps past the gun tower ... and I'm thinking, 'Goddam, I hope nobody saw me go into that bathroom; I'll be back in this jail in minutes' ...But I walked past the gun tower and into the waiting car that a friend had there for me. My last act at La Tuna was smuggling out those documents."

Upon my release, I, like Paul turned in a report to the ACLU in Denver about conditions in Safford and although I hadn't taken any formal surveys, one of the main emphases was on health care. "During my confinement," I wrote, "the med tech assistant misset a broken bone so that the victim had to be shipped to another prison where the bone could be rebroken and reset. He pulled out an ingrown toenail in such a manner that infection set in and a doctor had to be summoned to undo the damage. He refused to allow an inmate with a kidney infection to see a doctor until the case became so serious that the patient required emergency hospitalization outside the camp . . . (Moreover) the man holds prisoners in contempt. He hates Mexicans, draft objectors, and drug offenders who represent about 80 percent of the inmate population. The result of all this is that no one can enter the clinic with any assurance that he will receive medical attention. The MTA is the only man in the camp with authority to issue a 'lay-in'—a pass which excuses a sick man from work. Regularly, sick men must go to work, because (the MTA's) contempt for prisoners causes lay-ins to be practically unobtainable . . . Because of the mistrust he has inspired in the prisoners, many inmates feel safer just riding out their illnesses without ever going near the hospital."

Greg Nelson's story was typical of the medical care at Safford. "I'm still angry about it," he told me decades after our release. "Paul Barnes and I, we were horsing around on the handball court. Just being young fools, we started wrestling around and he grabbed me and kind of threw me to the ground. Somehow, my leg got caught up in between his, and my knee got ripped apart. I knew it was hurt; it was aching really bad, but I didn't know how bad. I limped off the handball court back to my dorm. My knee started to swell up—more and more swollen till it was like the size of a grapefruit. It was this huge swollen mess. I hobbled up to the control room with the help of some people and said, 'Man, my knee is really screwed up; I need something for it.'

"They had an EMT. He wasn't a real doctor, but he was basically in charge of the clinic . . . He was totally unsympathetic to any draft people . . . They called over to him from the control room and it turned out he was off bowling. He said he'd seen me limping across earlier and if I had a problem, I shoulda come then. He said they should give me a couple of aspirin and he'd see me in the morning . . . I remember having to pee that night and I literally had to crawl on my butt to get there; I mean my leg was in such pain. All I ever got for that knee was aspirin and a pair of crutches.

"My knees basically got destroyed while I was in jail—both of them. I was carrying rocks on the road crew one day and I twisted the other knee somehow ... That time the only help I got was from some of the guys from Mexico—some of the small village guys. They were untrained veterinarian-type guys who had owned horses. I don't know where they got it, but they had this incredibly hot horse liniment. I remember being in incredible pain and them putting it on my knee and just rubbing it and rubbing it. It (was so hot) it burned, but it worked. That was the only medicine I got—from other prisoners.

"By the time I left prison, I couldn't ride a bicycle ... It turned out part of the cartilage had calcified into this chip of bone about the size of a dime that was just floating around loose in my knee ... For years I was in terrible agony. I finally went to Kaiser when I was working in the printing industry and the guy said, 'You should have gotten this thing operated on years ago.' It was like an antiwar wound, but there was no help for an antiwar wound ... If the med tech was a real doctor who cared at all, he probably should have had me operated on right then ... I mean when your knee is the size of a grapefruit, they're supposed to do something ... Basically my knee was ruined for the rest of my life."

Between the Mexicans and the draft offenders, the med tech didn't much like anybody among the inmates at Safford. David Harris remembers several people trying to talk to Camp Administrator Benson about the problem. Nobody much sympathized with Tiny, the alleged snitch, but the tech's misdiagnosis of him in the clinic didn't instill any confidence about the quality of medical care. Then in February of 1970 a man with a history of epilepsy—it might have been the old man, Ronquillo—had a seizure in Dorm 4. When word got out that the tech stretched him out on the clinic floor and tested him for drugs instead of treating for epilepsy, the news sent a wave of anger through the prison. Any little incident afterwards could ignite some kind of action.

Scottish Woodcock

It was the mess hall that finally put the camp over the edge. Grumbling about prison food is, of course a time-honored tradition, but I think it was more the context of the food situation than the food itself. The food strike spurred some controversy among inmates—even between draft resisters—because there were differing attitudes toward the food's quality. Even those who spent long hours working in the kitchen expressed wide-ranging opinions.

Kendall, for instance, thought the food quite adequate. "I felt good about the food," he says. "The recipes were okay; it was tasty enough. There was never portion control except on meat. Bread, mashed potatoes, big #10 cans of vegetables . . . there was all you could eat. The main dishes—eggs, potatoes, meat they made enough for a serving per person. There was always plenty of milk. Plenty of bread. Desserts too. They weren't always nice but there was always desserts . . . I would often crack eggs for scrambled eggs and I remember inmates complaining about . . . all these powdered eggs. I said, 'No, these are real eggs . . . There are no powdered eggs in that kitchen.' I couldn't imagine anything less worthwhile than complaining about prison food. It was good food and there was always plenty . . . It's plain to see you've never been hungry . . . in your life if you think this is bad food."

As a baker, Bugsy, had somewhat different memories. Recalling that the Mexicans called him "El Torero" (the Bullfighter) because he used to wear his paper hat (required for sanitation) sideways, he says that "We were required each day to prepare a big vat of pudding—cornstarch pudding. I mean it was pretty awful stuff. Because he was such a fuck-up, we would assign E. to do the pudding. You couldn't do too much to screw it up because it was awful enough anyways. And we got him out of our hair. I mean we wanted to get our job done and out of the way and he would go wandering off and spacing out. So he would do the pudding.

"I decided that vegetable soup, stew, and meat loaf were essentially the same thing depending on how much water you put in. We used to claim that those of us in the bakery essentially made the meat loaf because it was so diluted with bread. A lot of old bread and a lot of leftover vegetables and the like all went into the meat loaf."

"One time Sexton came up to me with instructions on how to make sweet dough for cinnamon rolls without using so many eggs. I don't know whether it was because he wanted to take the eggs himself or he thought he was gonna save money. In any event, he came up and said 'You could do this and this and that and you only have to use half as many or a third as many eggs.' Then I pulled out the official Bureau of Prison recipe list. It was a file of cards you were supposed to look at daily. And I said, 'Oops. Nope. Here's the recipe. I'm required to follow the official Bureau of Prison recipe.' He was pretty pissed but there was nothing he could do."

Paul Barnes's memories of kitchen work weren't particularly positive either. "Very high starch and low protein," he recalls. "I remember the guards coming in when there was meat with their personal trucks riding high. Then they left with their trucks riding low. We couldn't prove it, but we knew (the theft) was happening. There were huge tubs in the kitchen and we'd open up gallon cans of canned vegetables; I mean ten- to fifteen-gallon cans of peas into a huge pot and you'd stir till they were hot. And there was always bread pudding which wasn't much beyond Elmer's glue in terms of taste or texture."

It wasn't the healthiest food, but there was plenty of it except for Greg and a few other vegetarians who truly suffered. Since much of the food was saturated with lard, their diets remained extremely limited. "They had boiled-out beans," says Greg. "String beans that had been boiled for two days and canned corn boiled out for two days. Whatever they gave you, it didn't have much nutritional value . . . It took me a while, and we had to fight for it, but I finally got them to let us have dried roasted soybeans in the commissary. That was my source of protein."

As for the rest of us, no one really went hungry, especially if you liked mashed potatoes, bread and gravy, cooked carrots, and canned peas. One standard fare was "shit on the shingle:" chipped beef—little morsels of low-grade meat—soaked abundantly in gravy. I happen to like gravy so I couldn't complain too much. I picked up a few pounds from a diet weighted towards starch and grease.

What was hard to take was the public-relations aspect. If you read the menu—which everybody did—it looked like we were dining in style. On paper, we had a different kind of potato every day: creamed potatoes, whipped potatoes, scalloped potatoes, Potatoes Delmonico, German potatoes, Holiday Potato Casserole. Translated into the reality of mess hall meals, we had mashed potatoes every day. Bugsy once wrote a poem about the thirty-seven different names they used for mashed potatoes. A little less starch and a little more honesty would have been greatly appreciated.

One provocation came late in 1969 when the menu was put to use publically as a propaganda tool. Wade Cavanaugh, a reporter for the *Arizona Republic* looked at one of Sexton's creatively written menus and utilized it as part of a hatchet job he wrote about conditions in Safford. One particular day the bakers made an ordinary run of flat cakes for dessert and topped them off with a few one-gallon cans of heavily syrupped strawberries. After conducting a couple of cursory interviews with the staff, Cavanaugh came out with his feature story: "It's a Strawberry Shortcake Life for Draft Dodgers." From snotty headline to final paragraph, the story was a piece of shabby reporting, transparently designed to reinforce the public's reservoir of resentment against draft resisters. It was a story that stuck in our craw for months.

And so the tension grew bit by bit. By February of 1970, any number of minor provocations might have set us off. The final spark was really a trivial thing: just one more overblown entry on the dinner menu. "Scottish Woodcock," it said. It certainly aroused our curiosity; we all wondered what Scottish Woodcock might taste like. After all, it sounded exotic; it sounded like some kind of wild fowl, a game bird, a delicacy from across the ocean.

When Dorm 4 got to the chow hall, they soon found out what Scottish Woodcock really was: one more variation of shit on the shingle. Some kind of stringy chicken substituted for the chipped beef, but basically it was shit on the shingle. If Sexton had just written "creamed chicken" or even better, "shit on the shingle" on the menu, I doubt there would have been any reaction at all. We would have grumbled and moved on. But somehow the picture of a Scottish Woodcock crowing to call attention to the gourmet chef in the Safford mess hall stood out as a symbol of hypocrisy.

Boycott

I'm not sure exactly how it began, but clearly it started among David Harris's circle of friends in Dorm 4. Harris later wrote that Jewell the barber opened the the discussion: "We don't got to take all this; you know that, man." They put out a call, not for a strict hunger strike, but for a boycott of the cafeteria. The demands: better food and a real doctor in the clinic.

By avoiding, on the one hand, a work strike, which would have brought down instant repression, and, on the other, a hunger strike, which required more suffering than necessary (especially considering the vagueness of the demands around food), the boycott's instigators hoped to encourage maximum participation among the camp's inmates.

The action clearly originated in David's circle, but it spread out in waves from there. I went over to Dorms 3 and 5—largely Mexican dorms—and talked to Ramirez and Cota, Flaco and Chato, and anyone else who was interested or who had questions. I explained as best I could the strategy and the issues. It felt good. It felt good to be able to contribute in such a concrete way. I wasn't sure how these guys might react to a call for a food strike. They had come—most of them—from the poorest ranches and most squalid colonias in Mexico and here in Safford, at least they were getting three squares a day. Would they see the food issue as a dead end?

I should have known better; I had heard some of their stories already. They tended to share among themselves a basic view of the U.S. justice system: a fast-moving train, flattening any hapless creature who wandered into its path. The court system for them bore no resemblance to that described in the civics textbooks or in the movies.

They told me, for example, what seemed to be standard operating procedure for prosecuting illegal entry cases: line up twenty or thirty defendants at a time, assign them all to a single public defender (invariably one who spoke no Spanish), advise them through an interpreter to plead guilty, sentence them, and return them all to lock-up within an hour or two. All very efficient.

No one bothered to explain the basics of courtroom procedure. They were all invisible. Shortly after his arrival in Safford in May of 1969, Carlos Romero Navarro told me about his courtroom experience. Arrested for smuggling "aliens" across the California border, he was instructed by the interpreter, he claimed, to "Say 'yes' to everything." "Will you accept a six-month sentence?" "Yes," he replied, figuring he'd "good-time" it out in four months. It was only after the return to his cell in San Diego County that he learned what really happened from his cell partner who spoke just enough English to understand the proceedings. The judge had actually given him a full year—double what he thought he had agreed to. Had he understood or had he been able to afford a lawyer, he would have argued for a sentence reduction on the grounds of hardship: he had twelve kids waiting for him in Oakland. Then again, had he the money for a lawyer, he wouldn't have been a hardship case to begin with. Romero knew the risks of smuggling and was no whiner. What he resented, however, was being misled—what he resented was being double-crossed and kept in the dark.

There was José Ronquillo's case, as well. He had been sentenced to probation in 1967 for illegal entry and deported to Mexico. When he got busted in Sacramento County two years later, they locked him up pending a probation hearing, or so he believed. Two weeks later, he found himself in Safford, summarily shipped off. It was only after his arrival here that he learned that he'd have to complete his three-year sentence in prison. No hearing, no communication, no explanation. Like Romero, his anger stemmed not from doing time, but from the fact that nobody told him a thing—that he had been shipped off like some kind of inert cargo.

The Mexicans in Dorms 1, 3, and 5—the bulk of the camp—they were tired. They were tired of the railroad system of justice, tired of the mass prosecutions. They were tired of hearing the word "wetback" uttered casually by the guards. They were tired of getting the pot-washing and mopping jobs while watching Anglos get the jobs as cooks and electricians. They were incensed hearing about one of their own—Ronquillo—accused of drug use while writhing on the clinic floor suffering an epileptic seizure. They were angry that their brothers who ran the burrito operation at El Restaurante de Tres Piedras had been busted and shipped off. They were tired of being invisible. And I'm sure they remembered, as well, the spirit of Doroteo Arango—the revolutionary of the North they all revered—the man who in 1917 had confounded an entire expeditionary force of the U.S. Army under General Pershing. They were ready to stand up over just about any issue that came down the road. It was a matter of self-respect.

The same was true—the quest for self-respect—for most of the rest of the population. "At some point," said Paul Barnes, "you say to yourself, 'I'm not gonna do this anymore. I'm gonna make some kind of stand, some kind of statement'. Really, what it is, is claiming sovereignty for yourself . . . reclaiming some sort of power for yourself . . . (The food strike) was the handle that (we) used; it was the means."

For draft resisters, the tensions were framed by the war and by our understanding of the political nature of the prison system. We understood full well that the Bureau of Prisons was no neutral player regarding Vietnam. Perhaps Kenski and Thomas, Lanier and Rios—maybe even Benson—failed to see any connection between their workaday lives and the killing in Southeast Asia. But we saw it. They were the enforcers. The BOP provided the unthinkable consequences for hundreds of thousands of young men who stood on the brink, who knew in their hearts that this particular war stunk—that this was a war for a president's ego, rather than the defense of the nation—but who saw no viable options. As the enforcer, the BOP was an active contributor to the war effort in Vietnam; the BOP was fair game.

There were certainly a few among us who believed we were just looking for trouble, looking for excuses to stir things up. I suppose they were right in their own way. But anyone trying to repair a shattered world, anyone looking toward social change, must necessarily search for tools and for issues that bring new realizations to the way people perceive the world. Perhaps a chow-hall boycott over Scottish Woodcock was not the most perfect issue. But given the political role of the justice system, given the yearning of so many inmates to engage in some kind of concerted action, given the heartfelt desire for self-respect, I have no regrets. You can bide your time for years waiting for exactly the right issue to take a stand on. I think for most of us, doing a year and a half, two years, three years without showing the slightest sign of concerted resistance would have been profoundly embarrassing.

Once the word got around, we had a day to prepare. The commissary was open on Thursday and many of us maxed out our accounts by spending $20 all in one shot on what food was available—soynuts, Tang, and candy bars—to be distributed throughout the camp and shared by everyone.

On the appointed day, the air was thick with tension as everyone watched—Snickers and Baby Ruths in hand—to see who would cross the invisible picket line. Dorm 6 went first. There was no support in Dorm 6 and almost all them crossed. It made us all uneasy. Then came Dorm 4. Hardly a soul moved. They were solid. Dorm 2: only a few trickled out down the compound to the mess hall. Dorms 1, then 3, then 5. Only a trickle from each of them. The kitchen crew had to report for work, but hardly any of them ate the food they had just prepared. Sexton was purple; Sexton was raging. He could be heard screaming at the guys on the compound who refused to go in. Fully 60 percent of the prisoners refused to cross the line and enter the mess hall.

David Harris claimed that the administration soon began to announce that anyone who chose to eat would be assured protection, presumably from the goons and thugs among the strike leaders. The hilarity of that announcement served to raise our numbers. Soon the boycott was 70 or 75 percent effective.

The contraband food ring stepped up to feed as many people as it could. Peanut butter appeared out of Bugsy's locker. The burrito kitchen made a speedy revival in the wake of the bust that sent the original chefs to La Tuna. Patrick Bryan who worked in the laundry recalls the hole at the top of the laundry wall. "There was a warehouse behind the laundry and back of the kitchen," he says. "Separating the food in the warehouse from the clothing in the laundry was a physical barrier—a grating like a fence that climbed up towards the ceiling. But it stopped before it got to the ceiling; there was hole at the top. That's where the kitchen crew liberated the cans of food out of the stockpile. We would cover the cans with clothing—surplus military clothes—and smuggle them through the hole at the top, through the laundry and then out to the dorms where we distributed them."

Everything was shared. Any walls still standing between the farm boys from Guanajuato, the street dealers from Albuquerque and East L.A., and the college boys from Stanford and UCLA momentarily dissolved. It was an object lesson in community self-organization and cooperation.

If only we could have kept it up. As quickly as it ignited, it burned out. In three or four days, the momentum began to fade—a basketball team gone cold. I'm not sure what happened; it just started to fizzle. We were strong on spontaneity and short on organization. Perhaps our goals were too vague; no one could really visualize what a victory might look like. At any rate, men began to drift back to the chow hall and only a small core remained true. Looking back the whole thing seems so anticlimactic now. Joan Baez came out and paraded along the perimeter wall. Benson definitely took notice.

It was on a Sunday afternoon that some of the inmates saw wisps of smoke whirling skyward from the direction of the lower mountain. No one knew what it might be until the next morning when the mountain crew returned to work. It was our hogan. The guards had burned it down in retaliation for the boycott. The painted canvas roof and the structure's sapling frames went up in flames; only the rock walls remained.

First on the scene were three resisters: Nick Reidy, David Harris, and Paul Barnes. "We were all milling around when Kenski came up," remembers Barnes. "Nick was sort of pacing and thinking about all this; you could tell he was agitated and pissed because they burned it down . . . David was looking at Nick and told him, 'We're with you.' Then Kenski said, 'Okay, it's time to get to work.' And Nick said, 'Yeah, I don't think I'm working today.' That's when Kenski pulled out his phone—his walkie-talkie—and made the call down to camp. Then David said, 'I'm not working either.' So Kenski made his call to . . . the office and says, 'Reidy refuses to work. Harris refuses to work'—So I completed his sentence, saying, 'And Barnes.' And Kenski repeated it on the phone. 'And Barnes refuses to work.' The next thing we know, he's off the phone and says, 'Come on, pick up your stuff and get in the truck.'"

I don't know what J.C. did to get himself involved. He never refused to work but at the end of the day, they took him along too. I didn't blame any of them. I think the boycott was pretty much over by then, anyway. Everyone has his own individual limits for what he's willing to put up with, and each of them—Nick, David, Paul—had reached his limit. Before dusk, they were all headed east to join Joe Maizlish in the segregation unit at La Tuna.

Chapter 14

Release

Dear Sam and Sarah,

They tell me they did some hard time in La Tuna. They remained in segregation for months and watched more than one friend self-destruct on drugs injected with discarded needles from the hospital clinic. The guards in La Tuna stepped up the harassment on Harris.

"Once they busted my visit," he said. "I had my son, Gabriel, out there—less than a year old. It was hot and the visiting yard at La Tuna had a couple of spigots for watering the lawn. I took my son's clothes off and put him under the spigot (to cool him off). They busted me for having a naked child. Closed my visit down. And they were always doing shit like that.

"I'd be sitting up in C-Block in my good khakis, my visiting-room clothes, and they'd call my number. They'd open my cell door and I'd step out, go down to the end of the cell block, go through another locked gate, go through a pat search, go down the stair to the gate that leads to the administrative area, go into a room, take all my clothes off, do the search, including the cavity search—you know, bend over and do the whole thing. And I'd get my clothes back on; I could see my people and they'd say, 'Oh, man. Look at those sideburns. You can't go out there lookin' like that.' I'd have to go back. Go through the cavity search again. Go through the whole process in reverse. Get back to my cell. Take a quarter off my sideburns or whatever and then turn around and do it all again.

"And there was always the threat: you fuck around and we're gonna take your visits away. They knew that was the one way to get to me because that was my relationship with my son—eight hours on a weekend in West Texas in a prison visiting yard—for the first fifteen months he was alive."

I reached my mandatory release date shortly after Reidy, Harris, Barnes, and Crampton were shipped out to Texas, having served a year and a half on Judge Arraj's two-year sentence. Through the mini work stoppage in October, through the control room confrontation with Sexton, through the Dorm 3 chow-line raid and the insolence charge, through the mess hall boycott, the prison authorities opted not to strip me of any good time. I was no threat and besides, I think they wanted us all out of jail as quickly as possible unless we outright refused every form of cooperation. In March of 1970, they gave me a pair of dress khakis, $30 dollars in cash, and a bus ticket home to Denver.

The anticipation had built up for weeks. I could just taste it: the air and the sunshine would be somehow different, more vibrant. Visions of fat juicy cheeseburgers danced around in my dreams. And girls! There would be girls in the free world!

The first letdown was the Greyhound station in Deming, New Mexico, just over the border from Arizona. The air was stuffy; I was exhausted from the sleepless nights of the last few weeks. I ordered a cheeseburger at the counter. The bun was stale, the inside soggy with surplus ketchup, the burger dry and barely edible, the melted American cheese cold. We had fifteen minutes; I gulped it down joylessly. Here I was in Paradise, in the land of the free, and all I felt was empty and lost. There was no one to talk to, no one who had a clue of what the last two years had been like. I missed the old buddies in Dorm 1, missed the camaraderie, missed the card games and the easy banter. I felt all alone.

"I don't think I realized (until I got out)," said Dana Rae "what kind of a unique brotherhood we had. Oh yeah, I was lonely when I got out . . . For one I was put up by my sister briefly and her husband kicked me out. At some point I remember not being welcome there anymore. I remember being passed along to various homes. And I remember having a hard time getting a job . . . When I began to travel and met other (former prisoners)—you, Paul, Ken, Nick—that time in prison just expanded again. We would talk, oh yeah, and everything was vibrant; everything was tingling; everything was alive. It was exciting, it was reinforcing of something that I'm glad I did—that little brotherhood that we had there and how unique it was and how precious it was at that time."

Kendall struggled for years before finding his way: "I was totally adrift. I got a job as a stagehand, but . . . they had to let me go. Apparently I couldn't perform . . . They said we need somebody who's here—whose mind is all here as well as his body . . . I was just drifting mentally, I guess. I was lost, confused; I didn't know what the hell was going on.

"I have no real memories for years after prison. Just odd jobs. For a few years I tried my best to be spiritual. I had read books in prison but I found I had zero spiritual aspects to my personality. I could never meditate worth a damn. I'd sit there quietly and say, 'Okay. Here I am. Sitting quietly. This is nice enough but is there anything out there? Anybody calling my name? Yoohoo, here I am. Well, I'll sit quietly a little bit longer maybe something will happen. Or maybe this is just it. Maybe this is it. Maybe that's all they're trying to do.' . . . It wasn't enough for me. I'm just not spiritually inclined."

I found out soon enough a lot of guys do better in prison than outside of it. I had even seen a short-timer, just two days shy of his release date take a swing at another inmate so he'd lose his good time and get shipped back to La Tuna. Deep down, perhaps subconsciously, he was scared to death of the streets. He preferred the routine, the predictability of prison. In the joint, he had few decisions to make; his life was in someone else's hands.

Freddy had just been released and had given me an address on Arno Street in Albuquerque. Since I had no "tail"— no obligation to report to a parole officer—I went to visit him on his own turf in the South Valley. Freddy had gone cold turkey in La Tuna, left the heroin habit behind, got his GED with Bugsy's help. He had acquired the first taste of political awareness—that his fall had not been his alone. He was a changed man. The "abrazos"—the hugs—were warm; it was so good to see a Safford brother.

Those Albuquerque streets were tough. We kicked around, went to a few bars, hooked up with his brother and some old friends. "Come on and trip with me," his brother kept telling him. "Come on, man." "No, man. I just got out of the joint. Leave me alone." "Come on, man, trip with me." For two days I saw Freddy hold his own as his brother kept up the pressure. I don't know what was going on in Freddy's mind; I don't know if he was sizing up his prospects on the street and coming to some grim conclusions. But on the third day I watched as he surrendered. "Come on, Freddy, trip with me." I watched as he tied the tourniquet tightly above the crook of his elbow. No, Freddy; don't do it! I watched as the needle found the vein and he pushed in on the plunger. Shaken, sick at heart and physically ill, I got on a Greyhound the next day and left "Alburque."

I had some savings from before my sentence so I figured I'd blow it all in one grand trip. In the tiny village of Villa Gonzales in Tamaulipas, I visited

Saul Ramirez who had also thrived in the prison environment. We had been quite close. Practically every day I visited him in Dorm 3 or he came over to Dorm 1 to trade vocabulary. He taught me three or four words in Spanish daily and I did the same for him in English. He was serious, disciplined, and sober. His aim was to improve his English, certainly enough to better blend in within the United States, and maybe get a better job. He was directed and had a plan. I'm afraid he caught on to English a lot quicker than I to Spanish.

Months after I saw him in Mexico, he jumped the border again around Brownsville, made his way up to Colorado, and pounded on my door one night on Eliot Street. He was obliterated on cheap wine, needed to be taken care of. When I moved to Moncrieff Avenue on the north side, he pounded once again on my door, once again, trashed, once again requiring painstaking care. He knocked on my row house door on East Dakota and practically fell over onto the living room floor. The streets for Ramirez were harder and more a struggle than jail.

J.C.'s story was the hardest to stomach. He had been, as Paul Barnes noted, a highly respected member of the Safford community, a father figure and mentor, a builder and farmer, a man who attracted a following. Upon his release, he hooked up with David and Paul in the San Joaquin Valley and helped run the People's Union Coop Farm, an offshoot of the Institute for the Study of Nonviolence. The farm fell apart after three years and Joe Crampton returned for a time to Albuquerque.

"He started dealing dope again in New Mexico," says David Harris. "Then he came back (to California) and was dealing a lot of dope out of West Marin . . . He fled from the cops and lived up in Oregon for a while. When he came back, it was kind of a downhill slide. This is when free-basing cocaine had come in and he had gotten into that. Then he started killing people. It was for a particular dope dealer. His son, Joe Junior, had been in a motorcycle accident and was brain-damaged. J.C. had taken his insurance settlement which was meager enough anyway and put it into a dope deal that went bad. We stayed friends, although I was like the last friend he had; he was a hard guy to be a friend with at that point."

"Joe always enjoyed young women, the younger the better," says Barnes. "I think he was about fifty and he was involved with a set of twins, young girls up near Tomales Bay. One of them was his girlfriend and the other sister had a boyfriend . . . The story goes that J.C. had a handgun and was threatening the boyfriend. A fight ensued—a struggle for the gun—and the sister's boyfriend ends up with the gun and shoots J.C. in the head in self-defense. I don't believe that story. You're never gonna get the truth about what really happened, but I've never met anybody who could take anything away from J.C. I mean Crampton was incredibly strong; it just couldn't happen."

Harris had a similar version: "He decided he wanted the second sister too, and he used to shove the boyfriend around. The boyfriend was kind of a little guy and you know J.C. was not a little guy. I talked to the cops and they said it was a struggle over the gun and I said, 'Bullshit.'... This was a guy J.C. could have handled with three fingers. And the guy is telling me he got the gun away from J.C. and got into position to shoot him behind the ear? People don't get shot behind the ear in that circumstance ... The guy just popped him. But it's not like J.C. had a lot of friends amongst the cops anyway."

Abandoned by his mom at age ten, on his own and on the street at age eleven, having spent most of his youthful years in prison, Joe Crampton was a hard man at the end. "Joe was just a violent person," says Barnes. "And not happy ... We spread his ashes near a favorite rock that overlooks the ocean over near Marshall on Tomales Bay. And that's where Joe's at."

I don't want to paint too harsh a post-prison picture because most us—certainly among the draft resisters—we did alright. Most of us went on and led pretty good lives. I didn't keep up with everyone, but I've heard a few stories over the years. I think almost everyone retained an abiding antiwar passion and a good number of us remained committed to political activism or to bringing some healing to a broken world.

Bugsy ended up going to law school at Rutgers. His passions never strayed far from those that filled his life prior to prison. He carried a caseload that centered on controversy, radical politics, and defense of the disenfranchised: immigrant rights, prisoner support, defense of soldiers who turned against war. For thirty years he represented the poor of Louisville through the Legal Aid Society and represented the lawyers themselves by organizing a United Auto Workers local for Legal Aid employees. A natural night owl, he's on his computer till the early hours of the morning, red-eyed like Marat, sipping occasionally, I suspect, on a bottle of Jack Daniels. Just as he did in Safford, he keeps me educated, sending a steady supply of e-mails with in-depth articles on topics rarely seen in the mainstream press: on labor unions and class analysis, Cuba and the Bolivarian Alliance, coup d'etats in Honduras, and a liberal sprinkling of Jewish jokes and cartoons. I still look back on him as a mentor.

David "basically walked out of prison into a divorce. For standard prisoner reasons," he says. "You don't spend time with someone—you grow apart. Especially when the two ends of the continuum are convict and singing star ... (But) there were a lot of other dynamics that had nothing to do with prison. We might never have gotten together if I weren't on my way to prison. It made it a safe relationship for her. There's an automatic exit. But then she had to do the childbirth ... by herself. And that's separation. That pushes you apart." The Wedding of the Century barely survived the '60s, failed outright to survive the awkward exchanges in the La Tuna visitation area.

David remained the most articulate of us, working against the war till the fighting stopped. When it finally ended, he ran in 1976 for the House of Representatives in Northern California. "We need a congressman," he explained to voters, "who went to jail before he went to Washington instead of after." As he was in jail, he was the most visible—the most public—of all of us and developed a successful career as a writer. He wrote for *Rolling Stone* and the *New York Times* before becoming the author of a long list of published books. Most notably: *Dreams Die Hard* and *Our War*, both of which explore the impact of Vietnam on our generation. Career success, however, could not stave off personal tragedy: he lost his second wife, Lacey Fosburgh, in 1993 when she succumbed to breast cancer. I think there's still a sense of melancholy in his life as he writes and practices Tibetan Buddhism in his Mill Valley home.

Like Harris, Paul Barnes got out and continued his activism against the war until the very end. He worked with the Institute for the Study of Nonviolence, went down to San Diego, tried to get an initiative on the California ballot that would formally place the whole state in opposition to the war. "We were signatures short of making it on to the ballot," he says. "We got hundreds of thousands of signatures, but we just didn't get enough. But again, it was just an opportunity to talk about the war and to present people with a direct way to participate ... But we didn't get it on the ballot."

Paul has worked as a carpenter for years in Chico, close to the wilderness areas where he loves to roam. "I still do a lot of talking," he says, "and sometimes folks get a little bit tired of listening to me talk politics."

After thirty months and a nationwide tour of the country's federal prisons, Joe Maizlish finally got out of the segregation unit in Texas and went home to L.A. He had time to mull over a lot of things in there. Like all of us he had witnessed firsthand the inequalities within the U.S. system of justice.

"I know a guy who had been part of a group," he explains, "that embezzled $8 million. Had a two-year sentence. There was another guy ... who had embezzled $2 million and had a four-year sentence. And then there was the guy who had done an unarmed robbery of a national bank and netted $6,000. He was doing thirteen years." Then there are the drug laws: "I thought those marijuana laws were ridiculous (before going in). But the really worse things are the heroin laws because ... it keeps it underground, it creates this whole underground culture that's more dangerous for people, and causes a lot of imprisonment. The drug laws were probably worse for society than the drugs ... Prison (provides) an impressive social education ... It turns something upside down in you."

With a history PhD in hand, Maizlish surprised everyone by going to mechanics school, and working fourteen years or so as an automotive mechanic and a service manager in a small garage. "There were different parts of me that I wanted to develop," he says. Eventually, he turned toward psychology and worked as a psychotherapist, specializing in trauma and trauma recovery, particularly in industrial environments.

Nevertheless, the politics of pacifism remained forever a primary focus. He connected with the *Catholic Worker*, the War Resisters League, and the Fellowship of Reconciliation, visited high schools, toured the Middle East, attended conferences, rallies, and peace parades. But his interest in psychology brought different perspectives to his politics.

"I wasn't satisfied because I felt like these movements just don't understand enough about human dynamics. Prison got me curious about what does make people tick, and what makes them tick one way and tock the other ... It's good to have these movements, but you also gotta have more understanding about how do you actually have an effect on people and how you have an effect on yourself. So you keep growing spiritually while you're doing this. For example, one of the main functions of political groups, although it's not often realized, is a kind of support group for people not to feel alone in their opposition to the existing system. And to actually talk about their feelings of despair and (what to do) to carry on ... And how do we handle frustration? It would be nice to be more conscious about that—about how we've been affected and how we've developed, what's satisfying about the group work and what isn't. And not to be guilt-tripping people. I tell groups, 'You know there are some people that actually don't like to come to meetings ... Are we gonna tell 'em they can't really be activists, or are we gonna figure out things that people can do that suits their own tastes and not be looking down on anybody for their choices?'

"So those are still some questions for me and I'm still trying to work on them. I'd like to see a little more freedom in those groups. I think they could be a little more attractive to the general public, although we'll still be maligned and insulted all the time. I guess that's the way it goes. That probably means we're contributing to society."

Dana Rae struggled some when he got out—struggled for a place to stay, struggled for a job. But there was some kindness also. He applied, for example, for a warehouse position at the local distributor in Honolulu for International Harvester. They turned him down initially because his criminal record would prevent his getting bonded. "But I remember my application got bounced up to the president," he recalls. "And I remember the president, Joe Volvo, I think his name was, going to bat for me; I don't know why. I remember him saying, 'Well, I don't see why this conviction should stop you from being bonded.' And he interceded on my behalf; I remember being in his office when he called the bonding company. And I eventually got the job. So there were people out there who were decent people."

Dana Rae later injured his back on one of his jobs and still suffers from the disability. I last saw him on Soda Bay Road in the little town of Kelseyville in Northern California. Residing on a hill above Clear Lake, he lives a somewhat hermetic life. As it was in Safford, his guitar is still his salvation. He sent me an audiotape a few years ago, a live performance—Dana Rae Park, folksinger. In his smooth tenor, he chose songs rich in political meaning: Bob Dylan's "Chimes of Freedom Flashing." Woody Guthrie's "Hobo's Lullabye": "Go to sleep you weary hobo, Let the towns drift slowly by, Can't you hear the steel rail humming That's a hobo's lullabye." Sara Grove's "Eyes on the Prize": "Paul and Silas began to shout, Jail door open and they walk on out. Keep your eyes on the prize, hold on."

Marty Harris turned his father's egg route into a small food distribution network, Heritage Produce Distributing in Torrance. He's wildly and unpredictably opinionated swerving from reverence for Ronald Reagan to respect for LBJ's Great Society. His blunt honesty made it all seem to make him all the more endearing to his L.A. compatriots. His marriage to Kathy has lasted all these years, since his proposal in 1969.

Patrick and Gayle Bryan are still together as well. He got his GED in Safford; then the two of them moved to Santa Rosa and eventually settled in Bellingham, Washington, where he worked some thirty years for the Rail Car Corporation.

Greg Nelson became a skilled printer at Peace Press in L.A. and then continued in the printing trade for the next three decades. Like Dana Rae, he's led somewhat of a solitary life, but has always kept himself well-informed on the newest twists in American foreign policy.

It was Bob Zaugh, however, who stayed with the Peace Press for the next twenty years. The press produced a remarkable diversity of posters, books, flyers, and pamphlets spanning the entire spectrum of progressive movements in Los Angeles. Although Zaugh harbored a lasting disdain for SDS chapters in L.A., the press published material for a whole collection of characters and organizations without getting caught up in political judgments. The Women's Strike for Peace, the Black Panthers, the Free Angela Davis Committee, Timothy Leary, the Chicano Moratorium, the Nicaraguan Sandinistas—they were all covered by the Peace Press.

Thayer (Thayer Ashton) wrote to me recently and maintains that his prison experience impacted him positively: "For one thing it enabled me to meet my wife . . . of forty years and therefore experience the joys of family life which I otherwise might not have known. Before entering prison, I had always lived a rather isolated, intellectual, and, I must say, aloof life. So I found interacting with both the other conscientious objectors and the general Mexican migrant population rather stimulating and refreshing—loud but lively.

"Shortly after leaving prison, I found myself self-employed in the fish business in order to support my family, and even though this was demanding physical work, it gave me a sense of self-sufficiency and the honest feeling of a day's work for a day's pay. Having formerly lived a financially secure and somewhat sheltered life, it was good for me to have to make my own way in the hard world. So, paradoxically, prison was actually a liberating time for me. I saw another side of life and people that I couldn't possibly have known otherwise, and it mentally and emotionally sustained me in my future career as a soon-to-be retired brain-dead bureaucrat. I wouldn't trade these memories for anything." Thayer's now in Boston, soon to be retired from the Social Security Administration.

Kendall saw things a little differently. "I understand more now," he says, "why people go into prison or the armed services and sometimes come out screwed up for the rest of their life . . . Looking back at it, I didn't grow that much . . . I was not a better person when I came out. I was less enfranchised, less capable of doing things. Socially, I was further behind than I was before . . . I was a screwed up kid to begin with, but this just did not help at all." Nevertheless, Kendall's life turned out nicely. He found he had a knack for computers, developed his tech skills, met a woman he got along with, and settled down comfortably close to the beach in Torrance. "All in all," he says, "I can't complain about my life. I've lived in peace. I've always had food. I've been poor at some points, but there's nothing wrong with that. I've known some nice people. This is a great country to live in. It's just a shame . . . that I couldn't give to my country more effectively than doing two years in prison."

Geoffrey Fishman lives with his wife in Irvine. A land planner in an architectural office in Orange County, he works on industrial and community design, placing the structures within the context of the surrounding environment.

Bill Garaway's turning was the most drastic. It began when the night before one of his trials he had a vision while walking in a canyon just outside of L.A. A voice told him not to fret about what he might say before the judge; it told him something along these lines: "If you are being persecuted for My Name's sake, I will put the words in your mouth." "I had no context for New Testament scripture," he says. "Zero. But it was clear as a bell . . . I was just gonna walk in the courtroom. I was gonna open my mouth in front of the jury and let God speak out of my mouth."

That experience set Garaway on a path leading to his embrace of evangelical Christianity. "After all that happened," he said, "my life straightened out a great deal . . . At a reunion years later, (there were) some people I couldn't be any more different from. It was bizarre and some of them have not changed at all. There was a hot tub there and there was a whole group . . . that spent the entire weekend without any clothes on. Back then, that's stuff that we did, but when you're in your sixties . . . it's probably not appropriate . . . It was just a whole different world." Garaway's friends in the L.A. Resistance were stunned enough when he became an evangelical pastor, but they were dumbfounded when—after devoting his youth to the peace movement—he came out in favor of the Iraq War.

Winter Dellenbach drove back to The Land in Beulah, a psychedelic school bus, and lived on the commune on Struggle Mountain in the upper Palo Alto foothills for twenty-three years before moving back to the city. She went to law school and became a public interest law attorney. Sherna Gluck stayed active in politics life long. In 1972 she co-founded the Feminist History Research Project connected with the Westside Women's Center. As an oral historian, she has interviewed women involved in the suffrage, birth control, labor, and other progressive movements of the early twentieth century. In 1977 she began teaching at California State University at Long Beach where she subsequently became the director of he Oral History and Women's History Programs. She was actively involved in the Socialist Feminist Network, the Feminist Forum. In 1987 she was a founding member of the Committee for Justice which worked to support the L.A. Eight, seven Palestinians and a Kenyan threatened with deportation.

I'd say the number-one factor for a happy and contented life is a long-lasting, enduring intimate relationship. On that score, we did about the same as everyone else in our generation. The 1970s, and the years after, could be tough on love and intimacy. We had our share of broken relationships and failed marriages—about the same rate as the rest of the country.

An Enormous Turning Point in My Life.

Except for marriage and family, the prison experience marked for me the most significant turning point of my life. It served as a rite of passage and transformed the lens through which I view the world. Convict. Outsider. During the years I spent teaching at an alternative high school, I worked with the custodian, Eddy Scott, who served for a couple of years in a reconnaissance unit near the DMZ. He would speak occasionally to my classes when I taught short six-week courses on Vietnam. I asked him once, knowing that he still carried shrapnel in his right leg, how often his memories brought him back to Vietnam. "Every day," he replied without hesitation. "And you? How often do you think of prison." I thought for a moment. "Every day," I answered. It's not that it's a painful memory or a traumatic one. It's just entwined/enmeshed into the deepest level of my identity. It's in my bones.

Upon my release, I spent the better part of a decade working factory assembly lines in Adams County and Montbello, dreaming of the great General Strike. Prison had made it painfully clear that any leap toward economic justice required the participation of a much broader swath of the population than the young people who had formed the basis of the draft resistance movement. And so I set out to apply what I had learned at the Bugsy Segal School of Revolution to an industrial setting. Along with a few others, I sought out young rebel workers, filed grievances as a shop steward, created underground newsletters mimeographed in blue ink, drank a lot of Miller Lites after swing shift at the Mapleton Lounge and the Silver Fox. We hoped to create a socialist presence within a foundering union movement and hoped even more to encourage our shop floor compatriots to consider the power they possessed at the core of the production process. We practiced for the General Strike—for the day the whole nation would shut down and propel the country into a new era.

So we each went our separate way. But each of us carried a common thread that linked us together back to a time of intense personal and historical transformation. We had each participated—body and soul—in the history of our times and for that, I believe, we are all thankful.

Chapter 15

After the War

Dear Sam and Sarah,

I had a guy in my cab the other day just back from several years in Cambodia. He'd been living the good life for pennies a day on the beaches along the Gulf of Thailand. There, he told me, all the twenty-year-olds love the Americans for their money and hate the Vietnamese because they have always done so. The irony escaped neither of us. No one ever told those young Cambodians it was Vietnam, not the United States, that, for whatever assorted motives, rescued them from the Khmer Rouge—the regime that had slaughtered their fathers and mothers by the million. No one ever told them, either, that American policy, with whatever intention, had bombed their country into oblivion and, consequently, handed it over to the Khmer Rouge on a silver platter. A generation after *The Killing Fields*, there is a gaping hole in these young people's history.

Looking Back at the War

Here in America, if you listened to Rush Limbaugh or Glenn Beck, you'd hear Vietnam described as some kind of a noble goddamn crusade. It was nothing of the sort.

I remember talking to Chester McQuery. After a stint in the Navy in the early '60s, he had dropped out of school to become a draft counselor for the American Friends Service Committee. "How could I write term papers," he had said, "when the world was blowing apart?" "We never saw much of the enemy," he wrote of the guerrillas. "We saw his handiwork—the ravaged outposts, the defenders with their heads blown off, their women lying dead beside them—but more often than not the guerrillas only showed themselves when they had superior strength. The first lesson that an American adviser in

Vietnam learned was that the enemy was good; if he stayed on a little longer he learned that this was wrong: the enemy was very good."

The war dragged on year after year until finally in the spring of 1975 the People's Army of Vietnam and the National Liberation Front marched into Saigon and raised the red flag. By that time, the American people were utterly weary. "My God, we're all tired of it," wrote one citizen. "We're sick to death of it." Sensing the national mood, Congress cut off all funding for U.S. operations late in 1973. It was the accumulation of the persistent moral persuasion of the antiwar movement, the weariness of the U.S. public of seeing the bodies of young Americans—58,000 of them—for no perceptible reason and with no credible end, and mostly the incredible endurance of the North Vietnamese Army and Viet Cong.

It was clear by the war's end, the vast majority of the country had come to realize what a swamp we had got ourselves into, how senseless and without purpose the bloodshed had become. Even our soldiers on the frontline suffered confusion and feelings of betrayal. Half the troops en route to Vietnam in 1971 openly labeled the war a "mistake." One author who interviewed hundreds of servicemen for his book, *When Can I Come Home?* found that "not one . . . was entirely free of doubt about the nature of the war and the American role in it."

By the war's end, Americans just wanted to forget about Vietnam and everything associated with it. I think the antiwar movement was pretty much forgotten and so were we—the resisters. Except for a few myth-creating movies I think most of the GIs were forgotten. Forgotten too were the Vietnamese people. Three million dead, lakes pockmarked the countryside from bombing raids, 20 percent of the country carcinogenic, the entire population uprooted.

During the time of the Vietnam War, forests, plantations, mangroves, brush lands, and other woody vegetation covered around twenty-five million acres of southern Vietnam, an area approximately the size of Vermont, New Hampshire, and Massachusetts combined. The dense forests that covered the uplands of southern Vietnam also provided cover for the enemy forces that the U.S. military and its allies were fighting. Hence, "Trees are our enemy." For ten years the U.S. air force flew nearly 20,000 herbicide spray missions to defoliating more than five million acres of forests (about 20 percent of the forest cover) as well as destroying 500,000 acres of cropland. Approximately 10 percent of the total land area of southern Vietnam was sprayed at least once. Loss of timber led to reduced sustainability of ecosystems, decreases in the biodiversity of plants and animals, poorer soil quality increased water contamination, heavier flooding and erosion, increased leaching of nutrients and reductions in their availability, invasions of less-desirable plant species.

We suffer no shortage of scholarly histories or riveting novels about our misadventure in Southeast Asia. Despite the information glut, I'm afraid it's popular culture (movies like *Forrest Gump* and *Rambo, Part II*) that has come to dominate our understanding. Now that the legends have had time to settle, doubts and memories of the war are frequently suppressed, lest a misplaced sense of national pride be offended.

Consider Lt. John Kerry, who stood in 1971 with a thousand other Vietnam veterans in front of a makeshift wooden fence erected to protect the Capitol from their angry approach. The men proceeded to cast their Bronze medals, their Purple Hearts, their ribbons earned in combat, their discharge papers—one of them even threw his walking cane—over that fence in a show of disgust for a policy they were no longer proud of. In front of a Senate investigative committee Kerry, a former Naval officer said, "We were given the opportunity to die for the biggest nothing in history." Over a quarter century later on the national stage of the 2004 presidential campaign, now Senator Kerry, fearful of the patriotic backlash, couldn't bring himself even to mention his opposition to the war. In such ways we create holes in our own historical memory just as surely as those Cambodian kids remain unaware of the ironies and complexities of their own past.

The war was a black hole in the American memory. We walked away. Some ultraconservatives tried to blame the war on us resisters. To those ultraconservatives, resisters gave the communists hope and they just didn't let us kill enough of the little motherfuckers.

Marx, Maslow, and the American Empire

I suppose it's fair to ask how I look back at those radical ideas that first crossed my path in Dorm 1 at the Safford Federal Prison. Only the most fossilized of us could have lived through these past forty years without some reassessment process.

Among the riveters, welders, punch press operators, and my fellow workers hanging out at the Mapleton Lounge, I easily accepted the labels of "Marxist," and "revolutionary." Long before my release from prison, Marxists in Europe and Chile had been charting new democratic paths toward a socialist vision.

You could be a Marxist without advocating the guillotine for the hedge fund managers at Merrill Lynch, without repudiating the First Amendment, and without defending the murderous and dishonest police states that characterized the Soviet Union or China.

For me now, Marx fails to answer near the number of questions he did when I was young but he provided some foundations that remain with me. The Marxists were right. America had transformed itself from a band of anticolonial revolutionists/rebels to the rulers of a global empire. The beast of the free market requires constant growth. It is Moloch. It is Tezcatlipoca. Without growth it will sputter and spit out its workers on to the streets. Yet continuous and endless growth is very likely utterly impossible. The problems of the unfettered market are systemic. You can change presidents to no avail.

My mother—your grandmother—was very fond of the views of Abraham Maslow and his hierarchy of needs that must be fulfilled on the path to "self-actualization." We all need a minimum of material things to thrive. Feed the face first. Give the body shelter. We need the roses, we need the finer things in life, but first we need the bread. This was common sense and not in conflict Marxist views.

Nevertheless, over the years, I've distanced myself, for a number of reasons, from those who who count themselves as Marxists. I no longer put my faith in the inevitability of a socialist revolution.

First there is of the dogma of many who call themselves Marxists. It is not so much disagreements over the sacred text—*Das Kapital*—which I must confess I've never read. But more because the dogmatic stance is in essence a type of fundamentalism. A parallel in religion: If much of the New Testament is attractive, what some of its followers did with the teachings was atrocious and unacceptable.

Second, Marx picked needlessly on religion and turned his materialism into a dogma that repelled millions of good people away from political movements. It alienated good-hearted people searching for higher meaning and sacredness. The critical nature of Marxism gave rise to culture of hairsplitting sectarianism. Forever critical and searching for the correct line.

Then there is the fact that we live always with uncertainty. Marxian science that claims the inevitability of the revolution relies too much on faith. We thought the revolution would follow inexorably from material conditions like the solution to some mathematical formula. Subsistence wages, overproduction, unemployment, economic depression, imperial wars, alienation—add all these together and they equal social revolution. We were riding the wave of natural laws into a new, more-just world; science or at least the social sciences were on our side. The whole world was poised for change: the general strike in France, the upheaval in Prague, the wars for independence in Angola and Mozambique, the insurgency in Guatemala, the election in Chile—we would see the revolution in our own lifetimes. Those conditions have surely existed numerous times in history—everything pointed towards revolutionary change—but when and where the revolution might happen were far less predictable than we imagined.

We children of the '60s who stood on the brink of social change, who dared to imagine social change in the heart of the empire, could not imagine the world would bring us Reagan and thirty years of conservative rule. This needn't reduce us to cynicism or despair, but for me, it required an acceptance that we live always with uncertainty, that neither revolution nor the march toward a brighter future are inevitable, as I once believed. Revolution in the heart of the empire is not inevitable nor is the better world. The class war—though generally one-sided—rages on. As a human race—as a world—there are many paths we might follow and not all of them bode well. It's our choice. At each juncture of choice, we could screw things up as easily as make them better. We have aching insecurity.

Lastly, we could not imagine the hold the American dream had on the American working class. Not only the working class, but many impoverished Americans are vehemently opposed to governmental policies and regulations that would limit the extreme disparities in income that we see. Is it that they imagine they could really become fabulously wealthy and do not want anything to inhibit that dream becoming reality? Is it an uncanny desire to be generous to the fabulously wealthy?

And yet with all these reasons for distancing myself from Marxism, I still subscribe to the main substance of what I learned in that revolutionary study group. I repudiate nothing. Though I no longer embrace Marxism as a core identity, Marxism and patriotism are by no means inconsistent. I never embraced the phrase "dictatorship of the proletariat" but given what has happened in the sorry dictatorships, both communist and otherwise, I am even more careful not to embrace the term.

The American empire though wounded and faltering staggers on. We are still the empire. Class conflict exists. Capitalism is dependent on impossible growth. We siphon the world's resources horrendously disproportionately into the United States. And ironically, as capitalism excoriates/scorns contemptuously the materialism of Marx, it has turned itself into a society that worships the acquisition of material things as the very purpose of life—a commodity fetish. It's ironic that American Christians are so attached to their material belongings. With all that I'm not cynical.

I can love America and not embrace the empire. I love the freedom. Even in an American prison I could get books that questioned the whole system. I love Denver, Queen City of the Plains with its sorry South Platte River cutting it in two. I love the faces of its diverse peoples. I remain astounded over the changes that have occurred in my lifetime. The Bull Connors, the Selma sheriff, the George Wallaces were the losers. I would like to say that national leaders reacted to this great swelling of the American people but it all started with a tiny minority. That the majority desired freedom for women, for blacks, for gays. Abrupt social change is also clearly possible; no one could have predicted the changes in the Soviet Union, the Prague spring, Tahrir Square, general strikes in France, anticolonial wars in Guinea, Angola, Guatemala, and Bolivia.

Where Were You During the War?

As a teacher, I never believed in stuffing my ideas down Englewood high school students' throats, but I think I exposed them to a vast spectrum of ideas they wouldn't get in the average classroom: they heard from Republicans and Democrats, Wobblies, Libertarians, Vietnam vets and draft resisters. They heard songs of Crosby with lines like "You've got to speak out against the madness" and "It appears to be a long time." Songs that questioned "what are they doing in our name?" "Blowin' in the Wind": "How many times can a man turn his head and pretend he just doesn't see?" Neil Young, Lynrd Skynrd, The Who, and Woody Guthrie. I think the passion I drew on in teaching stems in part from the prison experience, from the hope that education can lead us to a better world and more peaceful and loving world.

During the Vietnam War era, I was the lone wolf, related more to *Steppenwolf* than to new ideas about community. Besides I couldn't have organized my way out of a paper bag anyway, especially at that time. The thought of organizing wasn't in my mind-set. I suppose I still tend to be the lone wolf although your mom has tended to bring me into civilization.

I was no historian but I had enough of a sense of history to know that this was my war, my generation's war, and that if I were to participate in history this was the time to do it. I can remember reading books copyrighted 1943 and asking myself "What was this guy doing writing a book like this in 1943 in the midst of such a great historical cataclysm?" I wanted to be able to hold my head up in twenty years and say yes I was there and I was in prison. If this is individual morality or martyrdom so be it, although the boys who volunteered for the war were never accused of martyrdom.

I believe most resisters were readers. The power of the word, the power of the intellect to shape the thrust of history. Although our hopes to put a swift end to the war remained unfulfilled, we could count ourselves as part of a movement that put an end to the draft. Johnson had created the National Advisory Commission on Selective Service to look into inequities in the system. It found that America relied on working-class kids to fight the Vietnam War more than in any previous war of our history. However, the president ultimately kept the 2-S student deferment intact because he feared massive draft rebellions if it were eliminated.

Ultimately, the Selective Service could not endure what our generation put it through. But mostly, as resisters, we could answer proudly when our children asked us, "Where were you during the war?"

Chapter 16

Daughters and Fathers

Before he could finish the final pages of this book, my father, Richard Gould, died of a massive heart attack in January 2013. After all his commentary on the disconnect between the true story of the war and perceptions of younger generations, it is fitting and tragic that I, his daughter, born nearly twenty years after the end of the Vietnam era, will finish it.

At first it felt like a rare opportunity—not only to receive this gift, but to respond to it with the shocking and transformative intimacy of the page. But I now realize it is just a reminder that history is not a static thing—we are always in constant conversation with the voices that precede us, and we have just as much a say in our collective future as our ancestors ever have had.

The final chapter, after fifteen letters addressed to my older brother Sam and me, is, of course, my own letter in response to my father's writing. May this action serve as a bridging of generations, as an invitation for the young peacemakers and protesters of my own time to rise and carry on the legacy that has been left for us.

Dear Dad,

Your time in prison was always a ghost in our family. Sometimes we caught glimpses, but for the most part it was hidden from us, confined to the makeshift office behind the kitchen, that tiny nook scattered with papers and piles of notebooks filled with your sprawling cursive. I remember you staked out there late at night, furiously typing, enthralled by the limping rhythm of your old tape recorder as you transcribed interviews of your fellow resisters.

When I was fifteen or sixteen, I remember driving two hours from mom's hometown of Tucson to the prison in Safford, where you hoped the landscape might strike some somatic inspiration, the punch you needed to finish the book you'd been working on all those years. I remember how the town drooped inconsolably into the heat, how we peered up at your former residence from the parking lot, it's brick embroidered with barbed wire; definitively marked as outsiders. Driving back to Grandma's house, as the desert sun set over the sagebrush and spindly saguaro shadows cast on the highway, you were lost in thought; a distant, wandering story I wouldn't come to know until many years later.

For the most part, my inherited prison memories were all funny anecdotes—the food, the infamous handball incident—but nothing substantial about the war itself or the immense personal sacrifices you made. After reading your manuscript, it is now achingly clear to me that this narrative is very much the scaffolding of the man who raised me; who carried me on his shoulders at capitol building peace rallies in downtown Denver, who opted out of more age-appropriate movies for *Schindler's List* and documentaries about the Cuban Revolution. My childhood was infused with secret lessons about the nature of resistance, and for that, I am deeply thankful.

While reading your words, I was comforted to discover the many similarities between us; political persuasions and thought process, the pull between rage and compassion, and even the meticulous sentences of our shared writing style. But there is also the bitterness, that you left too soon, and there is so much of me that aches to ask you more. Still, here I am with this strange and tragic privilege of breathing life into history, of continuing the conversation, however lopsided and half-silent. You were the one who taught me, after all, that answers are not necessarily what we should spend our lives searching for. The power lies, instead, in our ability to ask relentless questions, to always think critically and creatively about the problems set before us.

In many ways, it seems you learned just as much about domestic injustice as you did about the war that put you there in the first place: migrant workers and labor rights, the political and economic conditions that blurred the border and drew your hermanos towards the north, how the draft targeted mostly poor and young men of color, the racial and class dimensions of the U.S. prison system itself—and how these same white-supremacist policies and instruments of subjugation affected the people of Vietnam. You saw how they wove together, reinforcing one another; that violence is never an isolated incident, but instead, part of a larger web of interconnected oppression.

Growing up, this same focus on holding complexity played a large role in our family life. In high school once, I asked if you were a pacifist. You didn't give a straight answer, but simply said that there were other wars in which you would have fought—particularly to end the Shoah—but that this one was fabricated on fear and profit, on Suits/Ties trying to cover up mistakes and miscalculations, the whole while our country, behind the curtains, the puppet-master. I remember a specific Pesach dinner, when you drew a giant map of Israel/Palestine on butcher paper, including both the supposed route of the Exodus from Egypt and the current state boundaries so crucial to the conflict today. As our friends and family crouched on pillows in our crowded living room, we discussed the implication of borders, of freedom, and renewed our commitment as Jews to fight for the emancipation from modern slavery of all kinds.

While studying in Costa Rica my freshman year of college, I became obsessed with the dirty history of U.S. economic and military intervention in Latin America. My class visited farms and factories, met with community leaders who shared their take on contemporary problems and their local solutions, the fight for sovereignty and survival. I learned to see the relationship between free trade agreements and north-bound migration, between climate change and the displacement of indigenous peoples, property rights and poverty, multinational corporations and the role of the U.S. government in protecting, above all else, their interests; the ensuing environmental degradation and disregard for human life.

Much like your own path to political consciousness, the act of witnessing became an entry point for my own outrage and education. You, having gone to Cuba in the 1980s and then to northern Nicaragua during the height of the Contra War, believed strongly in the power of bearing witness, of showing up and seeing for yourself an unbiased version of the events unfolding. And so, over the next four years on Skype and when I returned home on breaks, I turned to you for guidance on how to separate the self from the nation, to negotiate what it means to be a citizen of The Empire. Through our endless talks, you encouraged me to lean in, to struggle and wrestle, but never to turn away no matter how unnerving it was to confront the stark truth that so much of our own comfort was at the price of someone else's suffering. As I stitched together my view of the world and what I wished for it to be, you always stood by, introducing me to great thinkers (Eduardo Galleano's *The Open Veins of Latin America* stands as an especially memorable Hanukkah gift) and challenging me with new ideas I had not yet considered. Speaking with the grace and patience only a history teacher and father could, you held tight to the belief in the power of young people to carry the world forward and be a force for good. You lived this belief not by lecturing, but rather by listening.

Looking back, I see this capacity to listen not only as an attribute of a fantastically present father, but also as the foundation of your political consciousness, the very bones and balance of your fight to see the end of the war. Your concern for social change was born simply from talking to people, from your curiosity to know how they lived and survived, how they loved, what they did for themselves and their communities. I remember how you opened yourself to everyone, and with just a few-sentence entry, somehow got people to spill open their secret lives. Bus drivers, tour guides, fellow draft resisters, parents of my peers, the many people who passed through your classroom or cab. You were always armed with an endless supply of questions, tiny shovels to bring you closer to the heart of things. I saw you work your magic: how listening disarmed the ego, coaxed the story out, and invited you to see every human being as wonderfully and wholly human.

From this vantage point, your reading of history and political theory allowed you to draw links between the stories and experiences of the people you met and the policies and histories that shaped the material conditions of their lives. This smooth blend of Marxist thought and radically open empathy instilled in you a willingness to see all people (even prison guards and politicians) as prisoners of the insidious systems of power we've inherited. Maybe a little bit of this empathy, this humility, could have assuaged the tensions between rival SDS factions; could even be the very thing that keeps brilliant and necessary ideology from collapsing in on itself in contradiction. If we can't practice radical compassion and conflict resolution with our own comrades now in this moment, how in the hell will we ever achieve some semblance of a peaceful society when we finally reach the other side?

But with this incredible capacity to listen, also comes a quiet hesitation, an instinct towards observation over action. I see these moments of vulnerability surface throughout your writing; regret, fear of punishment, uncertainty of when to speak or stay silent. But what you sometimes saw in yourself as timid is actually the greatest measure of courage; to step out against your fear, and resist no matter how the hand trembles or the voice quivers. Resistance is not a polished thing. It is raw, often haphazard and improvised; stripping its conduits down to their most vulnerable, honest selves.

I think of myself, like you, as a quiet person. As an introvert and somewhat shy young woman, I find that I have difficulty showing up to do the work necessary to help heal the world. In most of my attempts to engage at different political meetings and protests, I slip to the back, overly aware of gaps in my knowledge of current events or my inability to speak articulately in public. I tend to think of successful social movements and campaigns as driven by surefooted, charismatic leaders—people magnets, who were, in some way, born to organize. But your words are a sharp reminder that movements call for everyone to step forward; not just the experienced and the experts, but the normal among us, the average, the curious, the hesitant. To take a public stand against injustice is to affirm a belief in our own power to affect change. This dovetails quite nicely with the Jewish concept of tikkun olam/tikkun hanefesh; "the healing of the world/the healing of the self"; a simultaneous, reciprocal transformation of the self and of society.

The power in your refusal to submit was the scathing simplicity of the act; your conviction untamed by political ideology or hours of strategic planning. Just a young man, unaffiliated, anchored by the flickering feeling that there was something profoundly immoral about this war; moved so deeply that inaction withered away and was simply no longer an option. Every human, flawed and ordinary, is capable of refusing to submit—to drafts, to complicity, to our own fear. Imagine entire armies deserting. Imagine people stepping down from office, no longer able to serve in good conscience knowing they're personally responsible for the death of fellow human beings. Imagine a culture in which accountability and genuine kindness are cultivated as the greatest measures of success. Stories of resistance such as yours call us to turn towards our own sense of capability and agency. This focus, inevitably, calls us to see violence as a choice, not a destiny.

Dad, I wish you were here to talk about these things. The uprising in Ferguson. The outrage and public mourning over the atrocious bombings of Gaza in the name of the Jewish people. The emergence of the Black Lives Matter movement, the solidarity between Palestinians and Ferguson activists. How the streets of Manhattan swelled with young people in the non-indictment of the cop who killed Eric Garner; the clergy and city council members who staged die-ins at the steps of City Hall. I wish you were here to have seen Bree Newsome's removal of the confederate flag from the capitol building in South Carolina, the grace with which she scaled the flagpole, the heartbreakingly beautiful and creative power and civil disobedience that will mark my generation.

Everyday, I will wake up and ask myself: How can I use the blunt gravity of my body to challenge these systems of subjugation? As a white person, as a woman, as a Jew, as a U.S. citizen—how can I confront my own complicity, how can I encourage my communities to be accountable, to choose resistance over the comforts of complacency and willful ignorance? It is easy to fill myself with knowledge, but it is an act of unparalleled courage to turn from the sheltered, safe world of the intellect into action.

On a sliver of doubt, you put your whole life on the line for justice. Choked the war machine, and let your body be, however tiny, a wrench. My blood and bravery who, even now, calls me to question, to love more deeply, to stop and listen to the rumble and rattle of the world's chains. You peace warrior, you shy hero, you fierce witness of history, my quiet and bespectacled father, may you rest in peace and in power.

Selected Letters and Documents

In this excerpt from his U.S. District Court of Colorado Presentence Report, Richard outlines his reasons for refusing to submit to induction.

DEFENDANT'S VERSION OF OFFENSE:

Defendant submits the following statement regarding the offense. "I cannot submit to induction into the United States Army. I cannot take an oath which subjects me to all orders issued by military officers, for in doing so, I would be violating my conscience in giving my tacit approval to this country's police in Viet Nam. I cannot give that approval.

I do not want to break the law. I am aware of the traditional argument against setting precedents of lawbreaking: that if the act of the lawbreaker is universalized, a society will fall back into chaos. But in this case, the situation is reversed. If I obey the law, if I submit to induction and obey military orders, I will contribute to the destruction of society in a nation which is in no way a threat to the United States. It is my belief that when such a conflict exists, one must choose to obey a law that is higher than civil law; that is, one much obey the law of his conscience. The dictates of my conscience are built upon several factors. First, they have their foundations in a set of moral values that were nurtured by my parents, by my reading and by my own experiences. The essence of this personal religious code is a respect for the life and rights of men, a feeling of kinship with the common aspirations, the common passions, the common ideals of mankind and a concern desire to help man better his condition.

Engulfed in this set of moral values is another factor nurtured by the fact that I am an American. Because of this background, the ideal of democracy, the ideal that each man must be respected simply because he is a man, is ingrained in my moral system."

"It follows from this democratic ideal that the state must be set up in order to benefit the individual and not vice-versa. It was within this context, then, that my decision concerning participation in the military was made. I am not a total pacifist. I believe that there are times when one must use force to protect himself from aggression, that there are certain cases when waging war is justifiable. However, I cannot believe that the American intervention in Viet Nam is such a case. To contribute to the military machine responsible for the senseless and unjustifiable multiplication of deaths in Viet Nam would violate all principles of a humanistic conscience. Our intervention, escalation and continued misuse of power has forced a communist-dominated, but essentially nationalistic revolution into ever tightening alliances with established communist governments. Our destruction of whole villages because there is the possibility that they harbor a few Viet Cong shows an incredible insensitivity to the worth of human life. Our continued support for oppressive, corrupt regimes interested more in maintaining their own power than in instituting needed reforms is completely alien to the American conscience.

I cannot view the Viet Cong as an inhuman devil intent on overthrowing all that is good in the world. I see him rather as a peasant-revolutionist who has at least a few just grievances against an entrenched aristocracy--an aristocracy which offers him little change through peaceful processes. I will not condone the Viet Cong's violence, and I deplore this terrorism. But since brutality is equally prevalent on both sides of the war, I cannot single out the Viet Cong as the only criminal; I cannot label him as my enemy. And I will not kill a man who is not my enemy.

I cannot contribute, or can I give my approval to a cause which results in mass killing in order to perpetuate a stagnant, incompetent and corrupt government in South Viet Nam. I cannot let the guise of "anti-communism" applied to a nationalistic social revolution cause me to support a South Vietnamese regime that has less concern for the welfare of its rural majority than the Viet Cong. In short, I will not be a mercenary for the Thieu government. Nor will I contribute to our effort in Viet Nam by submitting to military authority. To do so would be to disregard completely the dictates of my conscience. However, I am willing to serve my country in a non-military capacity. I, therefore, request that my 1-A draft classification be changed to 1-0 on the grounds of the selective conscientious objection described above"... (D)

Written shortly after his arrival to the Safford Federal Correctional Institution, a letter to his parents details Richard's first impressions of prison.

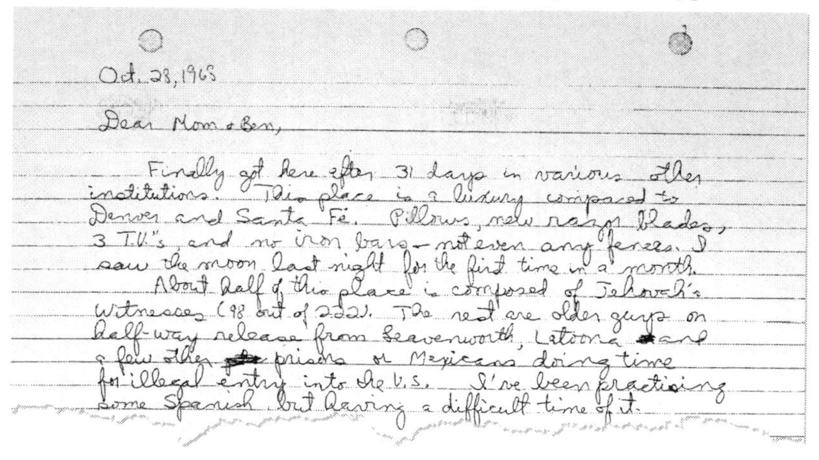

Oct. 28, 1968

Dear Mom & Ben,

Finally got here after 31 days in various other institutions. This place is a luxury compared to Denver and Santa Fé. Pillows, new razor blades, 3 T.V.'s, and no iron bars—not even any fences. I saw the moon last night for the first time in a month.

About half of this place is composed of Jehovah's Witnesses (98 out of 222). The rest are older guys on half-way release from Leavenworth, Latoona and a few other prisons or Mexicans doing time for illegal entry into the U.S. I've been practicing some Spanish but having a difficult time of it.

A letter from prison describes support from the L.A. Resistance.

The convictions on the Selective Service Act seems to be pouring in and the CO population is increasing. There are 16 or 17 here now (not including JW's). A group from LA Resistance came out last Sunday and serenaded the entire camp from across that small stone wall along the road. It was strange and in a way enjoyable, but in another way frustrating to communicate with people 100 yards away. For awhile they set up a rapport with the entire camp, not just the CO's, and when they yelled Viva Pancho Villa they got the whole Chicano population behind them.

In an excerpted letter, Richard gives more first impressions of the Safford prison conditions as well as explaining that his "mailing list" is filled up, so he won't be able to write to, or receive mail from, additional relatives.

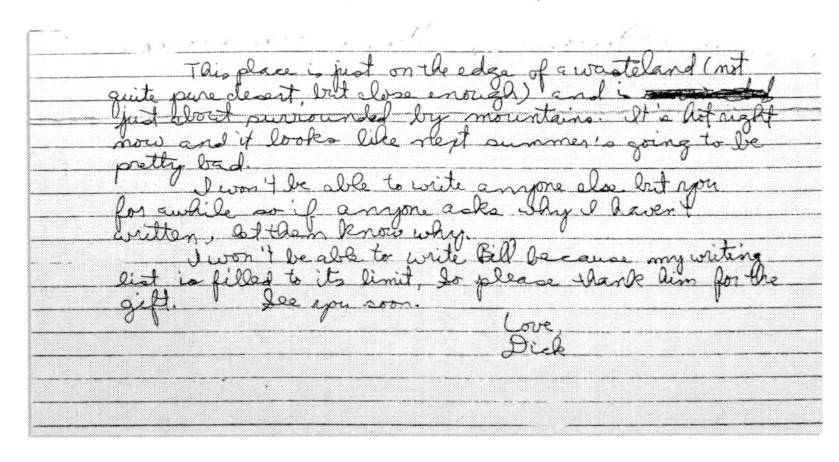

This place is just on the edge of a wasteland (not quite pure desert, but close enough) and is ~~[illegible]~~ just about surrounded by mountains. It's hot right now and it looks like next summer's going to be pretty bad.

I won't be able to write anyone else but you for awhile so if anyone asks why I haven't written, let them know why.

I won't be able to write Bill because my writing list is filled to its limit, so please thank him for the gift. See you soon.

Love,
Dick

Prison rules limited the number of people who could send mail to, or receive mail from, the prisoner.

Bob Tichy	~~Friend~~	235 Jersey, Denver, Colorado
Mr & Mrs Matt Wells	Friends	1099 Gilbert, Boulder, Colorado
~~Mr & Mrs Harold Goldberg~~		~~551 W. 185th St., Apt. 1C, New York, New York 10033~~
	Friend	4201 E. 2nd Ave., Denver, Colorado
Ann Silver	Friend	~~Pembroke East, Bryn Mawr College, Bryn Mawr, Pennsylvania~~
~~Dennis Darby~~	~~Friend~~	~~2819 Francis St., Los Angeles, California~~
Stevie Greenberg	Friend	1338 Amherst, Los Angeles, California
~~Jack Steiner~~	~~Friend~~	~~311 N. Market, Inglewood, California~~
Donna Smitherman	Friend	Box 834, Steamboat Springs, Colorado

ONLY 3 FRIENDS ARE ALLOWED ON YOUR MAILING LIST.

INDICATE THOSE FRIENDS THAT YOU WANT TO HAVE REMOVED.

ALL MR. & MRS. ENTRIES WILL COUNT AS TWO SEPARATE INDIVIDUALS.

INDICATE REMOVAL OF EITHER MR. OR MRS.

YOUR MAILING LIST WILL NOT EXCEED 12 INDIVIDUAL ENTRIES.

FOR EXAMPLE: YOUR MAILING LIST MAY CONSIST OF 3 FRIENDS AND 9 INDIVIDUAL RELATIVES.

OR YOU MAY HAVE 12 INDIVIDUAL RELATIVES IN ALL.

RETURN THIS SHEET WITH ALL CORRECTIONS TO THE PAROLE OFFICE.

After staying in the room of fellow prisoners to translate a memo into Spanish, Richard was disciplined for being in the wrong dorm.

Record Form No. 4
July 1938

UNITED STATES DEPARTMENT OF JUSTICE
BUREAU OF PRISONS

Institution FEDERAL PRISON CAMP

DISCIPLINARY REPORT

Name GOULD, Richard No. 4209-159

Living Quarters 1-46 Work Assignment M.O. # 2 How Long 11-20-69

Violation OUT OF BOUNDS, FAILURE TO DO ASSIGNED TASK, INSOLENT.

Each dormitory is sent to evening meal on a rotating basis. A problem had come about by inmates from other dormitories sneaking in to the dorm, whose turn it is to be first. GOULD and 11 other inmates where found in dorm 3 at evening meal time. The 12 inmates were assigned to clean the Adm. Bldg. corridor. 1 man went to school, 10 men worked in the corridor. GOULD refused saying he wouldn't work without a trial. His manner appeared to be one of great insolence, and he stated that I was to go ahead and write a report on him.

Reported By V. L. Thomas

Date 2-19-70 Title S. O. S.

Punishment or Action Taken

GOULD stated that he was in Dorm #3 interpreting a camp memo to the alien population which had not been translated to Spanish, not to be the chow line. Also he had never seen a regulation against being in another dormitory at chow time. Denied being insolent. He had a good attitude while appearing before the Adjustment Committee.

PUNISHMENT: One day extra duty in the messhall, Saturday, February 28, 1970

Age 23 Mental Age ? Total number of previous violations One (1)

Date February 25, 1970

T. E. Lanier Jr.
T. E. Lanier, Jr.
Correctional Supervisor

FPI-LPC-5-68-2M-3840

approved 2-17-70
C. L. Benson

An official pardon restored Richard's civil rights in 1975.

Gerald R. Ford

PRESIDENT OF THE UNITED STATES OF AMERICA

HAS THIS DAY GRANTED UNTO

Richard Gould

A

FULL PARDON

AND HAS DESIGNATED, DIRECTED AND EMPOWERED THE ATTORNEY GENERAL AS HIS REPRESENTATIVE TO SIGN THIS GRANT OF EXECUTIVE CLEMENCY TO THE ABOVE WHO WAS CONVICTED ON September 5, 1968 **OF AN OFFENSE AGAINST THE UNITED STATES IN THE** United States District Court for the District of Colorado.

IN ACCORDANCE WITH THESE INSTRUCTIONS AND AUTHORITY I HAVE SIGNED MY NAME AND CAUSED THE SEAL OF THE DEPARTMENT OF JUSTICE TO BE AFFIXED BELOW AND AFFIRM THAT THIS ACTION IS THE ACT OF THE PRESIDENT BEING PERFORMED AT HIS DIRECTION.

DONE AT THE CITY OF WASHINGTON, DISTRICT OF COLUMBIA

THIS fourth **DAY OF** August **1975**

BY DIRECTION OF THE PRESIDENT

Edward H. Levi

ATTORNEY GENERAL

Sarah, Susan, Sam and Richard on a family trip in 2004.

Epilogue

About the Author

When I asked Dick how he had learned to speak Spanish, it was not his words that drew me in. Humbly, with an unassuming attitude, he began to tell his story. As I watched over and over through the years, he never took sharing his story lightly. Many would put him up on a pedestal, expressing embarrassment as they compared his monumental act to their smaller political actions. Metaphorically stepping down, he always refocused the conversation by asking them questions and engaging them by listening. He believed that all intentional actions are important, rather than judging who is more "righteous."

Richard Gould, known to his family and friends as Dick, felt strongly about the distinction between his public and private names. Acknowledging this distinction, I will use the name I knew him as to honor a side of him that few may have seen.

Dick, my beloved husband, was a modest, soft-spoken man. He grew a beard after he left prison, and I watched the color of his hair gradually change from brown to flecks of gray to pure white. Although his involvement in the draft resistance movement and his prison time were pivotal in shaping his life of sixty-six years, he rarely spoke directly about that period. Hopefully you have gained a sense of who he was at that time. Since he can no longer speak for himself, my hope is to give you a glimpse of the person he became as a result of these experiences.

There was a subtle alchemy in his coming-of-age story, as he skillfully wove together the threads of his personal story, the biographical points of view of other draft resisters, the public narrative, and his in-depth historical research. All these accounts fused and put a new face on the Vietnam War for me.

As a lifelong social activist, Dick brought an intentionality to his daily life and work, melding values and action. His compassion, kindness, and capacity for deep listening are qualities that many people commented on at his funeral service. These qualities contributed to his ability to capture from each interview the essence of a person's story.

The Jewish concept of tikkun olam means taking action to repair, heal, and transform our world—starting with an individual's responsibility to pursue justice, making the world a better place for all. Tikkun olam recognizes our hidden interconnectedness, so that in concert with others, we collectively raise up our world. This principled intention holds a vision of equity, honesty, inclusion, and fair play. Dick's spirituality was always based in tikkun olam.

Dick began his "repair work" in 1964 as a high school senior, when he co-founded a magazine, *Tempo*, dedicated to social justice and the civil rights movement. After his release from prison, he went on to become a union organizer, activist and driver within the Denver Yellow Taxi Cab Coop, a field worker in Cuba in defiance of the U.S. travel ban, a journalist covering the Sandinista Revolution in Nicaragua, a social studies teacher in Colorado's Finest Alternative High School in Englewood, and a writer.

When our son, Sam, was born, Dick was forty-one years old. He insisted that our children receive a public education, as a form of social activism. Sometimes he was mistaken at school for their grandfather, which amused but never upset him. Dick did not lose his temper easily, always distinguishing between problems not worth wasting energy on and significant issues

A young Richard reads a copy of Tempo, *a magazine he co-founded in his high school years by and for young people about significant social issues.*

of fairness and justice. He was an exceptional father in our everyday family life, showing boundless patience and showing up for all the kids' activities.

Every night, we sang songs at bedtime. Sam and Sarah learned about history and peoples' struggles through Dick's passion for ballads and old labor and folk songs. Music chronicles everyday stories of resistance and ways to sustain one's spirit. Watching how gentle he was with our kids, I continually asked myself, "How could such a kind, trusting, and good-natured person survive prison life?"

The kids asked different questions as they were growing up. They asked if they could take his mug shot to school, laughing at how serious their father looked. When they saw his official pardon, signed by President Gerald Ford, they asked in disbelief, "Did the president know you when he signed this piece of paper?" This official pardon, given on August 4, 1975, restored Dick's civil rights, so he could vote in federal elections and, eventually, keep his position later, in his teaching career. All the draft resisters received a pardon that year.

Standing in Confluence Park in Denver, where Cherry Creek and the South Platte River come together, Dick explained the importance of knowing about our rivers as the kids threw stones into the current. Over the years, he had taken Sam and Sarah back to watch the rivers swell in the spring and contract in the winter. He felt strongly that one source of personal power arises from a knowledge of where things come from, like our water, food, and electricity, and then from advocating that everyone have access to our resources.

Sam says he feels it is hard to distinguish a single significant lesson from his dad. Because Dick was low-key and unobtrusive, he was more a role model than a giver of lectures to the kids. Sam watched and learned lessons about connecting values and action. He summarized this by saying, "His quiet presence, open attitude, and approach to life was to question authority and look for what is right."

As Sam grew older, he discussed registering for the draft with his father and what it means to choose to fight in a war. He has a draft folder to apply for conscientious objector status if he chooses, when and if the draft is reinstated. When Sam registered for Federal Student Aid for college, he had to register for the Selective Service, which brought home the fact that he, like all young adults, has little choice.

You may be wondering what happened to the draft, and whether there have been changes made to this tool of war. Formally known as the Induction Authority, the draft expired in 1973 and entered into a "deep standby." Selective Service Registration resumed in 1980 for an all-volunteer force, which exists to the present. Since the mid-1970s, the draft has been revamped in order to provide greater equity, such as limiting student deferments to the end of each semester; local draft boards that would better represent the racial and national origin of registrants in the area they served; a lottery system used to determine the order of who is called into service; and guaranteeing each registrant's right to a personal appearance before their draft board to appeal their classification.

Finding humor in the absurdities and insanity of current political issues reflected what he learned in prison. At one dinner-table discussion, laughing so hard he snorted, Dick fell from his dining room chair onto the floor. Laughing blunted the destructive power of despair and bitterness. His serious side was reflected in his abilities for sharp analysis, integrating many aspects of current politics, revealing essential questions and using history to cast light on the current situation.

A voracious reader, he was always reading books on history and politics. He read the Koran, Christian Bible, and Torah from front to back three times, developing his own understanding of their parallel values. He followed current events around the world and in the United States. To foster long-term change, he supported many organizations with values of transformative change similar to his own. In kindergarten, Sarah was asked to identify one thing that happened in the kitchen. While other children shared about the food they ate for breakfast, Sarah's contribution was NPR! In his makeshift office off the kitchen, Dick shifted the radio between National Public Radio news programs throughout the day, conservative talk radio shows, and music—funk, R&B, and rock. He often listened to conservative talk radio and read right-wing magazines, stretching himself to learn more about "the other side."

Dick believed in cooperative movements as an alternative to the blind materialism of our American society. Empowerment comes from working together as an intentional group or community, bringing a perspective of values and action to the world. He participated in our Bread & Roses Babysitting Cooperative, the Yellow Cab Taxi Cooperative, and our Havurah (a Jewish tradition of gathering like-minded individuals). At our Reconstructionist congregation, his bicycle, parked in the hallway opposite the sanctuary, was witness to his regular attendance at the musical Shabbat services. Later in life, he would call himself a spiritual progressive, conscious of the importance of bringing the spiritual values of tikkun olam to the political arena and everyday life.

Dick's intention to live a congruent life—matching values and action—was woven into his family, personal and professional life.

About the Book

As any activist knows, there is also another type of coming-of-age story that occurs when you enter into a social justice movement. Your original beliefs and imagination of what it looks like from the outside are transformed by actual experiences—the innumerable conversations and decisions; the people you learn to trust to do what they say they will do; and the fusing of intellectual, emotional, physical, and spiritual aspects of being a part of a collective effort. The testing of the spirit occurs on a communal as well as a personal level, finding how to sustain your spirit over time and not be broken by the power brokers.

The turning point for Dick, from thinking about his draft resistance experience to actually writing a book, came at a storytelling concert. Pat Mendoza, a proud veteran of the Vietnam War, introduced one of his stories with a personal tale. He spoke about two men who had fought in his unit in Vietnam and lost their lives one night in combat. With emotion, he declared, "We all carry ghosts—people whose lives have deeply impacted our own lives. We should never forget them . . . so I tell their stories to keep them alive." Dick's ghosts were all those he met along the way before and during prison. Their stories were in his bones—of sacrifice, resistance, and persistence—along with the telling of a good joke, cooking food in the hogan, gestures of kindness, distinct images, words that elicited fear, or watching the drum circle of the native peoples. Within those prison walls, they had sustained their spirits, individually and collectively, and he wanted to keep them alive.

Pulling at Dick's soul was a profound longing that our kids come to understand and know his own story. And because his story was bound up with those who walked this same path of resistance, the public narrative and the documentation of this historical time, he began braiding all these stories together into this book.

Thus began years of formal research and story-catching. He began to track down his "ghosts," finding most of the people he searched for. Jeff Segal, a fellow draft resister, helped him locate many of them. Everyone agreed to an interview, surprised and appreciative that Dick was going to record this period in history and had cared enough to include each of them.

Face-to-face conversations mattered to Dick. He crafted specific questions for each person, making no assumptions about their experiences and the personal meaning of those days in prison. He also heard about the consequential effect of prison on the rest of their lives. Like him, many remained politically active, left with a deep thirst for social justice and equity.

Just as Dick did in his life, most of the draft resisters lived their beliefs far after that time of clanging jail doors and dark nights of the soul, as they sat alone, separated from dear friends and family. Dick's letters to his mother and his lifelong friend Richard Frumess (along with other family and friends) show how so many aspects of prison life were designed to diminish their spirit. A prime example was the blacking out of paragraphs of their letters from home, so that prisoners could barely read their loved ones' comments. Small details like these helped me understand why Dick cared so fiercely about the right of free speech.

Many of the resisters, such as David Harris and Jeff Segal, are still politically active, working on current issues of social justice and equity. Others became writers, teachers, and artists, while a few had drifted into isolation by choice, deciding to live far away from mainstream culture. After six weeks of correspondence, one resister finally agreed to be interviewed. Dick flew to California and drove miles on backcountry roads until he was able to sit on his front deck and record his story. One man became an expatriate. A prison guard showed up in Dick's research, one who remembered Dick with some warmth. Although he declined to be interviewed, the prison guard was pleased and encouraging that Dick was writing a book about the draft resisters.

It can be difficult to narrow down the focus of such a writing project, given that the resistance movement occurred across the United States. Through his research, Dick spoke with members of the Los Angeles resistance movement, and attended their 2009 reunion. This is a current, active group, still interested in social action and justice. In 2013, the organization created a public archive of the draft resistance movement in the Los Angeles Public Library system. The recorded interviews in this book are an appropriate addition to this archive collection.

Dick loved a good story. His unusual capacity to listen and to hone his questions came from many years of practice. Apart from his addiction to York Peppermint patties, it was his fascination with and his love of humanity that led him to be a Yellow Taxi Cab driver for over thirty-six years. He collected stories from his riders. They were written on the back of old yellow credit slips and receipts, stashed for another book some day. Through a similar narrative interview and story-catching style, combined with research materials, he captured stories of the Colorado Chicano movement for his first book, published in 2007, *The Life and Times of Richard Castro—Bridging a Cultural Divide* (http://www.historycolorado.org/adult-visitors/buy-books). At the time of his death, he was using this narrative process for his unfinished third book, on Hispanic legislators in Colorado. That work was done for the Chicano Studies Department at Denver's Metropolitan State University, where he was teaching students how to conduct this type of narrative interview.

He traveled to big cities, small towns, and one small cabin, high up in the California woods, to record each draft resister—spending two to six hours taping their individual stories. In a painstaking process, Dick carefully transcribed the cassette tapes to record their stories accurately.

Being a Yellow Cab driver was his connection to the "working man." Driving was honest work. He saw himself, on one level, as that working man—someone whose work forms the often invisible foundation of our society: truck drivers, plumbers and electricians, waitresses, packinghouse workers, and the farmers in the San Luis Valley, to name a few. The relationships he formed with many working men he met in prison gave him an enduring regard for their work, rights, and stories. He listened and learned to recognize the patterns of structural oppression and disenfranchisement. He felt a moral responsibility to honor their stories. They were the witnesses inside the prison, watching the different treatment and public attention that draft resisters received.

His methodical research, interviewing, obtaining legal documents, and listening to the tapes was a slow dance of discernment and reflection. I noticed that as he became more engaged with the writing process, he became more isolated from friends and family, just as he had been in prison. Dick seemed to relive similar emotions as he wrote about them. He seemed to draw further into himself as he tried to give voice to his own story. When he was writing and researching, he had one foot in the past and one in the present—a delicate balance, as he grew in his understanding of his story and of those he was collecting. The threads of the collective story slowly emerged.

With enormous frustration, he made efforts to request documents under the Freedom of Information Act. In trying to locate the records covering key events, such as the prison hunger strike and the riot that occurred, he often felt he was chasing his own tail. Although he did obtain the documents he quotes in this book, there were many more that he requested but could not obtain. Supposedly, the boxes of documents covering the Stafford Prison were moved between two different government buildings and were lost. Ironically, he relived the same bureaucracy, inconsistencies, and lack of cooperation from the government institutions that he had experienced as a draft resister.

Beside his side of the bed were stacks of books on Vietnam, representing all the original sources he had read before he decided to resist the draft. All the books written since the war were stacked in another pile. His routine was to read in the morning and evening, burrowed down into the bed covers, taking notes in the front of each book cover. Nestled deeply into the blankets as he read, it was if he created a makeshift time-capsule back in time for his research.

Every professional storyteller will tell you that formulating your own story, the most challenging of all, takes practice. Dick had this practice as a teacher. Standing with one foot in the past and one in the present, he taught social studies for twenty years at Colorado's Finest Alternative High School (CFAHS). He joined an exemplary team of educators and staff, who envisioned and created innovative change in the public school system. His passion for bringing history alive for his students took him out of his comfort zone. Routinely nervous about speaking in front of his students, his passion to help students find meaning in history moved him beyond his soft-spoken manner.

Teaching was a form of social activism for Dick. Teaching critical thinking and how to discern the truth is often a cumbersome, time-consuming process of reading, reflecting, and asking questions. Using ingenious ways to inspire his students with music, movie clips, and his own story, he caught their interest. It was not his intention to write a book when he started teaching his "1960s" class at the high school, but it became instrumental in his writing.

Teaching served as practice for telling his story, a bigger feat for an introvert than you may realize. He was taken aback at times that they cared so deeply about what he had to say. Those who had family members in prison were stunned that someone would *choose* to go to prison.

In an effort towards reparation, he took fifteen students, our two young kids of five and three years old and myself, to the Diné (Navajo) reservation in northern Arizona. The trip was an effort to replant fruit trees in the San Juan River bed. This was the site of the 1864 U.S. Army war against the Diné people, using fire to destroy their homes and food supply. Guided by the Roanhorse family, we descended the cliff walls of the Canyon del Muerto to plant trees and acknowledge the invisible injustices done so many years ago. These "ghosts" reflected how easy it is to forget people's history, as their stories are forgotten and eventually disappear from the public collective memory. Just as he led the students on this path to remember the Diné peoples' struggles, so too does Dick help us remember the struggles of the draft resisters.

About Finding One's Voice

In the innumerable hours he took to write this book, I missed him. Dick was a beloved companion, with whom I shared a rich life on many levels. On our almost nightly evening walks with our golden retriever, Sparkles, he would quietly speak about what he was wrestling with that day. Research and interviewing came easy to him compared to the writing. As an author, he was deeply stirred to capture the essence of this struggle so that you, the reader, could feel, smell, hear and taste the experience for yourself. It took him close to ten years in total.

Yet this work went deeper, because it was soul work for him. Dick had to write his story, not just for our children and for his fellow draft resisters, but for himself. He found his own voice—his own power of expression—in this process.

His search for honesty and fairness also included something much more subtle—his sturdiness in telling a truth that honors his own story and simultaneously a larger struggle that was unfolding at the same time. It is like taking a continuous panorama picture on our modern-day phone cameras—picking up many more nuances than a simple shot.

Both Dick and Sarah have mentioned our family trip to Safford, Arizona. Dick's prison experience was still somewhat of a mystery to me until we went back to visit the prison. Here is a snapshot of that visit:

The East National Saguaro Park is to our north as we leave Tucson on Highway I-10. We travel through the stark yet beautiful desertscape of creosote bushes, mesquite trees, and prickly pear cacti. As we approach Safford, Dick, unflinching in his concentration, is unusually edgy. Not with the light nervousness of meeting someone new, but with the profound apprehension and uncertainty of returning to a place that has been imprinted on one's psychic memory. His trepidation is unnerving. A visceral anticipation fills our car.

I believe that when someone returns to a physical site where they have experienced distress and trauma, the nervous system is triggered, flooding the brain with a roller coaster of emotions and even imperceptible healing. Brain researchers tell us that something happens when we sense danger. The amygdala, our ever-diligent sentry, activates the hippocampus into a pattern of fight, flight, or freeze, to save our lives. This process happens in a split second.

Although Dick never labels his prison time as being traumatic, over the years I have seen signs of it, like his involuntary reaction to move out of closed-in spaces, his tracking police officers at protests and marches, and his comment that he thinks about being in prison almost every day.

Now, thirty-five years after his release from federal prison, we stand in the very same spot, the parking lot in front of the entrance. Without thinking, I take out my 35-millimeter camera to capture this moment: the looming rolls of barbed wire on top of the fences; the contrast of the spacious blue desert sky and the dense white concrete walls. A convergence occurs, my husband walking into his past with a sober expression and tilt of his head while I try to capture this present moment. I desperately want to catch glimpses of the young man who went to prison. The guard is out faster than I can take off the cap to my zoom lens.

"We don't allow any pictures," the guard announces, more loudly than I think is necessary. "NO pictures at ALL, ma'am, PUT your camera away NOW. What is your business here?"

As Dick starts to describe our pilgrimage, the guard cuts him off, abruptly directing us to go inside the main door. The guns, handcuffs, and nightstick strapped onto his belt jiggle as he walks away, turning to emphasize, "NO PICTURES ARE ALLOWED."

Holding my breath in, I realize how quickly fear can arise in my own body. The fierceness, control, and power of the guards, the lack of choice, and the starkness of the reality of being in prison are here, in front of me. You don't mess around with these clear lines of authority. Yet, my husband, like many others, stood up to the U.S. government by saying no to the Vietnam War.

I am beginning to understand this embodiment of fear and of the unknown from the frown lines etched into his forehead. I can't even imagine how he and the other prisoners could override this constant fear. They each did survive these high walls laced with barbed wire, symbolic of the sharp contempt and outrage some received from their own families and from the greater society. Somehow, the body remembers the feel of this fear and contempt.

Over the years, hearing Dick's research, interviews, and the written passages he would read to me, I conjured up images and emotions of this time. This fear and unknown—a mixture of anger, unease, agitation, uncertainty, boredom, and uncharted realms—were a common experience of draft resisters both in and out of prison. In actuality, it is similar to the fear and unknown that all Americans lived with during this time in history and that we experience in our own tumultuous times.

Dick freezes momentarily, seemingly unable to move forward to the prison door or back toward our car. For a nanosecond, I can see the shadow of this experience come over him. In this return trip he has found himself—again.

In January, 2013, Dick was feeling an extraordinary weight on his shoulders to finish this narrative. He had committed to all those interviewed that he would share their stories of resistance by publishing this book. To share what each person who was interviewed is now doing in their lives—well, that is another book. Once the book was completed, Dick had plans to visit Vietnam for the first time, exploring how this country and its people had impacted all our lives so profoundly. On January 4, he turned sixty-six years old. His last computer entry, finishing up work on the last chapter, is dated January 12, 2013, at 11:45 p.m. He died early the next morning, as his heart, dedicated to social justice and compassion, was silenced by a sudden heart attack. His gravestone reads:

A beloved b'shiert, father, brother, uncle, friend, teacher, tax-ista and Vietnam Draft Resister: a loving and loyal presence and a soldier of justice, peace and compassion.

Dick, we miss hearing your voice and your thoughtful responses to our questions and comments about *Refusal to Submit*. Your pensive replies and musings into how to affect change might have helped us understand our own questions about change today. We miss you greatly.

This is his story of how he entered this movement in an act of decency. Like anyone going through a formative transition, he held the tensions of knowing what he knew, yet he was also naïve. This was true then and true now. We still don't know how to hold tensions of differences without demonizing those who question the word of the U.S. government. These individual stories show insight into the layers of conflict that existed both in and out of prison. Dick valued each person he interviewed, was honored to record their experiences. He researched many traditional and nontraditional sources to provide in-depth perspective personally, socially, and politically. His perseverance in writing this book is, after all, just about truth telling.

Refusal to Submit is dedicated to bringing more in-depth understanding of this pivotal time in history. The local Safford Historical Society has very little material on the prison during the Vietnam War. It is as if draft resisters did not really exist. But they did and still do. We stand upon the shoulders of all our ancestors who have gone before us. Certainly, draft resisters, through their stories and learned wisdom, are ancestors who matter.

Dick is now a "ghost" and an ancestor, whose stories you can carry. May you be inspired by these stories to sustain an intentional life of working for repair, healing, and social justice in our world. Stand up for what is right.

Love and in peace,
Susan Kaplan
January 30, 2016

April 18, 1999

Dear Richard,

Thank you for all of your motivation. I was never interested in the social sciences until I took your classes. If it would not have been for you, I never would have found my passion for politics.

I have taken several History cources at CCD, along with Political Science & Economics. I find my self board in some of Humanities cources because I care more about the politics than the art.

I have been accepted to American University, and I plan to move away this August. I am planning to work on Al Gore's campaign while I am in D.C. I worked hard this last Fall for the Colorado Democrats, and even though the results of the Gov's race was devistating, I still enjoyed the experience & the people.

Take care of your self. I hope can keep in contact. I owe more to you, than I am sure you realize.

Thank you
Morgan

A letter from a former student shows Richard's impact during his career as a high school teacher.

Richard, far right, with a group of his high school students. As a high school teacher, he had a passion for helping students to find meaning in history.

Index

bold denotes photo

A

Abrams, Ivan, 39
Acheson, Dean, 182
ACLU (American Civil Liberties Union), 15, 17, 18, 19, 20, 299
Adams, Eddie, 91
Adams, John, 179
"Aggression From the North: The Record of North Vietnam's Campaign to Conquer South Vietnam" (white paper), 63
Ahimsa, 253
Akeson, John, 72
Alameda County Jail, 101, 161, 162, 166, 171, 176
Ali, Muhammad, 9–10, 16
Alice Cooper, 198
"Alice's Restaurant" (song), 240
Alinsky, Saul, 170
Allentown, 8
Alperovitz, Gar, 73
Alvirez, Rosita, 122
American apartheid, 43–44
American Civil Liberties Union (ACLU), 15, 17, 18, 19, 20, 299
American dream, 325
American empire, 179, 325–326
American Friends Service Committee, 207, 225, 248, 254, 321
anticommunism, 35, 36, 53, 69, 144, 235
antidraft movement
according to Kuchel, 78
and Crusade for Justice, 225
David Harris as darling of, 241
antidraft unions, 150, 151
antiwar movement
according to Lyndon Johnson and Richard Nixon, 283
as accused of being unpatriotic, 84
Century City as landmark event in history of, 15
characterization of, 159–160
Chicano Moratorium (1970), 227–228
Ernesto Vigil's sentence as success for, 227
first mass demonstration (April 1965), 145
great divides within, 178
impact of civil rights movement on, 40, 45
marriage with civil rights movement, 76
as opposing war on grounds of morality first and then politics, 52
antiwar sentiment, among "silent Americans," 73
Appell, Donald, 222
Arango, Doroteo, 121–122, 305
Arizona Republic, 302
Armstrong, Joel, 174, 223
Army of the Republic of Vietnam (ARVN) (South Vietnamese Army), 49, 50, 51, 64, 69, 83, 235, 236
Arraj, Alfred A., 91, 93, 94, 216, 224, 227, 310
Arraj, Sally, 91
The Arrogance of Power (Fulbright), 37, 69
Ashton, Thayer, 317
Aspen, Colorado, author's post-high school living/working in, 39
Atlas Shrugged (Rand), 107
Attica, 177, 206
Augustine, Saint, 69
The Autobiography of a Yogi (Yogananda), 187, 199, 200

B

Baez, Joan, 108, 141, 239, 247–248, 249, 250, 254, 255, 257, 258, 259, 272, 275, 291, 293, 296, 307
Banes, Wilhelm, 272
Banks, John, 131, 137
Bardacke, Frank, 155, 161
Barmack, Haim, 30
Barmack, Rose, 33
Barnes, Paul, 78, 87, 96, 187, 194, 195, 196–197, 199, 215, 218, 219, 220, 223, 278, 286, 289, 291, 296, 298, 299, 302, 305, 307, 309, 312, 313, 314
Baskir, Lawrence, 135
Beal, Ted, 208
Beatles, 96, 198, 228, 263
Beck, Glenn, 321
Begay, 140, 184
Beggar's Banquet (album), 231
Bell, Tom, 148
Beneath the Wheel (Hesse), 263
Benson, Charles, 293, 294, 300, 305, 307
Bentley, David, 80, 84
Benton, Gary Lane, 112
Ben-Veniste, Richard, 205
Berkeley, California, 60, 77, 146, 149, 150, 151, 152, 153, 154–155, 156–157, 160, 163, 164, 188, 242, 246, 276
Bernstein, Mal, 162
Berrigan, Dan, 136
Beveridge, Albert J., 181
Black Panther Party, 130, 140, 154, 162, 176, 201, 232, 255, 317
Blasi, Gary, 197
Blasi, Jeremy, 197
"Blowin' in the Wind" (song), 108, 326
Bolduc, David, 78, 191
Bond, Julian, 45, 147
Book of Exodus, 24, 28, 100, 114–115
books, author's reading of, 45–46, 48, 52, 59, 69, 70, 79, 81, 114, 129, 178, 244–245, 327, 332, 345, 349. *See also specific books*
BOP (Bureau of Prisons). *See* Bureau of Prisons (BOP)
Bosch, Juan, 183
Boston Five, 160
"Both Sides Now" (song), 111, 290
Bowart, Peggy Hitchcock, 271
Bowart, Walter, 271

Bracero Act (1942), 43, 115, 116, 117

Branch, Milton, 93, 94

Brink, Kent Ten, 209

Brotherhood of Eternal Love (Hippie Mafia), 277, 278

Brown, Robert (Bob), 288–289, 290

Bryan, Frank Dean, 168

Bryan, Gayle (née Garver), 169, 174, 316–317

Bryan, Patrick, 168–171, 173, 174, 175, 178, 202, 306, 316

Buchanon, John, 268

Buckley, Neil, 229, 230

Buddhist

crisis, in South Vietnam, 48

David Harris as, 196, 314

90 percent of South Vietnam as, 46

Buismato, Frank, 175

Bundy, William, 68

Bureau of Prisons (BOP)

author's reconsideration of relationship with, 213

author's seeking of archival information kept by, 288

author's two-year sentence with, 7

as enforcer, 305

Maizlish readjusting attitude toward, 204–205

number of refusers who served time in, 8

on treatment of resisters, 259

The Burners, 72, 147, 148, 178

Buttny, John, 70, 71, 72

The Byrds, 198

Byrne, Matthew, 209

C

cab driving (by author), 100, 281, 321, 332, 342, 345, 348

Café du Monde (New Orleans), 45–46, 48

Calhoun, John B., 87

"A Call to Resist Illegitimate Authority," 149

Calvert, Greg, 232

Calypso Joe, 195

Cambodia, invasion of, 190, 235

Cannon, Terry, 152, 161, 163

Cao, Huyn Van, 50

CAPIAS (Court Appointed Prisoner Is Awaiting Sentence), 90, 91, 95, 97, 100, 112, 118, 119

capitalism, 282, 325–326

Carmichael, Stokely, 130

Carney, Dr., 62

Carranza, Venustiano, 122

Carter, Special Agent, 134

Castro, Fidel, 183

Catholic Worker, 147, 315

Catonsville Nine, 136, 160

Cavanaugh, Wade, 302–303

Center for Constitutional Rights, 175

Central Committee for Conscientious Objectors (CCCO), 147, 169, 174, 175

Century City, 15–18, 20, 138, 192

Cervantes, 262

Chaparrito, 120, 124

Chato, 122, 123, 303

Chavez, Cesar, 170, 171

chess, author's playing of, 97–98, 100, 120

Cheviot Hills Park, 15, 17

Chicago Eight, 160, 231

Chicano Moratorium (1970), 227, 317

"Chimes of Freedom Flashing" (song), 316

Chinese communists, 36

Chomsky, Noam, 149, 187

Christianity

attachment of American Christians to material belongings, 326

Bill Garaway's embrace of evangelical Christianity, 318

on dark night of the soul, 198–199

influence of on Dana Rae Park, 107

Jehovah's Witnesses independence from mainstream Christianity, 129

Nietzsche's shocking of, 245

civil disobedience

call to, 76–79

Century City action intended as act of, 17

Greg Nelson's letter to draft board, 14–15

National Student Association (NSA) as called on to organize, 244

power of, 44

threat of, 10

as weighing heavily on Johnson's thoughts, 160

Civil Rights Act (1964), 43–44

civil rights movement, 20, 21, 40–41, 42, 45, 76, 79, 98, 138, 145, 169, 170, 175–176, 224, 241, 246, 342

class conflict/struggle/war, 213, 217, 325. *See also* social classes, clash between

Cleaver, Eldridge, 140, 154, 176

Clendening, J. B., 293

Coakley, Francis, 161

cocaine, 118, 273, 312

Coffin, William Sloane, 24, 149, 187, 188

Cold War, 30, 46, 144, 168, 177, 183

college campuses. *See also specific campuses*

antidraft unions on, 150, 154

L.A. Resistance members making rounds of, 195–196

as source of information/news about Vietnam War, 59

Colorado Daily, 60

communes, 159, 193, 210, 239, 244, 245, 246, 249, 250, 271, 273, 274, 275, 277, 318

communism

American's sentiment about, 37–38

author's exposure to, 35, 37, 55

as C-word, 70, 83

different shades of, 70

Nixon as obsessed about, 236

opposition to war in Chicano community as equated with, 225

in Vietnam, 68, 70

William Fulbright on, 38

Communist Manifesto, 267

Communist Party USA, 30, 35–36, 144, 167, 201, 283
Community Service Organization, 170
Community Storefront Law Office, 197
Confessions (Augustine), 69
Congo, U.S. involvement in, 183
Connor, Roy (Smilin' Roy), 213, 214
Connors, Bull, 326
conscientious objector status, 24, 78, 93, 128, 129, 137, 145, 175, 196, 225, 260, 270, 299, 317, 344
Containment and Change (Oglesby), 71
contemplative life, 280, 281
Cooley Street commune, 149, 159, 245, 246, 250
Coonan, Karen Jo, 152, 162
Cooper, Esther, 133
Cooper, Joe, 134
Cooper, Mendel, 72, 133–136, 147
Cooper, Thomas, 226
copout sheets, 108, 137, 215
Copperberg, Kendall (Ken), 105, 131–133, 138, 178, 214–215, 263–264, 266, 279, 301, 310–311, 317–318
Coronado National Forest, 105
Cota, Fernando, 117, 120–121, 122, 123, 124, 138, 297, 303
counterculture, 187, 249, 261, 268, 270, 274, 275, 276, 278
"Counterdraft" newsletter, 197
Country Joe and the Fish, 164, 276
county jails. *See also* Alameda County Jail; Denver County Jail; L.A. County Jail/Los Angeles County Jail
  author's learnings from, 100
  draft resisters in, 88, 90
  implied violence in, 100
  overcrowding in, 86, 87, 101
  reunions of prisoners in, 89
Court Appointed Prisoner Is Awaiting Sentence (CAPIAS), 90, 91, 95, 97, 100, 112, 118, 119
Crampton, Joe (J.C.), 218, 219–220, 222, 262, 279, 290, 307, 309, 312–313
Crampton, Joe, Jr., 312
Crane, Les, 258
Cranston, Alan, 292
Crosby, Stills, and Nash, 84, 326
Crumm, Robert, 268
Crusade for Justice, 224, 225, 227
The Crusade for Justice (Vigil), 225
CU (University of Colorado) (Boulder), 39, 57, 60, 69, 70, 71, 72
CU (University of Colorado) (Denver), 79, 80, 224
Cuba, U.S. involvement in, 183
Culbertson, William, 180
Curtis, Jesse William, 268–269, 270
Custer, George Armstrong, 232

D

Dali, Salvador, 139
Dancis, Bruce, 148, 192, 270
Das Kapital (Marx), 267, 324
Davidson, Carl, 70–71, 231
Davis, Hiawatha, 129–131, 138, 139, 142
Days of Rage, 231
DC Jail, 87
Deikman, Gene, 227
Dellenbach, Karen, 26
Dellenbach, Winter, 188–189, 190, 191, 193, 194, 197, 198, 269, 272, 274, 318
Dellinger, David, 232
Denver County Jail, 85, 90, 94–101, 112, 114, 118, 173
Denver Post, 135
Derrick, 172, 279
Deuteronomy 15:15, 184
Devillers, Philippe, 55–56
Diaz, Perfecto, 117, 120, 124, 138, 265
Diem, Ngo Dinh, 46–48, 50–51, 52, 53, 54, 55, 144, 287
Dirksen, Everett, 79
disciplinary report (of author), **339**
Dixon, Allen C., 81
Dominican Republic, U.S. involvement in, 183
The Doors, 198
Douglass, James, 136, 279–280
Doyle, William E., 133, 134, 135, 136
draft, terms to describe, 60
draft card, burning of, 72, 133, 134, 136, 148–149, 151, 155–156, 192. *See also* The Burners
draft card turn-in
  by David Harris, 245
  by Dick Roth, 73
  by Ernesto Vigil, 225
  national day of (October 16, 1967), 23, 72, 73, 133, 147, 149, 150, 151, 156, 159, 192, 248
draft dodgers, use of term, 8
draft law, defense system against, 197
draft objectors, as struggling individually with consciences, 129
draft prisoners, characterization of, 256
draft resistance movement
  author's coming into, 10, 71–72
  author's resistance as act of patriotism, 185
  disagreement about action in Oakland, 159
  early flyer from, 44–45
  founders of, 41
  as largely middle-class phenomenon, 60
  leading spokesmen of, 10, 26
  most resisters as readers, 327
  official pardons for participation in, **340**, 344
  opinions of Congress members about, 78–79
  overview, 60–61, 147
  public archive of, 347–348
  purpose of, 9
  SDS standard line about, 151
  Spring Antiwar Mobilization (1967), 148
  working-class participants in, 61
Draft Resistance Office (UCLA), 189, 191
draft resisters, most of acting as own attorneys, 197
Dreams Die Hard (Harris), 275, 314

drugs, 13, 31, 87, 172, 221, 225, 242, 244, 250, 261, 265, 266, 271, 272, 273, 276, 277, 279, 300, 309, 315. *See also specific drugs*
Duc, Quang, 48
Dulles, John Foster, 54, 182
Duncan, Donald, 69
Dundas, Malcolm, 191, 210
Dunphy, Don, 195
Durby, Dennis, 191
Dylan, Bob, 39, 72, 108, 196, 231, 239, 248, 316
Dzu, Truong Dinh, 68

E

East Village Other, 271
Eastern wisdom, 261, 271
economic justice, 319
economic system, 282, 283
Ed Sullivan Show, 96
Ehrlich, Reese, 161, 163
The Eighteenth Brumaire of Louis Napoleon (Marx), 276
Einstein, Albert, 138, 139, 177, 188
Eisenhower, Dwight D., 47, 54, 144, 194, 295
El Camino Junior College, 35, 62, 195, 196, 199
El Reno, 8, 95, 285, 287
El Restaurante de Tres Piedras (Three Rocks Restaurant), 221, 297, 305
The Electric Kool-Aid Acid Test (Wolfe), 270
Eliot, T. S., 97, 100
Ellsberg, Daniel, 75, 201, 287–288
Ellsberg, Patricia, 75
Emerson, Ralph Waldo, 77
Englewood (Colorado) draft board
author's decline of student deferment, 84
author's receipt of letter from, 57
author's registration at, 38
Enos, Dudley, 91, 97
Epicure Restaurant (Aspen), 39
Evans, Rowland, 145

F

Fall, Bernard, 69
FBI, 24, 35, 40, 42, 70, 72, 73, 93, 111, 113, 129–130, 194, 195, 240, 243
federal prisons
La Tuna Federal Correctional Institute. *See* La Tuna Federal Correctional Institute
Lompoc Federal Prison, 8, 208–210, 211, 212
Safford Federal Prison. *See* Safford Federal Prison
Terminal Island. *See* Terminal Island (TI)
Fellowship of Reconciliation, 315
Ferber, Michael, 10, 45, 152, 242, 245, 246
Ferkhins, Captain, 92
Fernandez, 123
Fielder, Lynn, 28, 29
First Amendment (U.S. Constitution), 28
Fischer, Louis, 202, 252, 253
Fishman, Geoffrey (Geoff), 187, 216, 261, 264, 290, 291, 296–297, 318
Fitzgerald, Frances, 234
Flaco, 121, 124, 262, 303
Flegler, Mr., 216
Florence state prison, 90, 110
Flores, Freddy, 172, 184, 282, 311
Florida, author's orange picking in, 42–43, 94, 115
Foisie, Jack, 63
folk music, as part of fabric of peace movement, 107–108
Folsom, 140, 177
food (in prison), 137, 221, 251, 300–303, 306, 330. *See also* El Restaurante de Tres Piedras (Three Rocks Restaurant)
"For What It's Worth" (song), 16
Ford, Gerald, 79, 344
Forrest Gump (film), 8, 323
Fosburgh, Lacey, 314
Fountainhead (Rand), 107
Franklin, Benjamin, 179
free market, 324
Free Press, 20
Free Speech Area (UCLA), 191
Free Speech Movement, 77, 169
"Freedom Summer" (1964), 40
The Freewheelin' Bob Dylan (album), 39
Friend, Tod, 187, 207, 220, 255, 259, 291
Frisch, Max, 117
Frumess, Richard, 39, 75, 80, 176, 347
Fulbright, J. William, 37–38, 62, 63, 69, 70
Fuller, Buckminster, 264

G

Galleano, Eduardo, 332
Gallegos, 114
Galloway, Joseph, 37–38
Gandhi, 37, 68, 77, 136–137, 138, 141, 170, 202, 213, 241–242, 248, 251–253, 255, 259, 261, 279
Gandhi: That Strange Little Brown Man of India, 241
Garaway, Bill, 26, 191–193, 197, 198, 199, 247, 268–271, 272–273, 274–275, 318
Garry, Charles, 162, 164, 165, 176
Garver, Gayle, 169. *See also* Bryan, Gayle (née Garver)
Gaskin, Stephen, 271
Gavin, James, 194
"Generals against the War" leaflet, 194
Geneva Accords, 47, 53, 54, 55, 62, 83
Genovese, Kitty, 79
Genovese, Vito, 286
Genovese family, 285
George Washington High School (Denver), 38, 88, 97, 120, 179, 224
Gerash, Walter, 133, 134, 135
Gettleman, Marvin, 52, 56
GI Forum, 224–225
Gibran, Kahlil, 264
Gibson, Bob, 248
Gila Valley, 104, 113
Ginsberg, Allen, 149–150, 233
GIs
disillusionment of, 68
as forgotten, 322
Gitman, Max, 184, 285

Gluck, Marvin, 190

Gluck, Sherna, 29, 190, 274, 318–319

Goldberg, Bruce, 70–71

Goldfarb, Ronald, 87

Gonzales, Corky, 225

"good German," 80

Goodman, Mitchell, 149

Gould, David, 33

Gould, Libby, 33, 285

Gould, Richard (Dick)

children of. *See* Gould, Sam; Gould, Sarah

disciplinary report of, **339**

letter from former student of, **354**

letters from prison, **337**, **338**

official pardon for, **340**, 344

parents of. *See* Gould, David; Gould, Libby

photos of, **351**, **355**

U.S. District Court of Colorado Presentence Report, **336**

wife of. *See* Kaplan, Susan

Gould, Sam, 7, 329, **341**, 342, 344

Gould, Sarah, 329–334, **341**, 344, 345, 351

Government of Vietnam (GVN), 234

Grace Episcopal Church (Los Angeles), 24, 27

The Grateful Dead, 276

Great Safford Chow-Line Raid, 297

Great Study Group Conspiracy, 178

Green Spider Coffee House (Denver), 38, 97

Greene, Michael, 197, 198, 268, 269, 272

Greene, Mike, 25

Griggs, John, 277

Guatemala, U.S. involvement in, 182–183

Gulf of Tonkin incident, 41, 54, 64, 287

Guthrie, Arlo, 240

Guthrie, Woody, 316, 326

GVN (Government of Vietnam), 234

H

Haifley, Allan, 71, 146, 147, 216

Haight-Ashbury, 130, 243, 251, 274–275, 276

Haiti, U.S. involvement in, 183

Halawa Jail (Honolulu), 85–86, 109

Halberstam, David, 45–46, 47, 48–49, 50, 51

Haldeman, H. R. (Bob), 236

hallucinogens, 221

Hamilton, Alexander, 258

Hamilton, George, 67

Hamilton, Steve, 149, 153, 159, 161, 246

Hamlin, Mildred, 129–130

Hampton, Fred, 232

handcuffs, sound of as triggering author's memory of prison, 111

hardship deferments, 67

Harkins, Paul, 50, 51

Harris, David, 26, 36, 41, 42, 44, 65–66, 77, 78, 79, 101, 138, 141, 149, 151, 153–154, 155, 156–157, 159, 191, 192, 193, 194, 196, 239–241, 242–244, 245–246, 247, 248, 249–251, 253, 254, 255–256, 257–260, 267, 274, 275, 276, 277, 280, 290–291, 296, 298, 300, 303, 306, 307, 309, 312, 313, 314, 347

Harris, Gabriel (Gabe), 291, 309

Harris, Kathy, 201, 202

Harris, Marty, 61, 62, 63, 69, 187, 194, 199, 201–202, 208, 258, 262, 263–264, 274, 276–277, 280, 288–289, 290, 316

hashish, 273

Hayden, Christian, 29, 30

Hayden, Sterling, 29–30

Helen of Troy (movie), 140

Heller, Lennie, 149, 159, 246

Henry, Lawrence, 130

Herren, Omar, 288

Hershey, Lewis B., 66–67

Hesse, Herman, 263, 280

"Hey, Jude" (song), 96–97

Hill, Joe, 241

hippie culture, 8, 16, 31, 46, 72, 135, 163, 187, 192, 229, 251, 264, 268, 270, 271, 273, 274, 276

Hippie Mafia (Brotherhood of Eternal Love), 277, 278

Ho, Mr., 204, 297

Ho Chi Minh, 52–53, 54, 62–63, 110, 236

Ho Chi Minh Trail, 235

"Hobo's Lullabye" (song), 316

Hodge, Dick, 162

Hoffman, Abbie, 150

the hole (in prison), 105, 208, 209, 210, 211, 212, 213, 217, 265, 293

Hollander, Emmett, 291, 292

Holocaust, 80, 133–134

Honolulu Advertiser, 86, 109

Hoover, J. Edgar, 35

Hornback, John, 269–270

House Un-American Activities Committee (HUAC), 30, 222, 223, 236

"Howl" (Ginsberg), 233

Hunt, Wanda, 288

I

I Ching, 271–272

inaction, impact of choice of, 84

Indonesia, U.S. involvement in, 183

induction centers

L.A. Induction Center, 194

numbers of men processed through, 9

Oakland Induction Center, 149, 150, 156, 162, 169, 249

Whitehall Induction Center, 147, 206, 240

inmate boycott, 263, 303–307, 310

inmate economy, 173

inmate strikes, 101, 203–204, 205, 255–256, 258, 290, 291, 293, 297–298, 300, 303, 305, 306, 349

inmate work stoppage, 296, 310

Institute for the Study of Nonviolence, 248, 312, 314

Institutional Revolutionary Party (PRI), 118

Iran, U.S. involvement in, 183

J

Jackson, Charles, 95–96, 97, 112
Jackson, George, 176
Jamie, 277, 278
Jefferson, Thomas, 179
Jefferson Airplane, 243
Jehovah's Witnesses, 14, 28, 125, 127–128, 288–289
Jensen, Lowell, 163, 165
Jewell, 277, 303
Jezer, Marty, 148, 150
John, Terry, 136, 261, 262, 264
Johnson, Lynda Bird, 67
Johnson, Lyndon, 10, 15, 19, 46, 64, 67, 72, 74, 78, 91, 154, 159, 160, 183, 208, 235, 283, 327
Johnson, Milton, 226
Jones, Mr., 163, 216
Jones, Tom, 224
Jordan, Mr., 179, 181
Judaism, relationship of with great empires, 184–185
Jung, Carl, 123, 242, 244, 245

K

Kalish, Donald (Don), 187, 188, 189
Kaplan, Susan
- epilogue by, 341–353
- memories of desert, 13
- photo of, **341**
- as witnessing author's reaction to hearing handcuff clicks, 111

Katzenbach, Chris, 208
Katzenbach, Nicholas, 146, 208
Kaukonen, Jor, 243
Kaukonen, Peter, 243
Kearns, Chris, 147
Kehler, Randy, 287, 288, 298
Kennedy, J.J., 108, 109, 176, 216, 259, 293
Kennedy, John F., 46
Kenski, Officer, 121, 176, 216, 266, 277, 296, 305, 307
Kerouac, Jack, 38, 39, 241
Kerry, John, 323
Kesey, Ken, 270
KGFJ Radio, 40
Kierkegaard, Søren, 244
The Killing Fields (film), 321
King, Martin Luther, 21, 68, 76, 77, 138, 189, 241–242, 248, 249
King William, 100, 119
Kissinger, Henry, 185, 236
KPFK Pacific Radio, 20, 40
KRHM Radio, 20, 22, 40
Ku Klux Klan, 222
Kuchel, Thomas H., 78
Kunkin, Art, 20
Ky, Nguyen Cao, 68

L

L.A. County Jail/Los Angeles County Jail, 26, 85, 86, 87, 89, 90, 96, 101, 110, 187
L.A. Induction Center, 194
L.A. Resistance
- activities of, 193–194
- author's prison letter as describing support from, **337**
- as core of resistance community in Safford, 187, 202
- and drugs, 273, 277
- lawyers' role in, 197–198
- leadership of, 26, 29
- legends within, 212
- The Medicine Show, 270–271, 274
- noncooperation as revered by, 207
- as the place to go, 191
- as plunging into counterculture, 267, 268, 270, 274
- reunion (2009), 347
- Sherna Gluck and Winter Dellenbach as soul of, 274
- slogan of, 193
- style of, 202
- UCLA peace movement as spawning early roots of, 187, 191

La Tuna Federal Correctional Institute, 8, 105, 119, 204, 205, 207, 217, 223, 259, 265, 278, 285–287, 288, 289, 290, 292, 293, 298, 306, 307, 309, 311, 314
Laird, Melvin, 234
Lane, John, 27, 29
Langdon, Susan, 18–19
Lanier, Thomas, 108, 109, 125, 136, 176, 259, 289, 290, 291, 292, 294, 297, 305
Lansdale, Edward, 75
Lansky, Meyer, 143
LAPD (Los Angeles Police Department), 16, 17, 18, 20
Lara, Johnny, 119, 120, 121, 124, 125
Larry, 263, 266, 267
Lausche, Frank J., 79
Law 10/59, 55
lawyers, role of in L.A. Resistance, 197–198
Leary, Timothy, 187, 201, 271, 273, 277, 317
Leech, Archibald, 28
Left, 150, 155, 156, 160, 179, 183, 233, 295. *See also* New Left; Old Left
LeMay, Curtis, 74
lending library (in prison), 177–180
Lenin, Vladimir, 187, 230, 233, 275
Lennon, John, 96
Les Crane Show, 258
Lester, Julius, 280
Levertov, Denise, 149
Lewis, Oscar, 121
liberals, 35, 110, 178, 196, 244, 257, 293
The Life and Times of Richard Castro—Bridging a Cultural Divide (Gould), 348
Life Magazine, 47, 147
Limbaugh, Rush, 321
Little Red Book (Mao Tse Tung), 228, 268
Littlefield, Bradley (Brad), 178, 179, 183, 295
Lockhart, Mrs., 35, 70
Lompoc Federal Prison, 8, 208–210, 211, 212
"Long Time Gone" (song), 84
Los Angeles Police Department (LAPD), 16, 17, 18, 20
Los Angeles Times (L.A. Times), 20, 25, 27, 63, 189
love-ins, 274
Lovely, Mr., 216, 278

LSD, 13, 164, 243, 263, 271, 273, 274, 276
Luce, Henry, 244
Luciano, Charles (Lucky), 285
Lynd, Staughton, 10
Lynrd Skynyrd, 326

M

MacArthur, Douglas, 53
MACV (Military Assistance Command, Vietnam), 49, 50, 51, 56, 83
Madison, James, 258
"Madman Theory," 235–236
Maizlish, Harry, 19–20, 21–22, 23, 32, 141–142, 205
Maizlish, Joe, 14, 15, 16, 17, 18, 19, 20–23, 29–32, 36, 40, 42, 44, 68–69, 86–87, 88–89, 90, 101, 104, 114, 126, 128, 136, 137, 138, 139, 141, 191, 199, 202, 203, 204–205, 206–207, 208, 213, 259, 272, 287, 288, 297, 307, 314, 315
Maizlish, Ruth, 20, 88, 141
The Making of a Quagmire (Halberstam), 45, 46, 56
Making of the English Working Class (Thompson), 276
Malcolm X, 9, 21
Malloy, Charles, 82
mandatory release date (of author), 309
Mandel, Bob, 161
Mansfield, Michael, 79
Mao Tse Tung, 228, 267–268
Maoists/Maoism, 151, 228, 232, 246
Marcuse, Herbert, 187
marijuana, 13, 118, 196, 226, 229, 272, 273, 315. *See also* weed
market capitalism, 282
market economy (in prison), 173
marriages
- broken relationships and failed marriages (of inmates), 319
- David Harris and Joan Baez, 251, 314
- Marty and Kathy Harris, 201–202, 316
- Patrick and Gayle Bryan, 202, 316–317

Marx, Karl, 231, 233, 276, 324, 326
Marxists/Marxism, 152, 167, 177, 184, 197, 213, 217, 230, 231, 261, 267, 268, 274, 279, 281, 282, 283, 323–324, 325, 332
masculinity, notions of, 36, 255
Maslow, Abraham, 324
Masters of Deceit: What the Communist Bosses Are Doing to Bring America to Its Knees (Hoover), 35
materialism, 324, 326, 345
McCarthy, Eugene, 224
McCarthy, Joe, 30, 64, 177, 236
McComb statement, 147
McGlaze, Greg, 64
McGlaze, Marcy, 64
McNamara, Robert, 75, 154, 208–209, 287
McQuery, Chester, 321
McReynolds, David, 192
medical care (in prison), 101, 204, 297–298, 299, 300
The Medicine Show, 270, 271, 272, 274
meditation, 31, 221, 263, 264, 311
Melville, Sam, 206
Mendoza, Pat, 346
Merlau-Ponty, Maurice, 71
Merrell, Mr., 216
mescaline, 265, 266, 269, 273
Mexicans. *See also* Bracero Act (1942)
- author's prison friendships with, 13, 99–100, 114, 120, 123
- immigration stories of, 115–116, 119
- impact of economic transformation on, 116, 117–118
- massacre at Tlatelolco (1968), 118
- in U.S. justice system, 305

Military Assistance Command, Vietnam (MACV), 49, 50, 51, 56, 83
military induction centers
- L.A. Induction Center, 194
- numbers of men processed through, 9
- Oakland Induction Center, 150, 156, 162, 169, 249
- Whitehall Induction Center, 147, 206, 240

Miller, David, 148
Mills, C. Wright, 187
Mink, Patsy, 110, 259
Mitchell, Joni, 110
Monthly Review Press, 177, 282
Moore, David, 196
Moorer, Thomas, 236
moral dilemmas, 79–81, 93
Moran, Warden, 292
Morris, Eugene, 288
Morse, Wayne, 63
Mousie, 143
The Movement, 152
Mt. Dora Growers Coop, 43, 116–117
Mt. Graham, 13, 103, 105, 121, 123, 215, 216, 219, 289
Munsat, Theodore, 15
music. *See also specific songs and artists*
- author's learning of gritos, 123
- as brought to Safford by Dana Rae Park, 107–108, 110
- folk music as part of fabric of peace movements, 107–108
- influence of on Dana Rae Park, 107–108
- in prison, 90, 96, 97, 114, 122, 224, 246, 262
- rock 'n' roll, 107, 198, 224

N

napalm, 74, 76, 136, 147, 148, 158, 169, 184, 188, 195
Narmad, 251
National Advisory Committee on Selective Service, 327
National Archives and Records Administration (NARA), 288
National Lawyers Guild, 197
National Liberation Front, 322
National Student Association (NSA), 244
The Nation, 64
Navarro, Carlos Romero, 222, 304
The Nazz, 198

Nelson, Greg, 14–15, 17, 19, 21, 23–29, 31, 33, 36, 37, 38, 64, 65, 67, 90, 125–126, 136, 168, 175, 191, 199, 202, 216, 223, 272, 277, 291, 299, 317

Nelson, Lois, 24, 27

Nelson, Richard, 23–24, 27–28, 33, 175

Neuschatz, 39

New Age, 261, 275

New Left, 143, 152, 157, 179, 184, 228

"New Left Notes," 157

New Orleans, author's time living in, 44, 45, 52, 59, 65, 113

The New Republic, 87

New York Times, 10, 46, 51, 74, 75, 79, 177, 235, 270, 287, 288, 314

The New Yorker, 81, 84

Newman, Becky, 140–141

Nguyen, Ngoc Loan, 91

Nhu, Madame, 47, 48, 49, 50, 51

Nhu, Ngo Dinh, 46, 47, 48–49, 50, 51, 52, 53, 54

Nicaragua, U.S. involvement in, 183

Nier, Harry, 227

Nietzsche, Friedrich, 242, 244–245

Nixon, Richard M., 64, 99, 136, 188, 234–237, 283

noncooperation

- according to David Harris, 244, 245
- according to Gandhi, 202–203, 213, 253, 259
- by Greg Nelson, 26
- by Jack Whitton, 211
- by Joe Maizlish, 203, 207

nonviolence. *See also* Gandhi

- according to Gandhi, 136, 202, 253
- Bill Garaway on, 270
- as core of alternative culture, 271
- current of, 136–138
- David Harris on, 151, 245, 249, 254–255, 281–282
- Institute for the Study of Nonviolence, 248, 312, 314
- as invoked by Martin Luther King, 241–242
- Joan Baez's study of, 248
- L.A. folks' inclination towards, 213
- as not sufficient to end war, 154

Novak, Robert, 145

NSA (National Student Association), 244

Nygaard, Olie, 67

O

Oakland Induction Center, 149, 150, 156, 162, 169, 249

Oakland Seven, 160–162, 166, 171, 176, 269

Oakland Tribune, 156

objectivist philosophy, 107, 198

October 16, 1967, draft card turn-in, 23, 72, 73, 133, 147, 149, 150, 151, 156, 159, 192, 248

official pardon (of author), **340**, 344

Oglesby, Carl, 71, 145

O'Keefe, Georgia, 104

O'Konski, Alvin, 67

Old Left, 144, 145, 171

omega, as symbol of The Resistance, 247

On the Road (Kerouac), 38

One-Tool-a-Day Plan, 217, 219

Open Door policy, 182

The Open Veins of Latin America (Galleano), 332

Operation Breakfast, 235

Operation Cedar Falls, 81, 83

Operation Dessert, 235

Operation Dinner, 235

Operation Duck Hook, 236

Operation Linebacker, 236

Operation Lunch, 235

Operation Phoenix, 235

Operation Rolling Thunder, 74

Operation Utah, 37

Operation Wetback, 116

Orange Sunshine, 277, 278

Oterman, Dale, 195

Our War (Harris), 36, 314

P

Pacheco, Norm, 67

pacifists/pacifism, 63, 80, 93, 107, 108, 128, 138, 145, 147, 148, 154, 155, 156, 190, 196, 237, 242, 248, 253, 254–255, 261, 281, 315, 331

Palmer, Jerry, 190, 194

Pancho Villa, 121–122

Panzer, Michael, 197, 198

Paradise Ranch, 271

pardon, for participation in draft resistance movement, **340**, 344

Park, Dana Rae, 37, 86, 90, 105–111, 112, 113, 125, 127, 136, 138, 139, 174, 187, 216, 219, 223, 255, 259, 266, 279–280, 290, 291, 310, 316, 317

Park, Noh Young, 36

Parkerson, C.W., 214

Parole Progress Report, 214

Parsons, James, 146

passive resistance, use of term, 253

Peace Action Council, 16, 17, 18, 19

peace movements

- Bill Garaway as devoting youth to, 318
- folk music as part of fabric of, 107–108
- Laird's hope for dividing of, 234
- participants in, 152
- at UCLA, 187

Peace Press, 190, 201, 267, 317

Pentagon Papers, 75–76, 287

People's Union Coop Farm, 312

Perkoff, Stuart Z., 206

Pershing, John J., 122, 305

"The Persistence of Memory" (Dali painting), 139

personal growth, quest for, 264

Peter, Paul, and Mary, 108

pets (in prison), 206–207

Philippines, U.S. involvement in, 183

PL (Progressive Labor Party), 151, 152, 190, 228–229, 230, 233, 246

political organizing (in prison), 171, 172, 173, 174, 176, 256, 258, 259, 274, 286, 288
poor man's crimes, 282
Port Chicago Peace Vigil, 169
Port Huron Statement, 144
Potter, Paul, 145
Pregerson, Harry, 200, 201, 208, 209–210
PRI (Institutional Revolutionary Party), 118
Prinzmetal, Irv, 22
Profumo, Rich, 89, 191, 196, 197, 199, 208, 209–210, 213
Progressive Labor Party (PL), 151, 152, 190, 228–229, 230, 233, 246
Psychedelic Experience (Leary), 187
psychedelics, 277

Q

"Qué buena es la vida," 123–124
Quintana, Gilbert, 226–227
Quotations from Chairman Mao Tse-tung, 228

R

racial issues
American apartheid, 43–45
bombings, 41, 223
in draft, 151, 330, 345
GI Forum and, 224–225
inequality, 184
preferences in cultural tastes, 96
Rader, Gary, 148
radicals, 45–46, 52, 148, 149, 150, 152, 154, 155, 156, 160, 167, 172, 178, 179, 184, 197, 225, 242, 244, 251, 280, 293
Rambo, Part II (film), 8, 323
Ramirez, Saul, 173, 184, 282, 297, 303, 312
Ramparts Magazine, 69, 76, 176, 177
Rand, Ayn, 107, 198
Rankin, Mr., 34–35, 36, 253
Raskin, Marcus, 149
Reagan, Ronald, 158, 316, 325
Real, Manuel, 31, 195, 200
Reddin, Tom, 18, 20
Regardie, Arnold, 31
Reidy, Nick, 136, 280, 290, 291, 307, 309, 310
Reidy, Pam, 290
religion, 28, 107, 128, 170, 233, 324. *See also* Buddhist; Christianity; Jehovah's Witnesses; Judaism
Resistance and Contemplation (Douglass), 136, 279
The Resistance
birth of, 149, 246
financial support for, 247–248, 249
founding document of, 246–247
iron rule of, 192, 258
naming of, 149, 246
SDS as clashing with, 71, 190
symbol of, 190
what made it different, 253–254
Resor, Stanley, 208
"Revolution" (song), 228
revolution, author's use of term, 185, 213, 279, 319, 323, 324–325
revolutionary study group, 64, 177, 282, 325
Revolutionary Youth Movement (RYM), 230, 233
Reynard, Bill, 93
Rhodes, Orlando, 17
rich man's crimes, 282
Rios, Omar, 106, 108, 109, 136, 176, 177, 259, 294, 305
rock 'n' roll, 107, 198, 224, 271
Rocky Mountain News, 51, 60, 72, 109
Rodriquez, Joe, 127, 138
Rolling Stone magazine, 314
Rolling Stones, 39, 231
Ronquillo, José, 300, 304, 305
Roosevelt, Franklin D., 64
Roosevelt University (Chicago), 167, 240
Rosenberg, Ethel, 36
Rosenberg, Julius, 36
Ross, Fred, 170
Roth, Dick, 73, 147
Royce, Miss, 120
Rubin, Jerry, 150
Rubio, 126
Rusk, Dean, 62, 63, 65–66, 154
Russell, Richard B., 79
RYM (Revolutionary Youth Movement), 230, 233

S

Sadagraha, 253
Safford, AZ, 8
Safford Federal Prison
acts of mischief/resistance at, 217–219
author and family's trip to, 330, 351–352
author's arrival at, 113
author's housing assignment at, 113
author's monthly work reports, 213
author's release from, 300–301
author's work assignments at, 113, 119, 215–219
cafeteria boycott, 303–307
censorship at, 176
the count in, 139, 290
criminalization of strangers at, 115
Dark Shadows, 295–296
demographics of prisoners at, 114
description of, 104–105
description of area around, 103–104
Great Safford Chow-Line Raid, 297
homebrew at, 114, 173, 177
inmate council, 294–295
inmate economy at, 173
inmates of, 13
L.A. Resistance as core of resistance community in, 187, 202
letters from author from, **337–338**
loneliness in, 140
med tech assistant (MTA) at, 172, 278, 299, 300
medical care at, 297–300
political organizing within. *See* political organizing (in prison)
power games, 296–297

prisoners' hogan at, 219–222, 307, 346
records from as missing and possibly destroyed, 288
resisters' post-imprisonment reflections/experiences, 313–319
reunions of prisoners in, 208, 210, 247, 318
rules limiting number of people who could send mail to or receive mail from, **338**
surrealism of, 261–262
threats of murder or physical harm in, 125
time as hanging over, 138
work stoppage, 296, 310
Sale, Kirkpatrick, 228–229, 231
Salisbury, Harrison, 74
Salter, 126, 138, 184
San Carlos Apache Reservation, 103
San Francisco Chronicle, 155, 164
San Quentin, 177
Sanchez, Oscar, 167, 173, 184, 276, 277
Sandperl, Ira, 248
Sandstone, 8
Sarnoff, Irving (Irv), 17, 19
Saturday Evening Post, 47
Satyagraha, 253
Savio, Mario, 77
Schell, Jonathan, 81–82
Schneider, Mark, 26
Scoggins, Robert, 222–223
Scott, Eddie, 67
Scott, Eddy, 319
SDS (Students for a Democratic Society). *See* Students for a Democratic Society (SDS)
Seale, Bobby, 130
Segal, Jeff (Bugsy), 142, 143, 150, 158, 160, 161, 167–168, 169, 171, 172–173, 174, 175–176, 177–178, 183, 184, 213, 214, 216, 217, 228, 229, 230, 232, 233, 239–241, 246, 256, 259, 267, 269, 276, 280, 282, 285, 293, 294, 295–296, 301, 302, 306, 311, 313, 319
Selective Service Law Panel (National Lawyers Guild), 197
Selective Service System (SSS)
author's classification, 57, 93
author's refusal to comply with, 93–94
author's registration with, 38
classifications of, 38, 57, 199, 345
Englewood (Colorado) draft board, 38, 57, 84
Form Number 2, 135
Form Number 150, 130
"Manpower Channeling," 66
numbers of men who clashed with, 8
qualifying tests, 9
student deferments. *See* student deferments
self-discoveries, 276, 279, 280
17th Parallel, 53, 55, 64, 74
Sexton, Sidney, 214, 215, 221, 291, 292, 293, 301, 302, 303, 306, 310
sexual freedom/sexual revolution, 252, 261
sexual identity, anticommunism as part of, 36
shackles, author's experience in, 112
Shaw, John D., 44
Shelton, Richard, 90, 104
Shelton, Robert, 222
Shoup, David, 194
Shurtleff, Jeffrey (Jeff), 196, 239, 244
Sickels, Bob, 67
Siddhartha (Hesse), 263, 280
Siegel, Benjamin (Bugsy), 143
Siegel, Robert (Bob), 187, 291
Sihanouk (prince), 235
Sikes, Robert F., 79
silent Americans, 73
Silver, Anne, 39
sing-ins, 274
Sisco, Jerry, 125–126, 133, 138, 167–168, 173, 216, 217, 282
sit-ins, 156, 188, 189
situationalism, 281
Smith, Bill, 197
Smith, Mike, 161
Smith, Walter Bedell, 54
Smitherman, Donna, 141
SNCC (Student Nonviolent Coordinating Committee), 42, 44, 45, 68, 147, 152
snitching, 95, 278, 279, 300
social change, 44, 144, 145, 160, 171, 233, 241, 255, 262, 305, 325, 326, 332
social classes, clash between, 98, 282. *See also* class conflict/struggle/war
socialists/socialism, 56, 134, 144, 152, 177, 231, 319, 320, 323, 324
Soledad, 176, 177
Soul on Ice (Cleaver), 176
space cadetism, 274–275
Spanish, author's speaking/learning of, 120–121, 214, 221, 312, 339, 341
Spires, Billy, 195, 271, 273
Spires, Evie, 273
spiritual journeys, 124, 195, 200, 210, 263, 271, 276, 279, 288, 311, 315, 342, 346
Spock, Benjamin, 149, 150, 188
Sporer, Louis, 18
Spray, Lisa, 174
Spring Antiwar Mobilization (1967), 148
Springfield, 8
Sri Baba, 264, 270, 271
Sri Rivan, 210, 211, 212, 264, 271, 293
SSS (Selective Service System). *See* Selective Service System (SSS)
Stalin, Joe, 35, 55, 145
Stanford Daily, 243, 245
Stanford University, 42, 65, 77, 154, 165, 208, 242–243, 245, 246, 276, 307
Stanley, Owsley, 276
Stark, Susie, 73–74
Starobin, Bob, 280
Stender, Fay, 176, 259
Stephens, Judge, 29, 31, 32
Steppenwolf (Hesse), 263, 326
Steppenwolf (rock group), 198
Stevenson, Albert, 25
Stewart, Sharon, 16
Stills, Stephen, 16
Stone, I. F. (Izzie), 64–65

Stop the Draft Week (STDW), 150–152, 154, 156, 159, 164, 169, 233, 258
Story, Wanda, 38, 57, 93
The Story of My Experiments with Truth (Gandhi), 136
Strategic Hamlet Program, 49
"Street Fighting Man" (song), 231
"the street," author's understanding of, 101
student deferments
author's, 57, 69
author's decline of, 84
availability of, 66
Bob Zaugh's rejection of, 78
of David Harris, 62
of Joe Maizlish, 14, 21, 23
Johnson as keeping intact, 327
limiting of, 345
opposition to, 146, 149, 151
Student Nonviolent Coordinating Committee (SNCC), 42, 44, 45, 68, 147, 152
Student Peace Union, 60
"A Student Syndicalist Movement" (Davidson), 70–71
Students for a Democratic Society (SDS), 60, 70, 71, 72, 73, 143–146, 150, 151, 152, 157, 161, 190, 228–233, 241, 267, 268, 273, 294, 296, 317, 332
study group, 64, 177, 282, 325
Study of History (Toynbee), 131
"Subterranean Homesick Blues" (song), 231
Sugar Bear, 99, 100
The Summer of Love, 155
Suu, Vo, 91
Swartz, Kelley, 210
Swartz, Mike, 191, 208, 210
Sweeney, Dennis, 41, 44, 45, 149, 159, 191, 192, 245, 246, 250, 257, 258, 274
Sweezy, Paul, 177
Swiers, Kathy, 39
Swift Trail Federal Prison Camp, 13, 103, 176, 237
systemic change, need for, 185, 282

T

T.C., 98–99, 100, 101, 119
Taylor, Kathy, 141
teach-ins, 60, 192, 242
Tempo magazine, 342, 343
Terminal Island (TI), 8, 141–142, 203, 204, 205, 206, 207, 297
Terrill, W. H., 112
Tet Offensive, 90–91
Thieu, Nguyen Van, 68, 93, 234
Thomas, Officer, 176, 277, 297, 305
Thompson, E.P., 276
Thompson, Misty, 288
Thoreau, Henry David, 68, 76–77
The Tibetan Book of the Dead, 210, 276
Tijerina, Reies, 286–287, 288
Time magazine, 244, 248, 251
"The Times They Are a Changin'" (song), 108
Tiny, 278–279
tobacco, as prison currency, 99–100, 114, 173–174
Toynbee, Arnold, 131
The Tragedy of American Diplomacy (Williams), 179
Tripp, Ed, 210
The Truth That Leads to Eternal Life, 129
Turner, Frederick Jackson, 181
Turner, George, 141

U

U Needa Comix (Crumm), 268
UCLA, 14, 21, 68, 69, 78, 137, 138, 187–188, 189, 190, 191–192, 199, 267, 307
United Farm Workers (UFW), 170, 171, 173, 175, 242
United States
involvement in Congo, 183
involvement in Cuba, 183
involvement in Dominican Republic, 183
involvement in Guatemala, 183
involvement in Haiti, 183
involvement in Indonesia, 183
involvement in Iran, 183
involvement in Nicaragua, 183
involvement in Philippines, 183
involvement in Vietnam, 183. *See also* Vietnam War
justice in, 184
University of Colorado (CU) (Boulder), 39, 57, 60, 69, 70, 71, 72
University of Colorado (CU) (Denver), 79, 80, 224
U.S. Constitution, First Amendment, 28
U.S. Customs House, 71, 91, 133
U.S. District Court of Colorado Presentence Report (of author), **336**
U.S. history, according to William Appleman Williams, 180–181
U.S. marshals, 13, 26–27, 32, 88, 90, 97, 106, 112, 113, 205, 209, 226–227, 239, 256
U.S. Supreme Court, *West Virginia State Board of Education vs. Barnette*, 28, 29

V

Valachi, Joe, 285, 286
Vane, Michael, 262
Vann, John Paul, 51
vegetarians (in prison), 137, 251, 302
Ventura County Jail, 90
Viet Cong, 9, 47, 49, 50, 51, 52, 64, 69, 74, 75, 79, 81, 91, 211, 234, 322
Viet Minh, 52, 53, 55, 62
Vietnam
author's plan to visit, 352
defending democracy in, 48–52
destruction of during war, 74, 83
Law 10/59, 55
longer view in, 52–53
subverting the peace in, 53–56
U.S. involvement in, 183
Vietnam (Gettleman), 52
Vietnam Day Committee (UCLA), 188, 189, 242
Vietnam Summer, 73, 169, 189
Vietnam War
air war, 74–76

author's research about, 46, 56, 67–68, 78–79, 349, 352
author's understanding of, 55–56, 63–64, 83–84
as black hole, 323
casualties in, 49, 50, 51, 224, 234
domestic opposition to, 159
Gulf of Tonkin incident, 41, 54, 64, 287
intersection of with race, 44
Lazarus project, 52
Operation Breakfast, 235
Operation Cedar Falls, 81, 83
Operation Dessert, 235
Operation Dinner, 235
Operation Duck Hook, 236
Operation Linebacker, 236
Operation Lunch, 235
Operation Phoenix, 235
Operation Rolling Thunder, 74
Operation Utah, 37
peace with honor, 234–237
post-war sentiments, 323
prisoned resisters as sharing common knowledge of roots of, 46
reasons for involvement in, 179
17th Parallel, 53, 55, 64, 74
sources of information/news about, 59
start of, 38
strain of as seeping into personal lives of many in positions of power, 208
strategy of Vietnamization, 234, 237
Tet Offensive, 90–91
troop levels late 1965, 40
turning of tide in, 52
weapons, 38, 50, 63–64, 65, 74, 236
working-class participants in, 327
Zippo Raids, 147
Vigil, Ernesto, 224–227
"The Village of Ben Suc" (Schell), 81–83
The Village Voice, 271
violence, author's views on, 281
virtual colleges (in prison system), 144
Vitale, Louie, 89, 191

W

Wald, Karen, 157
Walker, Mr., 179
Wallace, George, 326
War Resisters League, 147, 169, 192, 287, 315
Warren, Earl, 23
Washington, George, 54
Waskow, Arthur, 149
Watanabe, Jesus Uchira, 140
Watchtower Society, 129
Watkins, Don, 184, 282, 285
Wavy Gravy, 271
Wayne, John, 36, 253, 255, 295
"We Refuse to Serve," founding document of The Resistance, 146, 256
"We Shall Overcome" (song), 239, 249
"We Won't Go" statements, 45, 73, 150
Weather Underground, 232, 277
Weatherman, 231, 232, 233
weed, 221, 243, 250, 273. *See also* marijuana
Weekly, 64
Weitzel, Harlan, 26
Wells, Matt, 39
Wells, Tom, 60
West Virginia State Board of Education vs. Barnette, 28, 29
Western Prisoner and Support Service, 211
Westmoreland, William, 63, 160
Wheeler, Robert (Roster), 164
When Can I Come Home? (author unknown), 322
Whisenant, Alma, 29
White, Kenneth J., 82
Whitehall Induction Center, 147, 206, 240
Whitton, Jack, 191, 208, 210–212, 213
Whole Earth Catalog, 264
The Who, 326
"Why Socialism?" (Einstein), 177
Wicker, Tom, 10
Williams, William Appleman, 179, 180–181, 182
Wilson, Woodrow, 122, 181
Witte, Norman, 195
Wolfe, Tom, 270
work stoppage (in prison), 296, 310

Y

Yellow Cab, author's association with, 100, 281, 345, 348
yoga (in prison), 211, 212, 263–264, 271, 274, 293
Yogananda, Paramahansa, 200
Young, Nathan, 97–98
Young, Neil, 326
Young Americans for Freedom, 107
Youth Act, 106

Z

Zack, Art, 187, 291
Zaugh, Robert (Bob), 35, 36–37, 61, 62, 63, 78, 171, 190, 195, 199–200, 201, 267, 271, 274, 317
Zippo Raids, 147
Zip-Six sentence, 106, 109, 278, 290

Made in the USA
San Bernardino, CA
08 October 2017